THE OXFORD BOOK OF
SHORT STORIES

THE OXFORD
BOOK OF
SHORT STORIES

CHOSEN BY
V. S. PRITCHETT

NEW YORK
OXFORD UNIVERSITY PRESS
1981

103964

This edition published 1981 by Book Club Associates
by arrangement with Oxford University Press

Introduction and selection © V. S. Pritchett 1981

British Library Cataloguing in Publication Data
The Oxford book of short stories.
1. Short stories, English
I. Pritchett, Sir Victor Sawdon
823'.01'08   PR1309.S5
ISBN 0–19–214116–3

Printed in the United States of America

CONTENTS

vi *Contents*

viii *Contents*

INTRODUCTION

This anthology is a selection of short stories written in the much-travelled English language by authors whose roots are in five continents and are nourished by a variety of cultures. The period covered is from the early nineteenth century to the present day. There is no suggestion that they are 'the best'. All anthologies are a matter of personal taste: the only claim I can make for this one is that it has been formed by seventy years of passionate addiction to the short story and fifty years as a fellow writer in an art or craft that is distinctive and, for the writer, exquisitely difficult. The bond between all of us is our fascination not only with the 'story' but with its relatively new and still changing form wherever it appears; and I fancy that, as a body, we are more conscious of what other story writers have done in other languages, in France, Italy, Northern Europe, Russia, and Latin America and even in what is called the Third World, than our novelists commonly are. In private life, story-telling is a universal habit, and we think we have something that suits especially well with the temper of contemporary life.

For my purposes two stories in *English* literature by Sir Walter Scott – *The Two Drovers* and *The Highland Widow* – seem to establish the short story as a foundational form independent of the diffuse attractions of the novel: the novel tends to tell us everything whereas the short story tells us only one thing, and that, intensely. More important – in American literature, Washington Irving and, above all, Edgar Allan Poe and Nathaniel Hawthorne – defined where the significance of the short story would lie. It is, as some have said, a 'glimpse through' resembling a painting or even a song which we can take in at once, yet bring the recesses and contours of larger experience to the mind. If we move forward to the stories written, say, since 1910 I would say the picture is still there – but has less often the old elaborately gilded frame; or, if you like, the frame is now *inside* the picture. But, to go back to the nineteenth century after Scott, it is noticeable that American writers and those in young societies took to the new art with more alacrity than the British who were overwhelmed by the vitality of the great English novelists of that prolific age. The short stories of Dickens, Thackeray, Mrs Gaskell, Hardy, and many excellent minor writers, do read like crowded episodes of a continuing novel, or like novels that have been started and then given up. Hardy's stories could as well be novels; his genuine short stories are in his laconic poetry. Yet, the compulsively novelizing Trollope is an exception; he did discover the short story when he became a traveller. One remembers the Lotte Schmidt stories and the remarkable Cornish Tale, *Malachi's Cove*. If the British held a distinctive place it was chiefly in the stories of exotic travel. We had to get away from our closed doors and closely curtained windows. Not until Robert Louis Stevenson and Rudyard Kipling did we join the American fabulists. And, on reflection, we notice these two writers are on the move, restive when at home.

In saying the present volume is the expression of a personal taste I must add that constant difficulties of space and copyright are the anthologist's nightmares. One would need two or three volumes to do justice to the abundance of past talent and the new feeling for experiment in the youngest generation who are more given to the clinical document than to fable. One is forced to be arbitrary, to reject some masters because they have been over-anthologized. If Jack London, P. G. Wodehouse, Max Beerbohm, Saul Bellow, Bernard Malamud, and many others are omitted this implies no lack of admiration for their gifts and contribution.

There is also the special difficulty of the length of short stories. The short-story writer has always depended on periodicals. In the nineteenth century, newspapers in all countries published quite long stories every week and fat magazines published immensely long ones: stories that one has to call *novellas*, a delightful form that may run to thirty or forty thousand words. A master like Henry James gets longer and longer as the years go by. Not only are such writers lengthy; their prose is leisurely, often sententious and delights in cultivated circumlocution and in the ironies of euphemism. The break in prose style between ourselves and our elders that occurred in, say, 1900 is also a symptom of the conflict between long and short. It is painful to have to reject George Moore's *Albert Nobbs* (from *Celibate Lives*), a neglected work of genius, simply because it goes on and on. (It is still in print.) I have had to be sparing of other longer stories and have tended, where possible, to turn to the unusual or little-known examples of a talent. So, Henry James is not represented by *The Real Thing* – the well-known key to his art – nor by *The Pupil* or the admirable *Bench of Desolation*; but I do think the far briefer *Paste*, though it has a too obvious debt to Maupassant, is one of James's characteristic gems. There is a similar difficulty with Joyce: *The Dead* must surely be his most impressive and seminal story, but, again, it is very long and it has often appeared in anthologies: I have preferred therefore a shorter story from *Dubliners* where his genius was first signalled.

The variety of Kipling in scene and manner makes nonsense of the attempt to find the typical; I have chosen the Kipling of London's East End rather than the magical Indian scene, for this Cockney aspect of Kipling's work is often overlooked. In general, I have sought the surprising and perhaps uncharacteristic tale such as Katherine Mansfield's *The Woman at the Store* and in African, Canadian, Australian, and New Zealand writers I have looked less to the native scene than to what these writers have given to the art. They indeed require a volume to themselves. I go some way in supporting Frank O'Connor's view that the short story has flourished in what he calls 'anarchic' societies, in which social bonds are loose and where the traditional satisfactions of a culture are slack. However, the great French tradition is a clear exception to O'Connor's argument.

In the present century, now eighty years old, style, attitudes, and natural subject matter have changed. Strangely, we are now closer to the classic poetic conception of the short story as Hawthorne and Poe saw it, closer – in our mass societies – to fable and to the older vernacular writers. We are less bound by contrived plot, more intent on the theme buried in the heart. Readers used to speak of 'losing' themselves in a novel or a story: the contemporary addict turns to the short story to find himself. In a restless century which has lost its old assurances and in which our lives are fragmented, the nervous side-glance has replaced the steady confronting gaze. (Short-story writers – like painters – are now in something like the situation of Goya in *his* art.) In a mass society we have the sense of being anonymous: therefore we look for the silent moment in which our singularity breaks through, when emotions change, without warning, and reveal themselves. One remembers the terrible moment of passion in Kipling's *Mary Postgate*, the dumb response of the captured English soldiers in O'Connor's *Guests of the Nation* or the racing feet of the Borstal boy shaking his mind open in Alan Sillitoe's *Loneliness of the Long Distance Runner*.

Many of the great short-story writers have not succeeded as novelists: Kipling and Chekhov are examples and, to my mind, D.H. Lawrence's stories are superior to his novels. For myself, the short story springs from a spontaneously poetic as distinct from a prosaic impulse – yet is not 'poetical' in the sense of a shuddering sensibility. Because the short story has to be succinct and has to suggest things that have been 'left out', are, in fact, there all the time, the art calls for a mingling of the skills of the rapid reporter or traveller with an eye for incident and an ear for real speech, the instincts of the poet and ballad-maker, and the sonnet writer's concealed discipline of form. The writer has to cultivate the gift for aphorism and wit. A short story is always a disclosure, often an evocation – as in Lawrence or Faulkner – frequently the celebration of character at bursting point: it approaches the mythical. Above all, more than the novelist who is sustained by his discursive manner, the writer of short stories has to catch our attention at once not only by the novelty of his people and scene but by the distinctiveness of his voice, and to hold us by the ingenuity of his design: for what we ask for is the sense that our now restless lives achieve shape at times and that our emotions have their architecture. Particularly in the writers of this century we also notice the sense of people as strangers. A modern story comes to an open end. People are left carrying the aftermath of their tale into a new day of which, alarmingly, they can as yet know nothing.

V. S. PRITCHETT

The Two Drovers

I

It was the day after Doune Fair when my story commences. It had been a brisk market; several dealers had attended from the northern and midland counties in England, and English money had flown so merrily about as to gladden the hearts of the Highland farmers. Many large droves were about to set off for England, under the protection of their owners, or of the topsmen whom they employed in the tedious, laborious, and responsible office of driving the cattle for many hundred miles, from the market where they had been purchased, to the fields or farmyards where they were to be fattened for the shambles.

The Highlanders, in particular, are masters of this difficult trade of driving, which seems to suit them as well as the trade of war. It affords exercise for all their habits of patient endurance and active exertion. They are required to know perfectly the drove-roads, which lie over the wildest tracts of the country, and to avoid as much as possible the highways, which distress the feet of the bullocks, and the turnpikes, which annoy the spirit of the drover; whereas, on the broad green or grey track, which leads across the pathless moor, the herd not only move at ease and without taxation, but, if they mind their business, may pick up a mouthful of food by the way. At night, the drovers usually sleep along with their cattle, let the weather be what it will; and many of these hardy men do not once rest under a roof during a journey on foot from Lochaber to Lincolnshire. They are paid very highly, for the trust reposed is of the last importance, as it depends on their prudence, vigilance, and honesty, whether the cattle reach the final market in good order, and afford a profit to the grazier. But as they maintain themselves at their own expense, they are especially economical in that particular. At the period we speak of, a Highland drover was victualled for his long and toilsome journey with a few handfuls of oatmeal, and two or three onions, renewed from time to time, and a ram's horn filled with whisky, which he used regularly, but sparingly, every night and morning. His dirk, or *skene-dhu* (i.e. black-knife), so worn as to be concealed beneath the arm, or by the folds of the plaid, was his only weapon, excepting the cudgel with which he directed the movements of the cattle. A Highlander was never so happy as on these occasions. There was a variety in the whole journey, which exercised the Celt's natural curiosity and love of motion; there were the constant change of place and scene, the petty adventures incidental to the traffic, and the intercourse with the various farmers, graziers, and traders, intermingled with occasional merry-makings, not the less acceptable to Donald that they were void of expense; – and there was the consciousness of superior skill; for the Highlander, a child amongst flocks, is a prince amongst herds, and his natural habits induce him to disdain the shepherd's slothful life, so that he feels himself nowhere more at home than when following a gallant drove of his country cattle in the character of their guardian.

Of the number who left Doune in the morning, and with the purpose we described, not a *Glunamie* of them all cocked his bonnet more briskly, or gartered his tartan hose under knee over a pair of more promising *spiogs* (legs) than did Robin Oig M'Combich, called familiarly Robin Oig, that is, Young, or the Lesser, Robin. Though small of stature, as the epithet Oig implies, and not very strongly limbed, he was as light and alert as one of the deer of his mountains. He had an elasticity of step which, in the course of a long march, made many a stout fellow envy him; and the manner in which he busked his plaid and adjusted his bonnet, argued a consciousness that so smart a John Highlandman as himself would not pass unnoticed among the Lowland lasses. The ruddy cheek, red lips, and white teeth, set off a countenance which had gained by exposure to the weather a healthful and hardy rather than a rugged hue. If Robin Oig did not laugh, or even smile frequently, as indeed is not the practice among his countrymen, his bright eyes usually gleamed from under his bonnet with an expression of cheerfulness ready to be turned into mirth.

The departure of Robin Oig was an incident in the little town, in and near which he had many friends, male and female. He was a topping person in his way, transacted considerable business on his own behalf, and was entrusted by the best farmers in the Highlands, in preference to any other drover in that district. He might have increased his business to any extent had he condescended to manage it by deputy; but except a lad or two, sister's sons of his own, Robin rejected the idea of assistance, conscious, perhaps, how much his reputation depended upon his attending in person to the practical discharge of his duty in every instance. He remained, therefore, contented with the highest premium given to persons of his description, and comforted himself with the hopes that a few journeys to England might enable him to conduct business on his own account, in a manner becoming his birth. For Robin Oig's father, Lachlan M'Combich (or *son of my friend*, his actual clan-surname being M'Gregor), had been so called by the celebrated Rob Roy, because of the particular friendship which had subsisted between the grandsire of Robin and that renowned cateran. Some people even say that Robin Oig derived his Christian name from one as renowned in the wilds of Loch Lomond as ever was his namesake Robin Hood, in the precincts of merry Sherwood. 'Of such ancestry,' as James Boswell says, 'who would not be proud?' Robin Oig was proud accordingly; but his frequent visits to England and to the Lowlands had given him tact enough to know that pretensions, which still gave him a little right to distinction in his own lonely glen, might be both obnoxious and ridiculous if preferred elsewhere. The pride of birth, therefore, was like the miser's treasure, the secret subject of his contemplation, but never exhibited to strangers as a subject of boasting.

Many were the words of gratulation and good luck which were bestowed on Robin Oig. The judges commended his drove, especially Robin's own property, which were the best of them. Some thrust out their snuff-mulls for the parting pinch — others tendered the *doch-an-dorrach*, or parting cup. All cried — 'Good luck travel out with you and come home with you. — Give you luck in the Saxon market — brave notes in the *leabhar-dhu*' (black pocketbook), 'and plenty of English gold in the *sporran*' (pouch of goatskin).

The bonny lasses made their adieus more modestly, and more than one, it was said, would have given her best brooch to be certain that it was upon her that his eye last rested as he turned towards the road.

Robin Oig had just given the preliminary '*Hoo-hoo!*' to urge forward the loiterers of the drove, when there was a cry behind him.

'Stay, Robin – bide a blink. Here is Janet of Tomahourich – auld Janet, your father's sister.'

'Plague on her, for an auld Highland witch and spaewife,' said a farmer from the Carse of Stirling; 'she'll cast some of her cantrips on the cattle.'

'She canna do that,' said another sapient of the same profession – 'Robin Oig is no the lad to leave any of them, without tying St Mungo's knot on their tails, and that will put to her speed the best witch that ever flew over Dimayet upon a broomstick.'

It may not be indifferent to the reader to know, that the Highland cattle are peculiarly liable to be *taken*, or infected, by spells and witchcraft; which judicious people guard against by knitting knots of peculiar complexity on the tuft of hair which terminates the animal's tail.

But the old woman who was the object of the farmer's suspicion, seemed only busied about the drover, without paying any attention to the drove. Robin, on the contrary, appeared rather impatient of her presence.

'What auld-world fancy', he said, 'has brought you so early from the ingle-side this morning, Muhme? I am sure I bid you good-even, and had your God-speed, last night.'

'And left me more siller than the useless old woman will use till you come back again, bird of my bosom,' said the sibyl. 'But it is little I would care for the food that nourishes me, or the fire that warms me, or for God's blessed sun itself, if aught but weel should happen to the grandson of my father. So let me walk the *deasil* round you, that you may go safe out into the foreign land, and come safe home.'

Robin Oig stopped, half embarrassed, half laughing, and signing to those near that he only complied with the old woman to soothe her humour. In the meantime, she traced around him, with wavering steps, the propitiation, which some have thought has been derived from the Druidical mythology. It consists, as is well known, in the person who makes the *deasil* walking three times around the person who is the object of the ceremony, taking care to move according to the course of the sun. At once, however, she stopped short, and exclaimed, in a voice of alarm and horror, 'Grandson of my father, there is blood on your hand.'

'Hush, for God's sake, aunt,' said Robin Oig; 'you will bring more trouble on yourself with this *taishataragh*' (second sight) 'than you will be able to get out of for many a day.'

The old woman only repeated, with a ghastly look, 'There is blood on your hand, and it is English blood. The blood of the Gael is richer and redder. Let us see—let us' –

Ere Robin Oig could prevent her, which, indeed, could only have been done by positive violence, so hasty and peremptory were her proceedings, she had drawn from his side the dirk which lodged in the folds of his plaid, and held it up, exclaiming, although the weapon gleamed clear and bright in the sun, 'Blood, blood – Saxon blood again. Robin Oig M'Combich, go not this day to England!'

'Prutt trutt,' answered Robin Oig, 'that will never do neither – it would be next thing to running the country. For shame, Muhme – give me the dirk. You cannot tell by the colour the difference betwixt the blood of a black bullock and a white one, and you speak of knowing Saxon from Gaelic blood. All men have their blood from Adam, Muhme. Give me my skene-dhu, and let me go on my road. I should have been halfway to Stirling Brig by this time. – Give me my dirk, and let me go.'

'Never will I give it to you,' said the old woman – 'Never will I quit my hold on your plaid, unless you promise me not to wear that unhappy weapon.'

The women around him urged him also, saying few of his aunt's words fell to the ground; and as the Lowland farmers continued to look moodily on the scene, Robin Oig determined to close it at any sacrifice.

'Well, then,' said the young drover, giving the scabbard of the weapon to Hugh Morrison, 'you Lowlanders care nothing for these freats. Keep my dirk for me. I cannot give it to you, because it was my father's; but your drove follows ours, and I am content it should be in your keeping, not in mine. – Will this do, Muhme?'

'It must,' said the old woman – 'that is, if the Lowlander is mad enough to carry the knife.'

The strong westlandman laughed aloud.

'Goodwife,' said he, 'I am Hugh Morrison from Glenae, come of the Manly Morrisons of auld langsyne, that never took short weapon against a man in their lives. And neither needed they. They had their broadswords, and I have this bit supple,' showing a formidable cudgel – 'for dirking ower the board, I leave that to John Highlandman – Ye needna snort, none of you Highlanders, and you in especial, Robin. I'll keep the bit knife, if you are feared for the auld spaewife's tale, and give it back to you whenever you want it.'

Robin was not particularly pleased with some part of Hugh Morrison's speech; but he had learned in his travels more patience than belonged to his Highland constitution originally, and he accepted the service of the descendant of the Manly Morrisons without finding fault with the rather depreciating manner in which it was offered.

'If he had not had his morning in his head, and been but a Dumfriesshire hog into the boot, he would have spoken more like a gentleman. But you cannot have more of a sow than a grumph. It's shame my father's knife should ever slash a haggis for the like of him.'

Thus saying (but saying it in Gaelic), Robin drove on his cattle, and waved farewell to all behind him. He was in the greater haste, because he expected to join at Falkirk a comrade and brother in profession, with whom he proposed to travel in company.

Robin Oig's chosen friend was a young Englishman, Harry Wakefield by name, well known at every northern market, and in his way as much famed and honoured as our Highland driver of bullocks. He was nearly six feet high, gallantly formed to keep the rounds at Smithfield, or maintain the ring at a wrestling match; and although he might have been overmatched, perhaps, among the regular professors of the Fancy, yet, as a yokel, or rustic, or a chance customer, he was able to give a bellyful to any amateur of the pugilistic art. Doncaster races saw him in his glory, betting his guinea, and generally successfully; nor was there a main fought in Yorkshire, the feeders being persons of celebrity, at which he was not to be seen, if business permitted. But though a *sprack* lad, and fond of pleasure and its haunts, Harry Wakefield was steady, and not the cautious Robin Oig M'Combich himself was more attentive to the main chance. His holidays were holidays indeed; but his days of work were dedicated to steady and persevering labour. In countenance and temper, Wakefield was the model of old England's merry yeomen, whose clothyard shafts, in so many hundred battles, asserted her superiority over the nations, and whose good sabres, in our own time, are her cheapest and most assured defence. His mirth was readily excited; for, strong in limb and constitution, and fortunate in circumstances, he was disposed to be pleased with

everything about him; and such difficulties as he might occasionally
encounter were, to a man of his energy, rather matter of amusement
than serious annoyance. With all the merits of a sanguine temper,
our young English drover was not without his defects. He was iras-
cible, sometimes to the verge of being quarrelsome; and perhaps
not the less inclined to bring his disputes to a pugilistic decision,
because he found few antagonists able to stand up to him in the
boxing ring.

It is difficult to say how Harry Wakefield and Robin Oig first
became intimates; but it is certain a close acquaintance had taken
place betwixt them, although they had apparently few common
subjects of conversation or of interest, so soon as their talk ceased
to be of bullocks. Robin Oig, indeed, spoke the English language
rather imperfectly upon any other topics but stots and kyloes, and
Harry Wakefield could never bring his broad Yorkshire tongue to
utter a single word of Gaelic. It was in vain Robin spent a whole
morning, during a walk over Minch Moor, in attempting to teach
his companion to utter, with true precision, the shibboleth *Llhu*,
which is the Gaelic for a calf. From Traquair to Murder-cairn, the
hill rang with the discordant attempts of the Saxon upon the un-
manageable monosyllable, and the heartfelt laugh which followed
every failure. They had, however, better modes of awakening the
echoes; for Wakefield could sing many a ditty to the praise of Moll,
Susan, and Cicely, and Robin Oig had a particular gift at whistling
interminable pibrochs through all their involutions, and what was
more agreeable to his companion's southern ear, knew many of the
northern airs, both lively and pathetic, to which Wakefield learned
to pipe a bass. Thus, though Robin could hardly have compre-
hended his companion's stories about horse-racing, and cock-fight-
ing or fox-hunting, and although his own legends of clan-fights and
creaghs, varied with talk of Highland goblins and fairy folk, would
have been caviare to his companion, they contrived nevertheless to
find a degree of pleasure in each other's company, which had for
three years back induced them to join company and travel together,
when the direction of their journey permitted. Each, indeed, found
his advantage in his companionship; for where could the Englishman have found a guide through the Western Highlands like Robin
Oig M'Combich? and when they were on what Harry called the
right side of the Border, his patronage, which was extensive, and

his purse, which was heavy, were at all times at the service of his Highland friend, and on many occasions his liberality did him genuine yeoman's service.

II

Were ever two such loving friends! –
  How could they disagree?
Oh thus it was, he loved him dear,
  And thought how to requite him,
And having no friend left but he,
  He did resolve to fight him. — *Duke upon Duke*

The pair of friends had traversed with their usual cordiality the grassy wilds of Liddesdale, and crossed the opposite part of Cumberland, emphatically called The Waste. In these solitary regions, the cattle under the charge of our drovers derived their subsistence chiefly by picking their food as they went along the drove-road, or sometimes by the tempting opportunity of a *start and owerloup*, or invasion of the neighbouring pasture, where an occasion presented itself. But now the scene changed before them; they were descending towards a fertile and enclosed country, where no such liberties could be taken with impunity, or without a previous arrangement and bargain with the possessors of the ground. This was more especially the case, as a great northern fair was upon the eve of taking place, where both the Scotch and English drover expected to dispose of a part of their cattle, which it was desirable to produce in the market, rested and in good order. Fields were therefore difficult to be obtained, and only upon high terms. This necessity occasioned a temporary separation betwixt the two friends, who went to bargain, each as he could, for the separate accommodation of his herd. Unhappily it chanced that both of them, unknown to each other, thought of bargaining for the ground they wanted on the property of a country gentleman of some fortune, whose estate lay in the neighbourhood. The English drover applied to the bailiff on the property, who was known to him. It chanced that the Cumbrian squire, who had entertained some suspicions of his manager's honesty, was taking occasional measures to ascertain how far they were well founded, and had desired that any inquiries about his enclosures, with a view to occupy them for a temporary purpose, should be referred to himself. As, however, Mr Ireby had gone the day before upon a journey of some miles' distance to the northward, the bailiff chose to consider the check upon his full powers as for the time removed, and concluded that he should best consult his master's interest, and perhaps his own, in making an agreement with Harry Wakefield. Meanwhile, ignorant of what his comrade was doing, Robin Oig, on his side, chanced to be overtaken by a good-looking smart little man upon a pony, most knowingly hogged and cropped, as was then the fashion, the rider wearing tight leather breeches and long-necked bright spurs. This cavalier asked one or two pertinent questions about markets and the price of stock. So Robin, seeing him a well-judging civil gentleman, took the freedom to ask him whether he could let him know if there was any grassland to be let in that neighbourhood, for the temporary accommodation of his drove. He could not have put the question to more willing ears. The gentleman of the buckskin was the proprietor with whose bailiff Harry Wakefield had dealt or was in the act of dealing.

'Thou art in good luck, my canny Scot,' said Mr Ireby, 'to have spoken to me, for I see thy cattle have done their day's work, and I have at my disposal the only field within three miles that is to be let in these parts.'

'The drove can pe gang two, three, four miles very pratty weel indeed,' said the cautious Highlander; 'put what would his honour be axing for the peasts pe the head, if she was to tak the park for twa or three days?'

'We won't differ, Sawney, if you let me have six stots for winterers, in the way of reason.'

'And which peasts wad your honour pe for having?'

'Why – let me see – the two black – the dun one – yon doddy – him with the twisted horn – the brocket – How much by the head?'

'Ah,' said Robin, 'your honour is a shudge – a real shudge – I couldna have set off the pest six peasts petter mysell, me that ken them as if they were my pairns, puir things.'

'Well, how much per head, Sawney?' continued Mr Ireby.

'It was high markets at Doune and Falkirk,' answered Robin.

And thus the conversation proceeded, until they had agreed on the *prix juste* for the bullocks, the squire throwing in the temporary accommodation of the enclosure for the cattle into the boot, and

Robin making, as he thought, a very good bargain, provided the grass was but tolerable. The squire walked his pony alongside of the drove, partly to show him the way, and see him put into possession of the field, and partly to learn the latest news of the northern markets.

They arrived at the field, and the pasture seemed excellent. But what was their surprise when they saw the bailiff quietly inducting the cattle of Harry Wakefield into the grassy Goshen which had just been assigned to those of Robin Oig M'Combich by the proprietor himself! Squire Ireby set spurs to his horse, dashed up to his servant, and learning what had passed between the parties, briefly informed the English drover that his bailiff had let the ground without his authority, and that he might seek grass for his cattle wherever he would, since he was to get none there. At the same time he rebuked his servant severely for having transgressed his commands, and ordered him instantly to assist in ejecting the hungry and weary cattle of Harry Wakefield, which were just beginning to enjoy a meal of unusual plenty, and to introduce those of his comrade, whom the English drover now began to consider as a rival.

The feelings which arose in Wakefield's mind would have induced him to resist Mr Ireby's decision; but every Englishman has a tolerably accurate sense of law and justice, and John Fleecebumpkin, the bailiff, having acknowledged that he had exceeded his commission, Wakefield saw nothing else for it than to collect his hungry and disappointed charge, and drive them on to seek quarters elsewhere. Robin Oig saw what had happened with regret, and hastened to offer to his English friend to share with him the disputed possession. But Wakefield's pride was severely hurt, and he answered disdainfully, 'Take it all, man – take it all – never make two bites of a cherry – thou canst talk over the gentry, and blear a plain man's eye – Out upon you, man – I would not kiss any man's dirty latchets for leave to bake in his oven.'

Robin Oig, sorry but not surprised at his comrade's displeasure, hastened to entreat his friend to wait but an hour till he had gone to the squire's house to receive payment for the cattle he had sold, and he would come back and help him to drive the cattle into some convenient place of rest, and explain to him the whole mistake they had both of them fallen into. But the Englishman continued indignant: 'Thou hast been selling, hast thou? Aye, aye, – thou is a cunning lad for kenning the hours of bargaining. Go to the devil with thyself, for I will ne'er see thy fause loon's visage again – thou should be ashamed to look me in the face.'

'I am ashamed to look no man in the face,' said Robin Oig, something moved; 'and, moreover, I will look you in the face this blessed day, if you will bide at the clachan down yonder.'

'Mayhap you had as well keep away,' said his comrade; and turning his back on his former friend, he collected his unwilling associates, assisted by the bailiff, who took some real and some affected interest in seeing Wakefield accommodated.

After spending some time in negotiating with more than one of the neighbouring farmers, who could not, or would not, afford the accommodation desired, Henry Wakefield at last, and in his necessity, accomplished his point by means of the landlord of the alehouse at which Robin Oig and he had agreed to pass the night, when they first separated from each other. Mine host was content to let him turn his cattle on a piece of barren moor, at a price little less than the bailiff had asked for the disputed enclosure; and the wretchedness of the pasture, as well as the price paid for it, were set down as exaggerations of the breach of faith and friendship of his Scottish crony. This turn of Wakefield's passions was encouraged by the bailiff (who had his own reasons for being offended against poor Robin, as having been the unwitting cause of his falling into disgrace with his master), as well as by the innkeeper, and two or three chance guests, who stimulated the drover in his resentment against his quondam associate, – some from the ancient grudge against the Scots which, when it exists anywhere, is to be found lurking in the Border counties, and some from the general love of mischief, which characterizes mankind in all ranks of life, to the honour of Adam's children be it spoken. Good John Barleycorn also, who always heightens and exaggerates the prevailing passions, be they angry or kindly, was not wanting in his offices on this occasion; and confusion to false friends and hard masters was pledged in more than one tankard.

In the meanwhile Mr Ireby found some amusement in detaining the northern drover at his ancient hall. He caused a cold round of beef to be placed before the Scot in the butler's pantry, together with a foaming tankard of home-brewed, and took pleasure in seeing the hearty appetite with which these unwonted edibles were discussed by Robin Oig M'Combich. The squire himself lighting his pipe, compounded between his patrician dignity and his love of agricultural gossip, by walking up and down while he conversed with his guest.

'I passed another drove,' said the squire, 'with one of your countrymen behind them – they were something less beasts than your drove, doddies most of them – a big man was with them – none of your kilts though, but a decent pair of breeches – D'ye know who he may be?'

'Hout aye – that might, could, and would be Hughie Morrison – I didna think he could hae peen saw weel up. He has made a day on us; but his Argyleshires will have wearied shanks. How far was he pehind?'

'I think about six or seven miles,' answered the squire, 'for I passed them at the Christenbury Crag, and I overtook you at the Hollan Bush. If his beasts be leg-weary, he will be maybe selling bargains.'

'Na, na, Hughie Morrison is no the man for pargains – ye maun come to some Highland body like Robin Oig hersell for the like of these – put I maun pe wishing you goot night, and twenty of them let alane ane, and I maun down to the Clachan to see if the lad Harry Waakfelt is out of his humdudgeons yet.'

The party at the ale-house were still in full talk, and the treachery of Robin Oig still the theme of conversation, when the supposed culprit entered the apartment. His arrival, as usually happens in such a case, put an instant stop to the discussion of which he had furnished the subject, and he was received by the company assembled with that chilling silence which, more than a thousand exclamations, tells an intruder that he is unwelcome. Surprised and offended, but not appalled by the reception which he experienced, Robin entered with an undaunted and even a haughty air, attempted no greeting as he saw he was received with none, and placed himself by the side of the fire, a little apart from a table at which Harry Wakefield, the bailiff, and two or three other persons, were seated. The ample Cumbrian kitchen would have afforded plenty of room, even for a larger separation.

Robin, thus seated, proceeded to light his pipe, and call for a pint of twopenny.

'We have no twopence ale,' answered Ralph Heskett, the landlord; 'but as thou find'st thy own tobacco, it's like thou may'st find thy own liquor too – it's the wont of thy country, I wot.'

'Shame, goodman,' said the landlady, a blithe bustling housewife, hastening herself to supply the guest with liquor – 'Thou knowest well enow what the strange man wants, and it's thy trade to be civil, man. Thou shouldst know, that if the Scot likes a small pot, he pays a sure penny.'

Without taking any notice of this nuptial dialogue, the High-lander took the flagon in his hand, and addressing the company generally, drank the interesting toast of 'Good markets', to the party assembled.

'The better that the wind blew fewer dealers from the north,' said one of the farmers, 'and fewer Highland runts to eat up the English meadows.'

'Saul of my pody, put you are wrang there, my friend,' answered Robin, with composure; 'it is your fat Englishmen that eat up our Scots cattle, puir things.'

'I wish there was a summat to eat up their drovers,' said another; 'a plain Englishman canna make bread within a kenning of them.'

'Or an honest servant keep his master's favour, but they will come sliding in between him and the sunshine,' said the bailiff.

'If these pe jokes,' said Robin Oig, with the same composure, 'there is ower mony jokes upon one man.'

'It is no joke, but downright earnest,' said the bailiff. 'Harkye, Mr Robin Ogg, or whatever is your name, it's right we should tell you that we are all of one opinion, and that is, that you, Mr Robin Ogg, have behaved to our friend Mr Harry Wakefield here, like a raff and a blackguard.'

'Nae doubt, nae doubt,' answered Robin, with great compusure; 'and you are a set of very pretty judges, for whose prains or pehav-iour I wad not gie a pinch of sneeshing. If Mr Harry Waakfelt kens where he is wranged, he kens where he may be righted.'

'He speaks truth,' said Wakefield, who had listened to what passed, divided between the offence which he had taken at Robin's late behaviour, and the revival of his habitual feelings of regard.

He now arose, and went towards Robin, who got up from his seat as he aproached, and held out his hand.

'That's right, Harry – go it – serve him out,' resounded on all sides – 'tip him the nailer – show him the mill.'

'Hold your peace all of you, and be – ,' said Wakefield; and then addressing his comrade, he took him by the extended hand, with something alike of respect and defiance. 'Robin,' he said, 'thou hast used me ill enough this day; but if you mean, like a frank fellow, to shake hands, and make a tussle for love on the sod, why I'll forgie thee, man, and we shall be better friends than ever.'

'And would it not pe petter to pe cood friends without more of the matter?' said Robin; 'we will be much petter friendships with our panes hale than proken.'

Harry Wakefield dropped the hand of his friend, or rather threw it from him.

'I did not think I had been keeping company for three years with a coward.'

'Coward pelongs to none of my name,' said Robin, whose eyes began to kindle, but keeping the command of his temper. 'It was no coward's legs or hands, Harry Waakfelt, that drew you out of the fords of Frew, when you was drifting ower the plack rock, and every eel in the river expected his share of you.'

'And that is true enough, too,' said the Englishman, struck by the appeal.

'Adzooks!' exclaimed the bailiff – 'sure Harry Wakefield, the nattiest lad at Whitson Tryste, Wooler Fair, Carlisle Sands, or Stag-shaw Bank, is not going to show white feather? Ah, this comes of living so long with kilts and bonnets – men forget the use of their daddles.'

'I may teach you, Master Fleecebumpkin, that I have not lost the use of mine,' said Wakefield, and then went on. 'This will never do, Robin. We must have a turn-up, or we shall be the talk of the countryside. I'll be d—d if I hurt thee – I'll put on the gloves gin thou like. Come, stand forward like a man.'

'To pe peaten like a dog,' said Robin; 'is there any reason in that? If you think I have done you wrong, I'll go before your shudge, though I neither know his law nor his language.'

A general cry of 'No, no – no law, no lawyer! a bellyful and be friends,' was echoed by the bystanders.

'But,' continued Robin, 'if I am to fight, I've no skill to fight like a jackanapes, with hands and nails.'

'How would you fight, then,' said his antagonist; 'though I am thinking it would be hard to bring you to the scratch anyhow.'

'I would fight with proadswords, and sink point on the first plood drawn – like a gentlemans.'

A loud shout of laughter followed the proposal, which indeed had rather escaped from poor Robin's swelling heart, than been the dictate of his sober judgement.

'Gentleman, quotha!' was echoed on all sides, with a shout of unextinguishable laughter; 'a very pretty gentleman, God wot – Canst get two swords for the gentlemen to fight with, Ralph Heskett?'

'No, but I can send to the armoury at Carlisle, and lend them two forks, to be making shift with in the meantime.'

'Tush, man,' said another, 'the bonny Scots come into the world with the blue bonnet on their heads, and dirk and pistol at their belt.'

'Best send post,' said Mr Fleecebumpkin, 'to the squire of Corby Castle, to come and stand second to the *gentleman.*'

In the midst of this torrent of general ridicule, the Highlander instinctively griped beneath the folds of his plaid.

'But it's better not,' he said in his own language. 'A hundred curses on the swine-eaters, who know neither decency nor civility!'

'Make room, the pack of you,' he said, advancing to the door.

But his former friend interposed his sturdy bulk, and opposed his leaving the house; and when Robin Oig attempted to make his way by force, he hit him down on the floor, with as much ease as a boy bowls down a nine-pin.

'A ring, a ring!' was now shouted, until the dark rafters, and the hams that hung on them, trembled again, and the very platters on the *bink* clattered against each other. 'Well done, Harry,' – 'Give it him home, Harry,' – 'Take care of him now, – he sees his own blood!'

Such were the exclamations, while the Highlander, starting from the ground, all his coldness and caution lost in frantic rage, sprang at his antagonist with the fury, the activity, and the vindictive purpose, of an incensed tiger-cat. But when could rage encounter science and temper? Robin Oig again went down in the unequal contest; and as the blow was necessarily a severe one, he lay motionless on the floor of the kitchen. The landlady ran to offer some aid, but Mr Fleecebumpkin would not permit her to approach.

'Let him alone,' he said, 'he will come to within time, and come up to the scratch again. He has not got half his broth yet.'

'He has got all I mean to give him, though,' said his antagonist, whose heart began to relent towards his old associate; 'and I would rather by half give the rest to yourself, Mr Fleecebumpkin, for you pretend to know a thing or two, and Robin had not art enough even to peel before setting to, but fought with his plaid dangling about him. – Stand up, Robin, my man! all friends now; and let me hear the man that will speak a word against you, or your country, for your sake.'

Robin Oig was still under the dominion of his passion, and eager to renew the onset; but being withheld on the one side by the peace-making Dame Heskett, and on the other, aware that Wakefield no longer meant to renew the combat, his fury sank into gloomy sullenness.

'Come, come, never grudge so much at it, man,' said the brave-spirited Englishman, with the placability of his country, 'shake hands, and we will be better friends than ever.'

'Friends!' exclaimed Robin Oig, with strong emphasis – 'friends! – Never. Look to yourself, Harry Waakfelt.'

'Then the curse of Cromwell on your proud Scots stomach, as the man says in the play, and you may do your worst, and be d—d; for one man can say nothing more to another after a tussle, than that he is sorry for it.'

On these terms the friends parted; Robin Oig drew out, in silence, a piece of money, threw it on the table, and then left the ale-house. But turning at the door, he shook his hand at Wake-field, pointing with his forefinger upwards, in a manner which might imply either a threat or a caution. He then disappeared in the moonlight.

Some words passed after his departure, between the bailiff, who piqued himself on being a little of a bully, and Harry Wakefield, who, with generous inconsistency, was now not indisposed to begin a new combat in defence of Robin Oig's reputation, 'although he could not use his daddles like an Englishman, as it did not come natural to him'. But Dame Heskett prevented this second quarrel from coming to a head by her peremptory interference. 'There should be no more fighting in her house,' she said; 'there had been too much already. – And you, Mr Wakefield, may live to learn,' she added, 'what it is to make a deadly enemy out of a good friend.'

'Pshaw, dame! Robin Oig is an honest fellow, and will never keep malice.'

'Do not trust to that – you do not know the dour temper of the Scots, though you have dealt with them so often. I have a right to know them, my mother being a Scot.'

'And so is well seen on her daughter,' said Ralph Heskett.

This nuptial sarcasm gave the discourse another turn; fresh customers entered the tap-room or kitchen, and others left it. The conversation turned on the expected markets, and the report of prices from different parts both of Scotland and England – treaties were commenced, and Harry Wakefield was lucky enough to find a chap for a part of his drove, and at a very considerable profit; an event of consequence more than sufficient to blot out all remembrances of the unpleasant scuffle in the earlier part of the day. But there remained one party from whose mind that recollection could not have been wiped away by the possession of every head of cattle betwixt Esk and Eden.

This was Robin Oig M'Combich. – 'That I should have had no weapon,' he said, 'and for the first time in my life! – Blighted be the tongue that bids the Highlander part with the dirk – the dirk – ha! the English blood! – My Muhme's word – when did her word fall to the ground?'

The recollection of the fatal prophecy confirmed the deadly intention which instantly sprang up in his mind.

'Ha! Morrison cannot be many miles behind; and if it were a hundred, what then?'

His impetuous spirit had now a fixed purpose and motive of action, and he turned the light foot of his country towards the wilds, through which he knew, by Mr Ireby's report, that Morrison was advancing. His mind was wholly engrossed by the sense of injury – injury sustained from a friend; and by the desire of vengeance on one whom he now accounted his most bitter enemy. The treasured ideas of self-importance and self-opinion – of ideal birth and quality, had become more precious to him, like the hoard to the miser, because he could only enjoy them in secret. But that hoard was pillaged, the idols which he had secretly worshipped had been desecrated and profaned. Insulted, abused, and beaten, he was no longer worthy, in his own opinion, of the name he bore, or the lineage which he belonged to – nothing was left to him – nothing but revenge; and, as the reflection added a galling spur to every step, he determined it should be as sudden and signal as the offence.

When Robin Oig left the door of the ale-house, seven or eight English miles at least lay betwixt Morrison and him. The advance of the former was slow, limited by the sluggish pace of his cattle; the last left behind him stubble-field and hedgerow, crag and dark heath, all glittering with frost-rime in the broad November moonlight, at the rate of six miles an hour. And now the distant lowing of Morrison's cattle is heard; and now they are seen creeping like moles in size and slowness of motion on the broad face of the moor; and now he meets them – passes them, and stops their conductor.

'May good betide us,' said the Southlander – 'Is this you, Robin M'Combich, or your wraith?'

'It is Robin Oig M'Combich,' answered the Highlander, 'and it is not. – But never mind that, put pe giving me the skene-dhu.'

'What! you are for back to the Highlands – The devil! – Have you selt all off before the fair? This beats all for quick markets!'

'I have not sold – I am not going north – May pe I will never go north again. – Give me pack my dirk, Hugh Morrison, or there will pe words petween us.'

'Indeed, Robin, I'll be better advised before I gie it back to you – it is a wanchancy weapon in a Highlandman's hand, and I am thinking you will be about some barns-breaking.'

'Prutt, trutt! let me have my weapon,' said Robin Oig, impatiently.

'Hooly, and fairly,' said his well-meaning friend. 'I'll tell you what will do better than these dirking doings – Ye ken Highlander, and Lowlander, and Border-men, are a' ae man's bairns when you are over the Scots dyke. See, the Eskdale callants, and fighting Charlie of Liddesdale, and the Lockerby lads, and the four Dandies of Lustruther, and a wheen mair grey plaids, are coming up behind, and if you are wranged, there is the hand of a Manly Morrison, we'll see you righted, if Carlisle and Stanwix baith took up the feud.'

'To tell you the truth,' said Robin Oig, desirous of eluding the suspicions of his friend, 'I have enlisted with a party of the Black Watch, and must march off tomorrow morning.'

'Enlisted! Were you mad or drunk? – You must buy yourself off – I can lend you twenty notes, and twenty to that, if the drove sell.'

'I thank you – thank ye, Hughie; but I go with good will the gate that I am going, – so the dirk – the dirk!'

'There it is for you then, since less wunna serve. But think on what I was saying. – Waes me, it will be sair news in the braes of Balquidder, that Robin Oig M'Combich should have run an ill gate, and ta'en on.'

'Ill news in Balquidder, indeed!' echoed poor Robin. 'But Cot speed you, Hughie, and send you good marcats. Ye winna meet with Robin Oig again, either at tryste or fair.'

So saying, he shook hastily the hand of his acquaintance, and set out in the direction from which he had advanced, with the spirit of his former pace.

'There is something wrang with the lad,' muttered the Morrison to himself, 'but we'll maybe see better into it the morn's morning.'

But long ere the morning dawned, the catastrophe of our tale had taken place. It was two hours after the affray had happened, and it was totally forgotten by almost everyone, when Robin Oig returned to Heskett's inn. The place was filled at once by various sorts of men, and with noises corresponding to their character. There were the grave low sounds of men engaged in busy traffic, with the laugh, the song, and the riotous jest of those who had nothing to do but to enjoy themselves. Among the last was Harry Wakefield, who, amidst a grinning group of smock-frocks, hob-nailed shoes, and jolly English physiognomies, was trolling forth the old ditty,

> What though my name be Roger,
> Who drives the plough and cart –

when he was interrupted by a well-known voice saying in a high stern tone, marked by the sharp Highland accent, 'Harry Waakfelt – if you be a man, stand up!'

'What is the matter? – what is it?' the guests demanded of each other.

'It is only a d—d Scotsman,' said Fleecebumpkin, who was by this time very drunk, 'whom Harry Wakefield helped to his broth the day, who is now come to have *his cauld kail* het again.'

'Harry Waakfelt,' repeated the same ominous summons, 'stand up, if you be a man!'

There is something in the tone of deep and concentrated passion, which attracts attention and imposes awe, even by the very sound. The guests shrank back on every side, and gazed at the Highlander as he stood in the middle of them, his brows bent, and his features rigid with resolution.

'I will stand up with all my heart, Robin, my boy, but it shall be to shake hands with you, and drink down all unkindness. It is not the fault of your heart, man, that you don't know how to clench your hands.'

But this time he stood opposite to his antagonist; his open and unsuspecting look strangely contrasted with the stern purpose, which gleamed wild, dark, and vindictive in the eyes of the Highlander.

''Tis not thy fault, man, that, not having the luck to be an Englishman, thou canst not fight more than a schoolgirl.'

'I *can* fight,' answered Robin Oig sternly, but calmly, 'and you shall know it. You, Harry Waakfelt, showed me today how the Saxon churls fight – I show you now how the Highland Dunnie-wassel fights.'

He seconded the word with the action, and plunged the dagger, which he suddenly displayed, into the broad breast of the English yeoman, with such fatal certainty and force, that the hilt made a hollow sound against the breastbone, and the double-edged point split the very heart of his victim. Harry Wakefield fell and expired with a single groan. His assassin next seized the bailiff by the collar, and offered the bloody poniard to his throat, whilst dread and surprise rendered the man incapable of defence.

'It were very just to lay you beside him,' he said, 'but the blood of a base pickthank shall never mix on my father's dirk with that of a brave man.'

As he spoke, he cast the man from him with so much force that he fell on the floor, while Robin, with his other hand, threw the fatal weapon into the blazing turf-fire.

'There,' he said, 'take me who likes – and let fire cleanse blood if it can.'

The pause of astonishment still continuing, Robin Oig asked for a peace-officer, and a constable having stepped out, he surrendered himself to his custody.

'A bloody night's work you have made of it,' said the constable.

'Your own fault,' said the Highlander. 'Had you kept his hands off me twa hours since, he would have been now as well and merry as he was twa minutes since.'

'It must be sorely answered,' said the peace-officer.

'Never you mind that – death pays all debts; it will pay that too.'

The horror of the bystanders began now to give way to indignation; and the sight of a favourite companion murdered in the midst of them, the provocation being, in their opinion, so utterly inadequate to the excess of vengeance, might have induced them to kill the perpetrator of the deed even upon the very spot. The constable, however, did his duty on this occasion, and with the assistance of some of the more reasonable persons present, procured horses to guard the prisoner to Carlisle, to abide his doom at the next assizes. While the escort was preparing, the prisoner neither expressed the least interest nor attempted the slightest reply. Only, before he was carried from the fatal apartment, he desired to look at the dead body, which, raised from the floor, had been deposited upon the large table (at the head of which Harry Wakefield had presided but a few minutes before, full of life, vigour, and animation) until the surgeons should examine the mortal wound. The face of the corpse was decently covered with a napkin. To the surprise and horror of the bystanders, which displayed itself in a general *Ah!* drawn through clenched teeth and half-shut lips, Robin Oig removed the cloth, and gazed with a mournful but steady eye on the lifeless visage, which had been so lately animated, that the smile of good-humoured confidence in his own strength, of conciliation at once and contempt towards his enemy, still curled his lips. While those present expected that the wound, which had so lately flooded the apartment with gore, would send forth fresh streams at the touch of the homicide, Robin Oig replaced the covering, with the brief exclamation – 'He was a pretty man!'

My story is nearly ended. The unfortunate Highlander stood his trial at Carlisle. I was myself present, and as a young Scottish lawyer, or barrister at least, and reputed a man of some quality, the politeness of the Sheriff of Cumberland offered me a place on the bench. The facts of the case were proved in the manner I have related them; and whatever might be at first the prejudice of the audience against a crime so un-English as that of assassination from revenge, yet when the rooted national prejudices of the prisoner had been explained, which made him consider himself as stained with indelible dishonour when subjected to personal violence; when his previous patience, moderation, and endurance, were considered, the generosity of the English audience was inclined to regard his crime as the wayward aberration of a false idea of honour rather than as flowing from a heart naturally savage, or perverted by habitual vice. I shall never forget the charge of the venerable judge to the jury, although not at that time liable to be much affected either by that which was eloquent or pathetic.

'We have had,' he said, 'in the previous part of our duty' (alluding to some former trials) 'to discuss crimes which infer disgust and abhorrence, while they call down the well-merited vengeance of the law. It is now our still more melancholy task to apply its salutary though severe enactments to a case of a very singular character, in which the crime (for a crime it is, and a deep one) arose less out of the malevolence of the heart, than the error of the understanding – less from any idea of committing wrong, than from an unhappily perverted notion of that which is right. Here we have two men, highly esteemed, it has been stated, in their rank of life, and attached, it seems, to each other as friends, one of whose lives has been already sacrificed to a punctilio, and the other is about to prove the vengeance of the offended laws; and yet both may claim our commiseration at least, as men acting in ignorance of each other's national prejudices, and unhappily misguided rather than voluntarily erring from the path of right conduct.

'In the original cause of the misunderstanding, we must in justice give the right to the prisoner at the bar. He had acquired possession of the enclosure, which was the object of competition, by a legal contract with the proprietor, Mr Ireby; and yet, when accosted with reproaches undeserved in themselves, and galling doubtless to a temper at least sufficiently susceptible of passion, he offered notwithstanding to yield up half his acquisition for the sake of peace and good neighbourhood, and his amicable proposal was rejected with scorn. Then follows the scene at Mr Heskett the publican's, and you will observe how the stranger was treated by the deceased, and, I am sorry to observe, by those around, who seem to have urged him in a manner which was aggravating in the highest degree. While he asked for peace and for composition, and offered submission to a magistrate, or to a mutual arbiter, the prisoner was insulted by a whole company, who seem on this occasion to have forgotten the national maxim of "fair play"; and while attempting to escape from the place in peace, he was intercepted, struck down, and beaten to the effusion of his blood.

'Gentlemen of the jury, it was with some impatience that I heard my learned brother, who opened the case for the crown, give an unfavourable turn to the prisoner's conduct on this occasion. He said the prisoner was afraid to encounter his antagonist in fair fight, or to submit to the laws of the ring; and that therefore, like a cowardly Italian, he had recourse to his fatal stiletto, to murder the man whom he dared not meet in manly encounter. I observed the prisoner shrink from this part of the accusation with the abhorrence natural to a brave man; and as I would wish to make my words impressive when I point his real crime, I must secure his opinion of my impartiality, by rebutting everything that seems to me a false accusation. There can be no doubt that the prisoner is a man of resolution – too much resolution – I wish to Heaven that he had less, or rather that he had had a better education to regulate it.

'Gentlemen, as to the laws my brother talks of, they may be known in the bull-ring, or the bear-garden, or the cockpit, but they are not known here. Or, if they should be so far admitted as furnishing a species of proof that no malice was intended in this sort of combat, from which fatal accidents do sometimes arise, it can only be so admitted when both parties are *in pari casu*, equally acquainted with, and equally willing to refer themselves to, that species of arbitrement. But will it be contended that a man of superior rank and education is to be subjected, or is obliged to subject himself, to this coarse and brutal strife, perhaps in opposition to a younger, stronger, or more skilful opponent? Certainly even the pugilistic code, if founded upon the fair play of Merry Old England, as my brother alleges it to be, can contain nothing so preposterous. And, gentlemen of the jury, if the laws would support an English gentleman, wearing, we will suppose, his sword, in defending himself by force against a violent personal aggression of the nature offered to this prisoner, they will not less protect a foreigner and a stranger, involved in the same unpleasing circumstances. If, therefore, gentlemen of the jury, when thus pressed by a *vis major*, the object of obloquy to a whole company, and of direct violence from one at least, and, as he might reasonably apprehend, from more, the panel had produced the weapon which his countrymen, as we are informed, generally carry about their persons, and the same unhappy circumstance had ensued which you have heard detailed in evidence, I could not in my conscience have asked from you a verdict of murder. The prisoner's personal defence might, indeed, even in that case, have gone more or less beyond the *Mo-*

deramen inculpatae tutelae, spoken of by lawyers, but the punishment incurred would have been that of manslaughter, not of murder. I beg leave to add that I should have thought this milder species
of charge was demanded in the case supposed, notwithstanding the
statute of James I, cap. 8, which takes the case of slaughter by
stabbing with a short weapon, even without malice prepense, out
of the benefit of clergy. For this statute of stabbing, as it is termed,
arose out of a temporary cause; and as the real guilt is the same,
whether the slaughter be committed by the dagger, or by sword or
pistol, the benignity of the modern law places them all on the same,
or nearly the same footing.

'But, gentlemen of the jury, the pinch of the case lies in the interval of two hours interposed betwixt the reception of the injury and
the fatal retaliation. In the heat of affray and *chaude mêlée,* law,
compassionating the infirmities of humanity, makes allowance for
the passions which rule such a stormy moment – for the sense of
present pain, for the apprehension of further injury, for the difficulty of ascertaining with due accuracy the precise degree of violence which is necessary to protect the person of the individual,
without annoying or injuring the assailant more than is absolutely
requisite. But the time necessary to walk twelve miles, however
speedily performed, was an interval sufficient for the prisoner to
have recollected himself; and the violence with which he carried his
purpose into effect, with so many circumstances of deliberate determination, could neither be induced by the passion of anger, nor
that of fear. It was the purpose and the act of predetermined revenge, for which law neither can, will nor ought to have sympathy
or allowance.

'It is true, we may repeat to ourselves, in alleviation of this poor
man's unhappy action, that his case is a very peculiar one. The
country which he inhabits, was, in the days of many now alive,
inaccessible to the laws, not only of England, which have not even
yet penetrated thither, but to those to which our neighbours of
Scotland are subjected, and which must be supposed to be, and no
doubt actually are, founded upon the general principles of justice
and equity which pervade every civilized country. Amongst their
mountains, as among the North American Indians, the various
tribes were wont to make war upon each other, so that each man
was obliged to go armed for his own protection. These men, from
the ideas which they entertained of their own descent and of their

own consequence, regarded themselves as so many cavaliers or men-at-arms, rather than as the peasantry of a peaceful country. Those laws of the ring, as my brother terms them, were unknown to the race of the warlike mountaineers; that decision of quarrels by no other weapons than those which nature has given every man, must to them have seemed as vulgar and as preposterous as to the noblesse of France. Revenge, on the other hand, must have been as familiar to their habits of society as to those of the Cherokees or Mohawks. It is indeed, as described by Bacon, at bottom a kind of wild untutored justice; for the fear of retaliation must withhold the hands of the oppressor where there is no regular law to check daring violence. But though all this may be granted, and though we may allow that, such having been the case of the Highlands in the days of the prisoner's fathers, many of the opinions and sentiments must still continue to influence the present generation, it cannot, and ought not, even in this most painful case, to alter the administration of the law, either in your hands, gentlemen of the jury, or in mine. The first object of civilization is to place the general protection of the law, equally administered, in the room of that wild justice, which every man cut and carved for himself, according to the length of his sword and the strength of his arm. The law says to the subjects, with a voice only inferior to that of the Deity, "Vengeance is mine". The instant that there is time for passion to cool, and reason to interpose, an injured party must become aware that the law assumes the exclusive cognizance of the right and wrong betwixt the parties, and opposes her inviolable buckler to every attempt of the private party to right himself. I repeat, that this unhappy man ought personally to be the object rather of our pity than our abhorrence, for he failed in his ignorance, and from mistaken notions of honour. But his crime is not the less that of murder, gentlemen, and, in your high and important office, it is your duty so to find. Englishmen have their angry passions as well as Scots; and should this man's action remain unpunished, you may unsheath, under various pretences, a thousand daggers betwixt the Land's-end and the Orkneys.'

The venerable judge thus ended what, to judge by his apparent emotion, and by the tears which filled his eyes, was really a painful task. The jury, according to his instructions, brought in a verdict of Guilty; and Robin Oig M'Combich, *alias* M'Gregor, was sentenced to death and left for execution, which took place accordingly. He met his fate with great firmness, and acknowledged the justice of his sentence. But he repelled indignantly the observations of those who accused him of attacking an unarmed man. 'I give a life for the life I took,' he said, 'and what can I do more?'

The Birthmark

In the latter part of the last century there lived a man of science, an eminent proficient in every branch of natural philosophy, who not long before our story opens had made experience of a spiritual affinity more attractive than any chemical one. He had left his laboratory to the care of an assistant, cleared his fine countenance from the furnace smoke, washed the stain of acids from his fingers, and persuaded a beautiful woman to become his wife. In those days when the comparatively recent discovery of electricity and other kindred mysteries of Nature seemed to open paths into the region of miracle, it was not unusual for the love of science to rival the love of woman in its depth and absorbing energy. The higher intellect, the imagination, the spirit, and even the heart might all find their congenial aliment in pursuits which, as some of their ardent votaries believed, would ascend from one step of powerful intelligence to another, until the philosopher should lay his hand on the secret of creative force and perhaps make new worlds for himself. We know not whether Aylmer possessed this degree of faith in man's ultimate control over Nature. He had devoted himself, however, too unreservedly to scientific studies ever to be weaned from them by any second passion. His love for his young wife might prove the stronger of the two; but it could only be by intertwining itself with his love of science, and uniting the strength of the latter to his own.

Such a union accordingly took place, and was attended with truly remarkable consequences and a deeply impressive moral. One day, very soon after their marriage, Aylmer sat gazing at his wife with a trouble in his countenance that grew stronger until he spoke.

'Georgiana,' said he, 'has it never occurred to you that the mark upon your cheek might be removed?'

'No, indeed,' said she, smiling; but perceiving the seriousness of his manner, she blushed deeply. 'To tell you the truth it has been so often called a charm that I was simple enough to imagine it might be so.'

'Ah, upon another face perhaps it might,' replied her husband; 'but never on yours. No, dearest Georgiana, you came so nearly perfect from the hand of Nature that this slightest possible defect, which we hesitate whether to term a defect or a beauty, shocks me, as being the visible mark of earthly imperfection.'

'Shocks you, my husband!' cried Georgiana, deeply hurt; at first reddening with momentary anger, but then bursting into tears. 'Then why did you take me from my mother's side? You cannot love what shocks you!'

To explain this conversation it must be mentioned that in the centre of Georgiana's left cheek there was a singular mark, deeply interwoven, as it were, with the texture and substance of her face. In the usual state of her complexion – a healthy though delicate bloom – the mark wore a tint of deeper crimson, which imperfectly defined its shape amid the surrounding rosiness. When she blushed it gradually became more indistinct, and finally vanished amid the triumphant rush of blood that bathed the whole cheek with its brilliant glow. But if any shifting motion caused her to turn pale there was the mark again, a crimson stain upon the snow, in what Aylmer sometimes deemed an almost fearful distinctness. Its shape bore not a little similarity to the human hand, though of the smallest pygmy size. Georgiana's lovers were wont to say that some fairy at her birth hour had laid her tiny hand upon the infant's cheek, and left this impress there in token of the magic endowments that were to give her such sway over all hearts. Many a desperate swain would have risked life for the privilege of pressing his lips to the mysterious hand. It must not be concealed, however, that the impression wrought by this fairy sign manual varied exceedingly, according to the difference of temperament in the beholders. Some fastidious persons – but they were exclusively of her own sex – affirmed that the bloody hand, as they chose to call it, quite destroyed the effect of Georgiana's beauty, and rendered her countenance even hideous. But it would be as reasonable to say that one of those small blue stains which sometimes occur in the purest statuary marble would convert the Eve of Powers to a monster. Masculine observers, if the birthmark did not heighten their admiration, contented themselves with wishing it away, that the world might possess one living specimen of ideal loveliness without the semblance of a flaw. After his marriage, – for he thought little or nothing of the matter before, – Aylmer discovered that this was the case with himself.

Had she been less beautiful, – if Envy's self could have found aught else to sneer at, – he might have felt his affection heightened by the prettiness of this mimic hand, now vaguely portrayed, now lost, now stealing forth again and glimmering to and fro with every pulse of emotion that throbbed within her heart; but seeing her otherwise so perfect, he found this one defect grow more and more intolerable with every moment of their united lives. It was the fatal flaw of humanity which Nature, in one shape or another, stamps ineffaceably on all her productions, either to imply that they are temporary and finite, or that their perfection must be wrought by toil and pain. The crimson hand expressed the ineludible gripe in which mortality clutches the highest and purest of earthly mould, degrading them into kindred with the lowest, and even with the very brutes, like whom their visible frames return to dust. In this manner, selecting it as the symbol of his wife's liability to sin, sorrow, decay, and death, Aylmer's sombre imagination was not long in rendering the birthmark a frightful object, causing him more trouble and horror than ever Georgiana's beauty, whether of soul or sense, had given him delight.

At all the seasons which should have been their happiest, he invariably and without intending it, nay, in spite of a purpose to the contrary, reverted to this one disastrous topic. Trifling as it at first appeared, it so connected itself with innumerable trains of thought and modes of feeling that it became the central point of all. With the morning twilight Aylmer opened his eyes upon his wife's face and recognized the symbol of imperfection; and when they sat together at the evening hearth his eyes wandered stealthily to her cheek, and beheld, flickering with the blaze of the wood fire, the spectral hand that wrote mortality where he would fain have worshipped. Georgiana soon learned to shudder at his gaze. It needed but a glance with the peculiar expression that his face often wore to change the roses of her cheek into a deathlike paleness, amid which the crimson hand was brought strongly out, like a bas-relief of ruby on the whitest marble.

Late one night when the lights were growing dim, so as hardly to betray the stain on the poor wife's cheek, she herself, for the first time, voluntarily took up the subject.

'Do you remember, my dear Aylmer,' said she, with a feeble attempt at a smile, 'have you any recollection of a dream last night about this odious hand?'

'None! none whatever!' replied Aylmer, starting; but then he added, in a dry, cold tone, affected for the sake of concealing the real depth of his emotion, 'I might well dream of it; for before I fell asleep it had taken a pretty firm hold of my fancy.'

'And you did dream of it?' continued Georgiana, hastily; for she dreaded lest a gush of tears should interrupt what she had to say. 'A terrible dream! I wonder that you can forget it. Is it possible to forget this one expression? — "It is in her heart now; we must have it out!" Reflect, my husband; for by all means I would have you recall that dream.'

The mind is in a sad state when Sleep, the all-involving, cannot confine her spectres within the dim region of her sway, but suffers them to break forth, affrighting this actual life with secrets that perchance belong to a deeper one. Aylmer now remembered his dream. He had fancied himself with his servant Aminadab, attempting an operation for the removal of the birthmark; but the deeper went the knife, the deeper sank the hand, until at length its tiny grasp appeared to have caught hold of Georgiana's heart; whence, however, her husband was inexorably resolved to cut or wrench it away.

When the dream had shaped itself perfectly in his memory, Aylmer sat in his wife's presence with a guilty feeling. Truth often finds its way to the mind close muffled in robes of sleep, and then speaks with uncompromising directness of matters in regard to which we practise an unconscious self-deception during our waking moments. Until now he had not been aware of the tyrannizing influence acquired by one idea over his mind, and of the lengths which he might find in his heart to go for the sake of giving himself peace.

'Aylmer,' resumed Georgiana, solemnly, 'I know not what may be the cost to both of us to rid me of this fatal birthmark. Perhaps its removal may cause cureless deformity; or it may be the stain goes as deep as life itself. Again: do we know that there is a possibility, on any terms, of unclasping the firm gripe of this little hand which was laid upon me before I came into the world?'

'Dearest Georgiana, I have spent much thought upon the subject,' hastily interrupted Aylmer. 'I am convinced of the perfect practicability of its removal.'

'If there be the remotest possibility of it,' continued Georgiana, 'let the attempt be made at whatever risk. Danger is nothing to me; for life, while this hateful mark makes me the object of your horror and disgust, – life is a burden which I would fling down with joy. Either remove this dreadful hand, or take my wretched life! You have deep science. All the world bears witness of it. You have achieved great wonders. Cannot you remove this little, little mark, which I cover with the tips of two small fingers? Is this beyond your power, for the sake of your own peace, and to save your poor wife from madness?'

'Noblest, dearest, tenderest wife,' cried Aylmer, rapturously, 'doubt not my power. I have already given this matter the deepest thought – thought which might almost have enlightened me to create a being less perfect than yourself. Georgiana, you have led me deeper than ever into the heart of science. I feel myself fully competent to render this dear cheek as faultless as its fellow; and then, most beloved, what will be my triumph when I shall have corrected what Nature left imperfect in her fairest work! Even Pygmalion, when his sculptured woman assumed life, felt not greater ecstasy than mine will be.'

'It is resolved, then,' said Georgiana, faintly smiling. 'And, Aylmer, spare me not, though you should find the birthmark take refuge in my heart at last.'

Her husband tenderly kissed her cheek – her right cheek – not that which bore the impress of the crimson hand.

The next day Aylmer apprised his wife of a plan that he had formed whereby he might have opportunity for the intense thought and constant watchfulness which the proposed operation would require; while Georgiana, likewise, would enjoy the perfect repose essential to its success. They were to seclude themselves in the extensive apartments occupied by Aylmer as a laboratory, and where, during his toilsome youth, he had made discoveries in the elemental powers of Nature that had roused the admiration of all the learned societies in Europe. Seated calmly in this laboratory, the pale philosopher had investigated the secrets of the highest cloud region and of the profoundest mines; he had satisfied himself of the causes that kindled and kept alive the fires of the volcano; and had explained the mystery of fountains, and how it is that they gush forth, some so bright and pure, and others with such rich medicinal virtues, from the dark bosom of the earth. Here, too, at an earlier period, he had studied the wonders of the human frame, and attempted to fathom the very process by which Nature assimilates all her precious influences from earth and air, and from the spiritual world, to create and foster man, her masterpiece. The latter pursuit, however, Aylmer had long laid aside in unwilling recognition of the truth – against which all seekers sooner or later stumble – that our great creative Mother, while she amuses us with apparently working in the broadest sunshine, is yet severely careful to keep her own secrets, and, in spite of her pretended openness, shows us nothing but results. She permits us, indeed, to mar, but seldom to mend, and, like a jealous patentee, on no account to make. Now, however, Aylmer resumed these half-forgotten investigations; not, of course, with such hopes or wishes as first suggested them; but because they involved much physiological truth and lay in the path of his proposed scheme for the treatment of Georgiana.

As he led her over the threshold of the laboratory, Georgiana was cold and tremulous. Aylmer looked cheerfully into her face, with intent to reassure her, but was so startled with the intense glow of the birthmark upon the whiteness of her cheek that he could not restrain a strong convulsive shudder. His wife fainted.

'Aminadab! Aminadab!' shouted Aylmer, stamping violently on the floor.

Forthwith there issued from an inner apartment a man of low stature, but bulky frame, with shaggy hair hanging about his visage, which was grimed with the vapors of the furnace. This personage had been Aylmer's underworker during his whole scientific career, and was admirably fitted for that office by his great mechanical readiness, and the skill with which, while incapable of comprehending a single principle, he executed all the details of his master's experiments. With his vast strength, his shaggy hair, his smoky aspect, and the indescribable earthiness that incrusted him, he seemed to represent man's physical nature; while Aylmer's slender figure, and pale, intellectual face, were no less apt a type of the spiritual element.

'Throw open the door of the boudoir, Aminadab,' said Aylmer, 'and burn a pastil.'

'Yes, master,' answered Aminadab, looking intently at the lifeless form of Georgiana; and then he muttered to himself, 'If she were my wife, I'd never part with that birthmark.'

When Georgiana recovered consciousness she found herself breathing an atmosphere of penetrating fragrance, the gentle potency of which had recalled her from her deathlike faintness. The scene around her looked like enchantment. Aylmer had converted those smoky, dingy, sombre rooms, where he had spent his brightest years in recondite pursuits, into a series of beautiful apartments not unfit to be the secluded abode of a lovely woman. The walls were hung with gorgeous curtains, which imparted the combination of grandeur and grace that no other species of adornment can achieve; and as they fell from the ceiling to the floor, their rich and ponderous folds, concealing all angles and straight lines, appeared to shut in the scene from infinite space. For aught Georgiana knew, it might be a pavilion among the clouds. And Aylmer, excluding the sunshine, which would have interfered with his chemical processes, had supplied its place with perfumed lamps, emitting flames of various hue, but all uniting in a soft, impurpled radiance. He now knelt by his wife's side, watching her earnestly, but without alarm; for he was confident in his science, and felt that he could draw a magic circle round her within which no evil might intrude.

'Where am I? Ah, I remember,' said Georgiana, faintly; and she placed her hand over her cheek to hide the terrible mark from her husband's eyes.

'Fear not, dearest!' exclaimed he. 'Do not shrink from me! Believe me, Georgiana, I even rejoice in this single imperfection, since it will be such a rapture to remove it.'

'Oh, spare me!' sadly replied his wife. 'Pray do not look at it again. I never can forget that convulsive shudder.'

In order to soothe Georgiana, and, as it were, to release her mind from the burden of actual things, Aylmer now put in practice some of the light and playful secrets which science had taught him among its profounder lore. Airy figures, absolutely bodiless ideas, and forms of unsubstantial beauty came and danced before her, imprinting their momentary footsteps on beams of light. Though she had some indistinct idea of the method of these optical phenomena, still the illusion was almost perfect enough to warrant the belief that her husband possessed sway over the spiritual world. Then again, when she felt a wish to look forth from her seclusion, immediately, as if her thoughts were answered, the procession of external existence flitted across a screen. The scenery and the figures of actual life were perfectly represented, but with that bewitching, yet indescribable difference which always makes a picture, an image, or a shadow so much more attractive than the original. When wearied of this, Aylmer bade her cast her eyes upon a vessel containing a quantity of earth. She did so, with little interest at first; but was soon startled to perceive the germ of a plant shooting upward from the soil. Then came the slender stalk; the leaves gradually unfolded themselves; and amid them was a perfect and lovely flower.

'It is magical!' cried Georgiana. 'I dare not touch it.'

'Nay, pluck it,' answered Aylmer, – 'pluck it, and inhale its brief perfume while you may. The flower will wither in a few moments and leave nothing save its brown seed vessels; but thence may be perpetuated a race as ephemeral as itself.'

But Georgiana had no sooner touched the flower than the whole plant suffered a blight, its leaves turning coal-black as if by the agency of fire.

'There was too powerful a stimulus,' said Aylmer, thoughtfully.

To make up for this abortive experiment, he proposed to take her portrait by a scientific process of his own invention. It was to be effected by rays of light striking upon a polished plate of metal. Georgiana assented; but, on looking at the result, was affrighted to find the features of the portrait blurred and indefinable; while the minute figure of a hand appeared where the cheek should have been. Aylmer snatched the metallic plate and threw it into a jar of corrosive acid.

Soon, however, he forgot these mortifying failures. In the intervals of study and chemical experiment he came to her flushed and exhausted, but seemed invigorated by her presence, and spoke in glowing language of the resources of his art. He gave a history of the long dynasty of the alchemists, who spent so many ages in quest of the universal solvent by which the golden principle might be elicited from all things vile and base. Aylmer appeared to believe that, by the plainest scientific logic, it was altogether within the limits of possibility to discover this long-sought medium; 'but,' he added, 'a philosopher who should go deep enough to acquire the power would attain too lofty a wisdom to stoop to the exercise of it'. Not less singular were his opinions in regard to the elixir vitae. He more than intimated that it was at his option to concoct a liquid that should prolong life for years, perhaps interminably; but that it would produce a discord in Nature which all the world, and chiefly the quaffer of the immortal nostrum, would find cause to curse.

'Aylmer, are you in earnest?' asked Georgiana, looking at him with amazement and fear. 'It is terrible to possess such power, or even to dream of possessing it.'

'Oh, do not tremble, my love,' said her husband. 'I would not wrong either you or myself by working such inharmonious effects upon our lives; but I would have you consider how trifling, in comparison, is the skill requisite to remove this little hand.'

At the mention of the birthmark, Georgiana, as usual, shrank as if a red-hot iron had touched her cheek.

Again Aylmer applied himself to his labors. She could hear his voice in the distant furnace room giving directions to Aminadab, whose harsh, uncouth, misshapen tones were audible in response, more like the grunt or growl of a brute than human speech. After hours of absence, Aylmer reappeared and proposed that she should now examine his cabinet of chemical products and natural treasures of the earth. Among the former he showed her a small vial, in which, he remarked, was contained a gentle yet most powerful fragrance, capable of impregnating all the breezes that blow across a kingdom. They were of inestimable value, the contents of that little vial; and, as he said so, he threw some of the perfume into the air and filled the room with piercing and invigorating delight.

'And what is this?' asked Georgiana, pointing to a small crystal globe containing a gold-colored liquid. 'It is so beautiful to the eye that I could imagine it the elixir of life.'

'In one sense it is,' replied Aylmer; 'or, rather, the elixir of immortality. It is the most precious poison that ever was concocted in this world. By its aid I could apportion the lifetime of any mortal at whom you might point your finger. The strength of the dose would determine whether he were to linger out years, or drop dead in the midst of a breath. No king on his guarded throne could keep his life if I, in my private station, should deem that the welfare of millions justified me in depriving him of it.'

'Why do you keep such a terrific drug?' inquired Georgiana in horror.

'Do not mistrust me, dearest,' said her husband, smiling; 'its virtuous potency is yet greater than its harmful one. But see! here is a powerful cosmetic. With a few drops of this in a vase of water, freckles may be washed away as easily as the hands are cleansed. A stronger infusion would take the blood out of the cheek, and leave the rosiest beauty a pale ghost.'

'Is it with this lotion that you intend to bathe my cheek?' asked Georgiana, anxiously.

'Oh, no,' hastily replied her husband; 'this is merely superficial. Your case demands a remedy that shall go deeper.'

In his interviews with Georgiana, Aylmer generally made minute inquiries as to her sensations and whether the confinement of the rooms and the temperature of the atmosphere agreed with her. These questions had such a particular drift that Georgiana began to conjecture that she was already subjected to certain physical influences, either breathed in with the fragrant air or taken with her food. She fancied likewise, but it might be altogether fancy, that there was a stirring up of her system – a strange, indefinite sensation creeping through her veins, and tingling, half painfully, half pleasurably, at her heart. Still, whenever she dared to look into the mirror, there she beheld herself pale as a white rose and with the crimson birthmark stamped upon her cheek. Not even Aylmer now hated it so much as she.

To dispel the tedium of the hours which her husband found it necessary to devote to the processes of combination and analysis, Georgiana turned over the volumes of his scientific library. In many dark old tomes she met with chapters full of romance and poetry. They were the works of the philosophers of the middle ages, such as Albertus Magnus, Cornelius Agrippa, Paracelsus, and the famous friar who created the prophetic Brazen Head. All these antique naturalists stood in advance of their centuries, yet were imbued with some of their credulity, and therefore were believed, and perhaps imagined themselves to have acquired from the investigation of Nature a power above Nature, and from physics a sway over the spiritual world. Hardly less curious and imaginative were the early volumes of the Transactions of the Royal Society, in which the members, knowing little of the limits of natural possibility, were continually recording wonders or proposing methods whereby wonders might be wrought.

But to Georgiana the most engrossing volume was a large folio from her husband's own hand, in which he had recorded every experiment of his scientific career, its original aim, the methods adopted for its development, and its final success or failure, with the circumstances to which either event was attributable. The book, in truth, was both the history and emblem of his ardent, ambitious, imaginative, yet practical and laborious life. He handled physical details as if there were nothing beyond them; yet spiritualized them all, and redeemed himself from materialism by his strong and eager aspiration towards the infinite. In his grasp the veriest clod of earth assumed a soul. Georgiana, as she read, reverenced Aylmer and loved him more profoundly than ever, but with a less entire dependence on his judgment than heretofore. Much as he had accomplished, she could not but observe that his most splendid successes were almost invariably failures, if compared with the ideal at which he aimed. His brightest diamonds were the merest pebbles, and felt to be so by himself, in comparison with the inestimable gems which lay hidden beyond his reach. The volume, rich with achievements that had won renown for its author, was yet as melancholy a record as ever mortal hand had penned. It was the sad confession and continual exemplification of the shortcomings of the composite man, the spirit burdened with clay and working in matter, and of the despair that assails the higher nature at finding itself so miserably thwarted by the earthly part. Perhaps every man of genius in whatever sphere might recognize the image of his own experience in Aylmer's journal.

So deeply did these reflections affect Georgiana that she laid her face upon the open volume and burst into tears. In this situation she was found by her husband.

'It is dangerous to read in a sorcerer's books,' said he, with a smile, though his countenance was uneasy and displeased. 'Georgiana, there are pages in that volume which I can scarcely glance over and keep my senses. Take heed lest it prove as detrimental to you.'

'It has made me worship you more than ever,' said she.

'Ah, wait for this one success,' rejoined he, 'then worship me if you will. I shall deem myself hardly unworthy of it. But come, I have sought you for the luxury of your voice. Sing to me, dearest.'

So she poured out the liquid music of her voice to quench the thirst of his spirit. He then took his leave with a boyish exuberance of gayety, assuring her that her seclusion would endure but a little longer, and that the result was already certain. Scarcely had he departed when Georgiana felt irresistibly impelled to follow him. She had forgotten to inform Aylmer of a symptom which for two or three hours past had begun to excite her attention. It was a sensation in the fatal birthmark, not painful, but which induced a restlessness throughout her system. Hastening after her husband, she intruded for the first time into the laboratory.

The first thing that struck her eye was the furnace, that hot and feverish worker, with the intense glow of its fire, which by the quantities of soot clustered above it seemed to have been burning for ages. There was a distilling apparatus in full operation. Around the room were retorts, tubes, cylinders, crucibles, and other apparatus of chemical research. An electrical machine stood ready for immediate use. The atmosphere felt oppressively close, and was tainted with gaseous odors which had been tormented forth by the processes of science. The severe and homely simplicity of the apartment, with its naked walls and brick pavement, looked strange, accustomed as Georgiana had become to the fantastic elegance of her boudoir. But what chiefly, indeed almost solely, drew her attention, was the aspect of Aylmer himself.

He was pale as death, anxious and absorbed, and hung over the furnace as if it depended upon his utmost watchfulness whether the liquid which it was distilling should be the draught of immortal happiness or misery. How different from the sanguine and joyous mien that he had assumed for Georgiana's encouragement!

'Carefully now, Aminadab; carefully, thou human machine; carefully, thou man of clay!' muttered Aylmer, more to himself than his assistant. 'Now, if there be a thought too much or too little, it is all over.'

'Ho! ho!' mumbled Aminadab. 'Look, master! look!'

Aylmer raised his eyes hastily, and at first reddened, then grew paler than ever, on beholding Georgiana. He rushed towards her and seized her arm with a gripe that left the print of his fingers upon it.

'Why do you come hither? Have you no trust in your husband?' cried he, impetuously. 'Would you throw the blight of that fatal birthmark over my labors? It is not well done. Go, prying woman, go!'

'Nay, Aylmer,' said Georgiana with the firmness of which she possessed no stinted endowment, 'it is not you that have a right to complain. You mistrust your wife; you have concealed the anxiety with which you watch the development of this experiment. Think not so unworthily of me, my husband. Tell me all the risk we run,

and fear not that I shall shrink; for my share in it is far less than
your own.'

'No, no, Georgiana!' said Aylmer, impatiently, 'it must not be.'

'I submit,' replied she calmly. 'And, Aylmer, I shall quaff whatever draught you bring me; but it will be on the same principle that
would induce me to take a dose of poison if offered by your hand.'

'My noble wife,' said Aylmer, deeply moved, 'I knew not the
height and depth of your nature until now. Nothing shall be concealed. Know, then, that this crimson hand, superficial as it seems,
has clutched its grasp into your being with a strength of which I
had no previous conception. I have already administered agents
powerful enough to do aught except to change your entire physical
system. Only one thing remains to be tried. If that fail us we are
ruined.'

'Why did you hesitate to tell me this?' asked she.

'Because, Georgiana,' said Aylmer, in a low voice, 'there is
danger.'

'Danger? There is but one danger – that this horrible stigma shall
be left upon my cheek!' cried Georgiana. 'Remove it, remove it,
whatever be the cost, or we shall both go mad!'

'Heaven knows your words are too true,' said Aylmer, sadly.
'And now, dearest, return to your boudoir. In a little while all will
be tested.'

He conducted her back and took leave of her with a solemn tenderness which spoke far more than his words how much was now
at stake. After his departure Georgiana became rapt in musings.
She considered the character of Aylmer, and did it completer justice
than at any previous moment. Her heart exulted, while it trembled,
at his honorable love – so pure and lofty that it would accept nothing less than perfection nor miserably make itself contented with
an earthlier nature than he had dreamed of. She felt how much
more precious was such a sentiment than that meaner kind which
would have borne with the imperfection for her sake, and have
been guilty of treason to holy love by degrading its perfect idea to
the level of the actual; and with her whole spirit she prayed that,
for a single moment, she might satisfy his highest and deepest conception. Longer than one moment she well knew it could not be;
for his spirit was ever on the march, ever ascending, and each instant required something that was beyond the scope of the instant
before.

The sound of her husband's footsteps aroused her. He bore a crystal goblet containing a liquor colorless as water, but bright enough to be the draught of immortality. Aylmer was pale; but it seemed rather the consequence of a highly-wrought state of mind and tension of spirit than of fear or doubt.

'The concoction of the draught has been perfect,' said he, in answer to Georgiana's look. 'Unless all my science have deceived me, it cannot fail.'

'Save on your account, my dearest Aylmer,' observed his wife, 'I might wish to put off this birthmark of mortality by relinquishing mortality itself in preference to any other mode. Life is but a sad possession to those who have attained precisely the degree of moral advancement at which I stand. Were I weaker and blinder it might be happiness. Were I stronger, it might be endured hopefully. But, being what I find myself, methinks I am of all mortals the most fit to die.'

'You are fit for heaven without tasting death!' replied her husband. 'But why do we speak of dying? The draught cannot fail. Behold its effect upon this plant.'

On the window seat there stood a geranium diseased with yellow blotches, which had overspread all its leaves. Aylmer poured a small quantity of the liquid upon the soil in which it grew. In a little time, when the roots of the plant had taken up the moisture, the unsightly blotches began to be extinguished in a living verdure.

'There needed no proof,' said Georgiana, quietly. 'Give me the goblet. I joyfully stake all upon your word.'

'Drink, then, thou lofty creature!' exclaimed Aylmer, with fervid admiration. 'There is no taint of imperfection on thy spirit. Thy sensible frame, too, shall soon be all perfect.'

She quaffed the liquid and returned the goblet to his hand.

'It is grateful,' said she with a placid smile. 'Methinks it is like water from a heavenly fountain, for it contains I know not what of unobtrusive fragrance and deliciousness. It allays a feverish thirst that had parched me for many days. Now, dearest, let me sleep. My earthly senses are closing over my spirit like the leaves around the heart of a rose at sunset.'

She spoke the last words with a gentle reluctance, as if it required almost more energy than she could command to pronounce the faint and lingering syllables. Scarcely had they loitered through her lips ere she was lost in slumber. Aylmer sat by her side, watching her aspect with the emotions proper to a man the whole value of whose existence was involved in the process now to be tested. Mingled with this mood, however, was the philosophic investigation characteristic of the man of science. Not the minutest symptom escaped him. A heightened flush of the cheek, a slight irregularity of breath, a quiver of the eyelid, a hardly perceptible tremor through the frame, – such were the details which, as the moments passed, he wrote down in his folio volume. Intense thought had set its stamp upon every previous page of that volume, but the thoughts of years were all concentrated upon the last.

While thus employed, he failed not to gaze often at the fatal hand, and not without a shudder. Yet once, by a strange and unaccountable impulse, he pressed it with his lips. His spirit recoiled, however, in the very act; and Georgiana, out of the midst of her deep sleep, moved uneasily and murmured as if in remonstrance. Again Aylmer resumed his watch. Nor was it without avail. The crimson hand, which at first had been strongly visible upon the marble paleness of Georgiana's cheek, now grew more faintly outlined. She remained not less pale than ever; but the birthmark, with every breath that came and went, lost somewhat of its former distinctness. Its presence had been awful; its departure was more awful still. Watch the stain of the rainbow fading out of the sky, and you will know how that mysterious symbol passed away.

'By Heaven! it is well-nigh gone!' said Aylmer to himself, in almost irrepressible ecstasy. 'I can scarcely trace it now. Success! success! And now it is like the faintest rose color. The lightest flush of blood across her cheek would overcome it. But she is so pale!'

He drew aside the window curtain and suffered the light of natural day to fall into the room and rest upon her cheek. At the same time he heard a gross, hoarse chuckle, which he had long known as his servant Aminadab's expression of delight.

'Ah, clod! ah, earthly mass!' cried Aylmer, laughing in a sort of frenzy, 'you have served me well! Matter and spirit – earth and heaven – have both done their part in this! Laugh, thing of the senses! You have earned the right to laugh.'

These exclamations broke Georgiana's sleep. She slowly unclosed her eyes and gazed into the mirror which her husband had arranged for that purpose. A faint smile flitted over her lips when she recognized how barely perceptible was now that crimson hand which had once blazed forth with such disastrous brilliancy as to scare away all their happiness. But then her eyes sought Aylmer's face with a trouble and anxiety that he could by no means account for.

'My poor Aylmer!' murmured she.

'Poor? Nay, richest, happiest, most favored!' exclaimed he. 'My peerless bride, it is successful! You are perfect!'

'My poor Aylmer,' she repeated, with a more than human tenderness, 'you have aimed loftily; you have done nobly. Do not repent that with so high and pure a feeling, you have rejected the best the earth could offer. Aylmer, dearest Aylmer, I am dying!'

Alas! it was too true! The fatal hand had grappled with the mystery of life, and was the bond by which an angelic spirit kept itself in union with a mortal frame. As the last crimson tint of the birthmark — that sole token of human imperfection — faded from her cheek, the parting breath of the now perfect woman passed into the atmosphere, and her soul, lingering a moment near her husband, took its heavenward flight. Then a hoarse, chuckling laugh was heard again! Thus ever does the gross fatality of earth exult in its invariable triumph over the immortal essence which, in this dim sphere of half development, demands the completeness of a higher state. Yet, had Aylmer reached a profounder wisdom, he need not thus have flung away the happiness which would have woven his mortal life of the selfsame texture with the celestial. The momentary circumstance was too strong for him; he failed to look beyond the shadowy scope of time, and, living once for all in eternity, to find the perfect future in the present.

EDGAR ALLAN POE · 1809–1849

The Fall of the House of Usher

Son cœur est un luth suspendu;
Sitôt qu'on le touche il résonne. – *De Béranger*

During the whole of a dull, dark, and soundless day in the autumn
of the year, when the clouds hung oppressively low in the heavens,
I had been passing alone, on horseback, through a singularly
dreary tract of country; and at length found myself, as the shades
of evening drew on, within view of the melancholy House of Usher.
I know not how it was – but, with the first glimpse of the building,
a sense of insufferable gloom pervaded my spirit. I say insufferable;
for the feeling was unrelieved by any of that half-pleasurable, because poetic, sentiment, with which the mind usually receives even
the sternest natural images of the desolate or terrible. I looked upon
the scene before me – upon the mere house, and the simple landscape features of the domain – upon the bleak walls – upon the
vacant eye-like windows – upon a few rank sedges – and upon a
few white trunks of decayed trees – with an utter depression of soul
which I can compare to no earthly sensation more properly than to
the after dream of the reveler upon opium – the bitter lapse into
everyday life – the hideous dropping off of the veil. There was an
iciness, a sinking, a sickening of the heart – an unredeemed dreari-
ness of thought which no goading of the imagination could torture
into aught of the sublime. What was it – I paused to think – what
was it that so unnerved me in the contemplation of the House of
Usher? It was a mystery all insoluble; nor could I grapple with the
shadowy fancies that crowded upon me as I pondered. I was forced
to fall back upon the unsatisfactory conclusion, that while, beyond
doubt, there *are* combinations of very simple natural objects which
have the power of thus affecting us, still the analysis of this power
lies among considerations beyond our depth. It was possible, I reflected, that a mere different arrangement of the particulars of the
scene, of the details of the picture, would be sufficient to modify,

or perhaps to annihilate its capacity for sorrowful impression; and, acting upon this idea, I reined my horse to the precipitous brink of a black and lurid tarn that lay in unruffled luster by the dwelling, and gazed down – but with a shudder even more thrilling than before – upon the remodeled and inverted images of the gray sedge, and the ghastly tree-stems, and the vacant and eye-like windows.

Nevertheless, in this mansion of gloom I now proposed to myself a sojourn of some weeks. Its proprietor, Roderick Usher, had been one of my boon companions in boyhood; but many years had elapsed since our last meeting. A letter, however, had lately reached me in a distant part of the country – a letter from him – which, in its wildly importunate nature, had admitted of no other than the personal reply. The MS. gave evidence of nervous agitation. The writer spoke of acute bodily illness – of a mental disorder which oppressed him – and of an earnest desire to see me, as his best, and indeed his only personal friend, with a view to attempting, by the cheerfulness of my society, some alleviation of his malady. It was the manner in which all this, and much more, was said – it was the apparent *heart* that went with his request – which allowed me no room for hesitation; and I accordingly obeyed forthwith what I still considered a very singular summons.

Although, as boys, we had been even intimate associates, yet I really knew little of my friend. His reserve had always been excessive and habitual. I was aware, however, that his very ancient family had been noted, time out of mind, for a peculiar sensibility of temperament, displaying itself, through long ages, in many works of exalted art, and manifested of late in repeated deeds of munificent yet unobtrusive charity, as well as in a passionate devotion to the intricacies, perhaps even more than to the orthodox and easily recognizable beauties of musical science. I had learned, too, the very remarkable fact, that the stem of the Usher race, all time-honored as it was, had put forth at no period any enduring branch; in other words, that the entire family lay in the direct line of descent, and had always, with very trifling and very temporary variation, so lain. It was this deficiency, I considered, while running over in thought the perfect keeping of the character of the premises with the accredited character of the people, and while speculating upon the possible influence which the one, in the long lapse of centuries, might have exercised upon the other – it was this deficiency, perhaps, of collateral issue, and the consequent undeviating transmission from sire to son of the patrimony with the name, which had at length so identified the two as to merge the original title of the estate in the quaint and equivocal appellation of the 'House of Usher' – an appellation which seemed to include, in the minds of the peasantry who used it, both the family and the family mansion.

I have said that the sole effect of my somewhat childish experiment – that of looking down within the tarn – had been to deepen the first singular impression. There can be no doubt that the consciousness of the rapid increase of my superstition – for why should I not so term it? – served mainly to accelerate the increase itself. Such, I have long known, is the paradoxical law of all sentiments having terror as a basis. And it might have been for this reason only, that, when I again uplifted my eyes to the house itself from its image in the pool, there grew in my mind a strange fancy – a fancy so ridiculous, indeed, that I but mention it to show the vivid force of the sensations which oppressed me. I had so worked upon my imagination as really to believe that about the whole mansion and domain there hung an atmosphere peculiar to themselves and their immediate vicinity – an atmosphere which had no affinity with the air of heaven, but which had reeked up from the decayed trees, and the gray wall, and the silent tarn – a pestilent and mystic vapor, dull, sluggish, faintly discernible, and leaden-hued.

Shaking off from my spirit what *must* have been a dream, I scanned more narrowly the real aspect of the building. Its principal feature seemed to be that of an excessive antiquity. The discoloration of ages had been great. Minute fungi overspread the whole exterior, hanging in a fine tangled webwork from the eaves. Yet all this was apart from any extraordinary dilapidation. No portion of the masonry had fallen; and there appeared to be a wild inconsistency between its still perfect adaptation of parts and the crumbling condition of the individual stones. In this there was much that reminded me of the specious totality of old woodwork which has rotted for long years in some neglected vault, with no disturbance from the breath of the external air. Beyond this indication of extensive decay, however, the fabric gave little token of instability. Perhaps the eye of a scrutinizing observer might have discovered a barely perceptible fissure, which, extending from the roof of the building in front, made its way down the wall in a zigzag direction, until it became lost in the sullen waters of the tarn.

Noticing these things, I rode over a short causeway to the house. A servant in waiting took my horse, and I entered the Gothic archway of the hall. A valet, of stealthy step, thence conducted me, in silence, through many dark and intricate passages in my progress to the studio of his master. Much that I encountered on the way contributed, I know not how, to heighten the vague sentiments of which I have already spoken. While the objects around me – while the carvings of the ceilings, the somber tapestries of the walls, the ebon blackness of the floors, and the phantasmagoric armorial trophies which rattled as I strode, were but matters to which, or to such as which, I had been accustomed from my infancy – while I hesitated not to acknowledge how familiar was all this – I still wondered to find how unfamiliar were the fancies which ordinary images were stirring up. On one of the staircases I met the physician of the family. His countenance, I thought, wore a mingled expression of low cunning and perplexity. He accosted me with trepidation and passed on. The valet now threw open a door and ushered me into the presence of his master.

The room in which I found myself was very large and lofty. The windows were long, narrow, and pointed, and at so vast a distance from the black oaken floor as to be altogether inaccessible from within. Feeble gleams of encrimsoned light made their way through the trellised panes, and served to render sufficiently distinct the more prominent objects around; the eye, however, struggled in vain to reach the remoter angles of the chamber, or the recesses of the vaulted and fretted ceiling. Dark draperies hung upon the walls. The general furniture was profuse, comfortless, antique, and tattered. Many books and musical instruments lay scattered about, but failed to give any vitality to the scene. I felt that I breathed an atmosphere of sorrow. An air of stern, deep, and irredeemable gloom hung over and pervaded all.

Upon my entrance, Usher arose from a sofa on which he had been lying at full length, and greeted me with a vivacious warmth which had much in it, I at first thought, of an overdone cordiality – of the constrained effort of the *ennuyé* man of the world. A glance, however, at his countenance, convinced me of his perfect sincerity. We sat down; and for some moments, while he spoke not, I gazed upon him with a feeling half of pity, half of awe. Surely, man had never before so terribly altered, in so brief a period, as had Roderick Usher! It was with difficulty that I could bring myself to admit the identity of the wan being before me with the companion of my early boyhood. Yet the character of his face had been at all times remarkable. A cadaverousness of complexion; an eye large, liquid, and luminous beyond comparison; lips somewhat thin and very pallid, but of a surpassingly beautiful curve; a nose of a delicate Hebrew model, but with a breadth of nostril unusual in similar formations; a finely molded chin, speaking, in its want of prominence, of a want of moral energy; hair of a more than weblike softness and tenuity – these features, with an inordinate expansion above the regions of the temple, made up altogether a countenance not easily to be forgotten. And now in the mere exaggeration of the prevailing character of these features, and of the expression they were wont to convey, lay so much of change that I doubted to whom I spoke. The now ghastly pallor of the skin, and the now miraculous luster of the eye, above all things startled and even awed me. The silken hair, too, had been suffered to grow all unheeded, and as, in its wild gossamer texture, it floated rather than fell about the face, I could not, even with effort, connect its Arabesque expression with any idea of simple humanity.

In the manner of my friend I was at once struck with an incoherence – an inconsistency; and I soon found this to arise from a series of feeble and futile struggles to overcome an habitual trepidancy – an excessive nervous agitation. For something of this nature I had indeed been prepared, no less by his letter, than by reminiscences of certain boyish traits, and by conclusions deduced from his peculiar physical conformation and temperament. His action was alternately vivacious and sullen. His voice varied rapidly from a tremulous indecision (when the animal spirits seemd utterly in abeyance) to that species of energetic concision – that abrupt, weighty, unhurried, and hollow-sounding enunciation – that leaden, self-balanced, and perfectly modulated guttural utterance, which may be observed in the lost drunkard, or the irreclaimable eater of opium, during the periods of his most intense excitement.

It was thus that he spoke of the object of my visit, of his earnest desire to see me, and of the solace he expected me to afford him. He entered, at some length, into what he conceived to be the nature of his malady. It was, he said, a constitutional and a family evil, and one for which he despaired to find a remedy – a mere nervous affection, he immediately added, which would undoubtedly soon pass off. It displayed itself in a host of unnatural sensations. Some of these, as he detailed them, interested and bewildered me; although, perhaps, the terms and the general manner of the narration had their weight. He suffered much from a morbid acuteness of the senses; the most insipid food was alone endurable; he could wear only garments of certain texture; the odors of all flowers were oppressive; his eyes were tortured by even a faint light; and there were but peculiar sounds, and these from stringed instruments, which did not inspire him with horror.

To an anomalous species of terror I found him a bounden slave. 'I shall perish,' said he, 'I *must* perish in this deplorable folly. Thus, thus, and not otherwise, shall I be lost. I dread the events of the future, not in themselves, but in their results. I shudder at the thought of any, even the most trivial, incident, which may operate upon this intolerable agitation of soul. I have, indeed, no abhorrence of danger, except in its absolute effect – in terror. In this unnerved – in this pitiable condition – I feel that the period will sooner or later arrive when I must abandon life and reason together in some struggle with the grim phantasm, FEAR.'

I learned, moreover, at intervals, and through broken and equivocal hints, another singular feature of his mental condition. He was enchained by certain superstitious impressions in regard to the dwelling which he tenanted, and whence, for many years, he had never ventured forth – in regard to an influence whose suppositious force was conveyed in terms too shadowy here to be restated – an influence which some peculiarities in the mere form and substance of his family mansion had, by dint of long sufferance, he said, obtained over his spirit – an effect which the *physique* of the gray walls and turrets, and of the dim tarn into which they all looked down, had at length brought about upon the *morale* of his existence.

He admitted, however, although with hesitation, that much of the peculiar gloom which thus afflicted him could be traced to a more natural and far more palpable origin – to the severe and long-continued illness, indeed to the evidently approaching dissolution, of a tenderly beloved sister, his sole companion for long years, his last and only relative on earth. 'Her decease,' he said, with a bitterness which I can never forget, 'would leave him (him the hopeless and the frail) the last of the ancient race of the Ushers.' While he spoke, the Lady Madeline (for so was she called) passed slowly through a remote portion of the apartment, and, without having noticed my presence, disappeared. I regarded her with an utter astonishment not unmingled with dread – and yet I found it impossible to account for such feelings. A sensation of stupor oppressed me, as my eyes followed her retreating steps. When a door at length closed upon her, my glance sought instinctively and eagerly the countenance of the brother – but he had buried his face in his hands, and I could only perceive that a far more than ordinary wanness had overspread the emaciated fingers through which trickled many passionate tears.

The disease of the Lady Madeline had long baffled the skill of her physicians. A settled apathy, a gradual wasting away of the person, and frequent although transient affections of a partially cataleptical character, were the unusual diagnosis. Hitherto she had steadily borne up against the pressure of her malady, and had not betaken herself finally to bed; but, on the closing in of the evening of my arrival at the house, she succumbed (as her brother told me at night with inexpressible agitation) to the prostrating power of the destroyer; and I learned that the glimpse I had obtained of her person would thus probably be the last I should obtain – that the lady, at least while living, would be seen by me no more.

For several days ensuing, her name was unmentioned by either Usher or myself; and during this period I was busied in earnest endeavors to alleviate the melancholy of my friend. We painted and read together; or I listened, as if in a dream, to the wild improvisations of his speaking guitar. And thus, as a closer and still closer intimacy admitted me more unreservedly into the recesses of his spirit, the more bitterly did I perceive the futility of all attempt at cheering a mind from which darkness, as if an inherent positive quality, poured forth upon all objects of the moral and physical universe, in one unceasing radiation of gloom.

I shall ever bear about me a memory of the many solemn hours I thus spent alone with the master of the House of Usher. Yet I should fail in any attempt to convey an idea of the exact character of the studies, or of the occupations, in which he involved me, or led me the way. An excited and highly distempered ideality threw a sulphureous luster over all. His long improvised dirges will ring for ever in my ears. Among other things, I hold painfully in mind a certain singular perversion and amplification of the wild air of the last waltz of Von Weber. From the paintings over which his elaborate fancy brooded, and which grew, touch by touch, into vaguenesses at which I shuddered the more thrillingly, because I shuddered knowing not why – from these paintings (vivid as their images now are before me) I would in vain endeavor to educe more than a small portion which should lie within the compass of merely written words. By the utter simplicity, by the nakedness of his designs, he arrested and overawed attention. If ever mortal painted an idea, that mortal was Roderick Usher. For me at least – in the circumstances then surrounding me – there arose out of the pure abstractions which the hypochondriac contrived to throw upon his canvas, an intensity of intolerable awe, no shadow of which felt I ever yet in the contemplation of the certainly glowing yet too concrete reveries of Fuseli.

One of the phantasmagoric conceptions of my friend, partaking not so rigidly of the spirit of abstraction, may be shadowed forth, although feebly, in words. A small picture presented the interior of an immensely long and rectangular vault or tunnel, with low walls, smooth, white, and without interruption or device. Certain accessory points of the design served well to convey the idea that this excavation lay at an exceeding depth below the surface of the earth. No outlet was observed in any portion of its vast extent, and no torch, or other artificial source of light, was discernible; yet a flood of intense rays rolled throughout, and bathed the whole in a ghastly and inappropriate splendor.

I have just spoken of that morbid condition of the auditory nerve which rendered all music intolerable to the sufferer, with the exception of certain effects of stringed instruments. It was, perhaps, the narrow limits to which he thus confined himself upon the guitar, which gave birth, in great measure, to the fantastic character of his performances. But the fervid *facility* of his *impromptus* could not be so accounted for. They must have been, and were, in the notes as well as in the words of his wild fantasias (for he not unfrequently accompanied himself with rhymed verbal improvisations), the result of that intense mental collectedness and concentration to which I have previously alluded as observable only in particular moments of the highest artificial excitement. The words of one of these rhapsodies I have easily remembered. I was, perhaps, the more forcibly impressed with it as he gave it, because, in the under or mystic current of its meaning, I fancied that I perceived, and for the first time, a full consciousness on the part of Usher, of the tottering of his lofty reason upon her throne. The verses, which were entitled 'The Haunted Palace', ran very nearly, if not accurately, thus:

I

In the greenest of our valleys,
    By good angels tenanted,
Once a fair and stately palace —
    Radiant palace – reared its head.
In the monarch Thought's dominion —
    It stood there!
Never seraph spread a pinion
    Over fabric half so fair.

II

Banners yellow, glorious, golden,
    On its roof did float and flow
(This – all this – was in the olden
    Time long ago);
And every gentle air that dallied,
    In that sweet day,
Along the ramparts plumed and pallid,
    A winged odor went away.

III

Wanderers in that happy valley
    Through two luminous windows saw
Spirits moving musically
    To a lute's well-tunèd law,
Round about a throne, where sitting
    (Porphyrogene!)
In state his glory well befitting,
    The ruler of the realm was seen.

IV

And all with pearl and ruby glowing
    Was the fair palace door,
Through which came flowing, flowing, flowing,
    And sparkling evermore,
A troop of Echoes, whose sweet duty
    Was but to sing,
In voices of surpassing beauty,
    The wit and wisdom of their king.

V

But evil things, in robes of sorrow,
Assailed the monarch's high estate;
(Ah, let us mourn, for never morrow
Shall dawn upon him, desolate!)
And, round about his home, the glory
That blushed and bloomed
Is but a dim-remembered story
Of the old time entombed.

VI

And travelers now within that valley,
Through the red-litten windows, see
Vast forms that move fantastically
To a discordant melody;
While, like a rapid ghastly river,
Through the pale door,
A hideous throng rush out forever,
And laugh — but smile no more.

I well remember that suggestions arising from this ballad led us into a train of thought wherein there became manifest an opinion of Usher's, which I mention not so much on account of its novelty (for other men have thought thus), as on account of the pertinacity with which he maintained it. This opinion, in its general form, was that of the sentience of all vegetable things. But, in his disordered fancy, the idea had assumed a more daring character, and trespassed, under certain conditions, upon the kingdom of inorganization. I lack words to express the full extent, or the earnest *abandon* of his persuasion. The belief, however, was connected (as I have previously hinted) with the grey stones of the home of his forefathers. The conditions of the sentience had been here, he imagined, fulfilled in the method of collocation of these stones — in the order of their arrangement, as well as in that of the many fungi which overspread them, and of the decayed trees which stood around — above all, in the long undisturbed endurance of this arrangement, and in its reduplication in the still waters of the tarn. Its evidence — the evidence of the sentience — was to be seen, he said (and I here started as he spoke), in the gradual yet certain condensation of an atmosphere of their own about the waters and the walls. The result was discoverable, he added, in that silent, yet importunate and terrible influence which for centuries had molded the destinies of his family, and which made *him* what I now saw him – what he was. Such opinions need no comment, and I will make none.

Our books – the books which, for years, had formed no small portion of the mental existence of the invalid – were, as might be supposed, in strict keeping with this character of phantasm. We pored together over such works as the *Ververt et Chartreuse* of Gresset; the *Belphegor* of Machiavelli; the *Heaven and Hell* of Swedenborg; the *Subterranean Voyage of Nicholas Klimn* by Holberg; the *Chiromancy* of Robert Flud, of Jean D'Indaginé, and of De la Chambre; the *Journey into the Blue Distance* of Tieck; and the *City of the Sun* of Campanella. One favorite volume was a small octavo edition of the *Directorium Inquisitorum*, by the Dominican Eymeric de Gironne; and there were passages in Pomponius Mela, about the old African Satyrs and Aegipans, over which Usher would sit dreaming for hours. His chief delight, however, was found in the perusal of an exceedingly rare and curious book in quarto Gothic – the manual of a forgotten church – the *Vigiliae Mortuorum secundum Chorum Ecclesiae Maguntinae.*

I could not help thinking of the wild ritual of this work, and of its probable influence upon the hypochondriac, when, one evening, having informed me abruptly that the Lady Madeline was no more, he stated his intention of preserving her corpse for a fortnight (previously to its final interment), in one of the numerous vaults within the main walls of the building. The worldly reason, however, assigned for this singular proceeding, was one which I did not feel at liberty to dispute. The brother had been led to his resolution (so he told me) by consideration of the unusual character of the malady of the deceased, of certain obtrusive and eager inquiries on the part of her medical men, and of the remote and exposed situation of the burial-ground of the family. I will not deny that when I called to mind the sinister countenance of the person whom I met upon the staircase, on the day of my arrival at the house, I had no desire to oppose what I regarded as at best but a harmless, and by no means an unnatural, precaution.

At the request of Usher, I personally aided him in the arrangements for the temporary entombment. The body having been encoffined, we two alone bore it to its rest. The vault in which we placed it (and which had been so long unopened that our torches, half smothered in its oppressive atmosphere, gave us little opportunity for investigation) was small, damp, and entirely without means of admission for light; lying, at great depth, immediately beneath that portion of the building in which was my own sleeping apartment. It had been used, apparently, in remote feudal times, for the worst purposes of a donjonkeep, and, in later days, as a place of deposit for powder, or some other highly combustible substance, as a portion of its floor, and the whole interior of a long archway through which we reached it, were carefully sheathed with copper. The door, of massive iron, had been also similarly protected. Its immense weight caused an unusually sharp grating sound as it moved upon its hinges.

Having deposited our mournful burden upon tressels within this region of horror, we partially turned aside the yet unscrewed lid of the coffin, and looked upon the face of the tenant. A striking similitude between the brother and sister now first arrested my attention; and Usher, divining, perhaps, my thoughts, murmured out some few words from which I learned that the deceased and himself had been twins, and that sympathies of a scarcely intelligible nature had always existed between them. Our glances, however, rested not long upon the dead – for we could not regard her unawed. The disease which had thus entombed the lady in the maturity of youth, had left, as usual in all maladies of a strictly cataleptical character, the mockery of a faint blush upon the bosom and the face, and that suspiciously lingering smile upon the lip which is so terrible in death. We replaced and screwed down the lid, and, having secured the door of iron, made our way, with toil, into the scarcely less gloomy apartments of the upper portion of the house.

And now, some days of bitter grief having elapsed, an observable change came over the features of the mental disorder of my friend. His ordinary manner had vanished. His ordinary occupations were neglected or forgotten. He roamed from chamber to chamber with hurried, unequal, and objectless step. The pallor of his countenance had assumed, if possible, a more ghastly hue – but the luminousness of his eye had utterly gone out. The once occasional huskiness of his tone was heard no more; and a tremulous quaver, as if of extreme terror, habitually characterized his utterance. There were times, indeed, when I thought his unceasingly agitated mind was laboring with some oppressive secret, to divulge which he struggled for the necessary courage. At times, again, I was obliged to resolve all into the mere inexplicable vagaries of madness, for I beheld him gazing upon vacancy for long hours, in an attitude of the profoundest attention, as if listening to some imaginary sound. It was no wonder that his condition terrified – that it infected me. I felt creeping upon me, by slow yet certain degrees, the wild influences of his own fantastic yet impressive superstitions.

It was, especially, upon retiring to bed late in the night of the seventh or eighth day after the placing of the Lady Madeline within the donjon, that I experienced the full power of such feelings. Sleep came not near my couch, while the hours waned and waned away. I struggled to reason off the nervousness which had dominion over me. I endeavored to believe that much, if not all of what I felt, was due to the bewildering influence of the gloomy furniture of the room – of the dark and tattered draperies, which, tortured into motion by the breath of a rising tempest, swayed fitfully to and fro upon the walls, and rustled uneasily about the decorations of the bed. But my efforts were fruitless. An irrepressible tremor gradually pervaded my frame; and, at length, there sat upon my very heart an incubus of utterly causeless alarm. Shaking this off with a gasp and a struggle, I uplifted myself upon the pillows, and, peering earnestly within the intense darkness of the chamber, hearkened – I know not why, except that an instinctive spirit prompted me – to certain low and indefinite sounds which came, through the pauses of the storm, at long intervals, I knew not whence. Overpowered by an intense sentiment of horror, unaccountable yet unendurable, I threw on my clothes with haste (for I felt I should sleep no more during the night), and endeavored to arouse myself from the pitiable condition into which I had fallen, by pacing rapidly to and fro through the apartment.

I had taken but few turns in this manner, when a light step on an adjoining staircase arrested my attention. I presently recognized it as that of Usher. In an instant afterward he rapped, with a gentle touch, at my door, and entered bearing a lamp. His countenance was, as usual, cadaverously wan – but, moreover, there was a species of mad hilarity in his eyes – an evidently restrained hysteria in his whole demeanor. His air appalled me – but anything was preferable to the solitude which I had so long endured, and I even welcomed his presence as a relief.

'And you have not seen it?' he said abruptly, after having stared about him for some moments in silence – 'you have not then seen it? – but, stay! you shall.' Thus speaking, and having carefully shaded his lamp, he hurried to one of the casements, and threw it freely open to the storm.

The impetuous fury of the entering gust nearly lifted us from our feet. It was, indeed, a tempestuous yet sternly beautiful night, and one wildly singular in its terror and its beauty. A whirlwind had apparently collected its force in our vicinity, for there were frequent and violent alterations in the direction of the wind; and the exceeding density of the clouds (which hung so low as to press upon the turrets of the house) did not prevent our perceiving the life-like velocity with which they flew careering from all points against each other, without passing away into the distance. I say that even their exceeding density did not prevent our perceiving this; yet we had no glimpse of the moon or stars, nor was there any flashing forth of the lightning. But the under surfaces of the huge masses of agitated vapor, as well as all terrestrial objects immediately around us, were glowing in the unnatural light of a faintly luminous and distinctly visible gaseous exhalation which hung about and enshrouded the mansion.

'You must not – you shall not behold this!' said I, shudderingly, to Usher, as I led him with a gentle violence from the window to a seat. 'These appearances, which bewilder you, are merely electrical phenomena not uncommon – or it may be that they have their ghastly origin in the rank miasma of the tarn. Let us close this casement – the air is chilling and dangerous to your frame. Here is one of your favorite romances. I will read, and you shall listen – and so we will pass away this terrible night together.'

The antique volume which I had taken up was the *Mad Trist* of Sir Launcelot Canning, but I had called it a favorite of Usher's more in sad jest than in earnest; for, in truth, there is little in its uncouth and unimaginative prolixity which could have had interest for the lofty and spiritual ideality of my friend. It was, however, the only book immediately at hand; and I indulged a vague hope that the excitement which now agitated the hypochondriac, might find relief (for the history of mental disorder is full of similar anomalies) even in the extremeness of the folly which I should read. Could I have judged, indeed, by the wild overstrained air of vivacity with which he hearkened, or apparently hearkened, to the words of the tale, I might well have congratulated myself upon the success of my design.

I had arrived at that well-known portion of the story where Ethelred, the hero of the *Trist*, having sought in vain for peaceable admission into the dwelling of the hermit, proceeds to make good an entrance by force. Here, it will be remembered, the words of the narrative run thus:

'And Ethelred, who was by nature of a doughty heart, and who was now mighty withal, on account of the powerfulness of the wine which he had drunken, waited no longer to hold parley with the hermit, who, in sooth, was of an obstinate and maliceful turn, but, feeling the rain upon his shoulders, and fearing the rising of the tempest, uplifted his mace outright, and, with blows, made quickly room in the plankings of the door for his gauntleted hand; and now pulling therewith sturdily, he so cracked, and ripped, and tore all asunder, that the noise of the dry and hollow-sounding wood alarumed and reverberated throughout the forest.'

At the termination of this sentence I started, and for a moment paused; for it appeared to me (although I at once concluded that my excited fancy had deceived me) – it appeared to me that, from some very remote portion of the mansion, there came, indistinctly, to my ears, what might have been, in its exact similarity of character, the echo (but a stifled and dull one certainly) of the very cracking and ripping sound which Sir Launcelot had so particularly described. It was, beyond doubt, the coincidence alone which had arrested my attention; for, amid the rattling of the sashes of the casements, and the ordinary commingled noises of the still increasing storm, the sound, in itself, had nothing, surely, which should have interested or disturbed me. I continued the story:

'But the good champion Ethelred, now entering within the door, was sore enraged and amazed to perceive no signal of the maliceful hermit; but, in the stead thereof, a dragon of a scaly and prodigious demeanor, and of a fiery tongue, which sate in guard before a palace of gold, with a floor of silver; and upon the wall there hung a shield of shining brass with this legend enwritten:

Who entereth herein, a conqueror hath bin;
Who slayeth the dragon, the shield he shall win.

And Ethelred uplifted his mace, and struck upon the head of the dragon, which fell before him, and gave up his pesty breath, with a shriek so horrid and harsh, and withal so piercing, that Ethelred had fain to close his ears with his hands against the dreadful noise of it, the like whereof was never before heard.'

Here again I paused abruptly, and now with a feeling of wild amazement – for there could be no doubt whatever that, in this instance, I did actually hear (although from what direction it proceeded I found it impossible to say) a low and apparently distant, but harsh, protracted, and most unusual screaming or grating sound – the exact counterpart of what my fancy had already conjured up for the dragon's unnatural shriek as described by the romancer.

Oppressed as I certainly was, upon the occurrence of this second and most extraordinary coincidence, by a thousand conflicting sensations, in which wonder and extreme terror were predominant, I still retained sufficient presence of mind to avoid exciting, by any observation, the sensitive nervousness of my companion. I was by no means certain that he had noticed the sound in question; although, assuredly, a strange alteration had, during the last few minutes, taken place in his demeanor. From a position fronting my own, he had gradually brought round his chair, so as to sit with his face to the door of the chamber; and thus I could but partially perceive his features, although I saw that his lips trembled as if he were murmuring inaudibly. His head had dropped upon his breast – yet I knew that he was not asleep, from the wide and rigid opening of the eye as I caught a glance of it in profile. The motion of his body, too, was at variance with this idea – for he rocked from side to side with a gentle yet constant and uniform sway. Having rapidly taken notice of all this, I resumed the narrative of Sir Launcelot, which thus proceeded:

'And now, the champion, having escaped from the terrible fury of the dragon, bethinking himself of the brazen shield, and of the breaking up of the enchantment which was upon it, removed the carcass from out of the way before him, and approached valorously over the silver pavement of the castle to where the shield was upon the wall; which in sooth tarried not for his full coming, but fell down at his feet upon the silver floor, with a mighty great and terrible ringing sound.'

No sooner had these syllables passed my lips than – as if a shield of brass had indeed, at the moment, fallen heavily upon a floor of silver – I became aware of a distinct, hollow, metallic, and clangorous, yet apparently muffled reverberation. Completely unnerved, I leaped to my feet; but the measured rocking movement of Usher was undisturbed. I rushed to the chair in which he sat. His eyes were bent fixedly before him, and throughout his whole countenance there reigned a stony rigidity. But, as I placed my hand upon his shoulder, there came a strong shudder over his whole person; a sickly smile quivered about his lips; and I saw that he spoke in a low, hurried, and gibbering murmur, as if unconscious of my presence. Bending closely over him, I at length drank in the hideous import of his words.

'Not hear it? – yes, I hear it, and *have* heard it. Long – long – long – many minutes, many hours, many days, have I heard it – yet I dared not – oh, pity me, miserable wretch that I am! – I dared not – I *dared* not speak! *We have put her living in the tomb!* Said I not that my senses were acute? I *now* tell you that I heard her first feeble movements in the hollow coffin. I heard them – many, many days ago – yet I dared not – *I dared not speak!* And now – tonight – Ethelred – ha! ha! – the breaking of the hermit's door, and the death-cry of the dragon, and the clangor of the shield! – say, rather, the rending of her coffin, and the grating of the iron hinges of her prison, and her struggles within the coppered archway of the vault! Oh, whither shall I fly? Will she not be here anon? Is she not hurrying to upbraid me for my haste? Have I not heard her footstep on the stair? Do I not distinguish that heavy and horrible beating of her heart? Madman!' – here he sprang furiously to his feet, and shrieked out his syllables, as if in the effort he were giving up his soul – '*Madman! I tell you that she now stands without the door!*'

As if in the superhuman energy of his utterance there had been found the potency of a spell, the huge antique panels to which the speaker pointed threw slowly back, upon the instant, their ponderous and ebony jaws. It was the work of the rushing gust – but then without those doors there *did* stand the lofty and enshrouded figure of the Lady Madeline of Usher. There was blood upon her white robes, and the evidence of some bitter struggle upon every portion of her emaciated frame. For a moment she remained trembling and reeling to and fro upon the threshold – then, with a low moaning cry, fell heavily inward upon the person of her brother, and in her violent and now final death-agonies, bore him to the floor a corpse, and a victim to the terrors he had anticipated.

From that chamber, and from that mansion, I fled aghast. The storm was still abroad in all its wrath as I found myself crossing the old causeway. Suddenly there shot along the path a wild light, and I turned to see whence a gleam so unusual could have issued;

for the vast house and its shadows were alone behind me. The radiance was that of the full, setting, and blood-red moon, which now shone vividly through that once barely discernible fissure, of which I have before spoken as extending from the roof of the building, in a zigzag direction, to the base. While I gazed, this fissure rapidly widened – there came a fierce breath of the whirlwind – the entire orb of the satellite burst at once upon my sight – my brain reeled as I saw the mighty walls rushing asunder – there was a long tumultuous shouting sound like a voice of a thousand waters – and the deep and dank tarn at my feet closed sullenly and silently over the fragments of the 'House of Usher'.

The Celebrated Jumping Frog
of Calaveras County

In compliance with the request of a friend of mine, who wrote me from the East, I called on good-natured, garrulous old Simon Wheeler, and inquired after my friend's friend, *Leonidas W.* Smiley, as requested to do, and I hereunto append the result. I have a lurking suspicion that *Leonidas W.* Smiley is a myth; that my friend never knew such a personage; and that he only conjectured that, if I asked old Wheeler about him, it would remind him of his infamous *Jim* Smiley, and he would go to work and bore me nearly to death with some infernal reminiscence of him as long and tedious as it should be useless to me. If that was the design, it certainly succeeded.

I found Simon Wheeler dozing comfortably by the bar-room stove of the old, dilapidated tavern in the ancient mining camp of Angel's, and I noticed that he was fat, and bald-headed, and had an expression of winning gentleness and simplicity upon his tranquil countenance. He roused up and gave me good day. I told him a friend of mine had commissioned me to make some inquiries about a cherished companion of his boyhood, named *Leonidas W.* Smiley – Rev. *Leonidas W.* Smiley, a young minister of the gospel, who he had heard was at one time a resident of Angel's Camp. I added that, if Mr Wheeler could tell me anything about this Rev. Leonidas W. Smiley, I would feel under many obligations to him.

Simon Wheeler backed me into a corner, and blockaded me there with his chair, and then sat me down and reeled off the monotonous narrative which follows this paragraph. He never smiled, he never frowned, he never changed his voice from the gentle-flowing key to which he tuned the initial sentence, he never betrayed the slightest suspicion of enthusiasm; but all through the interminable narrative there ran a vein of impressive earnestness and sincerity, which showed me plainly that, so far from his imagining that there was anything ridiculous or funny about his story, he regarded it as a really important matter, and admired its two heroes as men of transcendent genius in *finesse*. To me, the spectacle of a man drifting serenely along through such a queer yarn without ever smiling, was exquisitely absurd. As I said before, I asked him to tell me what he knew of Rev. Leonidas W. Smiley, and he replied as follows. I let him go on in his own way, and never interrupted him once:

There was a feller here once by the name of *Jim* Smiley in the winter of '49 – or may be it was the spring of '50 – I don't recollect exactly, somehow, though what makes me think it was one or the other is because I remember the big flume wasn't finished when he first came to the camp; but anyway, he was the curiosest man about, always betting on anything that turned up you ever see, if he could get anybody to bet on the other side; and if he couldn't, he'd change sides. Anyway that suited the other man would suit him – anyway just so's he got a bet, *he* was satisfied. But still he was lucky, uncommon lucky; he most always come out winner. He was always ready and laying for a chance; there couldn't be no solit'ry thing mentioned but that feller'd offer to bet on it, and take any side you please, as I was just telling you. If there was a horse-race, you'd find him flush, or you'd find him busted at the end of it; if there was a dog-fight, he'd bet on it; if there was a cat-fight, he'd bet on it; if there was a chicken-fight, he'd bet on it; why, if there was two birds sitting on a fence, he would bet you which one would fly first; or if there was a camp-meeting, he would be there reg'lar, to bet on Parson Walker, which he judged to be the best exhorter about here, and so he was, too, and a good man. If he even seen a straddle-bug start to go anywheres, he would bet you how long it would take him to get wherever he was going to, and if you took him up, he would foller that straddle-bug to Mexico, but what he would find out where he was bound for and how long he was on the road. Lots of the boys here has seen that Smiley, and can tell you about him. Why, it never made no difference to *him* – he would bet on *any* thing – the dangdest feller. Parson Walker's wife laid very sick once, for a good while, and it seemed as if they warn't going to save her; but one morning he come in, and Smiley asked how she was, and he said she was considerable better – thank the Lord for his inf'nit mercy – and coming on so smart that, with the blessing of Prov'dence, she'd get well yet; and Smiley, before he thought, says, 'Well, I'll risk two-and-a-half that she don't, anyway.'

Thish-yer Smiley had a mare — the boys called her the fifteen-minute nag, but that was only in fun, you know, because, of course, she was faster than that — and he used to win money on that horse, for all she was so slow and always had the asthma, or the distemper, or the consumption, or something of that kind. They used to give her two or three hundred yards' start, and then pass her under way; but always at the fag-end of the race she'd get excited and desperate-like, and come cavorting and straddling up, and scattering her legs around limber, sometimes in the air, and sometimes out to one side amongst the fences, and kicking up m-o-r-e dust and raising m-o-r-e racket with her coughing and sneezing and blowing her nose — and always fetch up at the stand, just about a neck ahead, as near as you could cipher it down.

And he had a little small bull-pup, that to look at him you'd think he warn't worth a cent, but to set around and look ornery, and lay for a chance to steal something. But as soon as money was upon him, he was a different dog; his under-jaw'd begin to stick out like the fo'castle of a steamboat and his teeth would uncover, and shine savage like the furnaces. And a dog might tackle him, and bully-rag him, and bite him, and throw him over his shoulder two or three times, and Andrew Jackson — which was the name of the pup — Andrew Jackson would never let on but what *he* was satisfied, and hadn't expected nothing else — and the bets being doubled and doubled on the other side all the time, till the money was all up; and then all of a sudden he would grab that other dog jest by the j'int of his hind leg and freeze to it — not chaw, you understand, but only jest grip and hang on till they throwed up the sponge, if it was a year. Smiley always come out winner on that pup, till he harnessed a dog once that didn't have no hind legs, because they'd been saw'd off by a circular saw, and when the thing had gone along far enough, and the money was all up, and he come to make a snatch for his pet holt, he saw in a minute how he'd been imposed on, and how the other dog had him in the door, so to speak, and he 'peared surprised, and then he looked sorter discouraged-like, and didn't try no more to win the fight, and so he got shucked out bad. He gave Smiley a look, as much as to say his heart was broke, and it was *his* fault, for putting up a dog that hadn't no hind legs for him to take holt of, which was his main dependence in a fight, and then he limped off a piece and laid down and died. It was a good pup, was that Andrew Jackson, and would have made a name for hisself if he'd lived, for the stuff was in him, and he had genius – I know it, because he hadn't had no opportunities to speak of, and it don't stand to reason that a dog could make such a fight as he could under them circumstances, if he hadn't no talent. It always makes me feel sorry when I think of that last fight of his'n, and the way it turned out.

Well, thish-yer Smiley had rat-tarriers, and chicken-cocks, and tom-cats, and all them kind of things, till you couldn't rest, and you couldn't fetch nothing for him to bet on but he'd match you. He ketched a frog one day, and took him home, and said he cal'klated to edercate him; and so he never done nothing for three months but set in his back yard and learn that frog to jump. And you bet you he *did* learn him, too. He'd give him a little punch behind, and the next minute you'd see that frog whirling in the air like a doughnut – see him turn one summerset, or maybe a couple, if he got a good start, and come down flat-footed and all right, like a cat. He got him up so in the matter of catching flies, and kept him in practice so constant, that he'd nail a fly every time as far as he could see him. Smiley said all a frog wanted was education, and he could do most anything – and I believe him. Why, I've seen him set Dan'l Webster down here on this floor – Dan'l Webster was the name of the frog – and sing out, 'Flies, Dan'l, flies !' and quicker'n you could wink, he'd spring straight up, and snake a fly off'n the counter there, and flop down on the floor again as solid as a gob of mud, and fall to scratching the side of his head with his hind foot as indifferent as if he hadn't no idea he'd been doin' any more'n any frog might do. You never see a frog so modest and straight-for'ard as he was, for all he was so gifted. And when it come to fair and square jumping on a dead level, he could get over more ground at one straddle than any animal of his breed you ever see. Jumping on a dead level was his strong suit, you understand: and when it come to that, Smiley would ante up money on him as long as he had a red. Smiley was monstrous proud of his frog, and well he might be, for fellers that had travelled and been everywheres, all said he laid over any frog that ever *they* see.

Well, Smiley kept the beast in a little lattice box, and he used to fetch him down town sometimes and lay for a bet. One day a feller

— a stranger in the camp, he was — come across him with his box, and says:

'What might it be that you've got in the box?'

And Smiley says, sorter indifferent like, 'It might be a parrot, or it might be a canary, maybe, but it ain't — it's only just a frog.'

And the feller took it, and looked at it careful, and turned it round this way and that, and says, 'H'm — so 'tis. Well, what's *he* good for?'

'Well,' Smiley says, easy and careless, 'he's good enough for *one* thing, I should judge — he can outjump any frog in Calaveras County.'

The feller took the box again, and took another long, particular look, and gave it back to Smiley, and says, very deliberate, 'Well, I don't see no p'ints about that frog that's any better'n any other frog.'

'Maybe you don't,' Smiley says. 'Maybe you understand frogs, and maybe you don't understand 'em; maybe you've had experience, and maybe you ain't only a amateur, as it were. Anyways, I've got *my* opinion, and I'll risk forty dollars that he can outjump any frog in Calaveras County.'

And the feller studied a minute, and then says, kinder sad like, 'Well, I'm only a stranger here, and I ain't got no frog; but if I had a frog, I'd bet you.'

And then Smiley says, 'That's all right — that's all right — if you'll hold my box a minute, I'll go and get you a frog.' And so the feller took the box, and put up his forty dollars along with Smiley's, and set down to wait.

So he set there a good while thinking and thinking to hisself, and then he got the frog out and prized his mouth open and took a teaspoon and filled him full of quail shot — filled him pretty near up to his chin — and set him on the floor. Smiley he went to the swamp and slopped around in the mud for a long time, and finally he ketched a frog, and fetched him in, and gave him to this feller, and says:

'Now, if you're ready, set him alongside of Dan'l, with his forepaws just even with Dan'l's, and I'll give the word.' Then he says, 'One — two — three — jump!' and him and the feller touched up the frogs from behind, and the new frog hopped off, but Dan'l give a heave, and hysted up his shoulders — so — like a Frenchman, but it warn't no use – he couldn't budge; he was planted as solid as an anvil, and he couldn't no more stir than if he was anchored out. Smiley was a good deal surprised, and he was disgusted too, but he didn't have no idea what the matter was, of course.

The feller took the money and started away; and when he was going out at the door, he sorter jerked his thumb over his shoulder – this way – at Dan'l, and says again, very deliberate, 'Well, *I* don't see no p'ints about that frog that's any better'n any other frog.'

Smiley he stood scratching his head and looking down at Dan'l a long time, and at last he says, 'I do wonder what in the nation that frog throwed off for – I wonder if there ain't something the matter with him – he 'pears to look mighty baggy, somehow.' And he ketched Dan'l by the nap of the neck, and lifted him up and says, 'Why, blame my cats, if he don't weigh five pound!' and turned him upside down, and he belched out a double handful of shot. And then he see how it was, and he was the maddest man – he set the frog down and took out after that feller, but he never ketched him. And——

[Here Simon Wheeler heard his name called from the front yard, and got up to see what was wanted.] And turning to me as he moved away, he said: 'Just set where you are, stranger, and rest easy – I ain't going to be gone a second.'

But, by your leave, I did not think that a continuation of the history of the enterprising vagabond *Jim* Smiley would be likely to afford me much information concerning the *Rev. Leonidas W.* Smiley, and so I started away.

At the door I met the sociable Wheeler returning, and he button-holed me and recommenced:

'Well, thish-yer Smiley had a yaller one-eyed cow that didn't have no tail, only just a short stump like a bannanner, and —'

'Oh! hang Smiley and his afflicted cow!' I muttered, good-naturedly, and bidding the old gentleman good day, I departed.

The Iliad of Sandy Bar

Before nine o'clock it was pretty well known all along the river that the two parties of the 'Amity Claim' had quarreled and separated at daybreak. At that time the attention of their nearest neighbor had been attracted by the sounds of altercations and two consecutive pistol-shots. Running out, he had seen, dimly, in the grey mist that rose from the river, the tall form of Scott, one of the partners, descending the hill toward the cañon; a moment later, York, the other partner, had appeared from the cabin, and walked in an opposite direction toward the river, passing within a few feet of the curious watcher. Later it was discovered that a serious Chinaman, cutting wood before the cabin, had witnessed part of the quarrel. But John was stolid, indifferent, and reticent. 'Me choppee wood, me no fightee,' was his serene response to all anxious queries. 'But what did they *say*, John?' John did not '*sabe*'. Colonel Starbottle deftly ran over the various popular epithets which a generous public sentiment might accept as reasonable provocation for an assault. But John did not recognize them. 'And this yer's the cattle,' said the Colonel, with some severity, 'that some thinks oughter be allowed to testify agin' a White Man! Git – you heathen!'

Still the quarrel remained inexplicable. That two men, whose amiability and grave tact had earned for them the title of 'The Peacemakers', in a community not greatly given to the passive virtues – that these men, singularly devoted to each other, should suddenly and violently quarrel, might well excite the curiosity of the camp. A few of the more inquisitive visited the late scene of conflict, now deserted by its former occupants. There was no trace of disorder or confusion in the neat cabin. The rude table was arranged as if for breakfast; the pan of yellow biscuit still sat upon that hearth whose dead embers might have typified the evil passions that had raged there but an hour before. But Colonel Starbottle's eye – albeit, somewhat bloodshot and rheumy – was more intent on practical details.

On examination, a bullet-hole was found in the doorpost, and another, nearly opposite, in the casing of the window. The Colonel called attention to the fact that the one 'agreed with' the bore of Scott's revolver, and the other with that of York's derringer. 'They must hev stood about yer,' said the Colonel, taking position; 'not mor'n three feet apart, and – missed!' There was a fine touch of pathos in the falling inflection of the Colonel's voice, which was not without effect. A delicate perception of wasted opportunity thrilled his auditors.

But the Bar was destined to experience a greater disappointment. The two antagonists had not met since the quarrel, and it was vaguely rumored that, on the occasion of a second meeting, each had determined to kill the other 'on sight'. There was, consequently, some excitement – and, it is to be feared, no little gratification – when, at ten o'clock, York stepped from the Magnolia Saloon into the one, long straggling street of the camp, at the same moment that Scott left the blacksmith's shop at the forks of the road. It was evident, at a glance, that a meeting could only be avoided by the actual retreat of one or the other.

In an instant the doors and windows of the adjacent saloons were filled with faces. Heads unaccountably appeared above the river-banks and from behind boulders. An empty wagon at the crossroads was suddenly crowded with people, who seemed to have sprung from the earth. There was much running and confusion on the hillside. On the mountain road, Mr Jack Hamlin had reined up his horse and was standing upright on the seat of his buggy. And the two objects of this absorbing attention approached each other.

'York's got the sun,' 'Scott'll line him on that tree,' 'He's waiting to draw his fire,' came from the cart; and then it was silent. But above this human breathlessness the river rushed and sang, and the wind rustled the tree-tops with an indifference that seemed obtrusive. Colonel Starbottle felt it, and, in a moment of sublime pre-occupation, without looking around, waved his cane behind him warningly to all nature, and said, 'Shu!'

The men were now within a few feet of each other. A hen ran across the road before one of them. A feathery seed-vessel, wafted from a wayside tree, fell at the feet of the other. And, unheeding this irony of Nature, the two opponents came nearer, erect and rigid, looked in each other's eyes, and – passed!

Colonel Starbottle had to be lifted from the cart. 'This yer camp is played out,' he said, gloomily, as he affected to be supported into the 'Magnolia'. With what further expression he might have indicated his feelings it was impossible to say, for at that moment Scott joined the group. 'Did you speak to me?' he asked of the Colonel, dropping his hand, as if with accidental familiarity, on that gentleman's shoulder. The Colonel, recognizing some occult quality in the touch, and some unknown quantity in the glance of his questioner, contented himself by replying, 'No, sir,' with dignity. A few rods away, York's conduct was as characteristic and peculiar. 'You had a mighty fine chance; why didn't you plump him?' said Jack Hamlin, as York drew near the buggy. 'Because I hate him,' was the reply, heard by Jack. Contrary to popular belief, this reply was not hissed between the lips of the speaker, but was said in an ordinary tone. But Jack Hamlin, who was an observer of mankind, noticed that the speaker's hands were cold, and his lips dry, as he helped him into the buggy, and accepted the seeming paradox with a smile.

When Sandy Bar became convinced that the quarrel between York and Scott could not be settled after the usual local methods, it gave no further concern thereto. But presently it was rumored that the 'Amity Claim' was in litigation, and that its possession would be expensively disputed by each of the partners. As it was well known that the claim in question was 'worked out' and worthless, and that the partners, whom it had already enriched, had talked of abandoning it but a day or two before the quarrel, this proceeding could only be accounted for as gratuitous spite. Later, two San Francisco lawyers made their appearance in this guileless Arcadia, and were eventually taken into the saloons, and – what was pretty much the same thing – the confidences of the inhabitants. The results of this unhallowed intimacy were many subpoenas; and, indeed, when the 'Amity Claim' came to trial, all of Sandy Bar that was not in compulsory attendance at the county seat came there from curiosity. The gulches and ditches for miles around were deserted. I do not propose to describe that already famous trial. Enough that, in the language of the plaintiff's counsel, 'it was one of no ordinary significance, involving the inherent rights of that untiring industry which had developed the Pactolian resources of this golden land'; and, in the homelier phrase of Colonel Starbottle, 'A fuss that gentlemen might hev settled in ten minutes over a social glass, ef they meant business; or in ten seconds with a revolver, ef they meant fun.' Scott got a verdict, from which York instantly appealed. It was said that he had sworn to spend his last dollar in the struggle.

In this way Sandy Bar began to accept the enmity of the former partners as a lifelong feud, and the fact that they had ever been friends was forgotten. The few who expected to learn from the trial the origin of the quarrel were disappointed. Among the various conjectures, that which ascribed some occult feminine influence as the cause was naturally popular, in a camp given to dubious compliment of the sex. 'My word for it, gentlemen,' said Colonel Starbottle, who had been known in Sacramento as a Gentleman of the Old School, 'there's some lovely creature at the bottom of this.' The gallant Colonel then proceeded to illustrate his theory, by divers sprightly stories, such as Gentlemen of the Old School are in the habit of repeating, but which, from deference to the prejudices of gentlemen of a more recent school, I refrain from transcribing here. But it would appear that even the Colonel's theory was fallacious. The only woman who personally might have exercised any influence over the partners, was the pretty daughter of 'old man Folinsbee', of Poverty Flat, at whose hospitable house – which exhibited some comforts and refinements rare in that crude civilization – both York and Scott were frequent visitors. Yet into this charming retreat York strode one evening, a month after the quarrel, and beholding Scott sitting there, turned to the fair hostess with the abrupt query, 'Do you love this man?' The young woman thus addressed returned that answer – at once spirited and evasive – which would occur to most of my fair readers in such an exigency. Without another word, York left the house. 'Miss Jo' heaved the least possible sigh as the door closed on York's curls and square shoulders, and then, like a good girl, turned to her insulted guest. 'But would you believe it, dear?' she afterward related to an intimate friend, 'the other creature, after glowering at me for a moment, got upon its hind legs, took its hat, and left, too; and that's the last I've seen of either.'

The same hard disregard of all other interests or feelings in the gratification of their blind rancor characterized all their actions. When York purchased the land below Scott's new claim, and obliged the latter, at a great expense, to make a long detour to carry a 'tail-race' around it, Scott retaliated by building a dam that overflowed York's claim on the river. It was Scott who, in conjunction with Colonel Starbottle, first organized that active opposition to the Chinamen, which resulted in the driving off of York's Mongolian labourers; it was York who built the wagon-road and established the express which rendered Scott's mules and pack-trains obsolete; it was Scott who called into life the Vigilance Committee which expatriated York's friend, Jack Hamlin; it was York who created the *Sandy Bar Herald*, which characterized the act as 'a lawless outrage' and Scott as a 'Border Ruffian'; it was Scott, at the head of twenty masked men, who, one moonlight night, threw the offending 'forms' into the yellow river, and scattered the types in the dusty road. These proceedings were received in the distant and more civilized outlying towns as vague indications of progress and vitality. I have before me a copy of the *Poverty Flat Pioneer* for the week ending August 12, 1856, in which the editor, under the head of 'County Improvements', says: 'The new Presbyterian Church on C Street, at Sandy Bar, is completed. It stands upon the lot formerly occupied by the Magnolia Saloon, which was so mysteriously burnt last month. The temple, which now rises like a Phoenix from the ashes of the Magnolia, is virtually the free gift of H. J. York, Esq., of Sandy Bar, who purchased the lot and donated the lumber. Other buildings are going up in the vicinity, but the most noticeable is the "Sunny South Saloon", erected by Captain Mat. Scott, nearly opposite the church. Captain Scott has spared no expense in the furnishing of this saloon, which promises to be one of the most agreeable places of resort in old Tuolumne. He has recently imported two new, first-class billiard tables, with cork cushions. Our old friend, "Mountain Jimmy", will dispense liquors at the bar. We refer our readers to the advertisement in another column. Visitors to Sandy Bar cannot do better than give "Jimmy" a call.' Among the local items occurred the following: 'H. J. York, Esq., of Sandy Bar, has offered a reward of $100 for the detection of the parties who hauled away the steps of the new Presbyterian Church, C Street, Sandy Bar, during divine service on Sabbath evening last. Captain Scott adds another hundred for the capture of the miscreants who broke the magnificent plate-glass windows of the new saloon on the following evening. There is some talk of reorganizing the old Vigilance Committee at Sandy Bar.'

When, for many months of cloudless weather, the hard, unwinking sun of Sandy Bar had regularly gone down on the unpacified wrath of these men, there was some talk of mediation. In particular, the pastor of the church to which I have just referred – a sincere, fearless, but perhaps not fully enlightened man – seized gladly upon the occasion of York's liberality to attempt to reunite the former partners. He preached an earnest sermon on the abstract sinfulness of discord and rancor. But the excellent sermons of the Rev. Mr Daws were directed to an ideal congregation that did not exist at Sandy Bar – a congregation of beings of unmixed vices and .virtues, of single impulses, and perfectly logical motives, of preternatural simplicity, of childlike faith, and grown-up responsibilities. As, unfortunately, the people who actually attended Mr Daws's church were mainly very human, somewhat artful, more self-excusing than self-accusing, rather good-natured, and decidedly weak, they quietly shed that portion of the sermon which referred to themselves, and accepting York and Scott – who were both in defiant attendance – as curious examples of those ideal beings above referred to, felt a certain satisfaction – which, I fear, was not altogether Christian-like – in their 'raking-down'. If Mr Daws expected York and Scott to shake hands after the sermon, he was disappointed. But he did not relax his purpose. With that quiet fearlessness and determination which had won for him the respect of men who were apt to regard piety as synonymous with effeminacy, he attacked Scott in his own house. What he said has not been recorded, but it is to be feared that it was part of his sermon. When he had concluded, Scott looked at him, not unkindly, over the glasses of his bar, and said, less irreverently than the words might convey, 'Young man, I rather like your style; but when you know York and me as well as you do God Almighty, it'll be time to talk.'

And so the feud progressed; and so, as in more illustrious examples, the private and personal enmity of two representative men led gradually to the evolution of some crude, half-expressed principle or belief. It was not long before it was made evident that those beliefs were identical with certain principles laid down by the founders of the American Constitution, as expounded by the statesmanlike A., or were the fatal quicksands, on which the ship of state might be wrecked, warningly pointed out by the eloquent B. The practical result of all which was the nomination of York and Scott to represent the opposite factions of Sandy Bar in legislative councils.

For some weeks past, the voters of Sandy Bar and the adjacent camps had been called upon, in large type, to 'RALLY!' In vain the great pines at the crossroads – whose trunks were compelled to bear this and other legends – moaned and protested from their windy watchtowers. But one day, with fife and drum, and flaming transparency, a procession filed into the triangular grove at the head of the gulch. The meeting was called to order by Colonel Starbottle, who, having once enjoyed legislative functions, and being vaguely known as a 'war-horse', was considered to be a valuable partisan of York. He concluded an appeal for his friend, with an enunciation of principles, interspersed with one or two anecdotes so gratuitously coarse that the very pines might have been moved to pelt him with their cast-off cones, as he stood there. But he created a laugh, on which his candidate rode into popular notice; and when York rose to speak, he was greeted with cheers. But, to the general astonishment, the new speaker at once launched into bitter denunciation of his rival. He not only dwelt upon Scott's deeds and example, as known to Sandy Bar, but spoke of facts connected with his previous career, hitherto unknown to his auditors. To great precision of epithet and directness of statement, the speaker added the fascination of revelation and exposure. The crowd cheered, yelled, and were delighted, but when this astounding philippic was concluded, there was a unanimous call for 'Scott!' Colonel Starbottle would have resisted this manifest impropriety, but in vain. Partly from a crude sense of justice, partly from a meaner craving for excitement, the assemblage was inflexible; and Scott was dragged, pushed, and pulled upon the platform.

As his frowsy head and unkempt beard appeared above the railing, it was evident that he was drunk. But it was also evident, before he opened his lips, that the orator of Sandy Bar – the one man who could touch their vagabond sympathies (perhaps because he was not above appealing to them) – stood before them. A consciousness of this power lent a certain dignity to his figure, and I am not sure but that his very physical condition impressed them as a kind of regal unbending and large condescension. Howbeit, when this unexpected Hector arose from this ditch, York's myrmidons trembled.

'There's naught, gentlemen,' said Scott, leaning forward on the railing, – 'there's naught as that man hez said as isn't true. I was run outer Cairo; I did belong to the Regulators; I did desert from the army; I did leave a wife in Kansas. But thar's one thing he didn't charge me with, and, maybe, he's forgotten. For three years, gentlemen, I was that man's pardner! —' Whether he intended to say more, I cannot tell; a burst of applause artistically rounded and enforced the climax, and virtually elected the speaker. That Fall he went to Sacramento; York went abroad, and for the first time in many years, distance and a new atmosphere isolated the old antagonists.

With little of change in the green wood, grey rock, and yellow river, but with much shifting of human landmarks, and new faces in its habitations, three years passed over Sandy Bar. The two men, once so identified with its character, seemed to have been quite forgotten. 'You will never return to Sandy Bar,' said Miss Folinsbee, the 'Lily of Poverty Flat', on meeting York in Paris, 'for Sandy Bar is no more. They call it Riverside now; and the new town is built higher up on the river-bank. By the by, "Jo" says that Scott has won his suit about the "Amity Claim", and that he lives in the old cabin, and is drunk half his time. O, I beg your pardon,' added the lively lady, as a flush crossed York's sallow cheek; 'but, bless me, I really thought that old grudge was made up. I'm sure it ought to be.'

It was three months after this conversation, and a pleasant summer evening, that the Poverty Flat coach drew up before the veranda of the Union Hotel at Sandy Bar. Among its passengers was one, apparently a stranger, in the local distinction of well-fitting clothes and closely shaven face, who demanded a private room and retired early to rest. But before sunrise next morning he arose, and, drawing some clothes from his carpet-bag, proceeded to array himself in a pair of white duck trousers, a white duck overshirt, and straw hat. When this toilet was completed, he tied a red bandanna handkerchief in a loop and threw it loosely over his shoulders. The transformation was complete. As he crept softly down the stairs and stepped into the road, no one would have detected in him the elegant stranger of the previous night, and but few have recognized the face and figure of Henry York of Sandy Bar.

In the uncertain light of that early hour, and in the change that had come over the settlement, he had to pause for a moment to recall where he stood. The Sandy Bar of his recollection lay below him, nearer the river; the buildings around him were of later date and newer fashion. As he strode toward the river, he noticed here a schoolhouse and there a church. A little farther on, 'The Sunny South' came in view, transformed into a restaurant, its gilding faded and its paint rubbed off. He now knew where he was; and running briskly down a declivity, crossed a ditch, and stood upon the lower boundary of the Amity Claim.

The grey mist was rising slowly from the river, clinging to the tree-tops and drifting up the mountainside, until it was caught among these rocky altars, and held a sacrifice to the ascending sun. At his feet the earth, cruelly gashed and scarred by his forgotten engines, had, since the old days, put on a show of greenness here and there, and now smiled forgivingly up at him, as if things were not so bad after all. A few birds were bathing in the ditch with a pleasant suggestion of its being a new and special provision of Nature, and a hare ran into an inverted sluice-box, as he approached, as if it were put there for that purpose.

He had not yet dared to look in a certain direction. But the sun was now high enough to paint the little eminence on which the cabin stood. In spite of his self-control, his heart beat faster as he raised his eyes toward it. Its window and door were closed, no smoke came from its *adobe* chimney, but it was else unchanged. When within a few yards of it, he picked up a broken shovel, and shouldering it with a smile, strode toward the door and knocked. There was no sound from within. The smile died upon his lips as he nervously pushed the door open.

A figure started up angrily and came toward him, – a figure whose bloodshot eyes suddenly fixed into a vacant stare, whose arms were at first outstretched and then thrown up in warning gesticulation, – a figure that suddenly gasped, choked, and then fell forward in a fit.

But before he touched the ground, York had him out into the open air and sunshine. In the struggle, both fell and rolled over on the ground. But the next moment York was sitting up, holding the convulsed frame of his former partner on his knee, and wiping the foam from his inarticulate lips. Gradually the tremor became less frequent, and then ceased; and the strong man lay unconscious in his arms.

For some moments York held him quietly thus, looking in his face. Afar, the stroke of a woodman's axe – a mere phantom of sound – was all that broke the stillness. High up the mountain, a wheeling hawk hung breathlessly above them. And then came voices, and two men joined them.

'A fight?' No, a fit; and would they help him bring the sick man to the hotel?

And there, for a week, the stricken partner lay, unconscious of aught but the visions wrought by disease and fear. On the eighth day, at sunrise, he rallied, and, opening his eyes, looked upon York, and pressed his hand; then he spoke:

'And it's you. I thought it was only whiskey.'

York replied by taking both of his hands, boyishly working them backward and forward, as his elbow rested on the bed, with a pleasant smile.

'And you've been abroad. How did you like Paris?'

'So, so. How did *you* like Sacramento?'

'Bully!'

And that was all they could think to say. Presently Scott opened his eyes again.

'I'm mighty weak.'

'You'll get better soon.'

'Not much.'

A long silence followed, in which they could hear the sounds of wood-chopping, and that Sandy Bar was already astir for the coming day. Then Scott slowly and with difficulty turned his face to York, and said, —

'I might hev killed you once.'

'I wish you had.'

They pressed each other's hands again, but Scott's grasp was evidently failing. He seemed to summon his energies for a special effort.

'Old man!'

'Old chap.'

'Closer!'

York bent his head toward the slowly-fading face.

'Do ye mind that morning?'

'Yes.'

A gleam of fun slid into the corner of Scott's blue eye, as he whispered,

'Old man, thar *was* too much saleratus in that bread.'

It is said that these were his last words. For when the sun, which had so often gone down upon the idle wrath of these foolish men, looked again upon them reunited, it saw the hand of Scott fall cold and irresponsive from the yearning clasp of his former partner, and it knew that the feud of Sandy Bar was at an end.

The Coup de Grâce

The fighting had been hard and continuous, that was attested by all the senses. The very taste of battle was in the air. All was now over; it remained only to succor the wounded and bury the dead – to 'tidy up a bit', as the humorist of a burying squad put it. A good deal of 'tidying up' was required. As far as one could see through the forest, between the splintered trees, lay wrecks of men and horses. Among them moved the stretcher-bearers, gathering and carrying away the few who showed signs of life. Most of the wounded had died of exposure while the right to minister to their wants was in dispute. It is an army regulation that the wounded must wait; the best way to care for them is to win the battle. It must be confessed that victory is a distinct advantage to a man requiring attention, but many do not live to avail themselves of it.

The dead were collected in groups of a dozen or a score, and laid side by side in rows while the trenches were dug to receive them. Some, found at too great a distance from these rallying points, were buried where they lay. There was little attempt at identification, though in most cases, the burying parties being detailed to glean the same ground which they had assisted to reap, the names of the victorious dead were known and listed. The enemy's fallen had to be content with counting. But of that they got enough; many of them were counted several times, and the total, as given in the official report of the victorious commander, denoted rather a hope than a result.

At some little distance from the spot where one of the burying parties had established its 'bivouac of the dead', a man in the uniform of a Federal officer stood leaning against a tree. From his feet upward to his neck his attitude was that of weariness reposing; but he turned his head uneasily from side to side; his mind was apparently not at rest. He was perhaps uncertain in what direction to go; he was not likely to remain long where he was, for already the level rays of the setting sun struggled redly through the open spaces of the wood, and the weary soldiers were quitting their task for the day. He would hardly make a night of it alone there among the dead. Nine men in ten whom you meet after a battle inquire the way to some fraction of the army – as if anyone could know. Doubtless this officer was lost. After resting himself a moment, he would follow one of the retiring burial squads.

When all were gone, he walked straight away into the forest toward the red west, its light staining his face like blood. The air of confidence with which he now strode along showed that he was on familiar ground; he had recovered his bearings. The dead on his right and on his left were unregarded as he passed. An occasional low moan from some sorely stricken wretch whom the relief parties had not reached, and who would have to pass a comfortless night beneath the stars with his thirst to keep him company, was equally unheeded. What, indeed, could the officer have done, being no surgeon and having no water?

At the head of a shallow ravine, a mere depression of the ground, lay a small group of bodies. He saw, and, swerving suddenly from his course, walked rapidly toward them. Scanning each one sharply as he passed, he stopped at last above one which lay at a slight remove from the others, near a clump of small trees. He looked at it narrowly. It seemed to stir. He stooped and laid his hand upon its face. It screamed.

The officer was Captain Downing Madwell, of a Massachusetts regiment of infantry, a daring and intelligent soldier, an honorable man.

In the regiment were two brothers named Halcrow – Caffal and Creede Halcrow. Caffal Halcrow was a sergeant in Captain Madwell's company, and these two men, the sergeant and the captain, were devoted friends. In so far as disparity of rank, difference in duties, and considerations of military discipline would permit, they were commonly together. They had, indeed, grown up together from childhood. A habit of the heart is not easily broken off. Caffal Halcrow had nothing military in his taste or disposition, but the thought of separation from his friend was disagreeable; he enlisted in the company in which Madwell was second lieutenant. Each had taken two steps upward in rank, but between the highest non-commissioned and the lowest commissioned officer the social gulf is deep and wide, and the old relation was maintained with difficulty and a difference.

Creede Halcrow, the brother of Caffal, was the major of the regiment – a cynical, saturnine man, between whom and Captain Madwell there was a natural antipathy which circumstances had nourished and strengthened to an active animosity. But for the restraining influence of their mutual relation to Caffal, these two patriots would doubtless have endeavored to deprive their country of one another's services.

At the opening of the battle that morning, the regiment was performing outpost duty a mile away from the main army. It was attacked and nearly surrounded in the forest, but stubbornly held its ground. During a lull in the fighting, Major Halcrow came to Captain Madwell. The two exchanged formal salutes, and the major said: 'Captain, the colonel directs that you push your company to the head of this ravine and hold your place there until recalled. I need hardly apprise you of the dangerous character of the movement, but if you wish, you can, I suppose, turn over the command to your first lieutenant. I was not, however, directed to authorize the substitution; it is merely a suggestion of my own, unofficially made.'

To this deadly insult Captain Madwell coolly replied: —

'Sir, I invite you to accompany the movement. A mounted officer would be a conspicuous mark, and I have long held the opinion that it would be better if you were dead.'

The art of repartee was cultivated in military circles as early as 1862.

A half hour later Captain Madwell's company was driven from its position at the head of the ravine, with a loss of one-third its number. Among the fallen was Sergeant Halcrow. The regiment was soon afterward forced back to the main line, and at the close of the battle was miles away. The captain was now standing at the side of his subordinate and friend.

Sergeant Halcrow was mortally hurt. His clothing was deranged; it seemed to have been violently torn apart, exposing the abdomen. Some of the buttons of his jacket had been pulled off and lay on the ground beside him, and fragments of his other garments were strewn about. His leather belt was parted, and had apparently been dragged from beneath him as he lay. There had been no very great effusion of blood. The only visible wound was a wide, ragged opening in the abdomen. It was defiled with earth and dead leaves. Protruding from it was a lacerated end of the small intestine. In all his experience Captain Madwell had not seen a wound like this. He could neither conjecture how it was made nor explain the attendant circumstances – the strangely torn clothing, the parted belt, the besmirching of the white skin. He knelt and made a closer examination. When he rose to his feet, he turned his eyes in various directions as if looking for an enemy. Fifty yards away, on the crest of a low, thinly wooded hill, he saw several dark objects moving about among the fallen men – a herd of swine. One stood with its back to him, its shoulders sharply elevated. Its forefeet were upon a human body, its head was depressed and invisible. The bristly ridge of its chine showed black against the red west. Captain Madwell drew away his eyes and fixed them again upon the thing which had been his friend.

The man who had suffered these monstrous mutilations was alive. At intervals he moved his limbs; he moaned at every breath. He stared blankly into the face of his friend, and if touched screamed. In his giant agony he had torn up the ground on which he lay; his clenched hands were full of leaves and twigs and earth. Articulate speech was beyond his power; it was impossible to know if he were sensible to anything but pain. The expression of his face was an appeal; his eyes were full of prayer. For what?

There was no misreading that look; the captain had too frequently seen it in eyes of those whose lips had still the power to formulate it by an entreaty for death. Consciously or unconsciously, this writhing fragment of humanity, this type and example of acute sensation, this handiwork of man and beast, this humble, unheroic Prometheus, was imploring everything, all, the whole non-*ego*, for the boon of oblivion. To the earth and the sky alike, to the trees, to the man, to whatever took form in sense or consciousness, this incarnate suffering addressed its silent plea.

For what indeed? — For that which we accord to even the meanest creature without sense to demand it, denying it only to the wretched of our own race: for the blessed release, the rite of uttermost compassion, the *coup de grâce*.

Captain Madwell spoke the name of his friend. He repeated it over and over without effect until emotion choked his utterance. His tears plashed upon the livid face beneath his own and blinded himself. He saw nothing but a blurred and moving object, but the moans were more distinct than ever, interrupted at briefer intervals by sharper shrieks. He turned away, struck his hand upon his forehead, and strode from the spot. The swine, catching sight of him, threw up their crimson muzzles, regarding him suspiciously a second, and then, with a gruff, concerted grunt, raced away out of sight. A horse, its foreleg splintered horribly by a cannon shot, lifted its head sidewise from the ground and neighed piteously. Madwell stepped forward, drew his revolver and shot the poor beast between the eyes, narrowly observing its death struggle, which, contrary to his expectation, was violent and long; but at last it lay still. The tense muscles of its lips, which had uncovered the teeth in a horrible grin, relaxed; the sharp, clean-cut profile took on a look of profound peace and rest.

Along the distant thinly wooded crest to westward the fringe of sunset fire had now nearly burned itself out. The light upon the trunks of the trees had faded to a tender gray; the shadows were in their tops, like great dark birds aperch. The night was coming and there were miles of haunted forest between Captain Madwell and camp. Yet he stood there at the side of the dead animal, apparently lost to all sense of his surroundings. His eyes were bent upon the earth at his feet; his left hand hung loosely at his side, his right still held the pistol. Suddenly he lifted his face, turned it toward his dying friend, and walked rapidly back to his side. He knelt upon one knee, cocked the weapon, placed the muzzle against the man's forehead, turned away his eyes and pulled the trigger. There was no report. He had used his last cartridge for the horse. The sufferer moaned and his lips moved convulsively. The froth that ran from them had a tinge of blood.

Captain Madwell rose to his feet and drew his sword from the scabbard. He passed the fingers of his left hand along the edge from hilt to point. He held it out straight before him as if to test his nerves. There was no visible tremor of the blade; the ray of bleak skylight that it reflected was steady and true. He stooped, and with his left hand tore away the dying man's shirt, rose, and placed the point of the sword just over the heart. This time he did not withdraw his eyes. Grasping the hilt with both hands, he thrust downward with all his strength and weight. The blade sank into the man's body – through his body into the earth; Captain Madwell came near falling forward upon his work. The dying man drew up his knees and at the same time threw his right arm across his breast and grasped the steel so tightly that the knuckles of the hand visibly whitened. By a violent but vain effort to withdraw the blade, the wound was enlarged; a rill of blood escaped, running sinuously down into the deranged clothing. At that moment three men stepped silently forward from behind the clump of young trees which had concealed their approach. Two were hospital attendants and carried a stretcher.

The third was Major Creede Halcrow.

Paste

'I've found a lot more things,' her cousin said to her the day after the second funeral; 'they're up in her room – but they're things I wish *you'd* look at.'

The pair of mourners, sufficiently stricken, were in the garden of the vicarage together, before luncheon, waiting to be summoned to that meal, and Arthur Prime had still in his face the intention, she was moved to call it rather than the expression, of feeling something or other. Some such appearance was in itself of course natural within a week of his stepmother's death, within three of his father's; but what was most present to the girl, herself sensitive and shrewd, was that he seemed somehow to brood without sorrow, to suffer without what she in her own case would have called pain. He turned away from her after this last speech – it was a good deal his habit to drop an observation and leave her to pick it up without assistance. If the vicar's widow, now in her turn finally translated, had not really belonged to him it was not for want of her giving herself, so far as he ever would take her; and she had lain for three days all alone at the end of the passage, in the great cold chamber of hospitality, the dampish, greenish room where visitors slept and where several of the ladies of the parish had, without effect, offered, in pairs and successions, piously to watch with her. His personal connection with the parish was now slighter than ever, and he had really not waited for this opportunity to show the ladies what he thought of them. She felt that she herself had, during her doleful month's leave from Bleet, where she was governess, rather taken her place in the same snubbed order; but it was presently, none the less, with a better little hope of coming in for some remembrance, some relic, that she went up to look at the things he had spoken of, the identity of which, as a confused cluster of bright objects on a table in the darkened room, shimmered at her as soon as she had opened the door.

They met her eyes for the first time, but in a moment, before touching them, she knew them as things of the theatre, as very much too fine to have been, with any verisimilitude, things of the vicarage. They were too dreadfully good to be true, for her aunt had had no jewels to speak of, and these were coronets and girdles, diamonds, rubies and sapphires. Flagrant tinsel and glass, they looked strangely vulgar, but if, after the first queer shock of them, she found herself taking them up, it was for the very proof, never yet so distinct to her, of a far-off faded story. An honest widowed cleric with a small son and a large sense of Shakespeare had, on a brave latitude of habit as well as of taste – since it implied his having in very fact dropped deep into the 'pit' – conceived for an obscure actress, several years older than himself, an admiration of which the prompt offer of his reverend name and hortatory hand was the sufficiently candid sign. The response had perhaps, in those dim years, in the way of eccentricity, even bettered the proposal, and Charlotte, turning the tale over, had long since drawn from it a measure of the career renounced by the undistinguished *comédienne* – doubtless also tragic, or perhaps pantomimic, at a pinch – of her late uncle's dreams. This career could not have been eminent and must much more probably have been comfortless.

'You see what it is – old stuff of the time she never liked to mention.'

Our young woman gave a start; her companion had, after all, rejoined her and had apparently watched a moment her slightly scared recognition. 'So I said to myself,' she replied. Then, to show intelligence, yet keep clear of twaddle: 'How peculiar they look!'

'They look awful,' said Arthur Prime. 'Cheap gilt, diamonds as big as potatoes. These are trappings of a ruder age than ours. Actors do themselves better now.'

'Oh now,' said Charlotte, not to be less knowing, 'actresses have real diamonds.'

'Some of them.' Arthur spoke drily.

'I mean the bad ones – the nobodies too.'

'Oh, some of the nobodies have the biggest. But mamma wasn't of that sort.'

'A nobody?' Charlotte risked.

'Not a nobody to whom somebody – well, not a nobody with diamonds. It isn't all worth, this trash, five pounds.'

There was something in the old gewgaws that spoke to her, and she continued to turn them over. 'They're relics. I think they have their melancholy and even their dignity.'

Arthur observed another pause. 'Do you care for them?' he then asked. 'I mean,' he promptly added, 'as a souvenir.'

'Of you?' Charlotte threw off.

'Of me? What have I to do with it? Of your poor dead aunt who was so kind to you,' he said with virtuous sternness.

'Well, I would rather have them than nothing.'

'Then please take them,' he returned in a tone of relief which expressed somehow more of the eager than of the gracious.

'Thank you.' Charlotte lifted two or three objects up and set them down again. Though they were lighter than the materials they imitated they were so much more extravagant that they struck her in truth as rather an awkward heritage, to which she might have preferred even a matchbox or a penwiper. They were indeed shameless pinchbeck. 'Had you any idea she had kept them?'

'I don't at all believe she *had* kept them or knew they were there, and I'm very sure my father didn't. They had quite equally worked off any tenderness for the connection. These odds and ends, which she thought had been given away or destroyed, had simply got thrust into a dark corner and been forgotten.'

Charlotte wondered. 'Where then did you find them?'

'In that old tin box' – and the young man pointed to the receptacle from which he had dislodged them and which stood on a neighbouring chair. 'It's rather a good box still, but I'm afraid I can't give you *that*.'

The girl gave the box no look; she continued only to look at the trinkets. 'What corner had she found?'

'She hadn't "found" it,' her companion sharply insisted; 'she had simply lost it. The whole thing had passed from her mind. The box was on the top shelf of the old schoolroom closet, which, until one put one's head into it from a step-ladder, looked, from below, quite cleared out. The door is narrow and the part of the closet to the left goes well into the wall. The box had stuck there for years.'

Charlotte was conscious of a mind divided and a vision vaguely troubled, and once more she took up two or three of the subjects of this revelation; a big bracelet in the form of a gilt serpent with many twists and beady eyes, a brazen belt studded with emeralds and rubies, a chain, of flamboyant architecture, to which, at the Theatre Royal, Little Peddlington, Hamlet's mother had probably been careful to attach the portrait of the successor to Hamlet's father. 'Are you very sure they're not really worth something? Their mere weight alone — !' she vaguely observed, balancing a moment a royal diadem that might have crowned one of the creations of the famous Mrs Jarley.

But Arthur Prime, it was clear, had already thought the question over and found the answer easy. 'If they had been worth anything to speak of she would long ago have sold them. My father and she had unfortunately never been in a position to keep any considerable value locked up.' And while his companion took in the obvious force of this he went on with a flourish just marked enough not to escape her: 'If they're worth anything at all — why, you're only the more welcome to them.'

Charlotte had now in her hand a small bag of faded, figured silk — one of those antique conveniences that speak to us, in the terms of evaporated camphor and lavender, of the part they have played in some personal history; but, though she had for the first time drawn the string, she looked much more at the young man than at the questionable treasure it appeared to contain. 'I shall like them. They're all I have.'

'All you have — ?'

'That belonged to her.'

He swelled a little, then looked about him as if to appeal — as against her avidity — to the whole poor place. 'Well, what else do you want?'

'Nothing. Thank you very much.' With which she bent her eyes on the article wrapped, and now only exposed, in her superannuated satchel — a necklace of large pearls, such as might once have graced the neck of a provincial Ophelia and borne company to a flaxen wig. 'This perhaps *is* worth something. Feel it.' And she passed him the necklace, the weight of which she had gathered for a moment into her hand.

He measured it in the same way with his own, but remained quite detached. 'Worth at most thirty shillings.'

'Not more?'

'Surely not if it's paste?'

'But *is* it paste?'

He gave a small sniff of impatience. 'Pearls nearly as big as filberts?'

'But they're heavy,' Charlotte declared.

'No heavier than anything else.' And he gave them back with an allowance for her simplicity. 'Do you imagine for a moment they're real?'

She studied them a little, feeling them, turning them round. 'Mightn't they possibly be?'

'Of that size – stuck away with that trash?'

'I admit it isn't likely,' Charlotte presently said. 'And pearls are so easily imitated.'

'That's just what – to a person who knows – they're not. These have no lustre, no play.'

'No – they *are* dull. They're opaque.'

'Besides,' he lucidly inquired, 'how could she ever have come by them?'

'Mightn't they have been a present?'

Arthur stared at the question as if it were almost improper. 'Because actresses are exposed — ?' He pulled up, however, not saying to what, and before she could supply the deficiency had, with the sharp ejaculation of 'No, they mightn't!' turned his back on her and walked away. His manner made her feel that she had probably been wanting in tact, and before he returned to the subject, the last thing that evening, she had satisfied herself of the ground of his resentment. They had been talking of her departure the next morning, the hour of her train and the fly that would come for her, and it was precisely these things that gave him his effective chance. 'I really can't allow you to leave the house under the impression that my stepmother was at *any* time of her life the sort of person to allow herself to be approached — '

'With pearl necklaces and that sort of thing?' Arthur had made for her somehow the difficulty that she couldn't show him she understood him without seeming pert.

It at any rate only added to his own gravity. 'That sort of thing, exactly.'

'I didn't think when I spoke this morning – but I see what you mean.'

'I mean that she was beyond reproach,' said Arthur Prime.

'A hundred times yes.'

'Therefore if she couldn't, out of her slender gains, ever have paid for a row of pearls — '

'She couldn't, in that atmosphere, ever properly have had one? Of course she couldn't. I've seen perfectly since our talk,' Charlotte went on, 'that that string of beads isn't even, as an imitation, very good. The little clasp itself doesn't seem even gold. With false pearls, I suppose,' the girl mused, 'it naturally wouldn't be.'

'The whole thing's rotten paste,' her companion returned as if to have done with it. 'If it were *not*, and she had kept it all these years hidden — '

'Yes?' Charlotte sounded as he paused.

'Why, I shouldn't know what to think!'

'Oh, I see.' She had met him with a certain blankness, but adequately enough, it seemed, for him to regard the subject as dismissed; and there was no reversion to it between them before, on the morrow, when she had with difficulty made a place for them in her trunk, she carried off these florid survivals.

At Bleet she found small occasion to revert to them and, in an air charged with such quite other references, even felt, after she had laid them away, much enshrouded, beneath various piles of clothing, as if they formed a collection not wholly without its note of the ridiculous. Yet she was never, for the joke, tempted to show them to her pupils, though Gwendolen and Blanche, in particular, always wanted, on her return, to know what she had brought back; so that without an accident by which the case was quite changed they might have appeared to enter on a new phase of interment. The essence of the accident was the sudden illness, at the last moment, of Lady Bobby, whose advent had been so much counted on to spice the five days' feast laid out for the coming of age of the eldest son of the house; and its equally marked effect was the despatch of a pressing message, in quite another direction, to Mrs Guy, who, could she by a miracle be secured – she was always engaged ten parties deep – might be trusted to supply, it was believed, an element of exuberance scarcely less active. Mrs Guy was already known to several of the visitors already on the scene, but she was not yet known to our young lady, who found her, after many wires and counterwires had at last determined the triumph of her arrival, a strange, charming little red-haired, black-dressed woman, with the face of a baby and the authority of a commodore. She took on the spot the discreet, the exceptional young governess into the confidence of her designs and, still more, of her doubts; intimating that it was a policy she almost always promptly pursued.

'Tomorrow and Thursday are all right,' she said frankly to Charlotte on the second day, 'but I'm not half satisfied with Friday.'

'What improvement then do you suggest?'

'Well, my strong point, you know, is *tableaux vivants*.'

'Charming. And what is your favourite character?'

'Boss!' said Mrs Guy with decision; and it was very markedly under that ensign that she had, within a few hours, completely planned her campaign and recruited her troop. Every word she uttered was to the point, but none more so than, after a general survey of their equipment, her final inquiry of Charlotte. She had been looking about, but half appeased, at the muster of decoration and drapery. 'We shall be dull. We shall want more colour. You've nothing else?'

Charlotte had a thought. 'No – I've *some* things.'

'Then why don't you bring them?'

The girl hesitated. 'Would you come to my room?'

'No,' said Mrs Guy – 'bring them tonight to mine.'

So Charlotte, at the evening's end, after candlesticks had flickered through brown old passages bedward, arrived at her friend's door with the burden of her aunt's relics. But she promptly expressed a fear. 'Are they too garish?'

When she had poured them out on the sofa Mrs Guy was but a minute, before the glass, in clapping on the diadem. 'Awfully jolly – we can do Ivanhoe!'

'But they're only glass and tin.'

'Larger than life they are, *rather*! – which is exactly what, for tableaux, is wanted. *Our* jewels, for historic scenes, don't tell – the real thing falls short. Rowena must have rubies as big as eggs. Leave them with me,' Mrs Guy continued – 'they'll inspire me. Good night.'

The next morning she was in fact – yet very strangely – inspired. 'Yes, *I'll* do Rowena. But I don't, my dear, understand.'

'Understand what?'

Mrs Guy gave a very lighted stare. 'How you come to have such things.'

Poor Charlotte smiled. 'By inheritance.'

'Family jewels?'

'They belong to my aunt, who died some months ago. She was on the stage a few years in early life, and these are a part of her trappings.'

'She left them to you?'

'No; my cousin, her stepson, who naturally has no use for them, gave them to me for remembrance of her. She was a dear kind thing, always so nice to me, and I was fond of her.'

Mrs Guy had listened with visible interest. 'But it's *he* who must be a dear kind thing!'

Charlotte wondered. 'You think so?'

'Is *he*,' her friend went on, 'also "always so nice" to you?'

The girl, at this, face to face there with the brilliant visitor in the deserted breakfast-room, took a deeper sounding. 'What is it?'

'Don't you know?'

Something came over her. 'The pearls —?' But the question fainted on her lips.

'Doesn't *he* know?'

Charlotte found herself flushing. 'They're *not* paste?'

'Haven't you looked at them?'

She was conscious of two kinds of embarrassment. '*You* have?'

'Very carefully.'

'And they're real?'

Mrs Guy became slightly mystifying and returned for all answer: 'Come again, when you've done with the children, to my room.'

Our young woman found she had done with the children, that morning, with a promptitude that was a new joy to them, and when she reappeared before Mrs Guy this lady had already encircled a plump white throat with the only ornament, surely, in all the late Mrs Prime's — the effaced Miss Bradshaw's — collection, in the least qualified to raise a question. If Charlotte had never yet once, before the glass, tied the string of pearls about her own neck, this was because she had been capable of no such condescension to approved 'imitation'; but she had now only to look at Mrs Guy to see that, so disposed, the ambiguous objects might have passed for frank originals. 'What in the world have you done to them?'

'Only handled them, understood them, admired them and put them on. That's what pearls want; they want to be worn — it wakes them up. They're alive, don't you see? How *have* these been treated? They must have been buried, ignored, despised. They were half dead. Don't you *know* about pearls?' Mrs Guy threw off as she fondly fingered the necklace.

'How *should* I? Do *you*?'

'Everything. These were simply asleep, and from the moment I really touched them — well,' said their wearer lovingly, 'it only took one's eye!'

'It took more than mine — though I did just wonder; and then

Arthur's,' Charlotte brooded. She found herself almost panting. 'Then their value — ?'

'Oh, their value's excellent.'

The girl, for a deep moment, took another plunge into the wonder, the beauty and mystery, of them. 'Are you *sure?*'

Her companion wheeled round for impatience. 'Sure? For what kind of an idiot, my dear, do you take me?'

It was beyond Charlotte Prime to say. 'For the same kind as Arthur — and as myself,' she could only suggest. 'But my cousin didn't know. He thinks they're worthless.'

'Because of the rest of the lot? Then your cousin's an ass. But what — if, as I understood you, he gave them to you — had he to do with it?'

'Why, if he gave them to me as worthless and they turn out precious — '

'You must give them back? I don't see that — if he was such a fool. He took the risk.'

Charlotte fed, in fancy, on the pearls, which, decidedly, were exquisite, but which at the present moment somehow presented themselves much more as Mrs Guy's than either as Arthur's or as her own. 'Yes — he did take it; even after I had distinctly hinted to him that they looked to me different from the other pieces.'

'Well, then!' said Mrs Guy with something more than triumph — with a positive odd relief.

But it had the effect of making our young woman think with more intensity. 'Ah, you see he thought they couldn't be different, because — so peculiarly — they shouldn't be.'

'Shouldn't be? I don't understand.'

'Why, how would she have got them?' — so Charlotte candidly put it.

'She? Who?' There was a capacity in Mrs Guy's tone for a sinking of persons — !

'Why, the person I told you of: his stepmother, my uncle's wife — among whose poor old things, extraordinarily thrust away and out of sight, he happened to find them.'

Mrs Guy came a step nearer to the effaced Miss Bradshaw. 'Do you mean she may have stolen them?'

'No. But she had been an actress.'

'Oh, well then,' cried Mrs Guy, 'wouldn't that be just how?'

'Yes, except that she wasn't at all a brilliant one, nor in receipt of large pay.' The girl even threw off a nervous joke. 'I'm afraid she couldn't have been our Rowena.'

Mrs Guy took it up. 'Was she very ugly?'

'No. She may very well, when young, have looked rather nice.'

'Well, then!' was Mrs Guy's sharp comment and fresh triumph.

'You mean it was a present? That's just what he so dislikes the idea of her having received – a present from an admirer capable of going such lengths.'

'Because she wouldn't have taken it for nothing? *Speriamo* – that she wasn't a brute. The "length" her admirer went was the length of a whole row. Let us hope she was just a little kind!'

'Well,' Charlotte went on, 'that she was "kind" might seem to be shown by the fact that neither her husband, nor his son, nor I, his niece, knew or dreamed of her possessing anything so precious; by her having kept the gift all the rest of her life beyond discovery – out of sight and protected from suspicion.'

'As if, you mean' – Mrs Guy was quick – 'she had been wedded to it and yet was ashamed of it? Fancy,' she laughed while she manipulated the rare beads, 'being ashamed of *these*!'

'But you see she had married a clergyman.'

'Yes, she must have been "rum". But at any rate he had married *her*. What did he suppose?'

'Why, that she had never been of the sort by whom such offerings are encouraged.'

'Ah, my dear, the sort by whom they are *not* —!' But Mrs Guy caught herself up. 'And her stepson thought the same?'

'Overwhelmingly.'

'Was he, then, if only her stepson —'

'So fond of her as that comes to? Yes; he had never known, consciously, his real mother, and, without children of her own, she was very patient and nice with him. And *I* liked her so,' the girl pursued, 'that at the end of ten years, in so strange a manner, to "give her away" — '

'Is impossible to you? Then don't!' said Mrs Guy with decision.

'Ah, but if they're real I can't keep them!' Charlotte, with her eyes on them, moaned in her impatience. 'It's too difficult.'

'Where's the difficulty, if he has such sentiments that he would rather sacrifice the necklace than admit it, with the presumption it carries with it, to be genuine? You've only to be silent.'

'And keep it? How can *I* ever wear it?'

'You'd have to hide it, like your aunt?' Mrs Guy was amused. 'You can easily sell it.'

Her companion walked round her for a look at the affair from behind. The clasp was certainly, doubtless intentionally, misleading, but everything else was indeed lovely. 'Well, I must think. Why didn't *she* sell them?' Charlotte broke out in her trouble.

Mrs Guy had an instant answer. 'Doesn't that prove what they secretly recalled to her? You've only to be silent!' she ardently repeated.

'I must think – I must think!'

Mrs Guy stood with her hands attached but motionless. 'Then you want them back?'

As if with the dread of touching them Charlotte retreated to the door. 'I'll tell you tonight.'

'But may I wear them?'

'Meanwhile?'

'This evening – at dinner.'

It was the sharp, selfish pressure of this that really, on the spot, determined the girl; but for the moment, before closing the door on the question, she only said: 'As you like!'

They were busy much of the day with preparation and rehearsal, and at dinner, that evening, the concourse of guests was such that a place among them for Miss Prime failed to find itself marked. At the time the company rose she was therefore alone in the schoolroom, where, towards eleven o'clock, she received a visit from Mrs Guy. This lady's white shoulders heaved, under the pearls, with an emotion that the very red lips which formed, as if for the full effect, the happiest opposition of colour, were not slow to translate. 'My dear, you should have seen the sensation – they've had a success!'

Charlotte, dumb a moment, took it all in. 'It *is* as if they knew it – they're more and more alive. But so much the worse for both of us! I can't,' she brought out with an effort, 'be silent.'

'You mean to return them?'

'If I don't I'm a thief.'

Mrs Guy gave her a long, hard look: what was decidedly not of the baby in Mrs Guy's face was a certain air of established habit in the eyes. Then, with a sharp little jerk of her head and a backward reach of her bare beautiful arms, she undid the clasp and, taking off the necklace, laid it on the table. 'If you do, you're a goose.'

'Well, of the two — !' said our young lady, gathering it up with a sigh. And as if to get it, for the pang it gave, out of sight as soon as possible, she shut it up, clicking the lock, in the drawer of her own little table; after which, when she turned again, her companion, without it, looked naked and plain. 'But what will you say?' it then occurred to her to demand.

'Downstairs – to explain?' Mrs Guy was, after all, trying at least to keep her temper. 'Oh, I'll put on something else and say that clasp is broken. And you won't of course name *me* to him,' she added.

'As having undeceived me? No – I'll say that, looking at the thing more carefully, it's my own private idea.'

'And does he know how little you really know?'

'As an expert – surely. And he has much, always, the conceit of his own opinion.'

'Then he won't believe you – as he so hates to. He'll stick to his judgment and maintain his gift, and we shall have the darlings back!' With which reviving assurance Mrs Guy kissed for good night.

She was not, however, to be gratified or justified by any prompt event, for, whether or no paste entered into the composition of the ornament in question, Charlotte shrank from the temerity of despatching it to town by post. Mrs Guy was thus disappointed of the hope of seeing the business settled – 'by return', she had seemed to expect – before the end of the revels. The revels, moreover, rising to a frantic pitch, pressed for all her attention, and it was at last only in the general confusion of leave-taking that she made, parenthetically, a dash at her young friend.

'Come, what will you take for them?'

'The pearls? Ah, you'll have to treat with my cousin.'

Mrs Guy, with quick intensity, lent herself. 'Where then does he live?'

'In chambers in the Temple. You can find him.'

'But what's the use, if *you* do neither one thing nor the other?'

'Oh, I *shall* do the "other",' Charlotte said: 'I'm only waiting till I go up. You want them so awfully?' She curiously solemnly again sounded her.

'I'm dying for them. There's a special charm in them – I don't know what it is: they tell so their history.'

'But what do you know of that?'

'Just what they themselves say. It's all *in* them – and it comes out.

They breathe a tenderness – they have the white glow of it. My dear,' hissed Mrs Guy in supreme confidence and as she buttoned her glove – 'they're things of love!'

'Oh!' our young woman vaguely exclaimed.

'They're things of passion!'

'Mercy!' she gasped, turning short off. But these words remained, though indeed their help was scarce needed, Charlotte being in private face to face with a new light, as she by this time felt she must call it, on the dear dead, kind, colourless lady whose career had turned so sharp a corner in the middle. The pearls had quite taken their place as a revelation. She might have received them for nothing – admit that; but she couldn't have kept them so long and so unprofitably hidden, couldn't have enjoyed them only in secret, for nothing; and she had mixed them, in her reliquary, with false things, in order to put curiosity and detection off the scent. Over this strange fact poor Charlotte interminably mused: it became more touching, more attaching for her than she could now confide to any ear. How bad, or how happy – in the sophisticated sense of Mrs Guy and the young man at the Temple – the effaced Miss Bradshaw must have been to have had to be so mute! The little governess at Bleet put on the necklace now in secret sessions; she wore it sometimes under her dress; she came to feel, verily, a haunting passion for it. Yet in her penniless state she would have parted with it for money; she gave herself also to dreams of what in this direction it would do for her. The sophistry of her so often saying to herself that Arthur had after all definitely pronounced her welcome to any gain from his gift that might accrue – this trick remained innocent, as she perfectly knew it for what it was. Then there was always the possibility of his – as she could only picture it – rising to the occasion. Mightn't he have a grand magnanimous moment? – mightn't he just say: 'Oh, of course I couldn't have afforded to let you have it if I had known; but since you *have* got it, and have made out the truth by your own wit, I really can't screw myself down to the shabbiness of taking it back'?

She had, as it proved, to wait a long time – to wait till, at the end of several months, the great house of Bleet had, with due deliberation, for the season, transferred itself to town; after which, however, she fairly snatched at her first freedom to knock, dressed in her best and armed with her disclosure, at the door of her doubting kinsman. It was still with doubt and not quite with the face she had hoped that he listened to her story. He had turned pale, she thought, as she produced the necklace, and he appeared, above all, disagreeably affected. Well, perhaps there was reason, she more than ever remembered; but what on earth was one, in close touch with the fact, to do? She had laid the pearls on his table, where, without his having at first put so much as a finger to them, they met his hard, cold stare.

'I don't believe in them,' he simply said at last.

'That's exactly then,' she returned with some spirit, 'what I wanted to hear!'

She fancied that at this his colour changed; it was indeed vivid to her afterwards – for she was to have a long recall of the scene – that she had made him quite angrily flush. 'It's a beastly unpleasant imputation, you know!' – and he walked away from her as he had always walked at the vicarage.

'It's none of *my* making, I'm sure,' said Charlotte Prime. 'If you're afraid to believe they're real —'

'Well?' – and he turned, across the room, sharp round at her.

'Why, it's not my fault.'

He said nothing more, for a moment, on this; he only came back to the table. 'They're what I originally said they were. They're rotten paste.'

'Then I may keep them?'

'No. I want a better opinion.'

'Than your own?'

'Than *your* own.' He dropped on the pearls another queer stare, then, after a moment, bringing himself to touch them, did exactly what she had herself done in the presence of Mrs Guy at Bleet – gathered them together, marched off with them to a drawer, put them in and clicked the key. 'You say I'm afraid,' he went on as he again met her; 'but I shan't be afraid to take them to Bond Street.'

'And if the people say they're real — ?'

He hesitated – then had his strangest manner. 'They won't say it! They shan't!'

There was something in the way he brought it out that deprived poor Charlotte, as she was perfectly aware, of any manner at all. 'Oh!' she simply sounded, as she had sounded for her last word to Mrs Guy; and, within a minute, without more conversation, she had taken her departure.

A fortnight later she received a communication from him, and towards the end of the season one of the entertainments in Eaton Square was graced by the presence of Mrs Guy. Charlotte was not at dinner, but she came down afterwards, and this guest, on seeing her, abandoned a very beautiful young man on purpose to cross and speak to her. The guest had on a lovely necklace and had apparently not lost her habit of overflowing with the pride of such ornaments.

'Do you see?' She was in high joy.

They were indeed splendid pearls – so far as poor Charlotte could feel that she knew, after what had come and gone, about such mysteries. Charlotte had a sickly smile. 'They're almost as fine as Arthur's.'

'Almost? Where, my dear, are your eyes? They *are* "Arthur's!"' After which, to meet the flood of crimson that accompanied her young friend's start: 'I tracked them – after your folly, and, by miraculous luck, recognized them in the Bond Street window to which he had disposed of them.'

'*Disposed* of them?' the girl gasped. 'He wrote me that I had insulted his mother and that the people had shown him he was right – had pronounced them utter paste.'

Mrs Guy gave a stare. 'Ah, I told you he wouldn't bear it! No. But I had, I assure you,' she wound up, 'to drive my bargain!'

Charlotte scarce heard or saw; she was full of her private wrong. 'He wrote me', she panted, 'that he had smashed them.'

Mrs Guy could only wonder and pity. 'He's really morbid!' But it was not quite clear which of the pair she pitied; though Charlotte felt really morbid too after they had separated and she found herself full of thought. She even went the length of asking herself what sort of a bargain Mrs Guy had driven and whether the marvel of the recognition in Bond Street had been a veracious account of the matter. Hadn't she perhaps in truth dealt with Arthur directly? It came back to Charlotte almost luridly that she had had his address.

Thrawn Janet

The Reverend Murdoch Soulis was long minister of the moorland
parish of Balweary, in the vale of Dule. A severe, bleak-faced old
man, dreadful to his hearers, he dwelt in the last years of his life,
without relative or servant or any human company, in the small
and lonely manse under the Hanging Shaw. In spite of the iron
composure of his features, his eye was wild, scared, and uncertain;
and when he dwelt, in private admonitions, on the future of the
impenitent, it seemed as if his eye pierced through the storms of
time to the terrors of eternity. Many young persons, coming to prepare themselves against the season of the Holy Communion, were
dreadfully affected by his talk. He had a sermon on 1st Peter, v.
and 8th, 'The devil as a roaring lion', on the Sunday after every
seventeenth of August, and he was accustomed to surpass himself
upon that text both by the appalling nature of the matter and the
terror of his bearing in the pulpit. The children were frightened into
fits, and the old looked more than usually oracular, and were, all
that day, full of those hints that Hamlet deprecated. The manse
itself, where it stood by the water of Dule among some thick trees,
with the Shaw overhanging it on the one side, and on the other
many cold, moorish hilltops rising towards the sky, had begun, at
a very early period of Mr Soulis's ministry, to be avoided in the
dusk hours by all who valued themselves upon their prudence; and
guidmen sitting at the clachan ale-house shook their heads together
at the thought of passing late by that uncanny neighbourhood.
There was one spot, to be more particular, which was regarded
with special awe. The manse stood between the high road and the
water of Dule, with a gable to each; its back was towards the kirk-
town of Balweary, nearly half a mile away; in front of it, a bare
garden, hedged with thorn, occupied the land between the river
and the road. The house was two storeys high, with two large
rooms on each. It opened not directly on the garden, but on a
causewayed path, or passage, giving on the road on the one hand,

and closed on the other by the tall willows and elders that bordered on the stream. And it was this strip of causeway that enjoyed among the young parishioners of Balweary so infamous a reputation. The minister walked there often after dark, sometimes groaning aloud in the instancy of his unspoken prayers; and when he was from home, and the manse door was locked, the more daring schoolboys ventured, with beating hearts, to 'follow my leader' across the legendary spot.

This atmosphere of terror, surrounding, as it did, a man of God of spotless character and orthodoxy, was a common cause of wonder and subject of inquiry among the few strangers who were led by chance or business into that unknown, outlying country. But many even of the people of the parish were ignorant of the strange events which had marked the first year of Mr Soulis's ministrations; and among those who were better informed, some were naturally reticent, and others shy of that particular topic. Now and again, only, one of the older folk would warm into courage over his third tumbler, and recount the cause of the minister's strange looks and solitary life.

Fifty years syne, when Mr Soulis cam' first into Ba'weary, he was still a young man – a callant, the folk said – fu' o' book learnin' and grand at the exposition, but, as was natural in sae young a man, wi' nae leevin' experience in religion. The younger sort were greatly taken wi' his gifts and his gab; but auld, concerned, serious men and women were moved even to prayer for the young man, whom they took to be a self-deceiver, and the parish that was like to be sae ill-supplied. It was before the days o' the moderates — weary fa' them; but ill things are like guid – they baith come bit by bit, a pickle at a time; and there were folk even then that said the Lord had left the college professors to their ain devices, an' the lads that went to study wi' them wad hae done mair and better sittin' in a peat-bog, like their forebears of the persecution, wi' a Bible under their oxter and a speerit o' prayer in their heart. There was nae doubt, onyway, but that Mr Soulis had been ower lang at the college. He was careful and troubled for mony things besides the ae thing needful. He had a feck o' books wi' him – mair than had ever been seen before in a' that presbytery; and a sair wark the carrier had wi' them, for they were a' like to have smoored in the Deil's Hag between this and Kilmackerlie. They were books o' divinity, to be sure, or so they ca'd them; but the serious were o' opinion there was little service for sae mony, when the hail o' God's Word would gang in the neuk of a plaid. Then he wad sit half the day and half the nicht forbye, which was scant decent – writin', nae less; and first, they were feared he wad read his sermons; and syne it proved he was writin' a book himsel', which was surely no fittin' for ane of his years an' sma' experience.

Onyway it behoved him to get an auld, decent wife to keep the manse for him an' see to his bit denners; and he was recommended to an auld limmer – Janet M'Clour, they ca'd her – and sae far left to himsel' as to be ower persuaded. There was mony advised him to the contrar, for Janet was mair than suspeckit by the best folk in Ba'weary. Lang or that, she had had a wean to a dragoon; she hadnae come forrit* for maybe thretty year; and bairns had seen her mumblin' to hersel' up on Key's Loan in the gloamin', whilk was an unco time an' place for a God-fearin' woman. Howsoever, it was the laird himsel' that had first tauld the minister o' Janet; and in thae days he wad have gane a far gate to pleesure the laird. When folk tauld him that Janet was sib to the deil, it was a' super-stition by his way of it; an' when they cast up the Bible to him an' the witch of Endor, he wad threep it doun their thrapples that thir days were a' gane by, and the deil was mercifully restrained.

Weel, when it got about the clachan that Janet M'Clour was to be servant at the manse, the folk were fair mad wi' her an' him thegether; and some o' the guidwives had nae better to dae than get round her door cheeks and chairge her wi' a' that was ken't again her, frae the sodger's bairn to John Tamson's twa kye. She was nae great speaker; folk usually let her gang her ain gate, an' she let them gang theirs, wi' neither Fair-guid-een nor Fair-guid-day; but when she buckled to, she had a tongue to deave the miller. Up she got, an' there wasnae an auld story in Ba'weary but she gart somebody lowp for it that day; they couldnae say ae thing but she could say twa to it; till, at the hinder end, the guidwives up and claucht haud of her, and clawed the coats aff her back, and pu'd her doun the clachan to the water o' Dule, to see if she were a witch or no, soum or droun. The carline skirled till ye could hear her at the Hangin' Shaw, and she focht like ten; there was mony a guid-wife bure the mark of her neist day an' mony a lang day after; and just in the hettest o' the collieshangie, wha suld come up (for his

* To come forrit – to offer oneself as a communicant.

sins) but the new minister.

'Women,' said he (and he had a grand voice), 'I charge you in the Lord's name to let her go.'

Janet ran to him – she was fair wud wi' terror – an' clang to him, an' prayed him, for Christ's sake, save her frae the cummers; an' they, for their pairt, tauld him a' that was ken't, and maybe mair.

'Woman,' says he to Janet, 'is this true?'

'As the Lord sees me,' says she, 'as the Lord made me, no a word o't. Forbye the bairn,' says she, 'I've been a decent woman a' my days.'

'Will you,' says Mr Soulis, 'in the name of God, and before me, His unworthy minister, renounce the devil and his works?'

Weel, it wad appear that when he askit that, she gave a girn that fairly frichtit them that saw her, an' they could hear her teeth play dirl thegether in her chafts; but there was naething for it but the ae way or the ither; an' Janet lifted up her hand and renounced the deil before them a'.

'And now,' says Mr Soulis to the guidwives, 'home with ye, one and all, and pray to God for His forgiveness.'

And he gied Janet his arm, though she had little on her but a sark, and took her up the clachan to her ain door like a leddy of the land; an' her scrieghin' and laughin' as was a scandal to be heard.

There were mony grave folk lang ower their prayers that nicht; but when the morn cam' there was sic a fear fell upon a' Ba'weary that the bairns hid theirsels, and even the men folk stood and keekit frae their doors. For there was Janet comin' doun the clachan – her or her likeness, nane could tell – wi' her neck thrawn, and her heid on ae side, like a body that has been hangit, and a girn on her face like an unstreakit corp. By-an'-by they got used wi' it, and even speered at her to ken what was wrang; but frae that day forth she couldnae speak like a Christian woman, but slavered and played click wi' her teeth like a pair o' shears; and frae that day forth the name o' God cam' never on her lips. Whiles she would try to say it, but it michtnae be. Them that kenned best said least; but they never gied that Thing the name o' Janet M'Clour; for the auld Janet, by their way o't, was in muckle hell that day. But the minister was neither to haud nor to bind; he preached about naething but the folk's cruelty that had gi'en her a stroke of the palsy; he skelpt the bairns that meddled her; and he had her up to the manse that

same nicht, and dwalled there a' his lane wi' her under the Hangin'
Shaw.

Weel, time gaed by: and the idler sort commenced to think mair
lichtly o' that black business. The minister was weel thocht o'; he
was aye late at the writing, folk wad see his can'le doon by the
Dule water after twal' at e'en; and he seemed pleased wi' himsel'
and upsitten as at first, though a' body could see that he was dwin-
ing. As for Janet she cam' an' she gaed; if she didnae speak muckle
afore, it was reason she should speak less then; she meddled naebody; but she was an eldritch thing to see, an' nane wad hae mis-
trysted wi' her for Ba'weary glebe.

About the end o' July there cam' a spell o' weather, the like o't
never was in that country side; it was lown an' het an' heartless;
the herds couldnae win up the Black Hill, the bairns were ower
weariet to play; an' yet it was gousty too, wi' claps o' het wund
that rumm'led in the glens, and bits o' shouers that slockened naething. We aye thocht it but to thun'er on the morn; but the morn
cam', an' the morn's morning, and it was aye the same uncanny
weather, sair on folks and bestial. Of a' that were the waur, nane
suffered like Mr Soulis; he could neither sleep nor eat, he tauld his
elders; an' when he wasnae writin' at his weary book, he wad be
stravaguin' ower a' the countryside like a man possessed, when a'
body else was blythe to keep caller ben the house.

Abune Hangin' Shaw, in the bield o' the Black Hill, there's a bit
enclosed grund wi' an iron yett; and it seems, in the auld days, that
was the kirkyaird o' Ba'weary, and consecrated by the Papists before the blessed licht shone upon the kingdom. It was a great howff
o' Mr Soulis's, onyway; there he would sit an' consider his sermons; and indeed it's a bieldy bit. Weel, as he cam' ower the wast
end o' the Black Hill, ae day, he saw first twa, an syne fower, an'
syne seeven corbie craws fleein' round an' round abune the auld
kirkyaird. They flew laigh and heavy, an' squawked to ither as they
gaed; and it was clear to Mr Soulis that something had put them
frae their ordinar. He wasnae easy fleyed, an' gaed straucht up to
the wa's; an' what suld he find there but a man, or the appearance
of a man, sittin' in the inside upon a grave. He was of a great
stature, an' black as hell, and his e'en were singular to see.* Mr

* It was a common belief in Scotland that the devil appeared as a black man.
This appears in several witch trials and, I think, in Law's *Memorials*, that delightful
store-house of the quaint and grisly.

Soulis had heard tell o' black men, mony's the time; but there was something unco about this black man that daunted him. Het as he was, he took a kind o' cauld grue in the marrow o' his banes; but up he spak for a' that; an' says he: 'My friend, are you a stranger in this place?' The black man answered never a word; he got upon his feet, an' begude to hirsle to the wa' on the far side; but he aye lookit at the minister; an' the minister stood an' lookit back; till a' in a meenute the black man was ower the wa' an' rinnin' for the bield o' the trees. Mr Soulis, he hardly kenned why, ran after him; but he was sair forjaskit wi' his walk an' the het, unhalesome weather; and rin as he likit, he got nae mair than a glisk o' the black man amang the birks, till he won doun to the foot o' the hillside, an' there he saw him ance mair, gaun, hap, step, an' lowp, ower Dule water to the manse.

Mr Soulis wasnae well pleased that this fearsome gangrel suld mak' sae free wi' Ba'weary manse; an' he ran the harder, an', wet shoon, ower the burn, an' up the walk; but the deil a black man was there to see. He stepped out upon the road, but there was naebody there; he gaed a' ower the gairden, but na, nae black man. At the hinder end, and a bit feared as was but natural, he lifted the hasp and into the manse; and there was Janet M'Clour before his een, wi' her thrawn craig, and nane sae pleased to see him. And he aye minded sinsyne, when first he set his een upon her, he had the same cauld and deidly grue.

'Janet,' says he, 'have you seen a black man?'

'A black man?' quo' she. 'Save us a'! Ye're no wise, minister. There's nae black man in a' Ba'weary.'

But she didnae speak plain, ye maun understand; but yam-yammered, like a powney wi' the bit in its moo.

'Weel,' says he, 'Janet, if there was nae black man, I have spoken with the Accuser of the Brethren.'

And he sat down like ane wi' a fever, an' his teeth chittered in his heid.

'Hoots,' says she, 'think shame to yoursel', minister;' an' gied him a drap brandy that she keept aye by her.

Syne Mr Soulis gaed into his study amang a' his books. It's a lang, laigh, mirk chalmer, perishin' cauld in winter, an' no very dry even in the tap o' the simmer, for the manse stands near the burn. Sae doun he sat, and thocht of a' that had come an' gane since he was in Ba'weary, an' his hame, an' the days when he was a bairn an' ran daffin' on the braes; and that black man aye ran in his heid like the owercome of a sang. Aye the mair he thocht, the mair he thocht o' the black man. He tried the prayer, an' the words wouldnae come to him; an' he tried, they say, to write at his book, but he could nae mak' nae mair o' that. There was whiles he thocht the black man was at his oxter, an' the swat stood upon him cauld as well-water; and there was other whiles, when he cam' to himsel' like a christened bairn and minded naething.

The upshot was that he gaed to the window an' stood glowrin' at Dule water. The trees are unco thick, an' the water lies deep an' black under the manse; an' there was Janet washin' the cla'es wi' her coats kilted. She had her back to the minister, an' he, for his pairt, hardly kenned what he was lookin' at. Syne she turned round, an' shawed her face; Mr Soulis had the same cauld grue as twice that day afore, an' it was borne in upon him what folk said, that Janet was deid lang syne, an' this was a bogle in her clay-cauld flesh. He drew back a pickle and he scanned her narrowly. She was tramp-trampin' in the cla'es, croonin' to hersel'; and he! Gude guide us, but it was a fearsome face. Whiles she sang louder, but there was nae man born o' woman that could tell the words o' her sang; an' whiles she lookit side-lang doun, but there was naething there for her to look at. There gaed a scunner through the flesh upon his banes; and that was Heeven's advertisement. But Mr Soulis just blamed himsel', he said, to think sae ill of a puir, auld afflicted wife that hadnae a freend forbye himsel'; an' he put up a bit prayer for him and her, an' drank a little caller water – for his heart rose again the meat – an' gaed up to his naked bed in the gloaming.

That was a nicht that has never been forgotten in Ba'weary, the nicht o' the seventeenth of August, seventeen hun'er' an twal'. It had been het afore, as I hae said, but that nicht it was hetter than ever. The sun gaed doun amang unco-lookin' clouds; it fell as mirk as the pit; no a star, no a breath o' wund; ye couldnae see your han' afore your face, and even the auld folk cuist the covers frae their beds and lay pechin' for their breath. Wi' a' that he had upon his mind, it was gey and unlikely Mr Soulis wad get muckle sleep. He lay an' he tummled; the gude, caller bed that he got into brunt his very banes; whiles he slept, and whiles he waukened; whiles he heard the time o' nicht, and whiles a tyke yowlin' up the muir, as if somebody was deid; whiles he thocht he heard bogles claverin' in his lug, an' whiles he saw spunkies in the room. He behoved, he judged, to be sick; an' sick he was – little he jaloosed the sickness.

At the hinder end, he got a clearness in his mind, sat up in his sark on the bedside, and fell thinkin' ance mair o' the black man an' Janet. He couldnae well tell how – maybe it was the cauld to his feet – but it cam' in upon him wi' a spate that there was some connexion between thir twa, an' that either or baith o' them were bogles. And just at that moment, in Janet's room, which was neist to his, there cam' a stramp o' feet as if men were wars'lin', an' then a loud bang; an' then a wund gaed reishling round the fower quarters of the house; an' then a' was aince mair as seelent as the grave.

Mr Soulis was feared for neither man nor deevil. He got his tinder-box, an' lit a can'le, an' made three steps o't ower to Janet's door. It was on the hasp, an' he pushed it open, an' keeked bauldly in. It was a big room, as big as the minister's ain, an' plenished wi' grand, auld, solid gear, for he had naething else. There was a fower-posted bed wi' auld tapestry; and a braw cabinet of aik, that was fu' o' the minister's divinity books, an' put there to be out o' the gate; an' a wheen duds o' Janet's lying here and there about the floor. But nae Janet could Mr Soulis see; nor ony sign of a contention. In he gaed (an' there's few that wad ha'e followed him) an' lookit a' round, an' listened. But there was naethin' to be heard, neither inside the manse nor in a' Ba'weary parish, an' naethin' to be seen but the muckle shadows turnin' round the can'le. An' then a' at aince, the minister's heart played dunt an' stood stock-still; an' a cauld wund blew amang the hairs o' his heid. Whaten a weary sicht was that for the puir man's een! For there was Janet hangin' frae a nail beside the auld aik cabinet: her heid aye lay on her shoother, her een were steeked, the tongue projekit frae her mouth, and her heels were twa feet clear abune the floor.

'God forgive us all!' thocht Mr Soulis; 'poor Janet's dead.'

He cam' a step nearer to the corp; an' then his heart fair whammled in his inside. For by what cantrip it wad ill-beseem a man to judge, she was hingin' frae a single nail an' by a single wursted thread for darnin' hose.

It's an awfu' thing to be your lane at nicht wi' siccan prodigies o' darkness; but Mr Soulis was strong in the Lord. He turned an' gaed his ways oot o' that room, and lockit the door ahint him; and step by step, doon the stairs, as heavy as leed; and set doon the can'le on the table at the stairfoot. He couldnae pray, he couldnae think, he was dreepin' wi' caul' swat, an' naething could he hear but the dunt-dunt-duntin' o' his ain heart. He micht maybe have stood there an hour, or maybe twa, he minded sae little; when a' o' a sudden, he heard a laigh, uncanny steer upstairs; a foot gaed to an' fro in the cha'mer whaur the corp was hingin'; syne the door was opened, though he minded weel that he had lockit it; an' syne there was a step upon the landin', an' it seemed to him as if the corp was lookin' ower the rail and doun upon him whaur he stood.

He took up the can'le again (for he couldnae want the licht), and as saftly as ever he could, gaed straucht out o' the manse an' to the far end o' the causeway. It was aye pit-mirk; the flame o' the can'le, when he set it on the grund, brunt steedy and clear as in a room; naething moved, but the Dule water seepin' and sabbin' doun the glen, an' yon unhaly footstep that cam' ploddin' doun the stairs inside the manse. He kenned the foot over weel, for it was Janet's; and at ilka step that cam' a wee thing nearer, the cauld got deeper in his vitals. He commended his soul to Him that make an' keepit him; 'and O Lord,' said he, 'give me strength this night to war against the powers of evil'.

By this time the foot was comin' through the passage for the door; he could hear a hand skirt alang the wa', as if the fearsome thing was feelin' for its way. The saughs tossed an' maned thegether, a lang sigh cam' ower the hills, the flame o' the can'le was blawn aboot; an' there stood the corp of Thrawn Janet, wi' her grogram goun an' her black mutch, wi' the heid aye upon the shouther, an' the girn still upon the face o't – leevin', ye wad hae said – deid, as Mr Soulis weel kenned – upon the threshold o' the manse.

It's a strange thing that the saul of man should be that thirled into his perishable body; but the minister saw that, an' his heart didnae break.

She didnae stand there lang; she began to move again an' cam' slowly towards Mr Soulis whaur he stood under the saughs. A' the life o' his body, a' the strength o' his speerit, were glowerin' frae his een. It seemed she was gaun to speak, but wanted words, an' made a sign wi' the left hand. There cam' a clap o' wund, like a cat's fuff; oot gaed the can'le, the saughs skrieghed like folk; an' Mr Soulis kenned that, live or die, this was the end o't.

'Witch, beldame, devil!' he cried, 'I charge you, by the power of God, begone – if you be dead, to the grave – if you be damned, to hell.'

An' at that moment the Lord's ain hand out o' the Heevens struck the Horror whaur it stood; the auld, deid, desecrated corp o' the witch-wife, sae lang keepit frae the grave and hirsled round by deils, lowed up like a brunstane spunk and fell in ashes to the grund; the thunder followed, peal on dirling peal, the rairing rain upon the back o' that; and Mr Soulis lowped through the garden hedge, and ran, wi' skelloch upon skelloch, for the clachan.

That same mornin', John Christie saw the Black Man pass the Muckle Cairn as it was chappin' six; before eicht, he gaed by the change-house at Knockdow; an' no lang after, Sandy M'Lellan saw him gaun linkin' doun the braes frae Kilmackerlie. There's little doubt but it was him that dwalled sae lang in Janet's body; but he was awa' at last; and sinsyne the deil has never fashed us in Ba'weary.

But it was a sair dispensation for the minister; lang, lang he lay ravin' in his bed; and frae that hour to this, he was the man ye ken the day.

JOSEPH CONRAD · 1857–1924

The Secret Sharer

I

On my right hand there were lines of fishing-stakes resembling a mysterious system of half-submerged bamboo fences, incomprehensible in its division of the domain of tropical fishes, and crazy of aspect as if abandoned forever by some nomad tribe of fishermen now gone to the other end of the ocean; for there was no sign of human habitation as far as the eye could reach. To the left a group of barren islets, suggesting ruins of stone walls, towers, and blockhouses, had its foundations set in a blue sea that itself looked solid, so still and stable did it lie below my feet; even the track of light from the westering sun shone smoothly, without that animated glitter which tells of an imperceptible ripple. And when I turned my head to take a parting glance at the tug which had just left us anchored outside the bar, I saw the straight line of the flat shore joined to the stable sea, edge to edge, with a perfect and unmarked closeness, in one levelled floor half brown, half blue under the enormous dome of the sky. Corresponding in their insignificance to the islets of the sea, two small clumps of trees, one on each side of the only fault in the impeccable joint, marked the mouth of the river Meinam we had just left on the first preparatory stage of our homeward journey; and, far back on the inland level, a larger and loftier mass, the grove surrounding the great Paknam pagoda, was the only thing on which the eye could rest from the vain task of exploring the monotonous sweep of the horizon. Here and there gleams as of a few scattered pieces of silver marked the windings of the great river; and on the nearest of them, just within the bar, the tug steaming right into the land became lost to my sight, hull and funnel and masts, as though the impassive earth had swallowed her up without an effort, without a tremor. My eye followed the light cloud of her smoke, now here, now there, above the plain, according to the devious curves of the stream, but always fainter and farther away, till I lost it at last behind the mitre-shaped hill of the great pagoda. And then I was left alone with my ship, anchored at the head of the Gulf of Siam.

She floated at the starting-point of a long journey, very still in an immense stillness, the shadows of her spars flung far to the eastward by the setting sun. At that moment I was alone on her decks. There was not a sound in her – and around us nothing moved, nothing lived, not a canoe on the water, not a bird in the air, not a cloud in the sky. In this breathless pause at the threshold of a long passage we seemed to be measuring our fitness for a long and arduous enterprise, the appointed task of both our existences to be carried out, far from all human eyes, with only sky and sea for spectators and for judges.

There must have been some glare in the air to interfere with one's sight, because it was only just before the sun left us that my roaming eyes made out beyond the highest ridge of the principal islet of the group something which did away with the solemnity of perfect solitude. The tide of darkness flowed on swiftly; and with tropical suddenness a swarm of stars came out above the shadowy earth, while I lingered yet, my hand resting lightly on my ship's rail as if on the shoulder of a trusted friend. But, with all that multitude of celestial bodies staring down at one, the comfort of quiet communion with her was gone for good. And there were also disturbing sounds by this time – voices, footsteps forward; the steward flitted along the main-deck, a busily ministering spirit; a hand-bell tinkled urgently under the poop-deck. . . .

I found my two officers waiting for me near the supper table, in the lighted cuddy. We sat down at once, and as I helped the chief mate, I said:

'Are you aware that there is a ship anchored inside the islands? I saw her mastheads above the ridge as the sun went down.'

He raised sharply his simple face, overcharged by a terrible growth of whisker, and emitted his usual ejaculations: 'Bless my soul, sir! You don't say so!'

My second mate was a round-cheeked, silent young man, grave beyond his years, I thought; but as our eyes happened to meet I detected a slight quiver on his lips. I looked down at once. It was not my part to encourage sneering on board my ship. It must be said, too, that I knew very little of my officers. In consequence of certain events of no particular significance, except to myself, I had been appointed to the command only a fortnight before. Neither did I know much of the hands forward. All these people had been together for eighteen months or so, and my position was that of the only stranger on board. I mention this because it has some bearing on what is to follow. But what I felt most was my being a stranger to the ship; and if all the truth must be told, I was somewhat of a stranger to myself. The youngest man on board (barring the second mate), and untried as yet by a position of the fullest responsibility, I was willing to take the adequacy of the others for granted. They had simply to be equal to their tasks; but I wondered how far I should turn out faithful to that ideal conception of one's own personality every man sets up for himself secretly.

Meantime the chief mate, with an almost visible effect of collaboration on the part of his round eyes and frightful whiskers, was trying to evolve a theory of the anchored ship. His dominant trait was to take all things into earnest consideration. He was of a painstaking turn of mind. As he used to say, he 'liked to account to himself' for practically everything that came in his way, down to a miserable scorpion he had found in his cabin a week before. The why and the wherefore of that scorpion – how it got on board and came to select his room rather than the pantry (which was a dark place and more what a scorpion would be partial to), and how on earth it managed to drown itself in the inkwell of his writing-desk – had exercised him infinitely. The ship within the islands was much more easily accounted for; and just as we were about to rise from table he made his pronouncement. She was, he doubted not, a ship from home lately arrived. Probably she drew too much water to cross the bar except at the top of spring tides. Therefore she went into that natural harbour to wait for a few days in preference to remaining in an open roadstead.

'That's so,' confirmed the second mate, suddenly, in his slightly hoarse voice. 'She draws over twenty feet. She's the Liverpool ship *Sephora* with a cargo of coal. Hundred and twenty-three days from Cardiff.'

We looked at him in surprise.

'The tugboat skipper told me when he came on board for your letters, sir,' explained the young man. 'He expects to take her up the river the day after tomorrow.'

After thus overwhelming us with the extent of his information he slipped out of the cabin. The mate observed regretfully that he 'could not account for that young fellow's whims'. What prevented him telling us all about it at once, he wanted to know.

I detained him as he was making a move. For the last two days the crew had had plenty of hard work, and the night before they had very little sleep. I felt painfully that I – a stranger – was doing something unusual when I directed him to let all hands turn in without setting an anchor-watch. I proposed to keep on deck myself till one o'clock or thereabouts. I would get the second mate to relieve me at that hour.

'He will turn out the cook and the steward at four,' I concluded, 'and then give you a call. Of course at the slightest sign of any sort of wind we'll have the hands up and make a start at once.'

He concealed his astonishment. 'Very well, sir.' Outside the cuddy he put his head in the second mate's door to inform him of my unheard-of caprice to take a five hours' anchor-watch on myself. I heard the other raise his voice incredulously — 'What? The captain himself?' Then a few more murmurs, a door closed, then another. A few moments later I went on deck.

My strangeness, which had made me sleepless, had prompted that unconventional arrangement, as if I had expected in those solitary hours of the night to get on terms with the ship of which I knew nothing, manned by men of whom I knew very little more. Fast alongside a wharf, littered like any ship in port with a tangle of unrelated things, invaded by unrelated shore people, I had hardly seen her yet properly. Now, as she lay cleared for sea, the stretch of her main-deck seemed to me very fine under the stars. Very fine, very roomy for her size, and very inviting. I descended the poop and paced the waist, my mind picturing to myself the coming passage through the Malay Archipelago, down the Indian Ocean, and up the Atlantic. All its phases were familiar enough to me, every characteristic, all the alternatives which were likely to face me on the high seas – everything! . . . except the novel responsibility of command. But I took heart from the reasonable thought that the ship was like other ships, the men like other men, and that the sea was not likely to keep any special surprises expressly for my discomfiture.

Arrived at that comforting conclusion, I bethought myself of a cigar and went below to get it. All was still down there. Everybody at the after end of the ship was sleeping profoundly. I came out again on the quarterdeck, agreeably at ease in my sleeping-suit on that warm breathless night, barefooted, a glowing cigar in my teeth, and, going forward, I was met by the profound silence of the fore end of the ship. Only as I passed the door of the forecastle I heard a deep, quiet, trustful sigh of some sleeper inside. And suddenly I rejoiced in the great security of the sea as compared with the unrest of the land, in my choice of that untempted life presenting no disquieting problems, invested with an elementary moral beauty by the absolute straightforwardness of its appeal and by the singleness of its purpose.

The riding-light in the fore-rigging burned with a clear, untroubled, as if symbolic, flame, confident and bright in the mysterious shades of the night. Passing on my way aft along the other side of the ship, I observed that the rope side-ladder, put over, no doubt, for the master of the tug when he came to fetch away our letters, had not been hauled in as it should have been. I became annoyed at this, for exactitude in small matters is the very soul of discipline. Then I reflected that I had myself peremptorily dismissed my officers from duty, and by my own act had prevented the anchor-watch being formally set and things properly attended to. I asked myself whether it was wise ever to interfere with the established routine of duties even from the kindest of motives. My action might have made me appear eccentric. Goodness only knew how that absurdly whiskered mate would 'account' for my conduct, and what the whole ship thought of that informality of their new captain. I was vexed with myself.

Not from compunction certainly, but, as it were mechanically, I proceeded to get the ladder in myself. Now a side-ladder of that sort is a light affair and comes in easily, yet my vigorous tug, which should have brought it flying on board, merely recoiled upon my body in a totally unexpected jerk. What the devil! . . . I was so astounded by the immovableness of that ladder that I remained stockstill, trying to account for it to myself like that imbecile mate of mine. In the end, of course, I put my head over the rail.

The side of the ship made an opaque belt of shadow on the darkling glassy shimmer of the sea. But I saw at once something elongated and pale floating very close to the ladder. Before I could form a guess a faint flash of phosphorescent light, which seemed to issue suddenly from the naked body of a man, flickered in the sleeping water with the elusive, silent play of summer lightning in a night sky. With a gasp I saw revealed to my stare a pair of feet, the long legs, a broad livid back immersed right up to the neck in a greenish cadaverous glow. One hand, awash, clutched the bottom rung of the ladder. He was complete but for the head. A headless corpse! The cigar dropped out of my gaping mouth with a tiny plop and a short hiss quite audible in the absolute stillness of all things under heaven. At that I suppose he raised up his face, a dimly pale oval in the shadow of the ship's side. But even then I could only barely make out down there the shape of his black-haired head. However, it was enough for the horrid, frost-bound sensation which had gripped me about the chest to pass off. The moment of vain exclamations was past, too. I only climbed on the spare spar and leaned over the rail as far as I could, to bring my eyes nearer to that mystery floating alongside.

As he hung by the ladder, like a resting swimmer, the sea-lightning played about his limbs at every stir; and he appeared in it ghastly, silvery, fish-like. He remained as mute as a fish, too. He made no motion to get out of the water, either. It was inconceivable that he should not attempt to come on board, and strangely troubling to suspect that perhaps he did not want to. And my first words were prompted by just that troubled incertitude.

'What's the matter?' I asked in my ordinary tone, speaking down to the face upturned exactly under mine.

'Cramp,' it answered, no louder. Then slightly anxious, 'I say, no need to call anyone.'

'I was not going to,' I said.

'Are you alone on deck?'

'Yes.'

I had somehow the impression that he was on the point of letting go the ladder to swim away beyond my ken – mysterious as he came. But, for the moment, this being appearing as if he had risen from the bottom of the sea (it was certainly the nearest land to the ship) wanted only to know the time. I told him. And he, down there, tentatively:

'I suppose your captain's turned in?'

'I am sure he isn't,' I said.

He seemed to struggle with himself, for I heard something like the low, bitter murmur of doubt.

'What's the good?' His next words came out with a hesitating effort.

'Look here, my man. Could you call him out quietly?'

I thought the time had come to declare myself.

'*I* am the captain.'

I heard a 'By Jove!' whispered at the level of the water. The phosphorescence flashed in the swirl of the water all about his limbs, his other hand seized the ladder.

'My name's Leggatt.'

The voice was calm and resolute. A good voice. The self-possession of that man had somehow induced a corresponding state in myself. It was very quietly that I remarked:

'You must be a good swimmer.'

'Yes. I've been in the water practically since nine o'clock. The question for me now is whether I am to let go this ladder and go on swimming till I sink from exhaustion, or — to come on board here.'

I felt this was no mere formula of desperate speech, but a real alternative in the view of a strong soul. I should have gathered from this that he was young; indeed, it is only the young who are ever confronted by such clear issues. But at the time it was pure intuition on my part. A mysterious communication was established already between us two — in the face of that silent, darkened tropical sea. I was young, too; young enough to make no comment. The man in the water began suddenly to climb up the ladder, and I hastened away from the rail to fetch some clothes.

Before entering the cabin I stood still, listening in the lobby at the foot of the stairs. A faint snore came through the closed door of the chief mate's room. The second mate's door was on the hook, but the darkness in there was absolutely soundless. He, too, was young and could sleep like a stone. Remained the steward, but he was not likely to wake up before he was called. I got a sleeping-suit out of my room and, coming back on deck, saw the naked man from the sea sitting on the main-hatch, glimmering white in the darkness, his elbows on his knees and his head in his hands. In a moment he had concealed his damp body in a sleeping-suit of the same grey-stripe pattern as the one I was wearing and followed me like my double on the poop. Together we moved right aft, barefooted, silent.

'What is it?' I asked in a deadened voice, taking the lighted lamp out of the binnacle, and raising it to his face.

'An ugly business.'

He had rather regular features; a good mouth; light eyes under somewhat heavy, dark eyebrows; a smooth, square forehead; no growth on his cheeks; a small, brown moustache, and a well-shaped, round chin. His expression was concentrated, meditative, under the inspecting light of the lamp I held up to his face; such as a man thinking hard in solitude might wear. My sleeping-suit was just right for his size. A well-knit young fellow of twenty-five at most. He caught his lower lip with the edge of white, even teeth.

'Yes,' I said, replacing the lamp in the binnacle. The warm, heavy tropical night closed upon his head again.

'There's a ship over there,' he murmured.

'Yes, I know. The *Sephora*. Did you know of us?'

'Hadn't the slightest idea. I am the mate of her —' He paused and corrected himself. 'I should say I *was*.'

'Aha! Something wrong?'

'Yes. Very wrong indeed. I've killed a man.'

'What do you mean? Just now?'

'No, on the passage. Weeks ago. Thirty-nine south. When I say a man —'

'Fit of temper,' I suggested, confidently.

The shadowy, dark head, like mine, seemed to nod imperceptibly above the ghostly grey of my sleeping-suit. It was, in the night, as though I had been faced by my own reflection in the depths of a sombre and immense mirror.

'A pretty thing to have to own up to for a Conway boy,' murmured my double, distinctly.

'You're a Conway boy?'

'I am,' he said, as if startled. Then, slowly . . . 'Perhaps you too —'

It was so; but being a couple of years older I had left before he joined. After a quick interchange of dates a silence fell; and I thought suddenly of my absurd mate with his terrific whiskers and the 'Bless my soul – you don't say so' type of intellect. My double gave me an inkling of his thoughts by saying:

'My father's a parson in Norfolk. Do you see me before a judge and jury on that charge? For myself I can't see the necessity. There are fellows that an angel from heaven — And I am not that. He was one of those creatures that are just simmering all the time with a silly sort of wickedness. Miserable devils that have no business to live at all. He wouldn't do his duty and wouldn't let anybody else do theirs. But what's the good of talking! You know well enough the sort of ill-conditioned snarling cur —'

He appealed to me as if our experiences had been as identical as our clothes. And I knew well enough the pestiferous danger of such a character where there are no means of legal repression. And I knew well enough also that my double there was no homicidal ruffian. I did not think of asking him for details, and he told me the story roughly in brusque, disconnected sentences. I needed no more. I saw it all going on as though I were myself inside that other sleeping-suit.

'It happened while we were setting a reefed foresail, at dusk. Reefed foresail! You understand the sort of weather. The only sail we had left to keep the ship running; so you may guess what it had been like for days. Anxious sort of job, that. He gave me some of his cursed insolence at the sheet. I tell you I was overdone with this terrific weather that seemed to have no end to it. Terrific, I tell you – and a deep ship. I believe the fellow himself was half crazed with funk. It was no time for gentlemanly reproof, so I turned round and felled him like an ox. He up and at me. We closed just as an awful sea made for the ship. All hands saw it coming and took to the rigging, but I had him by the throat, and went on shaking him like a rat, the men above us yelling, "Look out! look out!" Then a crash as if the sky had fallen on my head. They say that for over ten minutes hardly anything was to be seen of the ship – just the three masts and a bit of the forecastle head and of the poop all awash driving along in a smother of foam. It was a miracle that they found us, jammed together behind the forebits. It's clear that I meant business, because I was holding him by the throat still when they picked us up. He was black in the face. It was too much for them. It seems they rushed us aft together, gripped as we were, screaming "Murder!" like a lot of lunatics, and broke into the cuddy. And the ship running for her life, touch-and-go all the time, any minute her last in a sea fit to turn your hair grey only a-looking at it. I understand that the skipper, too, started raving like the rest of them. The man had been deprived of sleep for more than a week, and to have this sprung on him at the height of a furious gale nearly drove him out of his mind. I wonder they didn't fling me overboard after getting the carcass of their precious shipmate out of my fingers. They had rather a job to separate us, I've been told. A sufficiently fierce story to make an old judge and a respectable jury sit up a bit. The first thing I heard when I came to myself was the maddening howling of that endless gale, and on that the voice of the old man. He was hanging on to my bunk, staring into my face out of his sou'wester.

' "Mr Leggatt, you have killed a man. You can act no longer as chief mate of the ship." '

His care to subdue his voice made it sound monotonous. He rested a hand on the end of the skylight to steady himself with, and all that time did not stir a limb, so far as I could see. 'Nice little tale for a quiet tea-party,' he concluded in the same tone.

One of my hands, too, rested on the end of the skylight; neither did I stir a limb, so far as I knew. We stood less than a foot from each other. It occurred to me that if old 'Bless my soul – you don't say so' were to put his head up the companion and catch sight of us, he would think he was seeing double, or imagine himself come upon a scene of weird witchcraft; the strange captain having a quiet confabulation by the wheel with his own grey ghost. I became very much concerned to prevent anything of the sort. I heard the other's soothing undertone.

'My father's a parson in Norfolk,' it said. Evidently he had forgotten he had told me this important fact before. Truly a nice little tale.

'You had better slip down into my stateroom now,' I said, moving off stealthily. My double followed my movements; our bare feet made no sound; I let him in, closed the door with care, and, after giving a call to the second mate, returned on deck for my relief.

'Not much sign of any wind yet,' I remarked when he approached.

'No, sir. Not much,' he assented, sleepily, in his hoarse voice, with just enough deference, no more, and barely suppressing a yawn.

'Well, that's all you have to look out for. You have got your orders.'

'Yes, sir.'

I paced a turn or two on the poop and saw him take up his position face forward with his elbow in the ratlines of the mizzen-rigging before I went below. The mate's faint snoring was still going on peacefully. The cuddy lamp was burning over the table on which stood a vase with flowers, a polite attention from the ship's provision merchant – the last flowers we should see for the next three months at the very least. Two bunches of bananas hung from the beam symmetrically, one on each side of the rudder-casing. Everything was as before in the ship – except that two of her captain's sleeping-suits were simultaneously in use, one motionless in the cuddy, the other keeping very still in the captain's stateroom.

It must be explained here that my cabin had the form of the capital letter L, the door being within the angle and opening into the short part of the letter. A couch was to the left, the bed-place to the right; my writing-desk and the chronometers' table faced the door. But anyone opening it, unless he stepped right inside, had no view of what I call the long (or vertical) part of the letter. It contained some lockers surmounted by a bookcase; and a few clothes, a thick jacket or two, caps, oilskin coat, and such like, hung on hooks. There was at the bottom of that part a door opening into my bathroom, which could be entered also directly from the saloon. But that way was never used.

The mysterious arrival had discovered the advantage of this particular shape. Entering my room, lighted strongly by a big bulkhead lamp swung on gimbals above my writing-desk, I did not see him anywhere till he stepped out quietly from behind the coats hung in the recessed part.

'I heard somebody moving about, and went in there at once,' he whispered.

I, too, spoke under my breath.

'Nobody is likely to come in here without knocking and getting permission.'

He nodded. His face was thin and the sunburn faded, as though he had been ill. And no wonder. He had been, I heard presently, kept under arrest in his cabin for nearly seven weeks. But there was nothing sickly in his eyes or in his expression. He was not a bit like me, really; yet, as we stood leaning over my bed-place, whispering side by side, with our dark heads together and our backs to the door, anybody bold enough to open it stealthily would have been treated to the uncanny sight of a double captain busy talking in whispers with his other self.

'But all this doesn't tell me how you came to hang on to our side-ladder,' I inquired, in the hardly audible murmurs we used, after he had told me something more of the proceedings on board the *Sephora* once the bad weather was over.

'When we sighted Java Head I had had time to think all those matters out several times over. I had six weeks of doing nothing else, and with only an hour or so every evening for a tramp on the quarterdeck.'

He whispered, his arms folded on the side of my bed-place, staring through the open port. And I could imagine perfectly the manner of this thinking out – a stubborn if not a steadfast operation; something of which I should have been perfectly incapable.

'I reckoned it would be dark before we closed with the land,' he continued, so low that I had to strain my hearing, near as we were to each other, shoulder touching shoulder almost. 'So I asked to speak to the old man. He always seemed very sick when he came to see me – as if he could not look me in the face. You know, that foresail saved the ship. She was too deep to have run long under bare poles. And it was I that managed to set it for him. Anyway, he came. When I had him in my cabin – he stood by the door looking at me as if I had the halter round my neck already – I asked him right away to leave my cabin door unlocked at night while the ship was going through Sunda Straits. There would be the Java coast within two or three miles, off Angier Point. I wanted nothing more. I've had a prize for swimming my second year in the Conway.'

'I can believe it,' I breathed out.

'God only knows why they locked me in every night. To see some of their faces you'd have thought they were afraid I'd go about at night strangling people. Am I a murdering brute? Do I look it? By Jove! if I had been he wouldn't have trusted himself like that into my room. You'll say I might have chucked him aside and bolted out, there and then – it was dark already. Well, no. And for the same reason I wouldn't think of trying to smash the door. There would have been a rush to stop me at the noise, and I did not mean to get into a confounded scrimmage. Somebody else might have got killed – for I would not have broken out only to get chucked back, and I did not want any more of that work. He refused, looking more sick than ever. He was afraid of the men, and also of that old second mate of his who had been sailing with him for years – a grey-headed old humbug; and his steward, too, had been with him devil knows how long – seventeen years or more – a dogmatic sort of loafer who hated me like poison, just because I was the chief mate. No chief mate ever made more than one voyage in the *Sephora*, you know. Those two old chaps ran the ship. Devil only knows what the skipper wasn't afraid of (all his nerve went to pieces altogether in that hellish spell of bad weather we had) – of what the law would do to him – of his wife, perhaps. Oh, yes! she's on board. Though I don't think she would have meddled. She would have been only too glad to have me out of the ship in any way. The "brand of Cain" business, don't you see. That's all right. I was ready enough to go off wandering on the face of the earth – and that was price enough to pay for an Abel of that sort. Anyhow, he wouldn't listen to me. "This thing must take its course. I represent the law here." He was shaking like a leaf. "So you won't?" "No!" "Then I hope you will be able to sleep on that," I said, and turned my back on him. "I wonder that *you* can," cries he, and locks the door.

'Well, after that, I couldn't. Not very well. That was three weeks ago. We have had a slow passage through the Java Sea; drifted about Carimata for ten days. When we anchored here they thought, I suppose, it was all right. The nearest land (and that's five miles) is the ship's destination; the consul would soon set about catching me; and there would have been no object in bolting to these islets there. I don't suppose there's a drop of water on them. I don't know how it was, but tonight that steward, after bringing me my supper, went out to let me eat it, and left the door unlocked. And I ate it – all there was, too. After I had finished I strolled out on the quarterdeck. I don't know that I meant to do anything. A breath of fresh air was all I wanted, I believe. Then a sudden temptation came over me. I kicked off my slippers and was in the water before I had made up my mind fairly. Somebody heard the splash and they raised an awful hullabaloo. "He's gone! Lower the boats! He's committed suicide! No, he's swimming." Certainly I was swimming. It's not so easy for a swimmer like me to commit suicide by drowning. I landed on the nearest islet before the boat left the ship's side. I heard them pulling about in the dark, hailing, and so on, but after a bit they gave up. Everything quieted down and the anchorage became as still as death. I sat down on a stone and began to think. I felt certain they would start searching for me at daylight. There was no place to hide on those stony things – and if there had been, what would have been the good? But now I was clear of that ship I was not going back. So after a while I took off all my clothes, tied them up in a bundle with a stone inside, and dropped them in the deep water on the outer side of that islet. That was suicide enough for me. Let them think what they liked, but I didn't mean to drown myself. I meant to swim till I sank – but that's not the same thing. I struck out for another of these little islands, and it was from that one that I first saw your riding-light. Something to swim for. I went on easily, and on the way I came upon a flat rock a foot or two above water. In the daytime, I dare say, you might make it out with a glass from your poop. I scrambled up on it and rested myself for a bit. Then I made another start. That last spell must have been over a mile.'

His whisper was getting fainter and fainter, and all the time he stared straight out through the porthole, in which there was not even a star to be seen. I had not interrupted him. There was something that made comment impossible in his narrative, or perhaps in himself; a sort of feeling, a quality, which I can't find a name for. And when he ceased, all I found was a futile whisper: 'So you swam for our light?'

'Yes – straight for it. It was something to swim for. I couldn't see any stars low down because the coast was in the way, and I couldn't see the land, either. The water was like glass. One might have been swimming in a confounded thousand-feet deep cistern with no place for scrambling out anywhere; but what I didn't like was the notion of swimming round and round like a crazed bullock before I gave out; and as I didn't mean to go back . . . No. Do you see me being hauled back, stark naked, off one of those little islands by the scruff of the neck and fighting like a wild beast? Somebody would have got killed for certain, and I did not want any of that. So I went on. Then your ladder —'

'Why didn't you hail the ship?' I asked, a little louder.

He touched my shoulder lightly. Lazy footsteps came right over our heads and stopped. The second mate had crossed from the other side of the poop and might have been hanging over the rail, for all we knew.

'He couldn't hear us talking – could he?' My double breathed into my very ear, anxiously.

His anxiety was an answer, a sufficient answer, to the question I had put to him. An answer containing all the difficulty of that situation. I closed the porthole quietly, to make sure. A louder word might have been overheard.

'Who's that?' he whispered then.

'My second mate. But I don't know much more of the fellow than you do.'

And I told him a little about myself. I had been appointed to take charge while I least expected anything of the sort, not quite a fort-night ago. I didn't know either the ship or the people. Hadn't had the time in port to look about me or size anybody up. And as to the crew, all they knew was that I was appointed to take the ship home. For the rest, I was almost as much of a stranger on board as himself, I said. And at the moment I felt it most acutely. I felt that it would take very little to make me a suspect person in the eyes of the ship's company.

He had turned about meantime; and we, the two strangers in the ship, faced each other in identical attitudes.

'Your ladder —' he murmured, after a silence. 'Who'd have thought of finding a ladder hanging over at night in a ship anchored out here! I felt just then a very unpleasant faintness. After the life I've been leading for nine weeks, anybody would have got out of condition. I wasn't capable of swimming round as far as your rud-der-chains. And, lo and behold! there was a ladder to get hold of. After I gripped it I said to myself, "What's the good?" When I saw a man's head looking over I thought I would swim away presently and leave him shouting – in whatever language it was. I didn't mind being looked at. I – I liked it. And then you speaking to me so quietly – as if you had expected me – made me hold on a little longer. It had been a confounded lonely time – I don't mean while swimming. I was glad to talk a little to somebody that didn't be-long to the *Sephora*. As to asking for the captain, that was a mere impulse. It could have been no use, with all the ship knowing about me and the other people pretty certain to be round here in the morning. I don't know – I wanted to be seen, to talk with some-body, before I went on. I don't know what I would have said. . . . "Fine night, isn't it?" or something of the sort.'

'Do you think they will be round here presently?' I asked with some incredulity.

'Quite likely,' he said, faintly.

He looked extremely haggard all of a sudden. His head rolled on his shoulders.

'H'm. We shall see then. Meantime get into that bed,' I whis-pered. 'Want help? There.'

It was a rather high bed-place with a set of drawers underneath. This amazing swimmer really needed the lift I gave him by seizing his leg. He tumbled in, rolled over on his back, and flung one arm across his eyes. And then, with his face nearly hidden, he must have looked exactly as I used to look in that bed. I gazed upon my other self for a while before drawing across carefully the two green serge curtains which ran on a brass rod. I thought for a moment of pinning them together for greater safety, but I sat down on the couch, and once there I felt unwilling to rise and hunt for a pin. I would do it in a moment. I was extremely tired, in a peculiarly intimate way, by the strain of stealthiness, by the effort of whispering, and the general secrecy of this excitement. It was three o'clock by now and I had been on my feet since nine, but I was not sleepy; I could not have gone to sleep. I sat there, fagged out, looking at the curtains, trying to clear my mind of the confused sensation of being in two places at once, and greatly bothered by an exasperating knocking in my head. It was a relief to discover suddenly that it was not in my head at all, but on the outside of the door. Before I could collect myself the words 'Come in' were out of my mouth, and the steward entered with a tray, bringing in my morning coffee. I had slept, after all, and I was so frightened that I shouted, 'This way! I am here, steward,' as though he had been miles away. He put down the tray on the table next the couch and only then said, very quietly, 'I can see you are here, sir.' I felt him give me a keen look, but I dared not meet his eyes just then. He must have wondered why I had drawn the curtains of my bed before going to sleep on the couch. He went out, hooking the door open as usual.

I heard the crew washing decks above me. I knew I would have been told at once if there had been any wind. Calm, I thought, and I was doubly vexed. Indeed, I felt dual more than ever. The steward reappeared suddenly in the doorway. I jumped up from the couch so quickly that he gave a start.

'What do you want here?'

'Close your port, sir – they are washing decks.'

'It is closed,' I said, reddening.

'Very well, sir.' But he did not move from the doorway and returned my stare in an extraordinary, equivocal manner for a time. Then his eyes wavered, all his expression changed, and in a voice unusually gentle, almost coaxingly:

'May I come in to take the empty cup away, sir?'

'Of course!' I turned my back on him while he popped in and out. Then I unhooked and closed the door and even pushed the bolt. This sort of thing could not go on very long. The cabin was as hot as an oven, too. I took a peep at my double, and discovered that he had not moved, his arm was still over his eyes; but his chest heaved; his hair was wet; his chin glistened with perspiration. I reached over him and opened the port.

'I must show myself on deck,' I reflected.

Of course, theoretically, I could do what I liked, with no one to say nay to me within the whole circle of the horizon; but to lock my cabin door and take the key away I did not dare. Directly I put my head out of the companion I saw the group of my two officers, the second mate barefooted, the chief mate in long indiarubber boots, near the break of the poop, and the steward halfway down the poop-ladder talking to them eagerly. He happened to catch sight of me and dived, the second ran down on the main-deck shouting some order or other, and the chief mate came to meet me, touching his cap.

There was a sort of curiosity in his eye that I did not like. I don't know whether the steward had told them that I was 'queer' only, or downright drunk, but I know the man meant to have a good look at me. I watched him coming with a smile which, as he got into point-blank range, took effect and froze his very whiskers. I did not give him time to open his lips.

'Square the yards by lifts and braces before the hands go to breakfast.'

It was the first particular order I had given on board that ship; and I stayed on deck to see it executed, too. I had felt the need of asserting myself without loss of time. That sneering young cub got taken down a peg or two on that occasion, and I also seized the opportunity of having a good look at the face of every foremast man as they filed past me to go to the after braces. At breakfast time, eating nothing myself, I presided with such frigid dignity that the two mates were only too glad to escape from the cabin as soon as decency permitted; and all the time the dual working of my mind distracted me almost to the point of insanity. I was constantly watching myself, my secret self, as dependent on my actions as my own personality, sleeping in that bed, behind that door which faced me as I sat at the head of the table. It was very much like being mad, only it was worse because one was aware of it.

I had to shake him for a solid minute, but when at last he opened his eyes it was in the full possession of his senses, with an inquiring look.

'All's well so far,' I whispered. 'Now you must vanish into the bathroom.'

He did so, as noiseless as a ghost, and I then rang for the steward, and facing him boldly, directed him to tidy up my stateroom while I was having my bath – 'and be quick about it'. As my tone admitted of no excuses, he said, 'Yes, sir,' and ran off to fetch his dustpan and brushes. I took a bath and did most of my dressing, splashing, and whistling softly for the steward's edification, while the secret sharer of my life stood drawn up bolt upright in that little space, his face looking very sunken in daylight, his eyelids lowered under the stern, dark line of his eyebrows drawn together by a slight frown.

When I left him there to go back to my room the steward was finishing dusting. I sent for the mate and engaged him in some insignificant conversation. It was, as it were, trifling with the terrific character of his whiskers; but my object was to give him an opportunity for a good look at my cabin. And then I could at last shut, with a clear conscience, the door of my stateroom and get my double back into the recessed part. There was nothing else for it. He had to sit still on a small folding stool, half smothered by the heavy coats hanging there. We listened to the steward going into the bathroom out of the saloon, filling the water-bottles there, scrubbing the bath, setting things to rights, whisk, bang, clatter – out again into the saloon – turn the key – click. Such was my scheme for keeping my second self invisible. Nothing better could be contrived under the circumstances. And there we sat; I at my writing-desk ready to appear busy with some papers, he behind me, out of sight of the door. It would not have been prudent to talk in daytime; and I could not have stood the excitement of that queer sense of whispering to myself. Now and then, glancing over my shoulder, I saw him far back there, sitting rigidly on the low stool, his bare feet close together, his arms folded, his head hanging on his breast – and perfectly still. Anybody would have taken him for me.

I was fascinated by it myself. Every moment I had to glance over my shoulder. I was looking at him when a voice outside the door said:

'Beg pardon, sir.'

'Well!' . . . I kept my eyes on him, and so, when the voice outside the door announced, 'There's a ship's boat coming our way, sir,' I saw him give a start – the first movement he had made for hours. But he did not raise his bowed head.

'All right. Get the ladder over.'

I hesitated. Should I whisper something to him? But what? His immobility seemed to have been never disturbed. What could I tell him he did not know already? . . . Finally I went on deck.

II

The skipper of the *Sephora* had a thin red whisker all round his face, and the sort of complexion that goes with hair of that colour; also the particular, rather smeary shade of blue in the eyes. He was not exactly a showy figure; his shoulders were high, his stature but middling – one leg slightly more bandy than the other. He shook hands, looking vaguely around. A spiritless tenacity was his main characteristic, I judged. I behaved with a politeness which seemed to disconcert him. Perhaps he was shy. He mumbled to me as if he were ashamed of what he was saying; gave his name (it was something like Archbold – but at this distance of years I hardly am sure), his ship's name, and a few other particulars of that sort, in the manner of a criminal making a reluctant and doleful confession. He had had terrible weather on the passage out – terrible – terrible – wife aboard, too.

By this time we were seated in the cabin and the steward brought in a tray with a bottle and glasses. 'Thanks! No.' Never took liquor. Would have some water, though. He drank two tumblerfuls. Terrible thirsty work. Ever since daylight had been exploring the islands round his ship.

'What was that for – fun?' I asked, with an appearance of polite interest.

'No!' He sighed. 'Painful duty.'

As he persisted in his mumbling and I wanted my double to hear every word, I hit upon the notion of informing him that I regretted to say I was hard of hearing.

'Such a young man, too!' he nodded, keeping his smeary blue, unintelligent eyes fastened upon me. What was the cause of it – some disease? he inquired, without the least sympathy and as if he thought that, if so, I'd got no more than I deserved.

'Yes; disease,' I admitted in a cheerful tone which seemed to shock him. But my point was gained, because he had to raise his

voice to give me his tale. It is not worth while to record that ver-
sion. It was just over two months since all this had happened, and
he had thought so much about it that he seemed completely muddled as to its bearings, but still immensely impressed.

'What would you think of such a thing happening on board your
own ship? I've had the *Sephora* for these fifteen years. I am a well-
known shipmaster.'

He was densely distressed – and perhaps I should have sympathized with him if I had been able to detach my mental vision from
the unsuspected sharer of my cabin as though he were my second
self. There he was on the other side of the bulkhead, four or five
feet from us, no more, as we sat in the saloon. I looked politely at
Captain Archbold (if that was his name), but it was the other I saw,
in a grey sleeping-suit, seated on a low stool, his bare feet close
together, his arms folded, and every word said between us falling
into the ears of his dark head bowed on his chest.

'I have been at sea now, man and boy, for seven-and-thirty years,
and I've never heard of such a thing happening in an English ship.
And that it should be my ship. Wife on board, too.'

I was hardly listening to him.

'Don't you think,' I said, 'that the heavy sea which, you told me,
came aboard just then might have killed the man? I have seen the
sheer weight of a sea kill a man very neatly, by simply breaking his
neck.'

'Good God!' he uttered, impressively, fixing his smeary blue eyes
on me. 'The sea! No man killed by the sea ever looked like that.'
He seemed positively scandalized at my suggestion. And as I gazed
at him, certainly not prepared for anything original on his part, he
advanced his head close to mine and thrust his tongue out at me so
suddenly that I couldn't help starting back.

After scoring over my calmness in this graphic way he nodded
wisely. If I had seen the sight, he assured me, I would never forget
it as long as I lived. The weather was too bad to give the corpse a
proper sea burial. So next day at dawn they took it up on the poop,
covering its face with a bit of bunting; he read a short prayer, and
then, just as it was, in its oilskins and long boots, they launched it
amongst those mountainous seas that seemed ready every moment
to swallow up the ship herself and the terrified lives on board
of her.

'That reefed foresail saved you,' I threw in.

'Under God – it did,' he exclaimed fervently. 'It was by a special mercy, I firmly believe, that it stood some of those hurricane squalls.'

'It was the setting of that sail which —' I began.

'God's own hand in it,' he interrupted me. 'Nothing less could have done it. I don't mind telling you that I hardly dared give the order. It seemed impossible that we could touch anything without losing it, and then our last hope would have been gone.'

The terror of that gale was on him yet. I let him go on for a bit, then said, casually – as if returning to a minor subject:

'You were very anxious to give up your mate to the shore people, I believe?'

He was. To the law. His obscure tenacity on that point had in it something incomprehensible and a little awful; something, as it were, mystical, quite apart from his anxiety that he should not be suspected of 'countenancing any doings of that sort'. Seven-and-thirty virtuous years at sea, of which over twenty of immaculate command, and the last fifteen in the *Sephora*, seemed to have laid him under some pitiless obligation.

'And you know,' he went on, groping shamefacedly amongst his feelings, 'I did not engage that young fellow. His people had some interest with my owners. I was in a way forced to take him on. He looked very smart, very gentlemanly, and all that. But do you know – I never liked him, somehow. I am a plain man. You see, he wasn't exactly the sort for the chief mate of a ship like the *Sephora*.'

I had become so connected in thoughts and impressions with the secret sharer of my cabin that I felt as if I, personally, were being given to understand that I, too, was not the sort that would have done for the chief mate of a ship like the *Sephora*. I had no doubt of it in my mind.

'Not at all the style of man. You understand,' he insisted, superfluously, looking hard at me.

I smiled urbanely. He seemed at a loss for a while.

'I suppose I must report a suicide.'

'Beg pardon?'

'Sui-cide! That's what I'll have to write to my owners directly I get in.'

'Unless you manage to recover him before tomorrow,' I assented, dispassionately. . . . 'I mean, alive.'

He mumbled something which I really did not catch, and I

turned my ear to him in a puzzled manner. He fairly bawled:

'The land – I say, the mainland is at least seven miles off my anchorage.'

'About that.'

My lack of excitement, of curiosity, of surprise, of any sort of pronounced interest, began to arouse his distrust. But except for the felicitous pretence of deafness I had not tried to pretend anything. I had felt utterly incapable of playing the part of ignorance properly, and therefore was afraid to try. It is also certain that he had brought some ready-made suspicions with him, and that he viewed my politeness as a strange and unnatural phenomenon. And yet how else could I have received him? Not heartily! That was impossible for psychological reasons, which I need not state here. My only object was to keep off his inquiries. Surlily? Yes, but surliness might have provoked a point-blank question. From its novelty to him and from its nature, punctilious courtesy was the manner best calculated to restrain the man. But there was the danger of his breaking through my defence bluntly. I could not, I think, have met him by a direct lie, also for psychological (not moral) reasons. If he had only known how afraid I was of his putting my feeling of identity with the other to the test! But, strangely enough – (I thought of it only afterwards) – I believe that he was not a little disconcerted by the reverse side of that weird situation, by something in me that reminded him of the man he was seeking – suggested a mysterious similitude to the young fellow he had distrusted and disliked from the first.

However that might have been, the silence was not very prolonged. He took another oblique step.

'I reckon I had no more than a two-mile pull to your ship. Not a bit more.'

'And quite enough, too, in this awful heat,' I said.

Another pause full of mistrust followed. Necessity, they say, is mother of invention, but fear, too, is not barren of ingenious suggestions. And I was afraid he would ask me point-blank for news of my other self.

'Nice little saloon, isn't it?' I remarked, as if noticing for the first time the way his eyes roamed from one closed door to the other. 'And very well fitted out, too. Here, for instance,' I continued, reaching over the back of my seat negligently and flinging the door open, 'is my bathroom.'

He made an eager movement, but hardly gave it a glance. I got up, shut the door of the bathroom, and invited him to have a look round, as if I were very proud of my accommodation. He had to rise and be shown round, but he went through the business without any raptures whatever.

'And now we'll have a look at my stateroom,' I declared, in a voice as loud as I dared to make it, crossing the cabin to the star-board side with purposely heavy steps.

He followed me in and gazed around. My intelligent double had vanished. I played my part.

'Very convenient – isn't it?'

'Very nice. Very comf ...' He didn't finish and went out brusquely as if to escape from some unrighteous wiles of mine. But it was not to be. I had been too frightened not to feel vengeful; I felt I had him on the run, and I meant to keep him on the run. My polite insistence must have had something menacing in it, because he gave in suddenly. And I did not let him off a single item; mate's room, pantry, store-rooms, the very sail-locker which was also un-der the poop – he had to look into them all. When at last I showed him out on the quarterdeck he drew a long, spiritless sigh, and mumbled dismally that he must really be going back to his ship now. I desired my mate, who had joined us, to see to the captain's boat.

The man of whiskers gave a blast on the whistle which he used to wear hanging round his neck, and yelled, '*Sephora*s away!' My double down there in my cabin must have heard, and certainly could not feel more relieved than I. Four fellows came running out from somewhere forward and went over the side, while my own men, appearing on deck too, lined the rail. I escorted my visitor to the gangway ceremoniously, and nearly overdid it. He was a tena-cious beast. On the very ladder he lingered, and in that unique, guiltily conscientious manner of sticking to the point:

'I say ... you ... you don't think that —'

I covered his voice loudly:

'Certainly not. . . . I am delighted. Good-bye.'

I had an idea of what he meant to say, and just saved myself by the privilege of defective hearing. He was too shaken generally to insist, but my mate, close witness of that parting, looked mystified, and his face took on a thoughtful cast. As I did not want to appear as if I wished to avoid all communication with my officers, he had the opportunity to address me.

'Seems a very nice man. His boat's crew told our chaps a very extraordinary story, if what I am told by the steward is true. I suppose you had it from the captain, sir?'

'Yes. I had a story from the captain.'

'A very horrible affair – isn't it, sir?'

'It is.'

'Beats all these tales we hear about murders in Yankee ships.'

'I don't think it beats them. I don't think it resembles them in the least.'

'Bless my soul – you don't say so! But of course I've no acquaintance whatever with American ships, not I, so I couldn't go against your knowledge. It's horrible enough for me. . . . But the queerest part is that those fellows seemed to have some idea the man was hidden aboard here. They had really. Did you ever hear of such a thing?'

'Preposterous – isn't it?'

We were walking to and fro athwart the quarterdeck. No one of the crew forward could be seen (the day was Sunday), and the mate pursued:

'There was some little dispute about it. Our chaps took offence. "As if we would harbour a thing like that," they said. "Wouldn't you like to look for him in our coal-hole?" Quite a tiff. But they made it up in the end. I suppose he did drown himself. Don't you, sir?'

'I don't suppose anything.'

'You have no doubt in the matter, sir?'

'None whatever.'

I left him suddenly. I felt I was producing a bad impression, but with my double down there it was most trying to be on deck. And it was almost as trying to be below. Altogether a nerve-trying situation. But on the whole I felt less torn in two when I was with him. There was no one in the whole ship whom I dared take into my confidence. Since the hands had got to know his story, it would have been impossible to pass him off for anyone else, and an accidental discovery was to be dreaded now more than ever. . . .

The steward being engaged in laying the table for dinner, we could talk only with our eyes when I first went down. Later in the afternoon we had a cautious try at whispering. The Sunday quietness of the ship was against us; the stillness of air and water around her was against us; the elements, the men were against us – everything was against us in our secret partnership; time itself – for this could not go on forever. The very trust in Providence was, I suppose, denied to his guilt. Shall I confess that this thought cast me down very much? And as to the chapter of accidents which counts for so much in the book of success, I could only hope that it was closed. For what favourable accident could be expected?

'Did you hear everything?' were my first words as soon as we took up our position side by side, leaning over my bed-place.

He had. And the proof of it was his earnest whisper, 'The man told you he hardly dared to give the order.'

I understood the reference to be to that saving foresail.

'Yes. He was afraid of it being lost in the setting.'

'I assure you he never gave the order. He may think he did, but he never gave it. He stood there with me on the break of the poop after the main-topsail blew away, and whimpered about our last hope – positively whimpered about it and nothing else – and the night coming on! To hear one's skipper go on like that in such weather was enough to drive any fellow out of his mind. It worked me up into a sort of desperation. I just took it into my own hands and went away from him, boiling, and — But what's the use telling you? *You* know! . . . Do you think that if I had not been pretty fierce with them I should have got the men to do anything? Not it! The bos'n perhaps? Perhaps! It wasn't a heavy sea – it was a sea gone mad! I suppose the end of the world will be something like that; and a man may have the heart to see it coming once and be done with it – but to have to face it day after day — I don't blame anybody. I was precious little better than the rest. Only – I was an officer of that old coal-wagon, anyhow —'

'I quite understand,' I conveyed that sincere assurance into his ear. He was out of breath with whispering; I could hear him pant slightly. It was all very simple. The same strung-up force which had given twenty-four men a chance, at least, for their lives, had, in a sort of recoil, crushed an unworthy mutinous existence.

But I had no leisure to weigh the merits of the matter – footsteps in the saloon, a heavy knock. 'There's enough wind to get under way with, sir.' Here was the call of a new claim upon my thoughts and even upon my feelings.

'Turn the hands up,' I cried through the door. 'I'll be on deck directly.'

I was going out to make the acquaintance of my ship. Before I left the cabin our eyes met – the eyes of the only two strangers on board. I pointed to the recessed part where the little camp-stool awaited him and laid my finger on my lips. He made a gesture – somewhat vague – a little mysterious, accompanied by a faint smile, as if of regret.

This is not the place to enlarge upon the sensations of a man who feels for the first time a ship move under his feet to his own independent word. In my case they were not unalloyed. I was not wholly alone with my command; for there was that stranger in my cabin. Or rather, I was not completely and wholly with her. Part of me was absent. That mental feeling of being in two places at once affected me physically as if the mood of secrecy had penetrated my very soul. Before an hour had elapsed since the ship had begun to move, having occasion to ask the mate (he stood by my side) to take a compass bearing of the pagoda, I caught myself reaching up to his ear in whispers. I say I caught myself, but enough had escaped to startle the man. I can't describe it otherwise than by saying that he shied. A grave, preoccupied manner, as though he were in possession of some perplexing intelligence, did not leave him henceforth. A little later I moved away from the rail to look at the compass with such a stealthy gait that the helmsman noticed it – and I could not help noticing the unusual roundness of his eyes. These are trifling instances, though it's to no commander's advantage to be suspected of ludicrous eccentricities. But I was also more seriously affected. There are to a seaman certain words, gestures, that should in given conditions come as naturally, as instinctively as the winking of a menaced eye. A certain order should spring on to his lips without thinking; a certain sign should get itself made, so to speak, without reflection. But all unconscious alertness had abandoned me. I had to make an effort of will to recall myself back (from the cabin) to the conditions of the moment. I felt that I was appearing an irresolute commander to those people who were watching me more or less critically.

And, besides, there were the scares. On the second day out, for instance, coming off the deck in the afternoon (I had straw slippers on my bare feet) I stopped at the open pantry door and spoke to the steward. He was doing something there with his back to me. At the sound of my voice he nearly jumped out of his skin, as the saying is, and incidentally broke a cup.

'What on earth's the matter with you?' I asked, astonished.

He was extremely confused. 'Beg your pardon, sir. I made sure you were in your cabin.'

'You see I wasn't.'

'No, sir. I could have sworn I had heard you moving in there not a moment ago. It's most extraordinary . . . very sorry, sir.'

I passed on with an inward shudder. I was so identified with my secret double that I did not even mention the fact in those scanty, fearful whispers we exchanged. I suppose he had made some slight noise of some kind or other. It would have been miraculous if he hadn't at one time or another. And yet, haggard as he appeared, he looked always perfectly self-controlled, more than calm – almost invulnerable. On my suggestion he remained almost entirely in the bathroom, which, upon the whole, was the safest place. There could be really no shadow of an excuse for anyone ever wanting to go in there, once the steward had done with it. It was a very tiny place. Sometimes he reclined on the floor, his legs bent, his head sustained on one elbow. At others I would find him on the camp-stool, sitting in his grey sleeping-suit and with his cropped dark hair like a patient, unmoved convict. At night I would smuggle him into my bed-place, and we would whisper together, with the regular footfalls of the officer of the watch passing and repassing over our heads. It was an infinitely miserable time. It was lucky that some tins of fine preserves were stowed in a locker in my state-room; hard bread I could always get hold of; and so he lived on stewed chicken, pâté de foie gras, asparagus, cooked oysters, sardines – on all sorts of abominable sham delicacies out of tins. My early morning coffee he always drank; and it was all I dared do for him in that respect.

Every day there was the horrible manœuvring to go through so that my room and then the bathroom should be done in the usual way. I came to hate the sight of the steward, to abhor the voice of that harmless man. I felt that it was he who would bring on the disaster of discovery. It hung like a sword over our heads.

The fourth day out, I think (we were then working down the east side of the Gulf of Siam, tack for tack, in light winds and smooth water) – the fourth day, I say, of this miserable juggling with the unavoidable, as we sat at our evening meal, that man, whose slightest movement I dreaded, after putting down the dishes ran up on deck busily. This could not be dangerous. Presently he came down again; and then it appeared that he had remembered a coat of mine which I had thrown over a rail to dry after having been wetted in a shower which had passed over the ship in the afternoon. Sitting stolidly at the head of the table I became terrified at the sight of the garment on his arm. Of course he made for my door. There was no time to lose.

'Steward,' I thundered. My nerves were so shaken that I could not govern my voice and conceal my agitation. This was the sort of thing that made my terrifically whiskered mate tap his forehead with his forefinger. I had detected him using that gesture while talking on deck with a confidential air to the carpenter. It was too far to hear a word, but I had no doubt that this pantomime could only refer to the strange new captain.

'Yes sir,' the pale-faced steward turned resignedly to me. It was this maddening course of being shouted at, checked without rhyme or reason, arbitrarily chased out of my cabin, suddenly called into it, sent flying out of his pantry on incomprehensible errands, that accounted for the growing wretchedness of his expression.

'Where are you going with that coat?'

'To your room, sir.'

'Is there another shower coming?'

'I'm sure I don't know, sir. Shall I go up again and see, sir?'

'No! never mind.'

My object was attained, as of course my other self in there would have heard everything that passed. During this interlude my two officers never raised their eyes off their respective plates; but the lip of that confounded cub, the second mate, quivered visibly.

I expected the steward to hook my coat on and come out at once. He was very slow about it; but I dominated my nervousness sufficiently not to shout after him. Suddenly I became aware (it could be heard plainly enough) that the fellow for some reason or other was opening the door of the bathroom. It was the end. The place was literally not big enough to swing a cat in. My voice died in my throat and I went stony all over. I expected to hear a yell of surprise and terror, and made a movement, but had not the strength to get on my legs. Everything remained still. Had my second self taken the poor wretch by the throat? I don't know what I would have done next moment if I had not seen the steward come out of my room, close the door, and then stand quietly by the sideboard.

'Saved,' I thought. 'But, no! Lost! Gone! He was gone!'

I laid my knife and fork down and leaned back in my chair. My head swam. After a while, when sufficiently recovered to speak in a steady voice, I instructed my mate to put the ship round at eight o'clock himself.

'I won't come on deck,' I went on. 'I think I'll turn in, and unless the wind shifts I don't want to be disturbed before midnight. I feel a bit seedy.'

'You did look middling bad a little while ago,' the chief mate remarked without showing any great concern.

They both went out, and I stared at the steward clearing the table. There was nothing to be read on that wretched man's face. But why did he avoid my eyes, I asked myself. Then I thought I should like to hear the sound of his voice.

'Steward!'

'Sir!' Startled as usual.

'Where did you hang up that coat?'

'In the bathroom, sir.' The usual anxious tone. 'It's not quite dry yet, sir.'

For some time longer I sat in the cuddy. Had my double vanished as he had come? But of his coming there was an explanation, whereas his disappearance would be inexplicable. . . . I went slowly into my dark room, shut the door, lighted the lamp, and for a time dared not turn round. When at last I did I saw him standing bolt upright in the narrow recessed part. It would not be true to say I had a shock, but an irresistible doubt of his bodily existence flitted through my mind. Can it be, I asked myself, that he is not visible to other eyes than mine? It was like being haunted. Motionless, with a grave face, he raised his hands slightly at me in a gesture which meant clearly, 'Heavens! what a narrow escape!' Narrow indeed. I think I had come creeping quietly as near insanity as any man who has not actually gone over the border. That gesture restrained me, so to speak.

The mate with the terrific whiskers was now putting the ship on the other tack. In the moment of profound silence which follows upon the hands going to their stations I heard on the poop his raised voice: 'Hard alee!' and the distant shout of the order repeated on the main-deck. The sails, in that light breeze, made but a faint fluttering noise. It ceased. The ship was coming round slowly; I held my breath in the renewed stillness of expectation; one wouldn't have thought that there was a single living soul on her decks. A sudden brisk shout, 'Mainsail haul!' broke the spell,

and in the noisy cries and rush overhead of the men running away
with the main brace we two, down in my cabin, came together in
our usual position by the bed-place.

He did not wait for my question. 'I heard him fumbling here and
just managed to squat myself down in the bath,' he whispered to
me. 'The fellow only opened the door and put his arm in to hang
the coat up. All the same —'

'I never thought of that,' I whispered back, even more appalled
than before at the closeness of the shave, and marvelling at that
something unyielding in his character which was carrying him
through so finely. There was no agitation in his whisper. Whoever
was being driven distracted, it was not he. He was sane. And the
proof of his sanity was continued when he took up the whispering
again.

'It would never do for me to come to life again.'

It was something that a ghost might have said. But what he was
alluding to was his old captain's reluctant admission of the theory
of suicide. It would obviously serve his turn – if I had understood
at all the view which seemed to govern the unalterable purpose of
his action.

'You must maroon me as soon as ever you can get amongst these
islands off the Cambodje shore,' he went on.

'Maroon you! We are not living in a boy's adventure tale,' I protested. His scornful whispering took me up.

'We aren't indeed! There's nothing of a boy's tale in this. But
there's nothing else for it. I want no more. You don't suppose I am
afraid of what can be done to me? Prison or gallows or whatever
they may please. But you don't see me coming back to explain such
things to an old fellow in a wig and twelve respectable tradesmen,
do you? What can they know whether I am guilty or not – or of
what I am guilty, either? That's my affair. What does the Bible say?
"Driven off the face of the earth." Very well. I am off the face of
the earth now. As I came at night so I shall go.'

'Impossible!' I murmured. 'You can't.'

'Can't? . . . Not naked like a soul on the Day of Judgement. I
shall freeze on to this sleeping-suit. The Last Day is not yet – and
. . . you have understood thoroughly. Didn't you?'

I felt suddenly ashamed of myself. I may say truly that I understood – and my hesitation in letting that man swim away from my
ship's side had been a mere sham sentiment, a sort of cowardice.

'It can't be done now till next night,' I breathed out. 'The ship is on the off-shore tack and the wind may fail us.'

'As long as I know that you understand,' he whispered. 'But of course you do. It's a great satisfaction to have got somebody to understand. You seem to have been there on purpose.' And in the same whisper, as if we two whenever we talked had to say things to each other which were not fit for the world to hear, he added, 'It's very wonderful.'

We remained side by side talking in our secret way – but sometimes silent or just exchanging a whispered word or two at long intervals. And as usual he stared through the port. A breath of wind came now and again into our faces. The ship might have been moored in dock, so gently and on an even keel she slipped through the water, that did not murmur even at our passage, shadowy and silent like a phantom sea.

At midnight I went on deck, and to my mate's great surprise put the ship round on the other tack. His terrible whiskers flitted round me in silent criticism. I certainly should not have done it if it had been only a question of getting out of that sleepy gulf as quickly as possible. I believe he told the second mate, who relieved him, that it was a great want of judgment. The other only yawned. That intolerable cub shuffled about so sleepily and lolled against the rails in such a slack, improper fashion that I came down on him sharply.

'Aren't you properly awake yet?'

'Yes, sir! I am awake.'

'Well, then, be good enough to hold yourself as if you were. And keep a look-out. If there's any current we'll be closing with some islands before daylight.'

The east side of the gulf is fringed with islands, some solitary, others in groups. On the blue background of the high coast they seem to float on silvery patches of calm water, arid and grey, or dark green and rounded like clumps of evergreen bushes, with the larger ones, a mile or two long, showing the outlines of ridges, ribs of grey rock under the dank mantle of matted leafage. Unknown to trade, to travel, almost to geography, the manner of life they harbour is an unsolved secret. There must be villages – settlements of fishermen at least – on the largest of them, and some communication with the world is probably kept up by native craft. But all that forenoon, as we headed for them, fanned along by the faintest of breezes, I saw no sign of man or canoe in the field of the telescope

I kept on pointing at the scattered group.

At noon I gave no orders for a change of course, and the mate's whiskers became much concerned and seemed to be offering themselves unduly to my notice. At last I said:

'I am going to stand right in. Quite in – as far as I can take her.'

The stare of extreme surprise imparted an air of ferocity also to his eyes, and he looked truly terrific for a moment.

'We're not doing well in the middle of the gulf,' I continued, casually. 'I am going to look for the land breezes tonight.'

'Bless my soul! Do you mean, sir, in the dark amongst the lot of all them islands and reefs and shoals?'

'Well – if there are any regular land breezes at all on this coast one must get close inshore to find them, mustn't one?'

'Bless my soul!' he exclaimed again under his breath. All that afternoon he wore a dreamy, contemplative appearance which in him was a mark of perplexity. After dinner I went into my stateroom as if I meant to take some rest. There we two bent our dark heads over a half-unrolled chart lying on my bed.

'There,' I said. 'It's got to be Koh-ring. I've been looking at it ever since sunrise. It has got two hills and a low point. It must be inhabited. And on the coast opposite there is what looks like the mouth of a biggish river – with some town, no doubt, not far up. It's the best chance for you that I can see.'

'Anything. Koh-ring let it be.'

He looked thoughtfully at the chart as if surveying chances and distances from a lofty height – and following with his eyes his own figure wandering on the blank land of Cochin-China, and then passing off that piece of paper clean out of sight into uncharted regions. And it was as if the ship had two captains to plan her course for her. I had been so worried and restless running up and down that I had not had the patience to dress that day. I had remained in my sleeping-suit, with straw slippers and a soft floppy hat. The closeness of the heat in the gulf had been most oppressive, and the crew were used to see me wandering in that airy attire.

'She will clear the south point as she heads now,' I whispered into his ear. 'Goodness only knows when, though, but certainly after dark. I'll edge her in to half a mile, as far as I may be able to judge in the dark —'

'Be careful,' he murmured, warningly – and I realized suddenly that all my future, the only future for which I was fit, would perhaps go irretrievably to pieces in any mishap to my first command.

I could not stop a moment longer in the room. I motioned him to get out of sight and made my way on the poop. That unplayful cub had the watch. I walked up and down for a while thinking things out, then beckoned him over.

'Send a couple of hands to open the two quarterdeck ports,' I said, mildly.

He actually had the impudence, or else so forgot himself in his wonder at such an incomprehensible order, as to repeat:

'Open the quarterdeck ports! What for, sir?'

'The only reason you need concern yourself about is because I tell you to do so. Have them open wide and fastened properly.'

He reddened and went off, but I believe made some jeering remark to the carpenter as to the sensible practice of ventilating a ship's quarterdeck. I know he popped into the mate's cabin to impart the fact to him because the whiskers came on deck, as it were by chance, and stole glances at me from below – for signs of lunacy or drunkenness, I suppose.

A little before supper, feeling more restless than ever, I rejoined, for a moment, my second self. And to find him sitting so quietly was surprising, like something against nature, inhuman.

I developed my plan in a hurried whisper.

'I shall stand in as close as I dare and then put her round. I shall presently find means to smuggle you out of here into the sail-locker, which communicates with the lobby. But there is an opening, a sort of square for hauling the sails out, which gives straight on the quarterdeck and which is never closed in fine weather, so as to give air to the sails. When the ship's way is deadened in stays and all the hands are aft at the main braces you shall have a clear road to slip out and get overboard through the open quarterdeck port. I've had them both fastened up. Use a rope's end to lower yourself into the water so as to avoid a splash – you know. It could be heard and cause some beastly complication.'

He kept silent for a while, then whispered, 'I understand.'

'I won't be there to see you go,' I began with an effort. 'The rest . . . I only hope I have understood, too.'

'You have. From first to last' – and for the first time there seemed to be a faltering, something strained in his whisper. He caught hold of my arm, but the ringing of the supper bell made me start. He didn't, though; he only released his grip.

After supper I didn't come below again till well past eight o'clock. The faint, steady breeze was loaded with dew; and the wet, darkened sails held all there was of propelling power in it. The night, clear and starry, sparkled darkly, and the opaque, lightless patches shifting slowly against the low stars were the drifting islets. On the port bow there was a big one more distant and shadowily imposing by the great space of sky it eclipsed.

On opening the door I had a back view of my very own self looking at a chart. He had come out of the recess and was standing near the table.

'Quite dark enough,' I whispered.

He stepped back and leaned against my bed with a level, quiet glance. I sat on the couch. We had nothing to say to each other. Over our heads the officer of the watch moved here and there. Then I heard him move quickly. I knew what that meant. He was making for the companion; and presently his voice was outside my door.

'We are drawing in pretty fast, sir. Land looks rather close.'

'Very well,' I answered. 'I am coming on deck directly.'

I waited till he was gone out of the cuddy, then rose. My double moved too. The time had come to exchange our last whispers, for neither of us was ever to hear each other's natural voice.

'Look here!' I opened a drawer and took out three sovereigns. 'Take this, anyhow. I've got six and I'd give you the lot, only I must keep a little money to buy some fruit and vegetables for the crew from native boats as we go through Sunda Straits.'

He shook his head.

'Take it,' I urged him, whispering desperately. 'No one can tell what —'

He smiled and slapped meaningly the only pocket of the sleeping-jacket. It was not safe, certainly. But I produced a large old silk handkerchief of mine, and tying the three pieces of gold in a corner, pressed it on him. He was touched, I suppose, because he took it at last and tied it quickly round his waist under the jacket, on his bare skin.

Our eyes met; several seconds elapsed, till, our glances still mingled, I extended my hand and turned the lamp out. Then I passed through the cuddy, leaving the door of my room wide open. . . .

'Steward!'

He was still lingering in the pantry in the greatness of his zeal, giving a rub-up to a plated cruet-stand the last thing before going to bed. Being careful not to wake up the mate, whose room was opposite, I spoke in an undertone.

He looked round anxiously. 'Sir!'

'Can you get me a little hot water from the galley?'

'I am afraid, sir, the galley fire's been out for some time now.'

'Go and see.'

He fled up the stairs.

'Now,' I whispered, loudly, into the saloon – too loudly, perhaps, but I was afraid I couldn't make a sound. He was by my side in an instant – the double captain slipped past the stairs – through a tiny dark passage . . . a sliding door. We were in the sail-locker, scrambling on our knees over the sails. A sudden thought struck me. I saw myself wandering barefooted, bareheaded, the sun beating on my dark poll. I snatched off my floppy hat and tried hurriedly in the dark to ram it on my other self. He dodged and fended off silently. I wonder what he thought had come to me before he understood and suddenly desisted. Our hands met gropingly, lingered united in a steady, motionless clasp for a second. . . . No word was breathed by either of us when they separated.

I was standing quietly by the pantry door when the steward returned.

'Sorry, sir. Kettle barely warm. Shall I light the spirit-lamp?'

'Never mind.'

I came out on deck slowly. It was now a matter of conscience to shave the land as close as possible – for now he must go overboard, whenever the ship was put in stays. Must! There could be no going back for him. After a moment I walked over to leeward and my heart flew into my mouth at the nearness of the land on the bow. Under any other circumstances I would not have held on a minute longer. The second mate had followed me anxiously.

I looked on till I felt I could command my voice.

'She will weather,' I said then in a quiet tone.

'Are you going to try that, sir?' he stammered out incredulously.

I took no notice of him and raised my tone just enough to be heard by the helmsman.

'Keep her good full.'

'Good full, sir.'

The wind fanned my cheek, the sails slept, the world was silent. The strain of watching the dark loom of the land grow bigger and denser was too much for me. I had shut my eyes – because the ship must go closer. She must! The stillness was intolerable. Were we standing still?

When I opened my eyes the second view started my heart with a thump. The black southern hill of Koh-ring seemed to hang right over the ship like a towering fragment of the everlasting night. On that enormous mass of blackness there was not a gleam to be seen, not a sound to be heard. It was gliding irresistibly toward us and yet seemed already within reach of the hand. I saw the vague figures of the watch grouped in the waist, gazing in awed silence.

'Are you going on, sir,' inquired an unsteady voice at my elbow.

I ignored it. I had to go on.

'Keep her full. Don't check her way. That won't do now,' I said, warningly.

'I can't see the sails very well,' the helmsman answered me, in strange, quavering tones.

Was she close enough? Already she was, I won't say in the shadow of the land, but in the very blackness of it, already swallowed up as it were, gone too close to be recalled, gone from me altogether.

'Give the mate a call,' I said to the young man who stood at my elbow as still as death. 'And turn all hands up.'

My tone had a borrowed loudness reverberated from the height of the land. Several voices cried out together: 'We are all on deck, sir.'

Then stillness again, with the great shadow gliding closer, towering higher, without a light, without a sound. Such a hush had fallen on the ship that she might have been a bark of the dead floating in slowly under the very gate of Erebus.

'My God! Where are we?'

It was the mate moaning at my elbow. He was thunderstruck, and as it were deprived of the moral support of his whiskers. He clapped his hands and absolutely cried out, 'Lost!'

'Be quiet,' I said, sternly.

He lowered his tone, but I saw the shadowy gesture of his despair. 'What are we doing here?'

'Looking for the land wind.'

He made as if to tear his hair, and addressed me recklessly.

'She will never get out. You have done it, sir. I knew it'd end in something like this. She will never weather, and you are too close now to stay. She'll drift ashore before she's round. O my God!'

I caught his arm as he was raising it to batter his poor devoted head, and shook it violently.

'She's ashore already,' he wailed, trying to tear himself away.

'Is she? . . . Keep good full there!'

'Good full, sir,' cried the helmsman in a frightened, thin, childlike voice.

I hadn't let go the mate's arm and went on shaking it. 'Ready about, do you hear? You go forward' – shake – 'and stop there' – shake – 'and hold your noise' – shake – 'and see these head-sheets properly overhauled' – shake, shake – shake.

And all the time I dared not look toward the land lest my heart should fail me. I released my grip at last and he ran forward as if fleeing for dear life.

I wondered what my double there in the sail-locker thought of this commotion. He was able to hear everything and perhaps he was able to understand why, on my conscience, it had to be thus close – no less. My first order 'Hard alee!' re-echoed ominously under the towering shadow of Koh-ring as if I had shouted in a mountain gorge. And then I watched the land intently. In that smooth water and light wind it was impossible to feel the ship coming-to. No! I could not feel her. And my second self was making now ready to slip out and lower himself overboard. Perhaps he was gone already . . . ?

The great black mass brooding over our very mast-heads began to pivot away from the ship's side silently. And now I forgot the. secret stranger ready to depart, and remembered only that I was a total stranger to the ship. I did not know her. Would she do it? How was she to be handled?

I swung the main yard and waited helplessly. She was perhaps stopped, and her very fate hung in the balance, with the black mass of Koh-ring like the gate of the everlasting night towering over her taffrail. What would she do now? Had she way on her yet? I stepped to the side swiftly, and on the shadowy water I could see nothing except a faint phosphorescent flash revealing the glassy smoothness of the sleeping surface. It was impossible to tell – and I had not learned yet the feel of my ship. Was she moving? What I needed was something easily seen, a piece of paper, which I could throw overboard and watch. I had nothing on me. To run down for it I didn't dare. There was no time. All at once my strained, yearning stare distinguished a white object floating within a yard of the ship's side. White on the black water. A phosphorescent flash passed under it. What was that thing? ... I recognized my own floppy hat. It must have fallen off his head ... and he didn't bother. Now I had what I wanted – the saving mark for my eyes. But I hardly thought of my other self, now gone from the ship, to be hidden for ever from all friendly faces, to be a fugitive and a vagabond on the earth, with no brand of the curse on his sane forehead to stay a slaying hand ... too proud to explain.

And I watched the hat – the expression of my sudden pity for his mere flesh. It had been meant to save his homeless head from the dangers of the sun. And now – behold – it was saving the ship, by serving me for a mark to help out the ignorance of my strangeness. Ha! It was drifting forward, warning me just in time that the ship had gathered sternway.

'Shift the helm,' I said in a low voice to the seaman standing still like a statue.

The man's eyes glistened wildly in the binnacle light as he jumped round to the other side and spun round the wheel.

I walked to the break of the poop. On the overshadowed deck all hands stood by the forebraces waiting for my order. The stars ahead seemed to be gliding from right to left. And all was so still in the world that I heard the quiet remark 'She's round,' passed in a tone of intense relief between two seamen.

'Let go and haul.'

The foreyards ran round with a great noise, amidst cheery cries. And now the frightful whiskers made themselves heard giving various orders. Already the ship was drawing ahead. And I was alone with her. Nothing! no one in the world should stand now between us, throwing a shadow on the way of silent knowledge and mute affection, the perfect communion of a seaman with his first command.

Walking to the taffrail, I was in time to make out, on the very edge of a darkness thrown by a towering black mass like the very gateway of Erebus – yes, I was in time to catch an evanescent glimpse of my white hat left behind to mark the spot where the secret sharer of my cabin and of my thoughts, as though he were my second self, had lowered himself into the water to take his punishment: a free man, a proud swimmer striking out for a new destiny.

The Record of Badalia Herodsfoot

The year's at the spring
And day's at the dawn;
Morning's at seven;
The hill-side's dew-pearled;
The lark's on the wing;
The snail's on the thorn:
God's in his heaven —
All's right with the world! – *Pippa Passes*

This is not that Badalia whose spare names were Joanna, Pugnacious, and M'Canna, as the song says, but another and a much nicer lady.

In the beginning of things she had been unregenerate; had worn the heavy fluffy fringe which is the ornament of the costermonger's girl, and there is a legend in Gunnison Street that on her wedding-day she, a flare-lamp in either hand, danced dances on a discarded lover's winkle-barrow, till a policeman interfered, and then Badalia danced with the Law amid shoutings. Those were her days of fatness, and they did not last long, for her husband after two years took to himself another woman, and passed out of Badalia's life, over Badalia's senseless body; for he stifled protest with blows. While she was enjoying her widowhood the baby that the husband had not taken away died of croup, and Badalia was altogether alone. With rare fidelity she listened to no proposals for a second marriage according to the customs of Gunnison Street, which do not differ from those of the Barralong. 'My man,' she explained to her suitors, ''e'll come back one o' these days, an' then, like as not, 'e'll take an' kill me if I was livin' 'long o' you. You don't know Tom; I do. Now you go. I can do for myself – not 'avin' a kid.' She did for herself with a mangle, some tending of babies, and an occasional sale of flowers. This latter trade is one that needs capital, and takes the vendor very far westward, insomuch that the return journey from, let us say, the Burlington Arcade to Gunnison Street, E, is an excuse for drink, and then, as Badalia pointed out, 'You come 'ome with your shawl arf off of your back, 'an your bonnick under your arm, and the price of nothing-at-all in your pocket, let alone a slop takin' care o' you.' Badalia did not drink, but she knew her sisterhood, and gave them rude counsel. Otherwise she kept herself to herself, and meditated a great deal upon Tom Herods-foot, her husband, who would come back some day, and the baby who would never return. In what manner these thoughts wrought upon her mind will not be known.

Her entry into society dates from the night when she rose literally under the feet of the Reverend Eustace Hanna, on the landing of No. 17 Gunnison Street, and told him that he was a fool without discernment in the dispensation of his district charities.

'You give Lascar Loo custids,' said she, without the formality of introduction; 'give her pork-wine. Garn! Give 'er blankits. Garn 'ome! 'Er mother, she eats 'em all, and drinks the blankits. Gits 'em back from the shop, she does, before you come visiting again, so as to 'ave 'em all handy an' proper; an' Lascar Loo she sez to you, "Oh, my mother's that good to me!" she do. Lascar Loo 'ad better talk so, bein' sick abed, 'r else 'er mother would kill 'er. Garn! you're a bloomin' gardener – you an' yer custids! Lascar Loo don't never smell of 'em even.'

Thereon the curate, instead of being offended, recognized in the heavy eyes under the fringe the soul of a fellow-worker, and so bade Badalia mount guard over Lascar Loo, when the next jelly or custard should arrive, to see that the invalid actually ate it. This Badalia did, to the disgust of Lascar Loo's mother, and the sharing of a black eye between the three; but Lascar Loo got her custard, and coughing heartily, rather enjoyed the fray.

Later on, partly through the Reverend Eustace Hanna's swift recognition of her uses, and partly through certain tales poured out with moist eyes and flushed cheeks by Sister Eva, youngest and most impressionable of the Little Sisters of the Red Diamond, it came to pass that Badalia, arrogant, fluffy-fringed, and perfectly unlicensed in speech, won a recognized place among such as labour in Gunnison Street.

These were a mixed corps, zealous or hysterical, faint-hearted or only very wearied of battle against misery, according to their lights. The most part were consumed with small rivalries and personal jealousies, to be retailed confidentially to their own tiny cliques in the pauses between wrestling with death for the body of a moribund laundress, or scheming for further mission-grants to re-sole a consumptive compositor's very consumptive boots. There was a rector that lived in dread of pauperizing the poor, would fain have held bazaars for fresh altar-cloths, and prayed in secret for a large new brass bird, with eyes of red glass, fondly believed to be carbuncles. There was Brother Victor, of the Order of Little Ease, who knew a great deal about altar-cloths but kept his knowledge in the background while he strove to propitiate Mrs Jessel, the Secretary of the Tea Cup Board, who had money to dispense but hated Rome – even though Rome would, on its honour, do no more than fill the stomach, leaving the dazed soul to the mercies of Mrs Jessel. There were all the Little Sisters of the Red Diamond, daughters of the horseleech, crying 'Give' when their own charity was exhausted, and pitifully explaining to such as demanded an account of their disbursements in return for one half-sovereign, that relief work in a bad district can hardly be systematized on the accounts' side without expensive duplication of staff. There was the Reverend Eustace Hanna, who worked impartially with Ladies' Committees, Androgynous Leagues and Guilds, Brother Victor, and anybody else who could give him money, boots, or blankets, or that more precious help that allows itself to be directed by those who know. And all these people learned, one by one, to consult Badalia on matters of personal character, right to relief, and hope of eventual reformation in Gunnison Street. Her answers were seldom cheering, but she possessed special knowledge and complete confidence in herself.

'I'm Gunnison Street,' she said to the austere Mrs Jessel. 'I know what's what, *I* do, an' they don't want your religion, Mum, not a single ——. Excuse me. It's all right when they comes to die, Mum, but till they die what they wants is things to eat. The men they'll shif' for themselves. That's why Nick Lapworth sez to you that 'e wants to be confirmed an' all that. 'E won't never lead no new life, nor 'is wife won't get no good out o' all the money you gives 'im. No more you can't pauperize them as 'asn't things to begin with. They're bloomin' well pauped. The women they can't shif' for themselves – 'specially bein' always confined. 'Ow should they? They wants things if they can get 'em anyways. If not they dies, and a good job too, for women is cruel put upon in Gunnison Street.'

'Do you believe that – that Mrs Herodsfoot is altogether a

proper person to trust funds to?' said Mrs Jessel to the curate after this conversation. 'She seems to be utterly godless in her speech at least.'

The curate agreed. She was godless according to Mrs Jessel's views, but did not Mrs Jessel think that since Badalia knew Gunnison Street and its needs, as none other knew it, she might in a humble way be, as it were, the scullion of charity from purer sources, and that if, say, the Tea Cup Board could give a few shillings a week, and the Little Sisters of the Red Diamond a few more, and, yes, he himself could raise yet a few more, the total, not at all likely to be excessive, might be handed over to Badalia to dispense among her associates. Thus Mrs Jessel herself would be set free to attend more directly to the spiritual wants of certain large-limbed hulking men who sat picturesquely on the lower benches of her gatherings and sought for truth – which is quite as precious as silver, when you know the market for it.

'She'll favour her own friends,' said Mrs Jessel. The curate refrained from mirth, and, after wise flattery, carried his point. To her unbounded pride Badalia was appointed the dispenser of a grant – a weekly trust, to be held for the benefit of Gunnison Street.

'I don't know what we can get together each week,' said the curate to her. 'But here are seventeen shillings to start with. You do what you like with them among your people, only let me know how it goes so that we shan't get muddled in the accounts. D'you see?'

'Ho yuss! 'Taint much though, is it?' said Badalia, regarding the white coins in her palm. The sacred fever of the administrator, only known to those who have tasted power, burned in her veins. 'Boots is boots, unless they're give you, an' then they ain't fit to wear unless they're mended top an' bottom; an' jellies is jellies; an' I don't think anything o' that cheap pork-wine, but it all comes to something. It'll go quicker 'n a quartern of gin – seventeen bob. An' I'll keep a book – same as I used to do before Tom went an' took up 'long o' that pan-faced slut in Hennessy's Rents. We was the only barrer that kep' regular books, me an' – 'im.'

She bought a large copy-book – her unschooled handwriting demanded room – and in it she wrote the story of her war; boldly, as befits a general, and for no other eyes than her own and those of the Reverend Eustace Hanna. Long ere the pages were full the mottled cover had been soaked in kerosene – Lascar Loo's mother, defrauded of her percentage on her daughter's custards, invaded Badalia's room in 17 Gunnison Street, and fought with her to the damage of the lamp and her own hair. It was hard, too, to carry the precious 'pork-wine' in one hand and the book in the other through an eternally thirsty land; so red stains were added to those of the oil. But the Reverend Eustace Hanna, looking at the matter of the book, never objected. The generous scrawls told their own tale, Badalia every Saturday night supplying the chorus between the written statements thus: —

Mrs Hikkey, very ill brandy 3d. Cab for hospital, she had to go, 1s. Mrs Poone confined. In money for tea (she took it I know, sir) 6d. Met her husband out looking for work.

'I slapped 'is face for a bone-idle beggar! 'E won't get no work becos 'e's — excuse me, sir. Won't you go on?' The curate continued —

Mrs Vincent. Confid. No linning for baby. Most untidy. In money 2s. 6d. Some cloths from Miss Evva.

'Did Sister Eva do that?' said the curate very softly. Now charity was Sister Eva's bounden duty, yet to one man's eyes each act of her daily toil was a manifestation of angelic grace and goodness – a thing to perpetually admire.

'Yes, sir. She went back to the Sisters' 'Ome an' took 'em off 'er own bed. Most beautiful marked too. Go on, sir. That makes up four and thruppence.'

Mrs Junnet to keep good fire coals is up. 7d.

Mrs Lockhart took a baby to nurse to earn a triffle but mother can'd pay husband summons over and over. He won't help. Cash 2s. 2d. Worked in a ketchin but had to leave. Fire, tea, and shin of beef 1s. 7½d.

'There was a fight there, sir,' said Badalia. 'Not me, sir. 'Er 'usband, o' course 'e come in at the wrong time, was wishful to 'ave the beef, so I calls up the next floor an' down comes that mulatter man wot sells the sword-stick canes, top o' Ludgate-'ill. "Muley," sez I, "you big black beast, you, take an' kill this big white beast 'ere." I knew I couldn't stop Tom Lockart 'alf drunk, with the beef in 'is 'ands. "I'll beef 'm," sez Muley, an' 'e did it, with that pore woman a-cryin' in the next room, an' the top banisters on that landin' is broke out, but she got 'er beef-tea, an' Tom 'e's got 'is gruel. Will you go on, sir?'

'No, I think it will be all right. I'll sign for the week,' said the curate. One gets so used to these things profanely called human documents.

'Mrs Churner's baby's got diptheery,' said Badalia, turning to go.

'Where's that? The Churners of Painter's Alley, or the other Churners in Houghton Street?'

'Houghton Street. The Painter's Alley people, they're sold out an' left.'

'Sister Eva's sitting one night a week with old Mrs Probyn in Houghton Street – isn't she?' said the curate uneasily.

'Yes; but she won't sit no longer. *I've* took up Mrs Probyn. I can't talk 'er no religion, but she don't want it; an' Miss Eva she don't want no diptheery, tho' she sez she does. Don't *you* be afraid for Miss Eva.'

'But – but you'll get it, perhaps.'

'Like as not.' She looked the curate between the eyes, and her own eyes flamed under the fringe. 'Maybe I'd like to get it, for aught you know.'

The curate thought upon these words for a little time till he began to think of Sister Eva in the gray cloak with the white bonnet ribbons under the chin. Then he thought no more of Badalia.

What Badalia thought was never expressed in words, but it is known in Gunnison Street that Lascar Loo's mother, sitting blind drunk on her own doorstep, was that night captured and wrapped up in the war-cloud of Badalia's wrath, so that she did not know whether she stood on her head or her heels, and after being soundly bumped on every particular stair up to her room, was set down on Badalia's bed, there to whimper and quiver till the dawn, protesting that all the world was against her, and calling on the names of children long since slain by dirt and neglect. Badalia, snorting, went out to war, and since the hosts of the enemy were many, found enough work to keep her busy till the dawn.

As she had promised, she took Mrs Probyn into her own care, and began by nearly startling the old lady into a fit with the announcement that 'there ain't no God like as not, an' if there *is* it don't matter to you or me, an' any'ow you take this jelly'. Sister Eva objected to being shut off from her pious work in Houghton Street, but Badalia insisted, and by fair words and the promise of favours to come so prevailed on three or four of the more sober men of the neighbourhood that they blockaded the door whenever Sister Eva attempted to force an entry, and pleaded the diphtheria as an excuse. 'I've got to keep 'er out o' 'arm's way,' said Badalia, 'an' out she keeps. The curick won't care a —— for me, but – he wouldn't any'ow.'

The effect of that quarantine was to shift the sphere of Sister Eva's activity to other streets, and notably those most haunted by the Reverend Eustace Hanna and Brother Victor, of the Order of Little Ease. There exists, for all their human bickerings, a very close brotherhood in the ranks of those whose work lies in Gunnison Street. To begin with, they have seen pain – pain that no word or deed of theirs can alleviate – life born into Death, and Death crowded down by unhappy life. Also they understand the full significance of drink, which is a knowledge hidden from very many well-meaning people, and some of them have fought with the beasts at Ephesus. They meet at unseemly hours in unseemly places, exchange a word or two of hasty counsel, advice, or suggestion, and pass on to their appointed toil, since time is precious and lives hang in the balance of five minutes. For many, the gas-lamps are their sun, and the Covent Garden wains the chariots of the twilight. They have all in their station begged for money, so that the freemasonry of the mendicant binds them together.

To all these influences there was added in the case of two workers that thing which men have agreed to call Love. The chance that Sister Eva might catch diphtheria did not enter into the curate's head till Badalia had spoken. Then it seemed a thing intolerable and monstrous that she should be exposed not only to this risk, but any accident whatever of the streets. A wain coming round a corner might kill her; the rotten staircases on which she trod daily and nightly might collapse and maim her; there was danger in the tottering coping-stones of certain crazy houses that he knew well; danger more deadly within those houses. What if one of a thousand drunken men crushed out that precious life? A woman had once flung a chair at the curate's head. Sister Eva's arm would not be strong enough to ward off a chair. There were also knives that were quick to fly. These and other considerations cast the soul of the Reverend Eustace Hanna into torment that no leaning upon Providence could relieve. God was indubitably great and terrible – one had only to walk through Gunnison Street to see that much – but it would be better, vastly better, that Eva should have the protection of his own arm. And the world that was not too busy to watch might have seen a woman, not too young, light-haired and light-eyed, slightly assertive in her speech, and very limited in such ideas as lay beyond the immediate sphere of her duty, where the eyes of the Reverend Eustace Hanna turned to follow the footsteps of a Queen crowned in a little gray bonnet with white ribbons under the chin.

If that bonnet appeared for a moment at the bottom of a court-yard, or nodded at him on a dark staircase, then there was hope yet for Lascar Loo, living on one lung and the memory of past excesses, hope even for whining sodden Nick Lapworth, blaspheming, in the hope of money, over the pangs of a 'true conversion this time, s'elp me Gawd, sir'. If that bonnet did not appear for a day, the mind of the curate was filled with lively pictures of horror, visions of stretchers, a crowd at some villainous crossing, and a policeman – he could see that policeman – jerking out over his shoulder the details of the accident, and ordering the man who would have set his body against the wheels – heavy dray wheels, he could see them – to 'move on'. Then there was less hope for the salvation of Gunnison Street and all in it.

This agony Brother Victor beheld one day when he was coming from a deathbed. He saw the light in the eye, the relaxing muscles of the mouth, and heard a new ring in the voice that had told flat all the forenoon. Sister Eva had turned into Gunnison Street after a forty-eight hours' eternity of absence. She had not been run over. Brother Victor's heart must have suffered in some human fashion, or he would never have seen what he saw. But the Law of his Church made suffering easy. His duty was to go on with his work until he died, even as Badalia went on. She, magnifying her office, faced the drunken husband; coaxed the doubly shiftless, thriftless girl-wife into a little forethought, and begged clothes when and where she could for the scrofulous babes that multiplied like the green scum on the untopped water-cisterns.

The story of her deeds was written in the book that the curate signed weekly, but she never told him any more of fights and tumults in the street. 'Mis' Eva does 'er work 'er way. I does mine mine. But I do more than Mis' Eva ten times over, an' "Thank yer, Badalia," sez 'e, "that'll do for this week." I wonder what Tom's doin' now long o' that – other woman. 'Seems like as if I'd go an' look at 'im one o' these days. But I'd cut 'er liver out – couldn't 'elp myself. Better not go, p'raps.'

Hennessy's Rents lay more than two miles from Gunnison Street, and were inhabited by much the same class of people. Tom had established himself there with Jenny Wabstow, his new woman, and for weeks lived in great fear of Badalia's suddenly descending upon him. The prospect of actual fighting did not scare him: but he objected to the police court that would follow, and the orders for maintenance and other devices of a law that cannot understand the simple rule that 'when a man's tired of a woman 'e ain't such a bloomin' fool as to live with 'er no more, an' that's the long an' short of it'. For some months his new wife wore very well, and kept Tom in a state of decent fear and consequent orderliness. Also work was plentiful. Then a baby was born, and, following the law of his kind, Tom, little interested in the children he helped to produce, sought distraction in drink. He had confined himself, as a rule, to beer, which is stupefying and comparatively innocuous: at least, it clogs the legs, and though the heart may ardently desire to kill, sleep comes swiftly, and the crime often remains undone. Spirits, being more volatile, allow both the flesh and the soul to work together – generally to the inconvenience of others. Tom discovered that there was merit in whisky – if you only took enough of it – cold. He took as much as he could purchase or get given him, and by the time that his woman was fit to go abroad again, the two rooms of their household were stripped of many valuable articles. Then the woman spoke her mind, not once, but several times, with point, fluency, and metaphor; and Tom was indignant at being deprived of peace at the end of his day's work, which included much whisky. He therefore withdrew himself from the solace and companionship of Jenny Wabstow, and she therefore pursued him with more metaphors. At the last, Tom would turn round and hit her – sometimes across the head, and sometimes across the breast, and the bruises furnished material for discussion on doorsteps among such women as had been treated in like manner by their husbands. They were not few.

But no very public scandal had occurred till Tom one day saw fit to open negotiations with a young woman for matrimony according to the laws of free selection. He was getting very tired of Jenny, and the young woman was earning enough from flower-selling to keep him in comfort, whereas Jenny was expecting another baby and most unreasonably expected consideration on this account. The shapelessness of her figure revolted him, and he said as much in the language of his breed. Jenny cried till Mrs Hart, lineal descendant, and Irish of the 'mother to Mike of the donkey-cart', stopped her on her own staircase and whispered: 'God be good to you, Jenny, my woman, for I see how 'tis with you.' Jenny wept more than ever, and gave Mrs Hart a penny and some kisses, while Tom was conducting his own wooing at the corner of the street.

The young woman, prompted by pride, not by virtue, told Jenny of his offers, and Jenny spoke to Tom that night. The altercation began in their own rooms, but Tom tried to escape; and in the end all Hennessy's Rents gathered themselves upon the pavement and formed a court to which Jenny appealed from time to time, her hair loose on her neck, her raiment in extreme disorder, and her steps astray from drink. 'When your man drinks, you'd better drink too! It don't 'urt so much when 'e 'its you then,' says the Wisdom of the Women. And surely they ought to know.

'Look at 'im!' shrieked Jenny. 'Look at 'im, standin' there without any word to say for himself, that 'ud smitch off and leave me an' never so much as a shillin' lef' be'ind! You call yourself a man – you call yourself the bleedin' shadow of a man? I've seen better men than you made outer chewed paper and spat out arterwards. Look at 'im! 'E's been drunk since Thursday last, an' 'e'll be drunk s' long's 'e can get drink. 'E's took all I've got, an' me – an' me – as you see —'

A murmur of sympathy from the women.

'Took it all, he did, an' atop of his blasted pickin' an' stealin' – yes, you, you thief – 'e goes off an' tries to take up long o' that' – here followed a complete and minute description of the young woman. Luckily, she was not on the spot to hear. ''E'll serve 'er as 'e served me! 'E'll drink every bloomin' copper she makes an' then leave 'er alone, same as 'e done me! O women, look you, I've bore 'im one an' there's another on the way, an' 'e'd up an' leave me as I am now – the stinkin' dorg. An' you *may* leave me. I don't want none o' your leavin's. Go away. Get away!' The hoarseness of passion overpowered the voice. The crowd attracted a policeman as Tom began to slink away.

'Look at 'im,' said Jenny, grateful for the new listener. 'Ain't there no law for such as 'im? 'E's took all my money, 'e's beat me once, twice an' over. 'E's swine drunk when 'e ain't mad drunk, an' now, an' now 'e's trying to pick up along o' another woman. 'Im I give up a four times better man for. Ain't there no law?'

'What's the matter now? You go into your 'ouse. I'll see to the man. 'As 'e been 'itting you?' said the policeman.

'Ittin' me? 'E's cut my 'eart in two, an' 'e stands there grinnin' as tho' 'twas all a play to 'im.'

'You go on into your 'ouse an' lie down a bit.'

'I'm a married woman, I tell you, an' I'll 'ave my 'usband!'

'I ain't done her no bloomin' 'arm,' said Tom from the edge of the crowd. He felt that public opinion was running against him.

'You ain't done me any bloomin' good, you dorg. I'm a married woman, I am, an' I won't 'ave my 'usband took from me.'

'Well, if you *are* a married woman, cover your breasts,' said the policeman soothingly. He was used to domestic brawls.

'Shan't – thank you for your impidence. Look 'ere!' She tore open her dishevelled bodice and showed such crescent-shaped bruises as are made by a well-applied chair-back. 'That's what 'e done to me acause my heart wouldn't break quick enough! 'E's tried to get in an' break it. Look at that, Tom, that you gave me last night; an' I made it up with you. But that was before I knew what you were tryin' to do long o' that woman —'

'D'you charge 'im?' said the policeman. ''E'll get a month for it, per'aps.'

'No,' said Jenny firmly. It was one thing to expose her man to the scorn of the street, and another to lead him to jail.

'Then you go in an' lie down, and you' – this to the crowd – 'pass along the pavement, there. Pass along. 'Taint nothing to laugh at.' To Tom, who was being sympathized with by his friends, 'It's good for you she didn't charge you, but mind this now, the next time,' etc.

Tom did not at all appreciate Jenny's forbearance, nor did his friends help to compose his mind. He had whacked the woman because she was a nuisance. For precisely the same reason he had cast about for a new mate. And all his kind acts had ended in a truly painful scene in the street, a most unjustifiable exposure by and of his woman, and a certain loss of caste – this he realized dimly – among his associates. Consequently, all women were nuisances, and consequently whisky was a good thing. His friends condoled with him. Perhaps he had been more hard on his woman than she deserved, but her disgraceful conduct under provocation excused all offence.

'I wouldn't 'ave no more to do with 'er – a woman like that

there,' said one comforter.

'Let 'er go an' dig for her bloomin' self. A man wears 'isself out to 'is bones shovin' meat down their mouths, while they sit at 'ome easy all day; an' the very fust time, mark you, you 'as a bit of a difference, an' very proper too for a man as *is* a man, she ups an' 'as you out into the street, callin' you Gawd knows what all. What's the good o' that, I arx you?' So spoke the second comforter.

The whisky was the third, and his suggestion struck Tom as the best of all. He would return to Badalia his wife. Probably she would have been doing something wrong while he had been away, and he could then vindicate his authority as a husband. Certainly she would have money. Single women always seemed to possess the pence that God and the Government denied to hard-working men. He refreshed himself with more whisky. It was beyond any doubt that Badalia would have done something wrong. She might even have married another man. He would wait till the new husband was out of the way, and, after kicking Badalia, would get money and a long absent sense of satisfaction. There is much virtue in a creed or a law, but when all is prayed and suffered, drink is the only thing that will make clean all a man's deeds in his own eyes. Pity it is that the effects are not permanent.

Tom parted with his friends, bidding them tell Jenny that he was going to Gunnison Street, and would return to her arms no more. Because this was the devil's message, they remembered and sev-erally delivered it, with drunken distinctness, in Jenny's ears. Then Tom took more drink till his drunkenness rolled back and stood off from him as a wave rolls back and stands off the wreck it will swamp. He reached the traffic-polished black asphalt of a side street and trod warily among the reflections of the shop lamps that burned in gulfs of pitchy darkness, fathoms beneath his boot heels. He was very sober indeed. Looking down his past, he beheld that he was justified of all his actions so entirely and perfectly that if Badalia had in his absence dared to lead a blameless life he would smash her for not having gone wrong.

Badalia at that moment was in her own room after the regular nightly skirmish with Lascar Loo's mother. To a reproof as stinging as a Gunnison Street tongue could make it, the old woman, de-tected for the hundredth time in the theft of the poor delicacies meant for the invalid, could only cackle and answer —

'D'you think Loo's never bilked a man in 'er life? She's dyin' now

— on'y she's so cunning long about it. Me! I'll live for twenty years yet.'

Badalia shook her, more on principle than in any hope of curing her, and thrust her into the night, where she collapsed on the pavement and called upon the devil to slay Badalia.

He came upon the word in the shape of a man with a very pale face who asked for her by name. Lascar Loo's mother remembered. It was Badalia's husband — and the return of a husband to Gunnison Street was generally followed by beatings.

'Where's my wife?' said Tom. 'Where's my slut of a wife?'

'Upstairs an' be —— to her,' said the old woman, falling over on her side. ' 'Ave you come back for 'er, Tom?'

'Yes. 'Oo's she took up while I bin gone?'

'All the bloomin' curicks in the parish. She's that set up you wouldn't know 'er.'

' 'Strewth she is!'

'Oh, yuss. Mor'n that, she's always round an' about with them sniffin' Sisters of Charity an' the curick. Mor'n that, 'e gives 'er money — pounds an' pounds a week. Been keepin' her that way for months, 'e 'as. No wonder you wouldn't 'ave nothin' to do with 'er when you left. An' she keeps me outer the foodstuff they gets for me lyin' dyin' out 'ere like a dorg. She's been a blazin' bad un has Badalia since you lef'.'

'Got the same room still, 'as she?' said Tom, striding over Lascar Loo's mother, who was picking at the chinks between the pavestones.

'Yes, but so fine you wouldn't know it.'

Tom went up the stairs and the old lady chuckled. Tom was angry. Badalia would not be able to bump people for some time to come, or to interfere with the heaven-appointed distribution of custards.

Badalia, undressing to go to bed, heard feet on the stair that she knew well. Ere they stopped to kick at her door she had, in her own fashion, thought over very many things.

'Tom's back,' she said to herself. 'An' I'm glad . . . spite o' the curick an' everythink.'

She opened the door, crying his name.

The man pushed her aside.

'I don't want none o' your kissin's an' slaverin's. I'm sick of 'em,' said he.

'You ain't 'ad so many neither to make you sick these two years past.'

'I've 'ad better. Got any money?'

'On'y a little – orful little.'

'That's a —— lie, an' you know it.'

"Taint – and, oh Tom, what's the use o' talkin' money the minute you come back? Didn't you like Jenny? I knowed you wouldn't.'

'Shut your 'ead. Ain't you got enough to make a man drunk fair?'

'You don't want bein' made more drunk any. You're drunk a'ready. You come to bed, Tom.'

'To you?'

'Ay, to me. Ain't I nothin' – spite o' Jenny?'

She put out her arms as she spoke. But the drink held Tom fast.

'Not for me,' said he, steadying himself against the wall. 'Don't I know 'ow you've been goin' on while I was away, yah!'

'Arsk about!' said Badalia indignantly, drawing herself together. "Oo sez anythink agin me 'ere?'

"Oo sez? W'y, everybody. I ain't come back more'n a minute fore I finds you've been with the curick Gawd knows where. Wot curick was 'e?'

'The curick that's 'ere always,' said Badalia hastily. She was thinking of anything rather than the Rev. Eustace Hanna at that moment. Tom sat down gravely in the only chair in the room. Badalia continued her arrangements for going to bed.

'Pretty thing that,' said Tom, 'to tell your own lawful married 'usband – an' I guv five bob for the weddin'-ring. Curick that's 'ere always! Cool as brass you are. Ain't you got no shame? Ain't 'e under the bed now?'

'Tom, you're bleedin' drunk. I ain't done nothin' to be 'shamed of.'

'You! You don't know wot shame is. But I ain't come 'ere to mess with you. Give me wot you've got, an' then I'll dress you down an' go to Jenny.'

'I ain't got nothin' 'cept some coppers an' a shillin' or so.'

'Wot's that about the curick keepin' you on five poun' a week?'

"Oo told you that?'

'Lascar Loo's mother, lyin' on the pavemint outside, an' more honest than you'll ever be. Give me wot you've got!'

Badalia passed over to a little shell pin-cushion on the mantelpiece, drew thence four shillings and threepence – the lawful earnings of her trade – and held them out to the man who was rocking in his chair and surveying the room with wide-opened rolling eyes.

'That ain't five poun',' said he drowsily.

'I ain't got no more. Take it an' go – if you won't stay.'

Tom rose slowly, gripping the arms of the chair. 'Wot about the curick's money that 'e guv you?' said he. 'Lascar Loo's mother told me. You give it over to me now, or I'll make you.'

'Lascar Loo's mother don't know anything about it.'

'She do, an' more than you want her to know.'

'She don't. I've bumped the 'eart out of 'er, and I can't give you the money. Anythin' else but that, Tom, an' everythin' else but that, Tom, I'll give willin' and true. 'Taint my money. Won't the dollar be enough? That money's my trust. There's a book along of it too.'

'Your trust? Wot are you doin' with any trust that your 'usband don't know of? You an' your trust! Take you that!'

Tom stepped towards her and delivered a blow of the clenched fist across the mouth. 'Give me wot you've got,' said he, in the thick abstracted voice of one talking in dreams.

'I won't,' said Badalia, staggering to the washstand. With any other man than her husband she would have fought savagely as a wild cat; but Tom had been absent two years, and, perhaps, a little timely submission would win him back to her. None the less, the weekly trust was sacred.

The wave that had so long held back descended on Tom's brain. He caught Badalia by the throat and forced her to her knees. It seemed just to him in that hour to punish an erring wife for two years of wilful desertion; and the more, in that she had confessed her guilt by refusing to give up the wage of sin.

Lascar Loo's mother waited on the pavement without for the sounds of lamentation, but none came. Even if Tom had released her gullet, Badalia would not have screamed.

'Give it up, you slut!' said Tom. 'Is that 'ow you pay me back for all I've done?'

'I can't. 'Tain't my money. Gawd forgive you, Tom, for wot you're ——,' the voice ceased as the grip tightened, and Tom heaved Badalia against the bed. Her forehead struck the bedpost, and she sank, half kneeling, on the floor. It was impossible for a self-respecting man to refrain from kicking her: so Tom kicked with the deadly intelligence born of whisky. The head drooped to the floor, and Tom kicked at that till the crisp tingle of hair striking through his nailed boot with the chill of cold water, warned him that it might be as well to desist.

'Where's the curick's money, you kep' woman?' he whispered in the blood-stained ear. But there was no answer – only a rattling at the door, and the voice of Jenny Wabstow crying ferociously, 'Come out o' that, Tom, an' come 'ome with me! An' you, Badalia, I'll tear your face off its bones!'

Tom's friends had delivered their message, and Jenny, after the first flood of passionate tears, rose up to follow Tom, and, if possible, to win him back. She was prepared even to endure an exemplary whacking for her performances in Hennessy's Rents. Lascar Loo's mother guided her to the chamber of horrors, and chuckled as she retired down the staircase. If Tom had not banged the soul out of Badalia, there would at least be a royal fight between that Badalia and Jenny. And Lascar Loo's mother knew well that Hell has no fury like a woman fighting above the life that is quick in her.

Still there was no sound audible in the street. Jenny swung back the unbolted door, to discover her man stupidly regarding a heap by the bed. An eminent murderer has remarked that if people did not die so untidily, most men, and all women, would commit at least one murder in their lives. Tom was reflecting on the present untidiness, and the whisky was fighting with the clear current of his thoughts.

'Don't make that noise,' he said. 'Come in quick.'

'My Gawd!' said Jenny, checking like a startled wild beast. 'Wot's all this 'ere? You ain't — '

'Dunno. 'Spose I did it.'

'Did it! You done it a sight too well this time.'

'She was aggravatin',' said Tom thickly, dropping back into the chair. 'That aggravatin' you'd never believe. Livin' on the fat o' the land among these aristocratic parsons an' all. Look at them white curtings on the bed. *We* ain't got no white curtings. What I want to know is —' The voice died as Badalia's had died, but from a different cause. The whisky was tightening its grip after the accomplished deed, and Tom's eyes were beginning to close. Badalia on the floor breathed heavily.

'No, nor like to 'ave,' said Jenny. 'You've done for 'er this time. You go!'

'Not me. She won't hurt. Do 'er good. I'm goin' to sleep. Look at those there clean sheets! Ain't you comin' too?'

Jenny bent over Badalia, and there was intelligence in the battered woman's eyes – intelligence and much hate.

'I never told 'im to do such,' Jenny whispered. ''Twas Tom's own doin' – none o' mine. Shall I get 'im took, dear?'

The eyes told their own story. Tom, who was beginning to snore, must not be taken by the Law.

'Go,' said Jenny. 'Get out! Get out of 'ere.'

'You – told – me – that – this afternoon,' said the man very sleepily. 'Lemme go asleep.'

'That wasn't nothing. You'd only 'it me. This time it's murder – murder – murder! Tom, you've killed 'er now.' She shook the man from his rest, and understanding with cold terror filled his fuddled brain.

'I done it for your sake, Jenny,' he whimpered feebly, trying to take her hand.

'You killed 'er for the money, same as you would ha' killed me. Get out o' this. Lay 'er on the bed first, you brute!'

They lifted Badalia on to the bed, and crept forth silently.

'I can't be took along o' you – and if you was took you'd say I made you do it, an' try to get me 'anged. Go away – anywhere outer 'ere,' said Jenny, and she dragged him down the stairs.

'Goin' to look for the curick?' said a voice from the pavement. Lascar Loo's mother was still waiting patiently to hear Badalia squeal.

'Wot curick?' said Jenny swiftly. There was a chance of salving her conscience yet in regard to the bundle upstairs.

''Anna – 63 Roomer Terrace – close 'ere,' said the old woman. She had never been favourably regarded by the curate. Perhaps, since Badalia had not squealed, Tom preferred smashing the man to the woman. There was no accounting for tastes.

Jenny thrust her man before her till they reached the nearest main road. 'Go away, now,' she gasped. 'Go off anywheres, but don't come back to me. I'll never go with you again; an', Tom – Tom, d'you 'ear me? – clean your boots.'

Vain counsel. The desperate thrust of disgust which she bestowed upon him sent him staggering face down into the kennel, where a policeman showed interest in his welfare.

'Took for a common drunk. Gawd send they don't look at 'is

boots! 'Anna, 63 Roomer Terrace!' Jenny settled her hat and ran.

The excellent housekeeper of the Roomer Chambers still remembers how there arrived a young person, blue-lipped and gasping, who cried only: 'Badalia, 17 Gunnison Street. Tell the curick to come at once – at once – at once!' and vanished into the night. This message was borne to the Rev. Eustace Hanna, then enjoying his beauty-sleep. He saw there was urgency in the demand, and unhesitatingly knocked up Brother Victor across the landing. As a matter of etiquette, Rome and England divided their cases in the district according to the creeds of the sufferers; but Badalia was an institution, and not a case, and there was no district-relief etiquette to be considered. 'Something has happened to Badalia,' the curate said, 'and it's your affair as well as mine. Dress and come along.'

'I am ready,' was the answer. 'Is there any hint of what's wrong?'

'Nothing beyond a runaway-knock and a call.'

'Then it's confinement or a murderous assault. Badalia wouldn't wake us up for anything less. I'm qualified for both, thank God.'

The two men raced to Gunnison Street, for there were no cabs abroad, and under any circumstances a cab fare means two days' good firing for such as are perishing with cold. Lascar Loo's mother had gone to bed, and the door was naturally on the latch. They found considerably more than they had expected in Badalia's room, and the Church of Rome acquitted itself nobly with bandages, while the Church of England could only pray to be delivered from the sin of envy. The Order of Little Ease, recognizing that the soul is in most cases accessible through the body, take their measures and train their men accordingly.

'She'll do now,' said Brother Victor, in a whisper. 'It's internal bleeding, I fear, and a certain amount of injury to the brain. She has a husband, of course?'

'They all have, more's the pity.'

'Yes, there's a domesticity about these injuries that shows their origin.' He lowered his voice. 'It's a perfectly hopeless business, you understand. Twelve hours at the most.'

Badalia's right hand began to beat on the counterpane, palm down.

'I think you are wrong,' said the Church of England. 'She is going.'

'No, that's not the picking at the counterpane,' said the Church of Rome. 'She wants to say something; you know her better than I.'

The curate bent very low.

'Send for Miss Eva,' said Badalia, with a cough.

'In the morning. She will come in the morning,' said the curate, and Badalia was content. Only the Church of Rome, who knew something of the human heart, knitted his brows and said nothing. After all, the law of his order was plain. His duty was to watch till the dawn while the moon went down.

It was a little before her sinking that the Rev. Eustace Hanna said, 'Hadn't we better send for Sister Eva? She seems to be going fast.'

Brother Victor made no answer, but as early as decency admitted there came one to the door of the house of the Little Sisters of the Red Diamond and demanded Sister Eva, that she might soothe the pain of Badalia Herodsfoot. That man, saying very little, led her to Gunnison Street, No. 17, and into the room where Badalia lay. Then he stood on the landing, and bit the flesh of his fingers in agony, because he was a priest trained to know, and knew how the hearts of men and women beat back at the rebound, so that Love is born out of horror, and passion declares itself when the soul is quivering with pain.

Badalia, wise to the last, husbanded her strength till the coming of Sister Eva. It is generally maintained by the Little Sisters of the Red Diamond that she died in delirium, but since one Sister at least took a half of her dying advice, this seems uncharitable.

She tried to turn feebly on the bed, and the poor broken human machinery protested according to its nature.

Sister Eva started forward, thinking that she heard the dread forerunner of the death-rattle. Badalia lay still conscious, and spoke with startling distinctness, the irrepressible irreverence of the street-hawker, the girl who had danced on the winkle-barrow, twinkling in her one available eye.

'Sounds jest like Mrs Jessel, don't it? Before she's 'ad 'er lunch an' 'as been talkin' all the mornin' to her classes.'

Neither Sister Eva nor the curate said anything. Brother Victor stood without the door, and the breath came harshly between his teeth, for he was in pain.

'Put a cloth over my 'ead,' said Badalia. 'I've got it good, an' I don't want Miss Eva to see. I ain't pretty this time.'

'Who was it?' said the curate.

'Man from outside. Never seed 'im no more'n Adam. Drunk, I s'pose. S'elp me Gawd that's truth! Is Miss Eva 'ere? I can't see under the towel. I've got it good, Miss Eva. Excuse my not shakin' 'ands with you, but I'm not strong, an' it's fourpence for Mrs Imeny's beef-tea, an' wot you can give 'er for baby-linning. Allus 'avin' kids, these people. I 'adn't oughter talk, for *my* 'usband 'e never come a-nigh me these two years, or I'd a-bin as bad as the rest; but 'e never come a-nigh me. . . . A man come and 'it me over the 'ead, an' 'e kicked me, Miss Eva; so it was just the same's if I had ha' had a 'usband, ain't it? The book's in the drawer, Mister 'Anna, an' it's all right, an' I never guv up a copper o' the trust money – not a copper. You look under the chist o' drawers – all wot isn't spent this week is there. . . . An', Miss Eva, don't you wear that gray bonnick no more. I kep' you from the diptheery, an' – an' I didn't want to keep you so, but the curick said it 'ad to be done. I'd a sooner ha' took up with 'im than any one, only Tom 'e come, an' then – you see, Miss Eva, Tom 'e never come a-nigh me for two years, nor I 'aven't seen 'im yet. S'elp me —, I 'aven't. Do you 'ear? But you two go along, and make a match of it. I've wished otherways often, but o' course it was not for the likes o' me. If Tom 'ad come back, which 'e never did, I'd ha' been like the rest – sixpence for beef-tea for the baby, an' a shilling for layin' out the baby. You've seen it in the books, Mister 'Anna. That's what it is; an' o' course, you couldn't never 'ave nothing to do with me. But a woman she wishes as she looks, an' never you 'ave no doubt about 'im, Miss Eva. I've seen it in 'is face time an' agin – time an' agin. . . . Make it a four pound ten funeral – with a pall.'

It was a seven pound fifteen shilling funeral, and all Gunnison Street turned out to do it honour. All but two; for Lascar Loo's mother saw that a Power had departed, and that her road lay clear to the custards. Therefore, when the carriages rattled off, the cat on the doorstep heard the wail of the dying prostitute who could not die —

'Oh, mother, mother, won't you even let me lick the spoon!'

O. HENRY · 1867–1910

Telemachus, Friend

Returning from a hunting trip, I waited at the little town of Los
Piños, in New Mexico, for the south-bound train, which was one
hour late. I sat on the porch of the Summit House and discussed
the functions of life with Telemachus Hicks, the hotel proprietor.

Perceiving that personalities were not out of order, I asked him
what species of beast had long ago twisted and mutilated his left
ear. Being a hunter, I was concerned in the evils that may befall one
in the pursuit of game.

'That ear,' said Hicks, 'is the relic of true friendship.'

'An accident?' I persisted.

'No friendship is an accident,' said Telemachus; and I was silent.

'The only perfect case of true friendship I ever knew', went on
my host, 'was a cordial intent between a Connecticut man and a
monkey. The monkey climbed palms in Barranquilla and threw
down coconuts to the man. The man sawed them in two and made
dippers, which he sold for two *reales* each and bought rum. The
monkey drank the milk of the nuts. Through each being satisfied
with his own share of the graft, they lived like brothers.

'But in the case of human beings, friendship is a transitory art,
subject to discontinuance without further notice.

'I had a friend once, of the entitlement of Paisley Fish, that I
imagined was sealed to me for an endless space of time. Side by
side for seven years we had mined, ranched, sold patent churns,
herded sheep, took photographs and other things, built wire fences,
and picked prunes. Thinks I, neither homicide nor flattery nor
riches nor sophistry nor drink can make trouble between me and
Paisley Fish. We was friends an amount you could hardly guess at.
We was friends in business, and we let our amicable qualities lap
over and season our hours of recreation and folly. We certainly had
days of Damon and nights of Pythias.

'One summer me and Paisley gallops down into these San Andrés
mountains for the purpose of a month's surcease and levity, dressed

in the natural store habiliments of man. We hit this town of Los Piños, which certainly was a roof-garden spot of the world, and flowing with condensed milk and honey. It had a street or two, and air, and hens, and a eating-house; and that was enough for us.

'We strikes the town after supper-time, and we concludes to sample whatever efficacy there is in this eating-house down by the railroad tracks. By the time we had set down and pried up our plates with a knife from the red oil-cloth, along intrudes Widow Jessup with the hot biscuit and the fried liver.

'Now, there was a woman that would have tempted an anchovy to forget his vows. She was not so small as she was large; and a kind of welcome air seemed to mitigate her vicinity. The pink of her face was the *in hoc signo* of a culinary temper and a warm disposition, and her smile would have brought out the dogwood blossoms in December.

'Widow Jessup talks to us a lot of garrulousness about the climate and history and Tennyson and prunes and the scarcity of mutton, and finally wants to know where we came from.

'"Spring Valley", says I.

'"Big Spring Valley," chips in Paisley, out of a lot of potatoes and knuckle-bone of ham in his mouth.

'That was the first sign I noticed that the old *fidus Diogenes* business between me and Paisley Fish was ended for ever. He knew how I hated a talkative person, and yet he stampedes into the conversation with his amendments and addendums of syntax. On the map it was Big Spring Valley; but I had heard Paisley himself call it Spring Valley a thousand times.

'Without saying any more, we went out after supper and set on the railroad track. We had been pardners too long not to know what was going on in each other's mind.

'"I reckon you understand," says Paisley, "that I've made up my mind to accrue that widow woman as part and parcel in and to my hereditaments for ever, both domestic, sociable, legal, and otherwise, until death us do part."

'"Why, yes," says I. "I read it between the lines, though you only spoke one. And I suppose you are aware," says I, "that I have a movement on foot that leads up to the widow's changing her name to Hicks, and leaves you writing to the society column to inquire whether the best man wears a japonica or seamless socks at the wedding!"

'"There'll be some hiatuses in your programme," says Paisley, chewing up a piece of a railroad tie. "I'd give in to you," says he, "in 'most any respect if it was secular affairs, but this is not so. The smiles of woman," goes on Paisley, "is the whirlpool of Squills and Chalybeates, into which vortex the good ship Friendship is often drawn and dismembered. I'd assault a bear that was annoying you," says Paisley, "Or I'd endorse your note, or rub the place between your shoulder-blades with opodeldoc the same as ever; but there my sense of etiquette ceases. In this fracas with Mrs Jessup we play it alone. I've notified you fair."

'And then I collaborates with myself, and offers the following resolutions and bye-laws—

'"Friendship between man and man," says I, "is an ancient historical virtue enacted in the days when men had to protect each other against lizards with eighty-foot tails and flying turtles. And they've kept up the habit to this day, and stand by each other till the bellboy comes up and tells them the animals are not really there. I've often heard," I says, "about ladies stepping in and breaking up a friendship between men. Why should that be? I'll tell you, Paisley, the first sight and hot bisuit of Mrs Jessup appears to have inserted a oscillation into each of our bosoms. Let the best man of us have her. I'll play you a square game, and won't do any underhanded work. I'll do all of my courting of her in your presence, so you will have an equal opportunity. With that arrangement I don't see why our steamboat of friendship should fall overboard in the medicinal whirlpools you speak of, whichever of us wins out."

'"Good old hoss!" says Paisley, shaking my hand. "And I'll do the same," says he. "We'll court the lady synonymously, and without any of the prudery and bloodshed usual to such occasions. And we'll be friends still, win or lose."

'At one side of Mrs Jessup's eating-house was a bench under some trees where she used to sit in the breeze after the south-bound had been fed and gone. And there me and Paisley used to congregate after supper and make partial payments on our respects to the lady of our choice. And we was so honorable and circuitous in our calls that if one of us got there first we waited for the other before beginning any gallivantery.

'The first evening that Mrs Jessup knew about our arrangement I got to the bench before Paisley did. Supper was just over, and Mrs

Jessup was out there with a fresh pink dress on, and almost cool enough to handle.

'I sat down by her and made a few specifications about the moral surface of nature as set forth by the landscape and the contiguous perspective. That evening was surely a case in point. The moon was attending to business in the section of the sky where it belonged, and the trees was making shadows on the ground according to science and nature, and there was a kind of conspicuous hullabaloo going on in the bushes between the bullbats and the orioles and the jack-rabbits and other feathered insects of the forest. And the wind out of the mountains was singing like a jew's harp in the pile of old tomato cans by the railroad track.

'I felt a kind of sensation in my left side – something like dough rising in a crock by the fire. Mrs Jessup had moved up closer.

'"Oh, Mr Hicks," says she, "when one is alone in the world, don't they feel it more aggravated on a beautiful night like this?"

'I rose up off of the bench at once.

'"Excuse me, ma'am," says I, "but I'll have to wait till Paisley comes before I can give a audible hearing to leading questions like that."

'And then I explained to her how we was friends cinctured by years of embarrassment and travel and complicity, and how we had agreed to take no advantage of each other in any of the more mushy walks of life, such as might be fomented by sentiment and proximity. Mrs Jessup appears to think serious about the matter for a minute and then she breaks into a species of laughter that makes the wild-wood resound.

'In a few minutes Paisley drops around, with oil of bergamot on his hair, and sits on the other side of Mrs Jessup, and inaugurates a sad tale of adventure in which him and Pieface Lumley has a skinning match of dead cows in '95 for a silver-mounted saddle in the Santa Rita valley during the nine months' drought.

'Now, from the start of that courtship I had Paisley Fish hobbled and tied to a post. Each one of us had a different system of reaching out for the easy places in the female heart. Paisley's scheme was to petrify 'em with wonderful relations of events that he had either come across personally or in large print. I think he must have got his idea of subjugation from one of Shakespeare's shows I see once called *Othello*. There is a colored man in it who acquires a duke's daughter by disbursing to her a mixture of the talk turned out by

Rider Haggard, Lew Dockstader, and Dr Parkhurst. But that style of courting don't work well off the stage.

'Now, I give you my own recipe for inveigling a woman into that state of affairs when she can be referred to as "*née* Jones". Learn how to pick up her hand and hold it, and she's yours. It ain't so easy. Some men grab at it so much like they was going to set a dislocation of the shoulder that you can smell the arnica and hear 'em tearing off bandages. Some take it up like a hot horseshoe, and hold it off at arm's length like a druggist pouring tincture of asafœtida in a bottle. And most of 'em catch hold of it and drag it right out before the lady's eyes like a boy finding a baseball in the grass, without giving her a chance to forget that the hand is growing on the end of her arm. Them ways are all wrong.

'I'll tell you the right way. Did you ever see a man sneak out in the back yard and pick up a rock to throw at a tom-cat that was sitting on a fence looking at him? He pretends he hasn't got a thing in his hand, and that the cat don't see him, and that he don't see the cat. That's the idea. Never drag her hand out where she'll have to take notice of it. Don't let her know that you think she knows you have the least idea she is aware you are holding her hand. That was my rule of tactics; and as far as Paisley's serenade about hostilities and misadventure went he might as well have been reading to her a timetable of the Sunday trains that stop at Ocean Grove, New Jersey.

'One night when I beat Paisley to the bench by one pipeful, my friendship gets subsidized for a minute, and I asks Mrs Jessup if she didn't think a "H" was easier to write than a "J". In a second her head was mashing the oleander flower in my buttonhole, and I leaned over and – but I didn't.

' "If you don't mind," says I, standing up, "we'll wait for Paisley to come before finishing this. I've never done anything dishonorable yet to our friendship, and this won't be quite fair."

' "Mr Hicks," says Mrs Jessup, looking at me peculiar in the dark, "if it wasn't for but one thing, I'd ask you to hike yourself down the gulch and never disresume your visits to my house."

' "And what is that, ma'am?" I asks.

' "You are too good a friend not to make a good husband," says she.

'In five minutes Paisley was on his side of Mrs Jessup.

' "In Silver City, in the summer of '98," he begins, "I see Jim

Bartholomew chew off a Chinaman's ear in the Blue Light Saloon on account of a cross-barred muslin shirt that – what was that noise?"

'I had resumed matters again with Mrs Jessup right where we had left off.

'"Mrs Jessup", says I, "has promised to make it Hicks. And this is another of the same sort."

'Paisley winds his feet around a leg of the bench and kind of groans.

'"Lem," says he, "we been friends for seven years. Would you mind not kissing Mrs Jessup quite so loud? I'd do the same for you."

'"All right," says I. "The other kind will do as well."

'"This Chinaman", goes on Paisley, "was the one that shot a man named Mullins in the spring of '97, and that was —"

'Paisley interrupted himself again.

'"Lem," says he, "if you was a true friend you wouldn't hug Mrs Jessup quite so hard. I felt the bench shake all over just then. You know you told me you would give me an even chance as long as there was any."

'"Mr Man," says Mrs Jessup turning around to Paisley, "if you was to drop in to the celebration of mine and Mr Hicks's silver wedding, twenty-five years from now, do you think you could get it into that Hubbard squash you call your head that you are *nix cum rous* in this business? I've put up with you a long time because you was Mr Hicks's friend; but it seems to me it's time for you to wear the willow and trot off down the hill."

'"Mrs Jessup," says I, without losing my grasp on the situation as fiancé, "Mr Paisley is my friend, and I offered him a square deal and a equal opportunity as long as there was a chance."

'"A chance!" says she. "Well, he may think he has a chance; but I hope he won't think he's got a cinch, after what he's been next to all the evening."

'Well, a month afterward me and Mrs Jessup was married in the Los Piños Methodist Church; and the whole town closed up to see the performance.

'When we lined up in front, and the preacher was beginning to sing out his rituals and observances, I looks around and misses Paisley. I calls time on the preacher. "Paisley ain't here," says I. "We've got to wait for Paisley. A friend once, a friend always –

that's Telemachus Hicks," says I. Mrs Jessup's eyes snapped some; but the preacher holds up the incantations according to instructions.

'In a few minutes Paisley gallops up the aisle, putting on a cuff as he comes. He explains that the only dry-goods store in town was closed for the wedding, and he couldn't get the kind of a boiled shirt that his taste called for until he had broke open the back window of the store and helped himself. Then he ranges up on the other side of the bride, and the wedding goes on. I always imagined that Paisley calculated as a last chance that the preacher might marry him to the widow by mistake.

'After the proceedings was over we had tea and jerked antelope and canned apricots, and then the populace hiked itself away. Last of all Paisley shook me by the hand and told me I'd acted square and on the level with him, and he was proud to call me a friend.

'The preacher had a small house on the side of the street that he'd fixed up to rent; and he allowed me and Mrs Hicks to occupy it till the ten-forty train the next morning, when we was going on a bridal tour to El Paso. His wife had decorated it all up with hollyhocks and poison ivy, and it looked real festal and bowery.

'About ten o'clock that night I sets down in the front door and pulls off my boots a while in the cool breeze, while Mrs Hicks was fixing around in the room. Right soon the light went out inside; and I sat there a while reverberating over old times and scenes. And then I heard Mrs Hicks call out, "Ain't you coming in soon, Lem?"

'"Well, well!" says I, kind of rousing up. "Durn me if I wasn't waiting for old Paisley to —— "

'But when I got that far,' concluded Telemachus Hicks, 'I thought somebody had shot this left ear of mine off with a forty-five. But it turned out to be only a lick from a broom-handle in the hands of Mrs Hicks.'

H. H. MUNRO ('SAKI') · 1870–1916

Sredni Vashtar

Conradin was ten years old, and the doctor had pronounced his professional opinion that the boy would not live another five years. The doctor was silky and effete, and counted for little, but his opinion was endorsed by Mrs De Ropp, who counted for nearly everything. Mrs De Ropp was Conradin's cousin and guardian, and in his eyes she represented those three-fifths of the world that are necessary and disagreeable and real; the other two-fifths, in perpetual antagonism to the foregoing, were summed up in himself and his imagination. One of these days Conradin supposed he would succumb to the mastering pressure of wearisome necessary things — such as illnesses and coddling restrictions and drawn-out dullness. Without his imagination, which was rampant under the spur of loneliness, he would have succumbed long ago.

Mrs De Ropp would never, in her honestest moments, have confessed to herself that she disliked Conradin, though she might have been dimly aware that thwarting him 'for his good' was a duty which she did not find particularly irksome. Conradin hated her with a desperate sincerity which he was perfectly able to mask. Such few pleasures as he could contrive for himself gained an added relish from the likelihood that they would be displeasing to his guardian, and from the realm of his imagination she was locked out — an unclean thing, which should find no entrance.

In the dull, cheerless garden, overlooked by so many windows that were ready to open with a message not to do this or that, or a reminder that medicines were due, he found little attraction. The few fruit-trees that it contained were set jealously apart from his plucking, as though they were rare specimens of their kind blooming in an arid waste; it would probably have been difficult to find a market-gardener who would have offered ten shillings for their entire yearly produce. In a forgotten corner, however, almost hidden behind a dismal shrubbery, was a disused tool-shed of respectable proportions, and within its walls Conradin found a haven, something that took on the varying aspects of a playroom and a cathedral. He had peopled it with a legion of familiar phantoms, evoked partly from fragments of history and partly from his own brain, but it also boasted two inmates of flesh and blood. In one corner lived a ragged-plumaged Houdan hen, on which the boy lavished an affection that had scarcely another outlet. Further back in the gloom stood a large hutch, divided into two compartments, one of which was fronted with close iron bars. This was the abode of a large polecat-ferret, which a friendly butcher-boy had once smuggled, cage and all, into its present quarters, in exchange for a long-secreted hoard of small silver. Conradin was dreadfully afraid of the lithe, sharp-fanged beast, but it was his most treasured possession. Its very presence in the tool-shed was a secret and fearful joy, to be kept scrupulously from the knowledge of the Woman, as he privately dubbed his cousin. And one day, out of Heaven knows what material, he spun the beast a wonderful name, and from that moment it grew into a god and a religion. The Woman indulged in religion once a week at a church near by, and took Conradin with her, but to him the church service was an alien rite in the House of Rimmon. Every Thursday, in the dim and musty silence of the tool-shed, he worshipped with mystic and elaborate ceremonial before the wooden hutch where dwelt Sredni Vashtar, the great ferret. Red flowers in their season and scarlet berries in the wintertime were offered at his shrine, for he was a god who laid some special stress on the fierce impatient side of things, as opposed to the Woman's religion, which, as far as Conradin could observe, went to great lengths in the contrary direction. And on great festivals powdered nutmeg was strewn in front of his hutch, an important feature of the offering being that the nutmeg had to be stolen. These festivals were of irregular occurrence, and were chiefly appointed to celebrate some passing event. On one occasion, when Mrs De Ropp suffered from acute toothache for three days, Conradin kept up the festival during the entire three days, and almost succeeded in persuading himself that Sredni Vashtar was personally responsible for the toothache. If the malady had lasted for another day the supply of nutmeg would have given out.

The Houdan hen was never drawn into the cult of Sredni Vashtar. Conradin had long ago settled that she was an Anabaptist. He did not pretend to have the remotest knowledge as to what an Anabaptist was, but he privately hoped that it was dashing and not very respectable. Mrs De Ropp was the ground plan on which he based and detested all respectability.

After a while Conradin's absorption in the tool-shed began to attract the notice of his guardian. 'It is not good for him to be pottering down there in all weathers,' she promptly decided, and at breakfast one morning she announced that the Houdan hen had been sold and taken away overnight. With her short-sighted eyes she peered at Conradin, waiting for an outbreak of rage and sorrow, which she was ready to rebuke with a flow of excellent precepts and reasoning. But Conradin said nothing: there was nothing to be said. Something perhaps in his white set face gave her a momentary qualm, for at tea that afternoon there was toast on the table, a delicacy which she usually banned on the ground that it was bad for him; also because the making of it 'gave trouble', a deadly offence in the middle-class feminine eye.

'I thought you liked toast,' she exclaimed, with an injured air, observing that he did not touch it.

'Sometimes,' said Conradin.

In the shed that evening there was an innovation in the worship of the hutch-god. Conradin had been wont to chant his praises, tonight he asked a boon.

'Do one thing for me, Sredni Vashtar.'

The thing was not specified. As Sredni Vashtar was a god he must be supposed to know. And choking back a sob as he looked at that other empty corner, Conradin went back to the world he so hated.

And every night, in the welcome darkness of his bedroom, and every evening in the dusk of the tool-shed, Conradin's bitter litany went up: 'Do one thing for me, Sredni Vashtar.'

Mrs De Ropp noticed that the visits to the shed did not cease, and one day she made a further journey of inspection.

'What are you keeping in that locked hutch?' she asked. 'I believe it's guinea-pigs. I'll have them all cleared away.'

Conradin shut his lips tight, but the Woman ransacked his bedroom till she found the carefully hidden key, and forthwith marched down to the shed to complete her discovery. It was a cold afternoon, and Conradin had been bidden to keep to the house. From the furthest window of the dining-room the door of the shed could just be seen beyond the corner of the shrubbery, and there Conradin stationed himself. He saw the Woman enter, and then he imagined her opening the door of the sacred hutch and peering down with her short-sighted eyes into the thick straw bed where his god lay hidden. Perhaps she would prod at the straw in her clumsy impatience. And Conradin fervently breathed his prayer for the last time. But he knew as he prayed that he did not believe. He knew that the Woman would come out presently with that pursed smile he loathed so well on her face, and that in an hour or two the gardener would carry away his wonderful god, a god no longer, but a simple brown ferret in a hutch. And he knew that the Woman would triumph always as she triumphed now, and that he would grow ever more sickly under her pestering and domineering and superior wisdom, till one day nothing would matter much more with him, and the doctor would be proved right. And in the sting and misery of his defeat, he began to chant loudly and defiantly the hymn of his threatened idol:

Sredni Vashtar went forth,
His thoughts were red thoughts and his teeth were white.
His enemies called for peace, but he brought them death.
Sredni Vashtar the Beautiful.

And then of a sudden he stopped his chanting and drew closer to the window-pane. The door of the shed still stood ajar as it had been left, and the minutes were slipping by. They were long minutes, but they slipped by nevertheless. He watched the starlings running and flying in little parties across the lawn; he counted them over and over again, with one eye always on that swinging door. A sour-faced maid came in to lay the table for tea, and still Conradin stood and waited and watched. Hope had crept by inches into his heart, and now a look of triumph began to blaze in his eyes that had only known the wistful patience of defeat. Under his breath, with a furtive exultation, he began once again the paean of victory and devastation. And presently his eyes were rewarded; out through that doorway came a long, low, yellow-and-brown beast, with eyes a-blink at the waning daylight, and dark wet stains around the fur of jaws and throat. Conradin dropped on his knees. The great polecat-ferret made its way down to a small brook at the foot of the garden, drank for a moment, then crossed a little plank bridge and was lost to sight in the bushes. Such was the passing of Sredni Vashtar.

'Tea is ready,' said the sour-faced maid; 'where is the mistress?'
'She went down to the shed some time ago,' said Conradin.

And while the maid went to summon her mistress to tea, Conradin fished a toasting-fork out of the sideboard drawer and proceeded to toast himself a piece of bread. And during the toasting of it and the buttering of it with much butter and the slow enjoyment of eating it, Conradin listened to the noises and silences which fell in quick spasms beyond the dining-room door. The loud foolish screaming of the maid, the answering chorus of wondering ejaculations from the kitchen region, the scuttering footsteps and hurried embassies for outside help, and then, after a lull, the scared sobbings and the shuffling tread of those who bore a heavy burden into the house.

'Whoever will break it to the poor child? I couldn't for the life of me!' exclaimed a shrill voice. And while they debated the matter among themselves, Conradin made himself another piece of toast.

The Open Boat

*A Tale intended to be after the fact: being the experience
of four men from the sunk steamer* Commodore

I

None of them knew the color of the sky. Their eyes glanced level,
and were fastened upon the waves that swept toward them. These
waves were of the hue of slate, save for the tops, which were of
foaming white, and all of the men knew the colors of the sea. The
horizon narrowed and widened, and dipped and rose, and at all
times its edge was jagged with waves that seemed thrust up in
points like rocks.

Many a man ought to have a bathtub larger than the boat which
here rode upon the sea. These waves were most wrongfully and
barbarously abrupt and tall, and each froth-top was a problem in
small-boat navigation.

The cook squatted in the bottom, and looked with both eyes at
the six inches of gunwale which separated him from the ocean. His
sleeves were rolled over his fat forearms, and the two flaps of his
unbuttoned vest dangled as he bent to bail out the boat. Often he
said, 'Gawd! that was a narrow clip.' As he remarked it he invariably gazed eastward over the broken sea.

The oiler, steering with one of the two oars in the boat, sometimes raised himself suddenly to keep clear of water that swirled in
over the stern. It was a thin little oar, and it seemed often ready to
snap.

The correspondent, pulling at the other oar, watched the waves
and wondered why he was there.

The injured captain, lying in the bow, was at this time buried in
that profound dejection and indifference which comes, temporarily
at least, to even the bravest and most enduring when, willy-nilly,
the firm fails, the army loses, the ship goes down. The mind of the
master of a vessel is rooted deep in the timbers of her, though he

command for a day or a decade; and this captain had on him the stern impression of a scene in the grays of dawn of seven turned faces, and later a stump of a topmast with a white ball on it, that slashed to and fro at the waves, went low and lower, and down. Thereafter there was something strange in his voice. Although steady, it was deep with mourning, and of a quality beyond oration or tears.

'Keep 'er a little more south, Billie,' said he.

'A little more south, sir,' said the oiler in the stern.

A seat in his boat was not unlike a seat upon a bucking broncho, and by the same token a broncho is not much smaller. The craft pranced and reared and plunged like an animal. As each wave came, and she rose for it, she seemed like a horse making at a fence outrageously high. The manner of her scramble over these walls of water is a mystic thing, and, moreover, at the top of them were ordinarily these problems in white water, the foam racing down from the summit of each wave requiring a new leap, and a leap from the air. Then, after scornfully bumping a crest she would slide and race and splash down a long incline, and arrive bobbing and nodding in front of the next menace.

A singular disadvantage of the sea lies in the fact that after successfully surmounting one wave you discover that there is another behind it just as important and just as nervously anxious to do something effective in the way of swamping boats. In a ten-foot dinghy one can get an idea of the resources of the sea in the line of waves that is not probable to the average experience which is never at sea in a dinghy. As each slaty wall of water approached, it shut all else from the view of the men in the boat, and it was not difficult to imagine that this particular wave was the final outburst of the ocean, the last effort of the grim water. There was a terrible grace in the move of the waves, and they came in silence, save for the snarling of the crests.

In the wan light the faces of the men must have been gray. Their eyes must have glinted in strange ways as they gazed steadily astern. Viewed from a balcony, the whole thing would doubtless have been weirdly picturesque. But the men in the boat had no time to see it, and if they had had leisure, there were other things to occupy their minds. The sun swung steadily up the sky, and they knew it was broad day because the color of the sea changed from slate to emerald green streaked with amber lights, and the foam was like tumbling snow. The process of the breaking day was unknown to them. They were aware only of this effect upon the color of the waves that rolled toward them.

In disjointed sentences the cook and the correspondent argued as to the difference between a life-saving station and a house of refuge. The cook had said: 'There's a house of refuge just north of the Mosquito Inlet Light, and as soon as they see us they'll come off in their boat and pick us up.'

'As soon as who see us?' said the correspondent.

'The crew,' said the cook.

'Houses of refuge don't have crews,' said the correspondent. 'As I understand them, they are only places where clothes and grub are stored for the benefit of shipwrecked people. They don't carry crews.'

'Oh, yes, they do,' said the cook.

'No, they don't,' said the correspondent.

'Well, we're not there yet, anyhow,' said the oiler, in the stern.

'Well,' said the cook, 'perhaps it's not a house of refuge that I'm thinking of as being near Mosquito Inlet Light; perhaps it's a life-saving station.'

'We're not there yet,' said the oiler in the stern.

II

As the boat bounced from the top of each wave the wind tore through the hair of the hatless men, and as the craft plopped her stern down again the spray slashed past them. The crest of each of these waves was a hill, from the top of which the men surveyed for a moment a broad tumultuous expanse, shining and wind-riven. It was probably splendid, it was probably glorious, this play of the free sea, wild with lights of emerald and white and amber.

'Bully good thing it's an onshore wind,' said the cook. 'If not, where would we be? Wouldn't have a show.'

'That's right,' said the correspondent.

The busy oiler nodded his assent.

Then the captain, in the bow, chuckled in a way that expressed humor, contempt, tragedy, all in one. 'Do you think we've got much of a show now, boys?' said he.

Whereupon the three were silent, save for a trifle of hemming and hawing. To express any particular optimism at this time they felt to be childish and stupid, but they all doubtless possessed this sense of the situation in their minds. A young man thinks doggedly at such times. On the other hand, the ethics of their condition was decidedly against any open suggestion of hopelessness. So they were silent.

'Oh, well,' said the captain, soothing his children, 'we'll get ashore all right.'

But there was that in his tone which made them think; so the oiler quoth, 'Yes! if this wind holds.'

The cook was bailing. 'Yes! if we don't catch hell in the surf.'

Canton-flannel gulls flew near and far. Sometimes they sat down on the sea, near patches of brown seaweed that rolled over the waves with a movement like carpets on a line in a gale. The birds sat comfortably in groups, and they were envied by some in the dinghy, for the wrath of the sea was no more to them than it was to a covey of prairie chickens a thousand miles inland. Often they came very close and stared at the men with black bead-like eyes. At these times they were uncanny and sinister in their unblinking scrutiny, and the men hooted angrily at them, telling them to be gone. One came, and evidently decided to alight on the top of the captain's head. The bird flew parallel to the boat and did not circle, but made short sidelong jumps in the air in chicken fashion. His black eyes were wistfully fixed upon the captain's head. 'Ugly brute,' said the oiler to the bird. 'You look as if you were made with a jackknife.' The cook and the correspondent swore darkly at the creature. The captain naturally wished to knock it away with the end of the heavy painter, but he did not dare do it, because anything resembling an emphatic gesture would have capsized this freighted boat; and so, with his open hand, the captain gently and carefully waved the gull away. After it had been discouraged from the pursuit the captain breathed easier on account of his hair, and others breathed easier because the bird struck their minds at this time as being somehow gruesome and ominous.

In the meantime the oiler and the correspondent rowed. And also they rowed. They sat together in the same seat, and each rowed an oar. Then the oiler took both oars; then the correspondent took both oars; then the oiler; then the correspondent. They rowed and they rowed. The very ticklish part of the business was when the time came for the reclining one in the stern to take his turn at the oars. By the very last star of truth, it is easier to steal eggs from under a hen than it was to change seats in the dinghy. First the man in the stern slid his hand along the thwart and moved with care, as if he were of Sèvres. Then the man in the rowing-seat slid his hand along the other thwart. It was all done with the most extraordinary care. As the two sidled past each other, the whole party kept watchful eyes on the coming wave, and the captain cried: 'Look out, now! Steady, there!'

The brown mats of seaweed that appeared from time to time were like islands, bits of earth. They were traveling, apparently, neither one way nor the other. They were, to all intents, stationary. They informed the men in the boat that it was making progress slowly toward the land.

The captain, rearing cautiously in the bow after the dinghy soared on a great swell, said that he had seen the lighthouse at Mosquito Inlet. Presently the cook remarked that he had seen it. The correspondent was at the oars then, and for some reason he too wished to look at the lighthouse but his back was toward the far shore, and the waves were important, and for some time he could not seize an opportunity to turn his head. But at last there came a wave more gentle than the others, and when at the crest of it he swiftly scoured the western horizon.

'See it?' said the captain.

'No,' said the correspondent, slowly; 'I didn't see anything.'

'Look again,' said the captain. He pointed. 'It's exactly in that direction.'

At the top of another wave the correspondent did as he was bid, and this time his eyes chanced on a small, still thing on the edge of the swaying horizon. It was precisely like the point of a pin. It took an anxious eye to find a lighthouse so tiny.

'Think we'll make it, Captain?'

'If this wind holds and the boat don't swamp, we can't do much else,' said the captain.

The little boat, lifted by each towering sea and splashed viciously by the crests, made progress that in the absence of seaweed was not apparent to those in her. She seemed just a wee thing wallowing, miraculously top up, at the mercy of five oceans. Occasionally a great spread of water, like white flames, swarmed into her.

'Bail her, cook,' said the captain, serenely.

'All right, Captain,' said the cheerful cook.

III

It would be difficult to describe the subtle brotherhood of men that was here established on the seas. No one said that it was so. No one mentioned it. But it dwelt in the boat, and each man felt it warm him. They were a captain, an oiler, a cook, and a correspondent, and they were friends – friends in a more curiously ironbound degree than may be common. The hurt captain, lying against the water jar in the bow, spoke always in a low voice and calmly; but he could never command a more ready and swiftly obedient crew than the motley three of the dinghy. It was more than a mere recognition of what was best for the common safety. There was surely in it a quality that was personal and heartfelt. And after this devotion to the commander of the boat, there was this comradeship, that the correspondent, for instance, who had been taught to be cynical of men, knew even at the time was the best experience of his life. But no one said that it was so. No one mentioned it.

'I wish we had a sail,' remarked the captain. 'We might try my overcoat on the end of an oar, and give you two boys a chance to rest.' So the cook and the correspondent held the mast and spread wide the overcoat; the oiler steered; and the little boat made good way with her new rig. Sometimes the oiler had to scull sharply to keep a sea from breaking into the boat, but otherwise sailing was a success.

Meanwhile the lighthouse had been growing slowly larger. It had now almost assumed color, and appeared like a little gray shadow on the sky. The man at the oars could not be prevented from turning his head rather often to try for a glimpse of this little gray shadow.

At last, from the top of each wave, the men in the tossing boat could see land. Even as the lighthouse was an upright shadow on the sky, this land seemed but a long black shadow on the sea. It certainly was thinner than paper. 'We must be about opposite New Smyrna,' said the cook, who had coasted this shore often in schooners. 'Captain, by the way, I believe they abandoned that life-saving station there about a year ago.'

'Did they?' said the captain.

The wind slowly died away. The cook and the correspondent were not now obliged to slave in order to hold high the oar. But the waves continued their old impetuous swooping at the dinghy, and the little craft, no longer under way, struggled woundily over them. The oiler or the correspondent took the oars again.

Shipwrecks are apropos of nothing. If men could only train for them and have them occur when the men had reached pink condition, there would be less drowning at sea. Of the four in the dinghy none had slept any time worth mentioning for two days and two nights previous to embarking in the dinghy, and in the excitement of clambering about the deck of a foundering ship they had also forgotten to eat heartily.

For these reasons, and for others, neither the oiler nor the correspondent was fond of rowing at this time. The correspondent wondered ingenuously how in the name of all that was sane could there be people who thought it amusing to row a boat. It was not an amusement; it was a diabolical punishment, and even a genius of mental aberrations could never conclude that it was anything but a horror to the muscles and a crime against the back. He mentioned to the boat in general how the amusement of rowing struck him, and the weary-faced oiler smiled in full sympathy. Previously to the foundering, by the way, the oiler had worked a double watch in the engine-room of the ship.

'Take her easy now, boys,' said the captain. 'Don't spend yourselves. If we have to run a surf you'll need all your strength, because we'll sure have to swim for it. Take your time.'

Slowly the land arose from the sea. From a black line it became a line of black and a line of white – trees and sand. Finally the captain said that he could make out a house on the shore. 'That's the house of refuge, sure,' said the cook. 'They'll see us before long, and come out after us.'

The distant lighthouse reared high. 'The keeper ought to be able to make us out now, if he's looking through a glass,' said the captain. 'He'll notify the life-saving people.'

'None of those other boats could have got ashore to give word of this wreck,' said the oiler, in a low voice, 'else the lifeboat would be out hunting us.'

Slowly and beautifully the land loomed out of the sea. The wind came again. It had veered from the north-east to the south-east. Finally a new sound struck the ears of the men in the boat. It was the low thunder of the surf on the shore. 'We'll never be able to make the lighthouse now,' said the captain. 'Swing her head a little more north, Billie.'

'A little more north, sir,' said the oiler.

Whereupon the little boat turned her nose once more down the wind, and all but the oarsman watched the shore grow. Under the influence of this expansion doubt and direful apprehension were leaving the minds of the men. The management of the boat was still most absorbing, but it could not prevent a quiet cheerfulness. In an hour, perhaps, they would be ashore.

Their backbones had become thoroughly used to balancing in the boat, and they now rode this wild colt of a dinghy like circus men. The correspondent thought that he had been drenched to the skin, but happening to feel in the top pocket of his coat, he found therein eight cigars. Four of them were soaked with sea-water; four were perfectly scatheless. After a search, somebody produced three dry matches; and thereupon the four waifs rode impudently in their little boat and, with an assurance of an impending rescue shining in their eyes, puffed at the big cigars, and judged well and ill of all men. Everybody took a drink of water.

IV

'Cook,' remarked the captain, 'there don't seem to be any signs of life about your house of refuge.'

'No,' replied the cook. 'Funny they don't see us!'

A broad stretch of lowly coast lay before the eyes of the men. It was of low dunes topped with dark vegetation. The roar of the surf was plain, and sometimes they could see the white lip of a wave as it spun up the beach. A tiny house was blocked out black upon the sky. Southward, the slim lighthouse lifted its little gray length.

Tide, wind, and waves were swinging the dinghy northward. 'Funny they don't see us,' said the men.

The surf's roar was here dulled, but its tone was nevertheless thunderous and mighty. As the boat swam over the great rollers the men sat listening to this roar. 'We'll swamp sure,' said everybody.

It is fair to say here that there was not a life-saving station within twenty miles in either direction; but the men did not know this fact, and in consequence they made dark and opprobrious remarks concerning the eyesight of the nation's life-savers. Four scowling men sat in the dinghy and surpassed records in the invention of epithets.

'Funny they don't see us.'

The light-heartedness of a former time had completely faded. To their sharpened minds it was easy to conjure pictures of all kinds of incompetency and blindness and, indeed, cowardice. There was the shore of the populous land, and it was bitter and bitter to them that from it came no sign.

'Well,' said the captain, ultimately, 'I suppose we'll have to make a try for ourselves. If we stay out here too long, we'll none of us have strength left to swim after the boat swamps.'

And so the oiler, who was at the oars, turned the boat straight for the shore. There was a sudden tightening of muscles. There was some thinking.

'If we don't all get ashore,' said the captain – 'if we don't all get ashore, I suppose you fellows know where to send news of my finish?'

They then briefly exchanged some addresses and admonitions. As for the reflections of the men, there was a great deal of rage in them. Perchance they might be formulated thus: 'If I am going to be drowned – if I am going to be drowned – if I am going to be drowned, why, in the name of the seven mad gods who rule the sea, was I allowed to come thus far and contemplate sand and trees? Was I brought here merely to have my nose dragged away as I was about to nibble the sacred cheese of life? It is preposterous. If this old ninny-woman, Fate, cannot do better than this, she should be deprived of the management of men's fortunes. She is an old hen who knows not her intention. If she has decided to drown me, why did she not do it in the beginning and save me all this trouble? The whole affair is absurd. – But no; she cannot mean to drown me. She dare not drown me. She cannot drown me. Not after all this work.' Afterward the man might have had an impulse to shake his fist at the clouds. 'Just you drown me, now, and then hear what I call you!'

The billows that came at this time were more formidable. They seemed always just about to break and roll over the little boat in a turmoil of foam. There was a preparatory and long growl in the speech of them. No mind unused to the sea would have concluded that the dinghy could ascend these sheer heights in time. The shore was still afar. The oiler was a wily surfman. 'Boys,' he said swiftly, 'she won't live three minutes more, and we're too far out to swim.

Shall I take her to sea again, Captain?'

'Yes; go ahead!' said the captain.

This oiler, by a series of quick miracles and fast and steady oarsmanship, turned the boat in the middle of the surf and took her safely to sea again.

There was a considerable silence as the boat bumped over the furrowed sea to deeper water. Then somebody in gloom spoke: 'Well, anyhow, they must have seen us from the shore by now.'

The gulls went in slanting flight up the wind toward the gray, desolate east. A squall, marked by dingy clouds and clouds brick-red like smoke from a burning building, appeared from the southeast.

'What do you think of those life-saving people? Ain't they peaches?'

'Funny they haven't seen us.'

'Maybe they think we're out here for sport! Maybe they think we're fishin'. Maybe they think we're damned fools.'

It was a long afternoon. A changed tide tried to force them southward, but wind and wave said northward. Far ahead, where coastline, sea, and sky formed their mighty angle, there were little dots which seemed to indicate a city on the shore.

'St Augustine?'

The captain shook his head. 'Too near Mosquito Inlet.'

And the oiler rowed, and then the correspondent rowed; then the oiler rowed. It was a weary business. The human back can become the seat of more aches and pains than are registered in books for the composite anatomy of a regiment. It is a limited area, but it can become the theatre of innumerable muscular conflicts, tangles, wrenches, knots, and other comforts.

'Did you ever like to row, Billie?' asked the correspondent.

'No,' said the oiler; 'hang it!'

When one exchanged the rowing-seat for a place in the bottom of the boat, he suffered a bodily depression that caused him to be careless of everything save an obligation to wiggle one finger. There was cold sea-water swashing to and fro in the boat, and he lay in it. His head, pillowed on a thwart, was within an inch of the swirl of a wave-crest, and sometimes a particularly obstreperous sea came inboard and drenched him once more. But these matters did not annoy him. It is almost certain that if the boat had capsized he would have tumbled comfortably out upon the ocean as if he felt sure that it was a great soft mattress.

'Look! There's a man on the shore!'

'Where?'

'There! See 'im? See 'im?'

'Yes, sure! He's walking along.'

'Now he's stopped. Look! He's facing us!'

'He's waving at us!'

'So he is! By thunder!'

'Ah, now we're all right! Now we're all right! There'll be a boat out here for us in half an hour.'

'He's going on. He's running. He's going up to that house there.'

The remote beach seemed lower than the sea, and it required a searching glance to discern the little black figure. The captain saw a floating stick, and they rowed to it. A bath towel was by some weird chance in the boat, and, tying this on the stick, the captain waved it. The oarsman did not dare turn his head, so he was obliged to ask questions.

'What's he doing now?'

'He's standing still again. He's looking, I think. – There he goes again – toward the house. – Now he's stopped again.'

'Is he waving at us?'

'No, not now; he was, though.'

'Look! There comes another man!'

'He's running.'

'Look at him go, would you!'

'Why, he's on a bicycle. Now he's met the other man. They're both waving at us. Look!'

'There comes something up the beach.'

'What the devil is that thing?'

'Why, it looks like a boat.'

'Why, certainly, it's a boat.'

'No; it's on wheels.'

'Yes, so it is. Well, that must be the lifeboat. They drag them along shore on a wagon.'

'That's the lifeboat, sure.'

'No, by God, it's – it's an omnibus.'

'I tell you it's a lifeboat.'

'It is not! It's an omnibus. I can see it plain. See? One of these big hotel omnibuses.'

'By thunder, you're right. It's an omnibus, sure as fate. What do

you suppose they are doing with an omnibus? Maybe they are
going around collecting the life-crew, hey?'
   'That's it, likely. Look! There's a fellow waving a little black flag.
He's standing on the steps of the omnibus. There come those other
two fellows. Now they're all talking together. Look at the fellow
with the flag. Maybe he ain't waving it!'
   'That ain't a flag, is it? That's his coat. Why, certainly, that's his
coat.'
   'So it is; it's his coat. He's taken it off and is waving it around his
head. But would you look at him swing it!'
   'Oh, say, there isn't any life-saving station there. That's just a
winter-resort hotel omnibus that has brought over some of the
boarders to see us drown.'
   'What's that idiot with the coat mean? What's he signaling, anyhow?'
   'It looks as if he were trying to tell us to go north. There must be
a life-saving station up there.'
   'No; he thinks we're fishing. Just giving us a merry hand. See?
Ah, there, Willie!'
   'Well, I wish I could make something out of those signals. What
do you suppose he means?'
   'He don't mean anything; he's just playing.'
   'Well, if he'd just signal us to try the surf again, or to go to sea
and wait, or go north, or go south, or go to hell, there would be
some reason in it. But look at him! He just stands there and keeps
his coat revolving like a wheel. The ass!'
   'There come more people.'
   'Now there's quite a mob. Look! Isn't that a boat?'
   'Where? Oh, I see where you mean. No, that's no boat.'
   'That fellow is still waving his coat.'
   'He must think we like to see him do that. Why don't he quit it?
It don't mean anything.'
   'I don't know. I think he is trying to make us go north. It must
be that there's a life-saving station there somewhere.'
   'Say, he ain't tired yet. Look at 'im wave!'
   'Wonder how long he can keep that up. He's been revolving his
coat ever since he caught sight of us. He's an idiot. Why aren't they
getting men to bring a boat out? A fishing-boat – one of those big
yawls – could come out here all right. Why don't he do something?'
   'Oh, it's all right now.'

'They'll have a boat out here for us in less than no time, now that they've seen us.'

A faint yellow tone came into the sky over the low land. The shadows on the sea slowly deepened. The wind bore coldness with it, and the men began to shiver.

'Holy smoke!' said one, allowing his voice to express his impious mood, 'if we keep on monkeying out here! If we've got to flounder out here all night!'

'Oh, we'll never have to stay here all night! Don't you worry. They've seen us now, and it won't be long before they'll come chasing out after us.'

The shore grew dusky. The man waving a coat blended gradually into this gloom, and it swallowed in the same manner the omnibus and the group of people. The spray, when it dashed uproariously over the side, made the voyagers shrink and swear like men who were being branded.

'I'd like to catch the chump who waved the coat. I feel like socking him one, just for luck.'

'Why? What did he do?'

'Oh, nothing, but then he seemed so damned cheerful.'

In the meantime the oiler rowed, and then the correspondent rowed, and then the oiler rowed. Gray-faced and bowed forward, they mechanically, turn by turn, plied the leaden oars. The form of the lighthouse had vanished from the southern horizon, but finally a pale star appeared, just lifting from the sea. The streaked saffron in the west passed before the all-merging darkness, and the sea to the east was black. The land had vanished, and was expressed only by the low and drear thunder of the surf.

'If I am going to be drowned – if I am going to be drowned – if I am going to be drowned, why, in the name of the seven mad gods who rule the sea, was I allowed to come thus far and contemplate sand and trees? Was I brought here merely to have my nose dragged away as I was about to nibble the sacred cheese of life?'

The patient captain, drooped over the water jar, was sometimes obliged to speak to the oarsman.

'Keep her head up! Keep her head up!'

'Keep her head up, sir.' The voices were weary and low.

This was surely a quiet evening. All save the oarsman lay heavily and listlessly in the boat's bottom. As for him, his eyes were just capable of noting the tall black waves that swept forward in a most sinister silence, save for an occasional subdued growl of a crest.

The cook's head was on a thwart, and he looked without interest at the water under his nose. He was deep in other scenes. Finally he spoke. 'Billie,' he murmured, dreamfully, 'what kind of pie do you like best?'

v

'Pie!' said the oiler and the correspondent, agitatedly. 'Don't talk about those things, blast you!'

'Well,' said the cook, 'I was just thinking about ham sandwiches and — '

A night on the sea in an open boat is a long night. As darkness settled finally, the shine of the light, lifting from the sea in the south, changed to full gold. On the northern horizon a new light appeared, a small bluish gleam on the edge of the waters. These two lights were the furniture of the world. Otherwise there was nothing but waves.

Two men huddled in the stern, and distances were so magnificent in the dinghy that the rower was enabled to keep his feet partly warm by thrusting them under his companions. Their legs indeed extended far under the rowing-seat until they touched the feet of the captain forward. Sometimes, despite the efforts of the tired oarsman, a wave came piling into the boat, an icy wave of the night, and the chilling water soaked them anew. They would twist their bodies for a moment and groan, and sleep the dead sleep once more, while the water in the boat gurgled about them as the craft rocked.

The plan of the oiler and the correspondent was for one to row until he lost the ability, and then arouse the other from his sea-water couch in the bottom of the boat.

The oiler plied the oars until his head drooped forward and the overpowering sleep blinded him; and he rowed yet afterward. Then he touched a man in the bottom of the boat, and called his name. 'Will you spell me for a little while?' he said, meekly.

'Sure, Billie,' said the correspondent, awaking and dragging himself to a sitting position. They exchanged places carefully, and the oiler, cuddling down in the sea-water at the cook's side, seemed to go to sleep instantly.

The particular violence of the sea had ceased. The waves came without snarling. The obligation of the man at the oars was to keep the boat headed so that the tilt of the rollers would not capsize her, and to preserve her from filling when the crests rushed past. The black waves were silent and hard to be seen in the darkness. Often one was almost upon the boat before the oarsman was aware.

In a low voice the correspondent addressed the captain. He was not sure that the captain was awake, although this iron man seemed to be always awake. 'Captain, shall I keep her making for that light north, sir?'

The same steady voice answered him. 'Yes. Keep it about two points off the port bow.'

The cook had tied a lifebelt around himself in order to get even the warmth which this clumsy cork contrivance could donate, and he seemed almost stove-like when a rower, whose teeth invariably chattered wildly as soon as he ceased his labour, dropped down to sleep.

The correspondent, as he rowed, looked down at the two men sleeping underfoot. The cook's arm was around the oiler's shoulders, and, with their fragmentary clothing and haggard faces, they were the babes of the sea – a grotesque rendering of the old babes in the wood.

Later he must have grown stupid at his work, for suddenly there was a growling of water, and a crest came with a roar and a swash into the boat, and it was a wonder that it did not set the cook afloat in his lifebelt. The cook continued to sleep, but the oiler sat up, blinking his eyes and shaking with the new cold.

'Oh, I'm awfully sorry, Billie,' said the correspondent, contritely.

'That's all right, old boy,' said the oiler, and lay down again and was asleep.

Presently it seemed that even the captain dozed, and the correspondent thought that he was the one man afloat on all the oceans. The wind had a voice as it came over the waves, and it was sadder than the end.

There was a long, loud swishing astern of the boat, and a gleaming trail of phosphorescence, like blue flame, was furrowed on the black waters. It might have been made by a monstrous knife.

Then there came a stillness, while the correspondent breathed with open mouth and looked at the sea.

Suddenly there was another swish and another long flash of bluish light, and this time it was alongside the boat, and might almost have been reached with an oar. The correspondent saw an enormous fin speed like a shadow through the water, hurling the crystalline spray and leaving the long glowing trail.

The correspondent looked over his shoulder at the captain. His face was hidden, and he seemed to be asleep. He looked at the babes of the sea. They certainly were asleep. So, being bereft of sympathy, he leaned a little way to one side and swore softly into the sea.

But the thing did not then leave the vicinity of the boat. Ahead or astern, on one side or the other, at intervals long or short, fled the long sparkling streak, and there was to be heard the *whirroo* of the dark fin. The speed and power of the thing was greatly to be admired. It cut the water like a gigantic and keen projectile.

The presence of this biding thing did not affect the man with the same horror that it would if he had been a picnicker. He simply looked at the sea dully and swore in an undertone.

Nevertheless, it is true that he did not wish to be alone with the thing. He wished one of his companions to awake by chance and keep him company with it. But the captain hung motionless over the water jar, and the oiler and the cook in the bottom of the boat were plunged in slumber.

VI

'If I am going to be drowned – if I am going to be drowned – if I am going to be drowned, why, in the name of the seven mad gods who rule the sea, was I allowed to come thus far and contemplate sand and trees?'

During this dismal night, it may be remarked that a man would conclude that it was really the intention of the seven mad gods to drown him, despite the abominable injustice of it. For it was certainly an abominable injustice to drown a man who had worked so hard, so hard. The man felt it would be a crime most unnatural. Other people had drowned at sea since galleys swarmed with painted sails, but still —

When it occurs to a man that nature does not regard him as important, and that she feels she would not maim the universe by disposing of him, he at first wishes to throw bricks at the temple, and he hates deeply the fact that there are no bricks and no temples. Any visible expression of nature would surely be pelleted with his jeers.

Then, if there be no tangible thing to hoot, he feels, perhaps, the desire to confront a personification and indulge in pleas, bowed to one knee, and with hands supplicant, saying, 'Yes, but I love myself.'

A high cold star on a winter's night is the word he feels that she says to him. Thereafter he knows the pathos of his situation.

The men in the dinghy had not discussed these matters, but each had, no doubt, reflected upon them in silence and according to his mind. There was seldom any expression upon their faces save the general one of complete weariness. Speech was devoted to the business of the boat.

To chime the notes of his emotion, a verse mysteriously entered the correspondent's head. He had even forgotten that he had forgotten this verse, but it suddenly was in his mind.

A soldier of the Legion lay dying in Algiers;
There was lack of woman's nursing, there was dearth of woman's tears;
But a comrade stood beside him, and he took that comrade's hand,
And he said, 'I never more shall see my own, my native land.'

In his childhood the correspondent had been made acquainted with the fact that a soldier of the Legion lay dying in Algiers, but he had never regarded the fact as important. Myriads of his school-fellows had informed him of the soldier's plight, but the dinning had naturally ended by making him perfectly indifferent. He had never considered it his affair that a soldier of the Legion lay dying in Algiers, nor had it appeared to him as a matter for sorrow. It was less to him than the breaking of a pencil's point.

Now, however, it quaintly came to him as a human, living thing. It was no longer merely a picture of a few throes in the breast of a poet, meanwhile drinking tea and warming his feet at the grate; it was an actuality – stern, mournful, and fine.

The correspondent plainly saw the soldier. He lay on the sand with his feet out straight and still. While his pale left hand was upon his chest in an attempt to thwart the going of his life, the blood came between his fingers. In the far Algerian distance, a city of low square forms was set against a sky that was faint with the last sunset hues. The correspondent, plying the oars and dreaming of the slow and slower movements of the lips of the soldier, was moved by a profound and perfectly impersonal comprehension. He was sorry for the soldier of the Legion who lay dying in Algiers.

The thing which had followed the boat and waited had evidently grown bored at the delay. There was no longer to be heard the slash of the cutwater, and there was no longer the flame of the long trail. The light in the north still glimmered, but it was apparently no nearer to the boat. Sometimes the boom of the surf rang in the correspondent's ears, and he turned the craft seaward then and rowed harder. Southward, someone had evidently built a watch-fire on the beach. It was too low and too far to be seen, but it made a shimmering, roseate reflection upon the bluff in back of it, and this could be discerned from the boat. The wind came stronger, and sometimes a wave suddenly raged out like a mountain cat, and there was to be seen the sheen and sparkle of a broken crest.

The captain, in the bow, moved on his water jar and sat erect. 'Pretty long night,' he observed to the correspondent. He looked at the shore. 'Those life-saving people take their time.'

'Did you see that shark playing around?'

'Yes, I saw him. He was a big fellow, all right.'

'Wish I had known you were awake.'

Later the correspondent spoke into the bottom of the boat. 'Billie!' There was a slow and gradual disentanglement. 'Billie, will you spell me?'

'Sure,' said the oiler.

As soon as the correspondent touched the cold, comfortable sea-water in the bottom of the boat and had huddled close to the cook's lifebelt he was deep in sleep, despite the fact that his teeth played all the popular airs. This sleep was so good to him that it was but a moment before he heard a voice call his name in a tone that demonstrated the last stages of exhaustion. 'Will you spell me?'

'Sure, Billie.'

The light in the north had mysteriously vanished, but the correspondent took his course from the wide-awake captain.

Later in the night they took the boat farther out to sea, and the captain directed the cook to take one oar at the stern and keep the boat facing the seas. He was to call out if he should hear the thunder of the surf. This plan enabled the oiler and the correspondent to get respite together. 'We'll give those boys a chance to get into shape again,' said the captain. They curled down and, after a few preliminary chatterings and trembles, slept once more the dead sleep. Neither knew they had bequeathed to the cook, the company of another shark, or perhaps the same shark.

As the boat caroused on the waves, spray occasionally bumped over the side and gave them a fresh soaking, but this had no power to break their repose. The ominous slash of the wind and the water affected them as it would have affected mummies.

'Boys,' said the cook, with the notes of every reluctance in his voice, 'she's drifted in pretty close. I guess one of you had better take her to sea again.' The correspondent, aroused, heard the crash of the toppled crests.

As he was rowing, the captain gave him some whiskey-and-water, and this steadied the chills out of him. 'If I ever get ashore and anybody shows me even a photograph of an oar — '

At last there was a short conversation.

'Billie! – Billie, will you spell me?'

'Sure,' said the oiler.

VII

When the correspondent again opened his eyes, the sea and the sky were each of the gray hue of the dawning. Later, carmine and gold was painted upon the waters. The morning appeared finally, in its splendor, with a sky of pure blue, and the sunlight flamed on the tips of the waves.

On the distant dunes were set many little black cottages, and a tall white windmill reared above them. No man, nor dog, nor bicycle appeared on the beach. The cottages might have formed a deserted village.

The voyagers scanned the shore. A conference was held in the boat. 'Well,' said the captain, 'if no help is coming, we might better try a run through the surf right away. If we stay out here much longer we will be too weak to do anything for ourselves at all.' The others silently acquiesced in this reasoning. The boat was headed for the beach. The correspondent wondered if none ever ascended the tall wind-tower, and if then they never looked seaward. This tower was a giant, standing with its back to the plight of the ants. It represented in a degree, to the correspondent, the serenity of nature amid the struggles of the individual – nature in the wind, and nature in the vision of men. She did not seem cruel to him then, nor beneficent, nor treacherous, nor wise. But she was indifferent, flatly indifferent. It is, perhaps, plausible that a man in this situation, impressed with the unconcern of the universe, should see the innumerable flaws of his life, and have them taste wickedly in his mind, and wish for another chance. A distinction between right and wrong seems absurdly clear to him, then, in this new ignorance of the grave-edge, and he understands that if he were given another opportunity he would mend his conduct and his words, and be better and brighter during an introduction or at a tea.

'Now, boys,' said the captain, 'she is going to swamp sure. All we can do is to work her in as far as possible, and then when she swamps, pile out and scramble for the beach. Keep cool now, and don't jump until she swamps sure.'

The oiler took the oars. Over his shoulders he scanned the surf. 'Captain,' he said, 'I think I'd better bring her about and keep her head-on to the seas and back her in.'

'All right, Billie,' said the captain. 'Back her in.' The oiler swung the boat then, and, seated in the stern, the cook and the correspondent were obliged to look over their shoulders to contemplate the lonely and indifferent shore.

The monstrous inshore rollers heaved the boat high until the men were again enabled to see the white sheets of water scudding up the slanted beach. 'We won't get in very close,' said the captain. Each time a man could wrest his attention from the rollers, he turned his glance toward the shore, and in the expression of the eyes during this contemplation there was a singular quality. The correspondent, observing the others, knew that they were not afraid, but the full meaning of their glances was shrouded.

As for himself, he was too tired to grapple fundamentally with the fact. He tried to coerce his mind into thinking of it, but the mind was dominated at this time by the muscles, and the muscles said they did not care. It merely occurred to him that if he should drown it would be a shame.

There were no hurried words, no pallor, no plain agitation. The men simply looked at the shore. 'Now, remember to get well clear of the boat when you jump,' said the captain.

Seaward the crest of a roller suddenly fell with a thunderous crash, and the long white comber came roaring down upon the boat.

'Steady now,' said the captain. The men were silent. They turned their eyes from the shore to the comber and waited. The boat slid up the incline, leaped at the furious top, bounced over it, and swung down the long back of the wave. Some water had been shipped, and the cook bailed it out.

But the next crest crashed also. The tumbling, boiling flood of white water caught the boat and whirled it almost perpendicular. Water swarmed in from all sides. The correspondent had his hands on the gunwale at this time, and when the water entered at that place he swiftly withdrew his fingers, as if he objected to wetting them.

The little boat, drunken with this weight of water, reeled and snuggled deeper into the sea.

'Bail her out, cook! Bail her out!' said the captain.

'All right, Captain,' said the cook.

'Now, boys, the next one will do us for sure,' said the oiler. 'Mind to jump clear of the boat.'

The third wave moved forward, huge, furious, implacable. It fairly swallowed the dinghy, and almost simultaneously the men tumbled into the sea. A piece of lifebelt had lain in the bottom of the boat, and as the correspondent went overboard he held this to his chest with his left hand.

The January water was icy, and he reflected immediately that it was colder than he had expected to find it off the coast of Florida. This appeared to his dazed mind as a fact important enough to be noted at the time. The coldness of the water was sad; it was tragic. This fact was somehow mixed and confused with his opinion of his own situation, so that it seemed almost a proper reason for tears. The water was cold.

When he came to the surface he was conscious of little but the noisy water. Afterward he saw his companions in the sea. The oiler was ahead in the race. He was swimming strongly and rapidly. Off to the correspondent's left, the cook's great white and corked back bulged out of the water; and in the rear the captain was hanging with his one good hand to the keel of the overturned dinghy.

There is a certain immovable quality to a shore, and the correspondent wondered at it amid the confusion of the sea.

It seemed also very attractive; but the correspondent knew that it was a long journey, and he paddled leisurely. The piece of life-preserver lay under him, and sometimes he whirled down the incline of a wave as if he were on a hand-sled.

But finally he arrived at a place in the sea where travel was beset with difficulty. He did not pause swimming to inquire what manner of current had caught him, but there his progress ceased. The shore was set before him like a bit of scenery on a stage, and he looked at it and understood with his eyes each detail of it.

As the cook passed, much farther to the left, the captain was calling to him, 'Turn over on your back, cook! Turn over on your back and use the oar.'

'All right, sir.' The cook turned on his back, and, paddling with an oar, went ahead as if he were a canoe.

Presently the boat also passed to the left of the correspondent, with the captain clinging with one hand to the keel. He would have appeared like a man raising himself to look over a board fence if it were not for the extraordinary gymnastics of the boat. The correspondent marveled that the captain could still hold to it.

They passed on nearer to shore – the oiler, the cook, the captain – and following them went the water jar, bouncing gaily over the seas.

The correspondent remained in the grip of this strange new enemy – a current. The shore, with its white slope of sand and its green bluff topped with little silent cottages, was spread like a picture before him. It was very near to him then, but he was impressed as one who, in a gallery, looks at a scene from Brittany or Algiers.

He thought: 'I am going to drown? Can it be possible? Can it be possible? Can it be possible?' Perhaps an individual must consider his own death to be the final phenomenon of nature.

But later a wave perhaps whirled him out of this small deadly current, for he found suddenly that he could again make progress toward the shore. Later still he was aware that the captain, clinging with one hand to the keel of the dinghy, had his face turned away from the shore and toward him, and was calling his name. 'Come to the boat! Come to the boat!'

In his struggle to reach the captain and the boat, he reflected that when one gets properly wearied drowning must really be a comfortable arrangement – a cessation of hostilities accompanied by a large degree of relief; and he was glad of it, for the main thing in his mind for some moments had been horror of the temporary agony. He did not wish to be hurt.

Presently he saw a man running along the shore. He was undressing with most remarkable speed. Coat, trousers, shirt, everything flew magically off him. 'Come to the boat!' called the captain.

'All right, Captain.' As the correspondent paddled, he saw the captain let himself down to bottom and leave the boat. Then the correspondent performed his one little marvel of the voyage. A large wave caught him and flung him with ease and supreme speed completely over the boat and far beyond it. It struck him even then as an event in gymnastics and a true miracle of the sea. An over-turned boat in the surf is not a plaything to a swimming man.

The correspondent arrived in water that reached only to his waist, but his condition did not enable him to stand for more than a moment. Each wave knocked him into a heap, and the undertow pulled at him.

Then he saw the man who had been running and undressing, and undressing and running, come bounding into the water. He dragged ashore the cook, and then waded toward the captain; but the captain waved him away and sent him to the correspondent. He was naked – naked as a tree in winter; but a halo was about his head, and he shone like a saint. He gave a strong pull, and a long drag, and a bully heave at the correspondent's hand. The correspondent, schooled in the minor formulæ, said, 'Thanks, old man.' But suddenly the man cried, 'What's that?' He pointed a swift finger. The correspondent said, 'Go.'

In the shallows, face downward, lay the oiler. His forehead touched sand that was periodically, between each wave, clear of the sea.

The correspondent did not know all that transpired afterward. When he achieved safe ground he fell, striking the sand with each particular part of his body. It was as if he had dropped from a roof, but the thud was grateful to him.

It seemed that instantly the beach was populated with men with blankets, clothes, and flasks, and women with coffee-pots and all the remedies sacred to their minds. The welcome of the land to the men from the sea was warm and generous; but a still and dripping shape was carried slowly up the beach, and the land's welcome for it could only be the different and sinister hospitality of the grave.

When it came night, the white waves paced to and fro in the moonlight, and the wind brought the sound of the great sea's voice to the men on the shore, and they felt that they could then be interpreters.

WALTER DE LA MARE · 1873–1956

An Ideal Craftsman

Away into secrecy frisked a pampered mouse. A scuffling of bed-clothes, the squeak of a dry castor followed, and then suddenly the boy sat up and set to piecing together reality with scraps of terrifying but half-forgotten dreams.

It was his ears had summoned him, they were still ringing with an obscure message, a faint *Qui vive*? But as he sat blinking and listening in the empty dark he could not satisfy himself what sound it was that had actually wakened him. Was it only a dying howl from out of one of his usual nightmares, or had some actual noise or cry sounded up from the vacancy of the house beneath? It was this uncertainty – as if his brain were a piece of mechanism wound up by sleep – that set working a vivid panorama of memories in the little theatre of his mind – cloaked men huddled together in some dark corner of the night, scoundrels plotting in the wind, the pause between rifle-click and the loose fall, finally to culminate in the adventure of glorious memory – raiding Jacobs.

He groped under his pillow for the treasures he had concealed there before blowing out his candle – a box of matches, a crumbling slice of pie-crust, and a dingy volume of the *Newgate Calendar*. This last usually lay behind the draughty chimney of his fireplace, because Jacobs had the habits of a ferret and nothing was safe from his nosings. He struck a match soundlessly on the edge of his mattress. Its flare lit up his lank-haired head, his sharp face and dazzled eyes. Then the flame drooped, went out. But he had had time to find the broad glossy belt he had cut out of a strip of mottled American cloth and the old sheathed poniard which he had months ago abstracted from his father's study. He buckled on the belt round his body in the dark over his nightshirt and dangled the rusty blood- or water-stained poniard coldly on his hip. He pulled on his stockings, tilted an old yachting cap over his eyes, and was fully equipped.

In this feverish haste he had had little time to ponder strategy.

But now he sat down again on the edge of his bed, and though he was. pretending to think, his brows wrinkled in a frown, he was actually listening. Even the stairs had ceased to creak. And the star that from a wraith of cloud glittered coldly in the night sky beyond the rift between his curtains made no sound. He drew open his door, inch by inch, still intent, then stepped out on to the landing.

The first danger to be encountered on the staircase below was his father's bedroom. Its door gaped half open, but was it empty? It was here on this very spot, he remembered with a qualm, that Jacobs had once leapt out on him. He saw in memory that agile shape stepping hastily and oddly in the dusk, furious at sight of the eavesdropper. And in an instant the tiny blue bead of gas on the landing had expanded into a white fan-shaped glare. Not so to-night. With a gasp and an oblique glance at the dusky bed and the spectral pendent clothes within, he slid by in safety on his stockinged feet, and so past yet another door – but this one tight shut, with its flower-painted panels – the door of his mother's gay little sitting-room, his real mother's, not the powdery eyebrowed stepmother who a few hours before had set out with his father, on pleasure bent.

A few paces beyond he trod even more cautiously, for here was a loose board. At the last loop of the staircase Jacobs' customary humming should issue up out of the gloom beneath – the faint tune which he rasped on and on and on, faint and shrill between his teeth, superciliously, ironically, in greasy good humour or sly facetiousness – he would hum it in his coffin perhaps. But no, not a sound. The raider hesitated. What next? Where now? He listened in vain.

And then, he suddenly remembered that this was 'silver' night. And doubtless – cook and housemaid long since snoring in their attic – a white glittering array of forks and spoons, soup ladles, and candlesticks were at this very moment spread out in bedaubed splendour before the aproned tyrant. For Jacobs was not only queer in his habits and nocturnal by nature but a glutton for work. But if it was silver night, why this prodigious hush? No clang of fork ringing against its neighbour; not a single rattle of whitening brush on metal reached his ears.

Slim as a ferret himself, he hung over the loop in the staircase as he might have hung over the Valley of Death; but still all was strangely quiet. And so, with a pang of disappointment, and at the same moment with a crow of relief, the boy came to the conclusion that Jacobs was out. And not for the first time either. He must have had a visitor – the woman in the black bonnet, with the silver locket dangling on her front, perhaps. As likely as not, they had gone off gallivanting together, and would reappear about eleven o'clock, Jacobs either swearing and quarrelsome or amiably garrulous.

But the boy was no fool. In spite of this sinister hush in the house – as if its walls were draped with the very darkness of night – Jacobs *might* perhaps be busy over his silver. Shammy, however hard you rub with it, makes little sound. And if he were, then too much confidence would mean not only a sudden pursuit, a heart-daunting scuttle up the stairs, and Jacobs with his cane cutting at his legs from behind, but the failure of his raid altogether. Nothing then but a bit of stale pie-crust for his midnight feast. So he trod on velvet down the stairs, his damp palm shunning the banister (*that* squeak would wake an army!), his lips dry and his tongue rolling in luxury of anticipation. And soon he was in the hall, with all the empty rooms of the house above his head, and minified in his own imagination to a mere atom of whiteness in the dusk, a mouse within smell of the cat. His rusty poniard clutched tight between his fingers, his stomach full of fear and his heart noisy as a cock-crow, he pushed on.

The staircase ran widely and shallowly into the hall; there was more light here, a thin faint glow of gaslight, turned low. He could distinguish the dark shapes of the heavy furniture, as he stalked on through this luminous twilight. But the back passage to the kitchen quarters was hidden from elegant visitors by a muffled door with a spring, which Jacobs, when it suited him, kept propped wide open. This passage, if followed to the end, turned abruptly at right angles; and at the inner angle near the fusty entry to the cellars he paused to breathe and then to listen again. Once round the corner, along the passage in front of him the kitchen door would come into view, ajar or wide open, on the right; and the larder itself a few paces further on, and exactly opposite the raider. But before reaching it, the boot cupboard, sour den of long-legged spiders and worse abominations, must be passed, and the window with the panes of coloured glass, looking out on a monstrous red, yellow, or blue garden of trees and stars.

The boy's lean dark face had in his progress become paler and leaner. His legs were now the skinny playthings of autumnal draughts, and at this moment a sound *had* actually reached his ears – the sound as of a lion panting over a meal. A sort of persistent half-choked snuffling. This was odd. This was surprising. Even when, with sleeves turned up and sharp elbows bared, Jacobs was engrossed in any job, he never breathed like that. In general, indeed, he scarcely seemed to be breathing at all; when for example, he stooped down close handing a dish of cabbage or blancmange at the Sunday dinner table of a taciturn father. *This* breathing was husky and unequal, almost like a snore through nostrils and mouth. Jacobs must be drunk, then; and that would mean either a sort of morose good humour, or a sullen drowsy malice, as dangerous as it was sly. The adventure was losing its edge. Even the hunger for romance in the boy's Scots-French blood died down within him at recollection of the dull, dull-lidded eyes of Jacobs half drunk.

There came a sudden *crkkk* and the squeak as of a boot. The boy bit hard on his lip. Yet another slow sliding step forward; the kitchen door *was* ajar. A spear of yellow light warned the intruder. But light – spear or no spear – was as vitalizing as a sip of wine. Red-capped, pock-marked faces, all sorts and conditions of criminals, buccaneers and highwaymen, gore and glory, flocked back again into the boy's fancy. An icy delicious shiver ran down his spine, for now Jacobs, tied with a tape round the middle, in his green baize apron, must be sitting at not much more than arm's length from the door. Or if not, who?

Inch by inch, courage restored, he slid on soundlessly, his stockinged foot first pushing forward into the light, then the white edge of his nightshirt. He pressed skin-close to the further side of the passage, and was actually half past the door ajar, when through a narrow chink he glanced into the kitchen, and so – suddenly found himself squinting full into the eyes of the fat woman in the black bonnet. Crouching a little, stiff and motionless, her eyes bolting out of her face, she stood there full in the light of the gas jet over her head, the faded brown hair that showed beneath her bonnet wreathing it as if with a nimbus. The boy stood frozen.

Not for an instant did he imagine he could be invisible to such a stare as that, to eyes which, though they were small and dark showed as round and shining as the silver locket that rose and fell jerkily upon her chest. His mouth opened – mute as a fish; every sinew in his body stiffened in readiness for flight. But the woman never so much as stirred. Every fibre and muscle in *her* body was at stretch to aid her ears. It looked as if she might be able to hear even his thoughts moving. So would a she-wolf stand at gaze under a white moon, with those unstirring eyes; famished and gaunt. And yet, what in the world was there for *her* to be afraid of? If anybody else was there she would have spoken. She was alone, then? His fingers suddenly relaxed, the scabbard of his poniard rattled against the wall behind him, and there slipped off his tongue the most unlikely question that would ever else have come into his mind. 'I say, where's Jacobs?'

The lids over the little black eyes fluttered and the woman's lips opened in a squawk. Her two rough red hands were suddenly clapped on either side of her mouth. For a moment he thought she was going to scream again, and was thankful when only a shuddering sob followed. 'Oh, sir, how you did startle me. Mr Jacobs, sir, why just as you was coming – he's gone, sir; he's gone.'

The boy pushed open the door and stood on the threshold. He had supposed it impossible that so stout a woman could speak in so small a voice. Sheer curiosity had banished all alarm. Besides, if Jacobs was out, there was no immediate danger. He looked about him, conscious that he was being closely watched from between those square red fingers, and that the forehead above them was deeply wrinkled almost as if the woman were helpless with laughter.

'Why, lor,' she was muttering as if to herself, 'it's only the little boy. My! I thought he was his pa, I did; God bless him. He's come down for a drink of water. That's what he wants. And all in his pretty nightgown too.'

Tears were now gushing down her round cheeks and gurgling in her voice. She walked in angles to a chair and sat there rocking her body to and fro and smiling at him – an odd contorted smile of blandishment and stupidity sicklied over with fear. He blushed, and stared back at her as hot and angry as when in days gone by bent-up wrinkled old ladies used to stop his nurse in the street to ask questions about him, and had even openly kissed him.

This end to his adventure, which seemed to be leading him into difficulties he had never dreamed of, was a bitter disappointment. A drink of water! He resented the presence of this fat woman in the kitchen. He resented even more his own embarrassment. He wriggled under his nightshirt, and was profoundly relieved when those flabby florid cheeks suddenly faded to a mottled mauve, the rocking ceased, and two heavy eyelids slowly descended upon the small black terrified eyes. Even if she *were* going to faint, she would at any rate have to stop staring.

But his troubles were only begun; ugly grunts were proceeding from that open mouth, and the woman's head was twitching oddly. Still, he had had experiences of this kind before. He knew what was to be done, and a scientific callousness gave his remedy zest. On the kitchen table beside some empty bottles of beer and a decanter stood a tumbler half full of water. This he liberally sprinkled on the woman's face and trickled a few drops, not without waste, between her teeth. Grunts expostulated, and the silver locket almost danced. She was coming to. Success stimulated him to fresh efforts; he snatched a scrap of brown paper from among the spoons and climbing up on to a chair lit it at the gas, and thrust it under her nose. It was enough. Such a smother would have stupefied an apiary.

But though the cure was now complete, and worthy of being proudly recorded, one pretty keepsake had been degraded for ever – the memory of his mother, lying on a sofa, and two blue eyes like dawn shining up amid the dewdrops sprinkling her fair cheeks. This fat stranger's petticoat was of coarse red dingy flannel. She was clammy and stupid and ridiculous. Nevertheless, the absurd fear of him or whatever it might be that had brought her to this pass seemed for the moment to be clean forgotten. For when her dazed eyes rolled down from under their lids again and looked out at him, precisely the same expression had come into her face as he had seen on it when he had watched her smiling mawkishly at Jacobs himself.

'Are you better now?' he asked coldly, flourishing the smouldering paper.

The woman smiled again, and nodded.

'I'm afraid I may have burnt you. But there's no other way, you see, though the smell's pretty beastly.' The woman went on vacantly smiling. Not that this stupid wrinkling up of her mouth and cheeks seemed to mean anything. She might have been made of wax. Further parleying, he decided, would be wasted.

'You needn't mention it to Jacobs, you know,' he began. '*I* shan't say anything. You see, I just happened to notice you through the door. I think I'll be going back now. Jacobs is a bit of a. . . .' Nothing very conciliatory could come after that 'bit'. At all events he decided to keep back the word that had so nearly slipped out. The silver locket began to jolt again, and clumsy fingers fumbled at it. The smile was beginning to crystallize into the familiar wrinkled stare.

'You *look* better, *much* better,' said the boy uneasily, edging towards the door. 'I remember once my mother . . . ' but his tongue refused for shame to say what he remembered. Also he found it difficult to turn his back on the woman, though when at last he reached the door he whipped round quickly.

'Little boy,' called the woman in a fulsome voice, 'come back! I say! – little *boy!*'

He frowned. Her eyes were now searching his face intently and suspiciously. She had begun to think again. And at sight of their hostility his own underlip drooped into a sullen obstinacy. He didn't mind *her*. If she decided to sneak to Jacobs, that was her look out; meanwhile he could easily manage her alone.

'What?' he said.

'I was took ill, wasn't I? The heat's something awful. *Phh!* But there isn't any need to stare, little boy. I shan't eat you.' Cunning peeped out of the unctuous face, and he merely waited for the trap. 'Not me; and what a pretty belt he's got on,' she continued, rolling her dingy handkerchief into a ball; 'and ain't he got a nice new dagger!'

But even such flatteries as these produced no response. The dagger wasn't new, and the belt was not meant to be pretty. 'I must be going now, thank you,' he repeated. 'Besides, I suppose he'll be back in a minute?'

Her hands stayed motionless, her head had suddenly jerked a little sideways like a thrush's intent on the stirrings of a worm.

'Going,' she repeated, 'why, of course, he must be going, poor lamb: he'll get his death of cold. And wasn't he *good* to me; *good* to me he was. And that clever! You'd have thought he was a doctor!'

Her glance meanwhile was roving in confusion into every corner of the room as though she were looking for something, and was afraid of what she might find. He could hardly keep his own from following them. 'That kind and gentle he was! Just like a doctor he was!' And again a menacing silence swallowed up her words. The boy's face reflected a distrust deepening into hostility. Was the whole thing a cheat then? Was Jacobs as usual playing the sneak? Would he suddenly leap out on him? In any case he knew he was only being cajoled, if not ridiculed.

'There, now!' she suddenly broke out, 'if he isn't *thinking* again. That's what he's doing. He's thinking about what I was saying to meself when that funny dream came over me. That's what he's doing. And why not, I should like to know. Eh?' She shot him a searching, ogling glance.

'I didn't notice,' he answered. 'Your *eyes* looked rather queer, with the whites gone up, and your skin twitched just as if the water burnt it. But *I* didn't mind.'

'How long was you there, then? Tell me that?' Her nails were now gripped uncomfortably sharp on his arm. 'You stand there frowning and sulking, my young soldier. And by what rights, may I ask? Just you tell me how long you was there!' Her face had grown hard and dangerous, but he shut his mouth tight and returned sullenly stare for stare. 'So help me,' she half whispered, releasing him, 'now I've been and frightened him again. That's it. He thinks I'm angry with him. Lord love you, my precious, I didn't mean anything like that. Not me. P'raps you just came down for a bit of fun, eh?'

She fixed her eyes on the dagger, and shuddered. 'What was I saying? Ah, yes. How long – *how long* was – you – there?' She stamped her foot. 'That's right, saucer-eyes, stare, stare! Didn't I *say* I'm old and ugly! Ain't *he* said it too? Oh, oh, oh! What shall I do, what shall I do?' She hid her face in her hands and her tears gushed out anew.

The boy stood stiffly at her side. This unexpected capitulation unnerved him, and his heart began to heave menacingly.

'I'm sorry; but I must go now,' he repeated, trying with as little obvious aversion as possible to drag his hand from her hot wet cheek. 'And I don't see what good crying will do.' As if by magic the snuffling ceased.

'Good! Who said, what "good"? It's *me* who must be going, my young man, and don't you make any mistake about *that*!' She shook out her skirts, and searched in vain for the bonnet on her head. He nearly laughed out loud, so absurd was the attempt – for the bunched-up old thing was dangling by its strings, behind her back. But this retrieved, she drew it on, pushing under it stragglings of her iron-grey hair. Then she opened a fat leather purse, stuffed with keys and dirty crumpled papers.

'Now what have I got here?' she began wheedlingly, as she pushed about with her finger and took out a sixpence. 'What have I got here? Why, a silver sixpence. And who's that for? Why, for any nice little boy what won't spy and pry. That's what that's for.' She stooped nearly double, holding it out to him with bolting eyes in her purpled face. 'What? He won't take it? Shakes his head? Too proud to take it. Oh, very well, very well.'

She opened her purse again and with shaking fingers pushed the sixpence back. She was not crying now, but her face had gone a deathly grey, and a blank, dreadful misery had crept into it. This woman was a very strange woman. He had never met anyone who behaved in such a queer way. He watched her as she went waddling off out of the kitchen and over the stone floor into the darkness beyond. Her footsteps ceased to sound. She was gone, then? And she must have left the garden door open behind her; the wind was bellying in his nightshirt and icy under his arms. Here was the cat come in, too, rolling in its sodden fur on the oilcloth at his feet. 'Puss, Puss,' he said. Where had *he* been to get in such a state. The boy stood dismayed and discomfited, while the cat rubbed its body and its purring jaws against his stockinged legs.

A stark unstirring silence had spread into the kitchen, though the gas was faintly singing – high and from very far away. And, as if to attract his attention, a wisp of hair was patting his forehead under his ridiculous cap brim. The silence entangled his thoughts in a medley of absurd misgivings productive only of chicken skin and perplexity. Something had gone wrong – the house was changed; and he didn't know how or why. He glanced up at the clock, which thereupon at once began to tick. His eyes dodged from side to side of the familiar kitchen and then it was as if a stealthy warning finger had been laid upon his thoughts, and chaos became unity.

His roving glance had fallen on the cupboard door. For there in the crack at the bottom of it, shut in and moving softly in the wind, showed a corner of green baize. Jacobs was there, then; bunched up there, then; smiling to himself and waiting, and listening in there, then? The boy stood appalled, his bright black eyes fixed on this flapping scrap of green baize apron. The whole thing *was* a trap. And yet, as he tried hard to keep his wits, he had known instantly there was something wrong – something he couldn't understand. That was just like one of Jacobs's jokes! – jokes that usually had so violent and humourless an ending. And yet. . . . Suddenly the hinges of the outer door had whinnied; he jerked round his head in alarm. It was the woman again. She had come back. Bead-bright raindrops glittered on the black of her jacket, on her bonnet, in her hair. That rigid awful stare of horror had come back into her face. He could move neither hand nor foot; could only stare at her.

'Eh, eh, now!' she was choking out at him. 'So you've *seen* now, my fine young gentleman, have you? That's what you've done. Then what do *I* say; *me*! Keep a civil tongue in your head, that's what *I* say. And tell me this —' The face thrust so close down to his had grown enormous and unspeakably dreadful. Her hot breath enveloped him. 'Where's the gate? Where's the gate, I say? I got lost there among them bushes. I can't get out. D'ye see? I've lost the gate. It's dark. It's come on raining. Where's the *gate*?'

Tiny beads of blood stood on her skin – she must have stumbled into the holly hedge at the foot of the garden by the cucumber frames. She smelt not only of her old clothes but of the night and the rain. And still he made no answer. He had been driven back by that awful and congealed look on her face – beyond fear. He was merely waiting – to find *his* way: this mystery, this horror.

'Eh, now'; she had turned away, her heavy head crooked down over one shoulder, and was speaking this time to herself: 'quiet and silly, that's what *he* is. Nothing much anybody could get out of *him*. But see you here!' She had twisted round. 'It's no good you playing the young innocent with me. You've seen and you know. That's what you've done. And you just tell me this. How *could* I have done it? how *should* I have done it? That's what I'm asking. Just you tell me that. Haven't I come of honest people? And didn't he promise me and promise me? And nothing but lies. And then, "You ain't the first," he says. And me as I am! "You ain't the first," he says. Ay, and meant it. "What, what!" I says. And then he hit me – here, with his clenched-up fist, *here*. "I shan't leave you," I said, "and you can't make me." And all I wanted was just to keep body and soul together. "And you can't make me," that's what I said. "That's all," I said. And then he laughed. "You ain't the first," he says, laughing. And me as I am! . . . Oh, my God, he *won't* understand. Listen, little boy. I didn't know what I was doing; everything went black and I couldn't see. And I put out my hands

– to push him off, and my fingers went stiff and a smudge of red
came over my eyes, and next thing he fell down like a bundle and
wouldn't speak, wouldn't speak. Mind you, I say *this*, if I hadn't
drunk the beer, if I hadn't drunk the beer, if I hadn't – done –
that. . . .' She faltered, her face went blank as she swayed.

Her listener was struggling hard to understand. These broken
words told him little that was clear and definite, and yet were brim-
ming over with sinister incomprehensible meanings. He frowned at
the contorted, dark-red moving face and loose lips. One fact and
one fact alone was plain. He had nothing to fear from Jacobs.
Jacobs was not going to pounce out on him. Simply because
Jacobs was gone. Then why . . . ? He twisted about, and kneeling
down on the floor by the cupboard beside the cooling kitchen
range – with scarcely a glint of drowsy red now in its ashy coals
– he struggled with the metal tongue that held back the door.
Usually loose, it now turned stiffly and hurt his fingers. Then suddenly it gave way.

And the boy's first quick thought was: Why, he's quite a little
man! And the next was one of supreme relief that all this wild
meaningless talk was now over. He leaned forward and peered into
the puckered-up clay-coloured face, with its blackened lips and
leaden-lidded eyes. The chin was dinted in with the claw pin in the
cravat. A gallipot stood near – a trap for crickets – touching one
limp hand, still smeared with pink plate powder. The door-tongue
was stiff, the boy supposed, because the corner of the baize apron
had got stuck to the varnish of the frame. You'd have hardly
thought, though, there'd be room in the cupboard. But the important thing, the illuminating, inspiring, and yet startlingly familiar
thing was the gallipot!

It had touched a spring, it had released a shutter in his mind and
set his thoughts winging back to a sooty, draughty chimney where
only a few minutes ago – minutes as vast and dark and empty as
the sea – he had hidden a book with a wedge of pie-crust on top of
it. In that book he had read of just such a gallipot as this – not as
a trap for crickets – but a gallipot with a handful of spade guineas
in it, which had belonged to an old man who had been brutally
strangled in the small hours by his two nephews. They had never
been caught either; nobody had even suspected them. They had
planned a means of escape – so vile and fantastic that even to watch
them at it had made his skin deliciously creep upon him and his

hair stir on his head. But it had succeeded, it had *worked*. To the dead old man's four-poster bed they had strung up the body of their victim, and until one of them, on his deathbed, had made confession, the old man's bones had lain beneath the tramplings of the crossroads. For everybody, even his own relatives, believed that he had hanged himself. This evilly romantic picture had flamed up with an ominous glow in the boy's imagination as he stood there contemplating his quiet enemy. The woman had become utterly unimportant. She was standing by the table, twisting, now up, now down, her dark-green bonnet-strings.

'How did you do it?' said the boy, looking up and leaning back, with a shuddering sigh, upon his heels. 'How on earth? Did he struggle? He couldn't have struggled *much*, I suppose. He's so small. He *looks* so small.'

The questions were unanswered and were unrepeated. He was merely drinking the scene in. That mole upon the bluish close-shaven cheek was certainly grown blacker than it had been in life, more conspicuous.

'But you aren't of course going to leave him like this?' he broke out sharply. 'You can't, you know; you simply can't.' But the woman was paying him no attention. 'Don't you *see*? They'd find it out in no time,' he added petulantly.

Yet even in the midst of this callous analysis, the woman's child-like attitude attracted his sympathy. At sight of the mute huddled contents of the cupboard, she seemed to have forgotten the danger she was in. A vacant immeasurable mournfulness quietened her face. She was crying. 'I'm sorry, but it's no good crying,' he went on, still kneeling on the cold oilcloth. '*That* won't be of any help; and I'd be awfully pleased to help you all I *can*. As a matter of fact I didn't much care for old Jacobs myself. But then, he's dead now. He *is* dead?'

The woman smothered his momentary fear with an eyeshot of horror. 'Well, if he is, I can't see why you shouldn't say so.' She remained motionless. 'Oh, dear,' he muttered impatiently, 'don't you under*stand*? We *must* do *some*thing.' A heavy frown had settled under the streak of dark hair on his forehead. 'You wouldn't stand the ghost of a chance as it is. They'd catch you easy.'

The woman nodded. 'I don't care; I hope they will. I don't care *what* happens now – because I can't think.'

'That's all rot,' said the boy stoutly. 'You've got to.'

The woman was irritating and paradoxical in this mood, and more than ever like a senseless wax model, which, with diabolical tremors, moves its glazed eyes and turns a glossy head. He peered again into the cupboard. Only once before had he seen Jacobs asleep – stretched out on a sofa in the dining-room one sultry afternoon in the streaming sunshine – gaping, sonorous. Then he had gone out as he had come in, on tiptoe. Now he stooped a little closer towards the cupboard, examining what was in it, stretching out even an experimental finger towards the small pallid hand.

He compared the woman's face and this other face, and found a fancy strangely contradictory of the facts. Jacobs was really and truly the man of blood; Jacobs was just the kind of person you'd expect to be a murderer. Not this woman, so fat and stupid. Nobody would be surprised to find *her* body in any cupboard. But Jacobs, small and ferrety, softly rasping his tune between his teeth, on and on. And now Jacobs was dead. So that's what *that* was like. He jerked his head aside, and his eyes became fixed once more on the gallipot. *That* was the real and eloquent thing. His mind had completed its circuit. He stood up convinced.

'It's no good going on like this,' he explained lucidly, almost cheerfully. 'This would be the very first place they would look into. I should look in here myself. But don't you see, you needn't be caught at all if you do what I tell you. It's something I read in a book of mine.'

The woman lifted a mechanical head and looked at him; and as if for the first time. She saw – a meagre boy with linnet legs and narrow shoulders, a lean clean-cut face of a rather bilious brown, and straight dark brown hair beneath a yachting cap; a boy in black stockings, a nightshirt and a shiny belt; his dark eyes, narrowed and intent, set steep in his head. This boy frightened her. She pushed on her bonnet and loosened her dress about her throat.

Manifestly she was preparing to go. He spoke more decisively. 'You don't *see*. That's all,' he said. 'Really, on my word of honour, it would be all right. I'm not just saying so. A baby could do it.'

The woman knelt down beside him in a posture not unlike the inmate's of the cupboard, and solemnly stared into his face. 'Tell me, tell me quick, you silly lamb. *What* did you say? A *baby* could do it?'

'Why, yes,' said the boy, outwardly cool, but inwardly ardent. 'It's as easy as A.B.C. You get a rope and make a noose, and you put it over his head and round his neck, you know, just as if he was going to be hanged. And then you hang him up on a nail or something. He mustn't touch the ground, of course. You throttled him, didn't you? You see there's no blood. They'll say he hanged himself, don't you see? They'd find old Jacobs strung up in the kitchen here and they'll say he's hanged himself. Don't you *see?*' he repeated.

'Oh, I couldn't do it,' she whimpered, 'not for worlds. I couldn't. I'd sooner stay here beside him till they come.' She began to sob in a stupid vacant fashion and then suddenly hiccuped.

'You *could*, I tell you. A baby could do it. You're afraid. That's what it is! I'm going to, I tell you: whether you like it or not.' He stamped his stockinged foot. 'Mind you, I'm not doing it for myself. It's nothing to do with me. You aren't taking the least trouble to understand.' He looked at her as if he couldn't believe any human being could by any possibility be so dense. 'It's just stupid,' he added over his shoulder, as he sallied out to the boot cupboard to fetch a rope.

Once more the tide of consciousness flowed in the woman's stolid, flattened brain. Two or three words of this young hero had at last fallen on good ground. And with consciousness, fear had come back. She came waddling after the boy. The vagrant crawling inmates of the cupboard had been swept carelessly from the corner, and now he was trailing a rope behind him as he went on into the larder for brandy. His match died down meanwhile, scorching his fingers, and he stayed on in the dark, the woman close behind him, rummaging gingerly among the bottles and dishes. And soon his fingertips touched the sharp-cut stopper. He returned triumphant, flipping from them the custard they had encountered in their search. The woman followed close behind him, stumbling ever and again upon his trailing rope, and thereby adding to her fears and docility. She was coming alive again. Brandy set her tongue gabbling faster. It gave the boy the strength and zeal of a stage villain.

He skipped hither and thither, now on to, now off the kitchen chair he had pushed nearer; then — having swept back the array of pink-smeared silver candlesticks and snuffers that were in his way, he scrambled up on to the table, and presently, after a few lasso-like flings of it, he had run the rope and made it fast over one of a few large hooks that curved down from the ceiling, hooks once used, as Jacobs had told him, to hang up hams on. His mouth was set, his face intent; his soldier grandfather's lower lip drawn in under the upper. The more active he was the more completely he became master of the ceremonies, the woman only an insignificant accomplice, as stupid as she was irresponsible. Even while she helped him drag out the body from the cupboard on to the flat arena of oilcloth, she continued to cry and snivel, as if *that* would be of any help. But a keen impassive will compelled her obedience. She followed the boy's every nod.

And presently she almost forgot the horror of the task, and found a partial oblivion in the intensity of it, though the boy was displeased by her maunderings. They were merely a doleful refrain to his troublesome grisly work. But he uttered no open reproof – not even when she buried her face in the baize apron and embraced the knees of the dead man. Only once she made any complaint against the limp heedless hung-up creature. 'If only,' she assured her young accomplice, 'if only he hadn't gone and *said* as how I wasn't the first. I ask you! As if I didn't know it.' But to this he paid no attention.

And now, at last, he drew back to view his handiwork. This he did with an inscrutable face, a face flattered at his own extra-ordinary ingenuity, a young face, almost angelic in its rapt gaslit look and yet one, maybe, of unsophisticated infamy. The dwarfish body seemed to be dangling naturally enough from its hook in the ceiling, its heels just free of the chair. And it did to some extent resemble the half-sinister, half-jocular cut that adorned his *Calendar*. Yet somehow he wasn't perfectly satisfied. Somehow the consum-mation was as yet incomplete. Some one thing was wanting, some blemish spoiled the effect and robbed it of unity. What? He stood hunting for it without success.

He followed the woman into the passage. She walked unsteadily, swaying bulkily to and fro, now and again violently colliding with the wall. 'Oh, it was crule, crule,' she was muttering.

After her stalked the boy, deep in thought. When she stopped, he stopped; when once more she set forward, as patiently he too set forward with her. Which of them was led, and which leader, it would be difficult to say. This dogged search after the one thing wanting continued to perplex and evade him. He decided that it was no good trying. It must be looked to when the woman was gone; when he was alone.

'I think you had better go now,' he said. 'He'll be coming home soon – my father, I mean, and. . . . It's just ten to twelve by Jacobs's clock.' The words conjured up in his mind a vision of his handsome dressed-up stepmother, standing there in the kitchen doorway half-hysterical before her swaying manservant. It faintly, and even a little sadly, tickled his fancy.

He opened the front door. It was still raining, and the smell of the damp earth and ivy leaves came washing into the house. The woman squatted down on the doorstep. 'Where shall I go?' she said. 'Where shall I go? What's the use? There ain't *nowhere*.' The boy scowled at the dripping trees. The house was surrounded by night – empty and silent but for the smothering soft small whisper of the rain, and the flat *drip, drip* of the drops from the porch.

'What's the use? There ain't *nowhere*,' again wailed his poor be-draggled confederate. He scrutinized her scornfully from under his tilted yachting cap. 'Wait a minute,' he said. He raced at full speed up the three dark flights of stairs to his bedroom. The book, the mouse-nibbled pie-crust were tossed on to the hearthrug and a florin was dug out of the gritty soot. Down he came again pell-mell.

Like a cat venturing into a busy street, the woman now stood peering out from the last of the three shallow crescent-shaped stone steps under the porch. 'I've brought you this,' he said superciliously.

'Thank you, sir,' said the woman.

She paused yet again, looking at him, in an attitude now familiar to the boy – the fingers of her knuckled left hand, with its thick brassy wedding-ring, pressed closely against mouth and cheek. He wondered for a moment what she was thinking about, and he was still wondering when she stepped finally off out into the rain.

A shrill shout followed her. 'I say! Mind that ditch there in the road!' But the only result of this was to bring the woman back again; she knelt and clasped him tightly to her bosom.

'I don't know why or anything. Oh, my lamb, my lamb, I didn't mean to do it and now I haven't got anywhere to go.' She bent low and hid her distorted miserable face on his shoulder. 'Oh, oh, I miss him so. The Lord God keep you safe! You've been very kind to me. But. . . .'

She released him, and waddled out once more under the flat-spread branches of the cedar tree, while the boy rubbed the smarting tears from his neck. He shut the door indignantly. This tame reaction was mawkish and silly. Then he paused, uncertain what to

do next. And suddenly memory rendered up the one thing wanting
– the master touch.

Why, of course, of course! Jacobs must have kicked a chair
down. You couldn't hang yourself like that without a drop. It was
impossible. The boy's valour, after all, was only a little shaken by
the embrace. Into the kitchen he walked victorious. The gas was
still singing, as it had sung all the evening, shedding its dismal flaring light on wall and clock and blind and ceiling and wide array of
glossy crockery. The puckered clay-coloured face looked stupidly
at him with bolting, dull, dull-lidded eyes. What was now to be
done must be done quickly. He ducked sharply and upset the chair
– a little too sharply, for a light spring-side boot had tapped him on
the cheek. He leapt back, hot and panting. The effect was masterly.
It was a triumph. And yet. . . . He stared, with clenched fists, and
whispered over his shoulder to a now absent accomplice. But no,
he was alone! Only Jacobs was there – with that drowsy slit of eye
– tremulously dangling. And as if, even for him, as if even for *his*
clear bold young spirit, this last repulsive spectacle, that last minute
assault of a helpless enemy, overwhelming some secret stronghold
in his mind, had suddenly proved intolerable, his energy, enterprise,
courage wilted within him. The whisper in the dark outside of the
uncertain wind, the soft bubbling whistle of the gas, the thousand
and one minute dumb things around him in the familiar kitchen –
nothing had changed. Yet *now* every object had become suddenly
real, stark, menacing, and hostile. Panic seized him. He ran out to
the front door and bawled into the dark after the woman.

No answer came. The rain was falling softly on the sodden turf;
and here, beneath the porch, in large ponderous drops. The wide-
spread palms of the cedar tree under the clouded midnight lay
prone and motionless. The whole world was gone out – black.
Nothing, nothing; he was alone.

He ran back again into the house – as if he had been awakened
out of a dream – leaving the door agape behind him, and whimper-
ing 'Mother!' Then louder – louder. And all the blind things of the
house took wooden voices. So up and down this white-shirted
raider ran, his clumsy poniard clapping against sudden corners, his
tongue calling in vain, and at last – as he went scuttling upstairs at
sound of cab-horse and wheels upon the sodden gravel – falling
dumb for very terror of its own noise.

An Official Position

He was a sturdy broad-shouldered fellow, of the middle height; though his bones were well covered as became his age, which was fifty, he was not fat; he had a ruddy complexion which neither the heat of the sun nor the unwholesomeness of the climate had affected. It was good rich blood that ran through his veins. His hair was brown and thick, and only at the temples touched with grey; he was very proud of his fair, handsome moustache and he kept it carefully brushed. There was a pleasant twinkle in his blue eyes. You would have said that this was a man whom life had treated well. There was in his appearance an air of good nature and in his vigour a glow of health that gave you confidence. He reminded you of one of those well-fed, rubicund burghers in an old Dutch picture, with their pink-cheeked wives, who made money and enjoyed the good things with which their industry provided them. He was, however, a widower. His name was Louis Remire, and his number 68763. He was serving a twelve-year sentence at St Laurent de Maroni, the great penal settlement of French Guiana, for killing his wife, but partly because he had served in the police force at Lyons, his native town, and partly on account of his good character, he had been given an official position. He had been chosen among nearly two hundred applicants to be the public executioner.

That was why he was allowed to sport the handsome moustache of which he took so much care. He was the only convict who wore one. It was in a manner of speaking his badge of office. That also was why he was allowed to wear his own clothes. The convicts wear pyjamas in pink and white stripes, round straw hats and clumsy boots with wooden soles and leather tops. Louis Remire wore espadrilles on his bare feet, blue cotton trousers, and a khaki shirt the open neck of which exposed to view his hairy and virile chest. When you saw him strolling about the public garden, with a kindly eye looking at the children, black or half-caste, who played there, you would have taken him for a respectable shopkeeper who was enjoying an hour's leisure. He had his own house. That was not only one of the perquisites of his office, but it was a necessity, since if he had lodged in the prison camp the convicts would have made short work of him. One morning he would have been found with his belly ripped open. It was true that the house was small, it was just a wooden shack of one room, with a lean-to that served as a kitchen; but it was surrounded by a tiny garden, within a palisade, and in the garden grew bananas, papaias and such vegetables as the climate allowed him to raise. The garden faced the sea and was surrounded by a coconut grove. The situation was charming. It was only a quarter of a mile from the prison, which was convenient for his rations. They were fetched by his assistant, who lived with him. The assistant, a tall, gawky, ungainly fellow, with deep-set, staring eyes and cavernous jaws, was serving a life sentence for rape and murder; he was not very intelligent, but in civil life he had been a cook and it was wonderful what, with the help of the vegetables they grew and such condiments as Louis Remire could afford to buy at the Chinese grocer's, he managed to do with the soup, potatoes and cabbage, and eternal beef, beef for three hundred and sixty-five days of the year, which the prison kitchens provided. It was on this account that Louis Remire had pressed his claim on the commandant when it had been found necessary to get a new assistant. The last one's nerves had given way and, absurdly enough, thought Louis Remire with a good-natured laugh, he had developed scruples about capital punishment; now, suffering from neurasthenia, he was on the Ile St Joseph, where the insane were confined.

His present assistant happened to be ill. He had high fever, and looked very much as if he were going to die. It had been necessary to send him to hospital. Louis Remire was sorry; he would not easily find so good a cook again. It was bad luck that this should have happened just now, for next day there was a job of work to be done. Six men were to be executed. Two were Algerians, one was a Pole, another a Spaniard from the mainland, and only two were French. They had escaped from prison in a band and gone up the river. For nearly twelve months, stealing, raping and killing they had spread terror through the colony. People scarcely dared move from their homesteads. Recaptured at last, they had all been sentenced to death, but the sentence had to be confirmed by the Minister of the Colonies, and the confirmation had only just arrived. Louis Remire could not manage without help, and besides there was a lot to arrange beforehand; it was particularly unfortunate that on this occasion of all others he should have to depend on an inexperienced man. The commandant had assigned to him one of the turnkeys. The turnkeys are convicts like the others, but they have been given their places for good behaviour and they live in separate quarters. They are on the side of the authorities and so are disliked by the other prisoners. Louis Remire was a conscientious fellow, and he was anxious that everything next day should go without a hitch. He arranged that his temporary assistant should come that afternoon to the place where the guillotine was kept so that he might explain to him thoroughly how it worked and show him exactly what he would have to do.

The guillotine, when not in use, stood in a small room which was part of the prison building, but which was entered by a separate door from the outside. When he sauntered along there at the appointed hour he found the man already waiting. He was a large-limbed, coarse-faced fellow. He was dressed in the pink and white stripes of the prison garb, but as turnkey he wore a felt hat instead of the straw of common convicts.

'What are you here for?'

The man shrugged his shoulders.

'I killed a farmer and his wife.'

'H'm. How long have you got?'

'Life.'

He looked a brute, but you could never be sure of people. He had himself seen a warder, a big, powerful man, faint dead away at an execution. He did not want his assistant to have an attack of nerves at the wrong moment. He gave him a friendly smile, and with his thumb pointed to the closed door behind which stood the guillotine.

'This is another sort of job,' he said. 'There are six of them, you know. They're a bad lot. The sooner they're out of the way the better.'

'Oh, that's all right. After what I've seen in this place I'm scared of nothing. It means no more to me than cutting the head off a chicken.'

Louis Remire unlocked the door and walked in. His assistant followed him. The guillotine in that small room, hardly larger than a cell, seemed to take up a great deal of space. It stood grim and sinister. Louis Remire heard a slight gasp and turning round saw that the turnkey was staring at the instrument with terrified eyes. His face was sallow and drawn from the fever and the hookworm from which all the convicts intermittently suffered, but now its pallor was ghastly. The executioner smiled good-naturedly.

'Gives you a turn, does it? Have you never seen it before?'

'Never.'

Louis Remire gave a little throaty chuckle.

'If you had, I suppose you wouldn't have survived to tell the tale. How did you escape it?'

'I was starving when I did my job. I'd asked for something to eat and they set the dogs on me. I was condemned to death. My lawyer went to Paris and he got the President to reprieve me.'

'It's better to be alive than dead, there's no denying that,' said Louis Remire, with that agreeable twinkle in his eyes.

He always kept his guillotine in perfect order. The wood, a dark hard native wood somewhat like mahogany, was highly polished; but there was a certain amount of brass, and it was Louis Remire's pride that this should be as bright and clean as the brasswork on a yacht. The knife shone as though it had just come out of the workshop. It was necessary not only to see that everything functioned properly, but to show his assistant how it functioned. It was part of the assistant's duty to refix the rope when the knife had dropped, and to do this he had to climb a short ladder.

It was with the satisfaction of a competent workman who knows his job from A to Z that Remire entered upon the necessary explanations. It gave him a certain quiet pleasure to point out the ingenuity of the apparatus. The condemned man was strapped to the bascule, a sort of shelf, and this by a simple mechanism was precipitated down and forwards so that the man's neck was conveniently under the knife. The conscientious fellow had brought with him a banana stem, about five feet long, and the turnkey had wondered why. He was now to learn. The stem was of about the same circumference and consistency as the human neck, so that it afforded a very good way, not only of showing a novice how the apparatus worked, but of making sure beforehand that it was in perfect order. Louis Remire placed the banana stem in position. He released the knife. It fell with incredible speed and with a great bang. From the time the man was attached to the bascule to the time his head was off only thirty seconds elapsed. The head fell in the basket. The executioner took it up by the ears and exhibited it to those whose duty it was to watch the execution. He uttered the solemn words:

'*Au nom du peuple français justice est faite.* In the name of the French people justice is done.'

Then he dropped the head back into the basket. Tomorrow, with six to be dispatched, the trunk would have to be unstrapped from the bascule and placed with the head on a stretcher, and the next man brought forward. They were taken in the order of their guilt. The least guilty, executed first, were spared the horror of seeing the death of their mates.

'We shall have to be careful that the right head goes with the right body,' said Louis Remire, in that rather jovial manner of his, 'or there may be no end of confusion at the Resurrection.'

He let down the knife two or three times in order to make quite sure that the assistant understood how to fix it, and then getting his cleaning materials from the shelf on which he kept them set him to work on the brass. Though it was spotless he thought that a final polish would do no harm. He leaned against the wall and idly smoked cigarettes.

Finally everything was in order and Louis Remire dismissed the assistant till midnight. At midnight they were moving the guillotine from the room in which it stood to the prison yard. It was always a bit of a job to set it up again, but it had to be in place an hour before dawn, at which time the execution took place. Louis Remire strolled slowly home to his shack. The afternoon was drawing to its close, and as he walked along he passed a working party who were returning to the prison. They spoke to one another in undertones and he guessed that they spoke of him; some looked down, two or three threw him a glance of hatred and one spat on the ground. Louis Remire, the end of a cigarette sticking to his lip, looked at them with irony. He was indifferent to the loathing, mingled with fear, with which they regarded him. It did not matter to him that not one of them would speak to him, and it only amused him to think that there was hardly one who would not gladly have thrust a knife into his guts. He had a supreme contempt for them all. He could take care of himself. He could use a knife as well as any of them, and he had confidence in his strength. The convicts knew that men were to be executed next day, and as always before an execution they were depressed and nervous. They went about their work in sullen silence, and the warders had to be more than usually on the alert.

'They'll settle down when it's all over,' said Louis Remire as he let himself into his little compound.

The dogs barked as he came along, and brave though he was, he listened to their uproar with satisfaction. With his own assistant ill, so that he was alone in the house, he was not sorry that he had the protection of those two savage mongrels. They prowled about the coconut grove outside his compound all night and they would give him good warning if anyone lurked there. They could be relied on to spring at the throat of any stranger who ventured too near. If his predecessor had had these dogs he wouldn't have come to his end.

The man who had been executioner before Louis Remire had only held the job a couple of years when one day he disappeared. The authorities thought he had run away; he was known to have a bit of money, and it was very probable that he had managed to make arrangements with the captain of a schooner to take him to Brazil. His nerves had given way. He had gone two or three times to the governor of the prison and told him that he feared for his life. He was convinced that the convicts were out to kill him. The governor felt pretty sure that his fears were groundless and paid no attention, but when the man was nowhere to be found he concluded that his terror had got the better of him and he had preferred to run the danger of escape, and the danger of being re-captured and put back into prison, rather than face the risk of an avenging convict's knife. About three weeks later the warder in charge of a working party in the jungle noticed a great flock of vultures clustered round a tree. These vultures, called urubus, are large black birds, of a horrible aspect, and they fly about the market-place of St Laurent, picking up the offal that is left there by the starving liberated convicts, and flit heavily from tree to tree in the neat, well-kept streets of the town. They fly in the prison yard to remind the convicts that if they attempt an escape into the jungle their end, ten to one, will be to have their bones picked clean by these loathsome creatures. They were fighting and screaming in such a mass round the tree that the warder thought there was something strange there. He reported it and the commandant sent a party to see. They found a man hanging by the neck from one of the branches, and when they cut him down discovered that he was the executioner. It was given out that he had committed suicide, but there was a knife-thrust in his back, and the convicts knew that he had been stabbed and then, still alive, taken to the jungle and hanged.

Louis Remire had no fear that anything of that sort would happen to him. He knew how his predecessor had been caught. The job had not been done by the convicts. By the French law when a man is sentenced to hard labour for a certain number of years he has at the expiration of his sentence to remain in the colony for the same number of years. He is free, but he may not stir from the spot that is assigned to him as a residence. In certain circumstances he can get a concession and if he works hard he manages to scrape a bare living from it, but after a long term of penal servitude, during which he has lost all power of initiative, what with the debilitating effect of fever, hookworm and so on, he is unfit for heavy and continuous labour, and so most of the liberated men subsist on begging, larceny, smuggling tobacco or money to the prisoners, and loading and unloading cargoes when two or three times a month a steamer comes into the harbour. It was the wife of one of these freed men that had been the means of the undoing of Louis Remire's predecessor. She was a coloured woman, young and pretty, with a neat little figure and mischievous eyes. The plot was well considered. The executioner was a burly, sanguine man, of ardent passions. She had thrown herself in his way, and when she caught his approving glance, had cast him a saucy look. He saw her a day or two later in the public garden. He did not venture to speak to her (no one, man, woman or child, would be seen speaking to him), but when he winked at her she smiled. One evening he met her walking through the coconut grove that surrounded his compound. No one was about. He got into conversation with her. They only exchanged a few words, for she was evidently terrified of being seen with him. But she came again to the coconut grove. She played him carefully till his suspicions were allayed; she teased his desires; she made him give her little presents, and at last on the promise of what was for both of them quite a sum of money she agreed to come one dark night to the compound. A ship had just come in and her husband would be working till dawn. It was when he opened the door for her and she hesitated to come in as though at the last moment she could not make up her mind, that he stepped outside to draw her in, and fell to the ground with the violence of the knife-thrust in his back.

'The fool,' muttered Louis Remire. 'He only got what he deserved. He should have smelt a rat. The eternal vanity of man.'

For his part he was through with women. It was on account of women that he found himself in the situation he was in now, at least on account of one woman; and besides, at his time of life, his passions were assuaged. There were other things in life and after a certain age a man, if he was sensible, turned his attention to them. He had always been a great fisherman. In the old days, at home in France before he had had his misfortune, as soon as he came off duty, he took his rod and line and went down to the Rhône. He got a lot of fishing now. Every morning, till the sun grew hot, he sat on his favourite rock and generally managed to get enough for the prison governor's table. The governor's wife knew the value of things and beat him down on the price he asked, but he did not blame her for that; she knew that he had to take what she was prepared to give and it would have been stupid of her to pay a penny more than she had to. In any case it brought in a little money useful for tobacco and rum and other odds and ends. But this evening he was going to fish for himself. He got his bait from the lean-to, and his rod, and settled down on his rock. No fish was so good as the fish you caught yourself, and by now he knew which were those that were good to eat and which were so tough and flavourless that you could only throw them back into the sea. There was one sort that, fried in real olive oil, was as good as mullet. He had not been sitting there five minutes when his float gave a sudden jerk, and when he pulled up his line, there, like an answer to prayer, was one of those very fish wriggling on the hook. He took it off, banged its head on the rock, and putting it down, replaced his bait. Four of them would make a good supper, the best a man could have, and with a night's hard work before him he needed a hearty meal. He would not have time to fish tomorrow morning. First of all the scaffold would have to be taken down and the pieces brought back to the room in which it was kept, and there would be a lot of cleaning to do. It was a bloody business; last time he had had his pants so soaked that he had been able to do nothing with them and had had to throw them away. The brass would have to be polished, the knife would have to be honed. He was not a man to leave a job half finished, and by the time it was through he would be pretty peckish. It would be worth while to catch a few more fish and put them in a cool place so that he could have a substantial breakfast. A cup of coffee, a couple of eggs and a bit of fried fish;

he could do with that. Then he would have a good sleep; after a
night on his feet, the anxiety of an inexperienced assistant, and the
clearing away of all the mess, God knew he would deserve it.

In front of him was spread the bay in a noble sweep, and in the
distance was a little island green with trees. The afternoon was
exquisitely still. Peace descended on the fisherman's soul. He
watched his float idly. When you came to think of it, he reflected,
he might be a great deal worse off; some of them, the convicts he
meant, the convicts who swarmed in the prison a few hundred
yards away from him, some of them had such a nostalgia for
France that they went mad with melancholy; but he was a bit of a
philosopher, so long as he could fish he was content; and did it
really matter if he watched his float on the southern sea or in the
Rhône? His thoughts wandered back to the past. His wife was an
intolerable woman and he did not regret that he had killed her. He
had never meant to marry her. She was a dressmaker, and he had
taken a fancy to her because she was always neatly and smartly
dressed. She seemed respectable and ladylike. He would not have
been surprised if she had looked upon herself as a cut above a policeman. But he had a way with him. She soon gave him to understand that she was no snob, and when he made the customary
advances he discovered to his relief, for he was not a man who
considered that resistance added a flavour to conquest, that she
was no prude. He liked to be seen with her when he took her out
to dinner. She talked intelligently, and she was economical. She
knew where they could dine well at the cheapest price. His situation was enviable. It added to his satisfaction that he could gratify
the sexual desires natural to his healthy temperament at so moder-
ate an expense. When she came to him and said she was going to
have a baby it seemed natural enough that they should get married.
He was earning good wages, and it was time that he should settle
down. He often grew tired of eating, *en pension*, at a restaurant,
and he looked forward to having his own home and home cooking.
Well, it turned out that it had been a mistake about the baby, but
Louis Remire was a good-natured fellow, and he didn't hold it up
against Adèle. But he found, as many men have found before, that
the wife was a very different woman from the mistress. She was
jealous and possessive. She seemed to think that on a Sunday afternoon he ought to take her for a walk instead of going out fishing,
and she made it a grievance that, on coming off duty, he would go

to the café. There was one café he frequented where other fishermen went and where he met men with whom he had a lot in common. He found it much pleasanter to spend his free evenings there over a glass or two of beer, whiling away the time with a game of cards, than to sit at home with his wife. She began to make scenes. Though sociable and jovial by nature he had a quick temper. There was a rough crowd at Lyons, and sometimes you could not manage them unless you were prepared to show a certain amount of firmness. When his wife began to make a nuisance of herself it never occurred to him that there was any other way of dealing with her than that he adopted. He let her know the strength of his hand. If she had been a sensible woman she would have learnt her lesson, but she was not a sensible woman. He found occasion more and more often to apply a necessary correction; she revenged herself by screaming the place down and by telling the neighbours – they lived in a two-roomed apartment on the fifth floor of a big house – what a brute he was. She told them that she was sure he would kill her one day. And yet never was there a more good-natured man than Louis Remire; she blamed him for the money he spent at the café, she accused him of wasting it on other women; well, in his position he had opportunities now and then, and as any man would he took them, and he was easy with his money, he never minded paying a round of drinks for his friends, and when a girl who had been nice to him wanted a new hat or a pair of silk stockings he wasn't the man to say no. His wife looked upon money that he did not spend on her as money stolen from her; she tried to make him account for every penny he spent, and when in his jovial way he told her he had thrown it out of the window, she was infuriated. Her tongue grew bitter and her voice was rasping. She was in a sullen rage with him all the time. She could not speak without saying something disagreeable. They led a cat-and-dog life. Louis Remire used to tell his friends what a harridan she was, he used to tell them that he wished ten times a day that he had never married her, and sometimes he would add that if an epidemic of influenza did not carry her off he would really have to kill her.

It was these remarks, made merely in jest, and the fact that she had so often told the neighbours that she knew he would murder her, that had sent him to St Laurent de Maroni with a twelve-year sentence. Otherwise he might very well have got off with three or four years in a French prison. The end had come one hot summer's day. He was, which was rare for him, in a bad temper. There was a strike in progress and the strikers had been violent. The police had had to make a good many arrests and the men had not submitted to this peaceably. Louis Remire had got a nasty blow on the jaw and he had had to make free use of his truncheon. To get the arrested men to the station had been a hot and tiring job. On coming off duty he had gone home to get out of his uniform and was intending to go to the café and have a glass of beer and a pleasant game of cards. His jaw was hurting him. His wife chose that moment to ask him for money and when he told her that he had none to give her she made a scene. He had plenty of money to go to the café, but none for her to buy a scrap of food with, she could starve for all he cared. He told her to shut up, and then the row began. She got in front of the door and swore that he should not pass till he gave her money. He told her to get out of the way and took a step towards her. She whipped out his service revolver which he had taken off when he removed his uniform and threatened that she would shoot him if he moved a step. He was used to dealing with dangerous criminals, and the words were hardly out of her mouth before he had sprung upon her and snatched the revolver out of her hand. She screamed and hit him in the face. She hit him exactly where his jaw most hurt him. Blind with rage and mad with pain, he fired, he fired twice and she fell to the floor. For a moment he stood and stared at her. He was dazed. She looked as if she were dead. His first feeling was one of indescribable relief. He listened. No one seemed to have heard the sound of the shot. The neighbours must be out. That was a bit of luck, for it gave him time to do what he had to do in his own way. He changed back into his uniform, went out, locking the door behind him and putting the key in his pocket; he stopped for five minutes at his familiar café to have a glass of beer and then returned to the police station he had lately left. On account of the day's disturbances the chief inspector was still there. Louis Remire went to his room and told him what had happened. He spent the night in a cell adjoining those of the strikers he had so recently himself arrested. Even at that tragic moment he was struck by the irony of the situation.

Louis Remire had on frequent occasions appeared as a police witness in criminal cases and he knew how eager are a man's companions to give any information that may damage him when he gets into trouble. It had caused him a certain grim amusement to realize how often it happened that a conviction was obtained only by the testimony of a prisoner's best friends. But notwithstanding his experience he was amazed, when his own case came up for trial, to listen to the evidence given by the proprietor of the little café he had so much frequented, and to that of the men who for years had fished with him, played cards with him and drunk with him. They seemed to have treasured every careless word he had ever uttered, the complaints he had made about his wife and the joking threats he had from time to time made that he would get even with her. He knew that at the time they had taken them no more seriously than he meant them. If he was able to do them a small service, and a man in the force often has it in his power to do one, he never hesitated. He had never been ungenerous with his money. You would have thought as you listened to them in the witness-box that it gave them the most intense satisfaction to disclose every trivial detail that could damage him.

From what appeared at the trial you would have thought that he was a bad man, dissolute, of violent temper, extravagant, idle and corrupt. He knew that he was nothing of the kind. He was just an ordinary, good-natured, easy-going fellow, who was willing to let you go your way if you would let him go his. It was true that he liked his game of cards and his glass of beer, it was true that he liked a pretty girl, but what of it? When he looked at the jury he wondered how many of them would come out of it any better than he if all their errors, all their rash words, all their follies were thus laid bare. He did not resent the long term of penal servitude to which he was sentenced. He was an officer of the law; he had committed a crime and it was right that he should be punished. But he was not a criminal; he was the victim of an unfortunate accident.

At St Laurent de Maroni, in the prison camp, wearing the pink and white stripe of the prison garb and the ugly straw hat, he remembered still that he had been a policeman and that the convicts with whom he must now consort had always been his natural enemies. He despised and disliked them. He had as little to do with them as he could. And he was not frightened of them. He knew them too well. Like all the rest he had a knife and he showed that he was prepared to use it. He did not want to interfere with anybody, but he was not going to allow anyone to interfere with him.

The chief of the Lyons police had liked him, his character while in the force had been exemplary, and the *fiche* which accompanied every prisoner spoke well of him. He knew that what officials like is a prisoner who gives no trouble, who accepts his position with cheerfulness and who is willing. He got a soft job; very soon he got a cell of his own and so escaped the horrible promiscuity of the dormitories; he got on well with the warders, they were decent chaps, most of them, and knowing that he had formerly been in the police they treated him more as a comrade than as a convict. The commandant of the prison trusted him. Presently he got the job of servant to one of the prison officials. He slept in the prison, but otherwise enjoyed complete freedom. He took the children of his master to school every day and fetched them at the end of their school hours. He made toys for them. He accompanied his mistress to market and carried back the provisions she bought. He spent long hours gossiping with her. The family liked him. They liked his chaffing manner and his good-natured smile. He was industrious and trustworthy. Life once more was tolerable.

But after three years his master was transferred to Cayenne. It was a blow. But it happened just then that the post of executioner fell free and he obtained it. Now once more he was in the service of the state. He was an official. However humble his residence it was his own. He need no longer wear the prison uniform. He could grow his hair and his moustache. He cared little if the convicts looked upon him with horror and contempt. That was how he looked upon them. Scum. When he took the bleeding head of an executed man from the basket and holding it by the ears pronounced those solemn words: *Au nom du peuple français justice est faite*, he felt that he did represent the Republic. He stood for law and order. He was the protector of society against that vast horde of ruthless criminals.

He got a hundred francs for each execution. That and what the governor's wife paid him for his fish provided him with many a pleasant comfort and not a few luxuries. And now as he sat on his rock in the peace of eventide he considered what he would do with the money he would earn next day. Occasionally he got a bite, now and then a fish; he drew it out of the water, took it off the hook and put on fresh bait; but he did this mechanically, and it did not disturb the current of his thoughts. Six hundred francs. It was a respectable sum. He scarcely knew what to do with it. He had everything he wanted in his little house, he had a good store of groceries and plenty of rum for one who was as little of a drinker as he was; he needed no fishing tackle; his clothes were good enough. The only thing was to put it aside. He already had a tidy little sum hidden in the ground at the root of a papaia tree. He chuckled when he thought how Adèle would have stared had she known that he was actually saving. It would have been balm to her avaricious soul. He was saving up gradually for when he was released. That was the difficult moment for the convicts. So long as they were in prison they had a roof over their heads and food to eat, but when they were released, with the obligation of staying for so many years more in the colony, they had to shift for themselves. They all said the same thing: it was at the expiration of their term that their real punishment began. They could not get work. Employers mistrusted them. Contractors would not engage them because the prison authorities hired out convict labour at a price that defied competition. They slept in the open, in the market-place, and for food were often glad to go to the Salvation Army. But the Salvation Army made them work hard for what they gave and besides forced them to listen to their services. Sometimes they committed a violent crime merely to get back to the safety of prison. Louis Remire was not going to take any risks. He meant to amass a sufficient capital to start in business. He ought to be able to get permission to settle in Cayenne, and there he might open a bar. People might hesitate to come at first because he had been the executioner, but if he provided good liquor they would get over their prejudice, and with his jovial manner, with his experience in keeping order, he ought to be able to make a go of it. Visitors came to Cayenne now and then and they would come out of curiosity. It would be something interesting to tell their friends when they got home that the best rum punch they had had in Cayenne was at the executioner's. But he had a good many years to go yet, and if there really was something he needed there was no reason why he shouldn't get it. He racked his brains. No, there wasn't a thing in the world he wanted. He was surprised. He allowed his eyes to wander from his float. The sea was wonderfully calm and now it was rich with all the colour of the setting sun. In the sky already a solitary star twinkled. A thought came to him that filled him with an extraordinary sensation.

'But if there's nothing in the world you want, surely that's happiness.' He stroked his handsome moustache and his blue eyes shone softly. 'There are no two ways about it, I'm a happy man and till this moment I never knew it.'

The notion was so unexpected that he did not know what to make of it. It was certainly a very odd one. But there it was, as obvious to anyone with a logical mind as a proposition of Euclid.

'Happy, that's what I am. How many men can say the same? In St Laurent de Maroni of all places, and for the first time in my life.'

The sun was setting. He had caught enough fish for his supper and enough for his breakfast. He drew in his line, gathered up his fish, and went back to his house. It stood but a few yards from the sea. It did not take him long to light his fire and in a little while he had four little fish cheerfully frizzling in a pan. He was always very particular about the oil he used. The best olive oil was expensive, but it was worth the money. The prison bread was good, and after he had fried his fish, he fried a couple of pieces of bread in the rest of the oil. He sniffed the savoury smell with satisfaction. He lit a lamp, washed a lettuce grown in his own garden, and mixed himself a salad. He had a notion that no one in the world could mix a salad better than he. He drank a glass of rum and ate his supper with appetite. He gave a few odds and ends to the two mongrel dogs who were lying at his feet, and then, having washed up, for he was by nature a tidy man, and when he came in to breakfast next morning did not want to find things in a mess, let the dogs out of the compound to wander about the coconut grove. He took the lamp into the house, made himself comfortable in his deck-chair, and smoking a cigar smuggled in from the neighbouring Dutch Colony settled down to read one of the French papers that had arrived by the last mail. Replete, his mind at ease, he could not but feel that life, with all its disadvantages, was good to live. He was still affected by the amused surprise that had overcome him when it suddenly occurred to him that he was a happy man. When you considered that men spent their lives seeking for happiness, it seemed hardly believable that he had found it. Yet the fact stared him in the face. A man who has everything he wants is happy, he had everything he wanted; therefore he was happy. He chuckled as a new thought crossed his mind.

'There's no denying it, I owe it to Adèle.'

Old Adèle. What a foul woman!

Presently he decided that he had better have a nap; he set his alarm clock for a quarter to twelve and lying down on his bed in a few minutes was fast asleep. He slept soundly and no dreams troubled him. He woke with a start when the alarm sounded, but in a moment remembered why he had set it. He yawned and stretched himself lazily.

'Ah, well, I suppose I must get to work. Every job has its inconveniences.'

He slipped from under his mosquito-net and relit his lamp. To freshen himself he washed his hands and face, and then as a protection against the night air drank a glass of rum. He thought for a moment of his inexperienced assistant and wondered whether it would be wise to take some rum in a flask with him.

'It would be a pretty business if his nerves went back on him.'

It was unfortunate that so many as six men had to be executed. If there had been only one, it wouldn't have mattered so much his assistant being new to the game; but with five others waiting there, it would be awkward if there were a hitch. He shrugged his shoulders. They would just have to do the best they could. He passed a comb through his tousled hair and carefully brushed his handsome moustache. He lit a cigarette. He walked through his compound, unlocked the door in the stout palisade that surrounded it, and locked it again behind him. There was no moon. He whistled for his dogs. He was surprised that they did not come. He whistled again. The brutes. They'd probably caught a rat and were fighting over it. He'd give them a good hiding for that; he'd teach them not to come when he whistled. He set out to walk in the direction of the prison. It was dark under the coconut trees and he would just as soon have had the dogs with him. Still there were only fifty yards to go and then he would be out in the open. There were lights in the governor's house, and it gave him confidence to see them. He smiled, for he guessed what those lights at that late hour meant; the governor, with the execution before him at dawn, was finding it hard to sleep. The anxiety, the malaise, that affected convicts and ex-convicts alike on the eve of an execution, had got on his nerves. It was true that there was always the chance of an outbreak then, and the warders went around with their eyes skinned and their hands ready to draw their guns at a suspicious movement.

Louis Remire whistled for his dogs once more, but they did not come. He could not understand it. It was a trifle disquieting. He was a man who habitually walked slowly, strolling along with a sort of roll, but now he hastened his pace. He spat the cigarette out of his mouth. It had struck him that it was prudent not to betray his whereabouts by the light it gave. Suddenly he stumbled against something. He stopped dead. He was a brave man, with nerves of steel, but on a sudden he felt sick with terror. It was something soft and rather large that he had stumbled against, and he was pretty sure what it was. He wore espadrilles, and with one foot he cautiously felt the object on the ground before him. Yes, he was right. It was one of his dogs. It was dead. He took a step backwards and drew his knife. He knew it was no good to shout. The only house in the neighbourhood was the prison governor's, it faced the clearing just beyond the coconut grove; but they would not hear him, or if they did would not stir. St Laurent de Maroni was not a place where you went out in the dead of night when you heard a man calling for help. If next day one of the freed convicts was found lying dead, well, it was no great loss. Louis Remire saw in a flash what had happened.

He thought rapidly. They had killed his dogs while he was sleeping. They must have got them when he had put them out of his compound after supper. They must have thrown them some poisoned meat and the brutes had snatched at it. If the one he had stumbled over was near his house it was because it tried to crawl home to die. Louis Remire strained his eyes. He could see nothing. The night was pitch black. He could hardly see the trunks of the coconut trees a yard away from him. His first thought was to make a rush for his shack. If he got back to the safety of that he could wait till the prison people, wondering why he did not come, sent to fetch him. But he knew he could never get back. He knew they were there in the darkness, the men who had killed his dogs; he would have to fumble with the key to find the lock and before he found it he would have a knife plunged in his back. He listened intently. There was not a sound. And yet he felt that there were men there, lurking behind the trees, and they were there to kill him. They would kill him as they had killed his dogs. And he would die like a dog. There was more than one certainly. He knew them, there were three or four of them at least, there might be more, convicts in service in private houses who were not obliged to get back to the camp till a late hour, or desperate and starving freed men who had nothing to lose. For a moment he hesitated what to do. He dared not make a run for it, they might easily have put a rope across the pathway that led from his house to the open, and if he tripped he was done for. The coconut trees were loosely planted and among them his enemies would see him as little as he saw them. He stepped over the dead dog and plunged into the grove. He stood with his back to a tree to decide how he should proceed. The silence was terrifying. Suddenly he heard a whisper and the horror of it was frightful. Again a dead silence. He felt he must move on, but his feet seemed rooted to the ground. He felt that they were peering at him out of the darkness and it seemed to him that he was as visible to them as though he stood in the broad light of day. Then from the other side was a little cough. It came as such a shock that Louis Remire nearly screamed. He was conscious now that they were all round him. He could expect no mercy from those robbers and murderers. He remembered the other executioner, his predecessor, whom they had carried still alive into the jungle, whose eyes they had gouged out, and whom they had left hanging for the vultures to devour. His knees began to tremble. What a fool he had been to take on the job! There were soft jobs he could have found in which you ran no risk. It was too late to think of that. He pulled himself together. He had no chance of getting out of the coconut grove alive, he knew that; he wanted to be sure that he would be dead. He tightened his grip on his knife. The awful part was that he could hear no one, he could see no one, and yet he knew that they were lurking there waiting to strike. For one moment he had a mad idea, he would throw his knife away and shout out to them that he was unarmed and they could come and kill him in safety. But he knew them; they would never be satisfied merely to kill him. Rage seized him. He was not the man to surrender tamely to a pack of criminals. He was an honest man and an official of the state; it was his duty to defend himself. He could not stay there all night. It was better to get it over quickly. Yet that tree at his back seemed to offer a sort of security, he could not bring himself to move. He stared at the trunk of a tree in front of him and suddenly it moved and he realized with horror that it was a man. That made up his mind for him and with a huge effort he stepped forwards. He advanced slowly and cautiously. He could hear nothing, he could see nothing. But he knew that as he advanced they advanced too. It was as though he were accompanied by an invisible bodyguard. He thought he could hear the sound of their naked feet on the ground. His fear had left him. He walked on, keeping as close to the trees as he could, so that they should have less chance of attacking him from behind; a wild hope sprang up in his breast that they would be afraid to strike, they knew him, they all knew him, and whoever struck the first blow would be lucky if he escaped a knife in his own guts; he had only another thirty yards to go, and once in the open, able to see, he could make a fight for it. A few yards more and then he would run for his life. Suddenly something happened that made him start out of his skin, and he stopped dead. A light was flashed and in that heavy darkness the sudden glare was terrifying. It was an electric torch. Instinctively he sprang to a tree and stood with his back to it. He could not see who held the light. He was blinded by it. He did not speak. He held his knife low, he knew that when they struck it was in the belly, and if someone flung himself at him he was prepared to strike back. He was going to sell his life dearly. For half a minute perhaps the light shone on his face, but it seemed to him an eternity. He thought now that he discerned dimly the faces of men. Then a word broke the horrible silence.

'Throw.'

At the same instant a knife came flying through the air and struck him on the breastbone. He threw up his hands and as he did so someone sprang at him and with a great sweep of the knife ripped up his belly. The light was switched off. Louis Remire sank to the ground with a groan, a terrible groan of pain. Five, six men gathered out of the gloom and stood over him. With his fall the knife that had stuck in his breastbone was dislodged. It lay on the ground. A quick flash of the torch showed where it was. One of the men took it and with a single, swift motion cut Remire's throat from ear to ear.

'*Au nom du peuple français justice est faite,*' he said.

They vanished into the darkness and in the coconut grove was the immense silence of death.

I Want to Know Why

We got up at four in the morning, that first day in the east. On the evening before we had climbed off a freight train at the edge of town, and with the true instinct of Kentucky boys had found our way across town and to the race track and stables at once. Then we knew we were all right. Hanley Turner right away found a nigger we knew. It was Bildad Johnson who in the winter works at Ed Becker's livery barn in our home town, Beckersville. Bildad is a good cook as almost all our niggers are and of course he, like everyone in our part of Kentucky who is anyone at all, likes the horses. In the spring Bildad begins to scratch around. A nigger from our country can flatter and wheedle anyone into letting him do most anything he wants. Bildad wheedles the stable men and the trainers from the horse farms in our country around Lexington. The trainers come into town in the evening to stand around and talk and maybe get into a poker game. Bildad gets in with them. He is always doing little favors and telling about things to eat, chicken browned in a pan, and how is the best way to cook sweet potatoes and corn bread. It makes your mouth water to hear him.

When the racing season comes on and the horses go to the races and there is all the talk on the streets in the evenings about the new colts, and everyone says when they are going over to Lexington or to the spring meeting at Churchill Downs or to Latonia, and the horsemen that have been down to New Orleans or maybe at the winter meeting at Havana in Cuba come home to spend a week before they start out again, at such a time when everything talked about in Beckersville is just horses and nothing else and the outfits start out and horse racing is in every breath of air you breathe, Bildad shows up with a job as cook for some outfit. Often when I think about it, his always going all season to the races and working in the livery barn in the winter where horses are and where men like to come and talk about horses, I wish I was a nigger. It's a foolish thing to say, but that's the way I am about being around horses, just crazy. I can't help it.

Well, I must tell you about what we did and let you in on what I'm talking about. Four of us boys from Beckersville, all whites and sons of men who live in Beckersville regular, made up our minds we were going to the races, not just to Lexington or Louisville, I don't mean, but to the big eastern track we were always hearing our Beckersville men talk about, to Saratoga. We were all pretty young then. I was just turned fifteen and I was the oldest of the four. It was my scheme. I admit that and I talked the others into trying it. There was Hanley Turner and Henry Rieback and Tom Tumberton and myself. I had thirty-seven dollars I had earned during the winter working nights and Saturdays in Enoch Myer's grocery. Henry Rieback had eleven dollars and the others, Hanley and Tom had only a dollar or two each. We fixed it all up and laid low until the Kentucky spring meetings were over and some of our men, the sportiest ones, the ones we envied the most, had cut out – then we cut out too.

I won't tell you the trouble we had beating our way on freights and all. We went through Cleveland and Buffalo and other cities and saw Niagara Falls. We bought things there, souvenirs and spoons and cards and shells with pictures of the falls on them for our sisters and mothers, but thought we had better not send any of the things home. We didn't want to put the folks on our trail and maybe be nabbed.

We got into Saratoga as I said at night and went to the track. Bildad fed us up. He showed us a place to sleep in hay over a shed and promised to keep still. Niggers are all right about things like that. They won't squeal on you. Often a white man you might meet, when you had run away from home like that, might appear to be all right and give you a quarter or a half dollar or something, and then go right and give you away. White men will do that, but not a nigger. You can trust them. They are squarer with kids. I don't know why.

At the Saratoga meeting that year there were a lot of men from home. Dave Williams and Arthur Mulford and Jerry Myers and others. Then there was a lot from Louisville and Lexington Henry Rieback knew but I didn't. They were professional gamblers and Henry Rieback's father is one too. He is what is called a sheet writer and goes away most of the year to tracks. In the winter when he is home in Beckersville he don't stay there much but goes away to cities and deals faro. He is a nice man and generous, is always sending Henry presents, a bicycle and a gold watch and a boy scout suit of clothes and things like that.

My own father is a lawyer. He's all right, but don't make much money and can't buy me things and anyway I'm getting so old now I don't expect it. He never said nothing to me against Henry, but Hanley Turner and Tom Tumberton's fathers did. They said to their boys that money so come by is no good and they didn't want their boys brought up to hear gamblers' talk and be thinking about such things and maybe embrace them.

That's all right and I guess the men know what they are talking about, but I don't see what it's got to do with Henry or with horses either. That's what I'm writing this story about. I'm puzzled. I'm getting to be a man and want to think straight and be O.K., and there's something I saw at the race meeting at the eastern track I can't figure out.

I can't help it, I'm crazy about thoroughbred horses. I've always been that way. When I was ten years old and saw I was growing to be big and couldn't be a rider I was so sorry I nearly died. Harry Hellinfinger in Beckersville, whose father is Postmaster, is grown up and too lazy to work, but likes to stand around in the street and get up jokes on boys like sending them to a hardware store for a gimlet to bore square holes and other jokes like that. He played one on me. He told me that if I would eat a half a cigar I would be stunted and not grow any more and maybe could be a rider. I did it. When father wasn't looking I took a cigar out of his pocket and gagged it down some way. It made me awful sick and the doctor had to be sent for, and then it did no good. I kept right on growing. It was a joke. When I told what I had done and why most fathers would have whipped me but mine didn't.

Well, I didn't get stunted and didn't die. It serves Harry Hellinfinger right. Then I made up my mind I would like to be a stable boy, but had to give that up too. Mostly niggers do that work and I knew father wouldn't let me go into it. No use to ask him.

If you've never been crazy about thoroughbreds it's because you've never been around where they are much and don't know any better. They're beautiful. There isn't anything so lovely and clean and full of spunk and honest and everything as some racehorses. On the big horse farms that are all around our town Beckersville there are tracks and the horses run in the early morning.

More than a thousand times I've got out of bed before daylight and walked two or three miles to the tracks. Mother wouldn't of let me go but father always says, 'Let him alone'. So I got some bread out of the bread box and some butter and jam, gobbled it and lit out.

At the tracks you sit on the fence with men, whites and niggers, and they chew tobacco and talk, and then the colts are brought out. It's early and the grass is covered with shiny dew and in another field a man is plowing and they are frying things in a shed where the track niggers sleep, and you know how a nigger can giggle and laugh and say things that make you laugh. A white man can't do it and some niggers can't but a track nigger can every time.

And so the colts are brought out and some are just galloped by stable boys, but almost every morning on a big track owned by a rich man who lives maybe in New York, there are always, nearly every morning, a few colts and some of the old racehorses and geldings and mares that are cut loose.

It brings a lump up into my throat when a horse runs. I don't mean all horses but some. I can pick them nearly every time. It's in my blood like in the blood of race-track niggers and trainers. Even when they just go slop-jogging along with a little nigger on their backs I can tell a winner. If my throat hurts and it's hard for me to swallow, that's him. He'll run like Sam Hill when you let him out. If he don't win every time it'll be a wonder and because they've got him in a pocket behind another or he was pulled or got off bad at the post or something. If I wanted to be a gambler like Henry Rieback's father I could get rich. I know I could and Henry says so too. All I would have to do is to wait 'til that hurt comes when I see a horse and then bet every cent. That's what I would do if I wanted to be a gambler, but I don't.

When you're at the tracks in the morning – not the race tracks but the training tracks around Beckersville – you don't see a horse, the kind I've been talking about, very often, but it's nice anyway. Any thoroughbred, that is sired right and out of a good mare and trained by a man that knows how, can run. If he couldn't what would he be there for and not pulling a plow?

Well, out of the stables they come and the boys are on their backs and it's lovely to be there. You hunch down on top of the fence and itch inside you. Over in the sheds the niggers giggle and sing. Bacon is being fried and coffee made. Everything smells lovely. Nothing smells better than coffee and manure and horses and niggers and bacon frying and pipes being smoked out of doors on a morning like that. It just gets you, that's what it does.

But about Saratoga. We was there six days and not a soul from home seen us and everything came off just as we wanted it to, fine weather and horses and races and all. We beat our way home and Bildad gave us a basket with fried chicken and bread and other eatables in, and I had eighteen dollars when we got back to Beckersville. Mother jawed and cried but Pop didn't say much. I told everything we done except one thing. I did and saw that alone. That's what I'm writing about. It got me upset. I think about it at night. Here it is.

At Saratoga we laid up nights in the hay in the shed Bildad had showed us and ate with the niggers early and at night when the race people had all gone away. The men from home stayed mostly in the grandstand and betting field, and didn't come out around the places where the horses are kept except to the paddocks just before a race when the horses are saddled. At Saratoga they don't have paddocks under an open shed as at Lexington and Churchill Downs and other tracks down in our country, but saddle the horses right out in an open place under trees on a lawn as smooth and nice as Banker Bohon's front yard here in Beckersville. It's lovely. The horses are sweaty and nervous and shine and the men come out and smoke cigars and look at them and the trainers are there and the owners, and your heart thumps so you can hardly breathe.

Then the bugle blows for post and the boys that ride come running out with their silk clothes on and you run to get a place by the fence with the niggers.

I always am wanting to be a trainer or owner, and at the risk of being seen and caught and sent home I went to the paddocks before every race. The other boys didn't but I did.

We got to Saratoga on a Friday and on Wednesday the next week the big Mullford Handicap was to be run. Middlestride was in it and Sunstreak. The weather was fine and the track fast. I couldn't sleep the night before.

What had happened was that both these horses are the kind it makes my throat hurt to see. Middlestride is long and looks awkward and is a gelding. He belongs to Joe Thompson, a little owner from home who only has a half dozen horses. The Mullford Handicap is for a mile and Middlestride can't untrack fast. He goes away slow and is always way back at the half, then he begins to run and if the race is a mile and a quarter he'll just eat up everything and get there.

Sunstreak is different. He is a stallion and nervous and belongs on the biggest farm we've got in our country, the Van Riddle place that belongs to Mr Van Riddle of New York. Sunstreak is like a girl you think about sometimes but never see. He is hard all over and lovely too. When you look at his head you want to kiss him. He is trained by Jerry Tillford who knows me and has been good to me lots of times, lets me walk into a horse's stall to look at him close and other things. There isn't anything as sweet as that horse. He stands at the post quiet and not letting on, but he is just burning up inside. Then when the barrier goes up he is off like his name, Sunstreak. It makes you ache to see him. It hurts you. He just lays down and runs like a bird dog. There can't anything I ever see run like him except Middlestride when he gets untracked and stretches himself.

Gee! I ached to see that race and those two horses run, ached and dreaded it too. I didn't want to see either of our horses beaten. We had never sent a pair like that to the races before. Old men in Beckersville said so and the niggers said so. It was a fact.

Before the race I went over to the paddocks to see. I looked a last look at Middlestride, who isn't such a much standing in a paddock that way, then I went to see Sunstreak.

It was his day. I knew when I see him. I forgot all about being seen myself and walked right up. All the men from Beckersville were there and no one noticed me except Jerry Tillford. He saw me and something happened. I'll tell you about that.

I was standing looking at that horse and aching. In some way, I can't tell how, I knew just how Sunstreak felt inside. He was quiet and letting the niggers rub his legs and Mr Van Riddle himself put the saddle on, but he was just a raging torrent inside. He was like the water in the river at Niagara Falls just before it goes plunk down. That horse wasn't thinking about running. He don't have to think about that. He was just thinking about holding himself back 'til the time for the running came. I knew that. I could just in a way see right inside him. He was going to do some awful running and I knew it. He wasn't bragging or letting on much or prancing or making a fuss, but just waiting. I knew it and Jerry Tillford his trainer knew. I looked up and then that man and I looked into each other's eyes. Something happened to me. I guess I loved the man as much as I did the horse because he knew what I knew. Seemed to me there wasn't anything in the world but that man and the horse and me. I cried and Jerry Tillford had a shine in his eyes. Then I came away to the fence to wait for the race. The horse was better than me, more steadier, and now I know better than Jerry. He was the quietest and he had to do the running.

Sunstreak ran first of course and he busted the world's record for a mile. I've seen that if I never see anything more. Everything came out just as I expected. Middlestride got left at the post and was way back and closed up to be second, just as I knew he would. He'll get a world's record too some day. They can't skin the Beckersville country on horses.

I watched the race calm because I knew what would happen. I was sure. Hanley Turner and Henry Rieback and Tom Tumberton were all more excited than me.

A funny thing had happened to me. I was thinking about Jerry Tillford the trainer and how happy he was all through the race. I liked him that afternoon even more than I ever liked my own father. I almost forgot the horses thinking that way about him. It was because of what I had seen in his eyes as he stood in the paddocks beside Sunstreak before the race started. I knew he had been watching and working with Sunstreak since the horse was a baby colt, had taught him to run and be patient and when to let himself out and not to quit, never. I knew that for him it was like a mother seeing her child do something brave or wonderful. It was the first time I ever felt for a man like that.

After the race that night I cut out from Tom and Hanley and Henry. I wanted to be by myself and I wanted to be near Jerry Tillford if I could work it. Here is what happened.

The track in Saratoga is near the edge of town. It is all polished up and trees around, the evergreen kind, and grass and everything painted and nice. If you go past the track you get to a hard road made of asphalt for automobiles, and if you go along this for a few miles there is a road turns off to a little rummy-looking farmhouse set in a yard.

That night after the race I went along that road because I had seen Jerry and some other men go that way in an automobile. I didn't expect to find them. I walked for a ways and then sat down by a fence to think. It was the direction they went in. I wanted to be as near Jerry as I could. I felt close to him. Pretty soon I went up the side road – I don't know why – and came to the rummy farm-house. I was just lonesome to see Jerry, like wanting to see your father at night when you are a young kid. Just then an automobile came along and turned in. Jerry was in it and Henry Rieback's father, and Arthur Bedford from home, and Dave Williams and two other men I didn't know. They got out of the car and went into the house, all but Henry Rieback's father who quarreled with them and said he wouldn't go. It was only about nine o'clock, but they were all drunk and the rummy-looking farmhouse was a place for bad women to stay in. That's what it was. I crept up along a fence and looked through a window and saw.

It's what give me the fantods. I can't make it out. The women in the house were all ugly mean-looking women, not nice to look at or be near. They were homely too, except one who was tall and looked a little like the gelding Middlestride, but not clean like him, but with a hard ugly mouth. She had red hair. I saw everything plain. I got up by an old rose-bush by an open window and looked. The women had on loose dresses and sat around in chairs. The men came in and some sat on the women's laps. The place smelled rot-ten and there was rotten talk, the kind a kid hears around a livery stable in a town like Beckersville in the winter but don't ever expect to hear talked when there are women around. It was rotten. A nig-ger wouldn't go into such a place.

I looked at Jerry Tillford. I've told you how I had been feeling about him on account of his knowing what was going on inside of Sunstreak in the minute before he went to the post for the race in which he made a world's record.

Jerry bragged in that bad woman house as I know Sunstreak wouldn't never have bragged. He said that he made that horse, that it was him that won the race and made the record. He lied and bragged like a fool. I never heard such silly talk.

And then, what do you suppose he did! He looked at the woman in there, the one that was lean and hard-mouthed and looked a little like the gelding Middlestride, but not clean like him, and his eyes began to shine just as they did when he looked at me and at Sunstreak in the paddocks at the track in the afternoon. I stood there by the window – gee! – but I wished I hadn't gone away from the tracks, but had stayed with the boys and the niggers and the horses. The tall rotten-looking woman was between us just as Sun-streak was in the paddocks in the afternoon.

Then, all of a sudden, I began to hate that man. I wanted to scream and rush in the room and kill him. I never had such a feeling before. I was so mad clean through that I cried and my fists were doubled up so my finger-nails cut my hands.

And Jerry's eyes kept shining and he waved back and forth, and then he went and kissed that woman and I crept away and went back to the tracks and to bed and didn't sleep hardly any, and then next day I got the other kids to start home with me and never told them anything I seen.

I been thinking about it ever since. I can't make it out. Spring has come again and I'm nearly sixteen and go to the tracks mornings as always, and I see Sunstreak and Middlestride and a new colt named Strident I'll bet will lay them all out, but no one thinks so but me and two or three niggers.

But things are different. At the tracks the air don't taste as good or smell as good. It's because a man like Jerry Tillford, who knows what he does, could see a horse like Sunstreak run, and kiss a woman like that the same day. I can't make it out. Darn him, what did he want to do like that for? I keep thinking about it and it spoils looking at horses and smelling things and hearing niggers laugh and everything. Sometimes I'm so mad about it I want to fight someone. It gives me the fantods. What did he do it for? I want to know why.

A. E. COPPARD · 1878–1957

The Field of Mustard

On a windy afternoon in November they were gathering kindling in the Black Wood, Dinah Lock, Amy Hardwick, and Rose Olliver, three sere disvirgined women from Pollock's Cross. Mrs Lock wore clothes of dull butcher's blue, with a short jacket that affirmed her plumpness, but Rose and Amy had on long grey ulsters. All of them were about forty years old, and the wind and twigs had tousled their gaunt locks, for none had a hat upon her head. They did not go far beyond the margin of the wood, for the forest ahead of them swept high over a hill and was gloomy; behind them the slim trunks of beech, set in a sweet ruin of hoar and scattered leaf, and green briar nimbly fluttering, made a sort of palisade against the light of the open, which was grey, and a wide field of mustard which was yellow. The three women peered up into the trees for dead branches, and when they found any Dinah Lock, the vivacious woman full of shrill laughter, with a bosom as massive as her haunches, would heave up a rope with an iron bolt tied to one end. The bolted end would twine itself around the dead branch, the three women would tug, and after a sharp crack the quarry would fall; as often as not the women would topple over too. By and by they met an old hedger with a round belly belted low, and thin legs tied at each knee, who told them the time by his ancient watch, a stout timepiece which the women sportively admired.

'Come Christmas I'll have me a watch like that!' Mrs Lock called out. The old man looked a little dazed as he fumblingly replaced his chronometer. 'I will,' she continued, 'if the Lord spares me and the pig don't pine.'

'You . . . you don't know what you're talking about,' he said. 'That watch was my uncle's watch.'

'Who was he? I'd like one like it.'

'Was a sergeant-major in the lancers, fought under Sir Garnet Wolseley, and it was given to him.'

'What for?'

The hedger stopped and turned on them, 'Doing of his duty.'

'That all?' cried Dinah Lock. 'Well, I never got no watch for that a-much. Do you know what I see when I went to London? I see'd a watch in a bowl of water, it was glass, and there was a fish swimming round it. . . .'

'I don't believe it.'

'There was a fish swimming round it. . . .'

'I tell you I don't believe it. . . .'

'And the little hand was going on like Clackford Mill. That's the sort of watch I'll have me; none of your Sir Garney Wolsey's!'

'He was a noble Christian man, that was.'

'Ah! I suppose he slept wid Jesus?' yawped Dinah.

'No, he didn't,' the old man disdainfully spluttered. 'He never did. What a God's the matter wid ye?' Dinah cackled with laughter. 'Pah!' he cried, going away, 'great fat thing! Can't tell your guts from your elbows.'

Fifty yards farther on he turned and shouted some obscenity back at them, but they did not heed him; they had begun to make three faggots of the wood they had collected, so he put his fingers to his nose at them and shambled out to the road.

By the time Rose and Dinah were ready, Amy Hardwick, a small slow silent woman, had not finished bundling her faggot together.

'Come on, Amy,' urged Rose.

'Come on,' Dinah said.

'All right, wait a minute,' she replied listlessly.

'O God, that's death!' cried Dinah Lock, and heaving a great faggot to her shoulders she trudged off, followed by Rose with a like burden. Soon they were out of the wood, and crossing a highway they entered a footpath that strayed in a diagonal wriggle to the far corner of the field of mustard. In silence they journeyed until they came to that far corner, where there was a hedged bank. Here they flung their faggots down and sat upon them to wait for Amy Hardwick.

In front of them lay the field they had crossed, a sour scent rising faintly from its yellow blooms that quivered in the wind. Day was dull, the air chill, and the place most solitary. Beyond the field of mustard the eye could see little but forest. There were hills there, a vast curving trunk, but the Black Wood heaved itself effortlessly upon them and lay like a dark pall over the outline of a corpse. Huge and gloomy, the purple woods draped it all completely. A white necklace of a road curved below, where a score of telegraph poles, each crossed with a multitude of white florets, were dwarfed by the hugeness to effigies that resembled hyacinths. Dinah Lock gazed upon this scene whose melancholy, and not its grandeur, had suddenly invaded her; with elbows sunk in her fat thighs, and nursing her cheeks in her hands, she puffed the gloomy air, saying:

'O God, cradle and grave is all there is for we.'

'Where's Amy got to?' asked Rose.

'I could never make a companion of her, you know,' Dinah declared.

'Nor I,' said Rose, 'she's too sour and slow.'

'Her disposition's too serious. Of course, your friends are never what you want them to be, Rose. Sometimes they're better – most often they're worse. But it's such a mercy to have a friend at all; I like you, Rose; I wish you was a man.'

'I might just as well ha' been,' returned the other woman.

'Well, you'd ha' done better; but if you had a tidy little family like me you'd wish you hadn't got 'em.'

'And if you'd never had 'em you'd ha' wished you had.'

'Rose, that's the cussedness of nature, it makes a mock of you. I don't believe it's the Almighty at all, Rose. I'm sure it's the devil, Rose. Dear heart, my corn's a-giving me what-for; I wonder what that bodes?'

'It's restless weather,' said Rose. She was dark, tall, and not unbeautiful still, though her skin was harsh and her limbs angular. 'Get another month or two over – there's so many of these long dreary hours.'

'Ah, your time's too long, or it's too short, or it's just right but you're too old. Cradle and grave's my portion. Fat old thing he called me!'

Dinah's brown hair was ruffled across her pleasant face and she looked a little forlorn, but corpulence dispossessed her of tragedy. 'I be thin enough a-summertimes, for I lives light and sweats like a bridesmaid, but winters I'm fat as a hog.'

'What all have you to grumble at then?' asked Rose, who had slid to the ground and lay on her stomach staring up at her friend.

'My heart's young, Rose.'

'You've your husband.'

'He's no man at all since he was ill. A long time ill, he was. When he coughed, you know, his insides come up out of him like coffee grouts. Can you ever understand the meaning of that? Coffee! I'm growing old, but my heart's young.'

'So is mine, too: but you got a family, four children grown or growing.' Rose had snapped off a sprig of the mustard flower and was pressing and pulling the bloom in and out of her mouth. 'I've none, and never will have.' Suddenly she sat up, fumbled in her pocket, and produced her purse. She slipped the elastic band from it, and it gaped open. There were a few coins there and a scrap of paper folded. Rose took out the paper and smoothed it open under Dinah's curious gaze. 'I found something lying about at home the other day, and I cut this bit out of it.' In soft tones she began to read:

The day was void, vapid; time itself seemed empty. Come evening it rained softly. I sat by my fire turning over the leaves of a book, and I was dejected, until I came upon a little old-fashioned engraving at the bottom of a page. It imaged a procession of some angelic children in a garden, little placidly-naked substantial babes, with tiny bird-wings. One carried a bow, others a horn of plenty, or a hamper of fruit, or a set of reed-pipes. They were garlanded and full of grave joys. And at the sight of them a strange bliss flowed into me such as I had never known, and I thought this world was all a garden, though its light was hidden and its children not yet born.

Rose did not fold the paper up; she crushed it in her hand and lay down again without a word.

'Huh, I tell you, Rose, a family's a torment. I never wanted mine. God love, Rose, I'd lay down my life for 'em; I'd cut myself into fourpenny pieces so they shouldn't come to harm; if one of 'em was to die I'd sorrow to my grave. But I know, I know, I know I never wanted 'em, they were not for me, I was just an excuse for their blundering into the world. Somehow I've been duped, and every woman born is duped so, one ways or another in the end. I had my sport with my man, but I ought never to have married. Now I'd love to begin all over again, and as God's my maker, if it weren't for those children, I'd be gone off out into the world again tomorrow, Rose. But I dunno what 'ud become o' me.'

The wind blew strongly athwart the yellow field, and the odour of mustard rushed upon the brooding women. Protestingly the breeze flung itself upon the forest; there was a gliding cry among the rocking pinions as of some lost wave seeking a forgotten shore. The angular faggot under Dinah Lock had begun to vex her; she too sunk to the ground and lay beside Rose Olliver, who asked:

'And what 'ud become of your old man?'

For a few moments Dinah Lock paused. She too took a sprig of the mustard and fondled it with her lips. 'He's no man now, the illness feebled him, and the virtue's gone; no man at all since two years, and bald as a piece of cheese – I like a hairy man, like . . . do you remember Rufus Blackthorn, used to be gamekeeper here?'

Rose stopped playing with her flower. 'Yes, I knew Rufus Blackthorn.'

'A fine bold man that was! Never another like him hereabouts, not in England neither; not in the whole world – though I've heard some queer talk of those foreigners, Australians, Chinymen. Well!'

'Well?' said Rose.

'He was a devil.' Dinah Lock began to whisper. 'A perfect devil; I can't say no fairer than that. I wish I could, but I can't.'

'O come,' protested Rose, 'he was a kind man. He'd never see anybody want for a thing.'

'No,' there was playful scorn in Dinah's voice; 'he'd shut his eyes first!'

'Not to a woman he wouldn't, Dinah.'

'Ah! Well – perhaps – he was good to women.'

'I can tell you things as would surprise you,' murmured Rose.

'You! But – well – no, no. I could tell *you* things as you wouldn't believe. Me and Rufus! We was – O my – yes!'

'He *was* handsome.'

'O, a pretty man!' Dinah acceded warmly. 'Black as coal and bold as a fox. I'd been married nigh on ten years when he first set foot in these parts. I'd got three children then. He used to give me a saucy word whenever he saw me, for I liked him and he knew it. One Whitsun Monday I was home all alone, the children were gone somewhere, and Tom was away boozing. I was putting some plants in our garden – I loved a good flower in those days – I wish the world was all a garden, but now my Tom he digs 'em up, digs everything up proper and never puts 'em back. Why, we had a crocus, once! And as I was doing that planting someone walked by the garden in such a hurry. I looked up and there was Rufus, all dressed up to the nines, and something made me call out to him. "Where be you off to in that flaming hurry," I says. "Going to a wedding," says he. "Shall I come with 'ee?" I says. "Ah yes," he says, very glad; "but hurry up, for I be sharp set and all." So I run in-a-doors and popped on my things and off we went to Jim Pickering's wedding over at Clackford Mill. When Jim brought the bride home from church that Rufus got hold of a gun and fired it off up chimney, and down come soot, the bushels of it! All over the room, and a chimney-pot burst and rattled down the tiles into a p'rambulator. What a rumbullion that was! But no one got angry – there was plenty of drink and we danced all the afternoon. Then we come home together again through the woods. O Lord – I said to myself – I shan't come out with you ever again, and that's what I said to Rufus Blackthorn. But I did, you know! I woke up in bed that night, and the moon shone on me dreadful – I thought the place was afire. But there was Tom snoring, and I lay and thought of me and Rufus in the wood, till I could have jumped out into the moonlight, stark, and flown over the chimney. I didn't sleep any more. And I saw Rufus the next night, and the night after that, often, often. Whenever I went out I left Tom the cupboardful – that's all he troubled about. I was mad after Rufus, and while that caper was on I couldn't love my husband. No.'

'No?' queried Rose.

'Well, I pretended I was ill, and I took my young Katey to sleep with me, and give Tom her bed. He didn't seem to mind, but after a while I found he was gallivanting after other women. Course, I soon put a stopper on that. And then – what do you think? Bless me if Rufus weren't up to the same tricks! Deep as the sea, that man. Faithless, you know, but such a bold one.'

Rose lay silent, plucking wisps of grass; there was a wry smile on her face.

'Did ever he tell you the story of the man who was drowned?' she asked at length. Dinah shook her head. Rose continued. 'Before he came here he was keeper over in that Oxfordshire, where the river goes right through the woods, and he slept in a boathouse moored to the bank. Some gentleman was drowned near there, an accident it was, but they couldn't find the body. So they offered a reward of ten pound for it to be found. . . .'

'Ten, ten pounds!'

'Yes. Well, all the watermen said the body wouldn't come up for ten days. . . .'

'No more they do.'

'It didn't. And so late one night – it was moonlight – some men in a boat kept on hauling and poking round the house where Rufus was, and he heard 'em say "It must be here, it must be here," and Rufus shouts out to them, "Course he's here! I got him in bed with me!" '

'Aw!' chuckled Dinah.

'Yes, and next day he got the ten pounds, because he *had* found the body and hidden it away.'

'Feared nothing,' said Dinah, 'nothing at all; he'd have been rude to Satan. But he was very delicate with his hands, sewing and things like that. I used to say to him, "Come, let me mend your coat," or whatever it was, but he never would, always did such things of himself. "I don't allow no female to patch my clothes," he'd say, " 'cos they works with a red-hot needle and a burning thread." And he used to make fine little slippers out of reeds.'

'Yes,' Rose concurred, 'he made me a pair.'

'You!' Dinah cried. 'What – were you . . . ?'

Rose turned her head away. 'We was all cheap to him,' she said softly, 'cheap as old rags; we was like chaff before him.'

Dinah Lock lay still, very still, ruminating; but whether in old grief or new rancour Rose was not aware, and she probed no further. Both were quiet, voiceless, recalling the past delirium. They shivered, but did not rise. The wind increased in the forest, its hoarse breath sorrowed in the yellow field, and swift masses of cloud flowed and twirled in a sky without end and full of gloom.

'Hallo!' cried a voice, and there was Amy beside them, with a faggot almost overwhelming her. 'Shan't stop now,' she said, 'for I've got this faggot perched just right, and I shouldn't ever get it up again. I found a shilling in the 'ood, you,' she continued shrilly and gleefully. 'Come along to my house after tea, and we'll have a quart of stout.'

'A shilling, Amy!' cried Rose.

'Yes,' called Mrs Hardwick, trudging steadily on. 'I tried to find the fellow to it, but no more luck. Come and wet it after tea!'

'Rose,' said Dinah, 'come on.' She and Rose with much circumstance heaved up their faggots and tottered after, but by then Amy was turned out of sight down the little lane to Pollock's Cross.

'Your children will be home,' said Rose as they went along, 'they'll be looking out for you.'

'Ah, they'll want their bellies filling!'

'It must be lovely a-winter's nights, you setting round your fire with 'em, telling tales, and brushing their hair.'

'Ain't you got a fire of your own indoors,' grumbled Dinah.

'Yes.'

'Well, why don't you set by it then!' Dinah's faggot caught the briars of a hedge that overhung, and she tilted round with a mild oath. A covey of partridges feeding beyond scurried away with ruckling cries. One foolish bird dashed into the telegraph wires and dropped dead.

'They're good children, Dinah, yours are. And they make you a valentine, and give you a ribbon on your birthday, I expect?'

'They're naught but a racket from cock-crow till the old man snores – and then it's worse!'

'Oh, but the creatures, Dinah!'

'You . . . you got your quiet trim house, and only your man to look after, a kind man, and you'll set with him in the evenings and play your dominoes or your draughts, and he'll look at you – the nice man – over the board and stroke your hand now and again.'

The wind hustled the two women closer together, and as they stumbled under their burdens Dinah Lock stretched out a hand and touched the other woman's arm. 'I like you, Rose, I wish you was a man.'

Rose did not reply. Again they were quiet, voiceless, and thus in fading light they came to their homes. But how windy, dispossessed and ravaged, roved the darkening world! Clouds were borne frantically across the heavens, as if in a rout of battle, and the lovely earth seemed to sigh in grief at some calamity all unknown to men.

Grace

Two gentlemen who were in the lavatory at the time tried to lift him up: but he was quite helpless. He lay curled up at the foot of the stairs down which he had fallen. They succeeded in turning him over. His hat had rolled a few yards away and his clothes were smeared with the filth and ooze of the floor on which he had lain, face downwards. His eyes were closed and he breathed with a grunting noise. A thin stream of blood trickled from the corner of his mouth.

These two gentlemen and one of the curates carried him up the stairs and laid him down again on the floor of the bar. In two minutes he was surrounded by a ring of men. The manager of the bar asked everyone who he was and who was with him. No one knew who he was, but one of the curates said he had served the gentleman with a small rum.

'Was he by himself?' asked the manager.

'No, sir. There was two gentlemen with him.'

'And where are they?'

No one knew; a voice said:

'Give him air. He's fainted.'

The ring of onlookers distended and closed again elastically. A dark medal of blood had formed itself near the man's head on the tessellated floor. The manager, alarmed by the grey pallor of the man's face, sent for a policeman.

His collar was unfastened and his necktie undone. He opened his eyes for an instant, sighed and closed them again. One of the gentlemen who had carried him upstairs held a dinged silk hat in his hand. The manager asked repeatedly did no one know who the injured man was or where had his friends gone. The door of the bar opened and an immense constable entered. A crowd which had followed him down the laneway collected outside the door, struggling to look in through the glass panels.

The manager at once began to narrate what he knew. The constable, a young man with thick immobile features, listened. He moved his head slowly to right and left and from the manager to the person on the floor, as if he feared to be the victim of some delusion. Then he drew off his glove, produced a small book from his waist, licked the lead of his pencil and made ready to indite. He asked in a suspicious provincial accent:

'Who is the man? What's his name and address?'

A young man in a cycling-suit cleared his way through the ring of bystanders. He knelt down promptly beside the injured man and called for water. The constable knelt down also to help. The young man washed the blood from the injured man's mouth and then called for some brandy. The constable repeated the order in an authoritative voice until a curate came running with the glass. The brandy was forced down the man's throat. In a few seconds he opened his eyes and looked about him. He looked at the circle of faces and then, understanding, strove to rise to his feet.

'You're all right now?' asked the young man in the cycling-suit.

'Sha, 's nothing,' said the injured man, trying to stand up.

He was helped to his feet. The manager said something about a hospital and some of the bystanders gave advice. The battered silk hat was placed on the man's head. The constable asked:

'Where do you live?'

The man, without answering, began to twirl the ends of his moustache. He made light of his accident. It was nothing, he said: only a little accident. He spoke very thickly.

'Where do you live?' repeated the constable.

The man said they were to get a cab for him. While the point was being debated a tall agile gentleman of fair complexion, wearing a long yellow ulster, came from the far end of the bar. Seeing the spectacle, he called out:

'Hallo, Tom, old man! What's the trouble?'

'Sha, 's nothing,' said the man.

The newcomer surveyed the deplorable figure before him and then turned to the constable, saying:

'It's all right, constable. I'll see him home.'

The constable touched his helmet and answered:

'All right, Mr Power!'

'Come now, Tom,' said Mr Power, taking his friend by the arm. 'No bones broken. What? Can you walk?'

The young man in the cycling-suit took the man by the other arm and the crowd divided.

'How did you get yourself into this mess?' asked Mr Power.

'The gentleman fell down the stairs,' said the young man.

'I' 'ery 'uch o'liged to you, sir,' said the injured man.

'Not at all.'

''an't we have a little . . .?'

'Not now. Not now.'

The three men left the bar and the crowd sifted through the doors into the laneway. The manager brought the constable to the stairs to inspect the scene of the accident. They agreed that the gentleman must have missed his footing. The customers returned to the counter, and a curate set about removing the traces of blood from the floor.

When they came out into Grafton Street, Mr Power whistled for an outsider. The injured man said again as well as he could:

'I' 'ery 'uch o'liged to you, sir. I hope we'll 'eet again. 'y na'e is Kernan.'

The shock and the incipient pain had partly sobered him.

'Don't mention it,' said the young man.

They shook hands. Mr Kernan was hoisted on to the car and, while Mr Power was giving directions to the carman, he expressed his gratitude to the young man and regretted that they could not have a little drink together.

'Another time,' said the young man.

The car drove off towards Westmoreland Street. As it passed the Ballast Office the clock showed half-past nine. A keen east wind hit them, blowing from the mouth of the river. Mr Kernan was huddled together with cold. His friend asked him to tell how the accident had happened.

'I 'an't 'an,' he said, ''y 'ongue is hurt.'

'Show.'

The other leaned over the wheel of the car and peered into Mr Kernan's mouth but he could not see. He struck a match and, sheltering it in the shell of his hands, peered again into the mouth which Mr Kernan opened obediently. The swaying movement of the car brought the match to and from the opened mouth. The lower teeth and gums were covered with clotted blood and a minute piece of the tongue seemed to have been bitten off. The match was blown out.

'That's ugly,' said Mr Power.

'Sha, 's nothing,' said Mr Kernan, closing his mouth and pulling the collar of his filthy coat across his neck.

Mr Kernan was a commercial traveller of the old school which believed in the dignity of its calling. He had never been seen in the city without a silk hat of some decency and a pair of gaiters. By grace of these two articles of clothing, he said, a man could always pass muster. He carried on the tradition of his Napoleon, the great Blackwhite, whose memory he evoked at times by legend and mimicry. Modern business methods had spared him only so far as to allow him a little office in Crowe Street, on the window blind of which was written the name of his firm with the address – London, E.C. On the mantelpiece of this little office a little leaden battalion of canisters was drawn up and on the table before the window stood four or five china bowls which were usually half full of a black liquid. From these bowls Mr Kernan tasted tea. He took a mouthful, drew it up, saturated his palate with it and then spat it forth into the grate. Then he paused to judge.

Mr Power, a much younger man, was employed in the Royal Irish Constabulary Office in Dublin Castle. The arc of his social rise intersected the arc of his friend's decline, but Mr Kernan's decline was mitigated by the fact that certain of those friends who had known him at his highest point of success still esteemed him as a character. Mr Power was one of these friends. His inexplicable debts were a byword in his circle; he was a debonair young man.

The car halted before a small house on the Glasnevin road and Mr Kernan was helped into the house. His wife put him to bed, while Mr Power sat downstairs in the kitchen asking the children where they went to school and what book they were in. The children – two girls and a boy, conscious of their father's helplessness and of their mother's absence, began some horseplay with him. He was surprised at their manners and at their accents, and his brow grew thoughtful. After a while Mrs Kernan entered the kitchen, exclaiming:

'Such a sight! Oh, he'll do for himself one day and that's the holy alls of it. He's been drinking since Friday.'

Mr Power was careful to explain to her that he was not responsible, that he had come on the scene by the merest accident. Mrs Kernan, remembering Mr Power's good offices during domestic quarrels, as well as many small, but opportune loans, said:

'O, you needn't tell me that, Mr Power. I know you're a friend of his, not like some of the others he does be with. They're all right so long as he has money in his pocket to keep him out from his wife and family. Nice friends! Who was he with tonight, I'd like to know?'

Mr Power shook his head but said nothing.

'I'm so sorry,' she continued, 'that I've nothing in the house to offer you. But if you wait a minute, I'll send round to Fogarty's, at the corner.'

Mr Power stood up.

'We were waiting for him to come home with the money. He never seems to think he has a home at all.'

'O, now, Mrs Kernan,' said Mr Power, 'we'll make him turn over a new leaf. I'll talk to Martin. He's the man. We'll come here one of these nights and talk it over.'

She saw him to the door. The carman was stamping up and down the footpath, and swinging his arms to warm himself.

'It's very kind of you to bring him home,' she said.

'Not at all,' said Mr Power.

He got up on the car. As it drove off he raised his hat to her gaily.

'We'll make a new man of him,' he said. 'Good-night, Mrs Kernan.'

Mrs Kernan's puzzled eyes watched the car till it was out of sight. Then she withdrew them, went into the house and emptied her husband's pockets.

She was an active, practical woman of middle age. Not long before she had celebrated her silver wedding and renewed her intimacy with her husband by waltzing with him to Mr Power's accompaniment. In her days of courtship, Mr Kernan had seemed to her a not ungallant figure: and she still hurried to the chapel door whenever a wedding was reported and, seeing the bridal pair, recalled with vivid pleasure how she had passed out of the Star of the Sea Church in Sandymount, leaning on the arm of a jovial well-fed man, who was dressed smartly in a frock-coat and lavender trousers and carried a silk hat gracefully balanced upon his other arm. After three weeks she had found a wife's life irksome and, later on, when she was beginning to find it unbearable, she had become a mother. The part of mother presented to her no insuperable difficulties and for twenty-five years she had kept house shrewdly for her husband. Her two eldest sons were launched. One was in a draper's shop in Glasgow and the other was clerk to a tea-merchant in Belfast. They were good sons, wrote regularly and sometimes sent home money. The other children were still at school.

Mr Kernan sent a letter to his office next day and remained in bed. She made beef-tea for him and scolded him roundly. She accepted his frequent intemperance as part of the climate, healed him dutifully whenever he was sick and always tried to make him eat a breakfast. There were worse husbands. He had never been violent since the boys had grown up, and she knew that he would walk to the end of Thomas Street and back again to book even a small order.

Two nights after, his friends came to see him. She brought them up to his bedroom, the air of which was impregnated with a personal odour, and gave them chairs at the fire. Mr Kernan's tongue, the occasional stinging pain of which had made him somewhat irritable during the day, became more polite. He sat propped up in the bed by pillows and the little colour in his puffy cheeks made them resemble warm cinders. He apologized to his guests for the disorder of the room, but at the same time looked at them a little proudly, with a veteran's pride.

He was quite unconscious that he was the victim of a plot which his friends, Mr Cunningham, Mr M'Coy and Mr Power had disclosed to Mrs Kernan in the parlour. The idea had been Mr Power's, but its development was entrusted to Mr Cunningham. Mr Kernan came of Protestant stock and, though he had been converted to the Catholic faith at the time of his marriage, he had not been in the pale of the Church for twenty years. He was fond, moreover, of giving side-thrusts at Catholicism.

Mr Cunningham was the very man for such a case. He was an elder colleague of Mr Power. His own domestic life was not very happy. People had great sympathy with him, for it was known that he had married an unpresentable woman who was an incurable drunkard. He had set up house for her six times; and each time she had pawned the furniture on him.

Everyone had respect for poor Martin Cunningham. He was a thoroughly sensible man, influential and intelligent. His blade of human knowledge, natural astuteness particularized by long association with cases in the police courts, had been tempered by brief immersions in the waters of general philosophy. He was well informed. His friends bowed to his opinions and considered that his face was like Shakespeare's.

When the plot had been disclosed to her, Mrs Kernan had said:

'I leave it all in your hands, Mr Cunningham.'

After a quarter of a century of married life, she had very few illusions left. Religion for her was a habit, and she suspected that a man of her husband's age would not change greatly before death. She was tempted to see a curious appropriateness in his accident and, but that she did not wish to seem bloody-minded, she would have told the gentlemen that Mr Kernan's tongue would not suffer by being shortened. However, Mr Cunningham was a capable man; and religion was religion. The scheme might do good and, at least, it could do no harm. Her beliefs were not extravagant. She believed steadily in the Sacred Heart as the most generally useful of all Catholic devotions and approved of the sacraments. Her faith was bounded by her kitchen, but, if she was put to it, she could believe also in the banshee and in the Holy Ghost.

The gentlemen began to talk of the accident. Mr Cunningham said that he had once known a similar case. A man of seventy had bitten off a piece of his tongue during an epileptic fit and the tongue had filled in again, so that no one could see a trace of the bite.

'Well, I'm not seventy,' said the invalid.

'God forbid,' said Mr Cunningham.

'It doesn't pain you now?' asked Mr M'Coy.

Mr M'Coy had been at one time a tenor of some reputation. His wife, who had been a soprano, still taught young children to play the piano at low terms. His line of life had not been the shortest distance between two points and for short periods he had been driven to live by his wits. He had been a clerk in the Midland Railway, a canvasser for advertisements for *The Irish Times* and for *The Freeman's Journal*, a town traveller for a coal firm on commission, a private inquiry agent, a clerk in the office of the Sub-Sheriff, and he had recently become secretary to the City Coroner. His new office made him professionally interested in Mr Kernan's case.

'Pain? Not much,' answered Mr Kernan. 'But it's so sickening. I feel as if I wanted to retch off.'

'That's the booze,' said Mr Cunningham firmly.

'No,' said Mr Kernan. 'I think I caught cold on the car. There's something keeps coming into my throat, phlegm or — '

'Mucus,' said Mr M'Coy.

'It keeps coming like from down in my throat; sickening thing.'

'Yes, yes,' said Mr M'Coy, 'that's the thorax.'

He looked at Mr Cunningham and Mr Power at the same time with an air of challenge. Mr Cunningham nodded his head rapidly and Mr Power said:

'Ah, well, all's well that ends well.'

'I'm very much obliged to you, old man,' said the invalid.

Mr Power waved his hand.

'Those other two fellows I was with — '

'Who were you with?' asked Mr Cunningham.

'A chap. I don't know his name. Damn it now, what's his name? Little chap with sandy hair. . . .'

'And who else?'

'Harford.'

'Hm,' said Mr Cunningham.

When Mr Cunningham made that remark, people were silent. It was known that the speaker had secret sources of information. In this case the monosyllable had a moral intention. Mr Harford sometimes formed one of a little detachment which left the city shortly after noon on Sunday with the purpose of arriving as soon as possible at some public house on the outskirts of the city where its members duly qualified themselves as bona fide travellers. But his fellow-travellers had never consented to overlook his origin. He had begun life as an obscure financier by lending small sums of money to workmen at usurious interest. Later on he had become the partner of a very fat, short gentleman, Mr Goldberg, in the Liffey Loan Bank. Though he had never embraced more than the Jewish ethical code, his fellow-Catholics, whenever they had smarted in person or by proxy under his exactions, spoke of him bitterly as an Irish Jew and an illiterate, and saw divine disapproval of usury made manifest through the person of his idiot son. At other times they remembered his good points.

'I wonder where did he go to,' said Mr Kernan.

He wished the details of the incident to remain vague. He wished his friends to think there had been some mistake, that Mr Harford and he had missed each other. His friends, who knew quite well Mr Harford's manners in drinking, were silent. Mr Power said again:

'All's well that ends well.'

Mr Kernan changed the subject at once.

'That was a decent young chap, that medical fellow,' he said. 'Only for him — '

'O, only for him,' said Mr Power, 'it might have been a case of seven days, without the option of a fine.'

'Yes, yes,' said Mr Kernan, trying to remember. 'I remember now there was a policeman. Decent young fellow, he seemed. How did it happen at all?'

'It happened that you were peloothered, Tom,' said Mr Cunningham gravely.

'True bill,' said Mr Kernan, equally gravely.

'I suppose you squared the constable, Jack,' said Mr M'Coy.

Mr Power did not relish the use of his Christian name. He was not straight-laced, but he could not forget that Mr M'Coy had recently made a crusade in search of valises and portmanteaus to enable Mrs M'Coy to fulfil imaginary engagements in the country. More than he resented the fact that he had been victimized, he resented such low playing of the game. He answered the question, therefore, as if Mr Kernan had asked it.

The narrative made Mr Kernan indignant. He was keenly conscious of his citizenship, wished to live with his city on terms mutually honourable and resented any affront put upon him by those whom he called country bumpkins.

'Is this what we pay rates for?' he asked. 'To feed and clothe these ignorant bostooms . . . and they're nothing else.'

Mr Cunningham laughed. He was a Castle official only during office hours.

'How could they be anything else, Tom?' he said.

He assumed a thick, provincial accent and said in a tone of command:

'65, catch your cabbage!'

Everyone laughed. Mr M'Coy, who wanted to enter the conversation by any door, pretended that he had never heard the story. Mr Cunningham said:

'It is supposed – they say, you know – to take place in the depot where they get these thundering big country fellows, omadhauns, you know, to drill. The sergeant makes them stand in a row against the wall and hold up their plates.' He illustrated the story by grotesque gestures.

'At dinner, you know. Then he has a bloody big bowl of cabbage before him on the table and a bloody big spoon like a shovel. He takes up a wad of cabbage on the spoon and pegs it across the room and the poor devils have to try and catch it on their plates:

65, *catch your cabbage.'*

Everyone laughed again: but Mr Kernan was somewhat indignant still. He talked of writing a letter to the papers.

'These yahoos coming up here,' he said, 'think they can boss the people. I needn't tell you, Martin, what kind of men they are.'

Mr Cunningham gave a qualified assent.

'It's like everything else in this world,' he said. 'You get some bad ones and you get some good ones.'

'O yes, you get some good ones, I admit,' said Mr Kernan, satisfied.

'It's better to have nothing to say to them,' said Mr M'Coy. 'That's my opinion!'

Mrs Kernan entered the room and, placing a tray on the table, said:

'Help yourselves, gentlemen.'

Mr Power stood up to officiate, offering her his chair. She declined it, saying she was ironing downstairs, and, after having exchanged a nod with Mr Cunningham behind Mr Power's back, prepared to leave the room. Her husband called out to her:

'And have you nothing for me, duckie?'

'O, you! The back of my hand to you!' said Mrs Kernan tartly.

Her husband called after her:

'Nothing for poor little hubby!'

He assumed such a comical face and voice that the distribution of the bottles of stout took place amid general merriment.

The gentlemen drank from their glasses, set the glasses again on the table and paused. Then Mr Cunningham turned towards Mr Power and said casually:

'On Thursday night, you said, Jack?'

'Thursday, yes,' said Mr Power.

'Righto!' said Mr Cunningham promptly.

'We can meet in M'Auley's,' said Mr M'Coy. 'That'll be the most convenient place.'

'But we mustn't be late,' said Mr Power earnestly, 'because it is sure to be crammed to the doors.'

'We can meet at half-seven,' said Mr M'Coy.

'Righto!' said Mr Cunningham.

'Half-seven at M'Auley's be it!'

There was a short silence. Mr Kernan waited to see whether he would be taken into his friends' confidence. Then he asked:

'What's in the wind?'

'O, it's nothing,' said Mr Cunningham. 'It's only a little matter that we're arranging about for Thursday.'

'The opera, is it?' said Mr Kernan.

'No, no,' said Mr Cunningham in an evasive tone, 'it's just a little . . . spiritual matter.'

'Oh,' said Mr Kernan.

There was silence again. Then Mr Power said, point-blank:

'To tell you the truth, Tom, we're going to make a retreat.'

'Yes, that's it,' said Mr Cunningham, 'Jack and I and M'Coy here – we're all going to wash the pot.'

He uttered the metaphor with a certain homely energy and, encouraged by his own voice, proceeded:

'You see, we may as well all admit we're a nice collection of scoundrels, one and all. I say, one and all,' he added with gruff charity and turning to Mr Power. 'Own up now!'

'I own up,' said Mr Power.

'And I own up,' said Mr M'Coy.

'So we're going to wash the pot together,' said Mr Cunningham.

A thought seemed to strike him. He turned suddenly to the invalid and said:

'D'ye know what, Tom, has just occurred to me? You might join in and we'd have a four-handed reel.'

'Good idea,' said Mr Power. 'The four of us together.'

Mr Kernan was silent. The proposal conveyed very little meaning to his mind, but, understanding that some spiritual agencies were about to concern themselves on his behalf, he thought he owed it to his dignity to show a stiff neck. He took no part in the conversation for a long while, but listened, with an air of calm enmity, while his friends discussed the Jesuits.

'I haven't such a bad opinion of the Jesuits,' he said, intervening at length. 'They're an educated order. I believe they mean well, too.'

'They're the grandest order in the Church, Tom,' said Mr Cunningham, with enthusiasm. 'The General of the Jesuits stands next to the Pope.'

'There's no mistake about it,' said Mr M'Coy, 'if you want a thing well done and no flies about, you go to a Jesuit. They're the boyos have influence. I'll tell you a case in point. . . .'

'The Jesuits are a fine body of men,' said Mr Power.

'It's a curious thing,' said Mr Cunningham, 'about the Jesuit Order. Every other order of the Church had to be reformed at some time or other, but the Jesuit Order was never once reformed. It never fell away.'

'Is that so?' asked Mr M'Coy.

'That's a fact,' said Mr Cunningham. 'That's history.'

'Look at their church, too,' said Mr Power. 'Look at the congregation they have.'

'The Jesuits cater for the upper classes,' said Mr M'Coy.

'Of course,' said Mr Power.

'Yes,' said Mr Kernan. 'That's why I have a feeling for them. It's some of those secular priests, ignorant, bumptious —'

'They're all good men,' said Mr Cunningham, 'each in his own way. The Irish priesthood is honoured all the world over.'

'O yes,' said Mr Power.

'Not like some of the other priesthoods on the continent,' said Mr M'Coy, 'unworthy of the name.'

'Perhaps you're right,' said Mr Kernan, relenting.

'Of course I'm right,' said Mr. Cunningham. 'I haven't been in the world all this time and seen most sides of it without being a judge of character.'

The gentlemen drank again, one following another's example. Mr Kernan seemed to be weighing something in his mind. He was impressed. He had a high opinion of Mr Cunningham as a judge of character and as a reader of faces. He asked for particulars.

'O, it's just a retreat, you know,' said Mr Cunningham. 'Father Purdon is giving it. It's for businessmen, you know.'

'He won't be too hard on us, Tom,' said Mr Power persuasively.

'Father Purdon? Father Purdon?' said the invalid.

'O, you must know him, Tom,' said Mr Cunningham, stoutly. 'Fine, jolly fellow! He's a man of the world like ourselves.'

'Ah, . . . yes. I think I know him. Rather red face; tall.'

'That's the man.'

'And tell me, Martin. . . . Is he a good preacher?'

'Munno. . . . It's not exactly a sermon, you know. It's just a kind of friendly talk, you know, in a commonsense way.'

Mr Kernan deliberated. Mr M'Coy said:

'Father Tom Burke, that was the boy!'

'O, Father Tom Burke,' said Mr Cunningham, 'that was a born orator. Did you ever hear him, Tom?'

'Did I ever hear him!' said the invalid, nettled. 'Rather! I heard him. . . .'

'And yet they say he wasn't much of a theologian,' said Mr Cunningham.

'Is that so?' said Mr M'Coy.

'O, of course, nothing wrong, you know. Only sometimes, they say, he didn't preach what was quite orthodox.'

'Ah! . . . he was a splendid man,' said Mr M'Coy.

'I heard him once,' Mr Kernan continued. 'I forget the subject of his discourse now. Crofton and I were in the back of the . . . pit, you know . . . the —'

'The body,' said Mr Cunningham.

'Yes, in the back near the door. I forget now what. . . . O yes, it was on the Pope, the late Pope. I remember it well. Upon my word it was magnificent, the style of the oratory. And his voice! God! hadn't he a voice! *The Prisoner of the Vatican*, he called him. I remember Crofton saying to me when we came out — '

'But he's an Orangeman, Crofton, isn't he?' said Mr Power.

''Course he is,' said Mr Kernan, 'and a damned decent Orangeman, too. We went into Butler's in Moore Street – faith, I was genuinely moved, tell you the God's truth – and I remember well his very words. *Kernan*, he said, *we worship at different altars*, he said, *but our belief is the same*. Struck me as very well put.'

'There's a good deal in that,' said Mr Power. 'There used always be crowds of Protestants in the chapel where Father Tom was preaching.'

'There's not much difference between us,' said Mr M'Coy. 'We both believe in — '

He hesitated for a moment.

' . . . in the Redeemer. Only they don't believe in the Pope and in the mother of God.'

'But, of course,' said Mr Cunningham quietly and effectively, 'our religion is *the* religion, the old, original faith.'

'Not a doubt of it,' said Mr Kernan warmly.

Mrs Kernan came to the door of the bedroom and announced:

'Here's a visitor for you!'

'Who is it?'

'Mr Fogarty.'

'O, come in! come in!'

A pale, oval face came forward into the light. The arch of its fair trailing moustache was repeated in the fair eyebrows looped above pleasantly astonished eyes. Mr Fogarty was a modest grocer. He had failed in business in a licensed house in the city because his financial condition had constrained him to tie himself to second-class distillers and brewers. He had opened a small shop on Glasnevin Road where, he flattered himself, his manners would ingratiate him with the housewives of the district. He bore himself with a certain grace, complimented little children and spoke with a neat enunciation. He was not without culture.

Mr Fogarty brought a gift with him, a half-pint of special whisky. He inquired politely for Mr Kernan, placed his gift on the table and sat down with the company on equal terms. Mr Kernan appreciated the gift all the more since he was aware that there was a small account for groceries unsettled between him and Mr Fogarty. He said:

'I wouldn't doubt you, old man. Open that, Jack, will you?'

Mr Power again officiated. Glasses were rinsed and five small measures of whisky were poured out. This new influence enlivened the conversation. Mr Fogarty, sitting on a small area of the chair, was specially interested.

'Pope Leo XIII,' said Mr Cunningham, 'was one of the lights of the age. His great idea, you know, was the union of the Latin and Greek Churches. That was the aim of his life.'

'I often heard he was one of the most intellectual men in Europe,' said Mr Power. 'I mean, apart from his being Pope.'

'So he was,' said Mr Cunningham, 'if not *the* most so. His motto, you know, as Pope, was *Lux upon Lux* – *Light upon Light.*'

'No, no,' said Mr Fogarty eagerly. 'I think you're wrong there. It was *Lux in Tenebris*, I think – *Light in Darkness.*'

'O yes,' said Mr M'Coy, '*Tenebrae.*'

'Allow me,' said Mr Cunningham positively, 'it was *Lux upon Lux*. And Pius IX his predecessor's motto was *Crux upon Crux* – that is, *Cross upon Cross* – to show the difference between their two pontificates.'

The inference was allowed. Mr Cunningham continued.

'Pope Leo, you know, was a great scholar and poet.'

'He had a strong face,' said Mr Kernan.

'Yes,' said Mr Cunningham. 'He wrote Latin poetry.'

'Is that so?' said Mr Fogarty.

Mr M'Coy tasted his whisky contentedly and shook his head

with a double intention, saying:

'That's no joke, I can tell you.'

'We didn't learn that, Tom,' said Mr Power, following Mr M'Coy's example, 'when we went to the penny-a-week school.'

'There was many a good man went to the penny-a-week school with a sod of turf under his oxter,' said Mr Kernan sententiously. 'The old system was the best: plain honest education. None of your modern trumpery. . . .'

'Quite right,' said Mr Power.

'No superfluities,' said Mr Fogarty.

He enunciated the word and then drank gravely.

'I remember reading,' said Mr Cunningham, 'that one of Pope Leo's poems was on the invention of the photograph – in Latin, of course.'

'On the photograph!' exclaimed Mr Kernan.

'Yes,' said Mr Cunningham.

He also drank from his glass.

'Well, you know,' said Mr M'Coy, 'isn't the photograph wonderful when you come to think of it?'

'O, of course,' said Mr Power, 'great minds can see things.'

'As the poet says: *Great minds are very near to madness*,' said Mr Fogarty.

Mr Kernan seemed to be troubled in mind. He made an effort to recall the Protestant theology on some thorny points and in the end addressed Mr Cunningham.

'Tell me, Martin,' he said. 'Weren't some of the popes – of course, not our present man, or his predecessor, but some of the old popes – not exactly . . . you know . . . up to the knocker?'

There was a silence. Mr Cunningham said:

'O, of course, there were some bad lots. . . . But the astonishing thing is this. Not one of them, not the biggest drunkard, not the most . . . out-and-out ruffian, not one of them ever preached *ex cathedra* a word of false doctrine. Now isn't that an astonishing thing?'

'That is,' said Mr Kernan.

'Yes, because when the Pope speaks *ex cathedra*,' Mr Fogarty explained, 'he is infallible.'

'Yes,' said Mr Cunningham.

'O, I know about the infallibility of the Pope. I remember I was younger then. . . . Or was it that — ?'

Mr Fogarty interrupted. He took up the bottle and helped the others to a little more. Mr M'Coy, seeing that there was not enough to go round, pleaded that he had not finished his first measure. The others accepted under protest. The light music of whisky falling into glasses made an agreeable interlude.

'What's that you were saying, Tom?' asked Mr M'Coy.

'Papal infallibility,' said Mr Cunningham, 'that was the greatest scene in the whole history of the Church.'

'How was that, Martin?' asked Mr Power.

Mr Cunningham held up two thick fingers.

'In the sacred college, you know, of cardinals and archbishops and bishops there were two men who held out against it while the others were all for it. The whole conclave except these two was unanimous. No! They wouldn't have it!'

'Ha!' said Mr M'Coy.

'And they were a German cardinal by the name of Dolling . . . or Dowling . . . or —'

'Dowling was no German, and that's a sure five,' said Mr Power, laughing.

'Well, this great German cardinal, whatever his name was, was one; and the other was John MacHale.'

'What?' cried Mr Kernan. 'Is it John of Tuam?'

'Are you sure of that now?' asked Mr Fogarty dubiously. 'I thought it was some Italian or American.'

'John of Tuam', repeated Mr Cunningham, 'was the man.'

He drank and the other gentlemen followed his lead. Then he resumed: 'There they were at it, all the cardinals and bishops and archbishops from all the ends of the earth and these two fighting dog and devil until at last the Pope himself stood up and declared infallibility a dogma of the Church *ex cathedra*. On the very moment John MacHale, who had been arguing and arguing against it, stood up and shouted out with the voice of a lion: "*Credo!*"'

'*I believe!*' said Mr Fogarty.

'*Credo!*' said Mr Cunningham. 'That showed the faith he had. He submitted the moment the Pope spoke.'

'And what about Dowling?' asked Mr M'Coy.

'The German cardinal wouldn't submit. He left the Church.'

Mr Cunningham's words had built up the vast image of the Church in the minds of his hearers. His deep, raucous voice had thrilled them as it uttered the word of belief and submission. When

Mrs Kernan came into the room, drying her hands, she came into a solemn company. She did not disturb the silence, but leaned over the rail at the foot of the bed.

'I once saw John MacHale,' said Mr Kernan, 'and I'll never forget it as long as I live.'

He turned towards his wife to be confirmed.

'I often told you that?'

Mrs Kernan nodded.

'It was at the unveiling of Sir John Gray's statue. Edmund Dwyer Gray was speaking, blathering away, and here was this old fellow, crabbed-looking old chap, looking at him from under his bushy eyebrows.'

Mr Kernan knitted his brows and, lowering his head like an angry bull, glared at his wife.

'God!' he exclaimed, resuming his natural face, 'I never saw such an eye in a man's head. It was as much as to say: *I have you properly taped, my lad.* He had an eye like a hawk.'

'None of the Grays was any good,' said Mr Power.

There was a pause again. Mr Power turned to Mrs Kernan and said with abrupt joviality:

'Well, Mrs Kernan, we're going to make your man here a good holy pious and God-fearing Roman Catholic.'

He swept his arm round the company inclusively.

'We're all going to make a retreat together and confess our sins – and God knows we want it badly.'

'I don't mind,' said Mr Kernan, smiling a little nervously.

Mrs Kernan thought it would be wiser to conceal her satisfaction. So she said:

'I pity the poor priest that has to listen to your tale.'

Mr Kernan's expression changed.

'If he doesn't like it,' he said bluntly, 'he can . . . do the other thing. I'll just tell him my little tale of woe. I'm not such a bad fellow —'

Mr Cunningham intervened promptly.

'We'll all renounce the devil', he said, 'together, not forgetting his works and pomps.'

'Get behind me, Satan!' said Mr Fogarty, laughing and looking at the others.

Mr Power said nothing. He felt completely outgeneralled. But a pleased expression flickered across his face.

'All we have to do,' said Mr Cunningham, 'is to stand up with lighted candles in our hands and renew our baptismal vows.'

'O, don't forget the candle, Tom,' said Mr M'Coy, 'whatever you do.'

'What?' said Mr Kernan. 'Must I have a candle?'

'O yes,' said Mr Cunningham.

'No, damn it all,' said Mr Kernan sensibly, 'I draw the line there. I'll do the job right enough. I'll do the retreat business and confession, and . . . all that business. But . . . no candles! No, damn it all, I bar the candles!'

He shook his head with farcical gravity.

'Listen to that!' said his wife.

'I bar the candles,' said Mr Kernan, conscious of having created an effect on his audience and continuing to shake his head to and fro. 'I bar the magic-lantern business.'

Everyone laughed heartily.

'There's a nice Catholic for you!' said his wife.

'No candles!' repeated Mr Kernan obdurately. 'That's off!'

The transept of the Jesuit Church in Gardiner Street was almost full; and still at every moment gentlemen entered from the side door and, directed by the lay brother, walked on tiptoe along the aisles until they found seating accommodation. The gentlemen were all well dressed and orderly. The light of the lamps of the church fell upon an assembly of black clothes and white collars, relieved here and there by tweeds, on dark mottled pillars of green marble and on lugubrious canvases. The gentlemen sat in the benches, having hitched their trousers slightly above their knees and laid their hats in security. They sat well back and gazed formally at the distant speck of red light which was suspended before the high altar.

In one of the benches near the pulpit sat Mr Cunningham and Mr Kernan. In the bench behind sat Mr M'Coy alone: and in the bench behind him sat Mr Power and Mr Fogarty. Mr M'Coy had tried unsuccessfully to find a place in the bench with the others, and, when the party had settled down in the form of a quincunx he had tried unsuccessfully to make comic remarks. As these had not been well received, he had desisted. Even he was sensible of the decorous atmosphere and even he began to respond to the religious stimulus. In a whisper, Mr Cunningham drew Mr Kernan's attention to Mr Harford, the moneylender, who sat some distance off, and to Mr Fanning, the registration agent and mayor maker of the city, who was sitting immediately under the pulpit beside one of the newly elected councillors of the ward. To the right sat old Michael Grimes, the owner of three pawnbroker's shops, and Dan Hogan's nephew, who was up for the job in the Town Clerk's office. Farther in front sat Mr Hendrick, the chief reporter of *The Freeman's Journal*, and poor O'Carroll, an old friend of Mr Kernan's, who had been at one time a considerable commercial figure. Gradually, as he recognized familiar faces, Mr Kernan began to feel more at home. His hat, which had been rehabilitated by his wife, rested upon his knees. Once or twice he pulled down his cuffs with one hand while he held the brim of his hat lightly, but firmly, with the other hand.

A powerful-looking figure, the upper part of which was draped with a white surplice, was observed to be struggling up into the pulpit. Simultaneously the congregation unsettled, produced handkerchiefs and knelt upon them with care. Mr Kernan followed the general example. The priest's figure now stood upright in the pulpit, two-thirds of its bulk, crowned by a massive red face, appearing above the balustrade.

Father Purdon knelt down, turned towards the red speck of light and, covering his face with his hands, prayed. After an interval, he uncovered his face and rose. The congregation rose also and settled again on its benches. Mr Kernan restored his hat to its original position on his knee and presented an attentive face to the preacher. The preacher turned back each wide sleeve of his surplice with an elaborate large gesture and slowly surveyed the array of faces. Then he said:

'For the children of this world are wiser in their generation than the children of light. Wherefore make unto yourselves friends out of the mammon of iniquity so that when you die they may receive you into everlasting dwellings. . . .'

Father Purdon developed the text with resonant assurance. It was one of the most difficult texts in all the Scriptures, he said, to interpret properly. It was a text which might seem to the casual observer at variance with the lofty morality elsewhere preached by Jesus Christ. But, he told his hearers, the text had seemed to him specially adapted for the guidance of those whose lot it was to lead the life of the world and who yet wished to lead that life not in the

manner of worldlings. It was a text for businessmen and professional men. Jesus Christ, with His divine understanding of every
cranny of our human nature, understood that all men were not
called to the religious life, that by far the vast majority were forced
to live in the world, and, to a certain extent, for the world: and in
this sentence He designed to give them a word of counsel, setting
before them as exemplars in the religious life those very worship-
pers of Mammon who were of all men the least solicitous in matters religious.

He told his hearers that he was there that evening for no terrifying, no extravagant purpose; but as a man of the world speaking
to his fellow-men. He came to speak to businessmen and he would
speak to them in a businesslike way. If he might use the metaphor,
he said, he was their spiritual accountant; and he wished each and
every one of his hearers to open his books, the books of his spiritual
life, and see if they tallied accurately with conscience.

Jesus Christ was not a hard taskmaster. He understood our little
failings, understood the weakness of our poor fallen nature, understood the temptations of this life. We might have had, we all had
from time to time, our temptations: we might have, we all had, our
failings. But one thing only, he said, he would ask of his hearers.
And that was: to be straight and manly with God. If their accounts
tallied in every point to say:

'Well, I have verified my accounts. I find all well.'

But if, as might happen, there were some discrepancies, to admit
the truth, to be frank and say like a man:

'Well, I have looked into my accounts. I find this wrong and this
wrong. But, with God's grace, I will rectify this and this. I will set
right my accounts.'

D. H. LAWRENCE · 1885–1930

The Rocking-Horse Winner

There was a woman who was beautiful, who started with all the advantages, yet she had no luck. She married for love, and the love turned to dust. She had bonny children, yet she felt they had been thrust upon her, and she could not love them. They looked at her coldly, as if they were finding fault with her. And hurriedly she felt she must cover up some fault in herself. Yet what it was that she must cover up she never knew. Nevertheless, when her children were present, she always felt the centre of her heart go hard. This troubled her, and in her manner she was all the more gentle and anxious for her children, as if she loved them very much. Only she herself knew that at the centre of her heart was a hard little place that could not feel love, no, not for anybody. Everybody else said of her: 'She is such a good mother. She adores her children.' Only she herself, and her children themselves, knew it was not so. They read it in each other's eyes.

There were a boy and two little girls. They lived in a pleasant house, with a garden, and they had discreet servants, and felt themselves superior to anyone in the neighbourhood.

Although they lived in style, they felt always an anxiety in the house. There was never enough money. The mother had a small income, and the father had a small income, but not nearly enough for the social position which they had to keep up. The father went in to town to some office. But though he had good prospects, these prospects never materialized. There was always the grinding sense of the shortage of money, though the style was always kept up.

At last the mother said, 'I will see if *I* can't make something.' But she did not know where to begin. She racked her brains, and tried this thing and the other, but could not find anything successful. The failure made deep lines come into her face. Her children were growing up, they would have to go to school. There must be more money, there must be more money. The father, who was always very handsome and expensive in his tastes, seemed as if he never *would* be able to do anything worth doing. And the mother, who had a great belief in herself, did not succeed any better, and her tastes were just as expensive.

And so the house came to be haunted by the unspoken phrase: *There must be more money! There must be more money!* The children could hear it all the time, though nobody said it aloud. They heard it at Christmas, when the expensive and splendid toys filled the nursery. Behind the shining modern rocking-horse, behind the smart doll's-house, a voice would start whispering: 'There *must* be more money! There *must* be more money!' And the children would stop playing, to listen for a moment. They would look into each other's eyes to see if they had all heard. And each one saw in the eyes of the other two that they too had heard. 'There *must* be more money! There *must* be more money!'

It came whispering from the springs of the still-swaying rocking-horse, and even the horse, bending his wooden, champing head, heard it. The big doll, sitting so pink and smirking in her new pram, could hear it quite plainly, and seemed to be smirking all the more self-consciously because of it. The foolish puppy, too, that took the place of the teddy-bear, he was looking so extraordinarily foolish for no other reason but that he heard the secret whisper all over the house: 'There *must* be more money!'

Yet nobody ever said it aloud. The whisper was everywhere, and therefore no one spoke it. Just as no one ever says: 'We are breathing!' in spite of the fact that breath is coming and going all the time.

'Mother,' said the boy Paul one day, 'why don't we keep a car of our own? Why do we always use uncle's, or else a taxi?'

'Because we're the poor members of the family,' said the mother.

'But why *are* we, mother?'

'Well – I suppose', she said slowly and bitterly, 'it's because your father has no luck.'

The boy was silent for some time.

'Is luck money, mother?' he asked, rather timidly.

'No, Paul. Not quite. It's what causes you to have money.'

'Oh!' said Paul vaguely. 'I thought when Uncle Oscar said *filthy lucker*, it meant money.'

'*Filthy lucre* does mean money,' said the mother. 'But it's lucre, not luck.'

'Oh!' said the boy, 'Then what *is* luck, mother?'

'It's what causes you to have money. If you're lucky you have money. That's why it's better to be born lucky than rich. If you're rich, you may lose your money. But if you're lucky, you will always get more money.'

'Oh! Will you? And is father not lucky?'

'Very unlucky, I should say,' she said bitterly.

The boy watched her with unsure eyes.

'Why?' he asked.

'I don't know. Nobody ever knows why one person is lucky and another unlucky.'

'Don't they? Nobody at all? Does *nobody* know?'

'Perhaps God. But He never tells.'

'He ought to, then. And aren't you lucky either, mother?'

'I can't be, if I married an unlucky husband.'

'But by yourself, aren't you?'

'I used to think I was, before I married. Now I think I am very unlucky indeed.'

'Why?'

'Well – never mind! Perhaps I'm not really,' she said.

The child looked at her, to see if she meant it. But he saw, by the lines of her mouth, that she was only trying to hide something from him.

'Well, anyhow,' he said stoutly, 'I'm a lucky person.'

'Why?' said his mother, with a sudden laugh.

He stared at her. He didn't even know why he had said it.

'God told me,' he asserted, brazening it out.

'I hope He did, dear!' she said, again with a laugh, but rather bitter.

'He did, mother!'

'Excellent!' said the mother, using one of her husband's exclamations.

The boy saw she did not believe him; or rather, that she paid no attention to his assertion. This angered him somewhere, and made him want to compel her attention.

He went off by himself, vaguely, in a childish way, seeking for the clue to 'luck'. Absorbed, taking no heed of other people, he went about with a sort of stealth, seeking inwardly for luck. He wanted luck, he wanted it, he wanted it. When the two girls were playing dolls in the nursery, he would sit on his big rocking-horse, charging madly into space, with a frenzy that made the little girls peer at him uneasily. Wildly the horse careered, the waving dark hair of the boy tossed, his eyes had a strange glare in them. The little girls dared not speak to him.

When he had ridden to the end of his mad little journey, he climbed down and stood in front of his rocking-horse, staring fixedly into its lowered face. Its red mouth was slightly open, its big eye was wide and glassy-bright.

'Now!' he would silently command the snorting steed. 'Now, take me to where there is luck! Now take me!'

And he would slash the horse on the neck with the little whip he had asked Uncle Oscar for. He *knew* the horse could take him to where there was luck, if only he forced it. So he would mount again, and start on his furious ride, hoping at last to get there. He knew he could get there.

'You'll break your horse, Paul!' said the nurse.

'He's always riding like that! I wish he'd leave off!' said his elder sister Joan.

But he only glared down on them in silence. Nurse gave him up. She could make nothing of him. Anyhow he was growing beyond her.

One day his mother and his Uncle Oscar came in when he was on one of his furious rides. He did not speak to them.

'Hallo, you young jockey! Riding a winner?' said his uncle.

'Aren't you growing too big for a rocking-horse? You're not a very little boy any longer, you know,' said his mother.

But Paul only gave a blue glare from his big, rather close-set eyes. He would speak to nobody when he was in full tilt. His mother watched him with an anxious expression on her face.

At last he suddenly stopped forcing his horse into the mechanical gallop, and slid down.

'Well, I got there!' he announced fiercely, his blue eyes still flaring, and his sturdy long legs straddling apart.

'Where did you get to?' asked his mother.

'Where I wanted to go,' he flared back at her.

'That's right, son!' said Uncle Oscar. 'Don't you stop till you get there. What's the horse's name?'

'He doesn't have a name,' said the boy.

'Gets on without all right?' asked the uncle.

'Well, he has different names. He was called Sansovino last week.'

'Sansovino, eh? Won the Ascot. How did you know his name?'

'He always talks about horse-races with Bassett,' said Joan.

The uncle was delighted to find that his small nephew was posted with all the racing news. Bassett, the young gardener, who had been wounded in the left foot in the war and had got his present job through Oscar Cresswell, whose batman he had been, was a perfect blade of the 'turf'. He lived in the racing events, and the small boy lived with him.

Oscar Cresswell got it all from Bassett.

'Master Paul comes and asks me, so I can't do more than tell him, sir,' said Bassett, his face terribly serious, as if he were speaking of religious matters.

'And does he ever put anything on a horse he fancies?'

'Well – I don't want to give him away – he's a young sport, a fine sport, sir. Would you mind asking him himself? He sort of takes a pleasure in it, and perhaps he'd feel I was giving him away, sir, if you don't mind.'

Bassett was serious as a church.

The uncle went back to his nephew, and took him off for a ride in the car.

'Say, Paul, old man, do you ever put anything on a horse?' the uncle asked.

The boy watched the handsome man closely.

'Why, do you think I oughtn't to?' he parried.

'Not a bit of it! I thought perhaps you might give me a tip for the Lincoln.'

The car sped on into the country, going down to Uncle Oscar's place in Hampshire.

'Honour bright?' said the nephew.

'Honour bright, son!' said the uncle.

'Well, then, Daffodil.'

'Daffodil! I doubt it, sonny. What about Mirza?'

'I only know the winner,' said the boy. 'That's Daffodil.'

'Daffodil, eh?'

There was a pause. Daffodil was an obscure horse comparatively.

'Uncle!'

'Yes, son?'

'You won't let it go any further, will you? I promised Bassett.'

'Bassett be damned, old man! What's he got to do with it?'

'We're partners. We've been partners from the first. Uncle, he lent me my first five shillings, which I lost. I promised him, honour bright, it was only between me and him; only you gave me that ten-shilling note I started winning with, so I thought you were lucky. You won't let it go any further, will you?'

The boy gazed at his uncle from those big, hot, blue eyes, set rather close together. The uncle stirred and laughed uneasily.

'Right you are, son! I'll keep your tip private. Daffodil, eh? How much are you putting on him?'

'All except twenty pounds,' said the boy. 'I keep that in reserve.'

The uncle thought it a good joke.

'You keep twenty pounds in reserve, do you, you young romancer? What are you betting, then?'

'I'm betting three hundred,' said the boy gravely. 'But it's between you and me, Uncle Oscar! Honour bright?'

The uncle burst into a roar of laughter.

'It's between you and me all right, you young Nat Gould,' he said, laughing. 'But where's your three hundred?'

'Bassett keeps it for me. We're partners.'

'You are, are you! And what is Bassett putting on Daffodil?'

'He won't go quite as high as I do, I expect. Perhaps he'll go a hundred and fifty.'

'What, pennies?' laughed the uncle.

'Pounds,' said the child, with a surprised look at his uncle. 'Bassett keeps a bigger reserve than I do.'

Between wonder and amusement Uncle Oscar was silent. He pursued the matter no further, but he determined to take his nephew with him to the Lincoln races.

'Now, son,' he said, 'I'm putting twenty on Mirza, and I'll put five for you on any horse you fancy. What's your pick?'

'Daffodil, uncle.'

'No, not the fiver on Daffodil!'

'I should if it was my own fiver,' said the child.

'Good! Good! Right you are! A fiver for me and a fiver for you on Daffodil.'

The child had never been to a race-meeting before, and his eyes were blue fire. He pursed his mouth tight, and watched. A Frenchman just in front had put his money on Lancelot. Wild with excitement, he flayed his arms up and down, yelling '*Lancelot! Lancelot!*' in his French accent.

Daffodil came in first, Lancelot second, Mirza third. The child, flushed and with eyes blazing, was curiously serene. His uncle brought him four five-pound notes, four to one.

'What am I to do with these?' he cried, waving them before the boy's eyes.

'I suppose we'll talk to Bassett,' said the boy. 'I expect I have fifteen hundred now; and twenty in reserve; and this twenty.'

His uncle studied him for some moments.

'Look here, son!' he said. 'You're not serious about Bassett and that fifteen hundred, are you?'

'Yes, I am. But it's between you and me, uncle. Honour bright!'

'Honour bright all right, son! But I must talk to Bassett.'

'If you'd like to be a partner, uncle, with Bassett and me, we could all be partners. Only, you'd have to promise, honour bright, uncle, not to let it go beyond us three. Bassett and I are lucky, and you must be lucky, because it was your ten shillings I started winning with. . . .'

Uncle Oscar took both Bassett and Paul into Richmond Park for an afternoon, and there they talked.

'It's like this, you see, sir,' Bassett said. 'Master Paul would get me talking about racing events, spinning yarns, you know, sir. And he was always keen on knowing if I'd made or if I'd lost. It's about a year since, now, that I put five shillings on Blush of Dawn for him: and we lost. Then the luck turned, with that ten shillings he had from you: that we put on Singhalese. And since that time, it's been pretty steady, all things considering. What do you say, Master Paul.'

'We're all right when we're sure,' said Paul. 'It's when we're not quite sure that we go down.'

'Oh, but we're careful then,' said Bassett.

'But when are you *sure*?' smiled Uncle Oscar.

'It's Master Paul, sir,' said Bassett, in a secret, religious voice. 'It's as if he had it from heaven. Like Daffodil, now, for the Lincoln. That was as sure as eggs.'

'Did you put anything on Daffodil?' asked Oscar Cresswell.

'Yes, sir. I made my bit.'

'And my nephew?'

Bassett was obstinately silent, looking at Paul.

'I made twelve hundred, didn't I, Bassett? I told uncle I was putting three hundred on Daffodil.'

'That's right,' said Bassett, nodding.

'But where's the money?' asked the uncle.

'I keep it safe locked up, sir. Master Paul he can have it any minute he likes to ask for it.'

'What, fifteen hundred pounds?'

'And twenty! And *forty*, that is, with the twenty he made on the course.'

'It's amazing!' said the uncle.

'If Master Paul offers you to be partners, sir, I would, if I were you: if you'll excuse me,' said Bassett.

Oscar Cresswell thought about it.

'I'll see the money,' he said.

They drove home again, and, sure enough, Bassett came round to the garden-house with fifteen hundred pounds in notes. The twenty pounds reserve was left with Joe Glee, in the Turf Commission deposit.

'You see, it's all right, uncle, when I'm *sure!* Then we go strong, for all we're worth. Don't we, Bassett?'

'We do that, Master Paul.'

'And when are you sure?' said the uncle, laughing.

'Oh, well, sometimes I'm *absolutely* sure, like about Daffodil,' said the boy; 'and sometimes I have an idea; and sometimes I haven't even an idea, have I, Bassett? Then we're careful, because we mostly go down.'

'You do, do you! And when you're sure, like about Daffodil, what makes you sure, sonny?'

'Oh, well, I don't know,' said the boy uneasily. 'I'm sure, you know, uncle; that's all.'

'It's as if he had it from heaven, sir,' Bassett reiterated.

'I should say so!' said the uncle.

But he became a partner. And when the Leger was coming on Paul was 'sure' about Lively Spark, which was a quite inconsiderable horse. The boy insisted on putting a thousand on the horse, Bassett went for five hundred, and Oscar Cresswell two hundred. Lively Spark came in first, and the betting had been ten to one against him. Paul had made ten thousand.

'You see,' he said, 'I was absolutely sure of him.'

Even Oscar Cresswell had cleared two thousand.

'Look here, son,' he said, 'this sort of thing makes me nervous.'

'It needn't, uncle! Perhaps I shan't be sure again for a long time.'

'But what are you going to do with your money?' asked the uncle.

'Of course,' said the boy, 'I started it for mother. She said she had no luck because father is unlucky, so I thought if *I* was lucky, it might stop whispering.'

'What might stop whispering?'

'Our house. I *hate* our house for whispering.'

'What does it whisper?'

'Why – why' – the boy fidgeted – 'why, I don't know. But it's always short of money, you know, uncle.'

'I know it, son, I know it.'

'You know people send mother writs, don't you, uncle?'

'I'm afraid I do,' said the uncle.

'And then the house whispers, like people laughing at you behind your back. It's awful, that is! I thought if I was lucky — '

'You might stop it,' added the uncle.

The boy watched him with big blue eyes, that had an uncanny cold fire in them, and he said never a word.

'Well, then!' said the uncle. 'What are we doing?'

'I shouldn't like mother to know I was lucky,' said the boy.

'Why not, son?'

'She'd stop me.'

'I don't think she would.'

'Oh!' – and the boy writhed in an odd way – 'I *don't* want her to know, uncle.'

'All right, son! We'll manage it without her knowing.'

They managed it very easily. Paul, at the other's suggestion, handed over five thousand pounds to his uncle, who deposited it with the family lawyer, who was then to inform Paul's mother that a relative had put five thousand pounds into his hands, which sum was to be paid out a thousand pounds at a time, on the mother's birthday, for the next five years.

'So she'll have a birthday present of a thousand pounds for five successive years,' said Uncle Oscar. 'I hope it won't make it all the harder for her later.'

Paul's mother had her birthday in November. The house had been 'whispering' worse than ever lately, and, even in spite of his luck, Paul could not bear up against it. He was very anxious to see the effect of the birthday letter, telling his mother about the thousand pounds.

When there were no visitors, Paul now took his meals with his parents, as he was beyond the nursery control. His mother went into town nearly every day. She had discovered that she had an odd knack of sketching furs and dress materials, so she worked secretly in the studio of a friend who was the chief 'artist' for the leading drapers. She drew the figures of ladies in furs and ladies in silk and sequins for the newspaper advertisements. This young woman artist earned several thousand pounds a year, but Paul's mother only made several hundreds, and she was again dissatisfied. She so wanted to be first in something, and she did not succeed, even in making sketches for drapery advertisements.

She was down to breakfast on the morning of her birthday. Paul watched her face as she read her letters. He knew the lawyer's letter. As his mother read it, her face hardened and became more expressionless. Then a cold, determined look came on her mouth. She hid the letter under the pile of others, and said not a word about it.

'Didn't you have anything nice in the post for your birthday, mother?' said Paul.

'Quite moderately nice,' she said, her voice cold and absent.

She went away to town without saying more.

But in the afternoon Uncle Oscar appeared. He said Paul's mother had had a long interview with the lawyer, asking if the whole five thousand could not be advanced at once, as she was in debt.

'What do you think, uncle?' said the boy.

'I leave it to you, son.'

'Oh, let her have it, then! We can get some more with the other,' said the boy.

'A bird in the hand is worth two in the bush, laddie!' said Uncle Oscar.

'But I'm sure to *know* for the Grand National; or the Lincolnshire; or else the Derby. I'm sure to know for *one* of them,' said Paul.

So Uncle Oscar signed the agreement, and Paul's mother touched the whole five thousand. Then something very curious happened. The voices in the house suddenly went mad, like a chorus of frogs on a spring evening. There were certain new furnishings, and Paul had a tutor. He was *really* going to Eton, his father's school, in the following autumn. There were flowers in the winter, and a blossoming of the luxury Paul's mother had been used to. And yet the voices in the house, behind the sprays of mimosa and almond-blossom, and from under the piles of iridescent cushions, simply trilled and screamed in a sort of ecstasy: 'There *must* be more money! Oh-h-h; there *must* be more money. Oh, now, now-w! Now-w-w – there *must* be more money! – more than ever! More than ever!'

It frightened Paul terribly. He studied away at his Latin and Greek with his tutors. But his intense hours were spent with Bassett. The Grand National had gone by: he had not 'known', and had lost a hundred pounds. Summer was at hand. He was in agony for the Lincoln. But even for the Lincoln he didn't 'know', and he lost fifty pounds. He became wild-eyed and strange, as if something were going to explode in him.

'Let it alone, son! Don't you bother about it!' urged Uncle Oscar. But it was as if the boy couldn't really hear what his uncle was saying.

'I've got to know for the Derby! I've got to know for the Derby!' the child reiterated, his big blue eyes blazing with a sort of madness.

His mother noticed how overwrought he was.

'You'd better go to the seaside. Wouldn't you like to go now to the seaside, instead of waiting? I think you'd better,' she said, looking down at him anxiously, her heart curiously heavy because of him.

But the child lifted his uncanny blue eyes.

'I couldn't possibly go before the Derby, mother!' he said. 'I couldn't possibly!'

'Why not?' she said, her voice becoming heavy when she was opposed. 'Why not? You can still go from the seaside to see the Derby with your Uncle Oscar, if that's what you wish. No need for you to wait here. Besides, I think you care too much about these races. It's a bad sign. My family has been a gambling family, and you won't know till you grow up how much damage it has done. But it has done damage. I shall have to send Bassett away, and ask Uncle Oscar not to talk racing to you, unless you promise to be reasonable about it: go away to the seaside and forget it. You're all nerves!'

'I'll do what you like mother, so long as you don't send me away till after the Derby,' the boy said.

'Send you away from where? Just from this house?'

'Yes,' he said, gazing at her.

'Why, you curious child, what makes you care about this house so much, suddenly? I never knew you loved it.'

He gazed at her without speaking. He had a secret within a secret, something he had not divulged, even to Bassett or to his Uncle Oscar.

But his mother, after standing undecided and a little bit sullen for some moments, said:

'Very well, then! Don't go to the seaside till after the Derby, if you don't wish it. But promise me you won't let your nerves go to pieces. Promise you won't think so much about horse-racing and *events*, as you call them!'

'Oh, no,' said the boy casually. 'I won't think much about them, mother. You needn't worry. I wouldn't worry, mother, if I were you.'

'If you were me and I were you,' said his mother, 'I wonder what we *should* do!'

'But you know you needn't worry, mother, don't you?' the boy repeated.

'I should be awfully glad to know it,' she said wearily.

'Oh, well, you *can*, you know. I mean, you *ought* to know you needn't worry,' he insisted.

'Ought I? Then I'll see about it,' she said.

Paul's secret of secrets was his wooden horse, that which had no name. Since he was emancipated from a nurse and a nursery-governess, he had had his rocking-horse removed to his own bedroom at the top of the house.

'Surely, you're too big for a rocking-horse!' his mother had remonstrated.

'Well, you see, mother, till I can have a *real* horse, I like to have *some* sort of animal about,' had been his quaint answer.

'Do you feel he keeps you company?' she laughed.

'Oh, yes! He's very good, he always keeps me company, when I'm there,' said Paul.

So the horse, rather shabby, stood in an arrested prance in the boy's bedroom.

The Derby was drawing near, and the boy grew more and more tense. He hardly heard what was spoken to him, he was very frail, and his eyes were really uncanny. His mother had sudden strange seizures of uneasiness about him. Sometimes, for half an hour, she would feel a sudden anxiety about him that was almost anguish. She wanted to rush to him at once, and know he was safe.

Two nights before the Derby, she was at a big party in town, when one of her rushes of anxiety about her boy, her first-born, gripped her heart till she could hardly speak. She fought with the feeling, might and main, for she believed in common sense. But it was too strong. She had to leave the dance and go downstairs to telephone to the country. The children's nursery-governess was terribly surprised and startled at being rung up in the night.

'Are the children all right, Miss Wilmot?'

'Oh, yes, they are quite all right.'

'Master Paul? Is he all right?'

'He went to bed as right as a trivet. Shall I run up and look at him?'

'No,' said Paul's mother reluctantly. 'No! Don't trouble. It's all right. Don't sit up. We shall be home fairly soon.' She did not want her son's privacy intruded upon.

'Very good,' said the governess.

It was about one o'clock when Paul's mother and father drove up to their house. All was still. Paul's mother went to her room and slipped off her white fur cloak. She had told her maid not to wait up for her. She heard her husband downstairs, mixing a whisky and soda.

And then, because of the strange anxiety at her heart, she stole upstairs to her son's room. Noiselessly she went along the upper corridor. Was there a faint noise? What was it?

She stood, with arrested muscles, outside his door, listening. There was a strange, heavy, and yet not loud noise. Her heart stood still. It was a soundless noise, yet rushing and powerful. Something huge, in violent, hushed motion. What was it? What in God's name was it? She ought to know. She felt that she knew the noise. She knew what it was.

Yet she could not place it. She couldn't say what it was. And on and on it went, like a madness.

Softly, frozen with anxiety and fear, she turned the door-handle. The room was dark. Yet in the space near the window, she heard and saw something plunging to and fro. She gazed in fear and amazement.

Then suddenly she switched on the light, and saw her son, in his green pyjamas, madly surging on the rocking-horse. The blaze of light suddenly lit him up, as he urged the wooden horse, and lit her up, as she stood, blonde, in her dress of pale green and crystal, in the doorway.

'Paul!' she cried, 'Whatever are you doing?'

'It's Malabar!' he screamed, in a powerful, strange voice. 'It's Malabar!'

His eyes blazed at her for one strange and senseless second, as he ceased urging his wooden horse. Then he fell with a crash to the ground, and she, all her tormented motherhood flooding upon her, rushed to gather him up.

But he was unconscious, and unconscious he remained, with some brain-fever. He talked and tossed, and his mother sat stonily by his side.

'Malabar! It's Malabar! Bassett, Bassett, I *know*! It's Malabar!'

So the child cried, trying to get up and urge the rocking-horse that gave him his inspiration.

'What does he mean by Malabar?' asked the heart-frozen mother.

'I don't know,' said the father stonily.

'What does he mean by Malabar?' she asked her brother Oscar.

'It's one of the horses running for the Derby,' was the answer.

And, in spite of himself, Oscar Cresswell spoke to Bassett, and himself put a thousand on Malabar: at fourteen to one.

The third day of the illness was critical: they were waiting for a change. The boy, with his rather long, curly hair, was tossing ceaselessly on the pillow. He neither slept nor regained consciousness, and his eyes were like blue stones. His mother sat, feeling her heart had gone, turned actually into a stone.

In the evening, Oscar Cresswell did not come, but Bassett sent a message, saying could he come up for one moment, just one moment? Paul's mother was very angry at the intrusion, but on second thoughts she agreed. The boy was the same. Perhaps Bassett might bring him to consciousness.

The gardener, a shortish fellow with a little brown moustache, and sharp little brown eyes, tiptoed into the room, touched his imaginary cap to Paul's mother, and stole to the bedside, staring with glittering, smallish eyes at the tossing, dying child.

'Master Paul!' he whispered. 'Master Paul! Malabar came in first all right, a clean win. I did as you told me. You've made over seventy thousand pounds, you have; you've got over eighty thousand. Malabar came in all right, Master Paul.'

'Malabar! Malabar! Did I say Malabar, mother? Did I say Malabar? Do you think I'm lucky, mother? I knew Malabar, didn't I? Over eighty thousand pounds! I call that lucky, don't you, mother? Over eighty thousand pounds! I knew, didn't I know I knew? Malabar came in all right. If I ride my horse till I'm sure, then I tell you, Bassett, you can go as high as you like. Did you go for all you were worth, Bassett?'

'I went a thousand on it, Master Paul.'

'I never told you, mother, that if I can ride my horse, and *get there*, then I'm absolutely sure – oh, absolutely! Mother, did I ever tell you? I *am* lucky!'

'No, you never did,' said the mother.

But the boy died in the night.

And even as he lay dead, his mother heard her brother's voice saying to her: 'My God, Hester, you're eighty-odd thousand to the good, and a poor devil of a son to the bad. But, poor devil, poor devil, he's best gone out of a life where he rides his rocking-horse to find a winner.'

Who Dealt?

You know, this is the first time Tom and I have been with real friends since we were married. I suppose you'll think it's funny for me to call you *my* friends when we've never met before, but Tom has talked about you so much and how much he thought of you and how crazy he was to see you and everything – well, it's just as if I'd known you all my life, like he has.

We've got our little crowd out there, play bridge and dance with them; but of course we've only been there three months, at least I have, and people you've known that length of time, well, it isn't like knowing people all your life, like you and Tom. How often I've heard Tom say he'd give any amount of money to be with Arthur and Helen, and how bored he was out there with just poor little me and his new friends!

Arthur and Helen, Arthur and Helen – he talks about you so much that it's a wonder I'm not jealous; especially of you, Helen. You must have been his real pal when you were kids.

Nearly all of his kid books, they have your name in front – to Thomas Cannon from Helen Bird Strong. This is a wonderful treat for him to see you! And a treat for me, too. Just think, I've at last met the wonderful Helen and Arthur! You must forgive me calling you by your first names; that's how I always think of you and I simply can't say Mr and Mrs Gratz.

No, thank you, Arthur; no more. Two is my limit and I've already exceeded it, with two cocktails before dinner and now this. But it's a special occasion, meeting Tom's best friends. I bet Tom wishes he could celebrate too, don't you, dear? Of course he could if he wanted to, but when he once makes up his mind to a thing, there's nothing in the world can shake him. He's got the strongest will-power of any person I ever saw.

I do think it's wonderful, him staying on the wagon this long, a man that used to – well, you know as well as I do; probably a whole lot better, because you were with him so much in the old days, and all I know is just what he's told me. He told me about once in Pittsburgh – All right, Tommie; I won't say another word. But it's all over now, thank heavens! Not a drop since we've been married; three whole months! And he says it's forever, don't you dear? Though I don't mind a person drinking if they do it in moderation. But you know Tom! He goes the limit in everything he does. Like he used to in athletics —

All right, dear; I won't make you blush. I know how you hate the limelight. It's terrible, though, not to be able to boast about your own husband; everything he does or ever has done seems so wonderful. But is that only because we've been married such a short time? Do you feel the same way about Arthur, Helen? You do? And you married him four years ago, isn't that right? And you eloped, didn't you? You see I know all about you.

Oh, are you waiting for me? Do we cut for partners? Why can't we play families? I don't feel so bad if I do something dumb when it's Tom I'm playing with. He never scolds, though he does give me some terrible looks. But not very often lately; I don't make the silly mistakes I used to. I'm pretty good now, aren't I, Tom? You better say so, because if I'm not, it's your fault. You know Tom had to teach me the game. I never played at all till we were engaged. Imagine! And I guess I was pretty awful at first, but Tom was a dear, so patient! I know he thought I never would learn, but I fooled you, didn't I, Tommie?

No, indeed, I'd rather play than do almost anything. But you'll sing for us, won't you, Helen? I mean after a while. Tom has raved to me about your voice and I'm dying to hear it.

What are we playing for? Yes, a penny's perfectly all right. Out there we generally play for half a cent a piece, a penny a family. But a penny a piece is all right. I guess we can afford it now, can't we, dear? Tom hasn't told you about his raise. He was – All right, Tommie; I'll shut up. I know you hate to be talked about, but your wife can't help being just a teeny bit proud of you. And I think your best friends are interested in your affairs, aren't you, folks?

But Tom is the most secretive person I ever knew. I believe he even keeps things from me! Not very many, though. I can usually tell when he's hiding something and I keep after him till he confesses. He often says I should have been a lawyer or a detective, the way I can worm things out of people. Don't you, Tom?

For instance, I never would have known about his experience

with those horrid football people at Yale if I hadn't just made him tell me. Didn't you know about that? No, Tom, I'm going to tell Arthur even if you hate me for it. I know you'd be interested, Arthur, not only because you're Tom's friend, but on account of you being such a famous athlete yourself. Let me see, how was it, Tom? You must help me out. Well, if I don't get it right, you correct me.

Well, Tom's friends at Yale had heard what a wonderful football player he was in high school so they made him try for a place on the Yale nine. Tom had always played half-back. You have to be a fast runner to be a half-back and Tom could run awfully fast. He can yet. When we were engaged we used to run races and the prize was – All right, Tommie, I won't give away our secrets. Anyway, he can beat me to pieces.

Well, he wanted to play half-back at Yale and he was getting along fine and the other men on the team said he would be a wonder and then one day they were having their practice and Tex Jones, no, Ted Jones – he's the main coach – he scolded Tom for having the signal wrong and Tom proved that Jones was wrong and he was right and Jones never forgave him. He made Tom quit playing half-back and put him tackle or end or some place like that where you can't do anything and being a fast runner doesn't count. So Tom saw that Jones had it in for him and he quit. Wasn't that it, Tom? Well, anyway, it was something.

Oh, are you waiting for me? I'm sorry. What did you bid, Helen? And you, Tom? You doubled her? And Arthur passed? Well, let's see. I wish I could remember what that means. I know that sometimes when he doubles he means one thing and sometimes another. But I always forget which is which. Let me see; it was two spades that he doubled, wasn't it? That means I'm to leave him in, I'm pretty sure. Well, I'll pass. Oh, I'm sorry, Tommie! I knew I'd get it wrong. Please forgive me. But maybe we'll set them anyway. Whose lead?

I'll stop talking now and try and keep my mind on the game. You needn't look that way, Tommie. I *can* stop talking if I try. It's kind of hard to concentrate though, when you're, well, excited. It's not only meeting you people, but I always get excited traveling. I was just terrible on our honeymoon, but then I guess a honeymoon's enough to make anybody nervous. I'll never forget when we went into the hotel in Chicago – All right, Tommie, I won't. But I can tell about meeting the Bakers.

They're a couple about our age that I've known all my life. They were the last people in the world I wanted to see, but we ran into them on State Street and they insisted on us coming to their hotel for dinner and before dinner they took us up to their room and Ken – that's Mr Baker – Ken made some cocktails, though I didn't want any and Tom was on the wagon. He said a honeymoon was a fine time to be on the wagon! Ken said.

'Don't tempt him, Ken,' I said. 'Tom isn't a drinker like you and Gertie and the rest of us. When he starts, he can't stop.' Gertie is Mrs Baker.

So Ken said why should he stop and I said there was good reason why he should because he had promised me he would and he told me the day we were married that if I ever saw him take another drink I would know that —

What did you make? Two odd? Well, thank heavens that isn't a game! Oh, that does make a game, doesn't it? Because Tom doubled and I left him in. Isn't that wicked! Oh, dearie, please forgive me and I'll promise to pay attention from now on! What do I do with these? Oh, yes, I make them for Arthur.

I was telling you about the Bakers. Finally Ken saw he couldn't make Tom take a drink, so he gave up in disgust. But imagine meeting them on our honeymoon, when we didn't want to see anybody! I don't suppose anybody does unless they're already tired of each other, and we certainly weren't, were we, Tommie? And aren't yet, are we, dear? And never will be. But I guess I better speak for myself.

There! I'm talking again! But you see it's the first time we've been with anybody we really cared about; I mean, you're Tom's best friends and it's so nice to get a chance to talk to somebody who's known him a long time. Out there the people we run around with are almost strangers and they don't talk about anything but themselves and how much money their husbands make. You never can talk to them about things that are worth while, like books. I'm wild about books, but I honestly don't believe half the women we know out there can read. Or at least they don't. If you mention some really worthwhile novel like, say, *Black Oxen*, they think you're trying to put on the Ritz.

You said a no-trump, didn't you, Tom? And Arthur passed. Let me see; I wish I knew what to do. I haven't any five-card – it's terrible! Just a minute. I wish somebody could – I know I ought to take – but – well, I'll pass. Oh, Tom, this is the worst you ever saw, but I don't know what I could have done.

I do hold the most terrible cards! I certainly believe in the saying, 'Unlucky at cards, lucky in love'. Whoever made it up must have been thinking of me. I hate to lay them down, dear. I know you'll say I ought to have done something. Well, there they are! Let's see your hand, Helen. Oh, Tom, she's – but I mustn't tell, must I? Anyway, I'm dummy. That's one comfort. I can't make a mistake when I'm dummy. I believe Tom overbids lots of times so I'll be dummy and can't do anything ridiculous. But at that I'm much better than I used to be, aren't I, dear?

Helen, do you mind telling me where you got that gown? Crandall and Nelsons's? I've heard of them, but I heard they were terribly expensive. Of course a person can't expect to get a gown like that without paying for it. I've got to get some things while I'm here and I suppose that's where I better go, if their things aren't too horribly dear. I haven't had a thing new since I was married and I've worn this so much I'm sick of it.

Tom's always after me to buy clothes, but I can't seem to get used to spending somebody else's money, though it was dad's money I spent before I did Tom's, but that's different, don't you think so? And of course at first we didn't have very much to spend, did we, dear? But now that we've had our raise – All right, Tommie, I won't say another word.

Oh, did you know they tried to get Tom to run for mayor? Tom is making faces at me to shut up, but I don't see any harm in telling it to his best friends. They know we're not the kind that brag, Tommie. I do think it was quite a tribute; he'd only lived there a little over a year. It came up one night when the Guthries were at our house, playing bridge. Mr Guthrie – that's A. L. Guthrie – he's one of the big lumbermen out there. He owns – just what does he own, Tom? Oh, I'm sorry. Anyway, he's got millions. Well, at least thousands.

He and his wife were at our house playing bridge. She's the queerest woman! If you just saw her, you'd think she was a janitor or something; she wears the most hideous clothes. Why, that night she had on a – honestly you'd have sworn it was a maternity gown, and for no reason. And the first time I met her – well, I just can't describe it. And she's a graduate of Bryn Mawr and one of the oldest families in Philadelphia. You'd never believe it!

She and her husband are terribly funny in a bridge game. He doesn't think there ought to be any conventions; he says a person might just as well tell each other what they've got. So he won't pay any attention to what-do-you-call-'em, informatory, doubles and so forth. And she plays all the conventions, so you can imagine how they get along. Fight! Not really fight, you know, but argue. That is, he does. It's horribly embarrassing to whoever is playing with them. Honestly, if Tom ever spoke to me like Mr Guthrie does to his wife, well – aren't they terrible, Tom? Oh, I'm sorry!

She was the first woman in Portland that called on me and I thought it was awfully nice of her, though when I saw her at the door I would have sworn she was a book agent or maybe a cook looking for work. She had on a – well, I can't describe it. But it was sweet of her to call, she being one of the real people there and me – well, that was before Tom was made a vice-president. What? Oh, I never dreamed he hadn't written you about that!

But Mrs Guthrie acted just like it was a great honor for her to meet me, and I like people to act that way even when I know it's all apple sauce. Isn't that a funny expression, 'apple sauce'? Some man said it in a vaudeville show in Portland the Monday night before we left. He was a comedian – Jack Brooks or Ned Frawley or something. It means – well, I don't know how to describe it. But we had a terrible time after the first few minutes. She is the silentest person I ever knew and I'm kind of bashful myself with strangers. What are you grinning about, Tommie? I am, too, bashful, when I don't know people. Not exactly bashful, maybe, but, well, bashful.

It was one of the most embarrassing things I ever went through. Neither of us could say a word and I could hardly help from laughing at what she had on. But after you get to know her you don't mind her clothes, though it's a terrible temptation all the time not to tell how much nicer – And her hair! But she plays a dandy game of bridge, lots better than her husband. You know he won't play conventions. He says it's just like telling you what's in each other's hand. And they have awful arguments in a game. That is, he does. She's nice and quiet and it's a kind of mystery how they ever fell in love. Though there's a saying or a proverb or something, isn't there, about like not liking like? Or is it just the other way?

But I was going to tell you about them wanting Tom to be mayor. Oh, Tom, only two down? Why, I think you did splendidly! I gave you a miserable hand and Helen had – what didn't you have,

Helen? You had the ace, king of clubs. No, Tom had the king. No, Tom had the queen. Or was it spades? And you had the ace of hearts. No, Tom had that. No, he didn't. What *did* you have, Tom? I don't exactly see what you bid on. Of course I was terrible, but – what's the difference anyway?

What was I saying? Oh, yes, about Mr and Mrs Guthrie. It's funny for a couple like that to get married when they are so different in every way. I never saw two people with such different tastes. For instance, Mr Guthrie is keen about motoring and Mrs Guthrie just hates it. She simply suffers all the time she's in a car. He likes a good time, dancing, golfing, fishing, shows, things like that. She isn't interested in anything but church work and bridge work.

'Bridge work'. I meant bridge, not bridge work. That's funny, isn't it? And yet they get along awfully well; that is when they're not playing cards or doing something else together. But it does seem queer that they picked each other out. Still, I guess hardly any husband and wife agree on anything.

You take Tom and me, though, and you'd think we were made for each other. It seems like we feel just the same about everything. That is, almost everything. The things we don't agree on are little things that don't matter. Like music. Tom is wild about jazz and blues and dance music. He adores Irving Berlin and Gershwin and Jack Kearns. He's always after those kind of things on the radio and I just want serious, classical things like 'Humoresque' and 'Indian Love Lyrics'. And then there's shows. Tom is crazy over Ed Wynn and I can't see anything in him. Just the way he laughs at his own jokes is enough to spoil him for me. If I'm going to spend time and money on a theater I want to see something worth while – *The Fool* or *Lightnin'*.

And things to eat. Tom insists, or that is he did insist, on a great big breakfast – fruit, cereal, eggs, toast, and coffee. All I want is a little fruit and dry toast and coffee. I think it's a great deal better for a person. So that's one habit I broke Tom of, was big breakfasts. And another thing he did when we were first married was to take off his shoes as soon as he got home from the office and put on bedroom slippers. I believe a person ought not to get sloppy just because they're married.

But the worst of all was pajamas! What's the difference, Tommie? Helen and Arthur don't mind. And I think it's kind of funny, you being so old-fashioned. I mean Tom had always worn a nightgown till I made him give it up. And it was a struggle, believe me! I had to threaten to leave him if he didn't buy pajamas. He certainly hated it. And now he's mad at me for telling, aren't you, Tommie? I just couldn't help it. I think it's so funny in this day and age. I hope Arthur doesn't wear them; nightgowns, I mean. You don't, do you, Arthur? I knew you didn't.

Oh, are you waiting for me? What did you say, Arthur? Two diamonds? Let's see what that means. When Tom makes an original bid of two it means he hasn't got the tops. I wonder – but of course you couldn't have the – heavens! What am I saying! I guess I better just keep still and pass.

But what was I going to tell you? Something about – oh, did I tell you about Tom being an author? I had no idea he was talented that way till after we were married and I was unpacking his old papers and things and came across a poem he'd written, the saddest, mushiest poem! Of course it was a long time ago he wrote it; it was dated four years ago, long before he met me, so it didn't make me very jealous, though it was about some other girl. You didn't know I found it, did you, Tommie?

But that wasn't what I refer to. He's written a story, too, and he's sent it to four different magazines and they all sent it back. I tell him though, that that doesn't mean anything. When you see some of the things the magazines do print, why, it's an honor to have them *not* like yours. The only thing is that Tom worked so hard over it and sat up nights writing and rewriting, it's kind of a disappointment to have them turn it down.

It's a story about two men and a girl and they were all brought up together and one of the men was awfully popular and well off and good-looking and a great athlete – a man like Arthur. There, Arthur! How is that for a T.L.? The other man was just an ordinary man with not much money, but the girl seemed to like him better and she promised to wait for him. Then this man worked hard and got money enough to see him through Yale.

The other man, the well-off one, went to Princeton and made a big hit as an athlete and everything and he was through college long before his friend because his friend had to earn the money first. And the well-off man kept after the girl to marry him. He didn't know she had promised the other one. Anyway she got tired waiting for the man she was engaged to and eloped with the other one. And the story ends up by the man she threw down welcoming the couple when they came home and pretending everything was all right, though his heart was broken.

What are you blushing about, Tommie? It's nothing to be ashamed of. I thought it was very well written and if the editors had any sense they'd have taken it.

Still, I don't believe the real editors see half the stories that are sent to them. In fact I know they don't. You've either got to have a name or a pull to get your things published. Or else pay the magazines to publish them. Of course if you are Robert Chambers or Irving R. Cobb, they will print whatever you write whether it's good or bad. But you haven't got a chance if you are an unknown like Tom. They just keep your story long enough so you will think they are considering it and then they send it back with a form letter saying it's not available for their magazine and they don't even tell why.

You remember, Tom, that Mr Hastings we met at the Hammonds'. He's a writer and knows all about it. He was telling me of an experience he had with one of the magazines; I forget which one, but it was one of the big ones. He wrote a story and sent it to them and they sent it back and said they couldn't use it.

Well, some time after that Mr Hastings was in a hotel in Chicago and a bell-boy went around the lobby paging Mr – I forget the name, but it was the name of the editor of this magazine that had sent back the story, Rungle, or Byers, or some such name. So the man, whatever his name was, he was really there and answered the page and afterwards Mr Hastings went up to him and introduced himself and told the man about sending a story to his magazine and the man said he didn't remember anything about it. And he was the editor! Of course he'd never seen it. No wonder Tom's story keeps coming back!

He says he is through sending it and just the other day he was going to tear it up, but I made him keep it because we may meet somebody some time who knows the inside ropes and can get a hearing with some big editor. I'm sure it's just a question of pull. Some of the things that get into the magazines sound like they had been written by the editor's friends or relatives or somebody whom they didn't want to hurt their feelings. And Tom really can write!

I wish I could remember that poem of his I found. I memorized it once, but – wait! I believe I can still say it! Hush, Tommie! What hurt will it do anybody? Let me see; it goes:

I thought the sweetness of her song
Would ever, ever more belong
To me; I thought (O thought divine!)
My bird was really mine!

But promises are made it seems,
Just to be broken. All my dreams
Fade out and leave me crushed, alone.
My bird, alas, has flown!

Isn't that pretty. He wrote it four years ago. Why, Helen, you revoked! And, Tom, do you know that's Scotch you're drinking? You said – *Why, Tom!*

KATHERINE MANSFIELD · 1888–1923

The Woman at the Store

All that day the heat was terrible. The wind blew close to the ground; it rooted among the tussock grass, slithered along the road, so that the white pumice dust swirled in our faces, settled and sifted over us and was like a dry skin itching for growth on our bodies. The horses stumbled along, coughing and chuffing. The pack-horse was sick – with a big open sore rubbed under the belly. Now and again she stopped short, threw back her head, looked at us as though she were going to cry, and whinnied. Hundreds of larks shrilled; the sky was slate colour, and the sound of the larks reminded me of slate pencils scraping over its surface. There was nothing to be seen but wave after wave of tussock grass, patched with purple orchids and manuka bushes covered with thick spider webs.

Jo rode ahead. He wore a blue galatea shirt, corduroy trousers and riding boots. A white handkerchief, spotted with red – it looked as though his nose had been bleeding on it – was knotted round his throat. Wisps of white hair straggled from under his wideawake – his moustache and eyebrows were called white – he slouched in the saddle, grunting. Not once that day had he sung

'I don't care, for don't you see,
My wife's mother was in front of me!'

It was the first day we had been without it for a month, and now there seemed something uncanny in his silence. Jim rode beside me, white as a clown; his black eyes glittered and he kept shooting out his tongue and moistening his lips. He was dressed in a Jaeger vest and a pair of blue duck trousers, fastened round the waist with a plaited leather belt. We had hardly spoken since dawn. At noon we had lunched off fly biscuits and apricots by the side of a swampy creek.

'My stomach feels like the crop of a hen,' said Jo. 'Now then, Jim, you're the bright boy of the party – where's this 'ere store you kep' on talking about. "Oh yes," you says, "I know a fine store, with a paddock for the horses and a creek runnin' through, owned by a friend of mine who'll give yer a bottle of whisky before 'e shakes hands with yer." I'd like ter see that place – merely as a matter of curiosity – not that I'd ever doubt yer word – as yer know very well – *but.* . . .'

Jim laughed. 'Don't forget there's a woman too, Jo, with blue eyes and yellow hair, who'll promise you something else before she shakes hands with you. Put that in your pipe and smoke it.'

'The heat's making you balmy,' said Jo. But he dug his knees into the horse. We shambled on. I half fell asleep and had a sort of uneasy dream that the horses were not moving forward at all – then that I was on a rocking-horse, and my old mother was scolding me for raising such a fearful dust from the drawing-room carpet. 'You've entirely worn off the pattern of the carpet,' I heard her saying, and she gave the reins a tug. I snivelled and woke to find Jim leaning over me, maliciously smiling.

'That was a case of all but,' said he. 'I just caught you. What's up? Been bye-bye?'

'No!' I raised my head. 'Thank the Lord we're arriving somewhere.'

We were on the brow of the hill, and below us there was a whare roofed with corrugated iron. It stood in a garden, rather far back from the road – a big paddock opposite, and a creek and a clump of young willow trees. A thin line of blue smoke stood up straight from the chimney of the whare; and as I looked a woman came out, followed by a child and a sheep dog – the woman carrying what appeared to me a black stick. She made gestures at us. The horses put on a final spurt, Jo took off his wideawake, shouted, threw out his chest, and began singing 'I don't care, for don't you see. . . .' The sun pushed through the pale clouds and shed a vivid light over the scene. It gleamed on the woman's yellow hair, over her flapping pinafore and the rifle she was carrying. The child hid behind her, and the yellow dog, a mangy beast, scuttled back into the whare, his tail between his legs. We drew rein and dismounted.

'Hallo,' screamed the woman. 'I thought you was three 'awks. My kid comes runnin' in ter me. "Mumma," says she, "there's three brown things comin' over the 'ill," says she. An' I comes out smart, I can tell yer. "They'll be 'awks," I says to her. Oh, the 'awks about 'ere, yer wouldn't believe.'

The 'kid' gave us the benefit of one eye from behind the woman's pinafore – then retired again.

'Where's your old man?' asked Jim.

The woman blinked rapidly, screwing up her face.

'Away shearin'. Bin away a month. I suppose ye're not goin' to stop, are yer? There's a storm comin' up.'

'You bet we are,' said Jo. 'So you're on your lonely, missus?'

She stood, pleating the frills of her pinafore, and glancing from one to the other of us, like a hungry bird. I smiled at the thought of how Jim had pulled Jo's leg about her. Certainly her eyes were blue, and what hair she had was yellow, but ugly. She was a figure of fun. Looking at her, you felt there was nothing but sticks and wires under that pinafore – her front teeth were knocked out, she had red, pulpy hands and she wore on her feet a pair of dirty Bluchers.

'I'll go and turn out the horses,' said Jim. 'Got any embrocation? Poi's rubbed herself to hell!'

''Arf a mo!' The woman stood silent a moment, her nostrils expanding as she breathed. Then she shouted violently, 'I'd rather you didn't stop. . . . You *can't*, and there's the end of it. I don't let out that paddock any more. You'll have to go on; I ain't got nothing!'

'Well, I'm blest!' said Jo heavily. He pulled me aside. 'Gone a bit off 'er dot,' he whispered. 'Too much alone, *you know*,' very significantly. 'Turn the sympathetic tap on 'er, she'll come round all right.'

But there was no need – she had come round by herself.

'Stop if yer like!' she muttered, shrugging her shoulders. To me – 'I'll give yer the embrocation if yer come along.'

'Right-o, I'll take it down to them.' We walked together up the garden path. It was planted on both sides with cabbages. They smelled like stale dish-water. Of flowers there were double poppies and sweet-williams. One little patch was divided off by pawa shells – presumably it belonged to the child – for she ran from her mother and began to grub in it with a broken clothes-peg. The yellow dog lay across the doorstep, biting fleas; the woman kicked him away.

'Gar-r, get away, you beast . . . the place ain't tidy. I 'aven't 'ad time ter fix things today – been ironing. Come right in.'

It was a large room, the walls plastered with old pages of English periodicals. Queen Victoria's Jubilee appeared to be the most recent number. A table with an ironing board and wash-tub on it, some wooden forms, a black horsehair sofa and some broken cane chairs pushed against the walls. The mantelpiece above the stove was draped in pink paper, further ornamented with dried grasses and ferns and a coloured print of Richard Seddon. There were four doors – one, judging from the smell, led into the 'Store', one on to the 'backyard', through a third I saw the bedroom. Flies buzzed in circles round the ceiling, and treacle papers and bundles of dried clover were pinned to the window curtains.

I was alone in the room; she had gone into the store for the embrocation. I heard her stamping about and muttering to herself: 'I got some, now where did I put that bottle?. . . . It's behind the pickles . . . no, it ain't.' I cleared a place on the table and sat there, swinging my legs. Down in the paddock I could hear Jo singing and the sound of hammer strokes as Jim drove in the tent pegs. It was sunset. There is no twilight in our New Zealand days, but a curious half-hour when everything appears grotesque – it frightens – as though the savage spirit of the country walked abroad and sneered at what it saw. Sitting alone in the hideous room I grew afraid. The woman next door was a long time finding that stuff. What was she doing in there? Once I thought I heard her bang her hands down on the counter, and once she half moaned, turning it into a cough and clearing her throat. I wanted to shout 'Buck up!' but I kept silent.

'Good Lord, what a life!' I thought. 'Imagine being here day in, day out, with that rat of a child and a mangy dog. Imagine bothering about ironing. *Mad*, of course she's mad! Wonder how long she's been here – wonder if I could get her to talk.'

At that moment she poked her head round the door.

'Wot was it yer wanted?' she asked.

'Embrocation.'

'Oh, I forgot. I got it, it was in front of the pickle jars.'

She handed me the bottle.

'My, you do look tired, you do! Shall I knock yer up a few scones for supper! There's some tongue in the store, too, and I'll cook yer a cabbage if you fancy it.'

'Right-o.' I smiled at her. 'Come down to the paddock and bring the kid for tea.'

She shook her head, pursing up her mouth.

'Oh no. I don't fancy it. I'll send the kid down with the things and a billy of milk. Shall I knock up a few extry scones to take with yer ter-morrow?'

'Thanks.'

She came and stood by the door.

'How old is the kid?'

'Six – come next Christmas. I 'ad a bit of trouble with 'er one way an' another. I 'adn't any milk till a month after she was born and she sickened like a cow.'

'She's not like you – takes after her father?' Just as the woman had shouted her refusal at us before, she shouted at me then.

'No, she don't! She's the dead spit of me. Any fool could see that. Come on in now, Else, you stop messing in the dirt.'

I met Jo climbing over the paddock fence.

'What's the old bitch got in the store?' he asked.

'Don't know – didn't look.'

'Well, of all the fools. Jim's slanging you. What have you been doing all the time?'

'She couldn't find this stuff. Oh, my shakes, you are smart!'

Jo had washed, combed his wet hair in a line across his forehead, and buttoned a coat over his shirt. He grinned.

Jim snatched the embrocation from me. I went to the end of the paddock where the willows grew and bathed in the creek. The water was clear and soft as oil. Along the edges held by the grass and rushes white foam tumbled and bubbled. I lay in the water and looked up at the trees that were still a moment, then quivered lightly and again were still. The air smelt of rain. I forgot about the woman and the kid until I came back to the tent. Jim lay by the fire watching the billy boil.

I asked where Jo was, and if the kid had brought our supper.

'Pooh,' said Jim, rolling over and looking up at the sky. 'Didn't you see how Jo had been titivating? He said to me before he went up to the whare, "Dang it! she'll look better by night light – at any rate, my buck, she's female flesh!"'

'You had Jo about her looks – you had me too.'

'No – look here. I can't make it out. It's four years since I came past this way and I stopped here two days. The husband was a pal of mine once, down the West Coast – a fine, big chap, with a voice on him like a trombone. She's been barmaid down the Coast – as pretty as a wax doll. The coach used to come this way then once a fortnight, that was before they opened the railway up Napier way, and she had no end of a time! Told me once in a confidential moment that she knew one hundred and twenty-five different ways of kissing!'

'Oh, go on, Jim! She isn't the same woman!'

''Course she is. . . . I can't make it out. What I think is the old man's cleared out and left her: that's all my eye about shearing. Sweet life! The only people who come through now are Maoris and sundowners!'

Through the dark we saw the gleam of the kid's pinafore. She trailed over to us with a basket in her hand, the milk billy in the other. I unpacked the basket, the child standing by.

'Come over here,' said Jim, snapping his fingers at her.

She went, the lamp from the inside of the tent cast a bright light over her. A mean, undersized brat, with whitish hair and weak eyes. She stood, legs wide apart and her stomach protruding.

'What do you do all day?' asked Jim.

She scraped out one ear with her little finger, looked at the result and said, 'Draw.'

'Huh! What do you draw? Leave your ears alone!'

'Pictures.'

'What on?'

'Bits of butter paper an' a pencil of my Mumma's.'

'Boh! What a lot of words at one time!' Jim rolled his eyes at her. 'Baa-lambs and moo-cows?'

'No, everything. I'll draw all of you when you're gone, and your horses and the tent, and that one' – she pointed to me – 'with no clothes on in the creek. I looked at her where she couldn't see me from.'

'Thanks very much. How ripping of you,' said Jim. 'Where's Dad?'

The kid pouted. 'I won't tell you because I don't like yer face!' She started operations on the other ear.

'Here,' I said. 'Take the basket, get along home and tell the other man supper's ready.'

'I don't want to.'

'I'll give you a box on the ear if you don't,' said Jim savagely.

'Hie! I'll tell Mumma. I'll tell Mumma.' The kid fled.

We ate until we were full, and had arrived at the smoke stage before Jo came back, very flushed and jaunty, a whisky bottle in his hand.

' 'Ave a drink – you two!' he shouted, carrying off matters with a high hand. ' 'Ere, shove along the cups.'

'One hundred and twenty-five different ways,' I murmured to Jim.

'What's that? Oh! stow it!' said Jo. 'Why 'ave you always got your knife into me. You gas like a kid at a Sunday School beano. She wants us to go there tonight and have a comfortable chat. I' – he waved his hand airily – 'I got 'er round.'

'Trust you for that,' laughed Jim. 'But did she tell you where the old man's got to?'

Jo looked up. 'Shearing! You 'eard 'er, you fool!'

The woman had fixed up the room, even to a light bouquet of sweet-williams on the table. She and I sat one side of the table, Jo and Jim the other. An oil lamp was set between us, the whisky bottle and glasses, and a jug of water. The kid knelt against one of the forms, drawing on butter paper; I wondered, grimly, if she was attempting the creek episode. But Jo had been right about night time. The woman's hair was tumbled – two red spots burned in her cheeks – her eyes shone – and we knew that they were kissing feet under the table. She had changed the blue pinafore for a white calico dressing-jacket and a black skirt – the kid was decorated to the extent of a blue sateen hair ribbon. In the stifling room, with the flies buzzing against the ceiling and dropping on to the table, we got slowly drunk.

'Now listen to me,' shouted the woman, banging her fist on the table. 'It's six years since I was married, and four miscarriages. I says to 'im, I says, what do you think I'm doin' up 'ere? If you was back at the Coast I'd 'ave you lynched for child murder. Over and over I tells 'im – you've broken my spirit and spoiled my looks, and wot for – that's wot I'm driving at.' She clutched her head with her hands and stared round at us. Speaking rapidly, 'Oh, some days – an' months of them – I 'ear them two words knockin' inside me all the time – "Wot for!" but sometimes I'll be cooking the spuds an' I lifts the lid off to give 'em a prong and I 'ears, quite suddin again, "Wot for!" Oh! I don't mean only the spuds and the kid – I mean – I mean,' she hiccoughed – 'you know what I mean, Mr Jo.'

'I know,' said Jo, scratching his head.

'Trouble with me is,' she leaned across the table, 'he left me too much alone. When the coach stopped coming, sometimes he'd go away days, sometimes he'd go away weeks, and leave me ter look after the store. Back 'e'd come – pleased as Punch. "Oh, 'allo," 'e'd say. " 'Ow are you gettin' on? Come and give us a kiss." Sometimes I'd turn a bit nasty, and then 'e'd go off again, and if I took it all right, 'e'd wait till 'e could twist me round 'is finger, then 'e'd say, "Well, so long, I'm off," and do you think I could keep 'im? – not me!'

'Mumma,' bleated the kid, 'I made a picture of them on the 'ill, an' you an' me an' the dog down below.'

'Shut your mouth!' said the woman.

A vivid flash of lightning played over the room – we heard the mutter of thunder.

'Good thing that's broke loose,' said Jo. 'I've 'ad it in me 'ead for three days.'

'Where's your old man now?' asked Jim slowly.

The woman blubbered and dropped her head on to the table. 'Jim, 'e's gone shearin' and left me alone again,' she wailed.

' 'Ere, look out for the glasses,' said Jo. 'Cheer-o, 'ave another drop. No good cryin' over spilt 'usbands! You, Jim, you blasted cuckoo!'

'Mr Jo,' said the woman, drying her eyes on her jacket frill, 'you're a gent, an' if I was a secret woman I'd place any confidence in your 'ands. I don't mind if I do 'ave a glass on that.'

Every moment the lightning grew more vivid and the thunder sounded nearer. Jim and I were silent – the kid never moved from her bench. She poked her tongue out and blew on her paper as she drew.

'It's the loneliness,' said the woman, addressing Jo – he made sheep's eyes at her – 'and bein' shut up 'ere like a broody 'en.' He reached his hand across the table and held hers, and though the position looked most uncomfortable when they wanted to pass the water and whisky, their hands stuck together as though glued. I pushed back my chair and went over to the kid, who immediately sat flat down on her artistic achievements and made a face at me.

'You're not to look,' said she.

'Oh, come on, don't be nasty!' Jim came over to us, and we were just drunk enough to wheedle the kid into showing us. And those drawings of hers were extraordinary and repulsively vulgar. The creations of a lunatic with a lunatic's cleverness. There was no doubt about it, the kid's mind was diseased. While she showed them to us, she worked herself up into a mad excitement, laughing and trembling, and shooting out her arms.

'Mumma,' she yelled. 'Now I'm going to draw them what you told me I never was to – now I am.'

The woman rushed from the table and beat the child's head with the flat of her hand.

'I'll smack you with yer clothes turned up if yer dare say that again,' she bawled.

Jo was too drunk to notice, but Jim caught her by the arm. The kid did not utter a cry. She drifted over to the window and began picking flies from the treacle paper.

We returned to the table – Jim and I sitting one side, the woman and Jo, touching shoulders, the other. We listened to the thunder, saying stupidly, 'That was a near one', 'There it goes again', and Jo, at a heavy hit, 'Now we're off', 'Steady on the brake', until rain began to fall, sharp as cannon shot on the iron roof.

'You'd better doss here for the night,' said the woman.

'That's right,' assented Jo, evidently in the know about this move.

'Bring up yer things from the tent. You two can doss in the store along with the kid – she's used to sleep in there and won't mind you.'

'Oh, Mumma, I never did,' interrupted the kid.

'Shut yer lies! An' Mr Jo can 'ave this room.'

It sounded a ridiculous arrangement, but it was useless to attempt to cross them, they were too far gone. While the woman sketched the plan of action, Jo sat, abnormally solemn and red, his eyes bulging and pulling at his moustache.

'Give us a lantern,' said Jim, 'I'll go down to the paddock.' We two went together. Rain whipped in our faces, the land was light as though a bush fire was raging. We behaved like two children let loose in the thick of an adventure, laughed and shouted to each other, and came back to the whare to find the kid already bedded in the counter of the store. The woman brought us a lamp. Jo took his bundle from Jim, the door was shut.

'Good night all,' shouted Jo.

Jim and I sat on two sacks of potatoes. For the life of us we could not stop laughing. Strings of onions and half-hams dangled from the ceiling – wherever we looked there were advertisements for 'Camp Coffee' and tinned meats. We pointed at them, tried to read them aloud – overcome with laughter and hiccoughs. The kid in the counter stared at us. She threw off her blanket and scrambled to the floor, where she stood in her grey flannel nightgown rubbing one leg against the other. We paid no attention to her.

'Wot are you laughing at?' she said uneasily.

'You!' shouted Jim. 'The red tribe of you, my child.'

She flew into a rage and beat herself with her hands. 'I won't be laughed at, you curs – you.' He swooped down upon the child and swung her on to the counter.

'Go to sleep, Miss Smarty – or make a drawing – here's a pencil – you can use Mumma's account book.'

Through the rain we heard Jo creak over the boarding of the next room – the sound of a door being opened – then shut to.

'It's the loneliness,' whispered Jim.

'One hundred and twenty-five different ways – alas! my poor brother!'

The kid tore out a page and flung it at me.

'There you are,' she said. 'Now I done it ter spite Mumma for shutting me up 'ere with you two. I done the one she told me I never ought to. I done the one she told me she'd shoot me if I did. Don't care! Don't care!'

The kid had drawn the picture of the woman shooting at a man with a rook rifle and then digging a hole to bury him in.

She jumped off the counter and squirmed about on the floor biting her nails.

Jim and I sat till dawn with the drawing beside us. The rain ceased, the little kid fell asleep, breathing loudly. We got up, stole out of the whare, down into the paddock. White clouds floated over a pink sky – a chill wind blew; the air smelled of wet grass. Just as we swung into the saddle Jo came out of the whare – he motioned to us to ride on.

'I'll pick you up later,' he shouted.

A bend in the road, and the whole place disappeared.

Flowering Judas

Braggioni sits heaped upon the edge of a straight-backed chair much too small for him, and sings to Laura in a furry, mournful voice. Laura has begun to find reasons for avoiding her own house until the latest possible moment, for Braggioni is there almost every night. No matter how late she is, he will be sitting there with a surly, waiting expression, pulling at his kinky yellow hair, thumbing the strings of his guitar, snarling a tune under his breath. Lupe the Indian maid meets Laura at the door, and says with a flicker of a glance towards the upper room, 'He waits.'

Laura wishes to lie down, she is tired of her hairpins and the feel of her long tight sleeves, but she says to him, 'Have you a new song for me this evening?' If he says yes, she asks him to sing it. If he says no, she remembers his favorite one, and asks him to sing it again. Lupe brings her a cup of chocolate and a plate of rice, and Laura eats at the small table under the lamp, first inviting Braggioni, whose answer is always the same: 'I have eaten, and besides, chocolate thickens the voice.'

Laura says, 'Sing, then,' and Braggioni heaves himself into song. He scratches the guitar familiarly as though it were a pet animal, and sings passionately off key, taking the high notes in a prolonged painful squeal. Laura, who haunts the markets listening to the ballad singers, and stops every day to hear the blind boy playing his reed-flute in Sixteenth of September Street, listens to Braggioni with pitiless courtesy, because she dares not smile at his miserable performance. Nobody dares to smile at him. Braggioni is cruel to everyone, with a kind of specialized insolence, but he is so vain of his talents, and so sensitive to slights, it would require a cruelty and vanity greater than his own to lay a finger on the vast cureless wound of his self-esteem. It would require courage, too, for it is dangerous to offend him, and nobody has this courage.

Braggioni loves himself with such tenderness and amplitude and eternal charity that his followers – for he is a leader of men, a skilled revolutionist, and his skin has been punctured in honorable warfare – warm themselves in the reflected glow, and say to each other: 'He has a real nobility, a love of humanity raised above mere personal affections.' The excess of this self-love has flowed out, inconveniently for her, over Laura, who, with so many others, owes her comfortable situation and her salary to him. When he is in a very good humor, he tells her, 'I am tempted to forgive you for being a *gringa. Gringita!*' and Laura, burning, imagines herself leaning forward suddenly, and with a sound back-handed slap wiping the suety smile from his face. If he notices her eyes at these moments he gives no sign.

She knows what Braggioni would offer her, and she must resist tenaciously without appearing to resist, and if she could avoid it she would not admit even to herself the slow drift of his intention. During these long evenings which have spoiled a long month for her, she sits in her deep chair with an open book on her knees, resting her eyes on the consoling rigidity of the printed page when the sight and sound of Braggioni singing threaten to identify themselves with all her remembered afflictions and to add their weight to her uneasy premonitions of the future. The gluttonous bulk of Braggioni has become a symbol of her many disillusions, for a revolutionist should be lean, animated by heroic faith, a vessel of abstract virtues. This is nonsense, she knows it now and is ashamed of it. Revolution must have leaders, and leadership is a career for energetic men. She is, her comrades tell her, full of romantic error, for what she defines as cynicism in them is merely 'a developed sense of reality'. She is almost too willing to say, 'I am wrong, I suppose I don't really understand the principles', and afterward she makes a secret truce with herself, determined not to surrender her will to such expedient logic. But she cannot help feeling that she has been betrayed irreparably by the disunion between her way of living and her feeling of what life should be, and at times she is almost contented to rest in this sense of grievance as a private store of consolation. Sometimes she wishes to run away, but she stays. Now she longs to fly out of this room, down the narrow stairs, and into the street where the houses lean together like conspirators under a single mottled lamp, and leave Braggioni singing to himself.

Instead she looks at Braggioni, frankly and clearly, like a good child who understands the rules of behavior. Her knees cling together under sound blue serge, and her round white collar is not

purposely nun-like. She wears the uniform of an idea, and has renounced vanities. She was born Roman Catholic, and in spite of
her fear of being seen by someone who might make a scandal of it,
she slips now and again into some crumbling little church, kneels
on the chilly stone, and says a Hail Mary on the gold rosary she
bought in Tehuantepec. It is no good and she ends by examining
the altar with its tinsel flowers and ragged brocades, and feels tender about the battered doll-shape of some real saint whose white,
lace-trimmed drawers hang limply around his ankles below the
hieratic dignity of his velvet robe. She has encased herself in a set
of principles derived from her early training, leaving no detail of
gesture or of personal taste untouched, and for this reason she will
not wear lace made on machines. This is her private heresy, for in
her special group the machine is sacred, and will be the salvation
of the workers. She loves fine lace, and there is a tiny edge of fluted
cobweb on this collar, which is one of twenty precisely alike, folded
in blue tissue paper in the upper drawer of her clothes chest.

Braggioni catches her glance solidly as if he had been waiting for
it, leans forward, balancing his paunch between his spread knees,
and sings with tremendous emphasis, weighing his words. He has,
the song relates, no father and no mother, nor even a friend to
console him; lonely as a wave of the sea he comes and goes, lonely
as a wave. His mouth opens round and yearns sideways, his balloon cheeks grow oily with the labor of song. He bulges marvel-
ously in his expensive garments. Over his lavender collar, crushed
upon a purple necktie, held by a diamond hoop: over his ammunition belt of tooled leather worked in silver, buckled cruelly around
his gasping middle: over the tops of his glossy yellow shoes Braggioni swells with ominous ripeness, his mauve silk hose stretched
taut, his ankles bound with the stout leather thongs of his shoes.

When he stretches his eyelids at Laura she notes again that his
eyes are the true tawny yellow cat's eyes. He is rich, not in money,
he tells her, but in power, and this power brings with it the blameless ownership of things, and the right to indulge his love of small
luxuries. 'I have a taste for the elegant refinements,' he said once,
flourishing a yellow silk handkerchief before her nose. 'Smell that?
It is Jockey Club, imported from New York.' Nonetheless he is
wounded by life. He will say so presently. 'It is true everything turns
to dust in the hand, to gall on the tongue.' He sighs and his leather
belt creaks like a saddle girth. 'I am disappointed in everything as

it comes. Everything.' He shakes his head. 'You, poor thing, you will be disappointed too. You are born for it. We are more alike than you realize in some things. Wait and see. Some day you will remember what I have told you, you will know that Braggioni was your friend.'

Laura feels a slow chill, a purely physical sense of danger, a warning in her blood that violence, mutilation, a shocking death, wait for her with lessening patience. She has translated this fear into something homely, immediate, and sometimes hesitates before crossing the street. 'My personal fate is nothing, except as the testimony of a mental attitude,' she reminds herself, quoting from some forgotten philosophic primer, and is sensible enough to add, 'Anyhow, I shall not be killed by an automobile if I can help it.'

'It may be true I am as corrupt, in another way, as Braggioni,' she thinks in spite of herself, 'as callous, as incomplete,' and if this is so, any kind of death seems preferable. Still she sits quietly, she does not run. Where could she go? Uninvited she has promised herself to this place; she can no longer imagine herself as living in another country, and there is no pleasure in remembering her life before she came here.

Precisely what is the nature of this devotion, its true motives, and what are its obligations? Laura cannot say. She spends part of her days in Xochimilco, near by, teaching Indian children to say in English, 'The cat is on the mat.' When she appears in the classroom they crowd about her with smiles on their wise, innocent, clay-colored faces, crying, 'Good morning, my titcher!' in immaculate voices, and they make of her desk a fresh garden of flowers every day.

During her leisure she goes to union meetings and listens to busy important voices quarreling over tactics, methods, internal politics. She visits the prisoners of her own political faith in their cells, where they entertain themselves with counting cockroaches, repenting of their indiscretions, composing their memoirs, writing out manifestoes and plans for their comrades who are still walking about free, hands in pockets, sniffing fresh air. Laura brings them food and cigarettes and a little money, and she brings messages disguised in equivocal phrases from the men outside who dare not set foot in the prison for fear of disappearing into the cells kept empty for them. If the prisoners confuse night and day, and complain, 'Dear little Laura, time doesn't pass in this infernal hole, and

I won't know when it is time to sleep unless I have a reminder,' she brings them their favorite narcotics, and says in a tone that does not wound them with pity, 'Tonight will really be night for you,' and though her Spanish amuses them, they find her comforting, useful. If they lose patience and all faith, and curse the slowness of their friends in coming to their rescue with money and influence, they trust her not to repeat everything, and if she inquires, 'Where do you think we can find money, or influence?' they are certain to answer, 'Well, there is Braggioni, why doesn't he do something?'

She smuggles letters from headquarters to men hiding from firing squads in back streets in mildewed houses, where they sit in tumbled beds and talk bitterly as if all Mexico were at their heels, when Laura knows positively they might appear at the band concert in the Alameda on Sunday morning, and no one would notice them. But Braggioni says, 'Let them sweat a little. The next time they may be careful. It is very restful to have them out of the way for a while.' She is not afraid to knock on any door in the street after midnight, and enter in the darkness, and say to one of these men who is really in danger: 'They will be looking for you – seriously – tomorrow morning after six. Here is some money from Vincente. Go to Vera Cruz and wait.'

She borrows money from the Romanian agitator to give to his bitter enemy the Polish agitator. The favor of Braggioni is their disputed territory, and Braggioni holds the balance nicely, for he can use them both. The Polish agitator talks love to her over café tables, hoping to exploit what he believes is her secret sentimental preference for him, and he gives her misinformation which he begs her to repeat as the solemn truth to certain persons. The Romanian is more adroit. He is generous with his money in all good causes, and lies to her with an air of ingenuous candor, as if he were her good friend and confidant. She never repeats anything they may say. Braggioni never asks questions. He has other ways to discover all that he wishes to know about them.

Nobody touches her, but all praise her gray eyes, and the soft, round under lip which promises gaiety, yet is always grave, nearly always firmly closed: and they cannot understand why she is in Mexico. She walks back and forth on her errands, with puzzled eyebrows, carrying her little folder of drawings and music and school papers. No dancer dances more beautifully than Laura walks, and she inspires some amusing, unexpected ardors, which cause little gossip, because nothing comes of them. A young captain who had been a soldier in Zapata's army attempted, during a horseback ride near Cuernavaca, to express his desire for her with the noble simplicity befitting a rude folk-hero: but gently, because he was gentle. This gentleness was his defeat, for when he alighted, and removed her foot from the stirrup, and essayed to draw her down into his arms, her horse, ordinarily a tame one, shied fiercely, reared and plunged away. The young hero's horse careered blindly after his stablemate, and the hero did not return to the hotel until rather late that evening. At breakfast he came to her table in full charro dress, gray buckskin jacket, and trousers with strings of silver buttons down the leg, and he was in a humorous, careless mood. 'May I sit with you?' and 'You are a wonderful rider. I was terrified that you might be thrown and dragged. I should never have forgiven myself. But I cannot admire you enough for your riding!'

'I learned to ride in Arizona,' said Laura.

'If you will ride with me again this morning, I promise you a horse that will not shy with you,' he said. But Laura remembered that she must return to Mexico City at noon.

Next morning the children made a celebration and spent their playtime writing on the blackboard, 'We lov ar titcher', and with tinted chalks they drew wreaths of flowers around the words. The young hero wrote her a letter: 'I am a very foolish, wasteful, impulsive man. I should have first said I love you, and then you would not have run away. But you shall see me again.' Laura thought, 'I must send him a box of colored crayons,' but she was trying to forgive herself for having spurred her horse at the wrong moment.

A brown, shock-haired youth came and stood in her patio one night and sang like a lost soul for two hours, but Laura could think of nothing to do about it. The moonlight spread a wash of gauzy silver over the clear spaces of the garden, and the shadows were cobalt blue. The scarlet blossoms of the Judas tree were dull purple, and the names of the colors repeated themselves automatically in her mind, while she watched not the boy, but his shadow, fallen like a dark garment across the fountain rim, trailing in the water. Lupe came silently and whispered expert counsel in her ear: 'If you will throw him one little flower, he will sing another song or two and go away.' Laura threw the flower, and he sang a last song and went away with the flower tucked in the band of his hat. Lupe said, 'He is one of the organizers of the Typographers Union, and before that he sold corridos in the Merced market, and before that, he came from Guanajuato, where I was born. I would not trust any man, but I trust least those from Guanajuato.'

She did not tell Laura that he would be back again the next night, and the next, nor that he would follow her at a certain fixed distance around the Merced market, through the Zócolo, up Francisco I Madero Avenue, and so along the Paseo de la Reforma to Chapultepec Park, and into the Philosopher's Footpath, still with that flower withering in his hat, and an indivisible attention in his eyes.

Now Laura is accustomed to him, it means nothing except that he is nineteen years old and is observing a convention with all propriety, as though it were founded on a law of nature, which in the end it might well prove to be. He is beginning to write poems which he prints on a wooden press, and he leaves them stuck like handbills in her door. She is pleasantly disturbed by the abstract, unhurried watchfulness of his black eyes which will in time turn easily towards another object. She tells herself that throwing the flower was a mistake, for she is twenty-two years old and knows better; but she refuses to regret it, and persuades herself that her negation of all external events as they occur is a sign that she is gradually perfecting herself in the stoicism she strives to cultivate against that disaster she fears, though she cannot name it.

She is not at home in the world. Every day she teaches children who remain strangers to her, though she loves their tender round hands and their charming opportunist savagery. She knocks at unfamiliar doors not knowing whether a friend or a stranger shall answer, and even if a known face emerges from the sour gloom of that unknown interior, still it is the face of a stranger. No matter what this stranger says to her, nor what her message to him, the very cells of her flesh reject knowledge and kinship in one monotonous word. No. No. No. She draws her strength from this one holy talismanic word which does not suffer her to be led into evil. Denying everything, she may walk anywhere in safety, she looks at everything without amazement.

No, repeats this firm unchanging voice of her blood; and she looks at Braggioni without amazement. He is a great man, he wishes to impress this simple girl who covers her great round breasts with thick dark cloth, and who hides long, invaluably beautiful legs under a heavy skirt. She is almost thin except for the incomprehensible fullness of her breasts, like a nursing mother's, and Braggioni, who considers himself a judge of women, speculates again on the puzzle of her notorious virginity, and takes the liberty of speech which she permits without a sign of modesty, indeed, without any sort of sign, which is disconcerting.

'You think you are so cold, *gringita*! Wait and see. You will surprise yourself some day! May I be there to advise you!' He stretches his eyelids at her, and his ill-humored cat's eyes waver in a separate glance for the two points of light marking the opposite ends of a smoothly drawn path between the swollen curve of her breasts. He is not put off by that blue serge, nor by her resolutely fixed gaze. There is all the time in the world. His cheeks are bellying with the wind of song. 'O girl with the dark eyes', he sings, and reconsiders. 'But yours are not dark. I can change all that. O girl with the green eyes, you have stolen my heart away!' then his mind wanders to the song, and Laura feels the weight of his attention being shifted elsewhere. Singing thus, he seems harmless, he is quite harmless, there is nothing to do but sit patiently and say 'No', when the moment comes. She draws a full breath, and her mind wanders also, but not far. She dares not wander too far.

Not for nothing has Braggioni taken pains to be a good revolutionist and a professional lover of humanity. He will never die of it. He has the malice, the cleverness, the wickedness, the sharpness of wit, the hardness of heart, stipulated for loving the world profitably. *He will never die of it.* He will live to see himself kicked out from his feeding trough by other hungry world-saviours. Traditionally he must sing in spite of his life which drives him to bloodshed, he tells Laura, for his father was a Tuscany peasant who drifted to Yucatan and married a Maya woman: a woman of race, an aristocrat. They gave him the love and knowledge of music, thus: and under the rip of his thumb-nail, the strings of the instrument complain like exposed nerves.

Once he was called Delgadito by all the girls and married women who ran after him; he was so scrawny all his bones showed under his thin cotton clothing, and he could squeeze his emptiness to the very backbone with his two hands. He was a poet and the revolution was only a dream then; too many women loved him and sapped away his youth, and he could never find enough to eat anywhere, anywhere! Now he is a leader of men, crafty men who whisper in his ear, hungry men who wait for hours outside his office for a word with him, emaciated men with wild faces who waylay him at the street gate with a timid, 'Comrade, let me tell you . . . ' and they blow the foul breath from their empty stomachs in his face.

He is always sympathetic. He gives them handfuls of small coins from his own pocket, he promises them work, there will be demonstrations, they must join the unions and attend the meetings, above all they must be on the watch for spies. They are closer to him than his own brothers, without them he can do nothing – until tomorrow, comrade!

Until tomorrow. 'They are stupid, they are lazy, they are treacherous, they would cut my throat for nothing,' he says to Laura. He has good food and abundant drink, he hires an automobile and drives in the Paseo on Sunday morning, and enjoys plenty of sleep in a soft bed beside a wife who dares not disturb him; and he sits pampering his bones in easy billows of fat, singing to Laura, who knows and thinks these things about him. When he was fifteen, he tried to drown himself because he loved a girl, his first love, and she laughed at him. 'A thousand women have paid for that,' and his tight little mouth turns down at the corners. Now he perfumes his hair with Jockey Club, and confides to Laura: 'One woman is really as good as another for me, in the dark. I prefer them all.'

His wife organizes unions among the girls in the cigarette factories, and walks in picket lines, and even speaks at meetings in the evening. But she cannot be brought to acknowledge the benefits of true liberty. 'I tell her I must have my freedom, net. She does not understand my point of view.' Laura has heard this many times. Braggioni scratches the guitar and meditates. 'She is an instinctively virtuous woman, pure gold, no doubt of that. If she were not, I should lock her up, and she knows it.'

His wife, who works so hard for the good of the factory girls, employs part of her leisure lying on the floor weeping because there are so many women in the world, and only one husband for her, and she never knows where nor when to look for him. He told her: 'Unless you can learn to cry when I am not here, I must go away for good.' That day he went away and took a room at the Hotel Madrid.

It is this month of separation for the sake of higher principles that has been spoiled not only for Mrs Braggioni, whose sense of reality is beyond criticism, but for Laura, who feels herself bogged in a nightmare. Tonight Laura envies Mrs Braggioni, who is alone, and free to weep as much as she pleases about a concrete wrong. Laura has just come from a visit to the prison, and she is waiting for tomorrow with a bitter anxiety as if tomorrow may not come, but time may be caught immovably in this hour, with herself transfixed, Braggioni singing on forever, and Eugenio's body not yet discovered by the guard.

Braggioni says: 'Are you going to sleep?' Almost before she can shake her head, he begins telling her about the May-day disturbances coming on in Morelia, for the Catholics hold a festival in honor of the Blessed Virgin, and the Socialists celebrate their martyrs on that day. 'There will be two independent processions starting from either end of town, and they will march until they meet, and the rest depends. . . .' He asks her to oil and load his pistols. Standing up, he unbuckles his ammunition belt, and spreads it laden across her knees. Laura sits with the shells slipping through the cleaning cloth dipped in oil, and he says again he cannot understand why she works so hard for the revolutionary idea unless she loves some man who is in it. 'Are you not in love with someone?' 'No,' says Laura. 'And no one is in love with you?' 'No.' 'Then it is your own fault. No woman need go begging. Why, what is the matter with you? The legless beggar woman in the Alameda has a perfectly faithful lover. Did you know that?'

Laura peers down the pistol barrel and says nothing, but a long, slow faintness rises and subsides in her; Braggioni curves his swollen fingers around the throat of the guitar and softly smothers the music out of it, and when she hears him again he seems to have forgotten her, and is speaking in the hypnotic voice he uses when talking in small rooms to a listening, close-gathered crowd. Some day this world, now seemingly so composed and eternal, to the edges of every sea shall be merely a tangle of gaping trenches, of crashing walls and broken bodies. Everything must be torn from its accustomed place where it has rotted for centuries, hurled skyward and distributed, cast down again clean as rain, without separate identity. Nothing shall survive that the stiffened hands of poverty have created for the rich and no one shall be left alive except the elect spirits destined to procreate a new world cleansed of cruelty and injustice, ruled by benevolent anarchy: 'Pistols are good, I love them, cannon are even better, but in the end I pin my faith to good dynamite,' he concludes, and strokes the pistol lying in her hands. 'Once I dreamed of destroying this city, in case it offered resistance to General Ortíz, but it fell into his hands like an over-ripe pear.'

He is made restless by his own words, rises and stands waiting. Laura holds up the belt to him: 'Put that on, and go kill somebody in Morelia, and you will be happier,' she says softly. The presence of death in the room makes her bold. 'Today, I found Eugenio going into a stupor. He refused to allow me to call the prison doctor. He had taken all the tablets I brought him yesterday. He said he took them because he was bored.'

'He is a fool, and his death is his own business,' says Braggioni, fastening his belt carefully.

'I told him if he had waited only a little while longer, you would have got him set free,' says Laura. 'He said he did not want to wait.'

'He is a fool and we are well rid of him,' says Braggioni, reaching for his hat.

He goes away. Laura knows his mood has changed, she will not see him any more for a while. He will send word when he needs her to go on errands into strange streets, to speak to the strange faces that will appear, like clay masks with the power of human speech, to mutter their thanks to Braggioni for his help. Now she is free, and she thinks, I must run while there is time. But she does not go.

Braggioni enters his own house where for a month his wife has spent many hours every night weeping and tangling her hair upon her pillow. She is weeping now, and she weeps more at the sight of him, the cause of all her sorrows. He looks about the room. Nothing is changed, the smells are good and familiar, he is well acquainted with the woman who comes toward him with no reproach except grief on her face. He says to her tenderly: 'You are so good, please don't cry any more, you dear good creature.' She says, 'Are you tired, my angel? Sit here and I will wash your feet.' She brings a bowl of water, and kneeling, unlaces his shoes, and when from her knees she raises her sad eyes under her blackened lids, he is sorry for everything, and bursts into tears. 'Ah, yes, I am hungry, I am tired, let us eat something together,' he says, between sobs. His wife leans her head on her arm and says, 'Forgive me!' and this time he is refreshed by the solemn, endless rain of her tears.

Laura takes off her serge dress and puts on a white linen nightgown and goes to bed. She turns her head a little to one side, and lying still, reminds herself that it is time to sleep. Numbers tick in her brain like little clocks, soundless doors close of themselves around her. If you would sleep, you must not remember anything, the children will say tomorrow, good morning, my teacher, the poor prisoners who come every day bringing flowers to their jailor. 1–2–3–4–5 – it is monstrous to confuse love with revolution, night with day, life with death – ah, Eugenio!

The tolling of the midnight bell is a signal, but what does it mean? Get up, Laura, and follow me: come out of your sleep, out of your bed, out of this strange house. What are you doing in this house? Without a word, without fear she rose and reached for Eugenio's hand, but he eluded her with a sharp, sly smile and drifted away. This is not all, you shall see – Murderer, he said, follow me, I will show you a new country, but it is far away and we must hurry. No, said Laura, not unless you take my hand, no; and she clung first to the stair rail, and then to the topmost branch of the Judas tree that bent down slowly and set her upon the earth, and then to the rocky ledge of a cliff, and then to the jagged wave of a sea that was not water but a desert of crumbling stone. Where are you taking me, she asked in wonder but without fear. To death, and it is a long way off, and we must hurry, said Eugenio. No, said Laura, not unless you take my hand. Then eat these flowers, poor prisoner, said Eugenio in a voice of pity, take and eat: and from the Judas tree he stripped the warm bleeding flowers, and held them to her lips. She saw that his hand was fleshless, a cluster of small white petrified branches, and his eye sockets were without light, but she ate the flowers greedily for they satisfied both hunger and thirst. Murderer! said Eugenio, and Cannibal! This is my body and my blood. Laura cried No! and at the sound of her own voice, she awoke trembling, and was afraid to sleep again.

The Tent

A sudden squall struck the tent. White glittering hailstones struck the shabby canvas with a wild noise. The tent shook and swayed slightly forward, dangling its tattered flaps. The pole creaked as it strained. A rent appeared near the top of the pole like a silver seam in the canvas. Water immediately trickled through the seam, making a dark blob.

A tinker and his two wives were sitting on a heap of straw in the tent, looking out through the entrance at the wild moor that stretched in front of it, with a snow-capped mountain peak rising like the tip of a cone over the ridge of the moor about two miles away. The three of them were smoking cigarettes in silence. It was evening, and they had pitched their tent for the night in a gravel pit on the side of the mountain road, crossing from one glen to another. Their donkey was tethered to the cart beside the tent.

When the squall came the tinker sat up with a start and looked at the pole. He stared at the seam in the canvas for several moments and then he nudged the two women and pointed upwards with a jerk of his nose. The women looked but nobody spoke. After a minute or so the tinker sighed and struggled to his feet.

'I'll throw a few sacks over the top,' he said.

He picked up two brown sacks from the heap of blankets and clothes that were drying beside the brazier in the entrance and went out. The women never spoke, but kept on smoking.

The tinker kicked the donkey out of his way. The beast had stuck his hindquarters into the entrance of the tent as far as possible, in order to get the heat from the wood burning in the brazier. The donkey shrank away sideways still chewing a wisp of the hay which the tinker had stolen from a haggard the other side of the mountain. The tinker scrambled up the bank against which the tent was pitched. The bank was covered with rank grass into which yesterday's snow had melted in muddy cakes.

The top of the tent was only about eighteen inches above the bank. Beyond the bank there was a narrow rough road, with a thick copse of pine trees on the far side, within the wired fence of a demesne, but the force of the squall was so great that it swept through the trees and struck the top of the tent as violently as if it were standing exposed on the open moor. The tinker had to lean against the wind to prevent himself being carried away. He looked into the wind with wide-open nostrils.

'It can't last,' he said, throwing the two sacks over the tent, where there was a rent in the canvas. He then took a big needle from his jacket and put a few stitches in them.

He was about to jump down from the bank when somebody hailed him from the road. He looked up and saw a man approaching, with his head thrust forward against the wind. The tinker scowled and shrugged his shoulders. He waited until the man came up to him.

The stranger was a tall, sturdily built man, with a long face and firm jaws and great sombre dark eyes, a fighter's face. When he reached the tinker he stood erect with his feet together and his hands by his sides like a soldier. He was fairly well dressed, his face was clean and well shaved, and his hands were clean. There was a blue figure of something or other tattooed on the back of his right hand. He looked at the tinker frankly with his sombre dark eyes. Neither spoke for several moments.

'Good evening,' the stranger said.

The tinker nodded without speaking. He was looking the stranger up and down, as if he were slightly afraid of this big, sturdy man, who was almost like a policeman or a soldier or somebody in authority. He looked at the man's boots especially. In spite of the muck of the roads, the melted snow and the hailstones, they were still fairly clean, and looked as if they were constantly polished.

'Travellin'?' he said at length.

'Eh,' said the stranger, almost aggressively. 'Oh! Yes, I'm lookin' for somewhere to shelter for the night.'

The stranger glanced at the tent slowly and then looked back to the tinker again.

'Goin' far?' said the tinker.

'Don't know,' said the stranger angrily. Then he almost shouted: 'I have no bloody place to go to . . . only the bloody roads.'

'All right, brother,' said the tinker, 'come on.'

He nodded towards the tent and jumped down into the pit. The stranger followed him, stepping carefully down to avoid soiling his clothes.

When he entered the tent after the tinker and saw the women he immediately took off his cap and said: 'Good evening.' The two women took their cigarettes from their mouths, smiled and nodded their heads.

The stranger looked about him cautiously and then sat down on a box to the side of the door near the brazier. He put his hands to the blaze and rubbed them. Almost immediately a slight steam rose from his clothes. The tinker handed him a cigarette, murmuring: 'Smoke?'

The stranger accepted the cigarette, lit it, and then looked at them. None of them were looking at him, so he 'sized them up' carefully, looking at each suspiciously with his sombre dark eyes. The tinker was sitting on a box opposite him, leaning languidly backwards from his hips, a slim, tall, graceful man, with a beautiful head poised gracefully on a brown neck, and great black lashes falling down over his half-closed eyes, just like a woman. A womanish-looking fellow, with that sensuous grace in the languid pose of his body which is found only among aristocrats and people who belong to a very small workless class, cut off from the mass of society, yet living at their expense. A young fellow with proud, contemptuous, closed lips and an arrogant expression in his slightly expanded nostrils. A silent fellow, blowing out cigarette smoke through his nostrils and gazing dreamily into the blaze of the wood fire. The two women were just like him in texture, both of them slatterns, dirty and unkempt, but with the same proud, arrogant, contemptuous look in their beautiful brown faces. One was dark-haired and black-eyed. She had rather a hard expression in her face and seemed very alert. The other woman was golden-haired, with a very small head and finely-developed jaw, that stuck out level with her forehead. She was surpassingly beautiful, in spite of her ragged clothes and the foul condition of her hair, which was piled on her tiny skull in knotted heaps, uncombed. The perfect symmetry and delicacy of her limbs, her bust and her long throat that had tiny freckles in the white skin, made the stranger feel afraid of her, of her beauty and her presence in the tent.

'Tinkers,' he said to himself. 'Awful bloody people.'

Then he turned to the tinker.

'Got any grub in the place ... eh ... mate?' he said brusquely, his thick lips rapping out every word firmly, like one accustomed to command inferiors. He hesitated before he added the word 'mate', obviously disinclined to put himself on a level of human intercourse with the tinker.

The tinker nodded and turned to the dark-haired woman.

'Might as well have supper now, Kitty,' he said softly.

The dark-haired woman rose immediately, and taking a blackened can that was full of water, she put it on the brazier. The stranger watched her. Then he addressed the tinker again.

'This is a hell of a way to be, eh?' he said. 'Stuck out on a mountain. Thought I'd make Roundwood tonight. How many miles is it from here?'

'Ten,' said the tinker.

'Good God!' said the stranger.

Then he laughed, and putting his hand in his breast pocket, he pulled out a half-pint bottle of whiskey.

'This is all I got left,' he said, looking at the bottle.

The tinker immediately opened his eyes wide when he saw the bottle. The golden-haired woman sat up and looked at the stranger eagerly, opening her brown eyes wide and rolling her tongue in her cheek. The dark-haired woman, rummaging in a box, also turned around to look. The stranger winked an eye and smiled.

'Always welcome,' he said. 'Eh? My curse on it, anyway. Anybody got a corkscrew?'

The tinker took a knife from his pocket, pulled out a corkscrew from its side and handed it to the man. The man opened the bottle.

'Here,' he said, handing the bottle to the tinker. 'Pass it round. I suppose the women'll have a drop.'

The tinker took the bottle and whispered to the dark-haired woman. She began to pass him mugs from the box.

'Funny thing,' said the stranger, 'when a man is broke and hungry, he can get whiskey but he can't get grub. Met a man this morning in Dublin and he knew bloody well I was broke, but instead of asking me to have a meal, or giving me some money, he gave me that. I had it with me all along the road and I never opened it.'

He threw the end of his cigarette out the entrance.

'Been drinkin' for three weeks, curse it,' he said.

'Are ye belongin' to these parts?' murmured the tinker, pouring out the whiskey into the tin mugs.

'What's that?' said the man, again speaking angrily, as if he resented the question. Then he added: 'No. Never been here in me life before. Question of goin' into the workhouse or takin' to the roads. Got a job in Dublin yesterday. The men downed tools when they found I wasn't a member of the union. Thanks. Here's luck.'

'Good health, sir,' the women said.

The tinker nodded his head only, as he put his own mug to his lips and tasted it. The stranger drained his at a gulp.

'Ha,' he said. 'Drink up, girls. It's good stuff.'

He winked at them. They smiled and sipped their whiskey.

'My name is Carney,' said the stranger to the tinker. 'What do they call you?'

'Byrne,' said the tinker. 'Joe Byrne.'

'Hm! Byrne,' said Carney. 'Wicklow's full o' Byrnes. Tinker, I suppose?'

'Yes,' murmured the tinker, blowing a cloud of cigarette smoke through his puckered lips. Carney shrugged his shoulders.

'Might as well,' he said. 'One thing is as good as another. Look at me. Sergeant-major in the army two months ago. Now I'm tramping the roads. That's boiling.'

The dark-haired woman took the can off the fire. The other woman tossed off the remains of her whiskey and got to her feet to help with the meal. Carney shifted his box back farther out of the way and watched the golden-haired woman eagerly. When she moved about her figure was so tall that she had to stoop low in order to avoid the roof of the tent. She must have been six feet in height, and she wore high-heeled shoes which made her look taller.

'There is a woman for ye,' thought Carney. 'Must be a gentleman's daughter. Lots o' these shots out of a gun in the county Wicklow. Half the population is illegitimate. Awful bloody people, these tinkers. I suppose the two of them belong to this Joe. More like a woman than a man. Suppose he never did a stroke o' work in his life.'

There was cold rabbit for supper, with tea and bread and butter. It was excellent tea, and it tasted all the sweeter on account of the storm outside which was still raging. Sitting around the brazier they could see the hailstones driving through a grey mist, sweeping the bleak black moor, and the cone-shaped peak of the mountain in the distance, with a whirling cloud of snow around it. The sky was rent here and there with a blue patch, showing through the blackness.

They ate the meal in silence. Then the women cleared it away. They didn't wash the mugs or plates, but put everything away, probably until morning. They sat down again after drawing out the straw, bed-shape, and putting the clothes on it that had been drying near the brazier. They all seemed to be in a good humour now with the whiskey and the food. Even the tinker's face had grown soft, and he kept puckering up his lips in a smile. He passed around cigarettes.

'Might as well finish that bottle,' said Carney. 'Bother the mugs. We can drink outa the neck.'

'Tastes sweeter that way,' said the golden-haired woman, laughing thickly, as if she were slightly drunk. At the same time she looked at Carney with her lips open.

Carney winked at her. The tinker noticed the wink and the girl's smile. His face clouded and he closed his lips very tightly. Carney took a deep draught and passed him the bottle. The tinker nodded his head, took the bottle and put it to his lips.

'I'll have a stretch,' said Carney. 'I'm done in. Twenty miles since mornin'. Eh?'

He threw himself down on the clothes beside the yellow-haired woman. She smiled and looked at the tinker. The tinker paused with the bottle to his lips and looked at her through almost closed eyes savagely. He took the bottle from his lips and bared his white teeth. The golden-headed woman shrugged her shoulders and pouted. The dark-haired woman laughed aloud, stretched back with one arm under her head and the other stretched out towards the tinker.

'Sht,' she whistled through her teeth. 'Pass it along, Joe.'

He handed her the bottle slowly, and as he gave it to her she clutched his hand and tried to pull him to her. But he tore his hand away, got up and walked out of the tent rapidly.

Carney had noticed nothing of this. He was lying close to the woman by his side. He could feel the softness of her beautiful body and the slight undulation of her soft side as she breathed. He became overpowered with desire for her and closed his eyes, as if to shut out the consciousness of the world and of the other people in the tent. Reaching down he seized her hand and pressed it. She answered the pressure. At the same time she turned to her companion and whispered:

'Where's he gone?'

'I dunno. Rag out.'

'What about?'

'Phst.'

'Give us a drop.'

'Here ye are.'

Carney heard the whispering, but he took no notice of it. He heard the golden-headed one drinking and then drawing a deep breath.

'Finished,' she said, throwing the bottle to the floor. Then she laughed softly.

'I'm going out to see where he's gone,' whispered the dark-haired one. She rose and passed out of the tent. Carney immediately turned around and tried to embrace the woman by his side. But she bared her teeth in a savage grin and pinioned his arms with a single movement.

'Didn't think I was strong,' she said, putting her face close to his and grinning at him.

He looked at her seriously, surprised and still more excited.

'What ye goin' to do in Roundwood?' she said.

'Lookin' for a job,' he muttered thickly.

She smiled and rolled her tongue in her cheek.

'Stay here,' she said.

He licked his lip and winked his right eye. 'With you?'

She nodded.

'What about him?' he said, nodding towards the door.

She laughed silently. 'Are ye afraid of Joe?'

He did not reply, but, making a sudden movement, he seized her around the body and pressed her to him. She did not resist, but began to laugh, and bared her teeth as she laughed. He tried to kiss her mouth, but she threw back her head and he kissed her cheek several times.

Then suddenly there was a hissing noise at the door. Carney sat up with a start. The tinker was standing in the entrance, stooping low, with his mouth open and his jaw twisted to the right, his two hands hanging loosely by his sides, with the fingers twitching. The dark-haired woman was standing behind him, peering over his shoulder. She was smiling.

Carney got to his feet, took a pace forward, and squared himself. He did not speak. The golden-headed woman uttered a loud peal of laughter, and, stretching out her arms, she lay flat on the bed, giggling.

'Come out here,' hissed the tinker.

He stepped back. Carney shouted and rushed at him, jumping the brazier. The tinker stepped aside and struck Carney a terrible blow on the jaw as he passed him. Carney staggered against the bank and fell in a heap. The tinker jumped on him like a cat, striking him with his hands and feet all together. Carney roared: 'Let me up, let me up. Fair play.' But the tinker kept on beating him until at last he lay motionless at the bottom of the pit.

'Ha,' said the tinker.

Then he picked up the prone body, as lightly as if it were an empty sack, and threw it to the top of the bank.

'Be off, you — ,' he hissed.

Carney struggled to his feet on the top of the bank and looked at the three of them. They were all standing now in front of the tent, the two women grinning, the tinker scowling. Then he staggered on to the road, with his hands to his head.

'Good-bye, dearie,' cried the golden-headed one.

Then she screamed. Carney looked behind and saw the tinker carrying her into the tent in his arms.

'God Almighty!' cried Carney, crossing himself.

Then he trudged away fearfully through the storm towards Roundwood.

'God Almighty!' he cried at every two yards. 'God Almighty!'

WILLIAM FAULKNER · 1897–1962

Dry September

I

Through the bloody September twilight, aftermath of sixty-two rainless days, it had gone like a fire in dry grass – the rumor, the story, whatever it was. Something about Miss Minnie Cooper and a Negro. Attacked, insulted, frightened: none of them, gathered in the barber shop on that Saturday evening where the ceiling fan stirred, without freshening it, the vitiated air, sending back upon them, in recurrent surges of stale pomade and lotion, their own stale breath and odors, knew exactly what had happened.

'Except it wasn't Will Mayes,' a barber said. He was a man of middle age; a thin, sand-colored man with a mild face, who was shaving a client. 'I know Will Mayes. He's a good nigger. And I know Miss Minnie Cooper, too.'

'What do you know about her?' a second barber said.

'Who is she?' the client said. 'A young girl?'

'No,' the barber said. 'She's about forty, I reckon. She ain't married. That's why I don't believe — '

'Believe, hell!' a hulking youth in a sweat-stained silk shirt said. 'Won't you take a white woman's word before a nigger's?'

'I don't believe Will Mayes did it,' the barber said. 'I know Will Mayes.'

'Maybe you know who did it, then. Maybe you already got him out of town, you damn niggerlover.'

'I don't believe anybody did anything. I don't believe anything happened. I leave it to you fellows if them ladies that get old without getting married don't have notions that a man can't — '

'Then you are a hell of a white man,' the client said. He moved under the cloth. The youth had sprung to his feet.

'You don't?' he said. 'Do you accuse a white woman of lying?'

The barber held the razor poised above the half-risen client. He did not look around.

'It's this durn weather,' another said. 'It's enough to make a man do anything. Even to her.'

Nobody laughed. The barber said in his mild, stubborn tone: 'I ain't accusing nobody of nothing. I just know and you fellows know how a woman that never — '

'You damn niggerlover!' the youth said.

'Shut up, Butch,' another said. 'We'll get the facts in plenty of time to act.'

'Who is? Who's getting them?' the youth said. 'Facts, hell! I — '

'You're a fine white man,' the client said. 'Ain't you?' In his frothy beard he looked like a desert rat in the moving pictures. 'You tell them, Jack,' he said to the youth. 'If there ain't any white men in this town, you can count on me, even if I ain't only a drummer and a stranger.'

'That's right, boys,' the barber said. 'Find out the truth first. I know Will Mayes.'

'Well, by God!' the youth shouted. 'To think that a white man in this town — '

'Shut up, Butch,' the second speaker said. 'We got plenty of time.'

The client sat up. He looked at the speaker. 'Do you claim that anything excuses a nigger attacking a white woman? Do you mean to tell me you are a white man and you'll stand for it? You better go back North where you came from. The South don't want your kind here.'

'North what?' the second said. 'I was born and raised in this town.'

'Well, by God!' the youth said. He looked about with a strained, baffled gaze, as if he was trying to remember what it was he wanted to say or to do. He drew his sleeve across his sweating face. 'Damn if I'm going to let a white woman — '

'You tell them, Jack,' the drummer said. 'By God, if they — '

The screen door crashed open. A man stood in the floor, his feet apart and his heavy-set body poised easily. His white shirt was open at the throat; he wore a felt hat. His hot, bold glance swept the group. His name was McLendon. He had commanded troops at the front in France and had been decorated for valor.

'Well,' he said, 'are you going to sit there and let a black son rape a white woman on the streets of Jefferson?'

Butch sprang up again. The silk of his shirt clung flat to his heavy shoulders. At each armpit was a dark half moon. 'That's what I been telling them! That's what I — '

'Did it really happen?' a third said. 'This ain't the first man scare she ever had, like Hawkshaw says. Wasn't there something about a man on the kitchen roof, watching her undress, about a year ago?'

'What?' the client said. 'What's that?' The barber had been slowly forcing him back into the chair; he arrested himself reclining, his head lifted, the barber still pressing him down.

McLendon whirled on the third speaker. 'Happen? What the hell difference does it make? Are you going to let the black sons get away with it until one really does it?'

'That's what I'm telling them!' Butch shouted. He cursed, long and steady, pointless.

'Here, here,' a fourth said. 'Not so loud. Don't talk so loud.'

'Sure,' McLendon said; 'no talking necessary at all. I've done my talking. Who's with me?' He poised on the balls of his feet, roving his gaze.

The barber held the drummer's face down, the razor poised. 'Find out the facts first, boys. I know Willy Mayes. It wasn't him. Let's get the sheriff and do this thing right.'

McLendon whirled upon him his furious, rigid face. The barber did not look away. They looked like men of different races. The other barbers had ceased also above their prone clients. 'You mean to tell me,' McLendon said, 'that you'd take a nigger's word before a white woman's? Why, you damn niggerloving — '

The third speaker rose and grasped McLendon's arm; he too had been a soldier. 'Now, now. Let's figure this thing out. Who knows anything about what really happened?'

'Figure out hell!' McLendon jerked his arm free. 'All that're with me get up from there. The ones that ain't — ' He roved his gaze, dragging his sleeve across his face.

Three men rose. The drummer in the chair sat up. 'Here,' he said, jerking at the cloth about his neck; 'get this rag off me. I'm with him. I don't live here, but by God, if our mothers and wives and sisters — ' He smeared the cloth over his face and flung it to the floor. McLendon stood in the floor and cursed the others. Another rose and moved toward him. The remainder sat uncomfortable, not looking at one another, then one by one they rose and joined him.

The barber picked the cloth from the floor. He began to fold it neatly. 'Boys, don't do that. Will Mayes never done it. I know.'

'Come on,' McLendon said. He whirled. From his hip pocket protruded the butt of a heavy automatic pistol. They went out. The screen door crashed behind them reverberant in the dead air.

The barber wiped the razor carefully and swiftly, and put it away, and ran to the rear, and took his hat from the wall. 'I'll be back as soon as I can,' he said to the other barbers. 'I can't let — ' He went out, running. The two other barbers followed him to the door and caught it on the rebound, leaning out and looking up the street after him. The air was flat and dead. It had a metallic taste at the base of the tongue.

'What can he do?' the first said. The second one was saying 'Jees Christ, Jees Christ' under his breath. 'I'd just as lief be Will Mayes as Hawk, if he gets McLendon riled.'

'Jees Christ, Jees Christ,' the second whispered.

'You reckon he really done it to her?' the first said.

II

She was thirty-eight or thirty-nine. She lived in a small frame house with her invalid mother and a thin, sallow, unflagging aunt, where each morning between ten and eleven she would appear on the porch in a lace-trimmed boudoir cap, to sit swinging in the porch swing until noon. After dinner she lay down for a while, until the afternoon began to cool. Then, in one of the three or four new voile dresses which she had each summer, she would go downtown to spend the afternoon in the stores with the other ladies, where they would handle the goods and haggle over the prices in cold, immediate voices, without any intention of buying.

She was of comfortable people – not the best in Jefferson, but good people enough – and she was still on the slender side of ordinary looking, with a bright, faintly haggard manner and dress. When she was young she had had a slender, nervous body and a sort of hard vivacity which had enabled her for a time to ride upon the crest of the town's social life as exemplified by the high school party and church social period of her contemporaries while still children enough to be unclassconscious.

She was the last to realize that she was losing ground; that those among whom she had been a little brighter and louder flame than any other were beginning to learn the pleasure of snobbery – male – and retaliation – female. That was when her face began to wear that bright, haggard look. She still carried it to parties on shadowy porticoes and summer lawns, like a mask or a flag, with that baf-flement of furious repudiation of truth in her eyes. One evening at a party she heard a boy and two girls, all schoolmates, talking. She never accepted another invitation.

She watched the girls with whom she had grown up as they mar-ried and got homes and children, but no man ever called on her steadily until the children of the other girls had been calling her 'aunty' for several years, the while their mothers told them in bright voices about how popular Aunt Minnie had been as a girl. Then the town began to see her driving on Sunday afternoons with the cashier in the bank. He was a widower of about forty – a high-colored man, smelling always faintly of the barber shop or of whiskey. He owned the first automobile in town, a red runabout; Minnie had the first motoring bonnet and veil the town ever saw. Then the town began to say: 'Poor Minnie.' 'But she is old enough to take care of herself,' others said. That was when she began to ask her old schoolmates that their children call her 'cousin' instead of 'aunty'.

It was twelve years now since she had been relegated into adul-tery by public opinion, and eight years since the cashier had gone to a Memphis bank, returning for one day each Christmas, which he spent at an annual bachelors' party at a hunting club on the river. From behind their curtains the neighbors would see the party pass, and during the over-the-way Christmas day visiting they would tell her about him, about how well he looked, and how they heard that he was prospering in the city, watching with bright, sec-ret eyes her haggard, bright face. Usually by that hour there would be the scent of whiskey on her breath. It was supplied her by a youth, a clerk at the soda fountain: 'Sure; I buy it for the old gal. I reckon she's entitled to a little fun.'

Her mother kept to her room altogether now; the gaunt aunt ran the house. Against that background Minnie's bright dresses, her idle and empty days, had a quality of furious unreality. She went out in the evenings only with women now, neighbors, to the moving pictures. Each afternoon she dressed in one of the new dresses and went downtown alone, where her young 'cousins' were already strolling in the late afternoons with their delicate, silken heads and thin, awkward arms and conscious hips, clinging to one another or shrieking and giggling with paired boys in the soda fountain when she passed and went on along the serried store fronts, in the doors of which the sitting and lounging men did not even follow her with their eyes any more.

III

The barber went swiftly up the street where the sparse lights, insect-swirled, glared in rigid and violent suspension in the lifeless air. The day had died in a pall of dust; above the darkened square, shrouded by the spent dust, the sky was as clear as the inside of a brass bell. Below the east was a rumor of the twice-waxed moon.

When he overtook them McLendon and three others were getting into a car parked in an alley. McLendon stooped his thick head, peering out beneath the top. 'Changed your mind, did you?' he said. 'Damn good thing; by God, tomorrow when this town hears about how you talked tonight — '

'Now, now,' the other ex-soldier said. 'Hawkshaw's all right. Come on, Hawk; jump in.'

'Will Mayes never done it, boys,' the barber said. 'If anybody done it. Why, you all know well as I do there ain't any town where they got better niggers than us. And you know how a lady will kind of think things about men when there ain't any reason to, and Miss Minnie anyway — '

'Sure, sure,' the soldier said. 'We're just going to talk to him a little; that's all.'

'Talk hell!' Butch said. 'When we're through with the — '

'Shut up, for God's sake!' the soldier said. 'Do you want everybody in town — '

'Tell them, by God!' McLendon said. 'Tell every one of the sons that'll let a white woman — '

'Let's go; let's go: here's the other car.' The second car slid squealing out of a cloud of dust at the alley mouth. McLendon started his car and took the lead. Dust lay like fog in the street. The street lights hung nimbused as in water. They drove on out of town.

A rutted lane turned at right angles. Dust hung above it too, and above all the land. The dark bulk of the ice plant, where the Negro Mayes was night-watchman, rose against the sky. 'Better stop here, hadn't we?' the soldier said. McLendon did not reply. He hurled the car up and slammed to a stop, the headlights glaring on the blank wall.

'Listen here, boys,' the barber said; 'if he's here, don't that prove he never done it? Don't it? If it was him, he would run. Don't you see he would?' The second car came up and stopped. McLendon got down; Butch sprang down beside him. 'Listen, boys,' the barber said.

'Cut the lights off!' McLendon said. The breathless dark rushed down. There was no sound in it save their lungs as they sought air in the parched dust in which for two months they had lived; then the diminishing crunch of McLendon's and Butch's feet, and a moment later McLendon's voice:

'Will! . . . Will!'

Below the east the wan haemorrhage of the moon increased. It heaved above the ridge, silvering the air, the dust, so that they seemed to breathe, live, in a bowl of molten lead. There was no sound of nightbird nor insect, no sound save their breathing and a faint ticking of contracting metal about the cars. Where their bodies touched one another they seemed to sweat dryly, for no more moisture came. 'Christ!' a voice said; 'let's get out of here.'

But they didn't move until vague noises began to grow out of the darkness ahead; then they got out and waited tensely in the breathless dark. There was another sound: a blow, a hissing expulsion of breath and McLendon cursing in undertone. They stood a moment longer, then they ran forward. They ran in a stumbling clump, as though they were fleeing something. 'Kill him, kill the son,' a voice whispered. McLendon flung them back.

'Not here,' he said. 'Get him into the car.' 'Kill him, kill the black son!' the voice murmured. They dragged the Negro to the car. The barber had waited beside the car. He could feel himself sweating and he knew he was going to be sick at the stomach.

'What is it, captains?' the Negro said. 'I ain't done nothing. 'Fore God, Mr John.' Someone produced handcuffs. They worked busily about the Negro as though he were a post, quiet, intent, getting in one another's way. He submitted to the handcuffs, looking swiftly and constantly from dim face to dim face. 'Who's here, captains?' he said, leaning to peer into the faces until they could feel his breath and smell his sweaty reek. He spoke a name or two. 'What you all say I done, Mr John?'

McLendon jerked the car door open. 'Get in!' he said.

The Negro did not move. 'What you all going to do with me, Mr John? I ain't done nothing. White folks, captains, I ain't done nothing: I swear 'fore God.' He called another name.

'Get in!' McLendon said. He struck the Negro. The others expelled their breath in a dry hissing and struck him with random blows and he whirled and cursed them, and swept his manacled hands across their faces and slashed the barber upon the mouth, and the barber struck him also. 'Get him in there,' McLendon said. They pushed at him. He ceased struggling and got in and sat quietly as the others took their places. He sat between the barber and the soldier, drawing his limbs in so as not to touch them, his eyes going swiftly and constantly from face to face. Butch clung to the running board. The car moved on. The barber nursed his mouth with his handkerchief.

'What's the matter, Hawk?' the soldier said.

'Nothing,' the barber said. They regained the highroad and turned away from town. The second car dropped back out of the dust. They went on, gaining speed; the final fringe of houses dropped behind.

'Goddamn, he stinks!' the soldier said.

'We'll fix that,' the drummer in front beside McLendon said. On the running board Butch cursed into the hot rush of air. The barber leaned suddenly forward and touched McLendon's arm.

'Let me out, John,' he said.

'Jump out, niggerlover,' McLendon said without turning his head. He drove swiftly. Behind them the sourceless lights of the second car glared in the dust. Presently McLendon turned into a narrow road. It was rutted with disuse. It led back to an abandoned brick kiln – a series of reddish mounds and weed- and vine-choked vats without bottom. It had been used for pasture once, until one day the owner missed one of his mules. Although he prodded carefully in the vats with a long pole, he could not even find the bottom of them.

'John,' the barber said.

'Jump out, then,' McLendon said, hurling the car along the ruts. Beside the barber the Negro spoke:

'Mr Henry.'

The barber sat forward. The narrow tunnel of the road rushed up and past. Their motion was like an extinct furnace blast: cooler, but utterly dead. The car bounded from rut to rut.

'Mr Henry,' the Negro said.

The barber began to tug furiously at the door. 'Look out, there!' the soldier said, but the barber had already kicked the door open and swung on to the running board. The soldier leaned across the

Negro and grasped at him, but he had already jumped. The car went on without checking speed.

The impetus hurled him crashing through dust-sheathed weeds, into the ditch. Dust puffed about him, and in a thin, vicious crackling of sapless stems he lay choking and retching until the second car passed and died away. Then he rose and limped on until he reached the highroad and turned toward town, brushing at his clothes with his hands. The moon was higher, riding high and clear of the dust at last, and after a while the town began to glare beneath the dust. He went on, limping. Presently he heard cars and the glow of them grew in the dust behind him and he left the road and crouched again in the weeds until they passed. McLendon's car came last now. There were four people in it and Butch was not on the running board.

They went on; the dust swallowed them; the glare and the sound died away. The dust of them hung for a while, but soon the eternal dust absorbed it again. The barber climbed back on to the road and limped on toward town.

IV

As she dressed for supper on that Saturday evening, her own flesh felt like fever. Her hands trembled among the hooks and eyes, and her eyes had a feverish look, and her hair swirled crisp and crackling under the comb. While she was still dressing the friends called for her and sat while she donned her sheerest underthings and stockings and a new voile dress. 'Do you feel strong enough to go out?' they said, their eyes bright too, with a dark glitter. 'When you have had time to get over the shock, you must tell us what happened. What he said and did; everything.'

In the leafed darkness, as they walked toward the square, she began to breathe deeply, something like a swimmer preparing to dive, until she ceased trembling, the four of them walking slowly because of the terrible heat and out of solicitude for her. But as they neared the square she began to tremble again, walking with her head up, her hands clenched at her sides, their voices about her murmurous, also with that feverish, glittering quality of their eyes.

They entered the square, she in the centre of the group, fragile in her fresh dress. She was trembling worse. She walked slower and slower, as children eat ice cream, her head up and her eyes bright in the haggard banner of her face, passing the hotel and the coatless drummers in chairs along the kerb looking around at her: 'That's the one: see? The one in pink in the middle.' 'Is that her? What did they do with the nigger? Did they — ?' 'Sure. He's all right.' 'All right, is he?' 'Sure. He went on a little trip.' Then the drugstore, where even the young men lounging in the doorway tipped their hats and followed with their eyes the motion of her hips and legs when she passed.

They went on, passing the lifted hats of the gentlemen, the suddenly ceased voices, deferent, protective. 'Do you see?' the friends said. Their voices sounded like long, hovering sighs of hissing exultation. 'There's not a Negro on the square. Not one.'

They reached the picture show. It was like a miniature fairyland with its lighted lobby and colored lithographs of life caught in its terrible and beautiful mutations. Her lips began to tingle. In the dark, when the picture began, it would be all right; she could hold back the laughing so it would not waste away so fast and so soon. So she hurried on before the turning faces, the undertones of low astonishment, and they took their accustomed places where she could see the aisle against the silver glare and the young men and girls coming in two and two against it.

The lights flicked away; the screen glowed silver, and soon life began to unfold, beautiful and passionate and sad, while still the young men and girls entered, scented and sibilant in the half dark, their paired backs in silhouette delicate and sleek, their slim, quick bodies awkward, divinely young, while beyond them the silver dream accumulated, inevitably on and on. She began to laugh. In trying to suppress it, it made more noise than ever; heads began to turn. Still laughing, her friends raised her and led her out, and she stood at the kerb, laughing on a high, sustained note, until the taxi came up and they helped her in.

They removed the pink voile and the sheer underthings and the stockings, and put her to bed, and cracked ice for her temples, and sent for the doctor. He was hard to locate, so they ministered to her with hushed ejaculations, renewing the ice and fanning her. While the ice was fresh and cold she stopped laughing and lay still for a time, moaning only a little. But soon the laughing welled again and her voice rose screaming.

'Shhhhhhhhhhh! Shhhhhhhhhhhhhhh!' they said, freshening the icepack, smoothing her hair, examining it for grey; 'poor girl!' Then to one another: 'Do you suppose anything really happened?'

their eyes darkly aglitter, secret and passionate. 'Shhhhhhhhhh! Poor girl! Poor Minnie!'

V

It was midnight when McLendon drove up to his neat new house. It was trim and fresh as a birdcage and almost as small, with its clean, green-and-white paint. He locked the car and mounted the porch and entered. His wife rose from a chair beside the reading lamp. McLendon stopped in the floor and stared at her until she looked down.

'Look at that clock,' he said, lifting his arm, pointing. She stood before him, her face lowered, a magazine in her hands. Her face was pale, strained, and weary-looking. 'Haven't I told you about sitting up like this, waiting to see when I come in?'

'John,' she said. She laid the magazine down. Poised on the balls of his feet, he glared at her with his hot eyes, his sweating face.

'Didn't I tell you?' He went toward her. She looked up then. He caught her shoulder. She stood passive, looking at him.

'Don't, John. I couldn't sleep. . . . The heat; something. Please, John. You're hurting me.'

'Didn't I tell you?' He released her and half struck, half flung her across the chair, and she lay there and watched him quietly as he left the room.

He went on through the house, ripping off his shirt, and on the dark, screened porch at the rear he stood and mopped his head and shoulders with the shirt and flung it away. He took the pistol from his hip and laid it on the table beside the bed, and sat on the bed and removed his shoes, and rose and slipped his trousers off. He was sweating again already, and he stopped and hunted furiously for the shirt. At last he found it and wiped his body again, and, with his body pressed against the dusty screen, he stood panting. There was no movement, no sound, not even an insect. The dark world seemed to lie stricken beneath the cold moon and the lidless stars.

Hills Like White Elephants

The hills across the valley of the Ebro were long and white. On this side there was no shade and no trees and the station was between two lines of rails in the sun. Close against the side of the station there was the warm shadow of the building and a curtain, made of strings of bamboo beads, hung across the open door into the bar, to keep out flies. The American and the girl with him sat at a table in the shade, outside the building. It was very hot and the express from Barcelona would come in forty minutes. It stopped at this junction for two minutes and went on to Madrid.

'What should we drink?' the girl asked. She had taken off her hat and put it on the table.

'It's pretty hot,' the man said.

'Let's drink beer.'

'Dos cervezas,' the man said into the curtain.

'Big ones?' a woman asked from the doorway.

'Yes. Two big ones.'

The woman brought two glasses of beer and two felt pads. She put the felt pads and the beer glasses on the table and looked at the man and the girl. The girl was looking off at the line of hills. They were white in the sun and the country was brown and dry.

'They look like white elephants,' she said.

'I've never seen one.' The man drank his beer.

'No, you wouldn't have.'

'I might have,' the man said. 'Just because you say I wouldn't have doesn't prove anything.'

The girl looked at the bead curtain. 'They've painted something on it,' she said 'What does it say?'

'Anis del Toro. It's a drink.'

'Could we try it?'

The man called 'Listen' through the curtain. The woman came out from the bar.

'Four reales.'

'We want two Anis del Toro.'

'With water?'

'Do you want it with water?'

'I don't know,' the girl said. 'Is it good with water?'

'It's all right.'

'You want them with water?' asked the woman.

'Yes, with water.'

'It tastes like licorice,' the girl said and put the glass down.

'That's the way with everything.'

'Yes,' said the girl. 'Everything tastes of licorice. Especially all the things you've waited so long for, like absinthe.'

'Oh, cut it out.'

'You started it,' the girl said. 'I was being amused. I was having a fine time.'

'Well, let's try and have a fine time.'

'All right. I was trying. I said the mountains looked like white elephants. Wasn't that bright?'

'That was bright.'

'I wanted to try this new drink. That's all we do, isn't it — look at things and try new drinks?'

'I guess so.'

The girl looked across at the hills.

'They're lovely hills,' she said. 'They don't really look like white elephants. I just meant the coloring of their skin through the trees.'

'Should we have another drink?'

'All right.'

The warm wind blew the bead curtain against the table.

'The beer's nice and cool,' the man said.

'It's lovely,' the girl said.

'It's really an awfully simple operation, Jig,' the man said. 'It's not really an operation at all.'

The girl looked at the ground the table legs rested on.

'I know you wouldn't mind it, Jig. It's really not anything. It's just to let the air in.'

The girl did not say anything.

'I'll go with you and I'll stay with you all the time. They just let the air in and then it's all perfectly natural.'

'Then what will we do afterward?'

'We'll be fine afterward. Just like we were before.'

'What makes you think so?'

'That's the only thing that bothers us. It's the only thing that's made us unhappy.'

The girl looked at the bead curtain, put her hand out and took hold of two of the strings of beads.

'And you think then we'll be all right and be happy?'

'I know we will. You don't have to be afraid. I've known lots of people that have done it.'

'So have I,' said the girl. 'And afterward they were all so happy.'

'Well,' the man said, 'if you don't want to you don't have to. I wouldn't have you do it if you didn't want to. But I know it's perfectly simple.'

'And you really want to?'

'I think it's the best thing to do. But I don't want you to do it if you don't really want to.'

'And if I do you'll be happy and things will be like they were and you'll love me?'

'I love you now. You know I love you.'

'I know. But if I do it, then it will be nice again if I say things are like white elephants, and you'll like it?'

'I'll love it. I love it now but I just can't think about it. You know how I get when I worry.'

'If I do it you won't ever worry?'

'I won't worry about that because it's perfectly simple.'

'Then I'll do it. Because I don't care about me.'

'What do you mean?'

'I don't care about me.'

'Well, I care about you.'

'Oh, yes. But I don't care about me. And I'll do it and then everything will be fine.'

'I don't want you to do it if you feel that way.'

The girl stood up and walked to the end of the station. Across, on the other side, were fields of grain and trees along the banks of the Ebro. Far away, beyond the river, were mountains. The shadow of a cloud moved across the field of grain and she saw the river through the trees.

'And we could have all this,' she said. 'And we could have everything and every day we make it more impossible.'

'What did you say?'

'I said we could have everything.'

'We can have everything.'

'No, we can't.'

'We can have the whole world.'

'No, we can't.'

'We can go everywhere.'

'No, we can't. It isn't ours any more.'

'It's ours.'

'No, it isn't. And once they take it away, you never get it back.'

'But they haven't taken it away.'

'We'll wait and see.'

'Come on back in the shade,' he said. 'You mustn't feel that way.'

'I don't feel any way,' the girl said. 'I just know things.'

'I don't want you to do anything that you don't want to do —'

'Nor that isn't good for me,' she said. 'I know. Could we have another beer?'

'All right. But you've got to realize —'

'I realize,' the girl said. 'Can't we maybe stop talking?'

They sat down at the table and the girl looked across at the hills on the dry side of the valley and the man looked at her and at the table.

'You've got to realize,' he said, 'that I don't want you to do it if you don't want to. I'm perfectly willing to go through with it if it means anything to you.'

'Doesn't it mean anything to you? We could get along.'

'Of course it does. But I don't want anybody but you. I don't want anyone else. And I know it's perfectly simple.'

'Yes, you know it's perfectly simple.'

'It's all right for you to say that, but I do know it.'

'Would you do something for me now?'

'I'd do anything for you.'

'Would you please please please please please please please stop talking?'

He did not say anything but looked at the bags against the wall of the station. There were labels on them from all the hotels where they had spent nights.

'But I don't want you to,' he said. 'I don't care anything about it.'

'I'll scream,' the girl said.

The woman came out through the curtains with two glasses of beer and put them down on the damp felt pads. 'The train comes in five minutes,' she said.

'What did she say?' asked the girl.

'That the train is coming in five minutes.'

The girl smiled brightly at the woman, to thank her.

'I'd better take the bags over to the other side of the station,' the man said. She smiled at him.

'All right. Then come back and we'll finish the beer.'

He picked up the two heavy bags and carried them around the station to the other tracks. He looked up the tracks but could not see the train. Coming back, he walked through the bar-room, where people waiting for the train were drinking. He drank an Anis at the bar and looked at the people. They were all waiting reasonably for the train. He went out through the bead curtain. She was sitting at the table and smiled at him.

'Do you feel better?' he asked.

'I feel fine,' she said. 'There's nothing wrong with me. I feel fine.'

ELIZABETH BOWEN · 1899–1973

The Demon Lover

Towards the end of her day in London Mrs Drover went round to her shut-up house to look for several things she wanted to take away. Some belonged to herself, some to her family, who were by now used to their country life. It was late August; it had been a steamy, showery day: at the moment the trees down the pavement glittered in an escape of humid yellow afternoon sun. Against the next batch of clouds, already piling up ink-dark, broken chimneys and parapets stood out. In her once familiar street, as in any unused channel, an unfamiliar queerness had silted up; a cat wove itself in and out of railings, but no human eye watched Mrs Drover's return. Shifting some parcels under her arm, she slowly forced round her latchkey in an unwilling lock, then gave the door, which had warped, a push with her knee. Dead air came out to meet her as she went in.

The staircase window having been boarded up, no light came down into the hall. But one door, she could just see, stood ajar, so she went quickly through into the room and unshuttered the big window in there. Now the prosaic woman, looking about her, was more perplexed than she knew by everything that she saw, by traces of her long former habit of life – the yellow smoke-stain up the white marble mantelpiece, the ring left by a vase on the top of the escritoire; the bruise in the wallpaper where, on the door being thrown open widely, the china handle had always hit the wall. The piano, having gone away to be stored, had left what looked like claw-marks on its part of the parquet. Though not much dust had seeped in, each object wore a film of another kind; and, the only ventilation being the chimney, the whole drawing-room smelled of the cold hearth. Mrs Drover put down her parcels on the escritoire and left the room to proceed upstairs; the things she wanted were in a bedroom chest.

She had been anxious to see how the house was – the part-time caretaker she shared with some neighbours was away this week on his holiday, known to be not yet back. At the best of times he did not look in often, and she was never sure that she trusted him. There were some cracks in the structure, left by the last bombing, on which she was anxious to keep an eye. Not that one could do anything —

A shaft of refracted daylight now lay across the hall. She stopped dead and stared at the hall table – on this lay a letter addressed to her.

She thought first – then the caretaker *must* be back. All the same, who, seeing the house shuttered, would have dropped a letter in at the box? It was not a circular, it was not a bill. And the post office redirected, to the address in the country, everything for her that came through the post. The caretaker (even if he *were* back) did not know she was due in London today – her call here had been planned to be a surprise – so his negligence in the manner of this letter, leaving it to wait in the dusk and the dust, annoyed her. Annoyed, she picked up the letter, which bore no stamp. But it cannot be important, or they would know . . . She took the letter rapidly upstairs with her, without a stop to look at the writing till she reached what had been her bedroom, where she let in light. The room looked over the garden and other gardens: the sun had gone in; as the clouds sharpened and lowered, the trees and rank lawns seemed already to smoke with dark. Her reluctance to look again at the letter came from the fact that she felt intruded upon – and by someone contemptuous of her ways. However, in the tenseness preceding the fall of rain she read it: it was a few lines.

Dear Kathleen,

You will not have forgotten that today is our anniversary, and the day we said. The years have gone by at once slowly and fast. In view of the fact that nothing has changed, I shall rely upon you to keep your promise. I was sorry to see you leave London, but was satisfied that you would be back in time. You may expect me, therefore, at the hour arranged.

Until then . . .

K.

Mrs Drover looked for the date: it was today's. She dropped the letter on to the bed-springs, then picked it up to see the writing again – her lips, beneath the remains of lipstick, beginning to go white. She felt so much the change in her own face that she went to the mirror, polished a clear patch in it and looked at once urgently and stealthily in. She was confronted by a woman of forty-four, with eyes starting out under a hat-brim that had been rather carelessly pulled down. She had not put on any more powder since she left the shop where she ate her solitary tea. The pearls her husband had given her on their marriage hung loose round her now rather thinner throat, slipping into the V of the pink wool jumper her sister knitted last autumn as they sat round the fire. Mrs Drover's most normal expression was one of controlled worry, but of assent. Since the birth of the third of her little boys, attended by a quite serious illness, she had had an intermittent muscular flicker to the left of her mouth, but in spite of this she could always sustain a manner that was at once energetic and calm.

Turning from her own face as precipitately as she had gone to meet it, she went to the chest where the things were, unlocked it, threw up the lid and knelt to search. But as rain began to come crashing down she could not keep from looking over her shoulder at the stripped bed on which the letter lay. Behind the blanket of rain the clock of the church that still stood struck six – with rapidly heightening apprehension she counted each of the slow strokes. 'The hour arranged . . . My God,' she said, '*what* hour? How should I . . . ? After twenty-five years. . . .'

The young girl talking to the soldier in the garden had not ever completely seen his face. It was dark; they were saying good-bye under a tree. Now and then – for it felt, from not seeing him at this intense moment, as though she had never seen him at all – she verified his presence for these few moments longer by putting out a hand, which he each time pressed, without very much kindness, and painfully, on to one of the breast buttons of his uniform. That cut of the button on the palm of her hand was, principally, what she was to carry away. This was so near the end of a leave from France that she could only wish him already gone. It was August 1916. Being not kissed, being drawn away from and looked at intimidated Kathleen till she imagined spectral glitters in the place of his eyes. Turning away and looking back up the lawn she saw, through branches of trees, the drawing-room window alight: she caught a breath for the moment when she could go running back there into the safe arms of her mother and sister, and cry: 'What shall I do, what shall I do? He has gone.'

Hearing her catch her breath, her fiancé said, without feeling: 'Cold?'

'You're going away such a long way.'

'Not so far as you think.'

'I don't understand?'

'You don't have to,' he said. 'You will. You know what we said.'

'But that was – suppose you – I mean, suppose.'

'I shall be with you,' he said, 'sooner or later. You won't forget that. You need do nothing but wait.'

Only a little more than a minute later she was free to run up the silent lawn. Looking in through the window at her mother and sister, who did not for the moment perceive her, she already felt that unnatural promise drive down between her and the rest of all humankind. No other way of having given herself could have made her feel so apart, lost and foresworn. She could not have plighted a more sinister troth.

Kathleen behaved well when, some months later, her fiancé was reported missing, presumed killed. Her family not only supported her but were able to praise her courage without stint because they could not regret, as a husband for her, the man they knew almost nothing about. They hoped she would, in a year or two, console herself – and had it been only a question of consolation things might have gone much straighter ahead. But her trouble, behind just a little grief, was a complete dislocation from everything. She did not reject other lovers, for these failed to appear: for years she failed to attract men – and with the approach of her thirties she became natural enough to share her family's anxiousness on this score. She began to put herself out, to wonder; and at thirty-two she was very greatly relieved to find herself being courted by William Drover. She married him, and the two of them settled down in this quiet, arboreal part of Kensington: in this house the years piled up, her children were born and they all lived till they were driven out by the bombs of the next war. Her movements as Mrs Drover were circumscribed, and she dismissed any idea that they were still watched.

As things were – dead or living the letter-writer sent her only a threat. Unable, for some minutes, to go on kneeling with her back exposed to the empty room, Mrs Drover rose from the chest to sit on an upright chair whose back was firmly against the wall. The desuetude of her former bedroom, her married London home's whole air of being a cracked cup from which memory, with its re-assuring power, had either evaporated or leaked away, made a cri-sis – and at just this crisis the letter-writer had, knowledgeably, struck. The hollowness of the house this evening cancelled years on years of voices, habits and steps. Through the shut windows she only heard rain fall on the roofs around. To rally herself, she said she was in a mood – and, for two or three seconds shutting her eyes, told herself that she had imagined the letter. But she opened them – there it lay on the bed.

On the supernatural side of the letter's entrance she was not per-mitting her mind to dwell. Who, in London, knew she meant to call at the house today? Evidently, however, this has been known. The caretaker, *had* he come back, had had no cause to expect her: he would have taken the letter in his pocket, to forward it, at his own time, through the post. There was no other sign that the care-taker had been in – but, if not? Letters dropped in at doors of deserted houses do not fly or walk to tables in halls. They do not sit on the dust of empty tables with the air of certainty that they will be found. There is needed some human hand – but nobody but the caretaker had a key. Under circumstances she did not care to con-sider, a house can be entered without a key. It was possible that she was not alone now. She might be being waited for, downstairs. Waited for – until when? Until 'the hour arranged'. At least that was not six o'clock: six has struck.

She rose from the chair and went over and locked the door.

The thing was, to get out. To fly? No, not that: she had to catch her train. As a woman whose utter dependability was the keystone of her family life she was not willing to return to the country, to her husband, her little boys and her sister, without the objects she had come up to fetch. Resuming work at the chest she set about making up a number of parcels in a rapid, fumbling-decisive way. These, with her shopping parcels, would be too much to carry; these meant a taxi – at the thought of the taxi her heart went up and her normal breathing resumed. I will ring up the taxi now; the taxi cannot come too soon: I shall hear the taxi out there running its engine, till I walk calmly down to it through the hall. I'll ring up — But no: the telephone is cut off. . . . She tugged at a knot she had tied wrong.

The idea of flight. . . . He was never kind to me, not really. I don't remember him kind at all. Mother said he never considered me. He was set on me, that was what it was – not love. Not love, not meaning a person well. What did he do, to make me promise like that? I can't remember — But she found that she could.

She remembered with such dreadful acuteness that the twenty-five years since then dissolved like smoke and she instinctively looked for the weal left by the button on the palm of her hand. She remembered not only all that he said and did but the complete suspension of *her* existence during that August week. I was not myself – they all told me so at the time. She remembered – but with one white burning blank as where acid has dropped on a photograph: *under no conditions* could she remember his face.

So, wherever he may be waiting, I shall not know him. You have no time to run from a face you do not expect.

The thing was to get to the taxi before any clock struck what could be the hour. She would slip down the street and round the side of the square to where the square gave on the main road. She would return in the taxi, safe, to her own door, and bring the solid driver into the house with her to pick up the parcels from room to room. The idea of the taxi driver made her decisive, bold: she unlocked her door, went to the top of the staircase and listened down.

She heard nothing – but while she was hearing nothing the *passé* air of the staircase was disturbed by a draught that travelled up to her face. It emanated from the basement: down there a door or window was being opened by someone who chose this moment to leave the house.

The rain had stopped; the pavements steamily shone as Mrs Drover let herself out by inches from her own front door into the empty street. The unoccupied houses opposite continued to meet her look with their damaged stare. Making towards the thoroughfare and the taxi, she tried not to keep looking behind. Indeed, the silence was so intense – one of those creeks of London silence exaggerated this summer by the damage of war – that no tread could have gained on hers unheard. Where her street debouched on the square where people went on living, she grew conscious of, and checked, her unnatural pace. Across the open end of the square two buses impassively passed each other: women, a perambulator, cyclists, a man wheeling a barrow signalized, once again, the ordinary flow of life. At the square's most populous corner should be – and was – the short taxi rank. This evening, only one taxi – but this, although it presented its blank rump, appeared already to be alertly waiting for her. Indeed, without looking round the driver started his engine as she panted up from behind and put her hand on the door. As she did so, the clock struck seven. The taxi faced the main road: to make the trip back to her house it would have to turn – she had settled back on the seat and the taxi *had* turned before she, surprised by its knowing movement, recollected that she had not 'said where'. She leaned forward to scratch at the glass panel that divided the driver's head from her own.

The driver braked to what was almost a stop, turned round and slid the glass panel back: the jolt of this flung Mrs Drover forward till her face was almost into the glass. Through the aperture driver and passenger, not six inches between them, remained for an eternity eye to eye. Mrs Drover's mouth hung open for some seconds before she could issue her first scream. After that she continued to scream freely and to beat with her gloved hands on the glass all round as the taxi, accelerating without mercy, made off with her into the hinterland of deserted streets.

Many Are Disappointed

Heads down to the wind from the hidden sea, the four men were cycling up a deserted road in the country. Bert, who was the youngest, dreamed:

'You get to the pub, and there's a girl at the pub, a dark girl with bare arms and bare legs in a white frock, the daughter of the house, or an orphan – maybe it's better she should be an orphan – and you say something to her, or, better still, you don't say anything to her – she just comes and puts her arms round you, and you can feel her skin through her frock and she brings you some beer and the other chaps aren't there and the people don't say anything except laugh and go away, because it's all natural and she doesn't have a baby. Same at the next place, same anywhere, different place, different girl, or same girl – same girl always turning up, always waiting. Dunno how she got there. Just slips along without you knowing it and waiting like all those songs . . .'

And there the pub was. It stood on the crown of the long hill, straight ahead of them, a small red-brick house with out-buildings and a single chimney trailing out smoke against the strong white light which seemed to be thrown up by great reflectors from the hidden sea.

'There's our beer, Mr Blake,' shouted Sid on his pink racing tyres, who was the first to see it, the first to see everything. The four men glanced up.

Yes, there's our beer, they said. Our ruddy beer. They had been thinking about it for miles. A pub at the crossroads, a pub where the old Roman road crossed this road that went on to the land's end, a funny place for a pub, but a pub all right, the only pub for ten miles at Harry's ruddy Roman road, marked on the map which stuck out of the backside pocket of Harry's breeches. Yes, that was the pub, and Ted, the oldest and the married one, slacked on the long hill and said all he hoped was that the Romans had left a drop in the bottom of the barrel for posterity.

When they had left in the morning there had been little wind. The skylarks were over the fields, and the sun itself was like one of their steel wheels flashing in the sky. Sid was the first, but Harry with the stubborn red neck and the close dull fair curls was the leader. In the week he sat in the office making the plan. He had this mania for Roman roads. 'Ask our Mr Newton,' they said, 'the man with the big head and the brain.' They had passed through the cream-walled villages and out again to pick up once more the singing of the larks; and then cloud had covered the sun like a grey hand, west of Handleyford the country had emptied, and it was astonishing to hear a bird. Reeds were in the small meadows. Hedges crawled uncut and there had been no villages, only long tablelands of common and bald wiry grass for sheep and the isolated farm with no ivy on the brick.

Well, they were there at last. They piled their bicycles against the wall of the house. They were shy before these country places. They waited for Ted. He was walking the last thirty yards. They looked at the four windows with their lace curtains and the varnished door. There was a chicken in the road and no sound but the whimper of the telegraph wire on the hill. In an open barn was a cart tipped down, its shaft white with the winter's mud, and last year's swallow nests, now empty, were under the eaves. Then Ted came and when he had piled his bicycle, they read the black sign over the door. 'Tavern,' it said. A funny old-fashioned word, Ted said, that you didn't often see.

'Well,' Sid said, 'a couple of pints all round?'

They looked to Harry. He always opened doors, but this door was so emphatically closed that he took off his fur gauntlet first and knocked before he opened it. The four men were surprised to see a woman standing behind the door, waiting there as if she had been listening to them. She was a frail, drab woman, not much past thirty, in a white blouse that drooped low over her chest.

'Good morning,' said Sid. 'This the bar?'

'The bar?' said the woman timidly. She spoke in a flat wondering voice and not in the singsong of this part of the country.

'Yes, the bar,' Ted said. 'It says "Tavern," ' he said, nodding up at the notice.

'Oh yes,' she said, hesitating. 'Come in. Come in here.'

She showed them not into the bar but into a sitting-room. There was a bowl of tomatoes in the window and a notice said 'Teas'.

The four men were tall and large beside her in the little room and she gazed up at them as if she feared they would burst its walls. And yet she was pleased. She was trying to smile.

'This is on me,' Sid said. 'Mild and bitter four times.'

'O.K., Mr Blake,' Ted said. 'Bring me my beer.'

'But let's get into the bar,' said Bert.

Seeing an armchair, Ted sank into it and now the woman was reassured. She succeeded in smiling but she did not go out of the room. Sid looked at her, and her smile was vacant and faint like the smile fading on an old photograph. Her hair was short, an impure yellow and the pale skin of her face and her neck and her breast seemed to be moist as if she had just got out of bed. The high strong light of this place drank all colour from her.

'There isn't a bar,' she said. 'This isn't a public-house. They call it the Tavern, but it isn't a tavern by rights.'

Very anxiously she raised her hands to her blouse.

'What!' they exclaimed. 'Not a pub! Here, Harry, it's marked on your map.' They were dumbfounded and angry.

'What you mean, don't sell beer,' they said.

Their voices were very loud.

'Yes,' said Harry. 'Here it is. See? Inn.'

He put the map before her face accusingly.

'You don't sell beer?' said Bert. He looked at the pale-blue-veined chest of the woman.

'No,' she said. She hesitated. 'Many are disappointed,' she said, and she spoke like a child reciting a piece without knowing its meaning. He lowered his eyes.

'You bet they ruddy well are,' said Ted from the chair.

'Where is the pub?' said Sid.

She put out her hand and a little girl came into the room and clung close to her mother. Now she felt happier.

'My little girl,' she said.

She was a tiny, frail child with yellow hair and pale-blue eyes like her mother's. The four men smiled and spoke more quietly because of the resemblance between the woman and her child.

'Which way did you come?' she asked, and her hand moving over the child's hair got courage from the child. 'Handleyford?' she said. 'That's it. It's ten miles. The Queen's Arms, Handleyford, the way you came. That's the nearest pub.'

'My God!' said Bert. 'What a country!'

'The Queen's Arms,' said Ted stupefied.

He remembered it. They were passing through Handleyford. He was the oldest, a flat wide man in loose clothes, loose in the chin too, with watery rings under his eyes and a small golden sun of baldness at the back of his head. 'Queen's Arms,' he had called. 'Here, what's the ruddy game?' But the others had grinned back at him. When you drop back to number four on the hills it comes back to you: they're single, nothing to worry about, you're married and you're forty. What's the hurry? Ease up, take what you can get. 'Queen's Arms' – he remembered looking back. The best things are in the past.

'Well, that's that!' said Sid.

'Queen's Arms, Harry,' Ted said.

And Bert looked at the woman. 'Let's go on,' he said fiercely. She was not the woman he had expected. Then he blushed and turned away from the woman.

She was afraid they were going and in a placating voice she said: 'I do teas.'

Sid was sitting on the arm of a chair, and the child was gazing at a gold ring he wore on his little finger. He saw the child was gazing and he smiled.

'What's wrong with tea?' Sid said.

'Ask the man with the brain,' said Ted. 'Ask the man with the map.'

Harry said: 'If you can't have beer, you'd better take what you can get, Mr Richards.'

'Tea,' nodded Sid to the woman. 'Make it strong.'

The woman looked at Sid as if he had performed a miracle.

'I'll get you tea,' she said eagerly. 'I always do teas for people.' She spoke with delight as if a bell had suddenly tinkled inside her. Her eyes shone. She would get them tea, she said, and bread and butter, but no eggs, because the man had not been that morning, and no ham. It was too early, she said, for ham. 'But there are tomatoes,' she said. And then, like a child: 'I put them in the window so as people can see.'

'O.K.,' Sid said. 'Four teas.'

She did not move at once but still, like a shy child, stood watching them, waiting for them to be settled and fearful that they would not stay. But at last she put out her hand to the child and hurried out to the kitchen.

'Well, Mr Blake,' said Ted, 'there's a ruddy sell.'

'Have a gasper, Mr Richards,' said Sid.

'Try my lighter,' said Ted.

He clicked the lighter, but no flame came.

'Wrong number,' said Ted. 'Dial O and try again.' A steak, said Sid, had been his idea. A couple of pints just to ease the passage and then some real drinking, Ted said. But Bert was drumming on a biscuit tin and was looking inside. There was nothing in it. 'Many,' said Bert, 'are disappointed.'

They looked at the room. There were two new treacle-coloured armchairs. There was a sofa with a pattern of black ferns on it. The new plush was damp and sticky to the hands from the air of the hidden sea. There was a gun-metal fender and there was crinkled, green paper in the fireplace. A cupboard with a glass door was empty except for the lowest shelf. On that was a thick book called *The Marvels of Science*.

The room was cold. They thought in the winter it must be damn cold. They thought of the ten drizzling miles to Handleyford.

They listened to the cold clatter of the plates in the kitchen and the sound of the woman's excited voice and the child's. There was the bare linoleum on the floor and the chill glass of the window. Outside was the road with blown sand at the edges and, beyond a wall, there were rows of cabbages, then a bit of field and the expressionless sky. There was no sound on the road. They – it occurred to them – had been the only sound on that road for hours.

The woman came in with a cup and then with a plate. The child brought a plate and the woman came in with another cup. She looked in a dazed way at the men, amazed that they were still there. It seemed to Ted, who was married, that she didn't know how to lay a table. 'And now I've forgotten the sugar,' she laughed. Every time she came into the room she glanced at Bert timidly and yet pityingly, because he was the youngest and had been the most angry. He lowered his eyes and avoided her look. But to Ted she said: 'That's right, you make yourselves comfortable,' and at Sid she smiled because he had been the kindest. At Harry she did not look at all.

She was very startled then when he stood at the door and said: 'Where's this Roman road?'

She was in the kitchen. She told him the road by the white gate and showed him from the doorway of the house.

'There he goes,' said Sid at the window. 'He's looking over the gate.'

They waited. The milk was put on the table. The woman came in at last with the bread and butter and the tea.

'He'll miss his tea next,' Ted said.

'Well,' Ted said, when Harry came back. 'See any Romans?'

'It's just grass,' Harry said. 'Nothing on it.' He stared in his baffled, bull-necked way.

'No beer and no Romans,' Ted said.

The woman, who was standing there, smiled. In a faltering voice, wishing to make them happy, she said:

'We don't often get no Romans here.'

'Oh God!' Bert laughed very loudly and Ted shook with laughter too. Harry stared.

'Don't take any notice of them, missus,' Sid said. And then to them: 'She means gypsies.'

'That come with brooms,' she said, bewildered by their laughter, wondering what she had done.

When she had gone and had closed the door, Bert and Ted touched their heads with their fingers and said she was dippy, but Sid told them to speak quietly.

Noisily they had drawn up their chairs and were eating and drinking. Ted cut up tomatoes, salted them, and put them on his bread. They were good for the blood, he told them, and Harry said they reckoned at home his granddad got the cancer he died of from eating tomatoes day after day. Bert, with his mouth full, said he'd read somewhere that tea was the most dangerous drink on earth. Then the child came in with a paper and said her mother had sent it. Sid looked at the door when it closed again.

'Funny thing,' he said. 'I think I've seen that woman before.'

That, they said, was Sid's trouble. He'd seen too many girls before.

He was a lanky man with a high forehead and a Hitler moustache and his lips lay over his mouth as if they were kissing the air or whispering to it. He was a dark, harsh-looking, cocksure man, but with a gentle voice and it was hard to see his eyes under his strong glasses. His lashes were long and his lids often half-lowered, which gave him an air of seriousness and shyness. But he stuck his thumbs in his waistcoat and stuck out his legs to show his loud check stockings and he had that ring on his finger. 'Move that up a couple and he'd be spliced,' they said. 'Not me,' he said, 'look at Ted.' A man with no ideals, Bert thought, a man whose life was hidden behind the syrup-thick lens of his glasses. Flash Sid. See the typists draw themselves up, tilt back their heads, and get their hands ready to keep him off. Not a man with ideals. See them watch his arms and his hands, see them start tapping hard on the typewriter keys and pretending to be busy when he leaned over to tell them a story. And then, when he was gone, see them peep through the Enquiry window to watch where he went, quarrel about him, and dawdle in the street when the office closed, hoping to see him.

'Well,' said Harry when they had cleared the table and got out the map.

Sid said: 'You gen'lemen settle it. I'll go and fix her up.'

Sid's off, they said. First on the road, always leading, getting the first of the air, licking the cream off everything.

He found her in the kitchen and he had to lower his head because of the ceiling. She was sitting drably at the table, which was covered with unwashed plates and the remains of a meal. There were unwashed clothes on the backs of the chairs and there was a man's waistcoat. The child was reading a comic paper at the table and singing in a high small voice.

A delicate stalk of neck, he thought, and eyes like the pale wild scabious you see in the ditches.

Four shillings, she said, would that be too much?

She put her hand nervously to her breast.

'That's all right,' Sid said, and put the money in her hand. It was coarsened by work. 'We cleared up everything,' he said.

'Don't get many people, I expect,' he said.

'Not this time of year.'

'A bit lonely,' he said.

'Some think it is,' she said.

'How long have you been here?' he said.

'Only three years. It seems,' she said with her continual wonder, 'longer.'

'I thought it wasn't long,' Sid said. 'I thought I seen you somewhere. You weren't in – in Horsham, were you?'

'I come from Ashford,' she said.

'Ashford,' he said. 'I knew you weren't from these parts.'

She brightened and she was fascinated because he took off his glasses and she saw the deep serious shadows of his eyes and the pale drooping of the naked lids. The eyes looked tired and as if they had seen many things and she was tired too.

'I bin ill,' she said. Her story came irresistibly to her lips. 'The doctor told us to come here. My husband gave up his job and everything. Things are different here. The money's not so good —' Her voice quickened. 'But I try to make it up with the teas.'

She paused, trying to read from his face if she should say any more. She seemed to be standing on the edge of another country. The pale-blue eyes seemed to be the pale sky of a far-away place where she had been living.

'I nearly died,' she said. She was a little amazed by this fact.

'You're O.K. now,' Sid said.

'I'm better,' she said. 'But it seems I get lonely now I'm better.'

'You want your health, but you want a bit of company,' Sid said.

'My husband says: "You got your health, what you want company for?"'

She put this to Sid in case her husband was not right, but she picked up her husband's waistcoat from the chair and looked over its buttons because she felt, timorously, she had been disloyal to her husband.

'A woman wants company,' said Sid.

He looked shy now to her, like Bert, the young one; but she was most astonished that someone should agree with her and not her husband.

Then she flushed and put out her hand to the little girl, who came to her mother's side, pressing against her. The woman felt safer and raised her eyes and looked more boldly at him.

'You and your friends going far?'

He told her. She nodded, counting the miles as if she were coming along with them. And then Sid felt a hand touch his.

It was the child's hand touching the ring on his finger.

'Ha!' laughed Sid. 'You saw that before.' He was quick. The child was delighted with his quickness. The woman put the waistcoat down at once. He took off the ring and put it in the palm of his hand and bent down so that his head nearly brushed the woman's arm. 'That's lucky,' he said. 'Here,' he said. He slipped the ring on the child's little finger. 'See,' he said. 'Keeps me out of mischief. Keep a ring on your little finger and you'll be lucky.'

The child looked at him without belief.

'Here y'are,' he said, taking back the ring. 'Your mother wants it,' he said, winking at the woman. 'She's got hers on the wrong finger. Little one luck, big one trouble.'

She laughed and she blushed and her eyes shone. He moved to the door and her pale lips pouted a little. Then, taking the child by the hand she hurried over to him as if both of them would cling to him. Excitedly, avidly, they followed him to the other room.

'Come on, Mr Blake,' said Ted. The three others rose to their feet.

The child clung to her mother's hand and danced up and down. She was in the midst of them. They zipped up their jackets, stubbed their cigarettes, folded up the map. Harry put on his gauntlets. He stared at the child and then slowly took off his glove and pulled out a sixpence. 'No,' murmured Ted, the married man, but the child was too quick.

They went out of the room and stood in the road. They stretched themselves in the open air. The sun was shining now on the fields. The woman came to the door to see them. They took their bicycles from the wall, looked up and down the road, and then swung on. To the sea, the coast road, and then perhaps a girl, some girl. But the others were shouting.

'Good-bye,' they called. 'Good-bye.'

And Bert, the last, remembered then to wave good-bye too, and glanced up at the misleading notice. When they were all together, heads down to the wind, they turned again. 'Good God,' they said. The woman and the child had come out into the middle of the road hand in hand and their arms were still raised and their hands were fluttering under the strong light of that high place. It was a long time before they went back into the house.

And now for a pub, a real pub, the three men called to Harry. Sid was ahead on his slim pink tyres getting the first of the new wind, with the ring shining on his finger.

Sinners

The canon, barely glancing at his two waiting penitents, entered the confessional. From inside he looked wearily across at the rows of penitents on each side of Father Deeley's box, all still as statues where they sat against the wall, or leaned forward to let the light of the single electric bulb, high up in the windy roof, fall on their prayer-books. Deeley would give each about ten minutes, and that meant he would not absolve the last until near midnight. 'More trouble with the sacristan,' sighed the canon, and closed the curtains and lifted his hands towards the slide of the grille.

He paused. To banish a sudden restiveness he said a prayer. He often said that prayer – an Aspiration against Anger. He had remembered that on the other side of the grille was a little serving-girl he had sent out of the box last Saturday night because she had been five years away from confession and did not seem to be a bit sorry for it. He lifted his hand, but paused again. To add to his difficulty – for it was no help to know what, under the *sigillum*, he must pretend not to know – he had just been told in the sacristy by her employer that a pair of her best boots was missing. Why on earth, he sighed, did people reveal such things to him? Did he *want* to know the sins of his penitents? Was the confession being made to him, or to God? Was it. . . . He lowered his hand, ashamed of his irritation, and repeated the prayer. Then he drew the slide, cupped his ear in his palm to listen, and saw her hands clasping and unclasping, as if her courage was a little bird between her palms trying to escape.

'My poor child,' he said, ever so gently, dutifully pretending to know nothing about her, 'tell me how long it is since your last confession.'

'It's a long time, father,' she whispered.

'How long?' To encourage her he added, 'Over a year?'

'Yes, father.'

'How much? Tell me, my poor child, tell me. Two years?'

'More, father.'

'Three years?'

'More, father.'

'Well, well, you must tell me, you know.'

In spite of himself his voice was a little pettish. The title 'father' instead of 'canon' was annoying him, too. She noted the change of voice, for she said, hurriedly:

' 'Tis that, father.'

' 'Tis what?' asked the canon a shade too loudly.

'Over three years, father,' she prevaricated.

He wondered if he could dare let the prevarication go; but his conscience would not let him.

'My dear child, how much over three years is it?'

' 'Tis, 'tis, father, 'tis . . . '

The canon forestalled the lie.

'My dear child, how much over three years is it? Is it four years? And would you mind calling me *canon*?'

The breathing became faster.

' 'Tis, father. I mean, 'tis more, *canon*, father.'

'Well, how much? I can't make your confession for you, you know.'

' 'Tis a bit more, father.'

'But how much?' broke from the canon.

'Two months,' lied the maid, and her hands made a flutter of whiteness in the dark.

The canon almost wished he could break the seal of the confessional and reveal to her that he knew exactly who she was, and how long she had been away; all he dared say was:

'I suspect you're telling me a lie.'

'Oh, God, father, it's gospel truth.'

'But,' the canon tapped the cushion, 'there's no use in telling me if it's not the truth. For God's sake, my poor child,' he controlled himself, 'maybe it's five years?'

' 'Tis five years,' admitted the maid in so low a voice that he barely heard it.

He sighed with satisfaction. He straightened his hair on his forehead. Then he leaned nearer to hear her sins, nearer and nearer until his ear was pressed against the lattice.

'Now,' he warned, 'that is a long time, my child. But, thank God, you have come back at last. You must try to remember all – all –

your sins. Let me help you. My poor little child! Take the first commandment.'

But when he heard the shudder of her breath he knew he had made a bad mistake; she would be seeing a long list of broken commandments before her and she would slur over many of her sins in order to shorten the ordeal.

'I mean to say,' went on the canon, annoyed with his own stupidity, 'that is one way of doing it. Do you wish to make your confession that way?'

'Yes, father.'

'Very well.'

'The first commandment . . . ' She stopped in confusion and he realized that she did not even know what the commandment was.

'Did you ever miss Mass on Sundays?' he helped her out, although his knees were beginning to dance with impatience.

'Oh, never, never in my whole life.'

'Good. Did you ever swear? Take the Lord's name in vain?'

'Tututut!' said the girl in horror at the very idea.

'Did you every disobey your parents, cause them pain in any way, give back-answers?'

'I have no parents, father. Mrs Higg – my mistress got me from the Orphanage.'

'Ah! Well . . . er . . . Lies? Anger? Have you told lies, or given way to anger?'

'Wisha, I suppose I did, father. I suppose I told a little lie now and again.'

'How often in those five years? On an average? I mean, is it a weakness you have? A habit?'

'God help us, father, I don't tell many. I only tell 'em when I do be afraid.'

'Well, we will say you told lies occasionally. Now the sixth commandment. Have you ever sinned in thought, word, or deed against Holy Purity? The opposite sex, for example. Have you ever misbehaved in any way with men?'

'Oh!' gasped the maid, and her voice thickened.

'Stealing?' prompted the canon, and he waited for her to say that she had stolen Mrs Higgins's boots.

'I never in my life, father, stole as much as the head off of a pin. Except when I was small I once stole an apple in the nuns' orchard. And then they caught me and gave me a flaking. And they took the last bite out of my mouth.'

'You never stole articles of dress?' threatened the canon, and he suddenly realized that there were only three very unlikely commandments left. 'Clothes? Hats? Gloves? Shoes?'

'Never, father.'

There was a long pause.

'Boots?' he whispered.

Suddenly the girl was sobbing violently.

'Father,' she wept, 'Mrs Higgins is telling you lies about me. I hate that wan. I . . . I . . . I hate her. I do. She's always prying and poking and prodding at me. She took me from the nuns five years ago and she never gave me a minute's rest. She calls me low names. She tells me I can't be good or wholesome to come out of an Orphanage. She is picking at me from dawn to dusk. She's an old bitch . . . '

'My child! My child!'

'I did take the boots. I took them. But I didn't steal them. Sure I haven't a boot on my foot and she has lashings and leavings of 'em. I was going to put them back.'

'My child, to take them is the same as to steal them.'

'What does she want them for? But she's that mean. Her own daughter ran away from her two years ago and married an Englishman who's half a Freemason. The poor girl told me with her own mouth, only last week, how she's half-starved by that husband of hers and they have no money to have a family. But do you think her mother would give her a penny?'

The girl sobbed on. The canon groaned and drew himself up to ease his chest. He could hear the wind whistling up in the roof and he could see the long queue on each side of Father Deeley's box, all still as statues in the dusk of the aisle. Seeing them he groaned again as much as to say, 'What's the use? They all deceive themselves. They all think everyone is sinful but themselves only. Or if they say they are sinners, and feel it – it only lasts while they are in the church. Then they go out and are filled with envy and pride and they have no charity.' He leaned back.

'My child, my child, my child! For five years you have stayed away from God. If you had died you would have died with that mortal sin on your soul and gone to hell for all eternity. It's the law of the Church, and the law of God, that you *must*, you *must* go to confession at least once a year. Why did you stay away? Look at the way your mind is deformed so that you can't even recognize a sin when you commit it. Is there some sin you haven't told me that you were ashamed to tell?'

'No, father.'

'Didn't your good mistress send you to confession at least every month during those five years?'

'She sent me every week. But it was always of a Saturday night. And one Saturday night I didn't go because I wanted to buy a blouse before the shops shut. Then it was six months before I knew it and I was afraid to go. And, anyway, sure what had I to tell?'

The canon waved his hands weakly and with great sarcasm he said:

'Did you *never* commit a sin?'

'I suppose I told a lie, father. And there was the apple in the nuns' orchard.'

Furiously the priest turned to her, determined to wring the truth from her. In her compartment he heard Lady Nolan-White, his second penitent, coughing impatiently.

'My dear child, you simply must have committed sins during those five years. Be honest with yourself. Come now! Look! Take the most common sin of all. Have you, ever, had what we, vulgarly, call a . . . er . . . call a, boy?'

'I had – once – father.'

'Well, now!' He rubbed his forehead like a man in a great heat and he strained towards her as if he were struggling with her demon. 'You were, what do we say . . . er . . . walking out with him?'

'Yes,' panted the girl. 'In the back-lane.'

'Well, what shall we say? Did, what do you say, did, er, did any intimacy take place with him?'

'I don't know, father.'

'You know what it is to be immodest, don't you?' cried the canon.

Her breath was panting in and out. She said nothing. She stared at him.

'My poor, poor child, you seem to have small experience of the world. But we must get at the truth. Did he – did you – did either of you ever go beyond the bounds of propriety?'

'I dunno, father.'

Loudly the canon expelled his breath. He was becoming exhausted, but he would not give in. He rubbed his hair all the wrong way, which gave him a wild look. He took off his pince-nez and wiped them.

'You understand plain English, don't you? Now, tell me, tell Almighty God the truth of the thing. Did you ever allow him to take liberties with you?'

'Yes, father. I mean no, father. We were in the lane. No, father. We didn't do nothing. Nothing much, I mean.'

'Five years,' moaned the canon, and he hammered his thigh with his fist. 'And nothing to tell. What kind of Christians . . . ' He determined to make one last effort – just one more effort. 'Did he ever touch your body?' he asked bluntly.

'No, father. Well, I mean – no, father.'

Seeing that she was beginning to whimper again he threw up his hands.

'All right, child,' he said gently. 'Say your Act of Contrition and I'll give you Absolution.'

'Father,' she whispered, her eyes black through the grille, 'I was in bed with him once.'

The canon looked at her. She drew back. He leaned away and looked from a distance at the criss-crossed face behind the grille. Then he began to smile, slowly expanding his mouth into a wide beam of relief.

'My child,' he whispered, 'did anyone ever tell you that you were a little deficient in the head? I mean, you weren't very smart at school, were you?'

'I was always at the top of the school, father. Mother Mary Gonzaga wanted to make a teacher of me.'

'And,' growled the canon, now utterly exasperated, and dancing his knees up and down on the balls of his feet like a man in the agony of toothache, 'do you kneel there and tell me that you think it no sin to go to bed with a man? Who,' he added, casually, 'isn't your husband?'

'I meant no harm, father,' she palpitated, 'and it's not what is in your mind at all, for we didn't do nothing, and if it wasn't for the thunder and lightning that terrified me, I wouldn't do it at all. Mrs Higgins was down in Crosshaven with Mrs Kinwall, that's her daughter, and I was all alone in the house, and I was afraid of the dark and the thunder, so Mikey said he'd stay with me, so he stayed, and then it was late and I was 'fraid to be by myself in the bed, so he said, "I'll mind you," so I said, "All right, Mikey, but none of that," and he said, "All right, Madgie, none of that," and there wasn't any of that, father.'

She stared at the canon, who was blowing and puffing and shaking his head as if the whole world were suddenly gone mad.

'It was no harm, father,' she wailed, seeing he did not believe her.

'Once?' asked the canon shortly. 'You did this once?'

'Yes, father.'

'Are you sorry for it?' he demanded briefly.

'If it was a sin. Was it, father?'

'It was,' he roared. 'People can't be allowed to do this kind of thing. It was a serious occasion of sin. Anything might have happened. Are you sorry?' – and he wondered if he should throw her out of the box again.

'I'm sorry, father.'

'Tell me a sin of your past life.'

'The apple in the orchard, father.'

'Say an Act of Contrition.'

She ran through it swiftly, staring at him all the while. There were beads of perspiration on her upper lip.

'Say three Rosarys for your penance.'

He shot the slide to and sank back, worn out. From force of habit he drew the opposite slide and at once he got the sweet scent of jasmine, but when Lady Nolan-White was in the middle of her *Confiteor* he waved his two hands madly in the air and said, hastily:

'Excuse me, one moment . . . I can't . . . It's all absurd . . . It's impossible. . . .'

And he drew the slide on her astonished, beautiful, rouged face. He put on his biretta, low down on his nose, and stalked out into the aisle. He parted the curtains on Lady Nolan-White and said:

'It's quite impossible. . . . You don't understand it. . . . Good night!'

He stalked up the dim aisle, and when he met two urchins gossiping in a corner he banged their little skulls together, and at once he became disgusted with himself to see them cowering from him in fright. He passed on, his hand under the tail of his surplice, dancing it up and down. When he saw two old women by the great Calvary, rubbing spittle into the Magdalen's foot and then rubbing the spittle to their eyes or throat, he groaned out, 'Oh, dear, oh dear,' and strode on towards Father Deeley's box. There he counted heads – fourteen penitents on one side and twelve on the other, looked at his gold watch and saw it was a quarter-past eight.

He strode back to the centre compartment and flung aside the curtains. Out of the dimness the warm, cherubic face of the young curate looked at him – a pink Italian saint. Slowly the glow of spiritual elevation died from his face as the canon's insistent whisper hissed down at him:

'Father Deeley, it won't do. I assure you it's absolutely impossible. Half-past eight and twenty-six people yet to hear confession. They're just deceiving you. They want to gabble. I am an old man and I understand them. Think of the sacristan. Electric light, too! And gas going until midnight. The organization of the Church . . . '

And so on. All the time he kept stretching and relaxing the mechanical bow of his genteel smile, and he spoke in the most polite voice. But Deeley's face grew troubled, and pained, and seeing it the canon groaned inwardly. He remembered a curate he had once who played the organ every day for hours on end, until the parishioners complained that they couldn't pray with the noise he made; the canon recalled how he had gone up into the loft to ask him to stop, and the curate had lifted to him a face like an angel, and how within one half-minute it had become the face of a cruel, bitter old man.

'All right, Father Deeley,' he said hastily, forestalling protests. 'You are young. I know. Still, you are young. . . .'

'I am not young,' hissed Deeley furiously. 'I know my duty. It's a matter of conscience. I can sit in the dark if you are so mean that you . . . '

'All right, all right, all right,' waved the canon, smiling furiously. 'We are all old nowadays. Experience counts for nothing . . . '

'Canon,' said Deeley, intensely, putting his two fists on his chest, 'when I was in the seminary, I used to say to myself, "Deeley," I used to say, "when you are a priest . . . " '

'Oh,' begged the canon, cracking his face in a smile, 'don't, I beg you, please don't tell me your life-story!'

Whereupon he whirled away, his head in the air, switching on and off the electric light of his smile to penitents he did not know and had never seen in his life before. He found himself before the high altar. He saw the sacristan standing on a step-ladder before it arranging the flowers for the morning, and he thought it would be well to apologize to him for Deeley's late hours. but the sacristan kept turning a vase round and round and round, and at last he realized that the little man was cross with him already, was deliberately delaying up there, and would not come down until he was gone.

Sighing, he went away, and after writing some letters he realized that his stomach had ceased to belong to him and would be out on its own devices until morning, like a hound that escapes from its kennel. Wearily he took his hat and cane and decided to take a long walk to calm his nerves.

It was tender night of floating moonlight, cosily damp, and it soothed him to look down on the city and see the roofs as white as if there was frost on them. More calm, he returned home. The river was like milk. The streets were asleep. He hummed quietly to himself and felt at peace with all men. The clocks of the city chimed at one another in a good-humoured mood, slow and with silvery, singing echoes. Then he heard a woman's voice talking from the high window of a cement-faced house, and he saw that it was Mrs Higgins's house. She was in a white nightdress.

'That's a fine story!' she cried down to the pavement. 'Ha! A cockalorum of a story! Wait until I see the canon. At confession, indeed! Wait until I see the nuns! Oh, you jade! You unfortunate, poor sinner!'

He saw the little girlish figure cowering down in the doorway.

'Mrs Higgins,' she wailed, 'it's gospel truth. The canon threw me out again. I told him all sorts of lies. I had to go to Father Deeley. He kept me half an hour. Oh, Mrs Higgins,' wailed the child. 'It's gospel truth.'

'Aha!' prated the nightdress. 'But you're a nice thing. Wait until I tell . . .'

The canon felt the hound of his stomach jump from the kennel again. His entrails came bodily up to his neck. He marched by, blowing and puffing.

'Oh, my God!' he whined. 'Have pity on me. Oh, my God! Have pity on me!'

He turned towards the dark presbytery deep among the darkest lanes.

FRANK O'CONNOR · 1903–1966

Guests of the Nation

I

At dusk the big Englishman Belcher would shift his long legs out of the ashes and ask, 'Well, chums, what about it?' and Noble or me would say, 'As you please, chum' (for we had picked up some of their curious expressions), and the little Englishman 'Awkins would light the lamp and produce the cards. Sometimes Jeremiah Donovan would come up of an evening and supervise the play, and grow excited over 'Awkins's cards (which he always played badly), and shout at him as if he was one of our own, 'Ach, you divil you, why didn't you play the tray?' But, ordinarily, Jeremiah was a sober and contented poor devil like the big Englishman Belcher, and was looked up to at all only because he was a fair hand at documents, though slow enough at these, I vow. He wore a small cloth hat and big gaiters over his long pants and seldom did I perceive his hands outside the pockets of that pants. He reddened when you talked to him, tilting from toe to heel and back and looking down all the while at his big farmer's feet. His uncommon broad accent was a great source of jest to me, I being from the town as you may recognize.

I couldn't at the time see the point of me and Noble being with Belcher and 'Awkins at all, for it was and is my fixed belief you could have planted that pair in any untended spot from this to Claregalway and they'd have stayed put and flourished like a native weed. I never seen in my short experience two men that took to the country as they did.

They were handed on to us by the Second Battalion to keep when the search for them became too hot, and Noble and myself, being young, took charge with a natural feeling of responsibility. But little 'Awkins made us look right fools when he displayed he knew the countryside as well as we did and something more. 'You're the bloke they calls Bonaparte?' he said to me. 'Well, Bonaparte, Mary Brigid Ho'Connell was arskin abaout you and said 'ow you'd a pair of socks belonging to 'er young brother.' For it seemed, as they explained it, that the Second used to have little evenings of their own, and some of the girls of the neighbourhood would turn in, and, seeing they were such decent fellows, our lads couldn't well ignore the two Englishmen, but invited them in and were hail-fellow-well-met with them. 'Awkins told me he learned to dance 'The Walls of Limerick' and 'The Siege of Ennis' and 'The Waves of Tory' in a night or two, though naturally he could not return the compliment, because our lads at that time did not dance foreign dances on principle.

So whatever privileges and favours Belcher and 'Awkins had with the Second they duly took with us, and after the first evening we gave up all pretence of keeping a close eye on their behaviour. Not that they could have got far, for they had a notable accent and wore khaki tunics and overcoats with civilian pants and boots. But it's my belief they never had an idea of escaping and were quite contented with their lot.

Now, it was a treat to see how Belcher got off with the old woman of the house we were staying in. She was a great warrant to scold, and crotchety even with us, but before ever she had a chance of giving our guests, as I may call them, a lick of her tongue, Belcher had made her his friend for life. She was breaking sticks at the time, and Belcher, who hadn't been in the house for more than ten minutes, jumped up out of his seat and went across to her.

'Allow me, madam,' he says, smiling his queer little smile; 'please allow me', and takes the hatchet from her hand. She was struck too parlatic to speak, and ever after Belcher would be at her heels carrying a bucket, or basket, or load of turf, as the case might be. As Noble wittily remarked, he got into looking before she leapt, and hot water or any little thing she wanted Belcher would have it ready before her. For such a huge man (and though I am five foot ten myself I had to look up to him) he had an uncommon shortness – or should I say lack – of speech. It took us some time to get used to him walking in and out like a ghost, without a syllable out of him. Especially because 'Awkins talked enough for a platoon, it was strange to hear big Belcher with his toes in the ashes come out with a solitary 'Excuse me, chum,' or 'That's right, chum.' His one and only abiding passion was cards, and I will say for him he was a good card-player. He could have fleeced me and Noble many a time; only if we lost to him, 'Awkins lost to us, and 'Awkins played with the money Belcher gave him.

'Awkins lost to us because he talked too much, and I think now we lost to Belcher for the same reason. 'Awkins and Noble would spit at one another about religion into the early hours of the morning; the little Englishman as you could see worrying the soul out of young Noble (whose brother was a priest) with a string of questions that would puzzle a cardinal. And to make it worse, even in treating of these holy subjects, 'Awkins had a deplorable tongue; I never in all my career struck across a man who could mix such a variety of cursing and bad language into the simplest topic. Oh, a terrible man was little 'Awkins, and a fright to argue! He never did a stroke of work, and when he had no one else to talk to he fixed his claws into the old woman.

I am glad to say that in her he met his match, for one day when he tried to get her to complain profanely of the drought she gave him a great comedown by blaming the drought upon Jupiter Pluvius (a deity neither 'Awkins nor I had ever even heard of, though Noble said among the pagans he was held to have something to do with rain). And another day the same 'Awkins was swearing at the capitalists for starting the German war, when the old dame laid down her iron, puckered up her little crab's mouth and said, 'Mr 'Awkins, you can say what you please about the war, thinking to deceive me because I'm an ignorant old woman, but I know well what started the war. It was that Italian count that stole the heathen divinity out of the temple in Japan, for believe me, Mr 'Awkins, nothing but sorrow and want follows them that disturbs the hidden powers!' Oh, a queer old dame, as you remark!

II

So one evening we had our tea together, and 'Awkins lit the lamp and we all sat in to cards. Jeremiah Donovan came in too, and sat down and watched us for a while. Though he was a shy man and didn't speak much, it was easy to see he had no great love for the two Englishmen, and I was surprised it hadn't struck me so clearly before. Well, like that in the story, a terrible dispute blew up late in the evening between 'Awkins and Noble, about capitalists and priests and love for your own country.

'The capitalists,' says 'Awkins, with an angry gulp, 'the capitalists pays the priests to tell you all abaout the next world, so's you waon't notice what they do in this!'

'Nonsense, man,' says Noble, losing his temper, 'before ever a capitalist was thought of people believed in the next world.'

'Awkins stood up as if he was preaching a sermon. 'Oh, they did, did they?' he says with a sneer. 'They believed all the things you believe, that's what you mean? And you believe that God created Hadam and Hadam created Shem and Shem created Jehoshophat? You believe all the silly hold fairy-tale abaout Heve and Heden and the happle? Well, listen to me, chum. If you're entitled to 'old to a silly belief like that, I'm entitled to 'old to my own silly belief – which is, that the fust thing your God created was a bleedin' capitalist with mirality and Rolls Royce complete. Am I right, chum?' he says then to Belcher.

'You're right, chum,' says Belcher, with his queer smile, and gets up from the table to stretch his long legs into the fire and stroke his moustache. So, seeing that Jeremiah Donovan was going, and there was no knowing when the conversation about religion would be over, I took my hat and went out with him. We strolled down towards the village together, and then he suddenly stopped, and blushing and mumbling, and shifting, as his way was, from toe to heel, he said I ought to be behind keeping guard on the prisoners. And I, having it put to me so suddenly, asked him what the hell he wanted a guard on the prisoners at all for, and said that so far as Noble and me were concerned we had talked it over and would rather be out with a column. 'What use is that pair to us?' I asked him.

He looked at me for a spell and said, 'I thought you knew we were keeping them as hostages.' 'Hostages — ?' says I, not quite understanding. 'The enemy', he says in his heavy way, 'have prisoners belong to us, and now they talk of shooting them. If they shoot our prisoners we'll shoot theirs, and serve them right.' 'Shoot them?' said I, the possibility just beginning to dawn on me. 'Shoot them, exactly,' said he. 'Now,' said I, 'wasn't it very unforeseen of you not to tell me and Noble that?' 'How so?' he asks. 'Seeing that we were acting as guards upon them, of course.' 'And hadn't you reason enough to guess that much?' 'We had not, Jeremiah Donovan, we had not. How were we to know when the men were on our hands so long?' 'And what difference does it make? The enemy have our prisoners as long or longer, haven't they?' 'It makes a great difference,' said I. 'How so?' said he sharply; but I couldn't tell him the difference it made, for I was struck too silly to speak.

'And when may we expect to be released from this anyway?' said I. 'You may expect it tonight,' says he. 'Or tomorrow or the next day at latest. So if it's hanging round here that worries you, you'll be free soon enough.'

I cannot explain it even now, how sad I felt, but I went back to the cottage, a miserable man. When I arrived the discussion was still on, 'Awkins holding forth to all and sundry that there was no next world at all and Noble answering in his best canonical style that there was. But I saw 'Awkins was after having the best of it. 'Do you know what, chum?' he was saying, with his saucy smile, 'I think you're jest as big a bleedin' hunbeliever as I am. You say you believe in the next world and you know jest as much abaout the next world as I do, which is sweet damn-all. What's 'Eaven? You dunno. Where's 'Eaven? You dunno. Who's in 'Eaven? You dunno. You know sweet damn-all! I arsk you again, do they wear wings?'

'Very well then,' says Noble, 'they do; is that enough for you? They do wear wings.' 'Where do they get them then? Who makes them? 'Ave they a fact'ry for wings? 'Ave they a sort of store where you 'ands in your chit and tikes your bleedin' wings? Answer me that.'

'Oh, you're an impossible man to argue with,' says Noble. 'Now listen to me — '. And off the pair of them went again.

It was long after midnight when we locked up the Englishmen and went to bed ourselves. As I blew out the candle I told Noble what Jeremiah Donovan had told me. Noble took it very quietly. After we had been in bed about an hour he asked me did I think we ought to tell the Englishmen. I having thought of the same thing myself (among many others) said no, because it was more than likely the English wouldn't shoot our men, and anyhow it wasn't to be supposed the Brigade who were always up and down with the second battalion and knew the Englishmen well would be likely to want them bumped off. 'I think so,' says Noble. 'It would be sort of cruelty to put the wind up them now.' 'It was very unforeseen of Jeremiah Donovan anyhow,' says I, and by Noble's silence I realized he took my meaning.

So I lay there half the night, and thought and thought, and picturing myself and young Noble trying to prevent the Brigade from shooting 'Awkins and Belcher sent a cold sweat out through me. Because there were men on the Brigade you daren't let nor hinder without a gun in your hand, and at any rate, in those days disunion between brothers seemed to me an awful crime. I knew better after. It was next morning we found it so hard to face Belcher and 'Awkins with a smile. We went about the house all day scarcely saying a word. Belcher didn't mind us much; he was stretched into the ashes as usual with his usual look of waiting in quietness for something unforeseen to happen, but little 'Awkins gave us a bad time with his audacious gibing and questioning. He was disgusted at Noble's not answering him back. 'Why can't you tike your beating like a man, chum?' he says. 'You with your Hadam and Heve! I'm a Communist – or an Anarchist. An Anarchist, that's what I am.' And for hours after he went round the house, mumbling when the fit took him, 'Hadam and Heve! Hadam and Heve!'

III

I don't know clearly how we got over that day, but get over it we did, and a great relief it was when the tea-things were cleared away and Belcher said in his peaceable manner, 'Well, chums, what about it?' So we all sat round the table and 'Awkins produced the cards, and at that moment I heard Jeremiah Donovan's footsteps up the path, and a dark presentiment crossed my mind. I rose quietly from the table and laid my hand on him before he reached the door. 'What do you want?' I asked him. 'I want those two soldier friends of yours,' he says reddening. 'Is that the way it is, Jeremiah Donovan?' I ask. 'That's the way. There were four of our lads went west this morning, one of them a boy of sixteen.' 'That's bad, Jeremiah,' says I.

At that moment Noble came out, and we walked down the path together talking in whispers. Feeney, the local intelligence officer, was standing by the gate. 'What are you going to do about it?' I asked Jeremiah Donovan. 'I want you and Noble to bring them out: you can tell them they're being shifted again; that'll be the quietest way.' 'Leave me out of that,' says Noble suddenly. Jeremiah Donovan looked at him hard for a minute or two. 'All right so,' he said peaceably. 'You and Feeney collect a few tools from the shed and dig a hole by the far end of the bog. Bonaparte and I'll be after you in about twenty minutes. But whatever else you do, don't let anyone see you with the tools. No one must know but the four of ourselves.'

We saw Feeney and Noble go round to the houseen where the

tools were kept, and sidled in. Everything if I can so express myself was tottering before my eyes, and I left Jeremiah Donovan to do the explaining as best he could, while I took a seat and said nothing. He told them they were to go back to the Second. 'Awkins let a mouthful of curses out of him at that, and it was plain that Belcher, though he said nothing, was duly perturbed. The old woman was for having them stay in spite of us, and she did not shut her mouth until Jeremiah Donovan lost his temper and said some nasty things to her. Within the house by this time it was pitch dark, but no one thought of lighting the lamp, and in the darkness the two Englishmen fetched their khaki topcoats and said good-bye to the woman of the house. 'Just as a man mikes a 'ome of a bleedin' place,' mumbles 'Awkins shaking her by the hand, 'some bastard at headquarters thinks you're too cushy and shunts you off.' Belcher shakes her hand very hearty. 'A thousand thanks, madam,' he says, 'a thousand thanks for everything . . . ' as though he'd made it all up.

We go round to the back of the house and down towards the fatal bog. Then Jeremiah Donovan comes out with what is in his mind. 'There were four of our lads shot by your fellows this morning so now you're to be bumped off.' 'Cut that stuff out,' says 'Awkins flaring up. 'It's bad enough to be mucked about such as we are without you plying at soldiers.' 'It's true,' says Jeremiah Donovan, 'I'm sorry, 'Awkins, but 'tis true,' and comes out with the usual rigmarole about doing our duty and obeying our superiors. 'Cut it out,' says 'Awkins irritably, 'Cut it out!'

Then, when Donovan sees he is not being believed he turns to me. 'Ask Bonaparte here,' he says. 'I don't need to arsk Bonaparte. Me and Bonaparte are chums.' 'Isn't it true, Bonaparte?' says Jeremiah Donovan solemnly to me. 'It is,' I say sadly, 'it is.' 'Awkins stops. 'Now, for Christ's sike. . . .' 'I mean it, chum,' I say. 'You daon't saound as if you mean it. You knaow well you don't mean it.' 'Well, if he don't I do,' says Jeremiah Donovan. 'Why the 'ell sh'd you want to shoot me, Jeremiah Donovan?' 'Why the hell should your people take out four prisoners and shoot them in cold blood upon a barrack square?' I perceive Jeremiah Donovan is trying to encourage himself with hot words.

Anyway, he took little 'Awkins by the arm and dragged him on, but it was impossible to make him understand that we were in earnest. From which you will perceive how difficult it was for me, as I kept feeling my Smith and Wesson and thinking what I would do if they happened to put up a fight or ran for it, and wishing in my heart they would. I knew if only they ran I would never fire on them. 'Was Noble in this?' 'Awkins wanted to know, and we said yes. He laughed. But why should Noble want to shoot him? Why should we want to shoot him? What had he done to us? Weren't we chums (the word lingers painfully in my memory)? Weren't we? Didn't we understand him and didn't he understand us? Did either of us imagine for an instant that he'd shoot us for all the so-and-so brigadiers in the so-and-so British Army? By this time I began to perceive in the dusk the desolate edges of the bog that was to be their last earthly bed, and, so great a sadness overtook my mind, I could not answer him. We walked along the edge of it in the darkness, and every now and then 'Awkins would call a halt and begin again, just as if he was wound up, about us being chums, and I was in despair that nothing but the cold and open grave made ready for his presence would convince him that we meant it all. But all the same, if you can understand, I didn't want him to be bumped off.

IV

At last we saw the unsteady glint of a lantern in the distance and made towards it. Noble was carrying it, and Feeney stood somewhere in the darkness behind, and somehow the picture of the two of them so silent in the boglands was like the pain of death in my heart. Belcher, on recognizing Noble, said ''Allo, chum' in his usual peaceable way, but 'Awkins flew at the poor boy immediately, and the dispute began all over again, only that Noble hadn't a word to say for himself, and stood there with the swaying lantern between his gaitered legs.

It was Jeremiah Donovan who did the answering. 'Awkins asked for the twentieth time (for it seemed to haunt his mind) if anybody thought he'd shoot Noble. 'You would,' says Jeremiah Donovan shortly. 'I wouldn't, damn you!' 'You would if you knew you'd be shot for not doing it.' 'I wouldn't, not if I was to be shot twenty times over; he's my chum. And Belcher wouldn't – isn't that right, Belcher?' 'That's right, chum,' says Belcher peaceably. 'Damned if I would. Anyway, who says Noble'd be shot if I wasn't bumped off? What d'you think I'd do if I was in Noble's place and we were out in the middle of a blasted bog?' 'What would you do?' 'I'd go with him wherever he was going. I'd share my last bob with him and stick by 'im through thick and thin.'

'We've had enough of this,' says Jeremiah Donovan, cocking his revolver. 'Is there any message you want to send before I fire?' 'No, there isn't, but . . . ' 'Do you want to say your prayers?' 'Awkins came out with a cold-blooded remark that shocked even me and turned to Noble again. 'Listen to me, Noble,' he said. 'You and me are chums. You won't come over to my side, so I'll come over to your side. Is that fair? Just you give me a rifle and I'll go with you wherever you want.'

Nobody answered him.

'Do you understand?' he said. 'I'm through with it all. I'm a deserter or anything else you like, but from this on I'm one of you. Does that prove to you that I mean what I say?' Noble raised his head, but as Donovan began to speak he lowered it again without answering. 'For the last time have you any messages to send?' says Donovan in a cold and excited voice.

'Ah, shut up, you, Donovan; you don't understand me, but these fellows do. They're my chums; they stand by me and I stand by them. We're not the capitalist tools you seem to think us.'

I alone of the crowd saw Donovan raise his Webley to the back of 'Awkins's neck, and as he did so I shut my eyes and tried to say a prayer. 'Awkins had begun to say something else when Donovan let fly, and, as I opened my eyes at the bang, I saw him stagger at the knees and lie out flat at Noble's feet, slowly, and as quiet as a child, with the lantern-light falling sadly upon his lean legs and bright farmer's boots. We all stood very still for a while watching him settle out in the last agony.

Then Belcher quietly takes out a handkerchief, and begins to tie it about his own eyes (for in our excitement we had forgotten to offer the same to 'Awkins), and, seeing it is not big enough, turns and asks for a loan of mine. I give it to him and as he knots the two together he points with his foot at 'Awkins. ' 'E's not quite dead,' he says, 'better give 'im another.' Sure enough 'Awkins's left knee as we see it under the lantern is rising again. I bend down and put my gun to his ear; then, recollecting myself and the company of Belcher, I stand up again with a few hasty words. Belcher understands what is in my mind. 'Give 'im 'is first,' he says. 'I don't mind. Poor bastard, we dunno what's 'appening to 'im now.' As by this time I am beyond all feeling I kneel down again and skilfully give 'Awkins the last shot so as to put him for ever out of pain.

Belcher who is fumbling a bit awkwardly with the handkerchiefs comes out with a laugh when he hears the shot. It is the first time I have heard him laugh, and it sends a shiver down my spine, coming as it does so inappropriately upon the tragic death of his old friend. 'Poor blighter,' he says quietly, 'and last night he was so curious abaout it all. It's very queer, chums, I always think. Naow, 'e knows as much abaout it as they'll ever let 'im know, and last night 'e was all in the dark.'

Donovan helps him to tie the handkerchiefs about his eyes. 'Thanks, chum,' he says. Donovan asks him if there are any messages he would like to send. 'Naow, chum,' he says, 'none for me. If any of you likes to write to 'Awkins's mother you'll find a letter from 'er in 'is pocket. But my missus left me eight years ago. Went away with another fellow and took the kid with her. I likes the feelin' of a 'ome (as you may 'ave noticed) but I couldn't start again after that.'

We stand around like fools now that he can no longer see us. Donovan looks at Noble and Noble shakes his head. Then Donovan raises his Webley again and just at that moment Belcher laughs his queer nervous laugh again. He must think we are talking of him; anyway, Donovan lowers his gun. ' 'Scuse me, chums,' says Belcher, 'I feel I'm talking the 'ell of a lot . . . and so silly . . ; abaout me being so 'andy abaout a 'ouse. But this thing come on me so sudden. You'll forgive me, I'm sure.' 'You don't want to say a prayer?' asks Jeremiah Donovan. 'No, chum,' he replies, 'I don't think that'd 'elp. I'm ready if you want to get it over.' 'You understand,' says Jeremiah Donovan, 'it's not so much our doing. It's our duty, so to speak.' Belcher's head is raised like a real blind man's, so that you can only see his nose and chin in the lamplight. 'I never could make out what duty was myself,' he said, 'but I think you're all good lads, if that's what you mean. I'm not complaining.' Noble, with a look of desperation, signals to Donovan, and in a flash Donovan raises his gun and fires. The big man goes over like a sack of meal, and this time there is no need of a second shot.

I don't remember much about the burying, but that it was worse than all the rest, because we had to carry the warm corpses a few yards before we sunk them in the windy bog. It was all mad lonely, with only a bit of lantern between ourselves and the pitch-blackness, and birds hooting and screeching all round disturbed by the guns. Noble had to search 'Awkins first to get the letter from his mother. Then having smoothed all signs of the grave away, Noble and I collected our tools, said good-bye to the others, and went back along the desolate edge of the treacherous bog without a word. We put the tools in the houseen and went into the house. The kitchen was pitch-black and cold, just as we left it, and the old woman was sitting over the hearth telling her beads. We walked past her into the room, and Noble struck a match to light the lamp. Just then she rose quietly and came to the doorway, being not at all so bold or crabbed as usual.

'What did ye do with them?' she says in a sort of whisper, and Noble took such a mortal start the match quenched in his trembling hand. 'What's that?' he asks without turning round. 'I heard ye,' she said. 'What did you hear?' asks Noble, but sure he wouldn't deceive a child the way he said it. 'I heard ye. Do you think I wasn't listening to ye putting the things back in the houseen?' Noble struck another match and this time the lamp lit for him. 'Was that what ye did with them?' she said, and Noble said nothing – after all what could he say?

So then, by God, she fell on her two knees by the door, and began telling her beads, and after a minute or two Noble went on his knees by the fireplace, so I pushed my way out past her, and stood at the door, watching the stars and listening to the damned shrieking of the birds. It is so strange what you feel at such moments, and not to be written afterwards. Noble says he felt he seen everything ten times as big, perceiving nothing around him but the little patch of black bog with the two Englishmen stiffening into it; but with me it was the other way, as though the patch of bog where the two Englishmen were was a thousand miles away from me, and even Noble mumbling just behind me and the old woman and the birds and the bloody stars were all far away, and I was somehow very small and very lonely. And anything that ever happened me after I never felt the same about again.

The Runaway

In the lumberyard by the lake there was an old brick building two storeys high and all around the foundations were heaped great piles of soft sawdust, softer than the thick moss in the woods. There were many of these golden mounds of dust covering that part of the yard right down to the blue lake. That afternoon all the fellows followed Michael up the ladder to the roof of the old building and they sat with their legs hanging over the edge looking out at the whitecaps on the water. Michael was younger than some of them but he was much bigger, his legs were long, his huge hands dangled awkwardly at his sides and his thick black hair curled up all over his head. 'I'll stump you all to jump down,' he said suddenly, and without thinking about it, he shoved himself off the roof and fell on the sawdust where he lay rolling around and laughing.

'You're all stumped,' he shouted, 'You're all yellow,' he said, coaxing them to follow him. Still laughing, he watched them looking down from the roof, white-faced and hesitant, and then one by one they jumped and got up grinning with relief.

In the hot afternoon sunlight they all lay on the sawdust pile telling jokes till at last one of the fellows said, 'Come on up on the old roof again and jump down.' There wasn't much enthusiasm among them, but they all went up to the roof again and began to jump off in a determined, desperate way till only Michael was left and the others were all down below grinning up at him and calling, 'Come on, Mike. What's the matter with you?' Michael longed to jump down there and be with them, but he remained on the edge of the roof, wetting his lips, with a silly grin on his face, wondering why it had not seemed such a long drop the first time. For a while they thought he was only kidding them, then they saw him clenching his fists. He was trying to count to ten and then jump, and when that failed, he tried to take a long breath and close his eyes.

In a while the fellows began to jeer at him; they were tired of waiting and it was getting on to dinner-time. 'Come on, you're yellow, do you think we're going to sit here all night?' they began to shout, and when he did not move they began to get up and walk away, still jeering. 'Who did this in the first place? What's the matter with you guys?' he shouted.

But for a long time he remained on the edge of the roof, staring unhappily and steadily at the ground. He remained all alone for nearly an hour while the sun like a great orange ball getting bigger and bigger rolled slowly over the gray line beyond the lake. His clothes were wet from nervous sweating. At last he closed his eyes, slipped off the roof, fell heavily on the pile of sawdust and lay there a long time. There were no sounds in the yard, the workmen had gone home. As he lay there he wondered why he had been unable to move; and then he got up slowly and walked home feeling deeply ashamed and wanting to avoid everybody.

He was so late for dinner that his stepmother said to him sarcastically, 'You're big enough by this time surely to be able to get home in time for dinner. But if you won't come home, you'd better try staying in tonight.' She was a well-built woman with a fair, soft skin and a little touch of gray in her hair and an eternally patient smile on her face. She was speaking now with a restrained, passionless severity, but Michael, with his dark face gloomy and sullen, hardly heard her; he was still seeing the row of grinning faces down below on the sawdust pile and hearing them jeer at him.

As he ate his cold dinner he was rolling his brown eyes fiercely and sometimes shaking his big black head. His father, who was sitting in the armchair by the window, a huge man with his hair nearly all gone so that his smooth wide forehead rose in a beautiful shining dome, kept looking at him steadily. When Michael had finished eating and had gone out to the veranda, his father followed, sat down beside him, lit his pipe and said gently, 'What's bothering you, son?'

'Nothing, Dad. There's nothing bothering me,' Michael said, but he kept on staring out at the gray dust drifting off the road.

His father kept coaxing and whispering in a voice that was amazingly soft for such a big man. As he talked, his long fingers played with the heavy gold watch fob on his vest. He was talking about nothing in particular and yet by the tone of his voice he was expressing a marvellous deep friendliness that somehow seemed to become a part of the twilight and then of the darkness. And Michael began to like the sound of his father's voice, and soon he blurted out, 'I guess by this time all the guys around here are saying I'm yellow. I'd like to be a thousand miles away.' He told how he could not force himself to jump off the roof the second time. But his father lay back in the armchair laughing in that hearty, rolling, easy way that Michael loved to hear; years ago when Michael had been younger and he was walking along the paths in the evening, he used to try and laugh like his father only his voice was not deep enough and he would grin sheepishly and look up at the trees over-hanging the paths as if someone hiding up there had heard him. 'You'll be all right with the bunch, son,' his father was saying. 'I'm betting you'll lick any boy in town that says you're yellow.'

But there was the sound of the screen door opening, and Michael's stepmother said in her mild, firm way, 'If I've rebuked the boy, Henry, as I think he ought to be rebuked, I don't know why you should be humoring him.'

'You surely don't object to me talking to Michael.'

'I simply want you to be reasonable, Henry.'

In his grave, unhurried way Mr Lount got up and followed his wife into the house and soon Michael could hear them arguing; he could hear his father's firm, patient voice floating clearly out to the street; then his stepmother's voice, mild at first, rising, becoming hysterical till at last she cried out wildly, 'You're setting the boy against me. You don't want him to think of me as his mother. The two of you are against me. I know your nature.'

As he looked up and down the street fearfully, Michael began to make prayers that no one would pass by who would think, 'Mr and Mrs Lount are quarrelling again.' Alert, he listened for faint sounds on the cinder path, but he heard only the frogs croaking under the bridge opposite Stevenson's place and the far-away cry of a freight train passing behind the hills. 'Why did Dad have to get married? It used to be swell on the farm,' he thought, remembering how he and his father had gone fishing down at the glen. And then while he listened to the sound of her voice, he kept thinking that his stepmother was a fine woman, only she always made him un-easy because she wanted him to like her, and then when she found out that he couldn't think of her as his mother, she had grown resentful. 'I like her and I like my father. I don't know why they quarrel. They're really such fine people. Maybe it's because Dad shouldn't have sold the farm and moved here. There's nothing for him to do.' Unable to get interested in town life, his father loafed all day down at the hotel or in Bailey's flour-and-feed store but he was such a fine-looking, dignified, reticent man that the loafers would not accept him as a crony. Inside the house now, Mrs Lount was crying quietly and saying, 'Henry, we'll kill each other. We seem to bring out all the very worst qualities in each other. I do all I can and yet you both make me feel like an intruder.'

'It's just your imagination, Martha. Now stop worrying.'

'I'm an unhappy woman. But I try to be patient. I try so hard, don't I, Henry?'

'You're very patient, dear, but you shouldn't be so suspicious of everyone and everybody, don't you see?' Mr Lount was saying in the soothing voice of a man trying to pacify an angry and hysterical wife.

Then Michael heard footsteps on the cinder path, and then he saw two long shadows flung across the road: two women were approaching, and one was a tall, slender girl. When Michael saw this girl, Helen Murray, he tried to duck behind the veranda post, for he had always wanted her for his girl. He had gone to school with her. At night-time he used to lie awake planning remarkable feats that would so impress her she would never want to be far away from him. Now the girl's mother was calling, 'Hello there, Michael,' in a very jolly voice.

'Hello, Mrs Murray,' he said glumly, for he was sure his father's or his mother's voice would rise again.

'Come on and walk home with us, Michael,' Helen called. Her voice sounded so soft and her face in the dusk light seemed so round, white and mysteriously far away that Michael began to ache with eagerness. Yet he said hurriedly, 'I can't. I can't to-night,' speaking almost rudely as if he believed they only wanted to tease him.

As they went on along the path and he watched them, he was really longing for that one bright moment when Helen would pass under the high corner light, though he was thinking with bitterness that he could already hear them talking, hear Mrs Murray saying, 'He's a peculiar boy, but it's not to be wondered at since his father and mother don't get along at all,' and the words were floating up to the verandas of all the houses: inside one of the houses someone had stopped playing a piano, maybe to hear one of the fellows who had been in the lumberyard that afternoon laughing and telling that young Lount was scared to jump off the roof.

Still watching the corner, Michael suddenly felt that the twisting and pulling in the life in the house was twisting and choking him. 'I'll get out of here. I'll go away,' and he began to think of going to the city. He began to long for freedom in strange places where everything was new and fresh and mysterious. His heart began to beat heavily at the thought of this freedom. In the city he had an uncle Joe who sailed the lake-boats in the summer months and in the winter went all over the south from one race track to another following the horses. 'I ought to go down to the city tonight and get a job,' he thought: but he did not move; he was still waiting for Helen Murray to pass under the light.

For most of the next day, too, Michael kept to himself. He was up-town once on a message, and he felt like running on the way home. With long sweeping strides he ran steadily on the paths past the shipyard, the church, the railway tracks, his face serious with determination.

But in the late afternoon when he was sitting on the veranda reading, Sammy Schwartz and Ike Hershfield came around to see him. 'Hello Mike, what's new with you?' they said, sitting on the steps very seriously.

'Hello, Sammy, hello, Ike. What's new with you?'

They began to talk to Michael about the colored family that had moved into the old roughcast shack down by the tracks. 'The big coon kid thinks he's tough,' Sammy said. 'He offered to beat up any of us so we said he wouldn't have a snowball's chance with you.'

'What did the nigger say?'

'He said he'd pop you one right on the nose if you came over his way.'

'Come on, guys. Let's go over there,' Michael said. 'I'll tear his guts out for you.'

They went out to the street, fell in step very solemnly, and walked over to the field by the tracks without saying a word. When they were about fifty paces away from the shack, Sammy said, 'Wait here. I'll go get the coon,' and he ran on to the unpainted door of the whitewashed house calling, 'Oh, Art, oh, Art, come on out.' A big colored boy with closely cropped hair came out and put his hand up, shading his eyes from the sun. Then he went back into the house and came out again with a big straw hat on his head. He was in his bare feet. The way he came walking across the field with

Sammy was always easy to remember because he hung back a little, talking rapidly, shrugging his shoulders and rolling the whites of his eyes. When he came close to Michael he grinned nervously, flashing his teeth, and said, 'What's the matter with you white boys? I don't want to do no fighting.' He looked scared.

'Come on. Get ready. I'm going to do a nice job on you,' Michael said.

The colored boy took off his big straw hat and with great care laid it on the ground while all the time he was looking mournfully across the field and at his house, hoping maybe that somebody would come out. Then they started to fight, and Michael knocked him down four times, but he, himself, got a black eye and a cut lip. The colored boy had been so brave and he seemed so alone, licked and lying on the ground, that they sat down around him, praising him, making friends with him and gradually finding out that he was a good ball player, a left-handed pitcher who specialized in a curve ball, and they agreed they could use him, maybe, on the town team.

Lying there in the field, flat on his back, Michael liked it so much that he almost did not want to go away. Art, the colored boy, was telling how he had always wanted to be a jockey but had got too big; he had a brother who could make the weight. So Michael began to boast about his Uncle Joe who went around to all the tracks in the winter making and losing money at places like Saratoga, Blue Bonnets and Tia Juana. It was a fine, friendly, eager discussion about far-away places.

It was nearly dinner-time when Michael got home; he went in the house sucking his cut lip and hoping his mother would not notice his black eye. But he heard no movement in the house. In the kitchen he saw his stepmother kneeling down in the middle of the floor with her hands clasped and her lips moving.

'What's the matter, Mother?' he asked.

'I'm praying,' she said.

'What for?'

'For your father. Get down and pray with me.'

'I don't want to pray, Mother.'

'You've got to,' she said.

'My lip's all cut. It's bleeding. I can't do it,' he said.

Late afternoon sunshine coming through the kitchen window shone on his stepmother's graying hair, on her soft smooth skin and on the gentle, patient expression that was on her face. At that moment Michael thought that she was desperately uneasy and terribly alone, and he felt sorry for her even while he was rushing out of the back door.

He saw his father walking toward the woodshed, walking slow and upright with his hands held straight at his side and with the same afternoon sunlight shining so brightly on the high dome of his forehead. He went right into the woodshed without looking back. Michael sat down on the steps and waited. He was afraid to follow. Maybe it was because of the way his father was walking with his head held up and his hands straight at his sides. Michael began to make a small desperate prayer that his father should suddenly appear at the woodshed door.

Time dragged slowly. A few doors away Mrs McCutcheon was feeding her hens who were clucking as she called them. 'I can't sit here till it gets dark,' Michael was thinking, but he was afraid to go into the woodshed and afraid to think of what he feared.

So he waited till he could not keep a picture of the interior of the shed out of his thoughts, a picture that included his father walking in with his hands as though strapped at his sides and his head stiff, like a man they were going to hang.

'What's he doing in there, what's he doing?' Michael said out loud, and he jumped up and rushed to the shed and flung the door wide.

His father was sitting on a pile of wood with his head on his hands and a kind of beaten look on his face. Still scared, Michael called out, 'Dad, Dad,' and then he felt such relief he sank down on the pile of wood beside his father and looked up at him.

'What's the matter with you, son?'

'Nothing. I guess I just wondered where you were.'

'What are you upset about?'

'I've been running. I feel all right.'

So they sat there quietly till it seemed time to go into the house. No one said anything. No one noticed Michael's black eye or his cut lip.

Even after they had eaten Michael could not get rid of the fear within him, a fear of something impending. In a way he felt that he ought to do something at once, but he seemed unable to move; it was like sitting on the edge of the roof yesterday, afraid to make the jump. So he went back of the house and sat on the stoop and for a long time looked at the shed till he grew even more uneasy. He heard the angry drilling of a woodpecker and the quiet rippling of the little water flowing under the street bridge and flowing on down over the rocks into the glen. Heavy clouds were sweeping up from the horizon.

He knew now that he wanted to run away, that he could not stay there any longer, only he couldn't make up his mind to go. Within him was that same breathless feeling he had had when he sat on the roof staring down, trying to move. Now he walked around to the front of the house and kept going along the path as far as Helen Murray's house. After going around to the back door, he stood for a long time staring at the lighted window, hoping to see Helen's shadow or her body moving against the light. He was breathing deeply and smelling the rich heavy odors from the flower garden. With his head thrust forward he whistled softly.

'Is that you, Michael?' Helen called from the door.

'Come on out, Helen.'

'What do you want?'

'Come on for a walk, will you?'

For a moment she hesitated at the door, then she came toward him, floating in her white organdie party dress over the grass toward him. She was saying, 'I'm dressed to go out. I can't go with you. I'm going down to the dance hall.'

'Who with?'

'Charlie Delaney.'

'Oh, all right,' he said. 'I just thought you might be doing nothing.' As he walked away he called back to her, 'So long, Helen.'

It was then, on the way back to the house, that he felt he had to go away at once. 'I've got to go. I'll die here. I'll write to Dad from the city.'

No one paid any attention to him when he returned to the house. His father and stepmother were sitting quietly in the living-room reading the paper. In his own room he took a little wooden box from the bottom drawer of his dresser and emptied it of twenty dollars and seventy cents, all that he had saved. He listened solemnly for sounds in the house, then he stuffed a clean shirt into his pocket, a comb, and a toothbrush.

Outside he hurried along with his great swinging strides, going past the corner house, on past the long fence and the bridge and the church, and the shipyard, and past the last of the town lights to the highway. He was walking stubbornly with his face looking solemn and dogged. Then he saw the moonlight shining on the hay stacked in the fields, and when he smelled the oats and the richer smell of sweet clover he suddenly felt alive and free. Headlights from cars kept sweeping by and already he was imagining he could see the haze of bright light hanging over the city. His heart began to thump with eagerness. He put out his hand for a lift, feeling full of hope. He looked across the fields at the dark humps, cows standing motionless in the night. Soon someone would stop and pick him up. They would take him among a million new faces, rumbling sounds, and strange smells. He got more excited. His Uncle Joe might get him a job on the boats for the rest of the summer; maybe, too, he might be able to move around with him in the winter. Over and over he kept thinking of places with beautiful names, places like Tia Juana, Woodbine, Saratoga and Blue Bonnets.

H. E. BATES · 1905–1974

Never

It was afternoon: great clouds stumbled across the sky. In the
drowsy, half-dark room the young girl sat in a heap near the window, scarcely moving herself, as if she expected a certain timed
happening, such as a visit, sunset, a command. Slowly she would
draw the fingers of one hand across the back of the other, in the
little hollows between the guides, and move her lips in the same
sad, vexed way in which her brows came together. And like this
too, her eyes would shift about, from the near, shadowed fields, to
the west hills, where the sun had dropped a strip of light, and to
the woods between, looking like black scars one minute, and like
friendly sanctuaries the next. It was all confused. There was the
room, too. The white keys of the piano would now and then exercise a fascination over her which would keep her whole body perfectly still for perhaps a minute. But when this passed, full of hesitation, her fingers would recommence the slow exploration of her
hands, and the restlessness took her again.

It was all confused. She was going away: already she had said a
hundred times during the afternoon – 'I am going away, I am going
away. I can't stand it any longer.' But she had made no attempt to
go. In this same position, hour after hour had passed her and all
she could think was: 'Today I'm going away. I'm tired here. I never
do anything. It's dead, rotten.'

She said, or thought it all without the slightest trace of exultation
and was sometimes even methodical when she began to consider:
'What shall I take? The blue dress with the rosette? Yes. What else?
what else?' And then it would all begin again: 'Today I'm going
away. I never do anything.'

It was true: she never did anything. In the mornings she got up
late, was slow over her breakfast, over everything – her reading,
her mending, her eating, her playing the piano, cards in the evening, going to bed. It was all slow – purposely done, to fill up the

day. And it was true, day succeeded day and she never did anything different.

But today something was about to happen: no more cards in the evening, every evening the same, with her father declaring: 'I never have a decent hand, I thought the ace of trumps had gone! It's too bad!!' and no more: 'Nellie, it's ten o'clock – Bed!' and the slow unimaginative climb of the stairs. Today she was going away: no one knew, but it was so. She was catching the evening train to London.

'I'm going away. What shall I take? The blue dress with the rosette? What else?'

She crept upstairs with difficulty, her body stiff after sitting. The years she must have sat, figuratively speaking, and grown stiff! And as if in order to secure some violent reaction against it all she threw herself into the packing of her things with a nervous vigour, throwing in the blue dress first and after it a score of things she had just remembered. She fastened her bag: it was not heavy. She counted her money a dozen times. It was all right! It was all right. She was going away!

She descended into the now dark room for the last time. In the dining-room someone was rattling tea-cups, an unbearable, horribly domestic sound! She wasn't hungry: she would be in London by eight – eating now meant making her sick. It was easy to wait. The train went at 6.18. She looked it up again: 'Elden 6.13, Olde 6.18, London 7.53.'

She began to play a waltz. It was a slow, dreamy tune, ta-tum, tum, ta-tum, tum, ta-tum, tum, of which the notes slipped out in mournful, sentimental succession. The room was quite dark, she could scarcely see the keys, and into the tune itself kept insinuating: 'Elden 6.13, Olde 6.18,' impossible to mistake or forget.

As she played on she thought: 'I'll never play this waltz again. It has the atmosphere of this room. It's the last time!' The waltz slid dreamily to an end: for a minute she sat in utter silence, the room dark and mysterious, the air of the waltz quite dead, then the tea-cups rattled again and the thought came back to her: 'I'm going away!'

She rose and went out quietly. The grass on the roadside moved under the evening wind, sounding like many pairs of hands rubbed softly together. But there was no other sound, her feet were light, no one heard her, and as she went down the road she told herself:

'It's going to happen! It's come at last!'

'Elden 6.13. Olde 6.18.'

Should she go to Elden or Olde? At the crossroads she stood to consider, thinking that if she went to Elden no one would know her. But at Olde someone would doubtless notice her and prattle about it. To Elden, then, not that it mattered. Nothing mattered now. She was going, was as good as gone!

Her breast, tremulously warm, began to rise and fall as her excitement increased. She tried to run over the things in her bag and could remember only 'the blue dress with the rosette', which she had thrown in first and had since covered over. But it didn't matter. Her money was safe, everything was safe, and with that thought she dropped into a strange quietness, deepening as she went on, in which she had a hundred emotions and convictions. She was never going to strum that waltz again, she had played cards for the last, horrible time, the loneliness, the slowness, the oppression were ended, all ended.

'I'm going away!'

She felt warm, her body tingled with a light delicious thrill that was like the caress of a soft night-wind. There were no fears now. A certain indignation, approaching fury even, sprang up instead, as she thought: 'No one will believe I've gone. But it's true – I'm going at last.'

Her bag grew heavy. Setting it down in the grass she sat on it for a brief while, in something like her attitude in the dark room during the afternoon, and indeed actually began to rub her gloved fingers over the backs of her hands. A phrase or two of the waltz came back to her. . . . That silly piano! Its bottom G was flat, had always been flat! How ridiculous! She tried to conjure up some sort of vision of London, but it was difficult and in the end she gave way again to the old cry: 'I'm going away.' And she was pleased more than ever deeply.

On the station a single lamp burned, radiating a fitful yellowness that only increased the gloom. And worse, she saw no one and in the cold emptiness traced and retraced her footsteps without the friendly assurance of another sound. In the black distance all the signals showed hard circles of red, looking as if they could never change. But she nevertheless told herself over and over again: 'I'm going away – I'm going away.' And later: 'I hate everyone. I've changed until I hardly know myself.'

Impatiently she looked for the train. It was strange. For the first time it occurred to her to know the time and she pulled back the sleeve of her coat. Nearly six-thirty! She felt cold. Up the line every signal displayed its red ring, mocking her. 'Six-thirty, of course, of course.' She tried to be careless. 'Of course, it's late, the train is late,' but the coldness, in reality her fear, increased rapidly, until she could no longer believe those words. . . .

Great clouds, lower and more than ever depressing, floated above her head as she walked back. The wind had a deep note that was sad too. These things had not troubled her before, now they, also, spoke failure and foretold misery and dejection. She had no spirit, it was cold, and she was too tired even to shudder.

In the absolutely dark, drowsy room she sat down, telling herself: 'This isn't the only day. Some day I shall go. Some day.'

She was silent. In the next room they were playing cards and her father suddenly moaned: 'I thought the ace had gone.' Somebody laughed. Her father's voice came again: 'I never have a decent hand! I never have a decent hand! Never!'

It was too horrible! She couldn't stand it! She must do something to stop it! It was too much. She began to play the waltz again and the dreamy, sentimental arrangement made her cry.

'This isn't the only day,' she reassured herself. 'I shall go. Some day!'

And again and again as she played the waltz, bent her head and cried, she would tell herself that same thing:

'Some day! Some day!'

A Horse and Two Goats

Of the seven hundred thousand villages dotting the map of India, in which the majority of India's five hundred million live, flourish, and die, Kritam was probably the tiniest, indicated on the district survey map by a microscopic dot, the map being meant more for the revenue official out to collect tax than for the guidance of the motorist, who in any case could not hope to reach it since it sprawled far from the highway at the end of a rough track furrowed up by the iron-hooped wheels of bullock carts. But its size did not prevent its giving itself the grandiose name Kritam, which meant in Tamil 'coronet' or 'crown' on the brow of this subcontinent. The village consisted of less than thirty houses, only one of them built with brick and cement. Painted a brilliant yellow and blue all over with gorgeous carvings of gods and gargoyles on its balustrade, it was known as the Big House. The other houses, distributed in four streets, were generally of bamboo thatch, straw, mud, and other unspecified material. Muni's was the last house in the fourth street, beyond which stretched the fields. In his prosperous days Muni had owned a flock of forty sheep and goats and sallied forth every morning driving the flock to the highway a couple of miles away. There he would sit on the pedestal of a clay statue of a horse while his cattle grazed around. He carried a crook at the end of a bamboo pole and snapped foliage from the avenue trees to feed his flock; he also gathered faggots and dry sticks, bundled them, and carried them home for fuel at sunset.

His wife lit the domestic fire at dawn, boiled water in a mud pot, threw into it a handful of millet flour, added salt, and gave him his first nourishment for the day. When he started out, she would put in his hand a packed lunch, once again the same millet cooked into a little ball, which he could swallow with a raw onion at midday. She was old, but he was older and needed all the attention she could give him in order to be kept alive.

His fortunes had declined gradually, unnoticed. From a flock of forty which he drove into a pen at night, his stock had now come down to two goats which were not worth the rent of a half rupee a month the Big House charged for the use of the pen in their back yard. And so the two goats were tethered to the trunk of a drumstick tree which grew in front of his hut and from which occasionally Muni could shake down drumsticks. This morning he got six. He carried them in with a sense of triumph. Although no one could say precisely who owned the tree, it was his because he lived in its shadow.

She said, 'If you were content with the drumstick leaves alone, I could boil and salt some for you.'

'Oh, I am tired of eating those leaves. I have a craving to chew the drumstick out of sauce, I tell you.'

'You have only four teeth in your jaw, but your craving is for big things. All right, get the stuff for the sauce, and I will prepare it for you. After all, next year you may not be alive to ask for anything. But first get me all the stuff, including a measure of rice or millet, and I will satisfy your unholy craving. Our store is empty today. Dhal, chili, curry leaves, mustard, coriander, gingelley oil, and one large potato. Go out and get all this.' He repeated the list after her in order not to miss any item and walked off to the shop in the third street.

He sat on an upturned packing case below the platform of the shop. The shopman paid no attention to him. Muni kept clearing his throat, coughing, and sneezing until the shopman could not stand it any more and demanded, 'What ails you? You will fly off that seat into the gutter if you sneeze so hard, young man.' Muni laughed inordinately, in order to please the shopman, at being called 'young man'. The shopman softened and said, 'You have enough of the imp inside to keep a second wife busy, but for the fact the old lady is still alive.' Muni laughed appropriately again at this joke. It completely won the shopman over; he liked his sense of humour to be appreciated. Muni engaged his attention in local gossip for a few minutes, which always ended with a reference to the postman's wife who had eloped to the city some months before.

The shopman felt most pleased to hear the worst of the postman, who had cheated him. Being an itinerant postman, he returned home to Kritam only once in ten days and every time managed to slip away again without passing the shop in the third street. By thus humouring the shopman, Muni could always ask for one or two items of food, promising repayment later. Some days the shopman was in a good mood and gave in, and sometimes he would lose his temper suddenly and bark at Muni for daring to ask for credit. This was such a day, and Muni could not progress beyond two items listed as essential components. The shopman was also displaying a remarkable memory for old facts and figures and took out an oblong ledger to support his observations. Muni felt impelled to rise and flee. But his self-respect kept him in his seat and made him listen to the worst things about himself. The shopman concluded, 'If you could find five rupees and a quarter, you would pay off an ancient debt and then could apply for admission to swarga. How much have you got now?'

'I will pay you everything on the first of the next month.'

'As always, and whom do you expect to rob by then?'

Muni felt caught and mumbled, 'My daughter has sent word that she will be sending me money.'

'Have you a daughter?' sneered the shopman. 'And she is sending you money! For what purpose, may I know?'

'Birthday, fiftieth birthday,' said Muni quietly.

'Birthday! How old are you?'

Muni repeated weakly, not being sure of it himself, 'Fifty'. He always calculated his age from the time of the great famine when he stood as high as the parapet around the village well, but who could calculate such things accurately nowadays with so many famines occurring? The shopman felt encouraged when other customers stood around to watch and comment. Muni thought helplessly, My poverty is exposed to everybody. But what can I do?

'More likely you are seventy,' said the shopman. 'You also forget that you mentioned a birthday five weeks ago when you wanted castor oil for your holy bath.'

'Bath! Who can dream of a bath when you have to scratch the tank-bed for a bowl of water? We would all be parched and dead but for the Big House, where they let us take a pot of water from their well.' After saying this Muni unobtrusively rose and moved off.

He told his wife, 'That scoundrel would not give me anything. So go out and sell the drumsticks for what they are worth.'

He flung himself down in a corner to recoup from the fatigue of his visit to the shop. His wife said, 'You are getting no sauce today, nor anything else. I can't find anything to give you to eat. Fast till the evening, it'll do you good. Take the goats and be gone now,' she cried and added, 'Don't come back before the sun is down.' He knew that if he obeyed her she would somehow conjure up some food for him in the evening. Only he must be careful not to argue and irritate her. Her temper was undependable in the morning but improved by evening time. She was sure to go out and work – grind corn in the Big House, sweep or scrub somewhere, and earn enough to buy foodstuff and keep a dinner ready for him in the evening.

Unleashing the goats from the drumstick tree, Muni started out, driving them ahead and uttering weird cries from time to time in order to urge them on. He passed through the village with his head bowed in thought. He did not want to look at anyone or be accosted. A couple of cronies lounging in the temple corridor hailed him, but he ignored their call. They had known him in the days of affluence when he lorded over a flock of fleecy sheep, not the miserable gawky goats that he had today. Of course he also used to have a few goats for those who fancied them, but real wealth lay in sheep; they bred fast and people came and bought the fleece in the shearing season; and then that famous butcher from the town came over on the weekly market days bringing him betel leaves, tobacco, and often enough some bhang, which they smoked in a hut in the coconut grove, undisturbed by wives and well-wishers. After a smoke one felt light and elated and inclined to forgive everyone including that brother-in-law of his who had once tried to set fire to his home. But all this seemed like the memoirs of a previous birth. Some pestilence afflicted his cattle (he could of course guess who had laid his animals under a curse) and even the friendly butcher would not touch one at half the price . . . and now here he was left with the two scraggy creatures. He wished someone would rid him of their company too. The shopman had said that he was seventy. At seventy, one only waited to be summoned by God. When he was dead what would his wife do? They had lived in each other's company since they were children. He was told on their day of wedding that he was ten years old and she was eight. During the wedding ceremony they had had to recite their respective ages and names. He had thrashed her only a few times in their career, and later she had the upper hand. Progeny, none. Perhaps a large progeny would have brought him the blessing of the gods. Fertility brought merit. People with fourteen sons were always so prosperous and at peace with the world and themselves. He recollected the thrill he had felt when he mentioned a daughter to that shopman; although it was not believed, what if he did not have a daughter? – his cousin in the next village had many daughters, and any one of them was as good as his; he was fond of them all and would buy them sweets if he could afford it. Still, everyone in the village whispered behind their backs that Muni and his wife were a barren couple. He avoided looking at anyone; they all professed to be so high up, and everyone else in the village had more money than he. 'I am the poorest fellow in our caste and no wonder that they spurn me, but I won't look at them either', and so he passed on with his eyes downcast along the edge of the street, and people left him also very much alone, commenting only to the extent, 'Ah, there he goes with his two great goats; if he slits their throats, he may have more peace of mind.' 'What has he to worry about anyway? They live on nothing and have nobody to worry about.' Thus people commented when he passed through the village. Only on the outskirts did he lift his head and look up. He urged and bullied the goats until they meandered along to the foot of the horse statue on the edge of the village. He sat on its pedestal for the rest of the day. The advantage of this was that he could watch the highway and see the lorries and buses pass through to the hills, and it gave him a sense of belonging to a larger world. The pedestal of the statue was broad enough for him to move around as the sun travelled up and westward; or he could also crouch under the belly of the horse, for shade.

The horse was nearly life-size, moulded out of clay, baked, burnt, and brightly coloured, and reared its head proudly, prancing its forelegs in the air and flourishing its tail in a loop; beside the horse stood a warrior with scythe-like mustachios, bulging eyes, and aquiline nose. The old image-makers believed in indicating a man of strength by bulging out his eyes and sharpening his moustache tips, and also had decorated the man's chest with beads which looked today like blobs of mud through the ravages of sun and wind and rain (when it came), but Muni would insist that he had known the beads to sparkle like the nine gems at one time in his life. The horse itself was said to have been as white as a dhobi-washed sheet, and had had on its back a cover of pure brocade of red and black lace, matching the multi-coloured sash around the waist of the warrior. But none in the village remembered the splendour as no one noticed its existence. Even Muni, who spent all his waking hours at its foot, never bothered to look up. It was untouched by the young vandals of the village who gashed tree trunks with knives and tried to topple off milestones and inscribed lewd designs on all the walls. This statue had been closer to the population of the village at one time, when this spot bordered the village; but when the highway was laid through (or perhaps when the tank and wells dried up completely here) the village moved a couple of miles inland.

Muni sat at the foot of the statue, watching his two goats graze in the arid soil among the cactus and lantana bushes. He looked at the sun; it had tilted westward no doubt, but it was not the time yet to go back home; if he went too early his wife would have no food for him. Also he must give her time to cool off her temper and feel sympathetic, and then she would scrounge and manage to get some food. He watched the mountain road for a time signal. When the green bus appeared around the bend he could leave, and his wife would feel pleased that he had let the goats feed long enough.

He noticed now a new sort of vehicle coming down at full speed. It looked both like a motor car and a bus. He used to be intrigued by the novelty of such spectacles, but of late work was going on at the source of the river on the mountain and an assortment of people and traffic went past him, and he took it all casually and described to his wife, later in the day, not everything as he once did, but only some things, only if he noticed anything special. Today, while he observed the yellow vehicle coming down, he was wondering how to describe it later when it sputtered and stopped in front of him. A red-faced foreigner who had been driving it got down and went round it, stooping, looking, and poking under the vehicle; then he straightened himself up, looked at the dashboard, stared in Muni's direction, and approached him. 'Excuse me, is there a gas station nearby, or do I have to wait until another car comes — ' He suddenly looked up at the clay horse and cried, 'Marvellous!' without completing his sentence. Muni felt he should get up and run away, and cursed his age. He could not readily put his limbs into action; some years ago he could outrun a cheetah, as happened once when he went to the forest to cut fuel and it was then that two of his sheep were mauled – a sign that bad times were coming. Though he tried, he could not easily extricate himself from his seat, and then there was also the problem of the goats. He could not leave them behind.

The red-faced man wore khaki clothes – evidently a policeman or a soldier. Muni said to himself, 'He will chase or shoot if I start running. Sometimes dogs chase only those who run – O Shiva protect me. I don't know why this man should be after me.' Meanwhile the foreigner cried, 'Marvellous!' again, nodding his head. He paced around the statue with his eyes fixed on it. Muni sat frozen for a while, and then fidgeted and tried to edge away. Now the other man suddenly pressed his palms together in a salute, smiled, and said, 'Namaste! How do you do?'

At which Muni spoke the only English expressions he had learnt, 'Yes, no.' Having exhausted his English vocabulary, he started in Tamil: 'My name is Muni. These two goats are mine, and no one can gainsay it – though our village is full of slanderers these days who will not hesitate to say that what belongs to a man doesn't belong to him.' He rolled his eyes and shuddered at the thought of evil-minded men and women peopling his village.

The foreigner faithfully looked in the direction indicated by Muni's fingers, gazed for a while at the two goats and the rocks, and with a puzzled expression took out his silver cigarette-case and lit a cigarette. Suddenly remembering the courtesies of the season, he asked, 'Do you smoke?' Muni answered, 'Yes, no.' Whereupon the red-faced man took a cigarette and gave it to Muni, who received it with surprise, having had no offer of a smoke from anyone for years now. Those days when he smoked bhang were gone with his sheep and the large-hearted butcher. Nowadays he was not able to find even matches, let alone bhang. (His wife went across and borrowed a fire at dawn from a neighbour.) He had always wanted to smoke a cigarette; only once had the shopman given him one on credit, and he remembered how good it had tasted. The other flicked the lighter open and offered a light to Muni. Muni felt so confused about how to act that he blew on it and put it out. The other, puzzled but undaunted, flourished his lighter, presented it again, and lit Muni's cigarette. Muni drew a deep puff and started coughing; it was racking, no doubt, but extremely pleasant. When his cough subsided he wiped his eyes and took stock of the situation, understanding that the other man was not an inquisitor of any kind. Yet, in order to make sure, he remained wary. No need to run away from a man who gave him such a potent smoke. His head was reeling from the effect of one of those strong American cigarettes made with roasted tobacco. The man said, 'I come from New York,' took out a wallet from his hip pocket, and presented his card.

Muni shrank away from the card. Perhaps he was trying to present a warrant and arrest him. Beware of khaki, one part of his mind warned. Take all the cigarettes or bhang or whatever is offered, but don't get caught. Beware of khaki. He wished he weren't seventy as the shopman had said. At seventy one didn't run, but surrendered to whatever came. He could only ward off trouble by talk. So he went on, all in the chaste Tamil for which Kritam was famous. (Even the worst detractors could not deny that the famous poetess Avvaiyar was born in this area, although no one could say whether it was in Kritam or Kuppam, the adjoining village.) Out of this heritage the Tamil language gushed through Muni in an unimpeded flow. He said, 'Before God, sir, Bhagwan, who sees everything, I tell you, sir, that we know nothing of the case. If the murder was committed, whoever did it will not escape. Bhagwan is all-seeing. Don't ask me about it. I know nothing.' A body had been found mutilated and thrown under a tamarind tree at the border between Kritam and Kuppam a few weeks before, giving rise to much gossip and speculation. Muni added an explanation, 'Anything is possible there. People over there will stop at nothing.' The foreigner nodded his head and listened courteously though he understood nothing.

'I am sure you know when this horse was made,' said the red man and smiled ingratiatingly.

Muni reacted to the relaxed atmosphere by smiling himself, and pleaded, 'Please go away, sir, I know nothing. I promise we will hold him for you if we see any bad character around, and we will bury him up to his neck in a coconut pit if he tries to escape; but our village has always had a clean record. Must definitely be the other village.'

Now the red man implored, 'Please, please, I will speak slowly, please try to understand me. Can't you understand even a simple word of English? Everyone in this country seems to know English. I have got along with English everywhere in this country, but you don't speak it. Have you any religious or spiritual scruples for avoiding the English speech?'

Muni made some indistinct sounds in his throat and shook his head. Encouraged, the other went on to explain at length, uttering each syllable with care and deliberation. Presently he sidled over and took a seat beside the old man, explaining, 'You see, last

August, we probably had the hottest summer in history, and I was working in shirt-sleeves in my office on the fortieth floor of the Empire State Building. You must have heard of the power failure, and there I was stuck for four hours, no elevator, no air conditioning. All the way in the train I kept thinking, and the minute I reached home in Connecticut, I told my wife Ruth, "We will visit India this winter, it's time to look at other civilizations." Next day she called the travel agent first thing and told him to fix it, and so here I am. Ruth came with me but is staying back at Srinagar, and I am the one doing the rounds and joining her later.'

Muni looked reflective at the end of this long peroration and said, rather feebly, 'Yes, no,' as a concession to the other's language, and went on in Tamil, 'When I was this high,' he indicated a foot high, 'I heard my uncle say . . . '

No one can tell what he was planning to say as the other interrupted him at this stage to ask, 'Boy, what is the secret of your teeth? How old are you?'

The old man forgot what he had started to say and remarked, 'Sometimes we too lose our cattle. Jackals or cheetahs may carry them off, but sometimes it is just theft from over in the next village, and then we will know who has done it. Our priest at the temple can see in the camphor flame the face of the thief, and when he is caught . . . ' He gestured with his hands a perfect mincing of meat.

The American watched his hands intently and said, 'I know what you mean. Chop something? Maybe I am holding you up and you want to chop wood? Where is your axe? Hand it to me and show me what to chop. I do enjoy it, you know, just a hobby. We get a lot of driftwood along the backwater near my house, and on Sundays I do nothing but chop wood for the fireplace. I really feel different when I watch the fire in the fireplace, although it may take all the sections of the Sunday *New York Times* to get a fire started,' and he smiled at this reference.

Muni felt totally confused but decided the best thing would be to make an attempt to get away from this place. He tried to edge out, saying, 'Must go home,' and turned to go. The other seized his shoulder and said desperately, 'Is there no one, absolutely no one here, to translate for me?' He looked up and down the road, which was deserted in this hot afternoon; a sudden gust of wind churned up the dust and dead leaves on the roadside into a ghostly column and propelled it towards the mountain road. The stranger almost pinioned Muni's back to the statue and asked, 'Isn't this statue yours? Why don't you sell it to me?'

The old man now understood the reference to the horse, thought for a second, and said in his own language, 'I was an urchin this high when I heard my grandfather explain this horse and warrior, and my grandfather himself was this high when he heard his grandfather, whose grandfather . . . '

The other man interrupted him with, 'I don't want to seem to have stopped here for nothing. I will offer you a good price for this,' he said, indicating the horse. He had concluded without the least doubt that Muni owned this mud horse. Perhaps he guessed by the way he sat at its pedestal, like other souvenir-sellers in this country presiding over their wares.

Muni followed the man's eyes and pointing fingers and dimly understood the subject matter and, feeling relieved that the theme of the mutilated body had been abandoned at least for the time being, said again, enthusiastically, 'I was this high when my grandfather told me about this horse and the warrior, and my grandfather was this high when he himself . . . ' and he was getting into a deeper bog of reminiscence each time he tried to indicate the antiquity of the statue.

The Tamil that Muni spoke was stimulating even as pure sound, and the foreigner listened with fascination. 'I wish I had my taperecorder here,' he said, assuming the pleasantest expression. 'Your language sounds wonderful. I get a kick out of every word you utter, here' – he indicated his ears – 'but you don't have to waste your breath in sales talk. I appreciate the article. You don't have to explain its points.'

'I never went to a school, in those days only Brahmin went to schools, but we had to go out and work in the fields morning till night, from sowing to harvest time . . . and when Pongal came and we had cut the harvest, my father allowed me to go out and play with others at the tank, and so I don't know the Parangi language you speak, even little fellows in your country probably speak the Parangi language, but here only learned men and officers know it. We had a postman in our village who could speak to you boldly in your language, but his wife ran away with someone and he does not speak to anyone at all nowadays. Who would if a wife did what she did? Women must be watched; otherwise they will sell themselves and the home,' and he laughed at his own quip.

The foreigner laughed heartily, took out another cigarette, and offered it to Muni, who now smoked with ease, deciding to stay on if the fellow was going to be so good as to keep up his cigarette supply. The American now stood up on the pedestal in the attitude of a demonstrative lecturer and said, running his finger along some of the carved decorations around the horse's neck, speaking slowly and uttering his words syllable by syllable, 'I could give a sales talk for this better than anyone else. . . . This is a marvellous combination of yellow and indigo, though faded now. . . . How do you people of this country achieve these flaming colours?'

Muni, now assured that the subject was still the horse and not the dead body, said, 'This is our guardian, it means death to our adversaries. At the end of Kali Yuga, this world and all other worlds will be destroyed, and the Redeemer will come in the shape of a horse called Kalki; this horse will come to life and gallop and trample down all bad men.' As he spoke of bad men the figures of his shopman and his brother-in-law assumed concrete forms in his mind, and he revelled for a moment in the predicament of the fellow under the horse's hoof: served him right for trying to set fire to his home. . . .

While he was brooding on this pleasant vision, the foreigner utilized the pause to say, 'I assure you that this will have the best home in the U.S.A. I'll push away the bookcase, you know I love books and am a member of five book clubs, and the choice and bonus volumes really mount up to a pile in our living-room, as high as this horse itself. But they'll have to go. Ruth may disapprove, but I will convince her. The T.V. may have to be shifted too. We can't have everything in the living-room. Ruth will probably say what about when we have a party? I'm going to keep him right in the middle of the room. I don't see how that can interfere with the party – we'll stand around him and have our drinks.'

Muni continued his description of the end of the world. 'Our pundit discoursed at the temple once how the oceans are going to close over the earth in a huge wave and swallow us – this horse will grow bigger than the biggest wave and carry on its back only the good people and kick into the floods the evil ones – plenty of them about,' he said reflectively. 'Do you know when it is going to happen?' he asked.

The foreigner now understood by the tone of the other that a question was being asked and said, 'How am I transporting it? I can push the seat back and make room in the rear. That van can take in an elephant' – waving precisely at the back of the seat.

Muni was still hovering on visions of avatars and said again, 'I never missed our pundit's discourses at the temple in those days during every bright half of the month, although he'd go on all night, and he told us that Vishnu is the highest god. Whenever evil men trouble us, he comes down to save us. He has come many times. The first time he incarnated as a great fish, and lifted the scriptures on his back when the floods and sea-waves . . . '

'I am not a millionaire, but a modest businessman. My trade is coffee.'

Amidst all this wilderness of obscure sound Muni caught the word 'coffee' and said, 'If you want to drink "kapi", drive further up, in the next town, they have Friday market, and there they open "kapi-otels" – so I learn from passers-by. Don't think I wander about. I go nowhere and look for nothing.' His thoughts went back to the avatars. 'The first avatar was in the shape of a little fish in a bowl of water, but every hour it grew bigger and bigger and became in the end a huge whale which the seas could not contain, and on the back of the whale the holy books were supported, saved, and carried.' Having launched on the first avatar it was inevitable that he should go on to the next, a wild boar on whose tusk the earth was lifted when a vicious conqueror of the earth carried it off and hid it at the bottom of the sea. After describing this avatar Muni concluded, 'God will always save us whenever we are troubled by evil beings. When we were young we staged at full moon the story of the avatars. That's how I know the stories; we played them all night until the sun rose, and sometimes the European collector would come to watch, bringing his own chair. I had a good voice and so they always taught me songs and gave me the women's roles. I was always Goddess Laxmi, and they dressed me in a brocade sari, loaned from the Big House . . . '

The foreigner said, 'I repeat I am not a millionaire. Ours is a modest business; after all, we can't afford to buy more than sixty minutes' T.V. time in a month, which works out to two minutes a day, that's all, although in the course of time we'll maybe sponsor a one-hour show regularly if our sales graph continues to go up . . . '

Muni was intoxicated by the memory of his theatrical days and was about to explain how he had painted his face and worn a wig and diamond earrings when the visitor, feeling that he had spent too much time already, said, 'Tell me, will you accept a hundred rupees or not for the horse? I'd love to take the whiskered soldier also but I've no space for him this year. I'll have to cancel my air ticket and take a boat home, I suppose. Ruth can go by air if she likes, but I will go with the horse and keep him in my cabin all the way if necessary,' and he smiled at the picture of himself voyaging across the seas hugging this horse. He added, 'I will have to pad it with straw so that it doesn't break . . . '

'When we played *Ramayana*, they dressed me as Sita,' added Muni. 'A teacher came and taught us the songs for the drama and we gave him fifty rupees. He incarnated himself as Rama, and he alone could destroy Ravana, the demon with ten heads who shook all the worlds; do you know the story of Ramayana?'

'I have my station-wagon as you see. I can push the seat back and take the horse in if you will just lend me a hand with it.'

'Do you know *Mahabharata*? Krishna was the eighth avatar of Vishnu, incarnated to help the Five Brothers regain their kingdom. When Krishna was a baby he danced on the thousand-hooded giant serpent and trampled it to death; and then he suckled the breasts of the demoness and left them flat as a disc though when she came to him her bosoms were large, like mounds of earth on the banks of a dug-up canal.' He indicated two mounds with his hands. The stranger was completely mystified by the gesture. For the first time he said, 'I really wonder what you are saying because your answer is crucial. We have come to the point when we should be ready to talk business.'

'When the tenth avatar comes, do you know where you and I will be?' asked the old man.

'Lend me a hand and I can lift off the horse from its pedestal after picking out the cement at the joints. We can do anything if we have a basis of understanding.'

At this stage the mutual mystification was complete, and there was no need even to carry on a guessing game at the meaning of words. The old man chattered away in a spirit of balancing off the credits and debits of conversational exchange, and said in order to be on the credit side, 'O honourable one, I hope God has blessed you with numerous progeny. I say this because you seem to be a good man, willing to stay beside an old man and talk to him, while all day I have none to talk to except when somebody stops by to ask for a piece of tobacco. But I seldom have it, tobacco is not what it used to be at one time, and I have given up chewing. I cannot afford it nowadays.' Noting the other's interest in his speech, Muni felt encouraged to ask, 'How many children have you?' with appropriate gestures with his hands. Realizing that a question was being asked, the red man replied, 'I said a hundred,' which encouraged Muni to go into details, 'How many of your children are boys and how many girls? Where are they? Is your daughter married? Is it difficult to find a son-in-law in your country also?'

In answer to these questions the red man dashed his hand into his pocket and brought forth his wallet in order to take immediate advantage of the bearish trend in the market. He flourished a hundred-rupee currency note and asked, 'Well, this is what I meant.'

The old man now realized that some financial element was entering their talk. He peered closely at the currency note, the like of which he had never seen in his life; he knew the five and ten by their colours although always in other people's hands, while his own earning at any time was in coppers and nickels. What was this man flourishing the note for? Perhaps asking for change. He laughed to himself at the notion of anyone coming to him for changing a thousand- or ten-thousand-rupee note. He said with a grin, 'Ask our village headman, who is also a moneylender; he can change even a lakh of rupees in gold sovereigns if you prefer it that way; he thinks nobody knows, but dig the floor of his puja room and your head will reel at the sight of the hoard. The man disguises himself in rags just to mislead the public. Talk to the headman yourself because he goes mad at the sight of me. Someone took away his pumpkins with the creeper and he, for some reason, thinks it was me and my goats . . . that's why I never let my goats be seen anywhere near the farms.' His eyes travelled to his goats nosing about, attempting to wrest nutrition from minute greenery peeping out of rock and dry earth.

The foreigner followed his look and decided that it would be a sound policy to show an interest in the old man's pets. He went up casually to them and stroked their backs with every show of courteous attention. Now the truth dawned on the old man. His dream of a lifetime was about to be realized. He understood that the red man was actually making an offer for the goats. He had reared them up in the hope of selling them some day and, with the capital, opening a small shop on this very spot. Sitting here, watching the hills, he had often dreamt how he would put up a thatched roof here, spread a gunny sack out on the ground, and display on it fried nuts, coloured sweets, and green coconut for the thirsty and famished wayfarers on the highway, which was sometimes very busy. The animals were not prize ones for a cattle show, but he had spent his occasional savings to provide them some fancy diet now and then, and they did not look too bad. While he was reflecting thus, the red man shook his hand and left on his palm one hundred rupees in tens now. 'It is all for you or you may share it if you have the partner.'

The old man pointed at the station-wagon and asked, 'Are you carrying them off in that?'

'Yes, of course,' said the other, understanding the transportation part of it.

The old man said, 'This will be their first ride in a motor car. Carry them off after I get out of sight, otherwise they will never follow you, but only me even if I am travelling on the path to Yama Loka.' He laughed at his own joke, brought his palms together in a salute, turned round and went off, and was soon out of sight beyond a clump of thicket.

The red man looked at the goats grazing peacefully. Perched on the pedestal of the horse, as the westerly sun touched the ancient faded colours of the statue with a fresh splendour, he ruminated, 'He must be gone to fetch some help, I suppose!' and settled down to wait. When a truck came downhill, he stopped it and got the help of a couple of men to detach the horse from its pedestal and place it in his station-wagon. He gave them five rupees each, and for a further payment they siphoned off gas from the truck and helped him to start his engine.

Muni hurried homeward with the cash securely tucked away at his waist in his dhoti. He shut the street door and stole up softly to his wife as she squatted before the lit oven wondering if by a miracle food would drop from the sky. Muni displayed his fortune for the day. She snatched the notes from him, counted them by the glow of the fire, and cried, 'One hundred rupees! How did you come by it? Have you been stealing?'

'I have sold our goats to a red-faced man. He was absolutely crazy to have them, gave me all this money and carried them off in his motor car!'

Hardly had these words left his lips when they heard bleating outside. She opened the door and saw the two goats at her door. 'Here they are!' she said. 'What's the meaning of all this?'

He muttered a great curse and seized one of the goats by its ears and shouted, 'Where is that man? Don't you know you are his? Why did you come back?' The goat only wriggled in his grip. He asked the same question of the other too. The goat shook itself off. His wife glared at him and declared, 'If you have thieved, the police will come tonight and break your bones. Don't involve me. I will go away to my parents. . . .'

A Visit of Charity

It was mid-morning – a very cold, bright day. Holding a potted plant before her, a girl of fourteen jumped off the bus in front of the Old Ladies' Home, on the outskirts of town. She wore a red coat, and her straight yellow hair was hanging down loose from the pointed white cap all the little girls were wearing that year. She stopped for a moment beside one of the prickly dark shrubs with which the city had beautified the Home, and then proceeded slowly toward the building, which was of whitewashed brick and reflected the winter sunlight like a block of ice. As she walked vaguely up the steps she shifted the small pot from hand to hand; then she had to set it down and remove her mittens before she could open the heavy door.

'I'm a Campfire Girl. . . . I have to pay a visit to some old lady,' she told the nurse at the desk. This was a woman in a white uniform who looked as if she were cold; she had close-cut hair which stood up on the very top of her head exactly like a sea wave. Marian, the little girl, did not tell her that this visit would give her a minimum of only three points in her score.

'Acquainted with any of our residents?' asked the nurse. She lifted one eyebrow and spoke like a man.

'With any old ladies? No – but – that is, any of them will do,' Marian stammered. With her free hand she pushed her hair behind her ears, as she did when it was time to study Science.

The nurse shrugged and rose. 'You have a nice *multiflora cineraria* there,' she remarked as she walked ahead down the hall of closed doors to pick out an old lady.

There was loose, bulging linoleum on the floor. Marian felt as if she were walking on the waves, but the nurse paid no attention to it. There was a smell in the hall like the interior of a clock. Everything was silent until, behind one of the doors, an old lady of some kind cleared her throat like a sheep bleating. This decided the nurse. Stopping in her tracks, she first extended her arm, bent her elbow, and leaned forward from the hips – all to examine the watch strapped to her wrist; then she gave a loud double-rap on the door.

'There are two in each room,' the nurse remarked over her shoulder.

'Two what?' asked Marian without thinking. The sound like a sheep's bleating almost made her turn around and run back.

One old woman was pulling the door open in short, gradual jerks, and when she saw the nurse a strange smile forced her old face dangerously awry. Marian, suddenly propelled by the strong, impatient arm of the nurse, saw next the side-face of another old woman, even older, who was lying flat in bed with a cap on and a counterpane drawn up to her chin.

'Visitor,' said the nurse, and after one more shove she was off up the hall.

Marian stood tongue-tied; both hands held the potted plant. The old woman, still with that terrible, square smile (which was a smile of welcome) stamped on her bony face, was waiting. . . . Perhaps she said something. The old woman in bed said nothing at all, and she did not look around.

Suddenly Marian saw a hand, quick as a bird claw, reach up in the air and pluck the white cap off her head. At the same time, another claw to match drew her all the way into the room, and the next moment the door closed behind her.

'My, my, my,' said the old lady at her side.

Marian stood enclosed by a bed, a washstand and a chair; the tiny room had altogether too much furniture. Everything smelled wet – even the bare floor. She held on to the back of the chair, which was wicker and felt soft and damp. Her heart beat more and more slowly, her hands got colder and colder, and she could not hear whether the old women were saying anything or not. She could not see them very clearly. How dark it was! The window shade was down, and the only door was shut. Marian looked at the ceiling. . . . It was like being caught in a robbers' cave, just before one was murdered.

'Did you come to be our little girl for a while?' the first robber asked.

Then something was snatched from Marian's hand – the little potted plant.

'Flowers!' screamed the old woman. She stood holding the pot in an undecided way. 'Pretty flowers,' she added.

Then the old woman in bed cleared her throat and spoke. 'They are not pretty,' she said, still without looking around, but very distinctly.

Marian suddenly pitched against the chair and sat down in it.

'Pretty flowers,' the first old woman insisted. 'Pretty – pretty . . . '

Marian wished she had the little pot back for just a moment – she had forgotten to look at the plant herself before giving it away. What did it look like?

'Stinkweeds,' said the other old woman sharply. She had a bunchy white forehead and red eyes like a sheep. Now she turned them toward Marian. The fogginess seemed to rise in her throat again, and she bleated, 'Who – are – you?'

To her surprise, Marian could not remember her name. 'I'm a Campfire Girl,' she said finally.

'Watch out for the germs,' said the old woman like a sheep, not addressing anyone.

'One came out last month to see us,' said the first old woman.

A sheep or a germ? wondered Marian dreamily, holding on to the chair.

'Did not!' cried the other old woman.

'Did so! Read to us out of the Bible, and we enjoyed it!' screamed the first.

'Who enjoyed it!' said the woman in bed. Her mouth was unexpectedly small and sorrowful, like a pet's.

'We enjoyed it,' insisted the other. 'You enjoyed it – I enjoyed it.'

'We all enjoyed it,' said Marian, without realizing that she had said a word.

The first old woman had just finished putting the potted plant high, high on the top of the wardrobe, where it could hardly be seen from below. Marian wondered how she had ever succeeded in placing it there, how she could ever have reached so high.

'You mustn't pay any attention to old Addie,' she now said to the little girl. 'She's ailing today.'

'Will you shut your mouth?' said the woman in bed. 'I am not.'

'You're a story.'

'I can't stay but a minute – really, I can't,' said Marian suddenly. She looked down at the wet floor and thought that if she were sick in here they would have to let her go.

With much to-do the first old woman sat down in a rocking chair – still another piece of furniture! – and began to rock. With the fingers of one hand she touched a very dirty cameo pin on her chest. 'What do you do at school?' she asked.

'I don't know . . . ' said Marian. She tried to think but she could not.

'Oh, but the flowers are beautiful,' the old woman whispered. She seemed to rock faster and faster; Marian did not see how anyone could rock so fast.

'Ugly,' said the woman in bed.

'If we bring flowers — ' Marian began, and then fell silent. She had almost said that if Campfire Girls brought flowers to the Old Ladies' Home, the visit would count one extra point, and if they took a Bible with them on the bus and read it to the old ladies, it counted double. But the old woman had not listened, anyway; she was rocking and watching the other one, who watched back from the bed.

'Poor Addie is ailing. She has to take medicine – see?' she said, pointing a horny finger at a row of bottles on the table, and rocking so high that her black comfort shoes lifted off the floor like a little child's.

'I am no more sick than you are,' said the woman in bed.

'Oh yes you are!'

'I just got more sense than you have, that's all,' said the other old woman, nodding her head.

'That's only the contrary way she talks when *you all* come,' said the first old lady with sudden intimacy. She stopped the rocker with a neat pat of her feet and leaned toward Marian. Her hand reached over – it felt like a petunia leaf, clinging and just a little sticky.

'Will you hush! Will you hush!' cried the other one.

Marian leaned back rigidly in her chair.

'When I was a little girl like you, I went to school and all,' said the old woman in the same intimate, menacing voice. 'Not here – another town. . . .'

'Hush!' said the sick woman. 'You never went to school. You never came and you never went. You never were anywhere – only here. You never were born! You don't know anything. Your head is empty, your heart and hands and your old black purse are all empty, even that little old box that you brought with you you brought empty – you showed it to me. And yet you talk, talk, talk, talk, talk all the time until I think I'm losing my mind! Who are you? You're a stranger – a perfect stranger! Don't you know you're a stranger? Is it possible that they have actually done a thing like this to anyone – sent them in a stranger to talk, and rock, and tell away her whole long rigmarole? Do they seriously suppose that I'll be able to keep it up, day in, day out, night in, night out, living in the same room with a terrible old woman – forever?'

Marian saw the old woman's eyes grow bright and turn toward her. This old woman was looking at her with despair and calculation in her face. Her small lips suddenly dropped apart, and exposed a half circle of false teeth with tan gums.

'Come here, I want to tell you something,' she whispered. 'Come here!'

Marian was trembling, and her heart nearly stopped beating altogether for a moment.

'Now, now, Addie,' said the first old woman. 'That's not polite. Do you know what's really the matter with old Addie today?' She, too, looked at Marian; one of her eyelids drooped low.

'The matter?' the child repeated stupidly. 'What's the matter with her?'

'Why, she's mad because it's her birthday!' said the first old woman, beginning to rock again and giving a little crow as though she had answered her own riddle.

'It is not, it is not!' screamed the old woman in bed. 'It is not my birthday, no one knows when that is but myself, and will you please be quiet and say nothing more, or I'll go straight out of my mind!' She turned her eyes toward Marian again, and presently she said in the soft, foggy voice, 'When the worst comes to the worst, I ring this bell, and the nurse comes.' One of her hands was drawn out from under the patched counterpane – a thin little hand with enormous black freckles. With a finger which would not hold still she pointed to a little bell on the table among the bottles.

'How old are you?' Marian breathed. Now she could see the old woman in bed very closely and plainly, and very abruptly, from all sides, as in dreams. She wondered about her – she wondered for a moment as though there was nothing else in the world to wonder about. It was the first time such a thing had happened to Marian.

'I won't tell!'

The old face on the pillow, where Marian was bending over it, slowly gathered and collapsed. Soft whimpers came out of the small open mouth. It was a sheep that she sounded like – a little lamb. Marian's face drew very close, the yellow hair hung forward.

'She's crying!' she turned a bright, burning face up to the first old woman.

'That's Addie for you,' the old woman said spitefully.

Marian jumped up and moved toward the door. For the second time, the claw almost touched her hair, but it was not quick enough. The little girl put her cap on.

'Well, it was a real visit,' said the old woman, following Marian through the doorway and all the way out into the hall. Then from behind she suddenly clutched the child with her sharp little fingers. In an affected, high-pitched whine she cried, 'Oh, little girl, have you a penny to spare for a poor old woman that's not got anything of her own? We don't have a thing in the world – not a penny for candy – not a thing! Little girl, just a nickel – a penny —'

Marian pulled violently against the old hands for a moment before she was free. Then she ran down the hall, without looking behind her and without looking at the nurse, who was reading *Field & Stream* at her desk. The nurse, after another triple motion to consult her wrist watch, asked automatically the question put to visitors in all institutions: 'Won't you stay and have dinner with *us*?'

Marian never replied. She pushed the heavy door open into the cold air and ran down the steps.

Under the prickly shrub she stooped and quickly, without being seen, retrieved a red apple she had hidden there.

Her yellow hair under the white cap, her scarlet coat, her bare knees all flashed in the sunlight as she ran to meet the big bus rocketing through the street.

'Wait for me!' she shouted. As though at an imperial command, the bus ground to a stop.

She jumped on and took a big bite out of the apple.

Various Temptations

His name unknown he had been strangling girls in the Victoria district. After talking no one knew what to them by the gleam of brass bedsteads; after lonely hours standing on pavements with people passing; after perhaps in those hot July streets, with blue sky blinding high above and hazed with burnt petrol, a dazzled headaching hatred of some broad scarlet cinema poster and the black leather taxis; after sudden hopeless ecstasies at some rounded girl's figure passing in rubber and silk, after the hours of slow crumbs in the empty milk-bar and the balneal reek of grim-tiled lavatories? After all the day-town's faceless hours, the evening town might have whirled quicker on him with the death of the day, the yellow-painted lights of the night have caused the minutes to accelerate and his fears to recede and a cold courage then to arm itself – until the wink, the terrible assent of some soft girl smiling towards the night . . . the beer, the port, the meat-pies, the bed-steads?

Each of the four found had been throttled with coarse thread. This, dry and the colour of hemp, had in each case been drawn from the frayed ends of the small carpet squares in those linoleum bedrooms. 'A man', said the papers, 'has been asked by the police to come forward in connection with the murders,' etc., etc. . . . 'Ronald Raikes – five foot nine, grey eyes, thin brown hair, brown tweed coat, grey flannel trousers. Black soft-brim hat.'

A girl called Clara, a plain girl and by profession an invisible mender, lay in her large white comfortable bed with its polished wood headpiece and its rose quilt. Faded blue curtains draped down their long soft cylinders, their dark recesses – and sometimes these columns moved, for the balcony windows were open for the hot July night. The night was still, airless; yet sometimes these queer causeless breezes, like the turning breath of a sleeper, came to rustle the curtains – and then as suddenly left them graven again in the stifling air like curtains that had never moved. And this girl Clara lay reading lazily the evening paper.

She wore an old wool bed-jacket, faded yet rich against her pale and bloodless skin; she was alone, expecting no one. It was a night of restitution, of early supper and washing underclothes and stockings, an early night for a read and a long sleep. Two or three magazines nestled in the eiderdowned bend of her knees. But saving for last the glossy, luxurious magazines, she lay now glancing through the paper – half reading, half tasting the quiet, sensing how secluded she was though the street was only one floor below, in her own bedroom yet with the heads of unsuspecting people passing only a few feet beneath. Unknown footsteps approached and retreated on the pavement beneath – footsteps that even on this still summer night sounded muffled, like footsteps heard on the pavement of a fog.

She lay listening for a while, then turned again to the paper, read again a bullying black headline relating the deaths of some hundreds of demonstrators somewhere in another hemisphere, and again let her eyes trail away from the weary greyish block of words beneath. The corner of the papers and its newsprint struck a harsh note of offices and tube-trains against the soft texture of the rose quilt – she frowned and was thus just about to reach for one of the more lustrous magazines when her eyes noted across the page a short, squat headline above a blackly-typed column about the Victoria murders. She shuffled more comfortably into the bed and concentrated hard to scramble up the delicious paragraphs.

But they had found nothing. No new murder, nowhere nearer to making an arrest. Yet after an official preamble, there occurred one of those theoretic dissertations, such as is often inserted to colour the progress of apprehension when no facts provide themselves. It appeared, it was *thought*, that the Victoria strangler suffered from a mania similar to that which had possessed the infamous Ripper; that is, the victims were mostly of a 'certain profession'; it might be thus concluded that the Victoria murderer bore the same maniacal grudge against such women.

At this Clara put the paper down – thinking, well for one thing she never did herself up like those sort, in fact she never did herself up at all, and what would be the use? Instinctively then she turned to look across to the mirror on the dressing-table, saw there her worn pale face and sack-coloured hair, and felt instantly neglected;

down in her plain-feeling body there stirred again that familiar envy, the impotent grudge that still came to her at least once every day of her life – that nobody had ever bothered to think deeply for her, neither loving, nor hating, nor in any way caring. For a moment then the thought came that whatever had happened in those bedrooms, however horrible, that murderer had at least felt deeply for his subject, the subject girl was charged with positive attractions that had forced him to act. There could hardly be such a thing, in those circumstances at least, as a disinterested murder. Hate and love were often held to be variations of the same obsessed emotion – when it came to murder, to the high impassioned pitch of murder, to such an intense concentration of one person on another, then it seemed that a divine paralysis, something very much like love, possessed the murderer.

Clara put the paper aside with finality, for whenever the question of her looks occurred then she forced herself to think immediately of something else, to ignore what had for some years groaned into an obsession leading only to hours wasted with self-pity and idle depression. So that now she picked up the first magazine, and scrutinized with a false intensity the large and laughing figure in several colours and few clothes of a motion-picture queen. However, rather than pointing her momentary depression, the picture comforted her. Had it been a real girl in the room, she might have been further saddened; but these pictures of fabulous people separated by the convention of the page and the distance of their world of celluloid fantasy instead represented the image of earlier personal dreams, comforting dreams of what then she hoped one day she might become, when that hope which is youth's unique asset outweighed the material attribute of what she in fact was.

In the quiet air fogging the room with such palpable stillness the turning of the brittle magazine page made its own decisive crackle. Somewhere outside in the summer night a car slurred past, changed its gear, rounded the corner and sped off on a petulant note of acceleration to nowhere. The girl changed her position in the bed, easing herself deeper into the security of the bedclothes. Gradually she became absorbed, so that soon her mind was again ready to wander, but this time within her own imagining, outside the plane of that bedroom. She was idly thus transported into a wished-for situation between herself and the owner of the shop where she worked: in fact, she spoke aloud her decision to take the following

Saturday off. This her employer instantly refused. Then still speaking aloud she presented her reasons, insisted – and at last, the blood beginning to throb in her forehead, handed in her notice! . . . This must have suddenly frightened her, bringing her back abruptly to the room – and she stopped talking. She laid the magazine down, looked round the room. Still that feeling of invisible fog – perhaps there was indeed mist; the furniture looked more than usually stationary. She tapped with her finger on the magazine. It sounded loud, too loud. Her mind returned to the murderer, she ceased tapping and looked quickly at the shut door. The memory of those murders must have lain at the back of her mind throughout the past minutes, gently elevating her with the compounding unconscious excitement that news sometimes brings, the sensation that somewhere something has happened, revitalizing life. But now she suddenly shivered. Those murders had happened in Victoria, the neighbouring district, only in fact – she counted – five, six streets away.

The curtains began to move. Her eyes were round and at them in the first flickering moment. This time they not only shuddered, but seemed to eddy, and then to belly out. A coldness grasped and held the ventricles of her heart. And the curtains, the whole length of the rounded blue curtains moved towards her across the carpet. Something was pushing them. They travelled out towards her, then the ends rose sailing, sailed wide, opened to reveal nothing but the night, the empty balcony – then as suddenly collapsed and receded back to where they had hung motionless before. She let out the deep breath that whitening she had held all that time. Only, then, a breath of wind again; a curious swell on the compressed summer air. And now again the curtains hung still. She gulped sickly, crumpled and decided to shut the window – better not to risk that sort of fright again, one never knew what one's heart might do. But, just then, she hardly liked to approach those curtains. As the atmosphere of a nightmare cannot be shaken off for some minutes after waking, so those curtains held for a while their ambience of dread. Clara lay still. In a few minutes those fears quietened, but now forgetting the sense of fright she made no attempt to leave the bed, it was too comfortable, she would read again for a little. She turned over and picked up her magazine. Then a short while later, stretching, she half-turned to the curtains again. They were wide open. A man was standing exactly in the centre, outlined against the night outside, holding the curtains apart with his two hands.

Ron Raikes, five foot nine, grey eyes, thin brown hair, brown sports jacket, black hat, stood on the balcony holding the curtains aside looking in at this girl twisted round in her white-sheeted bed. He held the curtains slightly behind him, he knew the street to be dark, he felt safe. He wanted to breathe deeply after the short climb of the painter's ladder – but instead held it, above all kept quite still. The girl was staring straight at him, terrified, stuck in the pose of an actress suddenly revealed on her bedroom stage in its flood of light; in a moment she would scream. But something here was unusual, some quality lacking from the scene he had expected – and he concentrated, even in that moment when he knew himself to be in danger, letting some self-assured side of his mind wander and wonder what could be wrong.

He thought hard, screwing up his eyes to concentrate against the other unsteady excitements aching in his head – he knew how he had got here, he remembered the dull disconsolate hours waiting round the station, following two girls without result, then walking away from the lighted crowds into these darker streets and suddenly seeing a glimpse of this girl through the lighted window. Then that curious, unreasoned idea had crept over him. He had seen the ladder, measured the distance, then scoffed at himself for risking such an escapade. Anyone might have seen him . . . and then what, arrest for house-breaking, burglary? He had turned, walked away. Then walked back. That extraordinary excitement rose and held him. He had gritted his teeth, told himself not to be such a fool, to go home. Tomorrow would be fresh, a fine day to spend. But then the next hours of the restless night exhibited themselves, sounding their emptiness – so that it had seemed too early to give in and admit the day worthless. A sensation then of ability, of dexterous clever power had taken him – he had loitered nearer the ladder, looking up and down the street. The lamps were dull, the street empty. Once a car came slurring past, changed gear, accelerated off petulantly into the night, away to nowhere. The sound emphasized the quiet, the protection of that deserted hour. He had put a hand on the ladder. It was then the same as any simple choice – taking a drink or not taking a drink. The one action might lead to some detrimental end – to more drinks, a night out, a headache in the morning – and would thus be best avoided; but the other, that action of taking, was pleasant and easy and the moral forehead argued that after all it could do no harm? So, quickly, telling himself that he would climb down again in a second, this man Raikes had prised himself above the lashed night-plank and had run up the ladder. On the balcony he had paused by the curtains, breathless, now exhilarated in his ability, agile and alert as an animal – and had heard the sound of the girl turning in bed and the flick of her magazine page. A moment later the curtains had moved, nimbly he had stepped aside. A wind. He had looked down at the street – the wind populated the kerbs with dangerous movement. He parted the curtains, saw the girl lying there alone, and silently stepped on to the threshold.

Now when at last she screamed – a hoarse diminutive sob – he knew he must move, and so soundlessly on the carpet went towards her. As he moved he spoke: 'I don't want to hurt you' – and then knowing that he must say something more than that, which she could hardly have believed, and knowing also that above all he must keep talking all the time with no pause to let her attention scream – 'Really I don't want to hurt you, you mustn't scream, let me explain – but don't you see if you scream I shall have to stop you. . . .' Even with a smile, as soft a gesture as his soft quick-speaking voice, he pushed forward his coat pocket, his hand inside, so that this girl might recognize what she must have seen in detective stories, and even believe it to be his hand and perhaps a pipe, yet not be sure: ' . . . but I won't shoot and you'll promise won't you to be good and not scream – while I tell you why I'm here. You think I'm a burglar, that's not true. It's right I need a little money, only a little cash, ten bob even, because I'm in trouble, not dangerous trouble, but let me tell you please, *please* listen to me, Miss.' His voice continued softly talking, talking all the time quietly and never stuttering nor hesitating nor leaving a pause. Gradually, though her body remained alert and rigid, the girl's face relaxed.

He stood at the foot of the bed, in the full light of the bedside lamp, leaning awkwardly on one leg, the cheap material of his coat ruffled and papery. Still talking, always talking, he took off his hat, lowered himself gently to sit on the end of the bed – rather to put her at her ease than to encroach further for himself. As she sat, he apologized. Then never pausing he told her a story, which was nearly true, about his escape from a detention camp, the cruelty of his long sentence for a trivial theft, the days thereafter of evasion, the furtive search for casual employment, and then worst of all the long hours of time on his hands, the vacuum of time wandering, time wasting on the café clocks, lamp-posts of time waiting on blind corners, time walking away from uniforms, time of the head-aching clocks loitering at the slow pace of death towards his sole refuge – sleep. And this was nearly true – only that he omitted that his original crime had been one of sexual assault; he omitted those other dark occasions during the past three weeks; but he omitted these events because in fact he had forgotten them, they could only be recollected with difficulty, as episodes of vague elation, dark and blurred as an undeveloped photograph of which the image should be known yet puzzles with its indeterminate shape, its hints of light in the darkness and always the feeling that it should be known, that it once surely existed. This was also like anyone trying to remember exactly what had been done between any two specific hours on some date of a previous month, two hours framed by known en-gagements yet themselves blurred into an exasperating and hungry screen of dots, dark, almost appearing, convolving, receding.

So gradually as he offered himself to the girl's pity, that bed-clothed hump of figure relaxed. Once her lips flexed their corners in the beginning of a smile. Into her eyes once crept that strange coquettish look, pained and immeasurably tender, with which a woman takes into her arms a strange child. The moment of danger was past, there would be no scream. And since now on her part she seemed to feel no danger from him, then it became very possible that the predicament might even appeal to her, to any girl nour-ished by the kind of drama that filled the magazines littering her bed. As well, he might look strained and ill – so he let his shoulders droop for the soft extraction of her last sympathy.

Yet as he talked on, as twice he instilled into the endless story a compliment to her and as twice her face seemed to shine for a mo-ment with sudden life – nevertheless he sensed that all was not right with this apparently well-contrived affair. For this, he knew, should be near the time when he would be edging nearer to her, dropping his hat, picking it up and shifting thus unostensibly his position. It was near the time when he would be near enough to attempt, in one movement, the risk that could never fail, either way, accepted or rejected. But . . . he was neither moving forward nor wishing to move. Still he talked, but now more slowly, with less purpose; he found that he was looking at her detachedly, no longer mixing her image with his words – and thus losing the words their energy; looking now not at the conceived image of something painted by the desiring brain – but as at something unexpected, not entirely known; as if instead of peering forward his head was leant back, surveying, listening, as a dog perhaps leans its head to one side listening for the whistled sign to regulate the bewildering moment. But – no such sign came. And through his words, straining at the diamond cunning that maintained him, he tried to reason out this perplexity, he annotated carefully what he saw. A white face, ill white, reddened faintly round the nostrils, pink and dry at the mouth; and a small fat mouth, puckered and fixed under its long upper lip: and eyes also small, yet full-irised and thus like brown pellets under eyebrows low and thick: and hair that colour of lustreless hemp, now tied with a bow so that it fell down either side of her cheeks as lank as string: and round her thin neck, a thin gold chain just glittering above the dull blue wool of that bed-jacket, blue brittle wool against the ill white skin: and behind, a white pillow and the dark wooden head of the bed curved like an inverted shield. Unattractive . . . not attractive as expected, not exciting . . . yet where? Where before had he remembered something like this, something impelling, strangely sympathetic and – there was no doubt – earnestly wanted?

Later, in contrast, there flashed across his memory the colour of other faces – a momentary reflection from the scarlet-lipped face on one of the magazine covers – and he remembered that these indeed troubled him, but in a different and accustomed way; these pricked at him in their busy way, lanced him hot, ached into his head so that it grew light, as in strong sunlight. And then, much later, long after this girl too had nervously begun to talk, after they had talked together they made a cup of tea in her kitchen. And then, since the July dawn showed through the curtains, she made a bed for him on the sofa in the sitting-room, a bed of blankets and a silk cushion for his head.

Two weeks later the girl Clara came home at five o'clock in the afternoon carrying three parcels. They contained two coloured ties, six yards of white material for her wedding dress, and a box of thin red candles.

As she walked toward her front door she looked up at the windows and saw that they were shut. As it should have been – Ron was out as he had promised. It was his birthday. Thirty-two. For a few hours Clara was to concentrate on giving him a birthday tea, forgetting for one evening the fabulous question of that wedding dress. Now she ran up the stairs, opened the second door and saw there in an instant that the flat had been left especially clean, tidied into a straight, unfamiliar rigour. She smiled (how thoughtful he was, despite his 'strangeness') and threw her parcels down on the sofa, disarranging the cushions, in her tolerant happiness delighting in this. Then she was up again and arranging things. First the lights – silk handkerchiefs wound over the tops of the shades, for they shone too brightly. Next the tablecloth, white and fresh, soon decorated with small tinsels left over from Christmas, red crackers with feathered paper ends, globes gleaming like crimson quick-silver, silver and copper snowflakes.

(He'll like this, a dash of colour. It's his birthday, perhaps we could have gone out, but in a way it's nicer in. Anyway, it must be in with him on the run. I wonder where he is now. I hope he went straight to the pictures. In the dark it's safe. We did have fun doing him up different – a nice blue suit, distinguished – and the moustache is nice. Funny how you get used to that, he looks just the same as that first night. Quite, a quiet one. Says he likes to be quiet too, a plain life and a peaceful one. But a spot of colour – oh, it'll do him good.)

Moving efficiently she hurried to the kitchen and fetched the hidden cake, placed it exactly in the centre of the table, wound a length of gold veiling round the bottom, undid the candle-parcel, and expertly set the candles – one to thirty-one – round the white-iced circle. She wanted to light them, but instead put down the matches and picked off the cake one silver pellet and placed this on the tip of her tongue: then impatiently went for the knives and forks. All these actions were performed with that economy and swiftness of movement peculiar to women who arrange their own houses, a movement so sure that it seems to suggest dislike, so that it brings with each adjustment a grimace of disapproval, though nothing by anyone could be more approved.

(Thirty-one candles – I won't put the other one, it's nicer for him to think he's still thirty-one. Or I suppose men don't mind – still, do it. You never know what he really likes. A quiet one – but ever so thoughtful. And tender. And that's a funny thing, you'd think he might have tried something, the way he is, on the loose. A regular Mr Proper. Doesn't like this, doesn't like that, doesn't like dancing, doesn't like the way the girls go about, doesn't like lipstick, nor the way some of them dress . . . of course he's right, they make themselves up plain silly, but you'd think a man . . . ?)

Now over to the sideboard, and from that polished oak cupboard take very carefully one, two, three, four fat quart bottles of black stout – and a half-bottle of port. Group them close together on the table, put the shining glasses just by, make it look like a real party. And the cigarettes, a coloured box of fifty. Crinkly paper serviettes. And last of all a long roll of paper, vivid green, on which she had traced, with a ruler and a pot of red paint: HAPPY BIRTHDAY RON!

This was now hung between two wall-lights, old gas-jets corded with electricity and shaded – and then she went to the door and switched on all the lights. The room warmed instantly, each light threw off a dark glow, as though it were part of its own shadow. Clara went to the curtains and half-drew them, cutting off some of the daylight. Then drew them altogether – and the table gleamed into sudden night-light, golden-white and warmly red, with the silver cake sparkling in the centre. She went into the other room to dress.

Sitting by the table with the mirror she took off her hat and shook her head; in the mirror the hair seemed to tumble about, not pinned severely as usual, but free and flopping – she had had it waved. The face, freckled with pin-points of the mirror's tarnish, looked pale and far away. She remembered she had much to do, and turned busily to a new silk blouse, hoping that Ron would still be in the pictures, beginning again to think of him.

She was not certain still that he might not be the man whom the police wanted in connection with those murders. She had thought it, of course, when he first appeared. Later his tender manner had dissipated such a first impression. He had come to supper the following night, and again had stayed; thus also for the next nights. It was understood that she was giving him sanctuary – and for his part, he insisted on paying her when he could again risk enquiring for work. It was an exciting predicament, of the utmost daring for anyone of Clara's way of life. Incredible – but the one important and overriding fact had been that suddenly, even in this shocking way, there had appeared a strangely attractive man who had expressed immediately an interest in her. She knew that he was also interested in his safety. But there was much more to his manner than simply this – his tenderness and his extraordinary preoccupation with *her*, staring, listening, striving to please and addressing to her all the attentions of which through her declining youth she had been starved. She knew, moreover, that these attentions were real and not affected. Had they been false, nevertheless she would have been flattered. But as it was, the new horizons became dreamlike, drunken impossible. To a normally frustrated, normally satisfied, normally hopeful woman – the immoral possibility that he might be that murderer would have frozen the relationship in its seed. But such was the waste and the want in lonely Clara that, despite every ingrained convention, the great boredom of her dull years had seemed to gather and move inside her, had heaved itself up like a monstrous sleeper turning, rearing and then subsiding on its other side with a flop of finality, a sigh of pleasure, welcoming now anything, anything but a return to the old dull days of nothing. There came the whisper: 'Now or never!' But there was no sense, as with other middle-aged escapists, of desperation; this chance had landed squarely on her doorstep, there was no striving, no doubt – it had simply happened. Then the instinctive knowledge of love – and finally to seal the atrophy of all hesitation, his proposal of marriage. So that now when she sometimes wondered whether he was the man the police wanted, her loyalty to him was so deeply assumed that it seemed she was really thinking of somebody else – or of him as another figure at a remove of time. The murders had certainly stopped – yet only two weeks ago? And anyway the man in the tweed coat was only wanted *in connection with* the murders . . . that in itself became indefinite . . . besides, there must be thousands of tweed coats and black hats . . . and besides there were thousands of coincidences of all kinds every day. . . .

So, shrugging her shoulders and smiling at herself for puzzling her mind so – when she knew there could be no answer – she returned to her dressing-table. Here her face grew serious, as again the lips pouted the down-drawn disapproval that meant she contemplated an act of which she approved. Her hand hesitated, then opened one of the dressing-table drawers. It disappeared inside, feeling to the very end of the drawer, searching there in the dark. Her lips parted, her eyes lost focus – as though she were scratching deliciously her back. At length the hand drew forth a small parcel.

Once more she hesitated, while the fingers itched at the knotted string. Suddenly they took hold of the knot and scrambled to untie it. The brown paper parted. Inside lay a lipstick and a box of powder.

(Just a little, a very little. I must look pretty, I *must* tonight.)

She pouted her lips and drew across them a thick scarlet smear, then frowned, exasperated by such extravagance. She started to wipe it off. But it left boldly impregnated already its mark. She shrugged her shoulders, looked fixedly into the mirror. What she saw pleased her, and she smiled.

As late as seven, when it was still light but the strength had left the day, when on trees and on the gardens of squares there extended a moist and cool shadow and even over the tram-torn streets a cooling sense of business past descended – Ronald Raikes left the cinema and hurried to get through the traffic and away into those quieter streets that led towards Clara's flat. After a day of gritted heat, the sky was clouding; a few shops and orange-painted snack-bars had turned on their electric lights. By these lights and the homing hurry of the traffic, Raikes felt the presence of the evening, and clenched his jaw against it. That restlessness, vague as the hot breath before a headache, lightly metallic as the taste of fever, must be avoided. He skirted the traffic dangerously, hurrying for the quieter streets away from that garish junction. Between the green and purple tiles of a public house and the red-framed window of a passport photographer's he entered at last into the duller, quieter perspective of a street of brown brick houses. Here was instant relief, as though a draught of wind had cooled physically his head. He thought of the girl, the calm flat, the safety, the rightness and the sanctuary there. Extraordinary, this sense of rightness and order that he felt with her; ease, relief, and constant need. Not at all like 'being in love'. Like being very young again, with a protective nurse. Looking down at the pavement cracks he felt pleasure in them, pleasure reflected from a sense of gratitude – and he started planning, to get a job next week, to end this hiding about, to do something for her in return. And then he remembered that even at that moment she was doing something more for him, arranging some sort of treat, a birthday supper. And thus tenderly grateful he slipped open the front door and climbed the stairs.

There were two rooms – the sitting-room and the bedroom. He tried the sitting-room door, which was regarded as his, but found it locked. But in the instant of rattling the knob Clara's voice came:

'Ron? . . . Ron, go in the bedroom, put your hat there – don't come in till you're quite ready. Surprise!'

Out in the dark passage, looking down at the brownish bare linoleum he smiled again, nodded, called a greeting and went into the bedroom. He washed, combed his hair, glancing now and then towards the closed connecting door. A last look in the mirror, a nervous washing gesture of his hands, and he was over at the door and opening it.

Coming from the daylit bedroom this room appeared like a picture of night, like some dimly-lit tableau recessed in a waxwork show. He was momentarily dazzled not by light but by a yellowed darkness, a promise of other unfocused light, the murky bewilderment of a room entered from strong sunlight. But a voice sang out to help him: 'Ron – HAPPY BIRTHDAY!' and, reassured, his eyes began to assemble the room – the table, crackers, shining cake, glasses and bottles, the green paper greeting, the glittering tinsel and those downcast shaded lights. Round the cake burned the little upright knives of those thirty-one candles, each yellow blade winking. The ceiling disappeared in darkness, all the light was lowered down upon the table and the carpet. He stood for a moment still shocked, robbed still of the room he had expected, its cold and clockless daylight, its motionless smell of dust.

An uncertain figure that was Clara came forward from behind the table, her waist and legs in light, then upwards in shadow. Her hands stretched towards him, her voice laughed from the darkness. And thus with the affirmation of her presence, the feeling of shock mysteriously cleared, the room fell into a different perspective – and instantly he saw with gratitude how carefully she had arranged that festive table, indeed how prettily reminiscent it was of festivity, old Christmases and parties held long ago in some separate life. Happier, he was able to watch the glasses fill with rich black stout, saw the red wink of the port dropped in to sweeten it, raised his glass in a toast. Then they stood in the half-light of that upper shadow, drank, joked, talked themselves into the climate of celebration. They moved round that table with its bright low centre-light like figures about a shaded gambling board – so vivid the clarity of their lowered hands, the sheen of his suit and the gleam of her stockings, yet with their faces veiled and diffused. Then, when two of the bottles were already empty, they sat down.

Raikes blinked in the new light. Everything sparkled suddenly,

all things round him seemed to wink. He laughed, abruptly too
excited. Clara was bending away from him, stretching to cut the
cake. As he raised his glass, he saw her back from the corner of his
eye, over the crystal rim of his glass – and held it then undrunk. He
stared at the shining white blouse, the concisely corrugated folds of
the knife-edge wave of her hair. Clara? The strangeness of the room
dropped its curtain round him again, heavily. Clara, a slow voice
mentioned in his mind, has merely bought herself a new blouse and
waved her hair. He nodded, accepting this automatically. But the
stout to which he was not used weighed inside his head, as though
some heavy circular hat was being pressed down, wreathing lead-
enly where its brim circled, forcing a lightness within that seemed
to balloon airily upwards. Unconsciously his hand went to his forehead – and at that moment Clara turned her face towards him,
setting it on one side in the full light, blowing out some of those
little red candles, laughing as she blew. The candle flames flickered
and winked like jewels close to her cheek. She blew her cheeks out,
so that they became full and rounded, then laughed so that her
white teeth gleamed between oil-rich red lips.

Thin candle-threads of black smoke needled curling by her hair.
She saw something strange in his eyes. Her voice said: 'Why Ron
– you haven't a headache? Not yet anyway . . . eh, dear?'

Now he no longer laughed naturally, but felt the stretch of his
lips as he tried to smile a denial of the headache. The worry was at
his head, he felt no longer at ease in that familiar chair, but rather
balanced on it alertly, so that under the table his calves were
braced, so that he moved his hands carefully for fear of encroach-
ing on what was not his, hands of a guest, hands uneasy at a
strange table.

Clara sat round now facing him – their chairs were to the same
side of that round table, and close. She kept smiling; those new
things she wore were plainly stimulating her, she must have felt
transformed and beautiful. Such a certainty together with the un-
accustomed alcohol brought a vivacity to her eye, a definition to
the movements of her mouth. Traces of faltering, of apology, of all
the wounded humilities of a face that apologizes for itself – all
these were gone, wiped away beneath the white powder; now her
face seemed to be charged with light, expressive, and in its new
self-assurance predatory. It was a face bent on effect, on making its
mischief. Instinctively it performed new tricks, attitudes learnt and

stored but never before used, the intuitive mimicry of the female seducer. She smiled now largely, as though her lips enjoyed the touch of her teeth; lowered her eyelids, then sprang them suddenly open; ended a laugh by tossing her head – only to shake the new curls in the light; raised her hand to her throat, to show the throat stretched back and soft, took a piece of butter-coloured marzipan and its marble-white icing between the tips of two fingers and laughing opened her mouth very wide, so that the tongue-tip came out to meet the icing, so that teeth and lips and mouth were wide and then suddenly shut in a coy gobble. And all this time, while they ate and drank and talked and joked, Raikes sat watching her, smiling his lips, but eyes heavily bright and fixed like pewter as the trouble roasted his brain.

He knew now fully what he wanted to do. His hand, as if it were some other hand not connected to his body, reached away to where the parcel of ties lay open; and its fingers were playing with the string. They played with it over-willingly, like the fingers guiding a paintbrush to over-decorate a picture, like fingers that pour more salt into a well-seasoned cook-pot. Against the knowledge of what he wanted the mind still balanced its danger, calculated the result and its difficult aftermath. Once again this was gluttonous, like deciding to take more drink. Sense of the moment, imagination of the result; the moment's desire, the mind's warning. Twice he leant towards her, measuring the distance then drawing back. His mind told him that he was playing, he was allowed such play, nothing would come of it.

Then abruptly it happened. That playing, like a swing pushing higher and then somersaulting the circle, mounted on its own momentum, grew huge and boundless, swelled like fired gas. Those fingers tautened, snapped the string. He was up off the chair and over Clara. The string, sharp and hempen, bit into her neck. Her lips opened in a wide laugh, for she thought he was clowning up suddenly to kiss her, and then stretched themselves wider, then closed into a bluish cough and the last little sounds.

My Vocation

I'm not married yet, but I'm still in hopes. One thing is certain though: I was never cut out to be a nun in the first place. Anyway, I was only thirteen when I got the Call, and I think if we were living out here in Crumlin at the time, in the new houses that the Government gave us, I'd never have got it at all, because we hardly ever see nuns out here, somehow, and a person wouldn't take so much notice of them out here anyway. It's so airy you know, and they blow along in their big white bonnets and a person wouldn't take any more notice of them than the seagulls that blow in from the sea. And then, too, you'd never get near enough to them out here to get the smell of them.

It was the smell of them I used to love in the Dorset Street days, when they'd stop us in the street to talk to us, when we'd be playing hopscotch on the path. I used to push up as close to them as possible and take big sniffs of them. But that was nothing to when they came up to the room to see Mother. You'd get it terribly strong then.

'What smell are you talking about?' said my father one day when I was going on about them after they went. 'That's no way to talk about people in Religious Orders,' he said. 'There's no smell at all off the like of them.'

That was right, of course, and I saw where I was wrong. It was the no-smell that I used to get, but there were so many smells fighting for place in Dorset Street, fried onions, and garbage, and the smell of old rags, that a person with no smell at all stood out a mile from everybody else. Anyone with an eye in their head could see that I didn't mean any disrespect. It vexed me shockingly to have my father think such a thing. I told him so, too, straight out.

'And if you want to know,' I finished up, 'I'm going to be a nun myself when I get big.'

But my father only roared laughing.

'Do you hear that?' he said, turning to mother. 'Isn't that a good one? She'll be joining the same order as you, I'm thinking.' And he roared out laughing again: a very common laugh I thought, even though he was my father.

And he was nothing to my brother Paudeen.

'We'll be all right if it isn't the Order of Mary Magdalen that one joins,' he said.

What do you make of that for commonness? Is it any wonder I wanted to get away from the lot of them?

He was always at me, that fellow, saying I was cheapening myself, and telling Ma on me if he saw me as much as lift my eye to a fellow passing me in the street.

'She's mad for boys, that one,' he used to say. And it wasn't true at all. It wasn't my fault if the boys were always after me, was it? And even if I felt a bit sparky now and then, wasn't that the kind that always became nuns? I never saw a plain-looking one, did you? I never did. Not in those days, I mean. The ones that used to come visiting us in Dorset Street were all gorgeous-looking, with pale faces and not a rotten tooth in their heads. They were twice as good-looking as the Tiller Girls in the Gaiety. And on Holy Thursday, when we were doing the Seven Churches, and we used to cross over the Liffey to the south side to make up the number, I used to go into the Convent of the Reparation just to look at the nuns. You see them inside in a kind of little golden cage, back of the altar in their white habits with blue sashes and their big silver beads dangling down by their side. They were like angels: honest to God. You'd be sure of it if you didn't happen to hear them give an odd cough now and again, or a sneeze.

It was in there with them I'd like to be, but Sis – she's my girlfriend – she told me they were all ladies, titled ladies too, some of them, and I'd have to be a lay sister. I wasn't having any of that, thank you. I could have gone away to domestic service any day if that was only all the ambition I had. It would have broken my mother's heart to see me scrubbing floors and the like. She never sank that low, although there were fourteen of them in the family, and only eleven of us. She was never anything less than a wards' maid in the Mater Hospital, and they're sort of nurses, if you like, and when she met my father she was after getting an offer of a great job as a barmaid in Geary's of Parnell Street. She'd never have held with me being a lay sister.

'I don't hold with there being any such things as lay sisters at all,' she said. 'They're not allowed a hot jar in their beds, I believe, and they have to sit at the back of the chapel with no red plush on their kneeler. If you ask me, it's a queer thing to see the Church making distinctions.'

She had a great regard for the Orders that had no lay sisters at all, like the Little Sisters of the Poor, and the Visiting Sisters.

'Oh, they're the grand women!' she said.

You'd think then, wouldn't you, that she'd be glad when I decided to join them. But she was as much against me as any of them.

'Is it you?' she cried. 'You'd want to get the impudent look taken off your face if that's the case!' she said, tightly.

I suppose it was the opposition that nearly drove me mad. It made me dead set on going ahead with the thing.

You see, they never went against me in any of the things I was going to be before that. The time I said I was going to be a Tiller Girl in the Gaiety, you should have seen the way they went on: all of them. They were dead keen on the idea.

'Are you tall enough though – that's the thing?' said Paudeen.

And the tears came into my mother's eyes.

'That's what I always wanted to be when I was a girl,' she said, and she dried her eyes and turned to my father. 'Do you think there is anyone you could ask to use his influence?' she said. Because she was always sure and certain that influence was the only thing that would get you any job.

But it wasn't influence in the Tiller Girls: it was legs. And I knew that, and my legs were never my strong point, so I gave up that idea.

Then there was the time I thought I'd like to be a waitress, even though I wasn't a blonde, said Paudeen morosely.

But you should see the way they went on then too.

'A packet of henna would soon settle the hair question,' said my mother.

'Although I'm sure some waitresses are good girls,' she said. 'It all depends on a girl herself, and the kind of a home she comes from.'

They were doubtful if I'd get any of these jobs, but they didn't raise any obstacles, and they didn't laugh at me like they did in this case.

'And what will I do for money,' said my father, 'when they come looking for your dowry? If you haven't an education you have to have money, going into those convents.'

But I turned a deaf ear to him.

'The Lord will provide,' I said. 'If it's His will for me to be a nun He'll find a way out of all difficulties,' I said grandly, and in a voice I imagined to be as near as I could make it to the ladylike voices of the Visiting Sisters.

But I hadn't much hope of getting into the Visiting Sisters. To begin with, they always seemed to take it for granted I'd get married.

'I hope you're a good girl,' they used to say to me, and you'd know by the way they said it what they meant. 'Boys may like a fast girl when it comes to having a good time, but it's the modest girl they pick when it comes to choosing a wife,' they said. And such-like things. They were always harping on the one string. Sure they'd never get over it if I told them what I had in mind. I'd never have the face to tell them!

And then one day what did I see but an advertisement in the paper.

'Wanted, Postulants,' it said, in big letters, and then underneath in small letters, there was the address of the Reverend Mother you were to apply to, and in smaller letters still, at the very bottom, were the words that made me sit up and take notice. 'No Dowry,' they said.

'That's me,' said I, and there and then I up and wrote off to them, without as much as saying a word to anyone only Sis.

Poor Sis: you should have seen how bad she took it.

'I can't believe it,' she said over and over again, and she threw her arms around me and burst out crying. She was always a good sort, Sis.

Every time she looked at me she burst out crying. And I must say that was more like the way I expected people to take me. But as a matter of fact Sis started the ball rolling, and it wasn't long after that everyone began to feel bad, because you see, the next thing that happened was a telegram arrived from the Reverend Mother in answer to my letter.

'It can't be for you,' said my mother, as she ripped it open. 'Who'd be sending you a telegram?'

And I didn't know who could have sent it either until I read the signature. It was Sister Mary Alacoque.

That was the name of the nun in the paper.

'It's for me all right,' I said then. 'I wrote to her,' I said and I felt a bit awkward.

My mother grabbed back the telegram.

'Glory be to God!' she said, but I don't think she meant it as a prayer. 'Do you see what it says? "Calling to see you this afternoon, Deo Gratias". What on earth is the meaning of all this?'

'Well,' I said defiantly, 'when I told you I was going to be a nun you wouldn't believe me. Maybe you'll believe it when I'm out among the savages!' I added. Because it was a missionary order: that's why they didn't care about the dowry. People are always leaving money in their wills to the Foreign Missions, and you don't need to be too highly educated to teach savages, I suppose.

'Glory be to God!' said my mother again. And then she turned on me. 'Get up out of that and we'll try and put some sort of front on things before they get here: there'll be two of them, I'll swear. Nuns never go out alone. Hurry up, will you?'

Never in your life did you see anyone carry on like my mother did that day. For the few hours that remained of the morning she must have worked like a lunatic, running mad around the room, shoving things under the bed, and ramming home the drawers of the chest, and sweeping things off the seats of the chairs.

'They'll want to see a chair they can sit on, anyway,' she said. 'And I suppose we'll have to offer them a bite to eat.'

'Oh, a cup of tea,' said my father.

But my mother had very grand ideas at times.

'Oh, I always heard you should give monks or nuns a good meal,' she said. 'They can eat things out in the world that they can't eat in the convent. As long as you don't ask them. Don't say will you or won't you! Just set it in front of them – that's what I always heard.'

I will say this for my mother, she has a sense of occasion, because we never heard any of this lore when the Visiting Sisters called, or even the Begging Sisters, although you'd think they could do with a square meal by the look of them sometimes.

But no: there was never before seen such a fuss as she made on this occasion.

'Run out to Mrs Mullins in the front room and ask her for the lend of her brass fender,' she cried, giving me a push out the door. 'And see if poor Mr Duffy is home from work – he'll be good enough to let us have a chair, I'm sure, the poor soul, the one with the plush seat,' she cried, coming out to the landing after me, and calling across the well of the stairs.

As I disappeared into Mrs Mullins's I could see her standing in the doorway as if she was trying to make up her mind about something. And sure enough, when I came out lugging the fender with me, she ran across and took it from me.

'Run down to the return room, like a good child,' she said, 'and ask old Mrs Dooley for her tablecloth – the one with the lace edging she got from America.' And as I showed some reluctance, she caught my arm. 'You might give her a wee hint of what's going on. Won't everyone know it as soon as the nuns arrive, and it'll give her the satisfaction of having the news ahead of everyone else.'

But it would be hard to say who had the news first because I was only at the foot of the steps leading to the return room when I could hear doors opening in every direction on our own landing, and the next minute you'd swear they were playing a new kind of postman's knock, in which each one carried a piece of furniture round with him, by the way our friends and neighbours were rushing back and forth across the landing; old Ma Dunne with her cuckoo clock, and young Mrs McBride, that shouldn't be carrying heavy things at all, with our old wicker chair that she was going to exchange for the time with a new one of her own. And I believe she wanted to get her piano rolled in to us too, only there wasn't time!

That was the great thing about Dorset Street: you could meet any and all occasions, you had so many friends at your back. And you could get anything you wanted, all in a few minutes, without anyone outside the landing being any the wiser.

My mother often said it was like one big happy family, that landing – including the return room, of course.

The only thing was everyone wanted to have a look at the room. 'We'll never get shut of them before the nuns arrive,' I thought.

'Isn't this the great news entirely,' said old Mrs Dooley, making her way up the stairs as soon as I told her. And she rushed up to my mother and kissed her. 'Not but that you deserve it,' she said. 'I never knew a priest or a nun yet that hadn't a good mother behind them!' And then Mrs McBride coming out, she drew her into it. 'Isn't that so, Mrs McBride?' she cried. 'I suppose you heard the news?'

'I did indeed,' said Mrs McBride. 'Not that I was surprised,' she said, but I think she only wanted to let on she was greater with us than she was, because as Sis could tell you, there was nothing of the Holy Molly about me – far from it.

What old Mr Duffy said was more like what you'd expect.

'Well, doesn't that beat all!' he cried, hearing the news as he came up the last step of the stairs. 'Ah, well, I always heard it's the biggest divils that make the best saints, and now I can believe it!'

He was a terribly nice old man.

'And is it the Foreign Missions?' he asked, calling me to one side, 'because if that's the case I want you to know you can send me raffle tickets for every draw you hold, and I'll sell the lot for you and get the stubs back in good time, with the money along with it in postal orders. And what's more—' he was going on, when Mrs Mullins let out a scream:

'You didn't tell me it was the Missions,' she cried. 'Oh, God help you, you poor child!' And she threw up her hands. 'How will any of us be saved at all at all with the like of you going to the ends of the earth where you'll never see a living soul only blacks till the day you die! Oh, glory be to God. And to think we never knew who we had in our midst!'

In some ways it was what I expected, but in another way I'd have liked if they didn't all look at me in such a pitying way.

And old Mrs Dooley put the lid on it.

'A saint – that's what you are, child,' she cried, and she caught my hand and pulled me down close to her – she was a low butt of a little woman. 'They tell me it's out to the poor lepers you're going?'

That was the first I heard about lepers, I can tell you. And I partly guessed the poor old thing had picked it up wrong, but all the same I put a knot in my handkerchief to remind me to ask where I was going.

And I may as well admit straight out, that I wasn't having anything to do with any lepers. I hadn't thought of backing out of the thing entirely at that time, but I was backing out of it if it was to be lepers!

The thought of the lepers gave me the creeps, I suppose. Did you ever get the feeling when a thing was mentioned that you *had* it? Well, that was the way I felt. I kept going over to the basin behind the screen (Mrs McBride's) and washing my hands every minute, and as for spitting out, my throat was raw by the time I heard the cab at the door.

'Here they come,' cried my father, raising his hand like the starter at the dog track.

'Out of this, all of you,' cried Mrs Mullins, rushing out and giving an example to everyone.

'Holy God!' said my mother, but I don't think that was meant to be a prayer either.

But she had nothing to be uneasy about: the room was gorgeous. That was another thing: I thought they'd be delighted with the room. We never did it up any way special for the Visiting Sisters, but they were always saying how nice we kept it: maybe that was only to encourage my mother, but all the same it was very nice of them. But when the two Recruiting Officers arrived (it was my father called them that after they went), they didn't seem to notice the room at all in spite of what we'd done to it.

And do you know what I heard one of them say to the other?

'It seems clean, anyway,' she said.

Now I didn't like that 'seems'. And what did she mean by the 'anyway' I'd like to know?

It sort of put me off from the start – would you believe that? That, and the look of them. They weren't a bit like the Visiting Sisters – or even the Begging Sisters; who all had lovely figures – like statues. One of them was thin all right, but I didn't like the look of her all the same. She didn't look thin in an ordinary way; she looked worn away, if you know what I mean? And the other one was fat. She was so fat I was afraid if she fell on the stairs she'd start to roll like a ball.

She was the boss: the fat one.

And do you know one of the first things she asked me? You'd never guess. I don't even like to mention it. She caught a hold of my hair.

'I hope you keep it nice and clean,' she said.

What do you think of that? I was glad my mother didn't hear her. My mother forgets herself entirely if she's mad about anything. She didn't hear it, though. But I began to think to myself that they must have met some very low-class girls if they had to ask *that* question. And wasn't that what you'd think?

Then the worn-looking one said a queer thing, not to me, but to the other nun.

'She seems strong, anyway,' she said. And there again I don't think she meant my health. I couldn't help putting her remark alongside the way she was so worn-looking, and I began to think I'd got myself into a nice pickle.

But I was prepared to go through with it all the same. That's me: I have great determination although you mightn't believe it. Sis often says I'd have been well able for the savages if I'd gone on with the thing.

But I didn't.

I missed it by a hair's breadth, though. I won't tell you all the interview, but at the end of it anyway they gave me the name of the Convent where I was to go for Probation, and they told me the day to go, and they gave me a list of clothes I was to get.

'Will you be able to pay for them?' they said, turning to my father. They hadn't taken much notice of him up to that.

I couldn't help admiring the way he answered.

'Well, I managed to pay for plenty of style for her up to now,' he said, 'and seeing that this mourning outfit is to be the last I'll be asked to pay for, I think I'll manage it all right. Why?'

I admired the 'why?'

'Oh, we have to be ready for all eventualities,' said the fat one.

Sis and I nearly died laughing afterwards thinking of those words. But I hardly noticed them at the time, because I was on my way out the door to order a cab. They had asked me to get one and they had given me so many instructions that I was nearly daft.

They didn't want a flighty horse, and they didn't want a cab that was too high up off the ground, and I was to pick a cabby that looked respectable.

Now at this time, although there were still cabs to be hired, you didn't have an almighty great choice, and I knew I had my work cut out for me to meet all their requirements.

But I seemed to be dead in luck in more ways than one, because when I went to the cab stand there, among the shiny black cabs, with big black horses that rolled their eyes at me, there was one old cab and it was all battered and green-mouldy. The cabby too looked about as mouldy as the cab. And as for the horse – well, wouldn't anyone think that he'd be mouldy too. But as a matter of fact the horse wasn't mouldy in any way. Indeed, it was due to the way he bucketed it about that the old cab was so racked-looking: it was newer than the others I believe, and as for the cabby, I believe it was the horse had him so bad-looking. That horse had the heart scalded in him.

But it was only afterwards I heard all this. I thought I'd done great work, and I went up and got the nuns, and put them into it and off they went, with the thin one waving to me.

It was while I was still waving that I saw the horse starting his capers.

My first thought was to run, but I thought I'd have to face them again, so I didn't do that. Instead, I ran after the cab and shouted to the driver to stop.

Perhaps that was what did the damage. Maybe I drove the horse clean mad altogether, because the next thing he reared up and let his hind legs fly. There was a dreadful crash and a sound of splintering, and the next thing I knew the bottom of the cab came down on the road with a clatter. I suppose it had got such abuse from that animal from time to time it was on the point of giving way all the time.

It was a miracle for them they weren't let down on the road – the two nuns. It was a miracle for me too in another way because if they did I'd have to go and pick them up and I'd surely be drawn deeper into the whole thing.

But that wasn't what happened. Off went the horse, as mad as ever down the street, rearing and leaping, but the nuns must have got a bit of a warning and held on to the sides, because the next thing I saw, along with the set of four feet under the horse, was four more feet showing out under the body of the cab, and running for dear life.

Honest to God, I started to laugh. Wasn't that awful? They could have been killed, and I knew it, although as a matter of fact someone caught hold of the cab before it got to Parnell Street and they were taken out of it and put into another cab. But once I started to laugh I couldn't stop, and in a way – if you can understand such a thing – I laughed away my vocation. Wasn't that awful?

Not but that I have a great regard for nuns even to this day, although, mind you, I sometimes think the nuns that are going nowadays are not the same as the nuns that were going in our Dorset Street days. I saw a terribly plain-looking one the other day in Cabra Avenue. But all the same, they're grand women! I'm going to make a point of sending all my kids to school with the nuns anyway, when I have them. But of course it takes a fellow with a bit of money to educate his kids nowadays. A girl has to have an eye to the future, as I always tell Sis – she's my girl-friend, you remember.

Well, we're going out to Dollymount this afternoon, Sis and me, and you'd never know who we'd pick up. So long for the present!

Five-Twenty

Most evenings, weather permitting, the Natwicks sat on the front veranda to watch the traffic. During the day the stream flowed, but towards five it began to thicken, it sometimes jammed solid like: the semi-trailers and refrigeration units, the decent old-style sedans, the mini-cars, the bombs, the Holdens and the Holdens. She didn't know most of the names. Royal did, he was a man, though never ever mechanical himself. She liked him to tell her about the vehicles, or listen to him take part in conversation with anyone who stopped at the fence. He could hold his own, on account of he was more educated, and an invalid has time to think.

They used to sit side by side on the tiled veranda, him in his wheelchair she had got him after the artheritis took over, her in the old cane. The old cane chair wasn't hardly presentable any more; she had torn her winter cardy on a nail and laddered several pair of stockings. You hadn't the heart to get rid of it, though. They brought it with them from Sarsaparilla after they sold the business. And now they could sit in comfort to watch the traffic, the big steel insects of nowadays, which put the wind up her at times.

Royal said, 'I reckon we're a shingle short to'uv ended up on the Parramatta Road.'

'You said we'd still see life,' she reminded, 'even if we lost the use of our legs.'

'But look at the traffic! Worse every year. And air. Rot a man's lungs quicker than the cigarettes. You should'uv headed me off. You who's supposed to be practical!'

'I thought it was what you wanted,' she said, keeping it soft; she had never been one to crow.

'Anyway, I already lost the use of me legs.'

As if she was to blame for that too. She was so shocked the chair sort of jumped. It made her blood run cold to hear the metal feet screak against the little draught-board tiles.

'Well, I 'aven't!' she protested. 'I got me legs, and will be able to get from 'ere to anywhere and bring 'ome the shopping. While I got me strength.'

She tried never to upset him by any show of emotion, but now she was so upset herself.

They watched the traffic in the evenings, as the orange light was stacked up in thick slabs, and the neon signs were coming on.

'See that bloke down there in the parti-coloured Holden?'

'Which?' she asked.

'The one level with our own gate.'

'The pink and brown?' She couldn't take all that interest tonight, only you must never stop humouring a sick man.

'Yairs. Pink. Fancy a man in a pink car!'

'Dusty pink is fashionable.' She knew that for sure.

'But a man!'

'Perhaps his wife chose it. Perhaps he's got a domineering wife.'

Royal laughed low. 'Looks the sort of coot who might like to be domineered, and if that's what he wants, it's none of our business, is it?'

She laughed to keep him company. They were such mates, everybody said. And it was true. She didn't know what she would do if Royal passed on first.

That evening the traffic had jammed. Some of the drivers began tooting. Some of them stuck their heads out, and yarned to one another. But the man in the pink-and-brown Holden just sat. He didn't look to either side.

Come to think of it, she had noticed him pass before. Yes. Though he wasn't in no way a noticeable man. Yes. She looked at her watch.

'Five-twenty,' she said. 'I seen that man in the pink-and-brown before. He's pretty regular. Looks like a business executive.'

Royal cleared his throat and spat. It didn't make the edge of the veranda. Better not to notice it, because he'd only create if she did. She'd get out the watering-can after she had pushed him inside.

'Business executives!' she heard. 'They're afraid people are gunner think they're poor class without they *execute*. In our day nobody was ashamed to *do*. Isn't that about right, eh?' She didn't answer because she knew she wasn't meant to. 'Funny sort of head that cove's got. Like it was half squashed. Silly-lookun bloody head!'

'Could have been born with it,' she suggested. 'Can't help what you're born with. Like your religion.'

There was the evening the Chev got crushed, only a young fellow too. Ahhh, it had stuck in her throat, thinking of the wife and kiddies. She ran in, and out again as quick as she could, with a couple of blankets, and the rug that was a present from Hazel. She had grabbed a pillow off their own bed.

She only faintly heard Royal shouting from the wheelchair.

She arranged the blankets and the pillow on the pavement, under the orange sky. The young fellow was looking pretty sick, kept on turning his head as though he recognized and wanted to tell her something. Then the photographer from the *Mirror* took his picture, said she ought to be in it to add a touch of human interest, but she wouldn't. A priest came, the *Mirror* took his picture, administering what Mrs Dolan said they call Extreme Unkshun. Well, you couldn't poke fun at a person's religion any more than the shape of their head, and Mrs Dolan was a decent neighbour, the whole family, and clean.

When she got back to the veranda, Royal, a big man, had slipped down in his wheelchair.

He said, or gasped, 'Wotcher wanter do that for, Ella? How are we gunner get the blood off?'

She hadn't thought about the blood, when of course she was all smeared with it, and the blankets, and Hazel's good Onkaparinka. Anyway, it was her who would get the blood off.

'You soak it in milk or something,' she said. 'I'll ask. Don't you worry.'

Then she did something. She bent down and kissed Royal on the forehead in front of the whole Parramatta Road. She regretted it at once, because he looked that powerless in his invalid chair, and his forehead felt cold and sweaty.

But you can't undo things that are done.

It was a blessing they could sit on the front veranda. Royal suffered a lot by now. He had his long-standing hernia, which they couldn't have operated on, on account of he was afraid of his heart. And then the artheritis.

'Arthritis.'

'All right,' she accepted the correction. 'Arth-er-itis.'

It was all very well for men, they could manage more of the hard words.

'What have we got for tea?' he asked.

'Well,' she said, fanning out her hands on the points of her elbows, and smiling, 'it's a surprise.'

She looked at her watch. It was five-twenty.

'It's a coupler nice little bits of fillet Mr Ballard let me have.'

'Wotcher mean let you have? Didn't you pay for them?'

She had to laugh. 'Anything I have I pay for!'

'Well? Think we're in the fillet-eating class?'

'It's only a treat, Royal,' she said. 'I got a chump chop for myself. I like a nice chop.'

He stopped complaining, and she was relieved.

'There's that gentleman,' she said, 'in the Holden.'

They watched him pass, as sober as their own habits.

Royal – he had been his mother's little king. Most of his mates called him 'Roy'. Perhaps only her and Mrs Natwick had stuck to the christened name, they felt it suited.

She often wondered how Royal had ever fancied her: such a big man, with glossy hair, black, and a nose like on someone historical. She would never have said it, but she was proud of Royal's nose. She was proud of the photo he had of the old family home in Kent, the thatch so lovely, and Grannie Natwick sitting in her apron on a rush-bottom chair in front, looking certainly not all that different from Mum, with the aunts gathered round in leggermutton sleeves, all big nosey women like Royal.

She had heard Mum telling Royal's mother, 'Ella's a plain little thing, but what's better than cheerful and willing?' She had always been on the mousey side, she supposed, which didn't mean she couldn't chatter with the right person. She heard Mum telling Mrs Natwick, 'My Ella can wash and bake against any comers. Clever with her needle too.' She had never entered any of the competitions, like they told her she ought to, it would have made her nervous.

It was all the stranger that Royal had ever fancied her.

Once as they sat on the veranda watching the evening traffic, she said, 'Remember how you used to ride out in the old days from "Bugilbar" to Cootramundra?'

'Cootamundra.'

'Yes,' she said. 'Cootramundra.' (That's why they'd called the house 'Coota' when they moved to the Parramatta Road.)

She had been so dazzled on one occasion by his parti-coloured forehead and his black hair, after he had got down from the saddle, after he had taken off his hat, she had run and fetched a duster, and dusted Royal Natwick's boots. The pair of new elastic-sides was white with dust from the long ride. It only occurred to her as she polished she might be doing something shameful, but when she looked up, it seemed as though Royal Natwick saw nothing peculiar in Ella McWhirter dusting his boots. He might even have expected it. She was so glad she could have cried.

Old Mr Natwick had come out from Kent when a youth, and after working at several uncongenial jobs, and studying at night, had been taken on as book-keeper at 'Bugilbar'. He was much valued in the end by the owners, and always made use of. The father would have liked his son to follow in his footsteps, and taught him how to keep the books, but Royal wasn't going to hang around any family of purse-proud squatters, telling them the things they wanted to hear. He had ideas of his own for becoming rich and important.

So when he married Ella McWhirter, which nobody could ever understand, not even Ella herself, perhaps only Royal, who never bothered to explain (why should he?) they moved to Juggerawa, and took over the general store. It was in a bad way, and soon was in a worse, because Royal's ideas were above those of his customers.

Fulbrook was the next stage. He found employment as book-keeper on a grazing property outside. She felt so humiliated on account of his humiliation. It didn't matter about herself because she always expected less. She took a job in Fulbrook from the start, at the 'Dixie Cafe' in High Street. She worked there several years as waitress, helping out with the scrubbing for the sake of the extra money. She had never hated anything, but got to hate the flies trampling in the sugar and on the necks of the tomato sauce bottles.

At weekends her husband usually came in, and when she wasn't needed in the shop, they lay on the bed in her upstairs room, listening to the corrugated iron and the warping white-washed weatherboard. She would have loved to do something for him, but in his distress he complained about 'wet kisses'. It surprised her. She had always been afraid he might find her a bit too dry in her show of affection.

Those years at the 'Dixie Cafe' certainly dried her up. She got those freckly patches and seams in her skin in spite of the lotions used as directed. Not that it matters so much in anyone born plain.

Perhaps her plainness helped her save. There was never a day when she didn't study her savings-book, it became her favourite recreation.

Royal, on the other hand, wasn't the type that dried up, being fleshier, and dark. He even put on weight out at the grazing property, where they soon thought the world of him. When the young ladies were short of a man for tennis the book-keeper was often invited, and to a ball once at the homestead. He was earning good money, and he too saved a bit, though his instincts weren't as mean as hers. For intance, he fancied a choice cigar. In his youth Royal was a natty dresser.

Sometimes the young ladies, if they decided to inspect the latest at Ryan's Emporium, or Mr Philup, if he felt like grogging up with the locals, would drive him in, and as he got out they would look funny at the book-keeper's wife they had heard about, they must have, serving out the plates of frizzled steak and limp chips. Royal always waited to see his employers drive off before coming in.

In spite of the savings, this might have gone on much longer than it did if old Mr Natwick hadn't died. It appeared he had been a very prudent man. He left them a nice little legacy. The evening of the news, Royal was driven in by Mr Philup and they had a few at the Imperial. Afterwards the book-keeper was dropped off, because he proposed to spend the night with his wife and catch the early train to attend his father's funeral.

They lay in the hot little room and discussed the future. She had never felt so hectic. Royal got the idea he would like to develop a grocery business in one of the posh outer suburbs of Sydney. 'Interest the monied residents in some of the luxury lines. Appeal to the imagination as well as the stomach.'

She was impressed, of course, but not as much as she should have been. She wasn't sure, but perhaps she was short on imagination. Certainly their prospects had made her downright feverish, but for no distinct, sufficient reason.

'And have a baby.' She heard her own unnatural voice.

'Eh?'

'We could start a baby.' Her voice grew word by word drier.

'There's no reason why we couldn't have a baby. Or two.' He laughed. 'But starting a new life isn't the time to start a baby.' He dug her in the ribs. 'And you the practical one!'

She agreed it would be foolish, and presently Royal fell asleep.

What could she do for him? As he lay there breathing she would have loved to stroke his nose she could see faintly in the light from the window. Again unpractical, she would have liked to kiss it. Or bite it suddenly off.

She was so disgusted with herself she got creaking off the bed and walked flat across the boards to the washstand and swallowed a couple of Aspros to put her solidly to sleep.

All their life together she had to try in some way to make amends to Royal, not only for her foolishness, but for some of the thoughts that got into her head. Because she hadn't the imagination, the thoughts couldn't have been her own. They must have been put into her.

It was easier of course in later life, after he had cracked up, what with his hernia, and heart, and the artheritis taking over. Fortunately she was given the strength to help him into the wheelchair, and later still, to lift, or drag him up on the pillows and over, to rub the bedsores, and stick the pan under him. But even during the years at Sarsaparilla she could make amends in many little ways, though with him still in his prime, naturally he mustn't know of them. So all her acts were mostly for her own self-gratification.

The store at Sarsaparilla, if it didn't exactly flourish, gave them a decent living. She had her problems, though. Some of the locals just couldn't accept that Royal was a superior man. Perhaps she had been partly to blame, she hardly dared admit it, for showing one or two 'friends' the photo of the family home in Kent. She couldn't resist telling the story of one of the aunts, Miss Ethel Natwick, who followed her brother to New South Wales. Ethel was persuaded to accept a situation at Government House, but didn't like it and went back, in spite of the Governor's lady insisting she valued Ethel as a close personal friend. When people began to laugh at Royal on account of his auntie and the family home, as you couldn't help finding out in a place like Sarsaparilla, it was her, she knew, it was her to blame. It hurt her deeply.

Of course Royal could be difficult. Said stockbrokers had no palate and less imagination. Royal said no Australian grocer could make a go of it if it wasn't for flour, granulated sugar, and tomato sauce. Some of the customers turned nasty in retaliation. This was where she could help, and did, because Royal was out on delivery more often than not. It embarrassed her only when some of them took it for granted she was on their side. As if he wasn't her husband. Once or twice she had gone out crying afterwards, amongst the wormy wattles and hens' droppings. Anyone across the gully could have heard her blowing her nose behind the store, but she didn't care. Poor Royal.

There was that Mr Ogburn said, 'A selfish, swollen-headed slob who'll chew you up and swallow you down.' She wouldn't let herself hear any more of what he had to say. Mr Ogburn had a harelip, badly sewn, opening and closing. There was nothing frightened her so much as even a well-disguised harelip. She got the palpitations after the scene with Mr Ogburn.

Not that there was anything wrong with her.

She only hadn't had the baby. It was her secret grief on black evenings as she walked slowly looking for the eggs a flighty hen might have hid in the bracken.

Dr Bamforth said, looking at the nib of his fountain pen, 'You know, don't you, it's sometimes the man?'

She didn't even want to hear, let alone think about it. In any case she wouldn't tell Royal, because a man's pride could be so easily hurt.

After they had sold out at Sarsaparilla and come to live at what they called 'Coota' on the Parramatta Road, it was both easier and more difficult, because if they were not exactly elderly they were getting on. Royal used to potter about in the beginning, while taking care, on account of the hernia and his heart. There was the business of the lawn-mowing, not that you could call it lawn, but it was what she had. She loved her garden. In front certainly there was only the two square of rather sooty grass which she would keep in order with the pushmower. The lawn seemed to get on Royal's nerves until the artheritis took hold of him. He had never liked mowing. He would lean against the veranda post, and shout, 'Don't know why we don't do what they've done down the street. Root the stuff out. Put down a green concrete lawn.'

'That would be copying,' she answered back.

She hoped it didn't sound stubborn. As she pushed the mower she bent her head, and smiled, waiting for him to cool off. The scent of grass and a few clippings flew up through the traffic fumes reminding you of summer.

While Royal shuffled along the veranda and leaned against another post. 'Or pebbles. You can buy clean, river pebbles. A few plastic shrubs, and there's the answer.'

He only gave up when his trouble forced him into the chair. You couldn't drive yourself up and down a veranda shouting at someone from a wheelchair without the passers-by thinking you was a nut. So he quietened.

He watched her, though. From under the peak of his cap. Because she felt he might still resent her mowing the lawn, she would try to reassure him as she pushed. 'What's wrong, *eh*? While I still have me health, me *strength* – I was always what they call *wiry* – why shouldn't I cut the *grass*?'

She would come and sit beside him, to keep him company in watching the traffic, and invent games to amuse her invalid husband.

'Isn't that the feller we expect?' she might ask. 'The one that passes at five-twenty,' looking at her watch, 'in the old pink-and-brown Holden?'

They enjoyed their snort of amusement all the better because no one else knew the reason for it.

Once when the traffic was particularly dense, and that sort of chemical smell from one of the factories was thickening in the evening air, Royal drew her attention. 'Looks like he's got something on his mind.'

Could have too. Or it might have been the traffic block. The way he held his hands curved listlessly around the inactive wheel reminded her of possums and monkeys she had seen in cages. She shifted a bit. Her squeaky old chair. She felt uneasy for ever having found the man, not a joke, but half of one.

Royal's chair moved so smoothly on its rubber-tyred wheels it was easy to push him, specially after her practice with the mower. There were ramps where necessary now, to cover steps, and she would sometimes wheel him out to the back, where she grew hollyhock and sunflower against the palings, and a vegetable or two on raised beds.

Royal would sit not looking at the garden from under the peak of his cap.

She never attempted to take him down the shady side, between them and Dolans, because the path was narrow from plants spilling over, and the shade might have lowered his spirits.

She loved her garden.

The shady side was where she kept her staghorn ferns, and fish-bones, and the pots of maidenhair. The water lay sparkling on the maidenhair even in the middle of the day. In the blaze of summer the light at either end of the tunnel was like you were looking through a sheet of yellow cellophane, but as the days shortened, the light deepened to a cold, tingling green, which might have made a person nervous who didn't know the tunnel by heart.

Take Mrs Dolan the evening she came in to ask for the loan of a cupful of sugar. 'You gave me a shock, Mrs Natwick. What ever are you up to?'

'Looking at the plants,' Mrs Natwick answered, whether Mrs Dolan would think it peculiar or not.

It was the season of cinerarias, which she always planted on that side, it was sheltered and cold-green. The wind couldn't bash the big spires and umbrellas of blue and purple. Visiting cats were the only danger, messing and pouncing. She disliked cats for the smell they left, but didn't have the heart to disturb their elastic forms curled at the cineraria roots, exposing their colourless pads, and sometimes pink, swollen teats. Blushing only slightly for it, she would stand and examine the details of the sleeping cats.

If Royal called she could hear his voice through the window. 'Where'uv you got to, Ella?'

After he was forced to take to his bed, his voice began to sort of dry up like his body. There were times when it sounded less like a voice than a breath of drowsiness or pain.

'Ella?' he was calling. 'I dropped the paper. Where are yer all this time? You know I can't pick up the paper.'

She knew. Guilt sent her scuttling to him, deliberately composing her eyes and mouth so as to arrive looking cheerful.

'I was in the garden,' she confessed, 'looking at the cinerarias.'

'The what?' It was a name Royal could never learn.

The room was smelling of sickness and the bottles standing on odd plates.

'It fell,' he complained.

She picked up the paper as quick as she could.

'Want to go la-la first?' she asked, because by now he depended on her to raise him and stick the pan under.

But she couldn't distract him from her shortcomings; he was shaking the paper at her. 'Haven't you lived with me long enough to know how to treat a newspaper?'

He hit it with his set hand, and certainly the paper looked a mess, like an old white battered brolly.

'Mucked up! You gotter keep the pages *aligned*. A paper's not readable otherwise. Of course you wouldn't understand because you don't read it, without it's to see who's died.' He began to cough.

'Like me to bring you some Bovril?' she asked him as tenderly as she knew.

'Bovril's the morning,' he coughed.

She knew that, but wanted to do something for him.

After she had rearranged the paper she walked out so carefully it made her go lopsided, out to the front veranda. Nothing would halt the traffic, not sickness, not death even.

She sat with her arms folded, realizing at last how they were aching.

'He hasn't been,' she had to call after looking at her watch.

'Who?' she heard the voice rustling back.

'The gentleman in the pink Holden.'

She listened to the silence, wondering whether she had done right.

When Royal called back, 'Could'uv had a blow-out.' Then he laughed. 'Could'uv stopped to get grogged up.' She heard the frail rustling of the paper. 'Or taken an axe to somebody like they do nowadays.'

She closed her eyes, whether for Royal, or what she remembered of the man sitting in the Holden.

Although it was cold she continued watching after dark. Might have caught a chill, when she couldn't afford to. She only went inside to make the bread-and-milk Royal fancied of an evening.

She watched most attentively, always at the time, but he didn't pass, and didn't pass.

'Who?'

'The gentleman in the Holden.'

'Gone on holiday.' Royal sighed, and she knew it was the point where a normal person would have turned over, so she went to turn him.

One morning she said on going in, 'Fancy, I had a dream, it was about that man! He was standing on the side path alongside the cinerarias. I know it was him because of his funny-shaped head.'

'What happened in the dream?' Royal hadn't opened his eyes yet; she hadn't helped him in with his teeth.

'I dunno,' she said, 'it was just a dream.'

That wasn't strictly truthful, because the Holden gentleman had looked at her, she had seen his eyes. Nothing was spoken, though.

'It was a sort of red and purple dream. That was the cinerarias,' she said.

'I don't dream. You don't when you don't sleep. Pills aren't sleep.'

She was horrified at her reverberating dream. 'Would you like a nice soft-boiled egg?'

'Eggs all have a taste.'

'But you gotter eat *something*!'

On another morning she told him – she could have bitten off her tongue – she *was* stupid, *stupid*, 'I had a dream.'

'What sort of dream?'

'Oh,' she said, 'a silly one. Not worth telling. I dreamed I dropped an egg on the side path, and it turned into two. Not two. A double-yolker.'

She never realized Royal was so much like Mrs Natwick. It was as she raised him on his pillows. Or he had got like that in his sickness. Old men and old women were not unlike.

'Wasn't that a silly one?' she coaxed.

Every evening she sat on the front veranda and watched the traffic as though Royal had been beside her. Looked at her watch. And turned her face away from the steady-flowing stream. The way she bunched her small chest she could have had a sour breath mounting in her throat. Sometimes she had, it was nervousness.

When she went inside she announced. 'He didn't pass.'

Royal said – he had taken to speaking from behind his eyelids. 'Something muster happened to 'im. He didn't go on holiday. He went and died.'

'Oh, no! He wasn't of an age!'

At once she saw how stupid she was, and went out to get the bread-and-milk.

She would sit at the bedside, almost crouching against the edge of the mattress, because she wanted Royal to feel she was close, and he seemed to realize, though he mostly kept his eyelids down.

Then one evening she came running, she felt silly, her calves felt silly, her voice, 'He's come! At five-twenty! In a new cream Holden!'

Royal said without opening his eyes, 'See? I said 'e'd gone on holiday.'

More than ever she saw the look of Mrs Natwick.

Now every evening Royal asked, 'Has he been, Ella?'

Trying not to make it sound irritable or superior, she would answer, 'Not yet. It's only five.'

Every evening she sat watching, and sometimes would turn proud, arching her back, as she looked down from the veranda. The man was so small and ordinary.

She went in on one occasion, into the more than electric light, lowering her eyelids against the dazzle. 'You know, Royal, you could feel prouder of men when they rode horses. As they looked down at yer from under the brim of their hats. Remember that hat you used to wear? Riding in to Cootramundra?'

Royal died quietly that same year before the cinerarias had folded, while the cold westerlies were still blowing; the back page of the *Herald* was full of those who had been carried off. She was left with his hand, already set, in her own. They hadn't spoken, except about whether she had put out the garbage.

Everybody was very kind. She wouldn't have liked to admit it was enjoyable being a widow. She sat around for longer than she had ever sat, and let the dust gather. In the beginning acquaintances and neighbours brought her little presents of food: a billy-can of giblet soup, moulded veal with hard-boiled egg making a pattern in the jelly, cakes so dainty you couldn't taste them. But when she was no longer a novelty they left off coming. She didn't care any more than she cared about the dust. Sometimes she would catch sight of her face in the glass, and was surprised to see herself looking so calm and white.

Of course she was calm. The feeling part of her had been removed. What remained was a slack, discardable eiderdown. Must have been the pills Doctor gave.

Well-meaning people would call to her over the front fence, 'Don't you feel lonely, Mrs Natwick?' They spoke with a restrained horror, as though she had been suffering from an incurable disease.

But she called back proud and slow, 'I'm under sedation.'

'Arrr!' They nodded thoughtfully. 'What's 'e given yer?'

She shook her head. 'Pills,' she called back. 'They say they're the ones the actress died of.'

The people walked on, impressed.

As the evenings grew longer and heavier she sat later on the front veranda watching the traffic of the Parramatta Road, its flow becoming syrupy and almost benign: big bulbous sedate buses, chrysalis cars still without a life of their own, clinging in line to the back of their host-articulator, trucks loaded for distances, empty loose-sounding jolly lorries. Sometimes women, looking out from the cabins of trucks from beside their men, shared her lack of curiosity. The light was so fluid nobody lasted long enough. You would never have thought boys could kick a person to death, seeing their long soft hair floating behind their sports models.

Every evening she watched the cream Holden pass. And looked at her watch. It was like Royal was sitting beside her. Once she heard herself, 'Thought he was gunner look round tonight, in our direction.' How could a person feel lonely?

She was, though. She came face to face with it walking through the wreckage of her garden in the long slow steamy late summer. The Holden didn't pass of course of a Saturday or Sunday. Something, something had tricked her, not the pills, before the pills. She couldn't blame anybody, probably only herself. Everything depended on yourself. Take the garden. It was a shambles. She would have liked to protest, but began to cough from running her head against some powdery mildew. She could only blunder at first, like a cow, or runty starved heifer, on breaking into a garden. She had lost her old wiriness. She shambled, snapping dead stems, uprooting. Along the bleached palings there was a fretwork of hollyhock, the brown fur of rotting sunflower. She rushed at a praying mantis, a big pale one, and deliberately broke its back, and was sorry afterwards for what was done so easy and thoughtless.

As she stood panting in her black, finally yawning, she saw all she had to repair. The thought of the seasons piling up ahead made her feel tired but necessary, and she went in to bathe her face. Royal's denture in a tumbler on top of the medicine cabinet, she ought to move, or give to the Sallies. In the meantime she changed the water. She never forgot it. The teeth looked amazingly alive.

All that autumn, winter, she was continually amazed, at the dust she had let gather in the house, at old photographs, books, clothes.

There was a feather she couldn't remember wearing, a scarlet feather, she *can't* have worn, and gloves with little fussy ruffles at the wrists, silver piping, like a snail had laid its trail round the edges. There was, she knew, funny things she had bought at times, and never worn, but she couldn't remember the gloves or the feather. And books. She had collected a few, though never a reader herself. Old people liked to give old books, and you took them so as not to hurt anybody's feelings. *Hubert's Crusade*, for instance. Lovely golden curls. Could have been Royal's father's book. Everybody was a child once. And almost everybody had one. At least if she had had a child she would have known it wasn't a white turnip, more of a praying mantis, which snaps too easy.

In the same box she had put away a coloured picture *Cities of the Plain*, she couldn't remember seeing it before. The people escaping from the burning cities had committed some sin or other nobody ever thought, let alone talked, about. As they hurried between rocks, through what must have been the 'desert places', their faces looked long and wooden. All they had recently experienced could have shocked the expression out of them. She was fascinated by what made her shiver. And the couples with their arms still around one another. Well, if you were damned, better hang on to your sin. She didn't blame them.

She put the box away. Its inlay as well as its contents made it something secret and precious.

The autumn was still and golden, the winter vicious only in fits. It was what you could call a good winter. The cold floods of air and more concentrated streams of dark-green light poured along the shady side of the house where her cinerarias had massed. She had never seen such cinerarias: some of the spired ones reached almost as high as her chin, the solid heads of others waited in the tunnel of dark light to club you with their colours, of purple and drenching blue, and what they called 'wine'. She couldn't believe wine would have made her drunker.

Just as she would sit every evening watching the traffic, evening was the time she liked best to visit the cinerarias, when the icy cold seemed to make the flowers burn their deepest, purest. So it was again evening when her two objects converged: for some blissfully confident reason she hadn't bothered to ask herself whether she had seen the car pass, till here was this figure coming towards her along the tunnel. She knew at once who it was, although she had never seen him on his feet; she had never seen him full-face, but knew from the funny shape of his head as Royal had been the first to notice. He was not at all an impressive man, not much taller than herself, but broad. His footsteps on the brickwork sounded purposeful.

'Will you let me use your phone, please, madam?' he asked in a prepared voice. 'I'm having trouble with the Holden.'

This was the situation she had always been expecting: somebody asking to use the phone as a way to afterwards murdering you. Now that it might be about to happen she couldn't care.

She said yes. She thought her voice sounded muzzy. Perhaps he would think she was drunk.

She went on looking at him, at his eyes. His nose, like the shape of his head, wasn't up to much, but his eyes, his eyes, she dared to think, were filled with kindness.

'Cold, eh? but clean cold!' He laughed friendly, shuffling on the brick paving because she was keeping him waiting.

Only then she noticed his mouth. He had a harelip, there was no mistaking, although it was well sewn. She felt so calm in the circumstances. She would have even liked to touch it.

But said, 'Why, yes – the telephone,' she said, 'it's this way,' she said, 'it's just off the kitchen – because that's where you spend most of your life. Or in bed,' she ended.

She wished she hadn't added that. For the first time since they had been together she felt upset, thinking he might suspect her of wrong intentions.

But he laughed and said, 'That's correct! You got something there!' It sounded manly rather than educated.

She realized he was still waiting, and took him to the telephone.

While he was phoning she didn't listen. She never listened when other people were talking on the phone. The sight of her own kitchen surprised her. While his familiar voice went on. It was the voice she had held conversations with.

But he was ugly, real ugly, *deformed*. If it wasn't for the voice, the eyes. She couldn't remember the eyes, but seemed to know about them.

Then she heard him laying the coins beside the phone, extra loud, to show.

He came back into the kitchen smiling and looking. She could smell him now, and he had the smell of a clean man.

She became embarrassed at herself, and took him quickly out.

'Fair bit of garden you got.' He stood with his calves curved through his trousers. A cocky little chap, but nice.

'Oh,' she said, 'this', she said, angrily almost, 'is nothing. You oughter see it. There's sunflower and hollyhock all along the palings. I'm famous for me hollyhocks!' She had never boasted in her life. 'But not now – it isn't the season. And I let it go. Mr Natwick passed on. You should'uv seen the cassia this autumn. Now it's only sticks, of course. And hibiscus. There's cream, gold, cerise, scarlet – double and single.'

She was dressing in them for him, revolving on high heels and changing frilly skirts.

He said, 'Gardening's not in my line,' turning his head to hide something, perhaps he was ashamed of his harelip.

'No,' she agreed. 'Not everybody's a gardener.'

'But like a garden.'

'My husband didn't even like it. He didn't have to tell me,' she added.

As they moved across the wintry grass, past the empty clothesline, the man looked at his watch, and said, 'I was reckoning on visiting somebody in hospital tonight. Looks like I shan't make it if the N.R.M.A. takes as long as usual.'

'Do they?' she said, clearing her throat. 'It isn't somebody close, I hope? The sick person?'

Yes he said they was close.

'Nothing serious?' she almost bellowed.

He said it was serious.

Oh she nearly burst out laughing at the bandaged figure they were sitting beside particularly at the bandaged face. She would have laughed at a brain tumour.

'I'm sorry,' she said. 'I understand. Mr Natwick was for many years an invalid.'

Those teeth in the tumbler on top of the medicine cabinet. Looking at her. Teeth can look, worse than eyes. But she couldn't help it, she meant everything she said, and thought.

At this moment they were pressing inside the dark-green tunnel, her sleeve rubbing his, as the crimson-to-purple light was dying.

'These are the cinerarias,' she said.

'The what?' He didn't know, any more than Royal.

As she was about to explain she got switched to another language. Her throat became a long palpitating funnel through which the words she expected to use were poured out in a stream of almost formless agonized sound.

'What is it?' he asked, touching her.

If it had happened to herself she would have felt frightened, it occurred to her, but he didn't seem to be.

'What is it?' he kept repeating in his familiar voice, touching, even holding her.

And for answer, in the new language, she was holding him. They were holding each other, his hard body against her eiderdowny one. As the silence closed round them again, inside the tunnel of light, his face, to which she was very close, seemed to be unlocking, the wound of his mouth, which should have been more horrible, struggling to open. She could see he had recognized her.

She kissed above his mouth. She kissed as though she might never succeed in healing all the wounds they had ever suffered.

How long they stood together she wasn't interested in knowing. Outside them the river of traffic continued to flow between its brick and concrete banks. Even if it overflowed it couldn't have drowned them.

When the man said in his gentlest voice, 'Better go out in front. The N.R.M.A. might have come.'

'Yes,' she agreed. 'The N.R.M.A.'

So they shuffled, still holding each other, along the narrow path. She imagined how long and wooden their faces must look. She wouldn't look at him now, though, just as she wouldn't look back at the still faintly smouldering joys they had experienced together in the past.

When they came out, apart, and into the night, there was the N.R.M.A., his pointed ruby of a light burning on top of the cabin.

'When will you come?' she asked.

'Tomorrow.'

'Tomorrow. You'll stay to tea.'

He couldn't stay.

'I'll make you a *pot* of tea?'

But he didn't drink it.

'Coffee, then?'

He said, 'I like a nice cup of coffee.'

Going down the path he didn't look back, or opening the gate. She would not let herself think of reasons or possibilities, she would not think, but stood planted in the path, swayed slightly by the motion of the night.

Mrs Dolan said, 'You bring the saucepan to the boil. You got that?'

'Yeeehs.' Mrs Natwick had never been a dab at coffee.

'Then you throw in some cold water. That's what sends the gravel to the bottom.' This morning Mrs Dolan had to laugh at her own jokes.

'That's the part that frightens me,' Mrs Natwick admitted.

'Well, you just do it, and see,' said Mrs Dolan; she was too busy.

After she had bought the coffee Mrs Natwick stayed in the city to muck around. If she had stayed at home her nerves might have wound themselves tighter, waiting for evening to come. Though mucking around only irritated in the end. She had never been an idle woman. So she stopped at the cosmetics as though she didn't have to decide, this was her purpose, and said to the young lady lounging behind one of the counters, 'I'm thinking of investing in a lipstick, dear. Can you please advise me?'

As a concession to the girl she tried to make it a laughing matter, but the young person was bored, she didn't bat a silver eyelid. 'Elderly ladies,' she said, 'go for the brighter stuff.'

Mrs Natwick ('my little Ella') had never felt so meek. Mum must be turning in her grave.

'This is a favourite.' With a flick of her long fingers the girl exposed the weapon. It looked too slippery-pointed, crimson-purple, out of its golden sheath.

Mrs Natwick's knees were shaking. 'Isn't it a bit noticeable?' she asked, again trying to make it a joke.

But the white-haired girl gave a serious laugh. 'What's wrong with noticeable?'

As Mrs Natwick tried it out on the back of her hand the way she had seen others do, the girl was jogging from foot to foot behind the counter. She was humming between her teeth, behind her white-smeared lips, probably thinking about a lover. Mrs Natwick blushed. What if she couldn't learn to get the tip of her lipstick back inside its sheath?

She might have gone quickly away without another word if the young lady hadn't been so professional and bored. Still humming, she brought out a little pack of rouge.

'Never saw myself with mauve cheeks!' It was at least dry, and easy to handle.

'It's what they wear.'

Mrs Natwick didn't dare refuse. She watched the long fingers with their silver nails doing up the parcel. The fingers looked as though they might resent touching anything but cosmetics; a lover was probably beneath contempt.

The girl gave her the change, and she went away without counting it.

She wasn't quiet, though, not a bit, booming and clanging in front of the toilet mirror. She tried to make a thin line, but her mouth exploded into a purple flower. She dabbed the dry-feeling pad on either cheek, and thick, mauve-scented shadows fell. She could hear and feel her heart behaving like a squeezed, rubber ball as she stood looking. Then she got at the lipstick again, still unsheathed. Her mouth was becoming enormous, so thick with grease she could hardly close her own lips underneath. A visible dew was gathering round the purple shadows on her cheeks.

She began to retch like, but dry, and rub, over the basin, scrubbing with the nailbrush. More than likely some would stay behind in the pores and be seen. Though you didn't have to see, to see.

There were Royal's teeth in the tumbler on top of the medicine cabinet. Ought to hide the teeth. What if somebody wanted to use the toilet? She must move the teeth. But didn't. In the present circumstances she couldn't have raised her arms that high.

Around five she made the coffee, throwing in the cold water at the end with a gesture copied from Mrs Dolan. If the gravel hadn't sunk to the bottom he wouldn't notice the first time, provided the coffee was hot. She could warm up the made coffee in a jiffy.

As she sat on the veranda waiting, the cane chair shifted and squealed under her. If it hadn't been for her weight it might have run away across the tiles, like one of those old planchette boards, writing the answers to questions.

There was an accident this evening down at the intersection. A head-on collision. Bodies were carried out of the crumpled cars, and she remembered a past occasion when she had run with blankets, and Hazel's Onkaparinka, and a pillow from their own bed. She had been so grateful to the victim. She could not give him enough, or receive enough of the warm blood. She had come back, she remembered, sprinkled.

This evening she had to save herself up. Kept on looking at her watch. The old cane chair squealing, ready to write the answers if she let it. Was he hurt? Was he killed, then? Was he – what?

Mrs Dolan it was, sticking her head over the palings. 'Don't like the accidents, Mrs Natwick. It's the blood. The blood turns me up.'

Mrs Natwick averted her face. Though unmoved by present blood. If only the squealing chair would stop trying to buck her off.

'Did your friend enjoy the coffee?' Mrs Dolan shouted; nothing nasty in her: Mrs Dolan was sincere.

'Hasn't been yet,' Mrs Natwick mumbled from glancing at her watch. 'Got held up.'

'It's the traffic. The traffic at this time of evenun.'

'Always on the dot before.'

'Working back. Or made a mistake over the day.'

Could you make a mistake? Mrs Natwick contemplated. Tomorrow had always meant tomorrow.

'Or he could'uv,' Mrs Dolan shouted, but didn't say it. 'I better go inside,' she said instead. 'They'll be wonderun where I am.'

Down at the intersection the bodies were lying wrapped in someone else's blankets, looking like the grey parcels of mice cats sometimes vomit up.

It was long past five-twenty, not all that long really, but drawing in. The sky was heaped with cold fire. Her city was burning.

She got up finally, and the chair escaped with a last squeal, writing its answer on the tiles.

No, it wasn't lust, not if the Royal God Almighty with bared teeth should strike her down. Or yes, though, it was. She was lusting after the expression of eyes she could hardly remember for seeing so briefly.

In the effort to see, she drove her memory wildly, while her body stumbled around and around the paths of the burning city there was now no point in escaping. You would shrivel up in time along with the polyanthers and out-of-season hibiscus. All the randy mouths would be stopped sooner or later with black.

The cinerarias seemed to have grown so luxuriant she had to force her way past them, down the narrow brick path. When she heard the latch click, and saw him coming towards her.

'Why,' she screamed laughing though it sounded angry, she *was*, 'I'd given you up, you know! It's long after five-twenty!'

As she pushed fiercely towards him, past the cinerarias, snapping one or two of those which were most heavily loaded, she realized he couldn't have known that she set her watch, her life, by his constant behaviour. He wouldn't have dawdled so.

'What is it?' she called at last, in exasperation at the distance which continued separating them.

He was far too slow, treading the slippery moss of her too shaded path. While she floundered on. She couldn't reach the expression of his eyes.

He said, and she could hardly recognize the faded voice, 'There's something – I been feeling off colour most of the day.' His mis-shapen head was certainly lolling as he advanced.

'Tell me!' She heard her voice commanding, like that of a man, or a mother, when she had practised to be a lover; she could still smell the smell of rouge. 'Won't you tell me – *dearest?*' It was thin and unconvincing now. (As a girl she had once got a letter from her cousin Kath Salter, who she hardly knew: *Dearest Ella . . .*)

Oh dear. She had reached him. And was given all strength – that of the lover she had aimed at being.

Straddling the path, unequally matched – he couldn't compete against her strength – she spoke with an acquired, a deafening soft-ness, as the inclining cinerarias snapped.

'You will tell me what is wrong – dear, dear.' She breathed with trumpets.

He hung his head. 'It's all right. It's the pain – here – in my arm – no, the shoulder.'

'Ohhhhh!' She ground her face into his shoulder forgetting it wasn't *her* pain.

Then she remembered, and looked into his eyes and said, 'We'll save you. You'll see.'

It was she who needed saving. She knew she was trying to enter by his eyes. To drown in them rather than be left.

Because, in spite of her will to hold him, he was slipping from her, down amongst the cinerarias, which were snapping off one by one around them.

A cat shot out. At one time she had been so poor in spirit she had wished she was a cat.

'It's all right,' either voice was saying.

Lying amongst the smashed plants, he was smiling at her dreadfully, not his mouth, she no longer bothered about that lip, but with his eyes.

'More air!' she cried. 'What you need is air!' hacking at one or two cinerarias which remained erect.

Their sap was stifling, their bristling columns callous.

'Oh! Oh!' she panted. 'Oh God! Dear love!' comforting with hands and hair and words.

Words.

While all he could say was, 'It's all right.'

Or not that at last. He folded his lips into a white seam. His eyes were swimming out of reach.

'Eh? Dear – dearest – darl – darlig – darling love – *love* – LOVE?' All the new words still stiff in her mouth, that she had heard so far only from the mouths of actors.

The words were too strong she could see. She was losing him. The traffic was hanging together only by charred silences.

She flung herself and covered his body, trying to force kisses – no, breath, into his mouth, she had heard about it.

She had seen turkeys, feathers sawing against each other's feathers, rising afterwards like new noisy silk.

She knelt up, and the wing-tips of her hair still dabbled limply in his cheeks. 'Eh? Ohh luff!' She could hardly breathe it.

She hadn't had time to ask his name, before she must have killed him by loving too deep, and too adulterously.

JOHN CHEEVER · 1912–

Goodbye, My Brother

We are a family that has always been very close in spirit. Our father was drowned in a sailing accident when we were young, and our mother has always stressed the fact that our familial relationships have a kind of permanence that we will never meet with again. I don't think about the family much, but when I remember its members and the coast where they lived and the sea salt that I think is in our blood, I am happy to recall that I am a Pommeroy – that I have the nose, the coloring, and the promise of longevity – and that while we are not a distinguished family, we enjoy the illusion, when we are together, that the Pommeroys are unique. I don't say any of this because I'm interested in family history or because this sense of uniqueness is deep or important to me but in order to advance the point that we are loyal to one another in spite of our differences, and that any rupture in this loyalty is a source of confusion and pain.

We are four children; there is my sister Diana and the three men – Chaddy, Lawrence, and myself. Like most families in which the children are out of their twenties, we have been separated by business, marriage, and war. Helen and I live on Long Island now, with our four children. I teach in a secondary school, and I am past the age where I expect to be made headmaster – or principal, as we say – but I respect the work. Chaddy, who has done better than the rest of us, lives in Manhattan, with Odette and their children. Mother lives in Philadelphia, and Diana, since her divorce, has been living in France, but she comes back to the States in the summer to spend a month at Laud's Head. Laud's Head is a summer place on the shore of one of the Massachusetts islands. We used to have a cottage there, and in the Twenties our father built the big house. It stands on a cliff above the sea and, excepting St Tropez and some of the Apennine villages, it is my favorite place in the world. We each have an equity in the place and we contribute some money to help keep it going.

Our youngest brother, Lawrence, who is a lawyer, got a job with a Cleveland firm after the war, and none of us saw him for four years. When he decided to leave Cleveland and go to work for a firm in Albany, he wrote Mother that he would, between jobs, spend ten days at Laud's Head, with his wife and their two children. This was when I had planned to take my vacation – I had been teaching summer school – and Helen and Chaddy and Odette and Diana were all going to be there, so the family would be together. Lawrence is the member of the family with whom the rest of us have least in common. We have never seen a great deal of him, and I suppose that's why we still call him Tifty – a nickname he was given when he was a child, because when he came down the hall toward the dining-room for breakfast, his slippers made a noise that sounded like 'Tifty, tifty, tifty.' That's what Father called him, and so did everyone else. When he grew older, Diana sometimes used to call him Little Jesus, and Mother often called him the Croaker. We had disliked Lawrence, but we looked forward to his return with a mixture of apprehension and loyalty, and with some of the joy and delight of reclaiming a brother.

Lawrence crossed over from the mainland on the four o'clock boat one afternoon late in the summer, and Chaddy and I went down to meet him. The arrivals and departures of the summer ferry have all the outward signs that suggest a voyage – whistles, bells, hand trucks, reunions, and the smell of brine – but it is a voyage of no import, and when I watched the boat come into the blue harbor that afternoon and thought that it was completing a voyage of no import, I realized that I had hit on exactly the kind of observation that Lawrence would have made. We looked for his face behind the windshields as the cars drove off the boat, and we had no trouble in recognizing him. And we ran over and shook his hand and clumsily kissed his wife and the children. 'Tifty!' Chaddy shouted. 'Tifty!' It is difficult to judge changes in the appearance of a brother, but both Chaddy and I agreed, as we drove back to Laud's Head, that Lawrence still looked very young. He got to the house first, and we took the suitcases out of his car. When I came in, he was standing in the living room, talking with Mother and Diana. They were in their best clothes and all their jewelry, and they were welcoming him extravagantly, but even then, when everyone was endeavoring to seem most affectionate and at a time when these endeavors come easiest, I was aware of a faint tension in the room. Thinking about this as I carried Lawrence's heavy suitcases up the stairs, I realized that our dislikes are as deeply ingrained as our better passions, and I remembered that once, twenty-five years ago, when I had hit Lawrence on the head with a rock, he had picked himself up and gone directly to our father to complain.

I carried the suitcases up to the third floor, where Ruth, Lawrence's wife, had begun to settle her family. She is a thin girl, and she seemed very tired from the journey, but when I asked her if she didn't want me to bring a drink upstairs to her, she said she didn't think she did.

When I got downstairs, Lawrence wasn't around, but the others were all ready for cocktails, and we decided to go ahead. Lawrence is the only member of the family who has never enjoyed drinking. We took our cocktails onto the terrace, so that we could see the bluffs and the sea and the islands in the east, and the return of Lawrence and his wife, their presence in the house, seemed to refresh our responses to the familiar view; it was as if the pleasure they would take in the sweep and the color of that coast, after such a long absence, had been imparted to us. While we were there, Lawrence came up the path from the beach.

'Isn't the beach fabulous, Tifty?' Mother asked. 'Isn't it fabulous to be back? Will you have a Martini?'

'I don't care,' Lawrence said. 'Whiskey, gin – I don't care what I drink. Give me a little rum.'

'We don't have any *rum*,' Mother said. It was the first note of asperity. She had taught us never to be indecisive, never to reply as Lawrence had. Beyond this, she is deeply concerned with the propriety of her house, and anything irregular by her standards, like drinking straight rum or bringing a beer can to the dinner table, excites in her a conflict that she cannot, even with her capacious sense of humor, surmount. She sensed the asperity and worked to repair it. 'Would you like some Irish, Tifty dear?' she said. 'Isn't Irish what you've always liked? There's some Irish on the sideboard. Why don't you get yourself some Irish?' Lawrence said that he didn't care. He poured himself a Martini, and then Ruth came down and we went in to dinner.

In spite of the fact that we had, through waiting for Lawrence, drunk too much before dinner, we were all anxious to put our best foot forward and to enjoy a peaceful time. Mother is a small woman whose face is still a striking reminder of how pretty she must have been, and whose conversation is unusually light, but she talked that evening about a soil-reclamation project that is going on up-island. Diana is as pretty as Mother must have been; she is an animated and lovely woman who likes to talk about the dissolute friends that she has made in France, but she talked that night about the school in Switzerland where she had left her two children. I could see that the dinner had been planned to please Lawrence. It was not too rich, and there was nothing to make him worry about extravagance.

After supper, when we went back onto the terrace, the clouds held that kind of light that looks like blood, and I was glad that Lawrence had such a lurid sunset for his homecoming. When we had been out there a few minutes, a man named Edward Chester came to get Diana. She had met him in France, or on the boat home, and he was staying for ten days at the inn in the village. He was introduced to Lawrence and Ruth, and then he and Diana left.

'Is that the one she's sleeping with now?' Lawrence asked.

'What a horrid thing to say!' Helen said.

'You ought to apologize for that, Tifty,' Chaddy said.

'I don't know,' Mother said tiredly. 'I don't know, Tifty. Diana is in a position to do whatever she wants, and I don't ask sordid questions. She's my only daughter. I don't see her often.'

'Is she going back to France?'

'She's going back the week after next.'

Lawrence and Ruth were sitting at the edge of the terrace, not in the chairs, not in the circle of chairs. With his mouth set, my brother looked to me then like a Puritan cleric. Sometimes, when I try to understand his frame of mind, I think of the beginnings of our family in this country, and his disapproval of Diana and her lover reminded me of this. The branch of the Pommeroys to which we belong was founded by a minister who was eulogized by Cotton Mather for his untiring abjuration of the Devil. The Pommeroys were ministers until the middle of the nineteenth century, and the harshness of their thought – man is full of misery, and all earthly beauty is lustful and corrupt – has been preserved in books and sermons. The temper of our family changed somewhat and became more lighthearted, but when I was of school age, I can remember a cousinage of old men and women who seemed to hark back to the dark days of the ministry and to be animated by perpetual guilt and the deification of the scourge. If you are raised in this atmosphere – and in a sense we were – I think it is a trial of the spirit to reject its habits of guilt, self-denial, taciturnity, and penitence, and it seemed to me to have been a trial of the spirit in which Lawrence had succumbed.

'Is that Cassiopeia?' Odette asked.

'No, dear,' Chaddy said. 'That isn't Cassiopeia.'

'Who was Cassiopeia?' Odette said.

'She was the wife of Cepheus and the mother of Andromeda,' I said.

'The cook is a Giants fan,' Chaddy said. 'She'll give you even money that they win the pennant.'

It had grown so dark that we could see the passage of light through the sky from the lighthouse at Cape Heron. In the dark below the cliff, the continual detonations of the surf sounded. And then, as she often does when it is getting dark and she has drunk too much before dinner, Mother began to talk about the improvements and additions that would someday be made on the house, the wings and bathrooms and gardens.

'This house will be in the sea in five years,' Lawrence said.

'Tifty the Croaker,' Chaddy said.

'Don't call me Tifty,' Lawrence said.

'Little Jesus,' Chaddy said.

'The sea wall is badly cracked,' Lawrence said. 'I looked at it this afternoon. You had it repaired four years ago, and it cost eight thousand dollars. You can't do that every four years.'

'Please, Tifty,' Mother said.

'Facts are facts,' Lawrence said, 'and it's a damned-fool idea to build a house at the edge of the cliff on a sinking coastline. In my lifetime, half the garden has washed away and there's four feet of water where we used to have a bathhouse.'

'Let's have a very *general* conversation,' Mother said bitterly. 'Let's talk about politics or the boat-club dance.'

'As a matter of fact,' Lawrence said, 'the house is probably in some danger now. If you had an unusually high sea, a hurricane sea, the wall would crumble and the house would go. We could all be drowned.'

'I can't *bear* it,' Mother said. She went into the pantry and came back with a full glass of gin.

I have grown too old now to think that I can judge the sentiments

of others, but I was conscious of the tension between Lawrence and
Mother, and I knew some of the history of it. Lawrence couldn't
have been more than sixteen years old when he decided that
Mother was frivolous, mischievous, destructive, and overly strong.
When he had determined this, he decided to separate himself from
her. He was at boarding school then, and I remember that he did
not come home for Christmas. He spent Christmas with a friend.
He came home very seldom after he had made his unfavorable
judgment on Mother, and when he did come home, he always tried,
in his conversation, to remind her of his estrangement. When he
married Ruth, he did not tell Mother. He did not tell her when his
children were born. But in spite of these principled and lengthy
exertions he seemed, unlike the rest of us, never to have enjoyed
any separation, and when they are together, you feel at once a tension, an unclearness.

And it was unfortunate, in a way, that Mother should have
picked that night to get drunk. It's her privilege, and she doesn't
get drunk often, and fortunately she wasn't bellicose, but we were
all conscious of what was happening. As she quietly drank her gin,
she seemed sadly to be parting from us; she seemed to be in the
throes of travel. Then her mood changed from travel to injury, and
the few remarks she made were petulant and irrelevant. When her
glass was nearly empty, she stared angrily at the dark air in front
of her nose, moving her head a little, like a fighter. I knew that
there was not room in her mind then for all the injuries that were
crowding into it. Her children were stupid, her husband was
drowned, her servants were thieves, and the chair she sat in was
uncomfortable. Suddenly she put down her empty glass and interrupted Chaddy, who was talking about baseball. 'I know one
thing,' she said hoarsely. 'I know that if there is an afterlife, I'm
going to have a very different kind of family. I'm going to have
nothing but fabulously rich, witty, and enchanting children.' She
got up and, starting for the door, nearly fell. Chaddy caught her
and helped her up the stairs. I could hear their tender good-nights,
and then Chaddy came back. I thought that Lawrence by now
would be tired from his journey and his return, but he remained on
the terrace, as if he were waiting to see the final malfeasance, and
the rest of us left him there and went swimming in the dark.

When I woke the next morning, or half woke, I could hear the sound of someone rolling the tennis court. It is a fainter and a deeper sound than the iron buoy bells off the point – an unrhythmic iron chiming – that belongs in my mind to the beginnings of a summer day, a good portent. When I went downstairs, Lawrence's two kids were in the living room, dressed in ornate cowboy suits. They are frightened and skinny children. They told me their father was rolling the tennis court but that they did not want to go out because they had seen a snake under the doorstep. I explained to them that their cousins – all the other children – ate breakfast in the kitchen and that they'd better run along in there. At this announcement, the boy began to cry. Then his sister joined him. They cried as if to go in the kitchen and eat would destroy their most precious rights. I told them to sit down with me. Lawrence came in, and I asked him if he wanted to play some tennis. He said no, thanks, although he thought he might play some singles with Chaddy. He was in the right here, because both he and Chaddy play better tennis than I, and he did play some singles with Chaddy after breakfast, but later on, when the others came down to play family doubles, Lawrence disappeared. This made me cross – unreasonably so, I suppose – but we play darned interesting family doubles and he could have played in a set for the sake of courtesy.

Late in the morning, when I came up from the court alone, I saw Tifty on the terrace, prying up a shingle from the wall with his jackknife. 'What's the matter, Lawrence?' I said. 'Termites?' There are termites in the wood and they've given us a lot of trouble.

He pointed out to me, at the base of each row of shingles, a faint blue line of carpenter's chalk. 'This house is about twenty-two years old,' he said. 'These shingles are about two hundred years old. Dad must have bought shingles from all the farms around here when he built the place, to make it look venerable. You can still see the carpenter's chalk put down where these antiques were nailed into place.'

It was true about the shingles, although I had forgotten it. When the house was built, our father, or his architect, had ordered it covered with lichened and weather-beaten shingles. I didn't follow Lawrence's reason for thinking that this was scandalous.

'And look at these doors,' Lawrence said. 'Look at these doors and window frames.' I followed him over to a big Dutch door that opens onto the terrace and looked at it. It was a relatively new door, but someone had worked hard to conceal its newness. The surface had been deeply scored with some metal implement, and white paint had been rubbed into the incisions to imitate brine, lichen, and weather rot. 'Imagine spending thousands of dollars to make a sound house look like a wreck,' Lawrence said. 'Imagine the frame of mind this implies. Imagine wanting to live so much in the past that you'll pay men carpenters' wages to disfigure your front door.' Then I remembered Lawrence's sensitivity to time and his sentiments and opinions about our feelings for the past. I had heard him say, years ago, that we and our friends and our part of the nation, finding ourselves unable to cope with the problems of the present, had, like a wretched adult, turned back to what we supposed was a happier and a simpler time, and that our taste for reconstruction and candlelight was a measure of this irremediable failure. The faint blue line of chalk had reminded him of these ideas, the scarified door had reinforced them, and now clue after clue presented itself to him – the stern light at the door, the bulk of the chimney, the width of the floorboards and the pieces set into them to resemble pegs. While Lawrence was lecturing me on these frailties, the others came up from the court. As soon as Mother saw Lawrence, she responded, and I saw that there was little hope of any rapport between the matriarch and the changeling. She took Chaddy's arm. 'Let's go swimming and have Martinis on the beach,' she said. 'Let's have a *fabulous* morning.'

The sea that morning was a solid color, like verd stone. Everyone went to the beach but Tifty and Ruth. 'I don't mind *him*,' Mother said. She was excited, and she tipped her glass and spilled some gin into the sand. 'I don't mind *him*. It doesn't matter to me how *rude* and *horrid* and *gloomy* he is, but what I can't bear are the faces of his wretched little children, those fabulously unhappy little children.' With the height of the cliff between us, everyone talked wrathfully about Lawrence; about how he had grown worse instead of better, how unlike the rest of us he was, how he endeavored to spoil every pleasure. We drank our gin; the abuse seemed to reach a crescendo, and then, one by one, we went swimming in the solid green water. But when we came out no one mentioned Lawrence unkindly; the line of abusive conversation had been cut, as if swimming had the cleansing force claimed for baptism. We dried our hands and lighted cigarettes, and if Lawrence was mentioned, it was only to suggest, kindly, something that might please him. Wouldn't he like to sail to Barin's cove, or go fishing?

And now I remember that while Lawrence was visiting us, we went swimming oftener than we usually do, and I think there was a reason for this. When the irritability that accumulated as a result of his company began to lessen our patience, not only with Lawrence but with one another, we would all go swimming and shed our animus in the cold water. I can see the family now, smarting from Lawrence's rebukes as they sat on the sand, and I can see them wading and diving and surface-diving and hear in their voices the restoration of patience and the rediscovery of inexhaustible good will. If Lawrence noticed this change – this illusion of purification – I suppose that he would have found in the vocabulary of psychiatry, or the mythology of the Atlantic, some circumspect name for it, but I don't think he noticed the change. He neglected to name the curative powers of the open sea, but it was one of the few chances for diminution that he missed.

The cook we had that year was a Polish woman named Anna Ostrovick, a summer cook. She was first-rate – a big, fat, hearty, industrious woman who took her work seriously. She liked to cook and to have the food she cooked appreciated and eaten, and whenever we saw her, she always urged us to eat. She cooked hot bread – crescents and brioches – for breakfast two or three times a week, and she would bring these into the dining-room herself and say, 'Eat, eat, eat!' When the maid took the serving dishes back into the pantry, we could sometimes hear Anna, who was standing there, say, 'Good! They eat.' She fed the garbage man, the milkman, and the gardener. 'Eat!' she told them. 'Eat, eat!' On Thursday afternoons, she went to the movies with the maid, but she didn't enjoy the movies, because the actors were all so thin. She would sit in the dark theatre for an hour and a half watching the screen anxiously for the appearance of someone who had enjoyed his food. Bette Davis merely left with Anna the impression of a woman who has not eaten well. 'They are all so skinny,' she would say when she left the movies. In the evenings, after she had gorged all of us, and washed the pots and pans, she would collect the table scraps and go out to feed the creation. We had a few chickens that year, and although they would have roosted by then, she would dump food into their troughs and urge the sleeping fowl to eat. She fed the songbirds in the orchard and the chipmunks in the yard. Her appearance at the edge of the garden and her urgent voice – we could hear her calling 'Eat, eat, eat' – had become, like the sunset gun at the boat club and the passage of light from Cape Heron, attached to that hour. 'Eat, eat, eat,' we could hear Anna say. 'Eat, eat . . . ' Then it would be dark.

When Lawrence had been there three days, Anna called me into the kitchen. 'You tell your mother,' she said, 'that *he* doesn't come into my kitchen. If *he* comes into my kitchen all the time, I go. *He* is always coming into my kitchen to tell me what a sad woman I am. He is always telling me that I work too hard and that I don't get paid enough and that I should belong to a union with vacations. Ha! He is so skinny but he is always coming into my kitchen when I am busy to pity me, but I am as good as him, I am as good as *anybody*, and I do not have to have people like that getting into my way all the time and feeling sorry for me. I am a famous and a wonderful cook and I have jobs everywhere and the only reason I come here to work this summer is because I was never before on an island, but I can have other jobs tomorrow, and if he is always coming into my kitchen to pity me, you tell your mother I am going. I am as good as *anybody* and I do not have to have that skinny all the time telling how poor I am.'

I was pleased to find that the cook was on our side, but I felt that the situation was delicate. If Mother asked Lawrence to stay out of the kitchen, he would make a grievance out of the request. He could make a grievance out of anything, and it sometimes seemed that as he sat darkly at the dinner table, every word of disparagement, wherever it was aimed, came home to him. I didn't mention the cook's complaint to anyone, but somehow there wasn't any more trouble from that quarter.

The next cause for contention that I had from Lawrence came over our backgammon games.

When we are at Laud's Head, we play a lot of backgammon. At eight o'clock, after we have drunk our coffee, we usually get out the board. In a way, it is one of our pleasantest hours. The lamps in the room are still unlighted, Anna can be seen in the dark garden, and in the sky above her head there are continents of shadow and fire. Mother turns on the light and rattles the dice as a signal. We usually play three games apiece, each with the others. We play for money, and you can win or lose a hundred dollars on a game, but the stakes are usually much lower. I think that Lawrence used to play – I can't remember – but he doesn't play any more. He doesn't gamble. This is not because he is poor or because he has any principles about gambling but because he thinks the game is foolish and a waste of time. He was ready enough, however, to waste his time watching the rest of us play. Night after night, when the game began, he pulled a chair up beside the board, and watched the checkers and the dice. His expression was scornful, and yet he watched carefully. I wondered why he watched us night after night, and, through watching his face, I think that I may have found out.

Lawrence doesn't gamble, so he can't understand the excitement of winning and losing money. He has forgotten how to play the game, I think, so that its complex odds can't interest him. His observations were bound to include the facts that backgammon is an idle game and a game of chance, and that the board, marked with points, was a symbol of our worthlessness. And since he doesn't understand gambling or the odds of the game, I thought that what interested him must be the members of his family. One night when I was playing with Odette – I had won thirty-seven dollars from Mother and Chaddy – I think I saw what was going on in his mind.

Odette has black hair and black eyes. She is careful never to expose her white skin to the sun for long, so the striking contrast of blackness and pallor is not changed in the summer. She needs and deserves admiration – it is the element that contents her – and she will flirt, unseriously, with any man. Her shoulders were bare that night, her dress was cut to show the division of her breasts and to show her breasts when she leaned over the board to play. She kept losing and flirting and making her losses seem like a part of the flirtation. Chaddy was in the other room. She lost three games, and when the third game ended, she fell back on the sofa and, looking at me squarely, said something about going out on the dunes to settle the score. Lawrence heard her. I looked at Lawrence. He seemed shocked and gratified at the same time, as if he had suspected all along that we were not playing for anything so insubstantial as money. I may be wrong, of course, but I think that Lawrence felt that in watching our backgammon he was observing the progress of a mordant tragedy in which the money we won and lost served as a symbol for more vital forfeits. It is like Lawrence to try to read significance and finality into every gesture that we make, and it is certain of Lawrence that when he finds the inner logic to our conduct, it will be sordid.

Chaddy came in to play with me. Chaddy and I have never liked to lose to each other. When we were younger, we used to be forbid-

den to play games together, because they always ended in a fight.
We think we know each other's mettle intimately. I think he is prudent; he thinks I am foolish. There is always bad blood when we
play anything – tennis or backgammon or softball or bridge – and
it does seem at times as if we were playing for the possession of
each other's liberties. When I lose to Chaddy, I can't sleep. All this
is only half the truth of our competitive relationship, but it was the
half-truth that would be discernible to Lawrence, and his presence
at the table made me so self-conscious that I lost two games. I tried
not to seem angry when I got up from the board. Lawrence was
watching me. I went out onto the terrace to suffer there in the dark
the anger I always feel when I lose to Chaddy.

When I came back into the room, Chaddy and Mother were
playing. Lawrence was still watching. By his lights, Odette had lost
her virtue to me, I had lost my self-esteem to Chaddy, and now I
wondered what he saw in the present match. He watched raptly, as
if the opaque checkers and the marked board served for an exchange of critical power. How dramatic the board, in its ring of
light, and the quiet players and the crash of the sea outside must
have seemed to him! Here was spiritual cannibalism made visible;
here, under his nose, were the symbols of the rapacious use human
beings make of one another.

Mother plays a shrewd, an ardent, and an interfering game. She
always has her hands in her opponent's board. When she plays with
Chaddy, who is her favorite, she plays intently. Lawrence would
have noticed this. Mother is a sentimental woman. Her heart is
good and easily moved by tears and frailty, a characteristic that,
like her handsome nose, has not been changed at all by age. Grief
in another provokes her deeply, and she seems at times to be trying
to divine in Chaddy some grief, some loss, that she can succor and
redress, and so re-establish the relationship that she enjoyed with
him when he was sickly and young. She loves defending the weak
and the childlike, and now that we are old, she misses it. The world
of debts and business, men and war, hunting and fishing has on her
an exacerbating effect. (When Father drowned, she threw away his
fly rods and his guns.) She has lectured us all endlessly on self-
reliance but when we come back to her for comfort and for help –
particularly Chaddy – she seems to feel most like herself. I suppose
Lawrence thought that the old woman and her son were playing
for each other's soul.

She lost. 'Oh *dear*,' she said. She looked stricken and bereaved, as she always does when she loses. 'Get me my glasses, get me my check-book, get me something to drink.' Lawrence got up at last and stretched his legs. He looked at us all bleakly. The wind and the sea had risen, and I thought that if he heard the waves, he must hear them only as a dark answer to all his dark questions; that he would think that the tide had expunged the embers of our picnic fires. The company of a lie is unbearable, and he seemed like the embodiment of a lie. I couldn't explain to him the simple and intense pleasures of playing for money, and it seemed to me hideously wrong that he should have sat at the edge of the board and concluded that we were playing for one another's soul. He walked restlessly around the room two or three times and then, as usual, gave us a parting shot. 'I should think you'd go crazy,' he said, 'cooped up with one another like this, night after night. Come on, Ruth. I'm going to bed.'

That night, I dreamed about Lawrence. I saw his plain face magnified into ugliness, and when I woke in the morning, I felt sick, as if I had suffered a great spiritual loss while I slept, like the loss of courage and heart. It was foolish to let myself be troubled by my brother. I needed a vacation. I needed to relax. At school, we live in one of the dormitories, we eat at the house table, and we never get away. I not only teach English winter and summer but I work in the principal's office and fire the pistol at track meets. I needed to get away from this and from every other form of anxiety, and I decided to avoid my brother. Early that day, I took Helen and the children sailing, and we stayed out until suppertime. The next day, we went on a picnic. Then I had to go to New York for a day, and when I got back, there was the costume dance at the boat club. Lawrence wasn't going to this, and it's a party where I always have a wonderful time.

The invitations that year said to come as you wish you were. After several conversations, Helen and I had decided what to wear. The thing she most wanted to be again, she said, was a bride, and so she decided to wear her wedding dress. I thought this was a good choice — sincere, lighthearted, and inexpensive. Her choice influenced mine, and I decided to wear an old football uniform. Mother decided to go as Jenny Lind, because there was an old Jenny Lind costume in the attic. The others decided to rent costumes, and when I went to New York, I got the clothes. Lawrence and Ruth didn't enter into any of this.

Helen was on the dance committee, and she spent most of Friday decorating the club. Diana and Chaddy and I went sailing. Most of the sailing that I do these days is in Manhasset, and I am used to setting a homeward course by the gasoline barge and the tin roofs of the boat shed, and it was a pleasure that afternoon, as we returned, to keep the bow on a white church spire in the village and to find even the inshore water green and clear. At the end of our sail, we stopped at the club to get Helen. The committee had been trying to give a submarine appearance to the ballroom, and the fact that they had nearly succeeded in accomplishing this illusion made Helen very happy. We drove back to Laud's Head. It had been a brilliant afternoon, but on the way home we could smell the east wind – the dark wind, as Lawrence would have said – coming in from the sea.

My wife, Helen, is thirty-eight, and her hair would be gray, I guess, if it were not dyed, but it is dyed an unobtrusive yellow – a faded color – and I think it becomes her. I mixed cocktails that night while she was dressing, and when I took a glass upstairs to her, I saw her for the first time since our marriage in her wedding dress. There would be no point in saying that she looked to me more beautiful than she did on our wedding day, but because I have grown older and have, I think, a greater depth of feeling, and because I could see in her face that night both youth and age, both her devotion to the young woman that she had been and the positions that she had yielded graciously to time, I think I have never been so deeply moved. I had already put on the football uniform, and the weight of it, the heaviness of the pants and the shoulder guards, had worked a change in me, as if in putting on these old clothes I had put off the reasonable anxieties and troubles of my life. It felt as if we had both returned to the years before our marriage, the years before the war.

The Collards had a big dinner party before the dance, and our family – excepting Lawrence and Ruth – went to this. We drove over to the club, through the fog, at about half-past nine. The orchestra was playing a waltz. While I was checking my raincoat, someone hit me on the back. It was Chucky Ewing, and the funny thing was that Chucky had on a football uniform. This seemed comical as hell to both of us. We were laughing when we went down the hall to the dance floor. I stopped at the door to look at the party, and it was beautiful. The committee had hung fish nets around the sides and over the high ceiling. The nets on the ceiling were filled with colored balloons. The light was soft and uneven, and the people – our friends and neighbors – dancing in the soft light to 'Three O'Clock in the Morning' made a pretty picture. Then I noticed the number of women dressed in white, and I realized that they, like Helen, were wearing wedding dresses. Patsy Hewitt and Mrs Gear and the Lackland girl waltzed by, dressed as brides. Then Pep Talcott came over to where Chucky and I were standing. He was dressed to be Henry VIII, but he told us that the Auerbach twins and Henry Barrett and Dwight MacGregor were all wearing football uniforms, and that by the last count there were ten brides on the floor.

This coincidence, this funny coincidence, kept everybody laughing, and made this one of the most lighthearted parties we've ever had at the club. At first I thought that the women had planned with one another to wear wedding dresses, but the ones that I danced with said it was a coincidence and I'm sure that Helen had made her decision alone. Everything went smoothly for me until a little before midnight. I saw Ruth standing at the edge of the floor. She was wearing a long red dress. It was all wrong. It wasn't the spirit of the party at all. I danced with her, but no one cut in, and I was darned if I'd spend the rest of the night dancing with her and I asked her where Lawrence was. She said he was out on the dock, and I took her over to the bar and left her and went out to get Lawrence.

The east fog was thick and wet, and he was alone on the dock. He was not in costume. He had not even bothered to get himself up as a fisherman or a sailor. He looked particularly saturnine. The fog blew around us like a cold smoke. I wished that it had been a clear night, because the easterly fog seemed to play into my misanthropic brother's hands. And I knew that the buoys – the groaners and bells that we could hear then – would sound to him like half-human, half-drowned cries, although every sailor knows that buoys are necessary and reliable fixtures, and I knew that the foghorn at the lighthouse would mean wanderings and losses to him and that he could misconstrue the vivacity of the dance music. 'Come on in, Tifty,' I said, 'and dance with your wife or get her some partners.'

'Why should I?' he said. 'Why should I?' And he walked to the window and looked in at the party. 'Look at it,' he said. 'Look at that . . .'

Chucky Ewing had got hold of a balloon and was trying to organize a scrimmage line in the middle of the floor. The others were dancing a samba. And I knew that Lawrence was looking bleakly at the party as he had looked at the weather-beaten shingles on our house, as if he saw here an abuse and a distortion of time; as if in wanting to be brides and football players we exposed the fact that, the lights of youth having been put out in us, we had been unable to find other lights to go by and, destitute of faith and principle, had become foolish and sad. And that he was thinking this about so many kind and happy and generous people made me angry, made me feel for him such an unnatural abhorrence that I was ashamed, for he is my brother and a Pommeroy. I put my arm around his shoulders and tried to force him to come in, but he wouldn't.

I got back in time for the Grand March, and after the prizes had been given out for the best costumes, they let the balloons down. The room was hot, and someone opened the big doors onto the dock, and the easterly wind circled the room and went out, carrying across the dock and out onto the water most of the balloons. Chucky Ewing went running out after the balloons, and when he saw them pass the dock and settle on the water, he took off his football uniform and dove in. Then Eric Auerbach dove in and Lew Phillips dove in and I dove in, and you know how it is at a party after midnight when people start jumping into the water. We recovered most of the balloons and dried off and went on dancing, and we didn't get home until morning.

The next day was the day of the flower show. Mother and Helen and Odette all had entries. We had a pickup lunch, and Chaddy drove the women and children over to the show. I took a nap, and in the middle of the afternoon I got some trunks and a towel and, on leaving the house, passed Ruth in the laundry. She was washing clothes. I don't know why she should seem to have so much more work to do than anyone else, but she is always washing or ironing or mending clothes. She may have been taught, when she was young, to spend her time like this, or she may be at the mercy of an expiatory passion. She seems to scrub and iron with a penitential fervor, although I can't imagine what it is that she thinks she's done wrong. Her children were with her in the laundry. I offered to take them to the beach, but they didn't want to go.

It was late in August, and the wild grapes that grow profusely all over the island made the land wind smell of wine. There is a little grove of holly at the end of the path, and then you climb the dunes, where nothing grows but that coarse grass. I could hear the sea, and I remember thinking how Chaddy and I used to talk mystically about the sea. When we were young, we had decided that we could never live in the West because we would miss the sea. 'It is very nice here,' we used to say politely when we visited people in the mountains, 'but we miss the Atlantic.' We used to look down our noses at people from Iowa and Colorado who had been denied this revelation, and we scorned the Pacific. Now I could hear the waves, whose heaviness sounded like a reverberation, like a tumult, and it pleased me as it had pleased me when I was young, and it seemed to have a purgative force, as if it had cleared my memory of, among other things, the penitential image of Ruth in the laundry.

But Lawrence was on the beach. There he sat. I went in without speaking. The water was cold, and when I came out, I put on a shirt. I told him that I was going to walk up to Tanners Point, and he said that he would come with me. I tried to walk beside him. His legs are no longer than mine, but he always likes to stay a little ahead of his companion. Walking along behind him, looking at his bent head and his shoulders, I wondered what he could make of that landscape.

There were the dunes and cliffs, and then, where they declined, there were some fields that had begun to turn from green to brown and yellow. The fields were used for pasturing sheep, and I guess Lawrence would have noticed that the soil was eroded and that the sheep would accelerate this decay. Beyond the fields there are a few coastal farms, with square and pleasant buildings, but Lawrence could have pointed out the hard lot of an island farmer. The sea, at our other side, was the open sea. We always tell guests that there, to the east, lies the coast of Portugal, and for Lawrence it would be an easy step from the coast of Portugal to the tyranny in Spain. The waves broke with a noise like a 'hurrah, hurrah, hurrah,' but to Lawrence they would say '*Vale, vale.*' I suppose it would have occurred to his baleful and incisive mind that the coast was terminal moraine, the edge of the prehistoric world, and it must have occurred to him that we walked along the edge of the known world in spirit as much as in fact. If he should otherwise have overlooked this, there were some Navy planes bombing an uninhabited island to remind him.

That beach is a vast and preternaturally clean and simple landscape. It is like a piece of the moon. The surf had pounded the floor solid, so it was easy walking, and everything left on the sand had been twice changed by the waves. There was the spine of a shell, a broomstick, part of a bottle and part of a brick, both of them milled and broken until they were nearly unrecognizable, and I suppose Lawrence's sad frame of mind – for he kept his head down – went from one broken thing to another. The company of his pessimism began to infuriate me, and I caught up with him and put a hand on his shoulder. 'It's only a summer day, Tifty,' I said. 'It's only a summer day. What's the matter? Don't you like it here?'

'I don't like it here,' he said blandly, without raising his eyes. 'I'm going to sell my equity in the house to Chaddy. I didn't expect to have a good time. The only reason I came back was to say goodbye.'

I let him get ahead again and I walked behind him, looking at his shoulders and thinking of all the goodbyes he had made. When Father drowned, he went to church and said goodbye to Father. It was only three years later that he concluded that Mother was frivolous and said goodbye to her. In his freshman year at college, he had been very good friends with his roommate, but the man drank too much, and at the beginning of the spring term Lawrence changed roommates and said goodbye to his friend. When he had been in college for two years, he concluded that the atmosphere was too sequestered and he said goodbye to Yale. He enrolled at Columbia and got his law degree there, but he found his first employer dishonest, and at the end of six months he said goodbye to a good job. He married Ruth in City Hall and said goodbye to the Protestant Episcopal Church; they went to live on a back street in Tuckahoe and said goodbye to the middle class. In 1938, he went to Washington to work as a government lawyer, saying goodbye to private enterprise, but after eight months in Washington he concluded that the Roosevelt administration was sentimental and he said goodbye to it. They left Washington for a suburb of Chicago, where he said goodbye to his neighbors, one by one, on counts of drunkenness, boorishness, and stupidity. He said goodbye to

Chicago and went to Kansas; he said goodbye to Kansas and went to Cleveland. Now he had said goodbye to Cleveland and come East again, stopping at Laud's Head long enough to say goodbye to the sea.

It was elegiac and it was bigoted and narrow, it mistook circumspection for character, and I wanted to help him. 'Come out of it,' I said. 'Come out of it, Tifty.'

'Come out of what?'

'Come out of this gloominess. Come out of it. It's only a summer day. You're spoiling your own good time and you're spoiling everyone else's. We need a vacation, Tifty. I need one. I need to rest. We all do. And you've made everything tense and unpleasant. I only have two weeks in the year. Two weeks. I need to have a good time and so do all the others. We need to rest. You think that your pessimism is an advantage, but it's nothing but an unwillingness to grasp realities.'

'What are the realities?' he said. 'Diana is a foolish and a promiscuous woman. So is Odette. Mother is an alcoholic. If she doesn't discipline herself, she'll be in a hospital in a year or two. Chaddy is dishonest. He always has been. The house is going to fall into the sea.' He looked at me and added, as an afterthought, 'You're a fool.'

'You're a gloomy son of a bitch,' I said. 'You're a gloomy son of a bitch.'

'Get your fat face out of mine,' he said. He walked along.

Then I picked up a root and, coming at his back – although I have never hit a man from the back before – I swung the root, heavy with sea water, behind me, and the momentum sped my arm and I gave him, my brother, a blow on the head that forced him to his knees on the sand, and I saw the blood come out and begin to darken his hair. Then I wished that he was dead, dead and about to be buried, not buried but about to be buried, because I did not want to be denied ceremony and decorum in putting him away, in putting him out of my consciousness, and I saw the rest of us – Chaddy and Mother and Diana and Helen – in mourning in the house on Belvedere Street that was torn down twenty years ago, greeting our guests and our relatives at the door and answering their mannerly condolences with mannerly grief. Nothing decorous was lacking so that even if he had been murdered on a beach, one would feel before the tiresome ceremony ended that he had come into the winter of his life and that it was a law of nature, and a beautiful one, that Tifty should be buried in the cold, cold ground.

He was still on his knees. I looked up and down. No one had seen us. The naked beach, like a piece of the moon, reached to invisibility. The spill of a wave, in a glancing run, shot up to where he knelt. I would still have liked to end him, but now I had begun to act like two men, the murderer and the Samaritan. With a swift roar, like hollowness made sound, a white wave reached him and encircled him, boiling over his shoulders, and I held him against the undertow. Then I led him to a higher place. The blood had spread all through his hair, so that it looked black. I took off my shirt and tore it to bind up his head. He was conscious, and I didn't think he was badly hurt. He didn't speak. Neither did I. Then I left him there.

I walked a little way down the beach and turned to watch him, and I was thinking of my own skin then. He had got to his feet and he seemed steady. The daylight was still clear, but on the sea wind fumes of brine were blowing in like a light fog, and when I had walked a little way from him, I could hardly see his dark figure in this obscurity. All down the beach I could see the heavy salt air blowing in. Then I turned my back on him and as I got near to the house, I went swimming again, as I seem to have done after every encounter with Lawrence that summer.

When I got back to the house, I lay down on the terrace. The others came back. I could hear Mother defaming the flower arrangements that had won prizes. None of ours had won anything. Then the house quieted, as it always does at that hour. The children went into the kitchen to get supper and the others went upstairs to bathe. Then I heard Chaddy making cocktails, and the conversation about the flower-show judges was resumed. Then Mother cried, 'Tifty! Tifty! Oh, Tifty!'

He stood in the door, looking half dead. He had taken off the bloody bandage and he held it in his hand. 'My brother did this,' he said. 'My brother did it. He hit me with a stone – something – on the beach.' His voice broke with self-pity. I thought he was going to cry. No one else spoke. 'Where's Ruth?' he cried. 'Where's Ruth? Where in hell is Ruth? I want her to start packing. I don't have any more time to waste here. I have important things to do. I have *important* things to do.' And he went up the stairs.

They left for the mainland the next morning, taking the six

o'clock boat. Mother got up to say goodbye, but she was the only one, and it is a harsh and an easy scene to imagine – the matriarch and the changeling, looking at each other with a dismay that would seem like the powers of love reversed. I heard the children's voices and the car go down the drive, and I got up and went to the window, and what a morning that was! Jesus, what a morning! The wind was northerly. The air was clear. In the early heat, the roses in the garden smelled like strawberry jam. While I was dressing, I heard the boat whistle, first the warning signal and then the double blast, and I could see the good people on the top deck drinking coffee out of fragile paper cups, and Lawrence at the bow, saying to the sea, '*Thalassa, thalassa,*' while his timid and unhappy children watched the creation from the encirclement of their mother's arms. The buoys would toll mournfully for Lawrence, and while the grace of the light would make it an exertion not to throw out your arms and swear exultantly, Lawrence's eyes would trace the black sea as it fell astern; he would think of the bottom, dark and strange, where full fathom five our father lies.

Oh, what can you do with a man like that? What can you do? How can you dissuade his eye in a crowd from seeking out the cheek with acne, the infirm hand; how can you teach him to respond to the inestimable greatness of the race, the harsh surface beauty of life; how can you put his finger for him on the obdurate truths before which fear and horror are powerless? The sea that morning was iridescent and dark. My wife and my sister were swimming – Diana and Helen – and I saw their uncovered heads, black and gold in the dark water. I saw them come out and I saw that they were naked, unshy, beautiful, and full of grace, and I watched the naked women walk out of the sea.

Mrs Fortescue

That autumn he became conscious all at once of a lot of things he had never thought about before.

Himself, for a start. . . .

His parents . . . whom he found he disliked, because they told lies. He discovered this when he tried to communicate to them something of his new state of mind and they pretended not to know what he meant.

His sister who, far from being his friend and ally, 'like two peas in a pod' – as people had been saying for years – seemed positively to hate him.

And Mrs Fortescue.

Jane, seventeen, had left school and went out every night. Fred, sixteen, loutish schoolboy, lay in bed and listened for her to come home, kept company by her imaginary twin self, invented by him at the end of summer. The tenderness of this lovely girl redeemed him from the shame, the squalor, the misery of his loneliness. Meanwhile, the parents ignorantly slept, not caring about the frightful battles their son was fighting with himself not six yards off. Sometimes Jane came home first; sometimes Mrs Fortescue. Fred listened to her going up over his head, and thought how strange he had never thought about her before, knew nothing about her.

The family lived in a small flat over the liquor shop that Mr and Mrs Danderlea had been managing for Sanko and Duke for twenty years. Above the shop, from where rose, day and night, a sickly, inescapable reek of beer and spirits, were the kitchen and the lounge. This layer of the house (it had been one once) was felt as an insulating barrier against the smell, but it reached up into the bedrooms above. Two bedrooms – the mother and father in one; while for years brother and sister had shared a room, until recently Mr Danderlea had put up a partition making two tiny boxes, giving at least the illusion of privacy for the boy and the girl.

On the top floor, the two rooms were occupied by Mrs Fortescue, and had been since before the Danderleas came. Ever since the boy could remember, grumbling went on that Mrs Fortescue had the part of the house where the liquor smell did not reach; though she, if remarks to this effect came to her, claimed that on hot nights she could not sleep for the smell. But on the whole relations were good. The Danderleas' energies were claimed by buying and selling liquor, while Mrs Fortescue went out a lot. Sometimes another old woman came to visit her, and an old man, small, shrunken and polite, came to see her most evenings, very late indeed, often after twelve.

Mrs Fortescue seldom went out during the day, but left every evening at about six, wearing furs: a pale, shaggy coat in winter, and in summer a stole over a costume. She always had a small hat on, with a veil that was drawn tight over her face and held with a bunch of flowers where the fur began. The furs changed often: Fred remembered half a dozen blonde fur coats, and a good many little animals biting their tails or dangling bright bead eyes and empty paws. From behind the veil, the dark made-up eyes of Mrs Fortescue had glimmered at him for years; and her small, old, reddened mouth had smiled.

One evening he postponed his homework, and slipped out past the shop where his parents were both at work, and took a short walk that led him to Oxford Street The exulting, fearful loneliness that surged through his blood with every heartbeat, making every stamp of shadow a reminder of death, each gleam of light a promise of his extraordinary future, drove him around and around the streets, muttering to himself, bringing tears to his eyes, or to his lips snatches of song which he had to suppress. For, while he knew himself to be crazy, and supposed he must have been all his life (he could no longer remember himself before this autumn), this was a secret he intended to keep for himself and the tender creature who shared the stuffy box he spent his nights in. Turning a corner probably (he would not have been able to say) already turned several times before that evening, he saw a woman walking ahead of him in a great fur coat that shone under the street lights, a small veiled hat, and with tiny sharp feet that took tripping steps towards Soho. Recognizing Mrs Fortescue, a friend, he ran forward to greet her, relieved that this frightening trap of streets was to be shared. Seeing him, she first gave him a smile never offered him before by a woman; then looked prim and annoyed; then nodded at him briskly and said as she always did: 'Well, Fred, and how are things with you?' He walked a few steps with her, said he had to do his homework, heard her old woman's voice say: 'That's right, son, you must work, your mum and dad are right, a bright boy like you, it would be a shame to let it go to waste,' – and watched her move on, across Oxford Street, into the narrow streets beyond.

He turned and saw Bill Bates coming toward him from the hard-ware shop, just closing. Bill was grinning, and he said: 'What, wouldn't she have you then?'

'It's Mrs Fortescue,' said Fred, entering a new world between one breath and the next, just because of the tone of Bill's voice.

'She's not a bad old tart,' said Bill. 'Bet she wasn't pleased to see you when she's on the job.'

'Oh, I don't know,' said Fred, trying out a new man-of-the-world voice for the first time, 'she lives over us, doesn't she?' (Bill must know this, everyone must know it, he thought, feeling sick.) 'I was just saying hullo, that's all.' It came off, he saw, for now Bill nodded and said: 'I'm off to the pictures, want to come?'

'Got to do homework,' said Fred, bitter.

'Then you've got to do it then, haven't you,' said Bill reasonably, going on his way.

Fred went home in a seethe of shame. How could his parents share their house with an old tart (whore, prostitute – but these were the only words he knew), how could they treat her like an ordinary decent person, even better (he understood, listening to them in his mind's ear, that their voices to her held something not far from respect), how could they put up with it? Justice insisted that they had not chosen her as a tenant, she was the company's tenant, but at least they should have told Sanko and Duke so that she could be evicted and . . .

Although it seemed as if his adventure through the streets had been as long as a night, he found when he got in that it wasn't yet eight, and his mother said no more than that he shouldn't forget his homework.

He went up to his box and set out his school-books. Through the ceiling-board he could hear his sister moving. There being no door between the rooms, he went out to the landing, through his parents' room (his sister had to creep past the sleeping pair when she came in late) and into hers. She stood in a black slip before the glass, making up her face. 'Do you mind?' she said daintily. 'Can't you knock?' He muttered something and felt a smile come on his face, aggressive and aggrieved, that seemed to switch on automatically these days if he even saw his sister at a distance. He sat on the edge of her bed. 'Do you *mind?*' she said again, moving away from him some black underwear. She slipped over her still puppy-fatted white shoulders a new dressing-gown in cherry-red and buttoned it up primly before continuing to work lipstick on to her mouth.

'Where are you going?'

'To the pictures, if you've got no objection,' she chipped out, in this new, jaunty voice that she had acquired when she left school, and which, he knew, she used as a weapon against all men. *But why against him?* He sat, feeling the ugly grin apparently painted on his face, for he couldn't remove it, and he looked at the pretty girl with her new hair-do, putting thick black rings around her eyes, and he thought of how they had been two peas in a pod. *In the summer* . . . yes, that is how it seemed to him now, through a year's long summer of visits to friends, the park, the zoo, the pictures, they had been friends, allies, then the dark came down suddenly and in the dark had been born this cool, flip girl who hated him.

'Who are you going with?'

'Jem Taylor, if you don't have any objection,' she said.

'Why should I have any objection? I just asked.'

'What you don't know won't hurt you,' she said, very pleased with herself because of her ease in this way of talking. He recognized his recent achievement in the exchange with Bill as the same step forward as she was making, with this tone, or style; and, out of a quite uncustomary feeling of equality with her, asked: 'How is old Jem? I haven't seen him for ages.'

'Oh Fred, I'm *late.*' This bad temper meant she had finished her face and wanted to put on her dress, which she would not do in front of him.

Silly cow, he thought, grinning and thinking of her alter ego, the girl of his nights, does she think I don't know what she looks like in a slip, or even less? Because of what went on behind the partition, in the dark, he banged his fist on it, laughing, and she whipped about and said: 'Oh Fred, you drive me crazy, you really do.' This being something from their brother-and-sister-past, admitting intimacy, even the possibility of real equality, she checked herself, put on a sweet contained smile, and said: 'If you don't *mind*, Fred, I want to get dressed.'

He went out, remembering only as he got through the parents' room and saw his mother's feathered mules by the bed, that he had wanted to talk about Mrs Fortescue. He realized his absurdity, because of course his sister would pretend she didn't understand what he meant . . . his fixed smile of shame changed into one of savagery as he thought: Well, Jem, you're not going to get anything out of her but *do you mind* and *have you any objection* and *please yourself*, I know that much about my sweet sister. . . . In his room he could not work, even after his sister had left, slamming three doors and making so much racket with her heels that the parents shouted at her from the shop. He was thinking of Mrs Fortescue. But she was old. She had always been old, as long as he could remember. And the old women who came up to see her in the afternoons, were they whores (tarts, prostitutes, *bad women*) too? And where did she, they, do it? And who was the nasty, smelly old man who came so late nearly every night?

He sat with the waves of liquor smell from the ground floor rising past him, thinking of the sourish smell of the old man, and of the scented smell of the old woman, feeling short-breathed because of the stuffy reek of this room and associating it (because of certain memories from his nights) with the reek from Mrs Fortescue's room which he could positively smell from where he sat, so strongly did he create it.

Bill must be wrong: she couldn't possibly be on the game still, who would want an old thing like that?

The family had a meal every night when the shop closed. It was usually about ten-thirty when they sat down. Tonight there was some boiled bacon, and baked beans. Fred brought out casually: 'I saw Mrs Fortescue going off to work when I came out.' He waited the results of this cheek, this effrontery, watching his parents' faces. They did not even exchange glances. His mother pushed tinted bronze hair back with a hand that had a stain of grease on it, and said: 'Poor old girl, I expect she's pleased about the Act, when you get down to it, in the winter it must have been bad sometimes.' The words, *the Act* hit Fred's outraged sense of propriety anew; he had to work them out; thinking that his parents did not even apologize for the years of corruption. Now his father said (his face inflamed, he must have been taking nips often from the glass under the counter), 'Once or twice, when I saw her on Frith Street before the Act I felt sorry for her. But I suppose she got used to it.'

'It must be nicer this way,' said Mrs Danderlea, pushing the crusting remains of the baked beans towards her husband.

He scooped them out of the dish with the edge of his fried bread, and she said: 'What's wrong with the spoon?'

'What's wrong with the bread?' he returned, with an unconvincing whisky glare, which she ignored.

'Where's her place, then?' asked Fred, casual, having worked out that she must have one.

'Over that new club in Panton Street. The rent's gone up again, so Mr Spencer told me, and there's the telephone she needs now, well I don't know how much you can believe of what *he* says, but he's said often enough that without him helping her out she'd do better at almost anything else.'

'Not a word he says,' said Mr Danderlea, pushing out his big whisky stomach as he sat back, replete. 'He told me he was door-man for the Greystock Hotel in Knightsbridge, well it turns out all this time he's been doorman for that strip-tease joint along the street from her new place, and that's where he's been for years, because it was a night-club before it was strip-tease.'

'Well there's no point in that, is there?' said Mrs Danderlea, pouring second cups. 'I mean, why tell fibs about it, I mean every-one knows, don't they?'

Fred again pushed down protest: that yes, Mr Spencer (Mrs Fortescue's 'regular', but he had never understood what they had meant by the ugly word before) was right to lie; he wished his parents would lie even now; anything rather than this casual back-and-forth chat about this horror, years-old, and right over their heads, part of their lives, inescapable.

He ducked down his face and shovelled beans into it fast, know-ing it was scarlet, and wanting a reason for it.

'You'll get heartburn, gobbling like that,' said his mother, as he had expected.

'I've got to finish my homework,' he said, and bolting, shaking his head at the cup of tea she was pushing over at him.

He sat in his room until his parents went to bed, marking off the routine of the house from his new knowledge. After an expected interval Mrs Fortescue came in, he could hear her moving about, taking her time about everything. Water ran, for a long time. He now understood that this sound, water running into and then out of a basin, was something he had heard at this hour all his life. He sat listening with the ashamed, fixed grin on his face. Then his sister came in; he could hear her sharp sigh of relief as she flumped on the bed and bent over to take off her shoes. He nearly called out 'Good-night, Jane', but thought better of it. Yet all through the summer they had whispered and giggled through the partition.

Mr Spencer, her regular, came up the stairs. He heard their voices together; listened to them as he undressed and went to bed; as he lay wakeful; as he at last went off to sleep, feeling savage with loneliness.

Next evening he waited until Mrs Fortescue went out, and followed her, careful she didn't see him. She walked fast and efficiently, like a woman on her way to the office, not looking at people. Why then the fur coat, the veil, the make-up? Of course, it was habit, because of all the years on the pavement; for it was a sure thing she didn't wear that outfit to receive customers in her place. But it turned out that he was wrong. Along the last hundred yards before her door, she slowed her pace, took a couple of quick glances left and right for the police, then looked at a large elderly man coming towards her. This man swung around, joined her, and they went side by side into her doorway, the whole operation so quick, so smooth, that even if there had been a policeman all he could have seen was a woman meeting someone she had expected to meet.

Fred then went home. Jane was dressing for the evening. He followed her too. She walked fast, not looking at people, her smart new coat flaring jade, emerald, dark green, as she moved through varying depths of light, her black puffy hair gleaming. She went into the underground. He followed her down the escalators, and on to the platform, at not much more than arm's distance, but quite safe because of her self-absorption. She stood on the edge of the platform, staring across the rails at a big advertisement. It was a very large dark-brown gleaming revolver holster, with a revolver in it, attached to a belt for bullets; but instead of bullets each loop had a lipstick, in all the pink-orange-scarlet-crimson shades it was possible to imagine lipstick in. Fred stood just behind his sister, and examined her sharp little face examining the advertisement and choosing which lipstick she would buy. She smiled – nothing like the appealing shamefaced smile that was stuck, for ever it seemed, on Fred's face, but a calm, triumphant smile. The train came streaming in, obscuring the advertisement. The doors slid open, receiving his sister, who did not look around. He stood close against the window, looking at her calm little face, willing her to look at him. But the train rushed her off again, and she would never know he had been there.

He went home, the ferment of his craziness breaking through his lips in an incredulous raw mutter: a revolver, a bloody revolver . . . his parents were at supper, taking in food, swilling in tea, like pigs, pigs, pigs, he thought, shovelling down his own supper to be rid of it. Then he said: 'I left a book in the shop, Dad, I want to get it,' and went down dark stairs through the sickly rising fumes. In a drawer under the till was a revolver which had been there for years, against the day when burglars broke in and Mr (or Mrs) Danderlea frightened them off with it. Many of Fred's dreams had been spun around that weapon. But it was broken somewhere in its black-gleaming interior. He carefully hid it under his sweater, and went up, to knock on his parents' door. They were already in bed, a large double bed at which, because of this hideous world he was now a citizen of, he was afraid to look. Two old people, with sagging faces and bulging mottled fleshy shoulders lay side by side, looking at him. 'I want to leave something for Jane,' he said, turning his gaze away from them. He laid the revolver on Jane's pillow, arranging half a dozen lipsticks of various colours as if they were bullets coming out of it. His parents' bedroom was in darkness. His father was snoring and his mother did not answer his good-night.

He went back to the shop. Under the counter stood the bottle of Black and White beside the glass stained sour with his father's tippling. He made sure the bottle was still half-full before turning the lights out and settling down to wait. Not for long. When he heard the key in the lock he set the door open wide so Mrs Fortescue must see him.

'Why, Fred, whatever are you doing?'

'I noticed Dad left the light on, so I came down.' Frowning with efficiency, he looked for a place to put the whisky bottle, while he rinsed the dirtied glass. Then casual, struck by a thought, he offered: 'Like a drink, Mrs Fortescue?' In the dim light she focussed, with difficulty, on the bottle. 'I never touch the stuff, dear. . . .' Bending his face down past hers, to adjust a wine bottle, he caught the liquor on her breath, and understood the vagueness of her good nature.

'Well all right, dear,' she went on, 'just a little one to keep you company. You're like your Dad, you know that?'

'Is that so?' He came out of the shop with the bottle under his arm, shutting the door behind him and locking it. The stairs glimmered dark. 'Many's the time he's offered me a nip on a cold night, though not when your mother could see.' She added a short triumphant titter, resting her weight on the stair-rail as if testing it.

'Let's go up,' he said insinuatingly, knowing he would get his way, because it had been so easy this far. He was shocked it was so easy. She should have said: 'What are you doing out of bed at this time?' Or: 'A boy of your age, drinking, what next!'

She obediently went up ahead of him, pulling herself up.

The small room she went into, vaguely smiling her invitation he should follow, was crammed with furniture and objects, all of which had the same soft glossiness of her clothes, which she now went to the next room to remove. He sat on an oyster-coloured satin sofa, looked at bluish brocade curtains, a cabinet full of china figures, thick, creamy rugs, pink cushions, pink-tinted walls. A table in a corner held photographs. Of her, so he understood, progressing logically back from those he could recognize to those that were inconceivable. The earliest was of a girl with yellow collar-bone-length curls, on which perched a top-hat. She wore a spangled bodice, in pink; pink satin pants, long black lace stockings, white gloves, and was roguishly pointing a walking-stick at the audience – at him, Fred. 'Like a bloody gun,' he thought, feeling the shameful derisive grin come on to his face. He heard the door shut behind him, but did not turn, wondering what he would see: he never had seen her, he realized, without hat, veil, furs. She said, pottering about behind his shoulder: 'Yes, that's me when I was a Gaiety Girl, a nice outfit, wasn't it?'

'Gaiety Girl?' he said, protesting, and she admitted: 'Well that was before your time, wasn't it?'

The monstrousness of this second *wasn't it*, made it easy for him to turn and look: she was bending over a cupboard, her back to him. It was a back whose shape was concealed by thick, soft, cherry-red, with a tufted pattern of whirls and waves. She stood up and faced him, displaying, without a trace of consciousness at the horror of the fact, his sister's dressing-gown. She carried glasses and a jug of water to the central table that was planted in a deep pink rug, and said: 'I hope you don't mind my getting into something comfortable, but we aren't strangers.' She sat opposite, having pushed the glasses towards him, as a reminder that the bottle was still in his hand. He poured the yellow, smelling liquid, watching her face to see when he must stop. But her face showed nothing, so he filled her tumbler half-full. 'Just a splash, dear . . . ' He splashed, and she lifted the glass and held it, in the vague tired way that went with her face, which, now that for the first time in his life he could look at it, was an old, shrunken face, with small black eyes deep in their sockets, and a small mouth pouting out of a tired mesh of lines. This old, rather kind face, at which he tried not to stare, was like a mask held between the cherry-red gown over a body whose shape was slim and young; and the hair, beautifully tinted a tactful silvery-blonde and waving softly into the hollows of an ancient neck.

'My sister's got a dressing-gown like that.'

'It's pretty isn't it? They've got them in at Richard's, down the street, I expect she got hers there too, did she?'

'I don't know.'

'Well the proof of the pudding's in the eating, isn't it?'

At this remark, which reminded him of nothing so much as his parents' idiotic pattering exchange at supper-time, when they were torpid before sleep, he felt the ridiculous smile leave his face. He was full of anger, but no longer of shame.

'Give me a cigarette, dear,' she went on, 'I'm too tired to get up.'

'I don't smoke.'

'If you could reach me my handbag.'

He handed her a large crocodile bag, that she had left by the photographs. 'I have nice things, don't I?' she agreed with his unspoken comment on it. 'Well, I always say, I always have nice things, whatever else . . . I never have anything cheap or nasty, my things are always nice. . . . Baby Batsby taught me that, never have anything cheap or nasty, he used to say. He used to take me on his yacht, you know, to Cannes and Nice. He was my friend for three years, and he taught me about having beautiful things.'

'Baby Batsby?'

'That was before your time, I expect, but he was in all the papers once, every week of the year. He was a great spender, you know, generous.'

'Is that a fact?'

'I've always been lucky that way, my friends were always generous. Take Mr Spencer now, he never lets me want for anything, only yesterday he said: Your curtains are getting a bit *passé*, I'll get you some new ones. And mark my words, he will, he's as good as his word.'

He saw that the whisky, coming on top of whatever she'd had earlier, was finishing her off. She sat blinking smeared eyes at him; and her cigarette, secured between thumb and forefinger six inches from her mouth, shed ash on her cherry-red gown. She took a gulp from the glass, and nearly set it down on air: Fred reached forward just in time.

'Mr Spencer's a good man, you know,' she told the air about a foot from her unfocussed brown gaze.

'Is he?'

'We're just old friends, now, you know. We're both getting on a bit. Not that I don't let him have a bit of a slap and a tickle sometimes to keep him happy, though I'm not interested, not really.'

Trying to insert the end of the cigarette inside her fumbling lips, she missed, and jammed the butt against her cheek. She leaned forward and stubbed it out. Sat back – with dignity. Stared at Fred, screwed up her eyes to see him, failed, offered the stranger in her room a social smile.

This smile trembled into a wrinkled pout, as she said: 'Take Mr Spencer now, he's a good spender, I'd never say he wasn't, but but but . . . ' She fumbled at the packet of cigarettes and he hastened to extract one for her and to light it. '*But*. Yes. Well, he may think I'm past it, but I'm not, and don't you think it. There's a good thirty years between us, do you know that?'

'Thirty years,' said Fred, politely, his smile now fixed by a cold determined loathing.

'What do you think, dear? He always makes out we're the same age, now he's past it, but – well, look at that then if you don't believe me.' She pointed her scarlet-tipped and shaking left hand at the table with the photographs. 'Yes, that one, just look at it, it's only from last summer.' Fred leaned forward and lifted towards him the image of her just indicated which, though she was sitting opposite him in the flesh, must prove her victory over Mr Spencer. She wore a full-skirted, tightly-belted, tightly-bodiced striped dress, from which her ageing bare arms hung down by her sides, and her old neck and face rose shameless under the beautiful gleaming hair.

'Well it stands to reason, doesn't it?' she said, as it were indignant: 'Well what do you think then?'

'When's Mr Spencer coming?' he asked.

'I'm not expecting him tonight, he's working. I admire him, I really do, holding down that job, three, four in the morning sometimes, and it's no joke, those layabouts you get at those places, and it's always Mr Spencer who has to fix them up with what they fancy, if you know what I mean, dear, or get rid of them if they make trouble, and he's not a big man, and he's not young any more, I don't know how he does it. But he's got tact. Tact. Yes, I often say to him, you've got tact, I say, it'll take a man anywhere.' Her glass was empty, and she was looking at it.

The news that Mr Spencer was not expected did not surprise Fred; he had known it, because of his secret brutal confidence born when she had said: 'I never touch the stuff, dear.'

He now got up, went behind her, stood a moment steeling himself, because the embarrassed shamefaced grin had come back on to his face, weakening his purpose – then put two hands firmly under her armpits, lifted her and supported her.

She at first struggled to remain sitting, but let herself be lifted. 'Time for byebyes?' she said. But as he began to push her, still supporting her, toward the bedroom, she said, suddenly coherent: 'But Fred, it's Fred, Fred, it's Fred . . . ' She twisted out of his grip, fell two steps back, and was stopped by the door to the bedroom. There she spread her two legs under the cherry gown, to hold her trembling weight, swayed, caught at Fred, held tight, and said: 'But it's *Fred.*'

'Why should you care,' he said, cold, grinning.

'But I don't work here, dear, you know that – no, let me go.' For he had put two great schoolboy hands on her shoulders.

He felt the shoulders tense, and then grow small and tender in his palms.

'You're like your father, you're the spitting image of your father, did you know that?'

He opened the door with his left hand; then spun her around by pushing at her left shoulder as she faced him; then, putting both hands under her armpits from behind, marched her into the bedroom, while she tittered, steadily.

The bedroom was mostly pink. Pink silk bedspread. Pink walls. A doll in a pink flounced skirt lolled against the pillow, its chin tucked into a white fichu over which it stared at the opposite wall where an eighteenth-century girl held a white rose to her lips. Fred pushed Mrs Fortescue over dark-red carpet, till her knees met the bed. He lifted her, dropped her on it, neatly moving the doll aside with one hand before she could crush it.

She lay, eyes closed, limp, breathing fast, her mouth slightly open. The black furrows beside the mouth were crooked; the eyelids shone blue in wells of black.

'Turn the lights out,' she tittered.

He turned out the pink-shaded lamp fixed to the headboard. She fumbled at her clothes. He stripped off his trousers, his underpants, pushed her hands aside, found silk in the opening of the gown that glowed cherry-red in the light from the next room. He stripped the silk pants off her so that her legs flew up, then flumped down. She was inert, he fumbled. Then her expertise revived in her, or at least in her tired hands, and he achieved the goal of his hot imaginings of these ugly autumn nights in one shattering spasm that filled him with no less disgust. Her old body stirred feebly under him, and he heard her irregular breathing. He sprang off her in a leap, tugged back pants, trousers. Then he switched on the light. She lay, eyes closed, her face blurred with woe, the upper part of her body nestled into the soft glossy cherry stuff, the white legs spread open, bare. She made an attempt to rouse herself, cover herself. He leaned over her, teeth bared in a hating grin, forcing her hands away from her body. They fell limp on the stained silk spread. Now he stripped off the gown, roughly, as if she were the doll. She whimpered, she tittered, she protested. He watched, with pleasure, tears welling out of the pits of dark and trickling crookedly down her face. She lay naked among the folds of cherry-colour. He looked at the greyish crinkles around the armpits, the small flat breasts, the loose stomach; then down, at the triangle of black hair where white hairs sprouted, obscene. She was attempting to fold her legs over each other. He forced them apart again, muttering: Look at yourself, look at yourself then . . . while he held his nausea, deepened by the miasmic smell which he had known was the air of this room. 'Filthy old whore, disgusting, that's what you are, disgusting. . . .' He let his grasp slacken on her thighs, saw red marks come up even as the legs flew together and she wriggled and burrowed to get under the cherry-red gown.

Then she opened her eyes and looked straight up at him. For the first time this evening she looked at him, straight in the eyes. He fell back a step, looking away from her, hearing his own breath coming in gasps of disgust.

She sat up, holding the gown around her – cherry-coloured gown, pink coverlet, pink walls, pink pink pink everywhere and the dark-red carpet: he felt as if the whole room flamed with disgust.

'That wasn't very nice, was it?' she said, quavering, but reproachful. Her voice broke in a titter, but she brought her lips together at last and said again: 'That wasn't at all nice, Fred, it wasn't nice at all.' Without looking at him, she let her feet down (he could see them trembling) over the edge of the bed, and she peered over to fit them into pink-feathered mules.

He noted that he had a need to *help* her fit her pathetic feet into the fancy mules; and with a muttered exclamation of horror, fear and shame, he fled out, down the stairs, into his box, where he flung himself face down on the bed. Through the ceiling-board an inch from his ear he heard his sister move. She had been waiting for him.

She said, low, so the parents couldn't hear, all the flip jauntiness of her voice gone, breathless with accusation and hurt: 'Very clever, I *don't* think . . . very clever.' She waited, but he did not answer. 'I know you're there, don't pretend.' He kept silent, waiting for her to tire. 'If I was as clever as you I'd go and drown myself, when I saw that gun on my pillow I thought I'd faint, I suppose you think you're just too clever to live. . . .' He waited until she got tired, and he heard her turn over and away from him. Then he put the back of his hand against his clenched teeth, and pulled the pillow down over his head so that no one could hear him.

Parker's Back

Parker's wife was sitting on the front porch floor, snapping beans. Parker was sitting on the step, some distance away, watching her sullenly. She was plain, plain. The skin on her face was thin and drawn as tight as the skin on an onion and her eyes were gray and sharp like the points of two icepicks. Parker understood why he had married her – he couldn't have got her any other way – but he couldn't understand why he stayed with her now. She was pregnant and pregnant women were not his favorite kind. Nevertheless, he stayed as if she had him conjured. He was puzzled and ashamed of himself.

The house they rented sat alone save for a single tall pecan tree on a high embankment overlooking a highway. At intervals a car would shoot past below and his wife's eyes would swerve suspiciously after the sound of it and then come back to rest on the newspaper full of beans in her lap. One of the things she did not approve of was automobiles. In addition to her other bad qualities, she was forever sniffing up sin. She did not smoke or dip, drink whiskey, use bad language or paint her face, and God knew some paint would have improved it, Parker thought. Her being against color, it was the more remarkable she had married him. Sometimes he supposed that she had married him because she meant to save him. At other times he had a suspicion that she actually liked everything she said she didn't. He could account for her one way or another; it was himself he could not understand.

She turned her head in his direction and said, 'It's no reason you can't work for a man. It don't have to be a woman.'

'Aw shut your mouth for a change,' Parker muttered.

If he had been certain she was jealous of the woman he worked for he would have been pleased but more likely she was concerned with the sin that would result if he and the woman took a liking to each other. He had told her that the woman was a hefty young blonde; in fact she was nearly seventy years old and too dried up to have an interest in anything except getting as much work out of him as she could. Not that an old woman didn't sometimes get an interest in a young man, particularly if he was as attractive as Parker felt he was, but this old woman looked at him the same way she looked at her old tractor – as if she had to put up with it because it was all she had. The tractor had broken down the second day Parker was on it and she had set him at once to cutting bushes, saying out of the side of her mouth to the nigger, 'Everything he touches, he breaks.' She also asked him to wear his shirt when he worked; Parker had removed it even though the day was not sultry; he put it back on reluctantly.

This ugly woman Parker married was his first wife. He had had other women but he had planned never to get himself tied up legally. He had first seen her one morning when his truck broke down on the highway. He had managed to pull it off the road into a neatly swept yard on which sat a peeling two-room house. He got out and opened the hood of the truck and began to study the motor. Parker had an extra sense that told him when there was a woman nearby watching him. After he had leaned over the motor a few minutes, his neck began to prickle. He cast his eye over the empty yard and porch of the house. A woman he could not see was either nearby beyond a clump of honeysuckle or in the house, watching him out the window.

Suddenly Parker began to jump up and down and fling his hand about as if he had mashed it in the machinery. He doubled over and held his hand close to his chest. 'God dammit!' he hollered, 'Jesus Christ in hell! Jesus God Almighty damm! God dammit to hell!' he went on, flinging out the same few oaths over and over as loud as he could.

Without warning a terrible bristly claw slammed the side of his face and he fell backwards on the hood of the truck. 'You don't talk no filth here!' a voice close to him shrilled.

Parker's vision was so blurred that for an instant he thought he had been attacked by some creature from above, a giant hawk-eyed angel wielding a hoary weapon. As his sight cleared, he saw before him a tall raw-boned girl with a broom.

'I hurt my hand,' he said. 'I HURT my hand.' He was so incensed that he forgot that he hadn't hurt his hand. 'My hand may be broke,' he growled although his voice was still unsteady.

'Lemme see it,' the girl demanded.

Parker stuck out his hand and she came closer and looked at it. There was no mark on the palm and she took the hand and turned it over. Her own hand was dry and hot and rough and Parker felt himself jolted back to life by her touch. He looked more closely at her. I don't want nothing to do with this one, he thought.

The girl's sharp eyes peered at the back of the stubby reddish hand she held. There emblazoned in red and blue was a tattooed eagle perched on a cannon. Parker's sleeve was rolled to the elbow. Above the eagle a serpent was coiled about a shield and in the spaces between the eagle and the serpent there were hearts, some with arrows through them. Above the serpent there was a spread hand of cards. Every space on the skin of Parker's arm, from wrist to elbow, was covered in some loud design. The girl gazed at this with an almost stupefied smile of shock, as if she had accidentally grasped a poisonous snake; she dropped the hand.

'I got most of my other ones in foreign parts,' Parker said. 'These here I mostly got in the United States. I got my first one when I was only fifteen year old.'

'Don't tell me,' the girl said, 'I don't like it. I ain't got any use for it.'

'You ought to see the ones you can't see,' Parker said and winked.

Two circles of red appeared like apples on the girl's cheeks and softened her appearance. Parker was intrigued. He did not for a minute think that she didn't like the tattoos. He had never yet met a woman who was not attracted to them.

Parker was fourteen when he saw a man in a fair, tattooed from head to foot. Except for his loins which were girded with a panther hide, the man's skin was patterned in what seemed from Parker's distance – he was near the back of the tent, standing on a bench – a single intricate design of brilliant color. The man, who was small and sturdy, moved about on the platform, flexing his muscles so that the arabesque of men and beasts and flowers on his skin appeared to have a subtle motion of its own. Parker was filled with emotion, lifted up as some people are when the flag passes. He was a boy whose mouth habitually hung open. He was heavy and earnest, as ordinary as a loaf of bread. When the show was over, he had remained standing on the bench, staring where the tattooed man had been, until the tent was almost empty.

Parker had never before felt the least motion of wonder in himself. Until he saw the man at the fair, it did not enter his head that there was anything out of the ordinary about the fact that he existed. Even then it did not enter his head, but a peculiar unease settled in him. It was as if a blind boy had been turned so gently in a different direction that he did not know his destination had been changed.

He had his first tattoo some time after — the eagle perched on the cannon. It was done by a local artist. It hurt very little, just enough to make it appear to Parker to be worth doing. This was peculiar too for before he had thought that only what did not hurt was worth doing. The next year he quit school because he was sixteen and could. He went to the trade school for a while, then he quit the trade school and worked for six months in a garage. The only reason he worked at all was to pay for more tattoos. His mother worked in a laundry and could support him, but she would not pay for any tattoo except her name on a heart, which he had put on, grumbling. However, her name was Betty Jean and nobody had to know it was his mother. He found out that the tattoos were attractive to the kind of girls he liked but who had never liked him before. He began to drink beer and get in fights. His mother wept over what was becoming of him. One night she dragged him off to a revival with her, not telling him where they were going. When he saw the big lighted church, he jerked out of her grasp and ran. The next day he lied about his age and joined the navy.

Parker was large for the tight sailor's pants but the silly white cap, sitting low on his forehead, made his face by contrast look thoughtful and almost intense. After a month or two in the navy, his mouth ceased to hang open. His features hardened into the features of a man. He stayed in the navy five years and seemed a natural part of the gray mechanical ship, except for his eyes, which were the same pale slate-color as the ocean and reflected the immense spaces around him as if they were a microcosm of the mysterious sea. In port Parker wandered about comparing the run-down places he was in to Birmingham, Alabama. Everywhere he went he picked up more tattoos.

He had stopped having lifeless ones like anchors and crossed rifles. He had a tiger and a panther on each shoulder, a cobra coiled about a torch on his chest, hawks on his thighs, Elizabeth II and Philip over where his stomach and liver were respectively. He did not care much what the subject was so long as it was colorful; on his abdomen he had a few obscenities but only because that seemed the proper place for them. Parker would be satisfied with each tattoo about a month, then something about it that had attracted him would wear off. Whenever a decent-sized mirror was available, he would get in front of it and study his overall look. The effect was not of one intricate arabesque of colors but of something haphazard and botched. A huge dissatisfaction would come over him and he would go off and find another tattooist and have another space filled up. The front of Parker was almost completely covered but there were no tattoos on his back. He had no desire for one anywhere he could not readily see it himself. As the space on the front of him for tattoos decreased, his dissatisfaction grew and became general.

After one of his furloughs, he didn't go back to the navy but remained away without official leave, drunk, in a rooming house in a city he did not know. His dissatisfaction, from being chronic and latent, had suddenly become acute and raged in him. It was as if the panther and the lion and the serpents and the eagles and the hawks had penetrated his skin and lived inside him in a raging warfare. The navy caught up with him, put him in the brig for nine months and then gave him a dishonorable discharge.

After that Parker decided that country air was the only kind fit to breathe. He rented the shack on the embankment and bought the old truck and took various jobs which he kept as long as it suited him. At the time he met his future wife, he was buying apples by the bushel and selling them for the same price by the pound to isolated homesteaders on back country roads.

'All that there', the woman said, pointing to his arm, 'is no better than what a fool Indian would do. It's a heap of vanity.' She seemed to have found the word she wanted. 'Vanity of vanities,' she said.

Well what the hell do I care what she thinks of it? Parker asked himself, but he was plainly bewildered. 'I reckon you like one of these better than another anyway,' he said, dallying until he thought of something that would impress her. He thrust the arm back at her. 'Which you like best?'

'None of them,' she said, 'but the chicken is not as bad as the rest.'

'What chicken?' Parker almost yelled.

She pointed to the eagle.

'That's an eagle,' Parker said. 'What fool would waste their time having a chicken put on themself?'

'What fool would have any of it?' the girl said and turned away. She went slowly back to the house and left him there to get going. Parker remained for almost five minutes, looking agape at the dark door she had entered.

The next day he returned with a bushel of apples. He was not one to be outdone by anything that looked like her. He liked women with meat on them, so you didn't feel their muscles, much less their old bones. When he arrived, she was sitting on the top step and the yard was full of children, all as thin and poor as herself; Parker remembered it was Saturday. He hated to be making up to a woman when there were children around, but it was fortunate he had brought the bushel of apples off the truck. As the children approached him to see what he carried, he gave each child an apple and told it to get lost; in that way he cleared out the whole crowd.

The girl did nothing to acknowledge his presence. He might have been a stray pig or goat that had wandered into the yard and she too tired to take up the broom and send it off. He set the bushel of apples down next to her on the step. He sat down on a lower step.

'Hep yourself,' he said, nodding at the basket; then he lapsed into silence.

She took an apple quickly as if the basket might disappear if she didn't make haste. Hungry people made Parker nervous. He had always had plenty to eat himself. He grew very uncomfortable. He reasoned he had nothing to say so why should he say it? He could not think now why he had come or why he didn't go before he wasted another bushel of apples on the crowd of children. He supposed they were her brothers and sisters.

She chewed the apple slowly but with a kind of relish of concentration, bent slightly but looking out ahead. The view from the porch stretched off across a long incline studded with iron weed and across the highway to a vast vista of hills and one small mountain. Long views depressed Parker. You look out into space like that and you begin to feel as if someone were after you, the navy or the government or religion.

'Who them children belong to, you?' he said at length.

'I ain't married yet,' she said. 'They belong to momma.' She said it as if it were only a matter of time before she would be married.

Who in God's name would marry her? Parker thought.

A large barefooted woman with a wide gap-toothed face appeared in the door behind Parker. She had apparently been there for several minutes.

'Good evening,' Parker said.

The woman crossed the porch and picked up what was left of the bushel of apples. 'We thank you,' she said and returned with it into the house.

'That your old woman?' Parker muttered.

The girl nodded. Parker knew a lot of sharp things he could have said like 'You got my sympathy,' but he was gloomily silent. He just sat there, looking at the view. He thought he must be coming down with something.

'If I pick up some peaches tomorrow I'll bring you some,' he said.

'I'll be much obliged to you,' the girl said.

Parker had no intention of taking any basket of peaches back there but the next day he found himself doing it. He and the girl had almost nothing to say to each other. One thing he did say was, 'I ain't got any tattoo on my back.'

'What you got on it?' the girl said.

'My shirt,' Parker said. 'Haw.'

'Haw, haw,' the girl said politely.

Parker thought he was losing his mind. He could not believe for a minute that he was attracted to a woman like this. She showed not the least interest in anything but what he brought until he appeared the third time with two cantaloups. 'What's your name?' she asked.

'O. E. Parker,' he said.

'What does the O. E. stand for?'

'You can just call me O. E.,' Parker said. 'Or Parker. Don't nobody call me by my name.'

'What's it stand for?' she persisted.

'Never mind,' Parker said. 'What's yours?'

'I'll tell you when you tell me what them letters are the short of,' she said. There was just a hint of flirtatiousness in her tone and it went rapidly to Parker's head. He had never revealed the name to any man or woman, only to the files of the navy and the government, and it was on his baptismal record which he got at the age of a month; his mother was a Methodist. When the name leaked out of the navy files, Parker narrowly missed killing the man who used it.

'You'll go blab it around,' he said.

'I'll swear I'll never tell nobody,' she said. 'On God's holy word I swear it.'

Parker sat for a few minutes in silence. Then he reached for the girl's neck, drew her ear close to his mouth and revealed the name in a low voice.

'Obadiah,' she whispered. Her face slowly brightened as if the name came as a sign to her. 'Obadiah,' she said.

The name still stank in Parker's estimation.

'Obadiah Elihue,' she said in a reverent voice.

'If you call me that aloud, I'll bust your head open,' Parker said. 'What's yours?'

'Sarah Ruth Cates,' she said.

'Glad to meet you, Sarah Ruth,' Parker said.

Sarah Ruth's father was a Straight Gospel preacher but he was away, spreading it in Florida. Her mother did not seem to mind his attention to the girl so long as he brought a basket of something with him when he came. As for Sarah Ruth herself, it was plain to Parker after he had visited three times that she was crazy about him. She liked him even though she insisted that pictures on the skin were vanity of vanities and even after hearing him curse, and even after she had asked him if he was saved and he had replied that he didn't see it was anything in particular to save him from. After that, inspired, Parker had said, 'I'd be saved enough if you was to kiss me.'

She scowled. 'That ain't being saved,' she said.

Not long after that she agreed to take a ride in his truck. Parker parked it on a deserted road and suggested to her that they lie down together in the back of it.

'Not until after we're married,' she said – just like that.

'Oh that ain't necessary,' Parker said and as he reached for her, she thrust him away with such force that the door of the truck came off and he found himself flat on his back on the ground. He made up his mind then and there to have nothing further to do with her.

They were married in the County Ordinary's office because Sarah Ruth thought churches were idolatrous. Parker had no opinion about that one way or the other. The Ordinary's office was lined with cardboard file boxes and record books with dusty yellow slips of paper hanging on out of them. The Ordinary was an old woman with red hair who had held office for forty years and looked as dusty as her books. She married them from behind the iron grill of a stand-up desk and when she finished, she said with a flourish, 'Three dollars and fifty cents and till death do you part!' and yanked some forms out of a machine.

Marriage did not change Sarah Ruth a jot and it made Parker gloomier than ever. Every morning he decided he had had enough and would not return that night; every night he returned. Whenever Parker couldn't stand the way he felt, he would have another tattoo, but the only surface left on him now was his back. To see a tattoo on his own back he would have to get two mirrors and stand between them in just the correct position and this seemed to Parker a good way to make an idiot of himself. Sarah Ruth who, if she had had better sense, could have enjoyed a tattoo on his back, would not even look at the ones he had elsewhere. When he attempted to point out especial details of them, she would shut her eyes tight and turn her back as well. Except in total darkness, she preferred Parker dressed and with his sleeves rolled down.

'At the judgement seat of God, Jesus is going to say to you, "What you been doing all your life besides have pictures drawn all over you?"' she said.

'You don't fool me none,' Parker said, 'you're just afraid that hefty girl I work for'll like me so much she'll say, "Come on, Mr Parker, let's you and me . . ."'

'You're tempting sin,' she said, 'and at the judgement seat of God you'll have to answer for that too. You ought to go back to selling the fruits of the earth.'

Parker did nothing much when he was at home but listen to what the judgement seat of God would be like for him if he didn't change his ways. When he could, he broke in with tales of the hefty girl he worked for. ' "Mr Parker," ' he said she said, ' "I hired you for your brains." ' (She had added, 'So why don't you use them?')

'And you should have seen her face the first time she saw me without my shirt,' he said. ' "Mr Parker," she said, "you're a walking panner-rammer!" ' This had, in fact, been her remark but it had been delivered out of one side of her mouth.

Dissatisfaction began to grow so great in Parker that there was no containing it outside of a tattoo. It had to be his back. There was no help for it. A dim half-formed inspiration began to work in his mind. He visualized having a tattoo put there that Sarah Ruth would not be able to resist – a religious subject. He thought of an open book with HOLY BIBLE tattooed under it and an actual verse printed on the page. This seemed just the thing for a while; then he began to hear her say, 'Ain't I already got a real Bible? What you think I want to read the same verse over and over for when I can read it all?' He needed something better even than the Bible! He thought about it so much that he began to lose sleep. He was already losing flesh – Sarah Ruth just threw food in the pot and let it boil. Not knowing for certain why he continued to stay with a woman who was both ugly and pregnant and no cook made him generally nervous and irritable, and he developed a little tic in the side of his face.

Once or twice he found himself turning around abruptly as if someone were trailing him. He had had a granddaddy who had ended in the state mental hospital, although not until he was seventy-five, but as urgent as it might be for him to get a tattoo, it was just as urgent that he get exactly the right one to bring Sarah Ruth to heel. As he continued to worry over it, his eyes took on a hollow preoccupied expression. The old woman he worked for told him that if he couldn't keep his mind on what he was doing, she knew where she could find a fourteen-year-old colored boy who could. Parker was too preoccupied even to be offended. At any time previous, he would have left her then and there, saying drily, 'Well, you go ahead on and get him then.'

Two or three mornings later he was baling hay with the old woman's sorry baler and her broken-down tractor in a large field, cleared save for one enormous old tree standing in the middle of it. The old woman was the kind who would not cut down a large old tree because it was a large old tree. She had pointed it out to Parker as if he didn't have eyes and told him to be careful not to hit it as the machine picked up hay near it. Parker began at the outside of the field and made circles inward toward it. He had to get off the tractor every now and then and untangle the baling cord or kick a rock out of the way. The old woman had told him to carry the rocks to the edge of the field, which he did when she was there watching. When he thought he could make it, he ran over them. As he circled the field his mind was on a suitable design for his back. The sun, the size of a golf ball, began to switch regularly from in front to behind him, but he appeared to see it both places as if he had eyes in the back of his head. All at once he saw the tree reaching out to grasp him. A ferocious thud propelled him into the air, and he heard himself yelling in an unbelievably loud voice, 'GOD ABOVE!'

He landed on his back while the tractor crashed upside-down into the tree and burst into flame. The first thing Parker saw were his shoes, quickly being eaten by the fire; one was caught under the tractor, the other was some distance away burning by itself. He was not in them. He could feel the hot breath of the burning tree on his face. He scrambled backwards, still sitting, his eyes cavernous, and if he had known how to cross himself he would have done it.

His truck was on a dirt road at the edge of the field. He moved toward it, still sitting, still backwards, but faster and faster; halfway to it he got up and began a kind of forward-bent run from which he collapsed on his knees twice. His legs felt like two old rusted rain gutters. He reached the truck finally and took off in it, zigzagging up the road. He drove past his house on the embankment and straight for the city, fifty miles distant.

Parker did not allow himself to think on the way to the city. He only knew that there had been a great change in his life, a leap forward into a worse unknown, and that there was nothing he could do about it. It was for all intents accomplished.

The artist had two large cluttered rooms over a chiropodist's office on a back street. Parker, still barefooted, burst silently in on him at a little after three in the afternoon. The artist, who was about Parker's own age – twenty-eight – but thin and bald, was behind a small drawing table, tracing a design in green ink. He looked up with an annoyed glance and did not seem to recognize Parker in the hollow-eyed creature before him.

'Let me see the book you got with all the pictures of God in it,' Parker said breathlessly. 'The religious one.'

The artist continued to look at him with his intellectual, superior stare. 'I don't put tattoos on drunks,' he said.

'You know me!' Parker cried indignantly. 'I'm O. E. Parker! You done work for me before and I always paid!'

The artist looked at him another moment as if he were not altogether sure. 'You've fallen off some,' he said. 'You must have been in jail.'

'Married,' Parker said.

'Oh,' said the artist. With the aid of mirrors the artist had tattooed on the top of his head a miniature owl, perfect in every detail.

It was about the size of a half-dollar and served him as a show piece. There were cheaper artists in town but Parker had never wanted anything but the best. The artist went over to a cabinet at the back of the room and began to look over some art books. 'Who are you interested in?' he said, 'saints, angels, Christs or what?'

'God,' Parker said.

'Father, Son or Spirit?'

'Just God,' Parker said impatiently. 'Christ. I don't care. Just so it's God.'

The artist returned with a book. He moved some papers off another table and put the book down on it and told Parker to sit down and see what he liked. 'The up-to-date ones are in the back,' he said.

Parker sat down with the book and wet his thumb. He began to go through it, beginning at the back where the up-to-date pictures were. Some of them he recognized – The Good Shepherd, Forbid Them Not, The Smiling Jesus, Jesus the Physician's Friend, but he kept turning rapidly backwards and the pictures became less and less reassuring. One showed a gaunt green dead face streaked with blood. One was yellow with sagging purple eyes. Parker's heart began to beat faster and faster until it appeared to be roaring inside him like a great generator. He flipped the pages quickly, feeling that when he reached the one ordained, a sign would come. He continued to flip through until he had almost reached the front of the book. On one of the pages a pair of eyes glanced at him swiftly. Parker sped on, then stopped. His heart too appeared to cut off; there was absolute silence. It said as plainly as if silence were a language itself, GO BACK.

Parker returned to the picture – the haloed head of a flat stern Byzantine Christ with all-demanding eyes. He sat there trembling; his heart began slowly to beat again as if it were being brought to life by a subtle power.

'You found what you want?' the artist asked.

Parker's throat was too dry to speak. He got up and thrust the book at the artist, opened at the picture.

'That'll cost you plenty,' the artist said. 'You don't want all those little blocks though, just the outline and some better features.'

'Just like it is,' Parker said, 'just like it is or nothing.'

'It's your funeral,' the artist said, 'but I don't do that kind of work for nothing.'

'How much?' Parker asked.

'It'll take maybe two days work.'

'How much?' Parker said.

'On time or cash?' the artist asked. Parker's other jobs had been on time, but he had paid.

'Ten down and ten for every day it takes,' the artist said.

Parker drew ten dollar bills out of his wallet; he had three left in.

'You come back in the morning,' the artist said, putting the money in his own pocket. 'First I'll have to trace that out of the book.'

'No no!' Parker said. 'Trace it now or gimme my money back,' and his eyes blared as if he were ready for a fight.

The artist agreed. Anyone stupid enough to want a Christ on his back, he reasoned, would be just as likely as not to change his mind the next minute, but once the work was begun he could hardly do so.

While he worked on the tracing, he told Parker to go wash his back at the sink with the special soap he used there. Parker did it and returned to pace back and forth across the room, nervously flexing his shoulders. He wanted to go look at the picture again but at the same time he did not want to. The artist got up finally and had Parker lie down on the table. He swabbed his back with ethyl chloride and then began to outline the head on it with his iodine pencil. Another hour passed before he took up his electric instrument. Parker felt no particular pain. In Japan he had had a tattoo of the Buddha done on his upper arm with ivory needles; in Burma, a little brown root of a man had made a peacock on each of his knees using thin pointed sticks, two feet long; amateurs had worked on him with pins and soot. Parker was usually so relaxed and easy under the hand of the artist that he often went to sleep, but this time he remained awake, every muscle taut.

At midnight the artist said he was ready to quit. He propped one mirror, four feet square, on a table by the wall and took a smaller mirror off the lavatory wall and put it in Parker's hands. Parker stood with his back to the one on the table and moved the other until he saw a flashing burst of color reflected from his back. It was almost completely covered with little red and blue and ivory and saffron squares; from them he made out the lineaments of the face – a mouth, the beginning of heavy brows, a straight nose, but the face was empty; the eyes had not yet been put in. The impression for the moment was almost as if the artist had tricked him and done the Physician's Friend.

'It don't have eyes,' Parker cried out.

'That'll come,' the artist said, 'in due time. We have another day to go on it yet.'

Parker spent the night on a cot at the Haven of Light Christian Mission. He found these the best places to stay in the city because they were free and included a meal of sorts. He got the last available cot and because he was still barefooted, he accepted a pair of second-hand shoes which, in his confusion, he put on to go to bed; he was still shocked from all that had happened to him. All night he lay awake in the long dormitory of cots with lumpy figures on them. The only light was from a phosphorescent cross glowing at the end of the room. The tree reached out to grasp him again, then burst into flame; the shoe burned quietly by itself; the eyes in the book said to him distinctly GO BACK and at the same time did not utter a sound. He wished that he were not in this city, not in this Haven of Light Mission, not in a bed by himself. He longed miserably for Sarah Ruth. Her sharp tongue and icepick eyes were the only comfort he could bring to mind. He decided he was losing it. Her eyes appeared soft and dilatory compared with the eyes in the book, for even though he could not summon up the exact look of those eyes, he could still feel their penetration. He felt as though, under their gaze, he was as transparent as the wing of a fly.

The tattooist had told him not to come until ten in the morning, but when he arrived at that hour, Parker was sitting in the dark hallway on the floor, waiting for him. He had decided upon getting up that, once the tattoo was on him, he would not look at it, that all his sensations of the day and night before were those of a crazy man and that he would return to doing things according to his own sound judgement.

The artist began where he left off. 'One thing I want to know,' he said presently as he worked over Parker's back, 'why do you want this on you? Have you gone and got religion? Are you saved?' he asked in a mocking voice.

Parker's throat felt salty and dry. 'Naw,' he said, 'I ain't got no use for none of that. A man can't save his self from whatever it is he don't deserve none of my sympathy.' These words seemed to leave his mouth like wraiths and to evaporate at once as if he had never uttered them.

'Then why . . . '

'I married this woman that's saved,' Parker said. 'I never should have done it. I ought to leave her. She's done gone and got pregnant.'

'That's too bad,' the artist said. 'Then it's her making you have this tattoo.'

'Naw,' Parker said, 'she don't know nothing about it. It's a surprise for her.'

'You think she'll like it and lay off you a while?'

'She can't hep herself,' Parker said. 'She can't say she don't like the looks of God.' He decided he had told the artist enough of his business. Artists were all right in their place but he didn't like them poking their noses into the affairs of regular people. 'I didn't get no sleep last night,' he said. 'I think I'll get some now.'

That closed the mouth of the artist but it did not bring him any sleep. He lay there, imagining how Sarah Ruth would be struck speechless by the face on his back and every now and then this would be interrupted by a vision of the tree of fire and his empty shoe burning beneath it.

The artist worked steadily until nearly four o'clock, not stopping to have lunch, hardly pausing with the electric instrument except to wipe the dripping dye off Parker's back as he went along. Finally he finished. 'You can get up and look at it now,' he said.

Parker sat up but he remained on the edge of the table.

The artist was pleased with his work and wanted Parker to look at it at once. Instead Parker continued to sit on the edge of the table, bent forward slightly but with a vacant look. 'What ails you?' the artist said. 'Go look at it.'

'Ain't nothing ails me,' Parker said in a sudden belligerent voice. 'That tattoo ain't going nowhere. It'll be there when I get there.' He reached for his shirt and began gingerly to put it on.

The artist took him roughly by the arm and propelled him between the two mirrors. 'Now *look*,' he said, angry at having his work ignored.

Parker looked, turned white and moved away. The eyes in the reflected face continued to look at him – still, straight, all-demanding, enclosed in silence.

'It was your idea, remember,' the artist said. 'I would have advised something else.'

Parker said nothing. He put on his shirt and went out the door while the artist shouted, 'I'll expect all of my money!'

Parker headed toward a package shop on the corner. He bought a pint of whiskey and took it into a nearby alley and drank it all in five minutes. Then he moved on to a pool hall nearby which he frequented when he came to the city. It was a well-lighted barn-like place with a bar up one side and gambling machines on the other and pool tables in the back. As soon as Parker entered, a large man in a red and black checkered shirt hailed him by slapping him on the back and yelling, 'Yeyyyyyy boy! O. E. Parker!'

Parker was not yet ready to be struck on the back. 'Lay off,' he said, 'I got a fresh tattoo there.'

'What you got this time?' the man asked and then yelled to a few at the machines. 'O. E.'s got him another tattoo.'

'Nothing special this time,' Parker said and slunk over to a machine that was not being used.

'Come on,' the big man said, 'let's have a look at O. E.'s tattoo,' and while Parker squirmed in their hands, they pulled up his shirt. Parker felt all the hands drop away instantly and his shirt fell again like a veil over the face. There was a silence in the pool room which seemed to Parker to grow from the circle around him until it extended to the foundations under the building and upward through the beams in the roof.

Finally someone said, 'Christ!' Then they all broke into noise at once. Parker turned around, an uncertain grin on his face.

'Leave it to O. E.!' the man in the checkered shirt said. 'That boy's a real card!'

'Maybe he's gone and got religion,' someone yelled.

'Not on your life,' Parker said.

'O. E.'s got religion and is witnessing for Jesus, ain't you, O. E.?' a little man with a piece of cigar in his mouth said wryly. 'An original way to do it if I ever saw one.'

'Leave it to Parker to think of a new one!' the fat man said.

'Yyeeeeeeyyyyyyy boy!' someone yelled and they all began to whistle and curse in compliment until Parker said, 'Aaa shut up.'

'What'd you do it for?' somebody asked.

'For laughs,' Parker said. 'What's it to you?'

'Why ain't you laughing then?' somebody yelled. Parker lunged into the midst of them and like a whirlwind on a summer's day there began a fight that raged amid overturned tables and swinging fists until two of them grabbed him and ran to the door with him and threw him out. Then a calm descended on the pool hall as nerve shattering as if the long barn-like room were the ship from which Jonah had been cast into the sea.

Parker sat for a long time on the ground in the alley behind the pool hall, examining his soul. He saw it as a spiderweb of facts and lies that was not at all important to him but which appeared to be necessary in spite of his opinion. The eyes that were now forever on his back were eyes to be obeyed. He was as certain of it as he had ever been of anything. Throughout his life, grumbling and sometimes cursing, often afraid, once in rapture, Parker had obeyed whatever instinct of this kind had come to him – in rapture when his spirit had lifted at the sight of the tattooed man at the fair, afraid when he had joined the navy, grumbling when he had married Sarah Ruth.

The thought of her brought him slowly to his feet. She would know what he had to do. She would clear up the rest of it, and she would at least be pleased. It seemed to him that, all along, that was what he wanted, to please her. His truck was still parked in front of the building where the artist had his place, but it was not far away. He got in it and drove out of the city and into the country night. His head was almost clear of liquor and he observed that his dissatisfaction was gone, but he felt not quite like himself. It was as if he were himself but a stranger to himself, driving into a new country though everything he saw was familiar to him, even at night.

He arrived finally at the house on the embankment, pulled the truck under the pecan tree and got out. He made as much noise as possible to assert that he was still in charge here, that his leaving her for a night without word meant nothing except it was the way he did things. He slammed the car door, stamped up the two steps and across the porch and rattled the door knob. It did not respond to his touch. 'Sarah Ruth!' he yelled, 'let me in.'

There was no lock on the door and she had evidently placed the back of a chair against the knob. He began to beat on the door and rattle the knob at the same time.

He heard the bed springs screak and bent down and put his head to the keyhole, but it was stopped up with paper. 'Let me in!' he hollered, bamming on the door again. 'What you got me locked out for?'

A sharp voice close to the door said, 'Who's there?'

'Me,' Parker said, 'O. E.'

He waited a moment.

'Me,' he said impatiently, 'O. E.'

Still no sound from inside.

He tried once more. 'O. E.,' he said, bamming the door two or three more times. 'O. E. Parker. You know me.'

There was a silence. Then the voice said slowly, 'I don't know no O. E.'

'Quit fooling,' Parker pleaded. 'You ain't got any business doing me this way. It's me, old O. E., I'm back. You ain't afraid of me.'

'Who's there?' the same unfeeling voice said.

Parker turned his head as if he expected someone behind him to give him the answer. The sky had lightened slightly and there were two or three streaks of yellow floating above the horizon. Then as he stood there, a tree of light burst over the skyline.

Parker fell back against the door as if he had been pinned there by a lance.

'Who's there?' the voice from inside said and there was a quality about it now that seemed final. The knob rattled and the voice said peremptorily, 'Who's there, I ast you?'

Parker bent down and put his mouth near the stuffed keyhole. 'Obadiah,' he whispered and all at once he felt the light pouring through him, turning his spiderweb soul into a perfect arabesque of colors, a garden of trees and birds and beasts.

'Obadiah Elihue!' he whispered.

The door opened and he stumbled in. Sarah Ruth loomed there, hands on her hips. She began at once, 'That was no hefty blonde woman you was working for and you'll have to pay her every penny on her tractor you busted up. She don't keep insurance on it. She came here and her and me had us a long talk and I . . . '

Trembling, Parker set about lighting the kerosene lamp.

'What's the matter with you, wasting that keresene this near daylight?' she demanded. 'I ain't got to look at you.'

A yellow glow enveloped them. Parker put the match down and began to unbutton his shirt.

'And you ain't going to have none of me this near morning,' she said.

'Shut your mouth,' he said quietly. 'Look at this and then I don't want to hear no more out of you.' He removed the shirt and turned his back to her.

'Another picture,' Sarah Ruth growled. 'I might have known you was off after putting some more trash on yourself.'

Parker's knees went hollow under him. He wheeled around and cried, 'Look at it! Don't just say that! *Look* at it!'

'I done looked,' she said.

'Don't you know who it is?' he cried in anguish.

'No, who is it?' Sarah Ruth said. 'It ain't anybody I know.'

'It's him,' Parker said.

'Him who?'

'God!' Parker cried.

'God? God don't look like that!'

'What do you know how he looks?' Parker moaned. 'You ain't seen him.'

'He don't *look*,' Sarah Ruth said. 'He's a spirit. No man shall see his face.'

'Aw listen,' Parker groaned, 'this is just a picture of him.'

'Idolatry!' Sarah Ruth screamed. 'Idolatry! Enflaming yourself with idols under every green tree! I can put up with lies and vanity but I don't want no idolator in this house!' and she grabbed up the broom and began to thrash him across the shoulders with it.

Parker was too stunned to resist. He sat there and let her beat him until she had nearly knocked him senseless and large welts had formed on the face of the tattooed Christ. Then he staggered up and made for the door.

She stamped the broom two or three times on the floor and went to the window and shook it out to get the taint of him off it. Still gripping it, she looked toward the pecan tree and her eyes hardened still more. There he was – who called himself Obadiah Elihue – leaning against the tree, crying like a baby.

Going Home

'Mulligatawny soup,' Carruthers said in the dining-car. 'Roast beef, roast potatoes, Yorkshire pudding, mixed vegetables.'

'And madam?' murmured the waiter.

Miss Fanshawe said she'd have the same. The waiter thanked her. Carruthers said:

'Miss Fanshawe'll take a medium dry sherry. Pale ale for me, please.'

The waiter paused. He glanced at Miss Fanshawe, shaping his lips.

'I'm sixteen and a half,' Carruthers said. 'Oh, and a bottle of Beaune. 1962.'

It was the highlight of every term and every holiday for Carruthers, coming like a no-man's-land between the two: the journey with Miss Fanshawe to their different homes. Not once had she officially complained, either to his mother or to the school. She wouldn't do that; it wasn't in Miss Fanshawe to complain officially. And as for him, he couldn't help himself.

'Always Beaune on a train,' he said now, 'because of all the burgundies it travels happiest.'

'Thank you, sir,' the waiter said.

'Thank *you*, old chap.'

The waiter went, moving swiftly in the empty dining-car. The train slowed and then gathered speed again. The fields it passed through were bright with sunshine; the water of a stream glittered in the distance.

'You shouldn't lie about your age,' Miss Fanshawe reproved, smiling to show she hadn't been upset by the lie. But lies like that, she explained, could get a waiter into trouble.

Carruthers, a sharp-faced boy of thirteen, laughed a familiar harsh laugh. He said he didn't like the waiter, a remark that Miss Fanshawe ignored.

'What weather!' she remarked instead. 'Just look at those weeping willows!' She hadn't ever noticed them before, she added, but Carruthers contradicted that, reminding her that she had often before remarked on those weeping willows. She smiled, with false vagueness in her face, slightly shaking her head. 'Perhaps it's just that everything looks so different this lovely summer. What will you do, Carruthers? Your mother took you to Greece last year, didn't she? It's almost a shame to leave England, I always think, when the weather's like this. So green in the long warm days —'

'Miss Fanshawe, why are you pretending nothing has happened?'

'Happened? My dear, what has happened?'

Carruthers laughed again, and looked through the window at cows resting in the shade of an oak tree. He said, still watching the cows, craning his neck to keep them in view:

'Your mind is thinking about what has happened and all the time you're attempting to make ridiculous conversation about the long warm days. Your heart is beating fast, Miss Fanshawe; your hands are trembling. There are two little dabs of red high up on your cheeks, just beneath your spectacles. There's a pink flush all over your neck. If you were alone, Miss Fanshawe, you'd be crying your heart out.'

Miss Fanshawe, who was thirty-eight, fair-haired and untouched by beauty, said that she hadn't the foggiest idea what Carruthers was talking about. He shook his head, implying that she lied. He said:

'Why are we being served by a man whom neither of us likes when we should be served by someone else? Just look at those weeping willows, you say.'

'Don't be silly, Carruthers.'

'What has become, Miss Fanshawe, of the other waiter?'

'Now please don't start any nonsense. I'm tired and —'

'It was he who gave me a taste for pale ale, d'you remember that? In your company, Miss Fanshawe, on this train. It was he who told us that Beaune travels best. Have a cig, Miss Fanshawe?'

'No, and I wish you wouldn't either.'

'Actually Mrs Carruthers allows me the odd smoke these days. Ever since my thirteenth birthday, May the twenty-sixth. How can she stop me, she says, when day and night she's at it like a factory chimney herself?'

'Your birthday's May the twenty-sixth? I never knew. Mine's two days later.' She spoke hastily, and with an eagerness that was as false as the vague expression her face had borne a moment ago.

'Gemini, Miss Fanshawe.'

'Yes: Gemini. Queen Victoria —'

'The sign of passion. Here comes the interloper.'

The waiter placed sherry before Miss Fanshawe and beer in front of Carruthers. He murmured deferentially, inclining his head.

'We've just been saying,' Carruthers remarked, 'that you're a new one on this line.'

'Newish, sir. A month — no, tell a lie, three weeks yesterday.'

'We knew your predecessor.'

'Oh yes, sir?'

'He used to say this line was as dead as a doornail. Actually, he enjoyed not having anything to do. Remember, Miss Fanshawe?'

Miss Fanshawe shook her head. She sipped her sherry, hoping the waiter would have the sense to go away. Carruthers said:

'In all the time Miss Fanshawe and I have been travelling together there hasn't been a solitary soul besides ourselves in this dining-car.'

The waiter said it hardly surprised him. You didn't get many, he agreed, and added, smoothing the tablecloth, that it would just be a minute before the soup was ready.

'Your predecessor', Carruthers said, 'was a most extraordinary man.'

'Oh yes, sir?'

'He had the gift of tongues. He was covered in freckles.'

'I see, sir.'

'Miss Fanshawe here had a passion for him.'

The waiter laughed. He lingered for a moment and then, since Carruthers was silent, went away.

'Now look here, Carruthers,' Miss Fanshawe began.

'Don't you think Mrs Carruthers is the most vulgar woman you've ever met?'

'I wasn't thinking of your mother. I will not have you talk like this to the waiter. Please now.'

'She wears a scent called "In Love", by Norman Hartnell. A woman of fifty, as thin as fuse wire. My God!'

'Your mother —'

'My mother doesn't concern you — oh, I agree. Still you don't want to deliver me to the female smelling of drink and tobacco smoke. I always brush my teeth in the lavatory, you know. For your sake, Miss Fanshawe.'

'Please don't engage the waiter in conversation. And please don't tell lies about the waiter who was here before. It's ridiculous the way you go on —'

'You're tired, Miss Fanshawe.'

'I'm always tired at the end of term.'

'That waiter used to say —'

'Oh, for heaven's sake, stop about that waiter!'

'I'm sorry.' He seemed to mean it, but she knew he didn't. And even when he spoke again, when his voice was softer, she knew that he was still pretending. 'What shall we talk about?' he asked, and with a weary cheerfulness she reminded him that she'd wondered what he was going to do in the holidays. He didn't reply. His head was bent. She knew that he was smiling.

'I'll walk beside her,' he said. 'In Rimini and Venice. In Zürich may be. By Lake Lugano. Or the Black Sea. New faces will greet her in an American Bar in Copenhagen. Or near the Spanish Steps – in Babbington's English Tea-Rooms. Or in Bandol or Cassis, the Ritz, the Hotel Excelsior in old Madrid. What shall we talk about, Miss Fanshawe?'

'You could tell me more. Last year in Greece —'

'I remember once we talked about guinea-pigs. I told you how I killed a guinea-pig that Mrs Carruthers gave me. Another time we talked about Rider Minor. D'you remember that?'

'Yes, but let's not —'

'McGullam was unpleasant to Rider Minor in the changing-room. McGullam and Travers went after Rider Minor with a little piece of wood.'

'You told me, Carruthers.'

He laughed.

'When I first arrived at Ashleigh Court the only person who spoke to me was Rider Minor. And of course the Sergeant-Major. The Sergeant-Major told me never to take to cigs. He described the lungs of a friend of his.'

'He was quite right.'

'Yes, he was. Cigs can give you a nasty disease.'

'I wish you wouldn't smoke.'

'I like your hat.'

'Soup, madam,' the waiter murmured. 'Sir.'

'Don't you like Miss Fanshawe's hat?' Carruthers smiled, pointing at Miss Fanshawe, and when the waiter said that the hat was very nice Carruthers asked him his name.

Miss Fanshawe dipped a spoon into her soup. The waiter offered her a roll. His name, he said, was Atkins.

'Are you wondering about us, Mr Atkins?'

'Sir?'

'Everyone has a natural curiosity, you know.'

'I see a lot of people in my work, sir.'

'Miss Fanshawe's an undermatron at Ashleigh Court Preparatory School for Boys. They use her disgracefully at the end of term – patching up clothes so that the mothers won't complain, packing trunks, sorting out laundry. From dawn till midnight Miss Fanshawe's on the trot. That's why she's tired.'

Miss Fanshawe laughed. 'Take no notice of him,' she said. She broke her roll and buttered a piece of it. She pointed at wheat ripening in a field. The harvest would be good this year, she said.

'At the end of each term,' Carruthers went on, 'she has to sit with me on this train because we travel in the same direction. I'm out of her authority really, since the term is over. Still, she has to keep an eye.'

The waiter, busy with the wine, said he understood. He raised his eyebrows at Miss Fanshawe and winked, but she did not encourage this, pretending not to notice it.

'Imagine, Mr Atkins,' Carruthers said, 'a country house in the mock Tudor style, with bits built on to it: a rackety old gymn and an art-room, and changing-rooms that smell of perspiration. There are a hundred and three boys at Ashleigh Court, in narrow iron beds with blue rugs on them, which Miss Fanshawe has to see are all kept tidy. She does other things as well: she wears a white overall and gives out medicines. She pours out cocoa in the dining-hall and at eleven o'clock every morning she hands each boy four *petit beurre* biscuits. She isn't allowed to say Grace. It has to be a master who says Grace: "For what we're about to receive . . . " Or the Reverend T. L. Edwards, who owns and runs the place, T.L.E., known to generations as a pervert. He pays boys, actually.'

The waiter, having meticulously removed a covering of red foil from the top of the wine bottle, wiped the cork with a napkin before attempting to draw it. He glanced quickly at Miss Fanshawe to see if he could catch her eye in order to put her at her ease with an understanding gesture, but she appeared to be wholly engaged with her soup.

'The Reverend Edwards is a law unto himself,' Carruthers said. 'Your predecessor was intrigued by him.'

'Please take no notice of him.' She tried to sound bracing, looking up suddenly and smiling at the waiter.

'The headmaster accompanied you on the train, did he, sir?'

'No, no, no, no. The Reverend Edwards was never on this train in his life. No, it was simply that your predecessor was interested in life at Ashleigh Court. He would stand there happily listening while we told him the details: you could say he was fascinated.'

At this Miss Fanshawe made a noise that was somewhere between a laugh and a denial.

'You could pour the Beaune now, Mr Atkins,' Carruthers suggested.

The waiter did so, pausing for a moment, in doubt as to which of the two he should offer a little of the wine to taste. Carruthers nodded to him, indicating that it should be he. The waiter complied and when Carruthers had given his approval he filled both their glasses and lifted from before them their empty soup plates.

'I've asked you not to behave like that,' she said when the waiter had gone.

'Like what, Miss Fanshawe?'

'You know, Carruthers.'

'The waiter and I were having a general conversation. As before, Miss Fanshawe, with the other waiter. Don't you remember? Don't you remember my telling him how I took forty of Hornsby's football cards? And drank the communion wine in the Reverend's cupboard?'

'I don't believe —'

'And I'll tell you another thing. I excused myself into Rider Minor's gum-boots.'

'Please leave the waiter alone. Please let's have no scenes this time, Carruthers.'

'There weren't scenes with the other waiter. He enjoyed everything we said to him. You could see him quite clearly trying to visualize Ashleigh Court, and Mrs Carruthers in her awful clothes.'

'He visualized nothing of the sort. You gave him drink that I had to pay for. He was obliged to listen to your fantasies.'

'He enjoyed our conversation, Miss Fanshawe. Why is it that

people like you and I are so unpopular?'

She didn't answer, but sighed instead. He would go on and on, she knew; and there was nothing she could do. She always meant not to protest, but when it came to the point she found it hard to sit silent, mile after mile.

'You know what I mean, Miss Fanshawe? At Ashleigh Court they say you have an awkward way of walking. And I've got no charm: I think that's why they don't much like me. But how for God's sake could any child of Mrs Carruthers have charm?'

'Please don't speak of your mother like that —'

'And yet men fancy her. Awful men arrive at weekends, as keen for sex as the Reverend Edwards is. "Your mother's a most elegant woman," a hard-eyed lecher remarked to me last summer, in the Palm Court of a Greek hotel.'

'Don't drink too much of that wine. The last time —'

'"You're staggering," she said the last time. I told her I had 'flu. She's beautiful, I dare say, in her thin way. D'you think she's beautiful?'

'Yes, she is.'

'She has men all over the place. Love flows like honey while you make do with waiters on a train.'

'Oh, don't be so *silly*, Carruthers.'

'She snaps her fingers and people come to comfort her with lust. A woman like that's never alone. While you —'

'Will you please stop talking about me!'

'You have a heart in your breast like anyone else, Miss Fanshawe.'

The waiter, arrived again, coughed. He leaned across the table and placed a warmed plate in front of Miss Fanshawe and a similar one in front of Carruthers. There was a silence while he offered Miss Fanshawe a silver-plated platter with slices of roast beef on it and square pieces of Yorkshire pudding. In the silence she selected what she wanted, a small portion, for her appetite on journeys with Carruthers was never great. Carruthers took the rest. The waiter offered vegetables.

'Miss Fanshawe ironed that blouse at a quarter to five this morning,' Carruthers said. 'She'd have ironed it last night if she hadn't been so tired.'

'A taste more carrots, sir?'

'I don't like carrots, Mr Atkins.'

'Peas, sir?'

'Thank you. She got up from her small bed, Mr Atkins, and her feet were chilly on the linoleum. She shivered, Mr Atkins, as she slipped her nightdress off. She stood there naked, thinking of another person. What became of your predecessor?'

'I don't know, sir. I never knew the man at all. All right for you, madam?'

'Yes, thank you.'

'He used to go back to the kitchen, Mr Atkins, and tell the cook that the couple from Ashleigh Court were on the train again. He'd lean against the sink while the cook poked about among his pieces of meat, trying to find us something to eat. Your predecessor would suck at the butt of a cig and occasionally he'd lift a can of beer to his lips. When the cook asked him what the matter was he'd say it was fascinating, a place like Ashleigh Court with boys running about in grey uniforms and an undermatron watching her life go by.'

'Excuse me, sir.'

The waiter went. Carruthers said: ' "She makes her own clothes," the other waiter told the cook. "She couldn't give a dinner party the way the young lad's mother could. She couldn't chat to this person and that, moving about among décolleté women and outshining every one of them." Why is she an undermatron at Ashleigh Court Preparatory School for Boys, owned and run by the Reverend T. L. Edwards, known to generations as a pervert?'

Miss Fanshawe, with an effort, laughed. 'Because she's qualified for nothing else,' she lightly said.

'I think that freckled waiter was sacked because he interfered with the passengers. "Vegetables?" he suggested, and before he could help himself he put the dish of cauliflowers on the table and put his arms around a woman. "All tickets please," cried the ticket-collector and then he saw the waiter and the woman on the floor. You can't run a railway company like that.'

'Carruthers —'

'Was it something like that, Miss Fanshawe? D'you think?'

'Of course it wasn't.'

'Why not?'

'Because you've just made it up. The man was a perfectly ordinary waiter on this train.'

'That's not true.'

'Of course it is.'

'I love this train, Miss Fanshawe.'

'It's a perfectly ordinary —'

'Of course it isn't.'

Carruthers laughed gaily, waiting for the waiter to come back, eating in silence until it was time again for their plates to be cleared away.

'Trifle, madam?' the waiter said. 'Cheese and biscuits?'

'Just coffee, please.'

'Sit down, why don't you, Mr Atkins? Join us for a while.'

'Ah no, sir, no.'

'Miss Fanshawe and I don't have to keep up appearances on your train. D'you understand that? We've been keeping up appearances for three long months at Ashleigh Court and it's time we stopped. Shall I tell you about my mother, Mr Atkins?'

'Your mother, sir?'

'Carruthers —'

'In 1960, when I was three, my father left her for another woman: she found it hard to bear. She had a lover at the time, a Mr Tennyson, but even so she found it hard to forgive my father for taking himself off.'

'I see, sir.'

'It was my father's intention that I should accompany him to his new life with the other woman, but when it came to the point the other woman decided against that. Why should she be burdened with my mother's child? she wanted to know: you can see her argument, Mr Atkins.'

'I must be getting on now, sir.'

'So my father arranged to pay my mother an annual sum, in return for which she agreed to give me house room. I go with her when she goes on holiday to a smart resort. My father's a thing of the past. What d'you think of all that, Mr Atkins? Can you visualize Mrs Carruthers at a resort? She's not at all like Miss Fanshawe.'

'I'm sure she's not —'

'Not at all.'

'Please let go my sleeve, sir.'

'We want you to sit down.'

'It's not my place, sir, to sit down with the passengers in the dining-car.'

'We want to ask you if you think it's fair that Mrs Carruthers should round up all the men she wants while Miss Fanshawe has only the furtive memory of a waiter on a train, a man who came to a sticky end, God knows.'

'Stop it!' cried Miss Fanshawe. 'Stop it! Stop it! Let go his jacket and let him go away —'

'I have things to do, sir.'

'He smelt of fried eggs, a smell that still comes back to her at night.'

'You're damaging my jacket. I must ask you to release me at once.'

'Are you married, Mr Atkins?'

'Carruthers!' Her face was crimson and her neck blotched with a flushing that Carruthers had seen before. 'Carruthers, for heaven's sake behave yourself!'

'The Reverend Edwards isn't married, as you might guess, Mr Atkins.'

The waiter tried to pull his sleeve out of Carruthers' grasp, panting a little from embarrassment and from the effort. 'Let go my jacket!' he shouted. 'Will you let me go!'

Carruthers laughed, but did not release his grasp. There was a sound of ripping as the jacket tore.

'Miss Fanshawe'll stitch it for you,' Carruthers said at once, and added more sharply when the waiter raised a hand to strike him: 'Don't do that please. Don't threaten a passenger, Mr Atkins.'

'You've ruined this jacket. You bloody little —'

'Don't use language in front of the lady.' He spoke quietly, and to a stranger entering the dining-car at that moment it might have seemed that the waiter was in the wrong, that the torn sleeve of his jacket was the just result of some attempted insolence on his part.

'You're mad,' the waiter shouted at Carruthers, his face red and sweating in his anger. 'That child's a raving lunatic,' he shouted as noisily at Miss Fanshawe.

Carruthers was humming a hymm. 'Lord, dismiss us', he softly sang, 'with Thy blessing.'

'Put any expenses on my bill,' whispered Miss Fanshawe. 'I'm very sorry.'

'Ashleigh Court'll pay,' Carruthers said, not smiling now, his face all of a sudden as sombre as the faces of the other two.

No one spoke again in the dining-car. The waiter brought coffee, and later presented a bill.

The train stopped at a small station. Three people got out as Miss Fanshawe and Carruthers moved down the corridor to their compartment. They walked in silence, Miss Fanshawe in front of Carruthers, he drawing his right hand along the glass of the windows. There'd been an elderly man in their compartment when they'd left it: to Miss Fanshawe's relief he was no longer there. Carruthers slid the door across. She found her book and opened it at once.

'I'm sorry,' he said when she'd read a page.

She turned the page, not looking up, not speaking.

'I'm sorry I tormented you,' he said after another pause.

She still did not look up, but spoke while moving her eyes along a line of print. 'You're always sorry,' she said.

Her face and neck were still hot. Her fingers tightly held the paperbacked volume. She felt taut and rigid, as though the unpleasantness in the dining-car had coiled some part of her up. On other journeys she'd experienced a similar feeling, though never as unnervingly as she experienced it now. He had never before torn a waiter's clothing.

'Miss Fanshawe?'

'I want to read.'

'I'm not going back to Ashleigh Court.'

She went on reading and then, when he'd repeated the statement, she slowly raised her head. She looked at him and thought, as she always did when she looked at him, that he was in need of care. There was a barrenness in his sharp face; his eyes reflected the tang of a bitter truth.

'I took the Reverend Edwards' cigarette-lighter. He's told me he won't have me back.'

'That isn't true, Carruthers —'

'At half-past eleven yesterday morning I walked into the Reverend's study and lifted it from his desk. Unfortunately he met me on the way out. Ashleigh Court, he said, was no place for a thief.'

'But why? Why did you do such a silly thing?'

'I don't know. I don't know why I do a lot of things. I don't know why I pretend you were in love with a waiter. This is the last horrid journey for you, Miss Fanshawe.'

'So you won't be coming back —'

'The first time I met you I was crying in a dormitory. D'you remember that? Do you, Miss Fanshawe?'

'Yes, I remember.'

'"Are you missing your mummy?" you asked me, and I said no. I was crying because I'd thought I'd like Ashleigh Court. I'd thought it would be heaven, a place without Mrs Carruthers. I didn't say that; not then.'

'No.'

'You brought me to your room and gave me liquorice allsorts. You made me blow my nose. You told me not to cry because the other boys would laugh at me. And yet I went on crying.'

In the fields men were making hay. Children in one field waved at the passing train. The last horrid journey, she thought; she would never see the sharp face again, nor the bitterness reflected in the eyes. He'd wept, as others occasionally had to; she'd been, for a moment, a mother to him. His own mother didn't like him, he'd later said – on a journey – because his features reminded her of his father's features.

'I don't know why I'm so unpleasant, Miss Fanshawe. The Reverend stared at me last night and said he had a feeling in his bones that I'd end up badly. He said I was a useless sort of person, a boy he couldn't ever rely on. I'd let him down, he said, thieving and lying like a common criminal. "I'm chalking you up as a failure for Ashleigh," he said. "I never had much faith in you, Carruthers."'

'He's a most revolting man.' She said it without meaning to, and yet the words came easily from her. She said it because it didn't matter any more, because he wasn't going to return to Ashleigh Court to repeat her words.

'You were kind to me that first day,' Carruthers said. 'I liked that holy picture in your room. You told me to look at it, I remember. Your white overall made a noise when you walked.'

She wanted to say that once she had told lies too, that at St Monica's School for Girls she'd said the King, the late George VI, had spoken to her when she stood in the crowd. She wanted to say that she'd stolen two rubbers from Elsie Grantham and poured ink all over the face of a clock, and had never been found out.

She closed her eyes, longing to speak, longing above all things in the world to fill the compartment with the words that had begun, since he'd told her, to pound in her brain. All he'd ever done on the train was to speak a kind of truth about his mother and the school, to speak in their no-man's-land, as now and then he'd called it. Tormenting her was incidental; she knew it was. Tormenting her was just by chance, a thing that happened.

His face was like a flint. No love had ever smoothed his face, and while she looked at it she felt, unbearably now, the urge to speak as he had spoken, so many times. He smiled at her. 'Yes,' he said. 'The Reverend's a most revolting man.'

'I'm thirty-eight,' she said and saw him nod as though, precisely, he'd guessed her age a long time ago. 'Tonight we'll sit together in the bungalow by the sea where my parents live and they'll ask me about the term at Ashleigh. "Begin at the beginning, Beryl," my mother'll say and my father'll set his deaf-aid. "The first day? What happened the first day, Beryl?" And I shall tell them. "Speak up," they'll say, and in a louder voice I'll tell them about the new boys, and the new members of staff. Tomorrow night I'll tell some more, and on and on until the holidays and the term are over. "Wherever are you going?" my mother'll say when I want to go out for a walk. "Funny time", she'll say, "to go for a walk." No matter what time it is.'

He turned his head away, gazing through the window as earlier she had gazed through the window of the dining-car, in awkwardness.

'I didn't fall in love with a freckled waiter,' he heard her say, 'but God knows the freckled waiter would have done.'

He looked at her again. 'I didn't mean, Miss Fanshawe —'

'If he had suddenly murmured while offering me the vegetables I'd have closed my eyes with joy. To be desired, to be desired in any way at all . . . '

'Miss Fanshawe —'

'Born beneath Gemini, the sign of passion, you said. Yet who wants to know about passion in the heart of an ugly undermatron? Different for your mother, Carruthers: your mother might weep and tear away her hair, and others would weep in pity because of all her beauty. D'you see, Carruthers? D'you understand me?'

'No, Miss Fanshawe. No, I don't think I do. I'm not as —'

'There was a time one Christmas, after a party in the staff-room, when a man who taught algebra took me up to a loft, the place where the Wolf Cubs meet. We lay down on an old tent, and then suddenly this man was sick. That was in 1954. I didn't tell them that in the bungalow: I've never told them the truth. I'll not say tonight, eating cooked ham and salad, that the boy I travelled with created a scene in the dining-car, or that I was obliged to pay for damage to a waiter's clothes.'

'Shall we read now, Miss Fanshawe?'

'How can we read, for God's sake, when we have other things to say? What was it like, d'you think, on all the journeys to see you so unhappy? Yes, you'll probably go to the bad. He's right: you have the look of a boy who'll end like that. The unhappy often do.'

'Unhappy, Miss Fanshawe? Do I seem unhappy?'

'Oh, for God's sake, tell the truth! The truth's been there between us on all our journeys. We've looked at one another and seen it, over and over again.'

'Miss Fanshawe, I don't understand you. I promise you, I don't understand —'

'How could I ever say in that bungalow that the algebra teacher laid me down on a tent and then was sick? Yet I can say it now to you, a thing I've never told another soul.'

The door slid open and a woman wearing a blue hat, a smiling, red-faced woman, asked if the vacant seats were taken. In a voice that amazed Carruthers further Miss Fanshawe told her to go away.

'Well, really!' said the woman.

'Leave us in peace, for God's sake!' shrieked Miss Fanshawe, and the woman, her smile all gone, backed into the corridor. Miss Fanshawe rose and shut the door again.

'It's different in that bungalow by the sea,' she then quite quietly remarked, as though no red-faced woman had backed away astonished. 'Not like an American Bar in Copenhagen or the Hotel Excelsior in Madrid. Along the walls the coloured geese stretch out their necks, the brass is polished and in its place. Inch by inch oppression fills the air. On the chintz covers in the sitting-room there's a pattern of small wild roses, the stair-carpet's full of fading lupins. *To W. F. Fanshawe on the occasion of his retirement*, says the plaque on the clock on the sitting-room mantelpiece, *from his friends in the Prudential*. The clock has a gold-coloured face and four black pillars of ersatz material: it hasn't chimed since 1958. At night, not far away, the sea tumbles about, seeming too real to be true. The seagulls shriek when I walk on the beach, and when I look at them I think they're crying out with happiness.'

He began to speak, only to speak her name, for there was nothing else he could think of to say. He changed his mind and said nothing at all.

'Who would take me from it now? Who, Carruthers? What freckled waiter or teacher of algebra? What assistant in a shop, what bank clerk, postman, salesman of cosmetics? They see a figure walking in the wind, discs of thick glass on her eyes, breasts as flat as paper. Her movement's awkward, they say, and when she's close enough they raise their hats and turn away: they mean no harm.'

'I see,' he said.

'In the bungalow I'm frightened of both of them: all my life I've been afraid of them. When I was small and wasn't pretty they made the best of things, and longed that I should be clever instead. "Read to us, Beryl," my father would say, rubbing his hands together when he came in from his office. And I would try to read. "Spell *merchant*," my father would urge as though his life depended upon it, and the letters would become jumbled in my mind. Can you see it, Carruthers, a child with glasses and an awkward way of walking and two angry figures, like vultures, unforgiving? They'd exchange a glance, turning their eyes away from me as though in shame. "Not bright," they'd think. "Not bright, to make up for the other."'

'How horrid, Miss Fanshawe.'

'No, no. After all, was it nice for them that their single child should be a gawky creature who blushed when people spoke? How could they help themselves, any more than your mother can?'

'Still, my mother —'

'"Going to the pictures?" he said the last time I was home. "What on earth are you doing that for?" And then she got the newspaper which gave the programme that was showing. "*Tarzan and the Apemen*", she read out. "My dear, at your age!" I wanted to sit in the dark for an hour or two, not having to talk about the term at Ashleigh Court. But how could I say that to them? I felt the redness coming in my face. "For children surely," my father said, "a film like that." And then he laughed. "Beryl's made a mistake," my mother explained, and she laughed too.'

'And did you go, Miss Fanshawe?'

'Go?'

'To *Tarzan and the Apemen*?'

'No, I didn't go. I don't possess courage like that: as soon as I enter the door of the bungalow I can feel their disappointment all round me and I'm terrified all over again. I've thought of not going back but I haven't even the courage for that: they've sucked everything out of me. D'you understand?'

'Well —'

'Why is God so cruel that we leave the ugly school and travel together to a greater ugliness when we could travel to something nice?'

'Nice, Miss Fanshawe? *Nice?*'

'You know what I mean, Carruthers.'

He shook his head. Again he turned it away from her, looking at the window, wretchedly now.

'Of course you do,' her voice said, 'if you think about it.'

'I really —'

'Funny our birthdays being close together!' Her mood was gayer suddenly. He turned to look at her and saw she was smiling. He smiled also.

'I've dreamed this train went on for ever,' she said, 'on and on until at last you stopped engaging passengers and waiters in fantastic conversation. "I'm better now," you said, and then you went to sleep. And when you woke I gave you liquorice allsorts. "I understand," I said: "it doesn't matter."'

'I know I've been very bad to you, Miss Fanshawe. I'm sorry — '

'I've dreamed of us together in my parents' bungalow, of my parents dead and buried and your thin mother gone too, and Ashleigh Court a thing of the nightmare past. I've seen us walking over the beaches together, you growing up, me cooking for you and mending your clothes and knitting you pullovers. I've brought you fresh brown eggs and made you apple dumplings. I've watched you smile over crispy chops.'

'Miss Fanshawe —'

'I'm telling you about a dream in which ordinary things are marvellous. Tea tastes nicer and the green of the grass is a fresher green than you've ever noticed before, and the air is rosy, and happiness runs about. I would take you to a cinema on a Saturday afternoon and we would buy chips on the way home and no one would mind. We'd sit by the fire and say whatever we liked to one another. And you would no longer steal things or tell lies, because you'd have no need to. Nor would you mock an unpretty undermatron.'

'Miss Fanshawe, I – I'm feeling tired. I think I'd like to read.'

'Why should they have a child and then destroy it? Why should your mother not love you because your face is like your father's face?'

'My mother —'

'Your mother's a disgrace,' she cried in sudden, new emotion. 'What life is it for a child to drag around hotels and lovers, a piece of extra luggage, alone, unloved?'

'It's not too bad. I get quite used to it —'

'Why can He not strike them dead?' she whispered. 'Why can't He make it possible? By some small miracle, surely to God?'

He wasn't looking at her. He heard her weeping and listened to the sound, not knowing what to do.

'You're a sorrowful mess, Carruthers,' she whispered. 'Yet you need not be.'

'Please. Please, Miss Fanshawe —'

'You'd be a different kind of person and so would I. You'd have my love, I'd care about the damage that's been done to you. You wouldn't come to a bad end: I'd see to that.'

He didn't want to turn his head again. He didn't want to see her, but in spite of that he found himself looking at her. She, too, was gazing at him, tears streaming on her cheeks. He spoke slowly and with as much firmness as he could gather together.

'What you're saying doesn't make any sense, Miss Fanshawe.'

'The waiter said that you were mad. Am I crazy too? Can people go mad like that, for a little while, on a train? Out of loneliness and locked-up love? Or desperation?'

'I'm sure it has nothing to do with madness, Miss Fanshawe —'

'The sand blows on to my face, and sometimes into my eyes. In my bedroom I shake it from my sandals. I murmur in the sitting-room. "Really, Beryl," my mother says, and my father sucks his breath in. On Sunday mornings we walk to church, all three of us. I go again, on my own, to Evensong: I find that nice. And yet I'm glad when it's time to go back to Ashleigh Court. Are you ever glad, Carruthers?'

'Sometimes I have been. But not always. Not always at all. I —'

'"Let's go for a stroll," the algebra teacher said. His clothes were stained with beer. "Let's go up there," he said. "It's nice up there." And in the pitch dark we climbed to the loft where the Wolf Cubs meet. He lit his cigarette-lighter and spread the tent out. I don't mind what happens, I thought. Anything is better than nothing happening all my life. And then the man was sick.'

'You told me that, Miss Fanshawe.'

'"You're getting fat," my mother might have said. "Look at Beryl, Dad, getting fat." And I would try to laugh. "A drunk has made me pregnant," I might have whispered in the bungalow, suddenly finding the courage for it. And they would look at me and see that I was happy, and I would kneel by my bed and pour my thanks out to God, every night of my life, while waiting for my child.' She paused and gave a little laugh. 'They are waiting for us, those people, Carruthers.'

'Yes.'

'The clock on the mantelpiece still will not chime. "Cocoa", my mother'll say at half-past nine. And when they die it'll be too late.'

He could feel the train slowing, and sighed within him, a gesture of thanksgiving. In a moment he would walk away from her: he would never see her again. It didn't matter what had taken place, because he wouldn't ever see her again. It didn't matter, all she had said, or all he had earlier said himself.

He felt sick in his stomach after the beer and the wine and the images she'd created of a life with her in a seaside bungalow. The food she'd raved about would be appalling; she'd never let him smoke. And yet, in the compartment now, while they were still alone, he was unable to prevent himself from feeling sorry for her. She was right when she spoke of her craziness: she wasn't quite sane beneath the surface, she was all twisted up and unwell.

'I'd better go and brush my teeth,' he said. He rose and lifted his overnight case from the rack.

'Don't go,' she whispered.

His hand, within the suitcase, had already grasped a blue spongebag. He released it and closed the case. He stood, not wishing to sit down again. She didn't speak. She wasn't looking at him now.

'Will you be all right, Miss Fanshawe?' he said at last, and repeated the question when she didn't reply. 'Miss Fanshawe?'

'I'm sorry you're not coming back to Ashleigh, Carruthers. I hope you have a pleasant holiday abroad.'

'Miss Fanshawe, will you —'

'I'll stay in England, as I always do.'

'We'll be there in a moment,' he said.

'I hope you won't go to the bad, Carruthers.'

They passed by houses now; the backs of houses, suburban gardens. Posters advertised beer and cigarettes and furniture. *Geo. Small. Seeds*, one said.

'I hope not, too,' he said.

'Your mother's on the platform. Where she always stands.'

'Goodbye, Miss Fanshawe.'

'Goodbye, Carruthers. Goodbye.'

Porters stood waiting. Mail-bags were on a trolley. A voice called out, speaking of the train they were on.

She didn't look at him. She wouldn't lift her head: he knew the tears were pouring on her cheeks now, more than before, and he wanted to say, again, that he was sorry. He shivered standing in the doorway, looking at her, and then he closed the door and went away.

She saw his mother greet him, smiling, in red as always she was. They went together to collect his luggage from the van, out of her sight, and when the train pulled away from the station she saw them once again, the mother speaking and Carruthers just as he always was, laughing his harsh laugh.

Lifeguard

Beyond doubt, I am a splendid fellow. In the autumn, winter, and spring, I execute the duties of a student of divinity; in the summer I disguise myself in my skin and become a lifeguard. My slightly narrow and gingerly hirsute but not necessarily unmanly chest becomes brown. My smooth back turns the color of caramel, which, in conjunction with the whipped cream of my white pith helmet, gives me, some of my teenage satellites assure me, a delightfully edible appearance. My legs, which I myself can study, cocked as they are before me while I repose on my elevated wooden throne, are dyed a lustreless maple walnut that accentuates their articulate strength. Correspondingly, the hairs of my body are bleached blond, so that my legs have the pointed elegance of, within the flower, umber anthers dusted with pollen.

For nine months of the year, I pace my pale hands and burning eyes through immense pages of biblical text barnacled with fudging commentary; through multi-volumed apologetics couched in a falsely friendly Victorian voice and bound in subtly abrasive boards of finely ridged, pre-faded red; through handbooks of liturgy and histories of dogma; through the bewildering duplicities of Tillich's divine politicking; through the suave table talk of Father D'Arcy, Étienne Gilson, Jacques Maritain, and other such moderns mistakenly put at their ease by the exquisite antique furniture and overstuffed larder of the hospitable St Thomas; through the terrifying attempts of Kierkegaard, Berdyaev, and Barth to scourge God into being. I sway appalled on the ladder of minus signs by which theologians would surmount the void. I tiptoe like a burglar into the house of naturalism to steal the silver. An acrobat, I swing from wisp to wisp. Newman's iridescent cobwebs crush in my hands. Pascal's blackboard mathematics are erased by a passing shoulder. The cave drawings, astoundingly vital by candlelight, of those aboriginal magicians, Paul and Augustine, in daylight fade into mere anthropology. The diverting productions of literary flirts like Chesterton, Eliot, Auden, and Greene – whether they regard Christianity as a pastel forest designed for a fairyland romp or a deliciously miasmic pit from which chiaroscuro can be mined with mechanical buckets – in the end all infallibly strike, despite the comic variety of gongs and mallets, the note of the rich young man who on the coast of Judaea refused in dismay to sell all that he had.

Then, for the remaining quarter of the solar revolution, I rest my eyes on a sheet of brilliant sand printed with the runes of naked human bodies. That there is no discrepancy between my studies, that the texts of the flesh complement those of the mind, is the easy burden of my sermon.

On the back rest of my lifeguard's chair is painted a cross – true, a red cross, signifying bandages, splints, spirits of ammonia, and sunburn unguents. Nevertheless, it comforts me. Each morning, as I mount into my chair, my athletic and youthfully fuzzy toes expertly gripping the slats that make a ladder, it is as if I am climbing into an immense, rigid, loosely fitting vestment.

Again, in each of my roles I sit attentively perched on the edge of an immensity. That the sea, with its multiform and mysterious hosts, its savage and senseless rages, no longer comfortably serves as a divine metaphor indicates how severely humanism has corrupted the apples of our creed. We seek God now in flowers and good deeds, and the immensities of blue that surround the little scabs of land upon which we draw our lives to their unsatisfactory conclusions are suffused by science with vacuous horror. I myself can hardly bear the thought of stars, or begin to count the mortalities of coral. But from my chair the sea, slightly distended by my higher perspective, seems a misty old gentleman stretched at his ease in an immense armchair which has for arms the arms of this bay and for an antimacassar the freshly laundered sky. Sailboats float on his surface like idle and unrelated but benevolent thoughts. The soughing of the surf is the rhythmic lifting of his ripple-stitched vest as he breathes. Consider. We enter the sea with a shock; our skin and blood shout in protest. But, that instant, that leap, past, what do we find? Ecstasy and buoyance. Swimming offers a parable. We struggle and thrash, and drown; we succumb, even in despair, and float, and are saved.

With what timidity, with what a sense of trespass, do I set forward even this obliquely a thought so official! Forgive me. I am not yet ordained; I am too disordered to deal with the main text. My competence is marginal, and I will confine myself to the gloss of flesh with which this particular margin, this one beach, is annotated each day.

Here the cinema of life is run backwards. The old are the first to arrive. They are idle, and have lost the gift of sleep. Each of our bodies is a clock that loses time. Young as I am, I can hear in myself the protein acids ticking; I wake at odd hours and in the shuddering darkness and silence feel my death rushing towards me like an express train. The older we get, and the fewer the mornings left to us, the more deeply dawn stabs us awake. The old ladies wear wide straw hats and, in their hats' shadows, smiles as wide, which they bestow upon each other, upon salty shells they discover in the morning-smooth sand, and even upon me, downy-eyed from my night of dissipation. The gentlemen are often incongruous; withered white legs support brazen barrel chests, absurdly potent, bustling with white froth. How these old roosters preen on their 'condition'! With what fatuous expertness they swim in the icy water – always, however, prudently parallel to the shore, at a depth no greater than their height.

Then come the middle-aged, burdened with children and aluminum chairs. The men are scarred with the marks of their vocation – the red forearms of the gasoline-station attendant, the pale X on the back of the overall-wearing mason or carpenter, the clammer's nicked ankles. The hair on their bodies has as many patterns as matted grass. The women are wrinkled but fertile, like the Iraqi rivers that cradled the seeds of our civilization. Their children are odious. From their gaunt faces leer all the vices, the greeds, the grating urgencies of the adult, unsoftened by maturity's reticence and fatigue. Except that here and there, a girl, the eldest daughter, wearing a knit suit striped horizontally with green, purple, and brown, walks slowly, carefully, puzzled by the dawn enveloping her thick smooth body, her waist not yet nipped but her throat elongated.

Finally come the young. The young matrons bring fat and fussing infants who gobble the sand like sugar, who toddle blissfully into the surf and bring me bolt upright on my throne. My whistle tweets. The mothers rouse. Many of these women are pregnant again, and sluggishly lie in their loose suits like cows tranced in a meadow. They gossip politics, and smoke incessantly, and lift their troubled eyes in wonder as a trio of flat-stomached nymphs parades past. These maidens take all our eyes. The vivacious redhead, freckled and white-footed, pushing against her boy and begging to be ducked; the solemn brunette, transporting the vase of herself with held breath; the dimpled blonde in the bib and diapers of her bikini, the lambent fuzz of her midriff shimmering like a cat's belly. Lust stuns me like the sun.

You are offended that a divinity student lusts? What prigs the unchurched are. Are not our assaults on the supernatural lascivious, a kind of indecency? If only you knew what de Sadian degradations, what frightful psychological spelunking, our gentle transcendentalist professors set us to, as preparation for our work, which is to shine in the darkness.

I feel that my lust makes me glow; I grow cold in my chair, like a torch of ice, as I study beauty. I have studied much of it, wearing all styles of bathing suit and facial expression, and have come to this conclusion: a woman's beauty lies, not in any exaggeration of the specialized zones, nor in any general harmony that could be worked out by means of the *sectio aurea* or a similar aesthetic superstition; but in the arabesque of the spine. The curve by which the back modulates into the buttocks. It is here that grace sits and rides a woman's body.

I watch from my white throne and pity women, deplore the demented judgement that drives them towards the braggart muscularity of the mesomorph and the prosperous complacence of the endomorph when it is we ectomorphs who pack in our scrawny sinews and exacerbated nerves the most intense gift, the most generous shelter, of love. To desire a woman is to desire to save her. Anyone who has endured intercourse that was neither predatory nor hurried knows how through it we descend, with a partner, into the grotesque and delicate shadows that until then have remained locked in the most guarded recess of our soul: into this harbor we bring her. A vague and twisted terrain becomes inhabited; each shadow, touched by the exploration, blooms into a flower of act. As if we are an island upon which a woman, tossed by her laboring vanity and blind self-seeking, is blown, and there finds security, until, an instant before the anticlimax, Nature with a smile thumps down her trump, and the island sinks beneath the sea.

There is great truth in those motion pictures which are slandered as true neither to the Bible nor to life. They are – written though they are by demons and drunks – true to both. We are all Solomons lusting for Sheba's salvation. The God-filled man is filled with a wilderness that cries to be populated. The stony chambers need jewels, furs, tints of cloth and flesh, even though, as in Samson's case, the temple comes tumbling. Women are an alien race of pagans set down among us. Every seduction is a conversion.

Who has loved and not experienced that sense of rescue? It is not true that our biological impulses are tricked out with ribands of chivalry; rather, our chivalric impulses go clanking in encumbering biological armor. Eunuchs love. Children love. I would love.

My chief exercise, as I sit above the crowds, is to lift the whole mass into immortality. It is not a light task; the throng is so huge, and its members so individually unworthy. No *memento mori* is so clinching as a photograph of a vanished crowd. Cheering Roosevelt, celebrating the Armistice, there it is, wearing its ten thousand straw hats and stiff collars, a fearless and wooden-faced bustle of life: it is gone. A crowd dies in the street like a derelict; it leaves no heir, no trace, no name. My own persistence beyond the last rim of time is easy to imagine; indeed, the effort of imagination lies the other way – to conceive of my ceasing. But when I study the vast tangle of humanity that blackens the beach as far as the sand stretches, absurdities crowd in on me. Is it as maiden, matron, or crone that the females will be eternalized? What will they do without children to watch and gossip to exchange? What of the thousand deaths of memory and bodily change we endure – can each be redeemed at a final Adjustments Counter? The sheer numbers involved make the mind scream. The race is no longer a tiny clan of simian aristocrats lording it over an ocean of grass; mankind is a plague racing like fire across the exhausted continents. This immense clot gathered on the beach, a fraction of a fraction – can we not say that this breeding swarm is its own immortality and end the suspense? The beehive in a sense survives; and is each of us not proved to be a hive, a galaxy of cells each of whom is doubtless praying, from its pew in our thumbnail or oesophagus, for personal resurrection? Indeed, to the cells themselves cancer may seem a revival of faith. No, in relation to other people oblivion is sensible and sanitary.

This sea of others exasperates and fatigues me most on Sunday mornings. I don't know why people no longer go to church –

whether they have lost the ability to sing or the willingness to listen. From eight-thirty onwards they crowd in from the parking lot, ants each carrying its crumb of baggage, until by noon, when the remote churches are releasing their gallant and gaily dressed minority, the sea itself is jammed with hollow heads and thrashing arms like a great bobbing backwash of rubbish. A transistor radio somewhere in the sand releases in a thin, apologetic gust the closing peal of a transcribed service. And right here, here at the very height of torpor and confusion, I slump, my eyes slit, and the blurred forms of Protestantism's errant herd seem gathered by the water's edge in impassioned poses of devotion. I seem to be lying dreaming in the infinite rock of space before Creation, and the actual scene I see is a vision of impossibility: a Paradise. For had we existed before the gesture that split the firmament, could we have conceived of our most obvious possession, our most platitudinous blessing, the moment, the single ever-present moment that we perpetually bring to our lips brimful?

So: be joyful. Be Joyful is my commandment. It is the message I read in your jiggle. Stretch your skins like pegged hides curing in the miracle of the sun's moment. Exult in your legs' scissoring, your waist's swivel. Romp; eat the froth; be children. I am here above you; I have given my youth that you may do this. I wait. The tides of time have treacherous undercurrents. You are borne continually towards the horizon. I have prepared myself; my muscles are instilled with everything that must be done. Someday my alertness will bear fruit; from near the horizon there will arise, delicious, translucent, like a green bell above the water, the call for help, the call, a call, it saddens me to confess, that I have yet to hear.

REFERENCES AND ACKNOWLEDGEMENTS

Sir Walter Scott: From *Chronicles of the Canongate* (1827).
Nathaniel Hawthorne: From *The Complete Works of Nathaniel Hawthorne*, Vol. II (1883).
Edgar Allan Poe: From *Tales of the Grotesque and Arabesque* (1839).
Mark Twain: From *The Celebrated Jumping Frog of Calaveras County and Other Sketches* (1867).
Bret Harte: From *Sandy Bar, &c* (1873).
Ambrose Bierce: From *In the Midst of Life* (1892).
Henry James: From *The Soft Side* (1900).
Robert Louis Stevenson: From *The Merry Men* (1887).
Joseph Conrad: From *'Twixt Land and Sea* (1912).
O. Henry: From *The Best of O. Henry* (1929).
H. H. Munro ('Saki'): From *The Chronicles of Clovis* (1911).
Stephen Crane: From *The Open Boat, and Other Tales of Adventure* (1898).

*

The editor and publishers wish to thank the following for their permission to reproduce copyright material:

Sherwood Anderson: From *The Triumph of the Egg* (Cape and B. W. Huebsch, Inc. 1921). Copyright 1921 by B. W. Huebsch, Inc., renewed 1948 by Eleanor Copenhaver Anderson. Reprinted by permission of Hughes Massie Ltd., Copyright Agents, and Harold Ober Associates Inc.
H. E. Bates: From *Day's End* (Cape, 1928). Reprinted by permission of Laurence Pollinger Limited on behalf of the Estate of the late H.E. Bates.
Elizabeth Bowen: 'The Demon Lover'. Copyright 1946 and renewed 1974 by Elizabeth Bowen. From *The Demon Lover* (Cape, 1945) and also in *Ivy Gripped the Steps and Other Stories* (Knopf). Reprinted by permission of Jonathan Cape Ltd. on behalf of the Estate of Elizabeth Bowen, and Alfred A. Knopf., Inc.
Morley Callaghan: From *Stories* (Macmillan Co. of Canada Ltd., 1959). Reprinted by permission of the author.
John Cheever: From *The Stories of John Cheever* (Knopf). © 1951 John Cheever. Originally in *The New Yorker*. Reprinted by permission of *The New Yorker*.

A. E. Coppard: From *Dusky Ruth and Other Stories* (Cape). Reprinted by permission of David Higham Associates Ltd.

William Faulkner: 'Dry September'. Copyright 1930 and renewed 1958 by William Faulkner. From *These Thirteen* (Chatto) and also in *Collected Stories of William Faulkner* (Random House). Reprinted by permission of Curtis Brown Ltd., and Random House Inc.

Ernest Hemingway: From *The First Forty-Nine Stories* (Cape, 1939), and also in *Men without Women*. Copyright 1927 by Charles Scribner's Sons, renewal copyright © 1955 by Ernest Hermingway. Reprinted by permission of Jonathan Cape Ltd., on behalf of the Executors of the Ernest Hemingway Estate, and Charles Scribner's Sons.

James Joyce: From *Dubliners* (Cape, 1914). Copyright © 1967 by the Estate of James Joyce. Reprinted by permission of Jonathan Cape Ltd. on behalf of the Executors of the James Joyce Estate; The Society of Authors as the literary representatives of the Estate of James Joyce; and Viking Penguin Inc.

Rudyard Kipling: From *Many Inventions* (Macmillan). Reprinted by permission of A. P. Watt Ltd. on behalf of the National Trust and Macmillan London Ltd.

Ring Lardner: From *The Best Short Stories of Ring Lardner* (Chatto, 1974). Reprinted by permission of Chatto & Windus Ltd. on behalf of the Author's Literary Estate, and Charles Scribner's Sons.

Mary Lavin: From *Collected Stories* (Vol. 2, Constable, 1964). Reprinted by permission of Constable Publishers and the author.

Doris Lessing: 'Mrs Fortescue'. Copyright © 1963, 1978 by Doris Lessing. From *Stories* (Knopf, 1978). Reprinted by permission of Alfred A. Knopf Inc., and Curtis Brown Ltd.

Katherine Mansfield: 'The Woman at the Store'. Copyright 1924 by Alfred A. Knopf, Inc. and renewed 1952 by J. Middleton Murry. From *The Short Stories of Katherine Mansfield*. Reprinted by permission of Alfred A. Knopf, Inc.

Walter de la Mare: From *Best Stories of de la Mare* (Faber, 1942). Reprinted by permission of The Literary Trustees of Walter de la Mare and the Society of Authors as their representative.

W. Somerset Maugham: From *Complete Short Stories*. Copyright 1937 by Hearst Magazines Inc. Reprinted by permission of A. P. Watt Ltd on behalf of the estate of W. Somerset Maugham and William Heinemann Ltd., and Doubleday & Company, Inc.

R. K. Narayan: From *A Horse and Two Goats* (Bodley Head, 1970). Reprinted by permission of David Higham Associates Ltd.

Flannery O'Connor: From *Everything that Rises Must Converge* (F.S. & G. 1965/Faber 1966). Copyright © 1965 by the Estate of Mary Flannery O'Connor. Reprinted by permission of A. D. Peters & Co. Ltd. and Farrar, Straus and Giroux, Inc.

Frank O'Connor: From *Guests of the Nation* (Macmillan, 1931). Reprinted by permission of A. D. Peters & Co. Ltd.

Seán O'Faoláin: From *A Purse of Coppers* (Cape, 1937). Reprinted by permission of A. P. Watt Ltd. for the author.

Liam O'Flaherty: From *The Short Stories of Liam O'Flaherty* (Cape, 1937) and also in *The Stories of Liam O'Flaherty*. Copyright © 1956 by the Devin-Adair Co. Reprinted by permission of Jonathan Cape Ltd. and the Devin-Adair Co., Old Greenwich, Conn. 06870.

Katherine Anne Porter: From *The Collected Stories of Katherine Anne Porter* (Cape, 1964) and also in *Flowering Judas and Other Stories* (Harcourt Brace Jovanovich). Copyright 1930, 1958 by Katherine Anne Porter. Reprinted by permission of Jonathan Cape Ltd. and Harcourt Brace Jovanovich Inc.

V. S. Pritchett: From *The Sailor, Sense of Humour and Other Stories*. Reprinted by permission of the author.

William Sansom: From *The Stories of William Sansom* (Hogarth Press, 1963). Copyright © William Sansom 1963. Reprinted by permission of Elaine Greene Ltd.

William Trevor: From *The Ballroom of Romance* (Bodley Head, 1972). Reprinted by permission of John Johnson, Author's Agents.

John Updike: From *Pigeon Feathers and Other Stories* (Deutsch, 1962/ Knopf 1962). Copyright © 1961 by John Updike. Reprinted by permission of André Deutsch Ltd. and Alfred A. Knopf, Inc.

Eudora Welty: From *A Curtain of Green and Other Stories*. Copyright 1941, 1969 by Eudora Welty. Reprinted by permission of Harcourt Brace Jovanovich, Inc., and Russell & Volkening.

Patrick White: From *The Cockatoos* (Cape, 1974). Reprinted by permission of Curtis Brown (Aust) Pty Ltd, Sydney.

While every effort has been made to secure permission, we may have failed in a few cases to trace the copyright holder. We apologize for any apparent negligence.

INDEX OF AUTHORS